AGATHA CHRISTIE'S DETECTIVES

Five Complete Novels

AGATHA CHRISTIE'S DETECTIVES

Five Complete Novels

THE MURDER AT THE VICARAGE
DEAD MAN'S FOLLY
SAD CYPRESS
TOWARDS ZERO
N or M?

WINGS BOOKS
NEW YORK

Previously published in separate volumes under
the titles:

The Murder at the Vicarage copyright 1930 by Dodd,
Mead & Company, Inc., © renewed 1958 by Agatha
Christie Mallowan
Dead Man's Folly copyright © 1956 by Agatha Christie
Limited
Sad Cypress copyright 1939, 1940, © renewed 1967,
1968 by Agatha Christie Mallowan
Towards Zero copyright 1944, © renewed 1972 by
Agatha Christie Mallowan
N or M? copyright 1941, © renewed 1969 by Agatha
Christie Mallowan

This 1982 edition is published by Wings Books,
distributed by Outlet Book Company, Inc., a
Random House Company, 225 Park Avenue South,
New York, NY 10003, by arrangement with Dodd,
Mead & Company.

Manufactured in the United States of America

Library of Congress Cataloging in Publication Data
Christie, Agatha, 1890–1976.
    Agatha Christie's detectives.

    1. Detective and mystery stories, English. 1. Title.
PR6005.H66A6 1982   823′.912   82-1765
                                        AACR2
ISBN 0-517-03581-2
8   7   6   5   4   3   2

CONTENTS

The Murder at the Vicarage

1

IT IS DIFFICULT to know quite where to begin this story, but I have fixed my choice on a certain Wednesday at luncheon at the Vicarage. The conversation, though in the main irrelevant to the matter in hand, yet contained one or two suggestive incidents which influenced later developments.

I had just finished carving some boiled beef (remarkably tough by the way) and on resuming my seat I remarked, in a spirit most unbecoming to my cloth, that anyone who murdered Colonel Protheroe would be doing the world at large a service.

My young nephew, Dennis, said instantly:

"That'll be remembered against you when the old boy is found bathed in blood. Mary will give evidence, won't you, Mary? And describe how you brandished the carving knife in a vindictive manner."

Mary, who is in service at the Vicarage as a stepping-stone to better things and higher wages, merely said in a loud, businesslike voice, "Greens," and thrust a cracked dish at him in a truculent manner.

My wife said in a sympathetic voice: "Has he been *very* trying?"

I did not reply at once, for Mary, setting the greens on the table with a bang, proceeded to thrust a dish of singularly moist and unpleasant dumplings under my nose. I said, "No, thank you," and she deposited the dish with a clatter on the table and left the room.

"It is a pity that I am such a shocking housekeeper," said my wife, with a tinge of genuine regret in her voice.

I was inclined to agree with her. My wife's name is Griselda—a highly suitable name for a parson's wife. But there the suitability ends. She is not in the least meek.

I have always been of the opinion that a clergyman should be unmarried. Why I should have urged Griselda to marry me at the end of twenty-four hours' acquaintance is a mystery to me. Marriage, I have always held, is a serious affair, to be entered into only after long deliberation and forethought, and suitability of tastes and inclinations is the most important consideration.

Griselda is nearly twenty years younger than myself. She is most distractingly pretty and quite incapable of taking anything seriously. She is incompetent in every way, and extremely trying to live with. She treats the parish as a kind of huge joke arranged for her amusement. I have endeavored to form her mind and failed. I am more than ever convinced that celibacy is desirable for the clergy. I have frequently hinted as much to Griselda, but she has only laughed.

"My dear," I said, "if you would only exercise a little care—"

"I do sometimes," said Griselda. "But, on the whole, I think things go worse when I'm trying. I'm evidently *not* a housekeeper by nature. I find it better to leave things to Mary and just make up my mind to be uncomfortable and have nasty things to eat."

"And what about your husband, my dear?" I said reproachfully, and proceeding to follow the example of the devil in quoting Scripture for his own ends I added: "She looketh to the ways of her household . . ."

"Think how lucky you are not to be torn to pieces by lions," said Griselda, quickly interrupting. "Or burnt at the stake. Bad food and lots of dust and dead wasps is really nothing to make a fuss about. Tell me more about Colonel Protheroe. At any rate the early Christians were lucky enough not to have churchwardens."

"Pompous old brute," said Dennis. "No wonder his first wife ran away from him."

"I don't see what else she could do," said my wife.

"Griselda," I said sharply. "I will not have you speaking in that way."

"Darling," said my wife affectionately. "Tell me about him. What was the trouble? Was it Mr. Hawes's becking and nodding and crossing himself every other minute?"

Hawes is our new curate. He has been with us just over three weeks. He has High Church views and fasts on Fridays. Colonel Protheroe is a great opposer of ritual in any form.

"Not this time. He did touch on it in passing. No, the whole trouble arose out of Mrs. Price Ridley's wretched pound note."

Mrs. Price Ridley is a devout member of my congregation. Attending early service on the anniversary of her son's death, she put a pound note into the offertory bag. Later, reading the amount of the collection posted up, she was pained to observe that one ten-shilling note was the highest item mentioned.

She complained to me about it, and I pointed out, very reasonably, that she must have made a mistake.

"We're none of us so young as we were," I said, trying to turn it off tactfully. "And we must pay the penalty of advancing years."

Strangely enough, my words only seemed to incense her further. She said that things had a very odd look and that she was surprised I didn't think so also. And she flounced away and, I gather, took her troubles to Colonel Protheroe. Protheroe is the kind of man who enjoys making a fuss on every conceivable occasion. He made a fuss. It is a pity he made it on a Wednesday. I teach in the Church Day School on Wednesday mornings, a proceeding that causes me acute nervousness and leaves me unsettled for the rest of the day.

"Well, I suppose he must have some fun," said my wife, with the air of trying to sum up the position impartially. "Nobody flutters round him and calls him the dear vicar, and embroiders awful slippers for him, and gives him bed-socks for Christmas. Both his wife and his daughter are fed to the teeth with him. I suppose it makes him happy to feel important somewhere."

"He needn't be offensive about it," I said with some heat. "I don't think he quite realized the implications of what he was saying. He wants to go over all the Church accounts—in case of defalcations—that was the word he used. Defalcations! Does he suspect me of embezzling the Church funds?"

"Nobody would suspect you of anything, darling," said Griselda. "You're so transparently above suspicion that really it would be a marvellous opportunity. I wish you'd embezzle the SPG funds. I hate missionaries—I always have."

I would have reproved her for that sentiment, but Mary entered at that moment with a partially cooked rice pudding. I made a mild protest, but Griselda said that the Japanese always ate half-cooked rice and had marvellous brains in consequence.

"I dare say," she said, "that if you had a rice pudding like this every day till Sunday, you'd preach the most marvellous sermon."

"Heaven forbid," I said with a shudder.

"Protheroe's coming over tomorrow evening and we're going over the accounts together," I went on. "I must finish preparing my talk for the CEMS today. Looking up a reference, I became so engrossed in Canon Shirley's *Reality* that I haven't got on as well as I should. What are you doing this afternoon, Griselda?"

"My duty," said Griselda. "My duty as the Vicaress. Tea and scandal at four-thirty."

"Who is coming?'

Griselda ticked them off on her fingers with a glow of virtue on her face.

"Mrs. Price Ridley, Miss Wetherby, Miss Hartnell, and that terrible Miss Marple."

"I rather like Miss Marple," I said. "She has, at least, a sense of humor."

"She's the worst cat in the village," said Griselda. "And she always knows every single thing that happens—and draws the worst inferences from it."

Griselda, as I have said, is much younger than I am. At my time of life, one knows that the worst is usually true.

"Well, don't expect *me* in for tea, Griselda," said Dennis.

"Beast!" said Griselda.

"Yes, but look here, the Protheroes really *did* ask me for tennis today."

"Beast!" said Griselda again.

Dennis beat a prudent retreat and Griselda and I went together into my study.

"I wonder what we shall have for tea," said Griselda, seating herself on my writing-table. "Dr. Stone and Miss Cram, I suppose, and perhaps Mrs. Lestrange. By the way, I called on her yesterday, but she was out. Yes, I'm sure we shall have Mrs. Lestrange for tea. It's so mysterious, isn't it, her arriving like this and taking a house down here, and hardly ever going outside it? Makes one think of detective stories. You know— '*Who was she, the mysterious woman with the pale, beautiful face? What was her past history? Nobody knew. There was something faintly sinister about her.*' I believe Dr. Haydock knows something about her."

"You read too many detective stories, Griselda," I observed mildly.

"What about you?" she retorted. "I was looking everywhere for *The Stain on the Stairs* the other day when you were in here writing a sermon. And at last I came in to ask you if you'd seen it anywhere, and what did I find?"

I had the grace to blush.

"I picked it up at random. A chance sentence caught my eye and—"

"I know those chance sentences," said Griselda. She quoted impressively, " '*And then a very curious thing happened—Griselda rose, crossed the room and kissed her elderly husband affectionately.*' " She suited the action to the word.

"Is that a very curious thing?" I inquired.

"Of course it is," said Griselda. "Do you realize, Len, that I might have married a Cabinet Minister, a Baronet, a rich Company Promoter, three subalterns and a ne'er-do-weel with attractive manners, and that instead I chose you? Didn't it astonish you very much?"

"At the time it did," I replied. "I have often wondered why you did it."

Griselda laughed.

"It made me feel so powerful," she murmured. "The others thought me simply wonderful and of course it would have been very nice for *them* to have *me*. But I'm everything you most dislike and disapprove of, and yet you couldn't withstand me! My vanity couldn't hold out against that. It's so much nicer to be a secret and delightful sin to anybody than to be a feather in their cap. I make you frightfully uncomfortable and stir you up the wrong way the whole time, and yet you adore me madly. You adore me madly, don't you?"

"Naturally I am very fond of you, my dear."

"Oh! Len, you adore me. Do you remember that day when I stayed up in town and sent you a wire you never got because the postmistress's sister was having twins and she forgot to send it round? The state you got into and you telephoned Scotland Yard and made the most frightful fuss."

There are things one hates being reminded of. I had really been strangely foolish on the occasion in question. I said:

"If you don't mind, dear, I want to get on with the CEMS."

Griselda gave a sigh of intense irritation, ruffled my hair up on end, smoothed it down again, said:

"You don't deserve me. You really don't. I'll have an affair with the artist. I will—really and truly. And then think of the scandal in the parish."

"There's a good deal already," I said mildly.

Griselda laughed, blew me a kiss, and departed through the window.

2

GRISELDA IS A very irritating woman. On leaving the luncheon table, I had felt myself to be in a good mood for preparing a really forceful address for the Church of England Men's Society. Now I felt restless and disturbed.

Just when I was really settling down to it, Lettice Protheroe drifted in.

I use the word drifted advisedly. I have read novels in which young people are described as bursting with energy—*joie de vivre*, the magnificent vitality of youth . . . Personally, all the young people I come across have the air of animal wraiths.

Lettice was particularly wraith-like this afternoon. She is a pretty girl, very tall and fair and completely vague. She drifted through the French window, absently pulled off the yellow beret she was wearing and murmured vaguely with a kind of far-away surprise: "Oh! it's you."

There is a path from Old Hall through the woods which comes out by our garden gate, so that most people coming from there come in at that gate and up to the study window instead of going a long way round by the road and coming to the front door. I was not surprised at Lettice coming in this way, but I did a little resent her attitude.

If you come to a Vicarage, you ought to be prepared to find a Vicar.

She came in and collapsed in a crumpled heap in one of my big armchairs. She plucked aimlessly at her hair, staring at the ceiling.

"Is Dennis anywhere about?"

"I haven't seen him since lunch. I understand he was going to play tennis at your place."

"Oh!" said Lettice. "I hope he isn't. He won't find anybody there."

"He said you asked him."

"I believe I did. Only that was Friday. And today's Tuesday."

"It's Wednesday," I said.

"Oh! how dreadful," said Lettice. "That means that I've forgotten to go to lunch with some people for the third time."

Fortunately it didn't seem to worry her much.

"Is Griselda anywhere about?"

"I expect you'll find her in the studio in the garden—sitting to Lawrence Redding."

"There's been quite a shemozzle about him," said Lettice. "With father, you know. Father's dreadful."

"What was the she— whatever it was about?" I inquired.

"About his painting me. Father found out about it. Why shouldn't I be painted in my bathing dress? If I go on a beach in it, why shouldn't I be painted in it?"

Lettice paused and then went on.

"It's really absurd—father forbidding a young man the house. Of course, Lawrence and I simply shriek about it. I shall come and be done here in your studio."

"No, my dear," I said. "Not if your father forbids it."

"Oh! dear," said Lettice, sighing. "How tiresome everyone is. I feel shattered. Definitely. If only I had some money I'd go away, but without it I can't. If only father would be decent and die, I should be all right."

"You must not say things like that, Lettice."

"Well, if he doesn't want me to want him to die, he shouldn't be so horrible over money. I don't wonder mother left him. Do you know, for years I believed she was dead. What sort of a young man did she run away with? Was he nice?"

"It was before your father came to live here."

"I wonder what's become of her. I expect Anne will have an affair with someone soon. Anne hates me—she's quite decent to me, but she hates me. She's getting old and she doesn't like it. That's the age you break out, you know."

I wondered if Lettice was going to spend the entire afternoon in my study.

"You haven't seen my gramophone records, have you?" she asked.

"No."

"How tiresome. I know I've left them somewhere. And I've lost the dog. And my wrist watch is somewhere, only it doesn't much matter because it won't go. Oh! dear, I am so sleepy. I can't think why, because I didn't get up till eleven. But life's very shattering, don't you think? Oh! dear, I must go. I'm going to see Dr. Stone's barrow at three o'clock."

I glanced at the clock and remarked that it was now five-and-twenty to four.

"Oh! is it? How dreadful. I wonder if they've waited or if they've gone without me. I suppose I'd better go down and do something about it."

She got up and drifted out again, murmuring over her shoulder:

"You'll tell Dennis, won't you?"

I said "Yes" mechanically, only realizing too late that I had no idea what it was I was to tell Dennis. But I reflected that in all probability it did not matter. I fell to cogitating on the subject of Dr. Stone, a well-known archaeologist who had recently come to stay at the Blue Boar, whilst he superintended the excavation of a barrow situated on Colonel Protheroe's property. There had already been several disputes between him and the Colonel. I was amused at his appointment to take Lettice to see the operations.

It occurred to me that Lettice Protheroe was something of a minx. I wondered how she would get on with the archaeologist's secretary, Miss Cram. Miss Cram is a healthy young woman of twenty-five, noisy in manner, with a high color, fine animal spirits and a mouth that always seems to have more than its full share of teeth.

Village opinion is divided as to whether she is no better than she should be, or else a young woman of iron virtue who purposes to become Mrs. Stone at an early opportunity. She is in every way a great contrast to Lettice.

I could imagine that the state of things at Old Hall might not be too happy. Colonel Protheroe had married again some five years previously. The second Mrs. Protheroe was a remarkably handsome woman in a rather unusual style. I had always guessed that the relations between her and her stepdaughter were not too happy.

I had one more interruption. This time, it was my curate, Hawes. He wanted to know the details of my interview with Protheroe. I told him that the colonel had deplored his "Romish tendencies" but that the real purpose of his visit had been on quite another matter. At the same time, I entered a protest of my own, and told him plainly that he must conform to my ruling. On the whole, he took my remarks very well.

I felt rather remorseful when he had gone for not liking him better. These irrational likes and dislikes that one takes to people are, I am sure, very unchristian.

With a sigh, I realized that the hands of the clock on my writing-table pointed to a quarter to five, a sign that it was really half-past four, and I made my way to the drawing-room.

Four of my parishioners were assembled there with teacups. Griselda sat behind the tea table trying to look natural in her environment, but only succeeded in looking more out of place than usual.

I shook hands all round and sat down between Miss Marple and Miss Wetherby.

Miss Marple is a white-haired old lady with a gentle, appealing manner— Miss Wetherby is a mixture of vinegar and gush. Of the two Miss Marple is much the more dangerous.

"We were just talking," said Griselda in a honeysweet voice, "about Dr. Stone and Miss Cram."

A ribald rhyme concocted by Dennis shot through my head.

"Miss Cram doesn't give a damn."

I had a sudden yearning to say it out loud and observe the effect, but fortunately I refrained. Miss Wetherby said tersely:

"No nice girl would do it," and shut her thin lips disapprovingly.

"Do what?" I inquired.

"Be a secretary to an unmarried man," said Miss Wetherby in a horrified tone.

"Oh! my dear," said Miss Marple. "*I* think married ones are the worst. Remember poor Mollie Carter."

"Married men living apart from their wives are, of course, notorious," said Miss Wetherby.

"And even some of the ones living with their wives," murmured Miss Marple. "I remember—"

I interrupted these unsavory reminiscences.

"But surely," I said, "in these days a girl can take a post in just the same way as a man does."

"To come away to the country? And stay at the same hotel?" said Mrs. Price Ridley in a severe voice.

Miss Wetherby murmured to Miss Marple in a low voice.

"And all the bedrooms on the same floor . . ."

Miss Hartnell, who is weather-beaten and jolly and much dreaded by the poor, observed in a loud, hearty voice:

"The poor man will be caught before he knows where he is. He's as innocent as a babe unborn, you can see that."

Curious what turns of phrase we employ. None of the ladies present would have dreamed of alluding to an actual baby till it was safely in the cradle, visible to all.

"Disgusting, I call it," continued Miss Hartnell, with her usual tactlessness. "The man must be at least twenty-five years older than she is."

Three female voices rose at once making disconnected remarks about the Choirboys' Outing, the regrettable incident at the last Mothers' Meeting, and the drafts in the church. Miss Marple twinkled at Griselda.

"Don't you think," said my wife, "that Miss Cram may just like having an interesting job? And that she considers Dr. Stone just as an employer?"

There was a silence. Evidently none of the four ladies agreed. Miss Marple broke the silence by patting Griselda on the arm.

"My dear," she said, "you are very young. The young have such innocent minds."

Griselda said indignantly that she hadn't got at all an innocent mind.

"Naturally," said Miss Marple, unheeding of the protest, "you think the best of everyone."

"Do you really think she wants to marry that bald-headed dull man?"

"I understand he is quite well off," said Miss Marple. "Rather a violent temper, I'm afraid. He had quite a serious quarrel with Colonel Protheroe the other day."

Everyone leaned forward interestedly.

"Colonel Protheroe accused him of being an ignoramus."

"How like Colonel Protheroe, and how absurd," said Mrs. Price Ridley.

"Very like Colonel Protheroe, but I don't know about it being absurd," said Miss Marple. "You remember the woman who came down here and said she represented Welfare, and after taking subscriptions she was never heard of again and proved to have nothing whatever to do with Welfare. One is so inclined to be trusting and take people at their own valuation."

I should never have dreamed of describing Miss Marple as trusting.

"There's been some fuss about that young artist, Mr. Redding, hasn't there?" asked Miss Wetherby.

Miss Marple nodded.

"Colonel Protheroe turned him out of the house. It appears he was painting Lettice in her bathing dress."

"I always *thought* there was something between them," said Mrs. Price Ridley. "That young fellow is always mouching off up there. Pity the girl hasn't got a mother. A stepmother is never the same thing."

"I dare say Mrs. Protheroe does her best," said Miss Hartnell.

"Girls are so sly," deplored Mrs. Price Ridley.

"Quite a romance, isn't it?" said the softer-hearted Miss Wetherby. "He's a very good-looking young fellow."

"But loose," said Miss Hartnell. "Bound to be. An artist! Paris! Models! The Altogether!"

"Painting her in her bathing dress," said Mrs. Price Ridley. "Not quite nice."

"He's painting me too," said Griselda.

"But not in your bathing dress, dear," said Miss Marple.

"It might be worse," said Griselda solemnly.

"Naughty girl," said Miss Hartnell, taking the joke broadmindedly. Everybody else looked slightly shocked.

"Did dear Lettice tell you of the trouble?" asked Miss Marple of me.

"Tell me?"

"Yes. I saw her pass through the garden and go round to the study window."

Miss Marple always sees everything. Gardening is as good as a smoke screen, and the habit of observing birds through powerful glasses can always be turned to account.

"She mentioned it, yes," I admitted.

"Mr. Hawes looked worried," said Miss Marple. "I hope he hasn't been working too hard."

"Oh!" cried Miss Wetherby excitedly. "I quite forgot. I knew I had some news for you. I saw Dr. Haydock coming out of Mrs. Lestrange's cottage."

Everyone looked at each other.

"Perhaps she's ill," suggested Mrs. Price Ridley.

"It must have been very sudden, if so," said Miss Hartnell. "For I saw her walking round her garden at three o'clock this afternoon, and she seemed in perfect health."

"She and Dr. Haydock must be old acquaintances," said Mrs. Price Ridley. "He's been very quiet about it."

"It's curious," said Miss Wetherby, "that he's never *mentioned* it."

"As a matter of fact—" said Griselda in a low, mysterious voice, and stopped. Everyone leaned forward excitedly.

"I happen to *know*," said Griselda impressively. "Her husband was a missionary. Terrible story. *He was eaten,* you know. Actually eaten. And she was forced to become the chief's head wife. Dr. Haydock was with an expedition and rescued her."

For a moment excitement was rife, then Miss Marple said reproachfully, but with a smile: "Naughty girl!"

She tapped Griselda reprovingly on the arm.

"Very unwise thing to do, my dear. If you make up these things, people are quite likely to believe them. And sometimes that leads to complications."

A distinct frost had come over the assembly. Two of the ladies rose to take their departure.

"I wonder if there *is* anything between young Lawrence Redding and Lettice Protheroe," said Miss Wetherby. "It certainly looks like it. What do you think, Miss Marple?"

Miss Marple seemed thoughtful.

"I shouldn't have said so myself. Not *Lettice*. *Quite* another person I should have said."

"But Colonel Protheroe must have thought—"

"He has always struck me as rather a stupid man," said Miss Marple. "The kind of man who gets the wrong idea into his head and is obstinate about it. Do you remember Joe Bucknell who used to keep the Blue Boar? Such a to-do about his daughter carrying on with young Bailey. And all the time it was that minx of a wife of his."

She was looking full at Griselda as she spoke, and I suddenly felt a wild surge of anger.

"Don't you think, Miss Marple," I said, "that we're all inclined to let our tongues run away with us too much. Charity thinketh no evil, you know. Inestimable harm may be done by foolish wagging of tongues in ill-natured gossip."

"Dear vicar," said Miss Marple, "you are so unworldly. I'm afraid that observing human nature for as long as I have done, one gets not to expect very much from it. I dare say the idle tittle-tattle is very wrong and unkind, but it is so often true, isn't it?"

That last Parthian shot went home.

3

"NASTY OLD CAT," said Griselda, as soon as the door was closed.

She made a face in the direction of the departing visitors and then looked at me and laughed.

"Len, do you really suspect me of having an affair with Lawrence Redding?"

"My dear, of course not."

"But you thought Miss Marple was hinting at it. And you rose to my defense simply beautifully. Like—like an angry tiger."

A momentary uneasiness assailed me. A clergyman of the Church of England ought never to put himself in the position of being described as an angry tiger.

"I felt the occasion could not pass without a protest," I said. "But Griselda, I wish you would be a little more careful in what you say."

"Do you mean the cannibal story?" she asked. "Or the suggestion that Lawrence was painting me in the nude! If they only knew that he was painting me in a thick cloak with a very high fur collar—the sort of thing that you could go quite purely to see the Pope in—not a bit of sinful flesh showing anywhere! In fact, it's all marvellously pure. Lawrence never even attempts to make love to me—I can't think why."

"Surely, knowing that you're a married woman—"

"Don't pretend to come out of the ark, Len. You know very well that an attractive young woman with an elderly husband is a kind of gift from heaven to a young man. There must be some other reason—it's not that I'm unattractive—I'm not."

"Surely you don't want him to make love to you?"

"N-n-o," said Griselda, with more hesitation than I thought becoming.

"If he's in love with Lettice Protheroe—"

"Miss Marple didn't seem to think he was."

"Miss Marple may be mistaken."

"She never is. That kind of old cat is always right." She paused a minute and then said, with a quick sidelong glance at me: "You do believe me, don't you? I mean, that there's nothing between Lawrence and me."

"My dear Griselda," I said, surprised. "Of course."

My wife came across and kissed me.

"I wish you weren't so terribly easy to deceive, Len. You'd believe me whatever I said."

"I should hope so. But, my dear, I do beg of you to guard your tongue and be careful what you say. These women are singularly deficient in humor, remember, and take everything seriously."

"What they need," said Griselda, "is a little immorality in their lives. Then they wouldn't be so busy looking for it in other people's."

And on this she left the room, and glancing at my watch I hurried out to pay some visits that ought to have been made earlier in the day.

The Wednesday evening service was sparsely attended as usual, but when I came out through the church, after disrobing in the vestry, it was empty save for a woman who stood staring up at one of our windows. We have some rather fine old stained glass, and indeed the church itself is well worth looking at. She turned at my footsteps, and I saw that it was Mrs. Lestrange.

We both hesitated a moment, and then I said:

"I hope you like our little church."

"I've been admiring the screen," she said.

Her voice was pleasant, low, yet very distinct, with a clear-cut enunciation. She added:

"I'm so sorry to have missed your wife yesterday."

We talked a few minutes longer about the church. She was evidently a cultured woman who knew something of Church history and architecture. We left the building together and walked down the road, since one way to the Vicarage led past her house. As we arrived at the gate, she said pleasantly:

"Come in, won't you? And tell me what you think of what I have done."

I accepted the invitation. Little Gates had formerly belonged to an Anglo-Indian colonel, and I could not help feeling relieved by the disappearance of the brass tables and Burmese idols. It was furnished now very simply, but in exquisite taste. There was a sense of harmony and rest about it.

Yet I wondered more and more what had brought such a woman as Mrs. Lestrange to St. Mary Mead. She was so very clearly a woman of the world that it seemed a strange taste to bury herself in a country village.

In the clear light of her drawing-room I had an opportunity of observing her closely for the first time.

She was a very tall woman. Her hair was gold with a tinge of red in it. Her eyebrows and eyelashes were dark, whether by art or by nature I could not decide. If she was, as I thought, made up, it was done very artistically. There was something Sphinxlike about her face when it was in repose and she had the most curious eyes I have ever seen—they were almost golden in shade.

Her clothes were perfect and she had all the ease of manner of a well-bred woman, and yet there was something about her that was incongruous and baffling. You felt that she was a mystery. The word Griselda had used occurred to me—*sinister*. Absurd, of course, and yet—was it so absurd? The thought sprang unbidden into my mind: "This woman would stick at nothing."

Our talk was on most normal lines—pictures, books, old churches. Yet somehow I got very strongly the impression that there was something else—something of quite a different nature that Mrs. Lestrange wanted to say to me.

I caught her eyes on me once or twice, looking at me with a curious hesitancy, as though she were unable to make up her mind. She kept the talk, I noticed, strictly to impersonal subjects. She made no mention of a husband or of friends or relations.

But all the time there was that strange urgent appeal in her glance. It seemed to say: "Shall I tell you? I want to. Can't you help me?"

Yet in the end it died away—or perhaps it had all been my fancy. I had the feeling that I was being dismissed. I rose and took my leave. As I went out of the room, I glanced back and saw her staring after me with a puzzled, doubtful expression. On an impulse I came back:

"If there is anything I can do—"

She said doubtfully: "It's very kind of you—"

We were both silent. Then she said:

"I wish I knew. It's very difficult. No, I don't think anyone can help me. But thank you for offering to do so."

That seemed final, so I went. But as I did so, I wondered. We are not used to mysteries in St. Mary Mead.

So much is this the case that as I emerged from the gate I was pounced upon. Miss Hartnell is very good at pouncing in a heavy and cumbrous way.

"*I* saw you!" she exclaimed with ponderous humor. "And I *was* so excited. Now can you tell us all about it."

"About what?'

"The mysterious lady! Is she a widow or has she a husband somewhere?"

"I really couldn't say. She didn't tell me."

"How very peculiar. One would think she would be certain to mention something casually. It almost looks, doesn't it, as though she had a reason for not speaking?"

"I really don't see that."

"Ah! but as dear Miss Marple says, you are so unworldly, dear vicar. Tell me, has she known Dr. Haydock long?"

"She didn't mention him, so I don't know."

"Really? But what did you talk about then?"

"Pictures, music, books," I said truthfully.

Miss Hartnell, whose only topics of conversation are the purely personal, looked suspicious and unbelieving. Taking advantage of a momentary hesitation on her part as to how to proceed next, I bade her good night and walked rapidly away.

I called in at a house farther down the village and returned to the Vicarage by the garden gate, passing, as I did so, the danger point of Miss Marple's garden. However, I did not see how it was humanly possible for the news of my visit to Mrs. Lestrange to have yet reached her ears, so I felt reasonably safe.

As I latched the gate, it occurred to me that I would just step down to the shed in the garden which young Lawrence Redding was using as a studio, and see for myself how Griselda's portrait was progressing.

I append a rough sketch here which will be useful in the light of after happenings, only sketching in such details as are necessary.

I had no idea there was anyone in the studio. There had been no voices from within to warn me, and I suppose that my own footsteps made no noise upon the grass.

I opened the door and then stopped awkwardly on the threshold. For there were two people in the studio, and the man's arms were round the woman and he was kissing her passionately.

The two people were the artist, Lawrence Redding, and Mrs. Protheroe.

I backed out precipitately and beat a retreat to my study. There I sat down in a chair, took out my pipe, and thought things over. The discovery had come as a great shock to me. Especially since my conversation with Lettice that afternoon, I had felt fairly certain that there was some kind of understanding growing up between her and the young man. Moreover, I was convinced that she herself thought so. I felt positive that she had no idea of the artist's feelings for her stepmother.

A nasty tangle. I paid a grudging tribute to Miss Marple. She had not

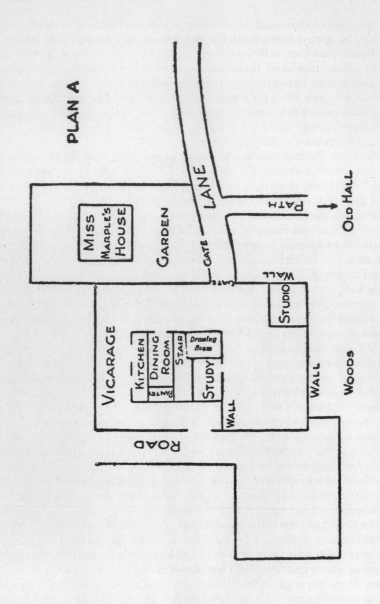

PLAN A

LANE

PATH → OLD HALL

GATE

Miss Marple's House

GARDEN

GATE

WALL

STUDIO

VICARAGE

KITCHEN

DINING ROOM

PANTRY

STAIR

Drawing Room

STUDY

WALL

WALL

WOODS

ROAD

been deceived but had evidently suspected the true state of things with a fair amount of accuracy. I had entirely misread her meaning glance at Griselda.

I had never dreamed of considering Mrs. Protheroe in the matter. There has always been rather a suggestion of Caesar's wife about Mrs. Protheroe—a quiet, self-contained woman whom one would not suspect of any great depths of feeling.

I had got to this point in my meditations when a tap on my study window aroused me. I got up and went to it. Mrs. Protheroe was standing outside. I opened the window and she came in, not waiting for an invitation on my part. She crossed the room in a breathless sort of way and dropped down on the sofa.

I had the feeling that I had never really seen her before. The quiet self-contained woman that I knew had vanished. In her place was a quick-breathing, desperate creature. For the first time I realized that Anne Protheroe was beautiful.

She was a brown-haired woman with a pale face and very deep set gray eyes. She was flushed now and her breast heaved. It was as though a statue had suddenly come to life. I blinked my eyes at the transformation.

"I thought it best to come," she said. "You—you saw just now?" I bowed my head.

She said very quietly: "We love each other . . ."

And even in the middle of her evident distress and agitation she could not keep a little smile from her lips. The smile of a woman who sees something very beautiful and wonderful.

I still said nothing, and she added presently:

"I suppose to you that seems very wrong?"

"Can you expect me to say anything else, Mrs. Protheroe?"

"No—no, I suppose not."

I went on, trying to make my voice as gentle as possible:

"You are a married woman—"

She interrupted me.

"Oh! I know—I know. Do you think I haven't gone over all that again and again? I'm not a bad woman really—I'm not. And things aren't—aren't—as you might think they are."

I said gravely: "I'm glad of that."

She asked rather timorously:

"Are you going to tell my husband?"

I said rather dryly:

"There seems to be a general idea that a clergyman is incapable of behaving like a gentleman. That is not true."

She threw me a grateful glance.

"I'm so unhappy. Oh! I'm so dreadfully unhappy. I can't go on. I simply can't go on. And I don't know what to do." Her voice rose with a slightly hysterical note in it. "You don't know what my life is like. I've been miserable with Lucius from the beginning. No woman could be happy with him. I wish he were dead ... It's awful, but I do ... I'm desperate. I tell you, I'm desperate." She started and looked over at the window.

"What was that? I thought I heard someone? Perhaps it's Lawrence."

I went over to the window which I had not closed as I had thought. I stepped out and looked down the garden, but there was no one in sight. Yet I was almost convinced that I, too, had heard someone. Or perhaps it was her certainty that had convinced me.

When I re-entered the room she was leaning forward, drooping her head down. She looked the picture of despair. She said again:

"I don't know what to do. I don't know what to do."

I came and sat down beside her. I said the things I thought it was my duty to say, and tried to say them with the necessary conviction, uneasily conscious all the time that that same morning I had given voice to the sentiment that a world without Colonel Protheroe in it would be improved for the better.

Above all, I begged her to do nothing rash. To leave her home and her husband was a very serious step.

I don't suppose I convinced her. I have lived long enough in the world to know that arguing with anyone in love is next door to useless, but I do think my words brought to her some measure of comfort.

When she rose to go, she thanked me, and promised to think over what I had said.

Nevertheless, when she had gone, I felt very uneasy. I felt that hitherto I had misjudged Anne Protheroe's character. She impressed me now as a very desperate woman, the kind of woman who would stick at nothing once her emotions were aroused. And she was desperately, wildly, madly in love with Lawrence Redding, a man several years younger than herself. I didn't like it.

4

I HAD ENTIRELY forgotten that we had asked Lawrence Redding to dinner that night. When Griselda burst in and scolded me, pointing out that it lacked two minutes to dinner time, I was quite taken aback.

"I hope everything will be all right," Griselda called up the stairs after me. "I've thought over what you said at lunch, and I've really thought of some quite good things to eat."

I may say, in passing, that our evening meal amply bore out Griselda's assertion that things went much worse when she tried than when she didn't. The menu was ambitious in conception, and Mary seemed to have taken a perverse pleasure in seeing how best she could alternate undercooking and overcooking. Some oysters which Griselda had ordered, and which would seem to be beyond the reach of incompetence, we were, unfortunately, not able to sample as we had nothing in the house to open them with—an omission which was discovered only when the moment for eating them arrived.

I had rather doubted whether Lawrence Redding would put in an appearance. He might very easily have sent an excuse.

However, he arrived punctually enough, and the four of us went in to dinner.

Lawrence Redding has an undeniably attractive personality. He is, I suppose, about thirty years of age. He has dark hair, but his eyes are of a brilliant, almost startling blue. He is the kind of young man who does everything well. He is good at games, an excellent shot, a good amateur actor, and can tell a first-rate story. He is capable of making any party go. He has, I think, Irish blood in his veins. He is not, at all, one's idea of the typical artist. Yet I believe he is a clever painter in the modern style. I know very little of painting myself.

It was only natural that on this particular evening he should appear a shade *distrait*. On the whole, he carried off things very well. I don't think Griselda or Dennis noticed anything wrong. Probably I should not have noticed anything myself if I had not known beforehand.

Griselda and Dennis were particularly gay—full of jokes about Dr. Stone and Miss Cram—the Local Scandal! It suddenly came home to me with something of a pang that Dennis is nearer Griselda's age than I am. He calls me Uncle Len, but her Griselda. It gave me, somehow, a lonely feeling.

I must, I think, have been upset by Mrs. Protheroe. I'm not usually given to such unprofitable reflections.

Griselda and Dennis went rather far now and then, but I hadn't the heart to check them. I have always thought it a pity that the mere presence of a clergyman should have a damping effect.

Lawrence took a gay part in the conversation. Nevertheless I was aware of his eyes continually straying to where I sat, and I was not surprised when after dinner he maneuvered to get me into the study.

As soon as we were alone his manner changed.

"You've surprised our secret, sir," he said. "What are you going to do about it?"

I could speak far more plainly to Redding than I could to Mrs. Protheroe, and I did so. He took it very well.

"Of course," he said, when I had finished, "you're bound to say all this. You're a parson. I don't mean that in any way offensively. As a matter of fact I think you're probably right. But this isn't the usual sort of thing between Anne and me."

I told him that people had been saying that particular phrase since the dawn of time, and a queer little smile creased his lips.

"You mean everyone thinks their case is unique? Perhaps so. But one thing you must believe."

He assured me that so far—"there was nothing wrong in it." Anne, he said, was one of the truest and most loyal women that ever lived. What was going to happen he didn't know.

"If this were only a book," he said gloomily, "the old man would die—and a good riddance to everybody."

I reproved him.

"Oh! I didn't mean I was going to stick him in the back with a knife, though I'd offer my best thanks to anyone else who did so. There's not a soul in the world who's got a good word to say for him. I rather wonder the first Mrs. Protheroe didn't do him in. I met her once, years ago, and she looked quite capable of it. One of those calm dangerous women. He goes blustering along, stirring up trouble everywhere, mean as the devil, and with a particularly nasty temper. You don't know what Anne has had to stand from him. If I had a penny in the world I'd take her away without any more ado."

Then I spoke to him very earnestly. I begged him to leave St. Mary Mead. By remaining there, he could only bring greater unhappiness on Anne Protheroe than was already her lot. People would talk, the matter would get to Colonel Protheroe's ears—and things would be made infinitely worse for her.

Lawrence protested.

"Nobody knows a thing about it except you, padre."

"My dear young man, you underestimate the detective instinct of village life. In St. Mary Mead everyone knows your most intimate affairs. There is no detective in England equal to a spinster lady of uncertain age with plenty of time on her hands."

He said easily that that was all right. Everyone thought it was Lettice.

"Has it occurred to you," I asked, "that possibly Lettice might think so herself?"

He seemed quite surprised by the idea. Lettice, he said, didn't care a hang about him. He was sure of that.

"She's a queer sort of girl," he said. "Always seems in a kind of dream, and yet underneath I believe she's really rather practical. I believe all that vague stuff is a pose. Lettice knows jolly well what she's doing. And there's a funny vindictive streak in her. The queer thing is that she hates Anne. Simply loathes her. And yet Anne's been a perfect angel to her always."

I did not, of course, take his word for this last. To infatuated young men, their inamorata always behaves like an angel. Still, to the best of my observation, Anne had always behaved to her stepdaughter with kindness and fairness. I had been surprised myself that afternoon at the bitterness of Lettice's tone.

We had to leave the conversation there, because Griselda and Dennis burst in upon us and said I was not to make Lawrence behave like an old fogy.

"Oh! dear," said Griselda, throwing herself into an arm-chair. "How I would like a thrill of some kind. A murder—or even a burglary."

"I don't suppose there's anyone much worth burgling," said Lawrence, trying to enter into her mood. "Unless we stole Miss Hartnell's false teeth."

"They do click horribly," said Griselda. "But you're wrong about there being no one worth while. There's some marvellous old silver at Old Hall. Trencher salts and a Charles II Tazza—all kinds of things like that. Worth thousands of pounds, I believe."

"The old man would probably shoot you with an army revolver," said Dennis. "Just the sort of thing he'd enjoy doing."

"Oh! we'd get in first and hold him up," said Griselda. "Who's got a revolver?"

"I've got a Mauser pistol," said Lawrence.

"Have you? How exciting. Why do you have it?"

"Souvenir of the war," said Lawrence briefly.

"Old Protheroe was showing the silver to Stone today," volunteered Dennis. "Old Stone was pretending to be no end interested in it."

"I thought they'd quarrelled about the barrow," said Griselda.

"Oh! they've made that up," said Dennis. "I can't think what people want to grub about in barrows for, anyway."

"That man Stone puzzles me," said Lawrence. "I think he must be very absent-minded. You'd swear sometimes he knew nothing about his own subject."

"That's love," said Dennis. "Sweet Gladys Cram, you are no sham. Your teeth are white and fill me with delight. Come, fly with me, my bride to be. And at the Blue Boar, on the bedroom floor—"

"That's enough, Dennis," I said.

"Well," said Lawrence Redding, "I must be off. Thank you very much, Mrs. Clement, for a very pleasant evening."

Griselda and Dennis saw him off. Dennis returned to the study alone. Something had happened to ruffle the boy. He wandered about the room aimlessly, frowning and kicking the furniture.

Our furniture is so shabby already that it can hardly be damaged further, but I felt impelled to utter a mild protest.

"Sorry," said Dennis.

He was silent for a moment and then burst out:

"What an absolutely rotten thing gossip is!"

I was a little surprised. "What's the matter?" I asked.

"I don't know whether I ought to tell you."

I was more and more surprised.

"It's such an absolutely rotten thing," Dennis said again. "Going round and saying things. Not even saying them. Hinting them. No, I'm damned— sorry—if I tell you! It's too absolutely rotten."

I looked at him curiously, but I did not press him further. I wondered very much, though. It is very unlike Dennis to take anything to heart.

Griselda came in at that moment.

"Miss Wetherby's just rung up," she said. "Mrs. Lestrange went out at a quarter-past eight and hasn't come in yet. Nobody knows where she's gone."

"Why should they know?"

"But it isn't to Dr. Haydock's. Miss Wetherby does know that, because she telephoned to Miss Hartnell who lives next door to him and who would have been sure to see her."

"It is a mystery to me," I said, "how anyone ever gets any nourishment in this place. They must eat their meals standing up by the window so as to be sure of not missing anything."

"And that's not all," said Griselda, bubbling with pleasure. "They've found out about the Blue Boar. Dr. Stone and Miss Cram have got rooms next door to each other, BUT"—she waved an impressive forefinger—"*no communicating door!*"

"That," I said, "must be very disappointing to everybody."

At which Griselda laughed.

Thursday started badly. Two of the ladies of my parish elected to quarrel about the church decorations. I was called in to adjudicate between two middle-aged ladies, each of whom was literally trembling with rage. If it had not been so painful, it would have been quite an interesting physical phenomenon.

Then I had to reprove two of our choirboys for persistent sweet-sucking during the hours of divine service, and I had an uneasy feeling that I was not doing the job as wholeheartedly as I should have done.

Then our organist, who is distinctly "touchy", had taken offense and had to be smoothed down.

And four of my poorer parishioners declared open rebellion against Miss Hartnell, who came to me bursting with rage about it.

I was just going home when I met Colonel Protheroe. He was in high good-humor, having sentenced three poachers, in his capacity as magistrate.

"Firmness," he shouted in his stentorian voice. He is slightly deaf and raises his voice accordingly as deaf people often do. "That's what's needed nowadays—firmness! Make an example. That rogue Archer came out yesterday and is vowing vengeance against me, I hear. Impudent scoundrel. Threatened men live long, as the saying goes. I'll show him what his vengeance is worth next time I catch him taking my pheasants. Lax! We're too lax nowadays! I believe in showing a man up for what he is. You're always being asked to consider a man's wife and children. Damned nonsense. Fiddlesticks. Why should a man escape the consequences of his acts just because he whines about his wife and children? It's all the same to me—no matter what a man is—doctor, lawyer, clergyman, poacher, drunken wastrel—if you catch him on the wrong side of the law, let the law punish him. You agree with me, I'm sure."

"You forget," I said. "My calling obliges me to respect one quality above all others—the quality of mercy."

"Well, I'm a just man. No one can deny that."

I did not speak, and he said sharply:

"Why don't you answer? A penny for your thoughts, man."

I hesitated, then I decided to speak.

"I was thinking," I said, "that when my time comes, I should be sorry if the only plea I had to offer was that of justice. Because it might mean that only justice would be meted out to me . . ."

"Pah! What we need is a little militant Christianity. I've always done my duty, I hope. Well, no more of that. I'll be along this evening, as I said. We'll make it a quarter-past six instead of six, if you don't mind. I've got to see a man in the village."

"That will suit me quite well."

He flourished his stick and strode away. Turning, I ran into Hawes. I thought he looked distinctly ill this morning. I had meant to upbraid him mildly for various matters in his province which had been muddled or shelved, but seeing his white strained face, I felt that the man was ill.

I said as much, and he denied it, but not very vehemently. Finally he confessed that he was not feeling too fit, and appeared ready to accept my advice of going home to bed.

I had a hurried lunch and went out to do some visits. Griselda had gone to London by the cheap Thursday train.

I came in about a quarter to four with the intention of sketching the outline of my Sunday sermon, but Mary told me that Mr. Redding was waiting for me in the study.

I found him pacing up and down with a worried face. He looked white and haggard.

He turned abruptly at my entrance.

"Look here, sir. I've been thinking over what you said yesterday. I've had a sleepless night thinking about it. You're right. I've got to cut and run."

"My dear boy," I said.

"You were right in what you said about Anne. I'll only bring trouble on her by staying here. She's—she's too good for anything else. I see I've got to go. I've made things hard enough for her as it is, Heaven help me."

"I think you have made the only decision possible," I said. "I know that it is a hard one, but believe me, it will be for the best in the end."

I could see that he thought that that was the kind of thing easily said by someone who didn't know what he was talking about.

"You'll look after Anne? She needs a friend."

"You can rest assured that I will do everything in my power."

"Thank you, sir." He wrung my hand. "You're a good sort, padre. I shall see her to say goodbye this evening, and I shall probably pack up and go tomorrow. No good prolonging the agony. Thanks for letting me have the shed to paint in. I'm sorry not to have finished Mrs. Clement's portrait."

"Don't worry about that, my dear boy. Goodbye, and God bless you."

When he had gone I tried to settle down to my sermon, but with very poor success. I kept thinking of Lawrence and Anne Protheroe.

I had rather an unpalatable cup of tea, cold and black, and at half-past five the telephone rang. I was informed that Mr. Abbott of Lower Farm was dying and would I please come at once.

I rang up Old Hall immediately, for Lower Farm was nearly two miles away and I could not possibly get back by six-fifteen. I have never succeeded in learning to ride a bicycle.

I was told, however, that Colonel Protheroe had just started out in the car, so I departed, leaving word with Mary that I had been called away, but would try to be back by six-thirty or soon after.

5

IT WAS NEARER seven than half-past six when I approached the Vicarage gate on my return. Before I reached it, it swung open and Lawrence Redding came out. He stopped dead on seeing me, and I was immediately struck by his appearance. He looked like a man who was on the point of going mad. His eyes stared in a peculiar manner, he was deathly white, and he was shaking and twitching all over.

I wondered for a moment whether he could have been drinking, but repudiated the idea immediately.

"Hullo," I said, "have you been to see me again? Sorry I was out. Come back now. I've got to see Protheroe about some accounts—but I dare say we shan't be long."

"Protheroe," he said. He began to laugh. "Protheroe? You're going to see Protheroe? Oh! you'll see Protheroe all right. Oh! my God—yes."

I stared. Instinctively I stretched out a hand towards him. He drew sharply aside.

"No," he almost cried out. "I've got to get away—to think. I've got to think. I must think."

He broke into a run and vanished rapidly down the road towards the village, leaving me staring after him, my first idea of drunkenness recurring.

Finally I shook my head, and went on to the Vicarage. The front door is always left open, but nevertheless I rang the bell. Mary came, wiping her hands on her apron.

"So you're back at last," she observed.

"Is Colonel Protheroe here?" I asked.

"In the study. Been here since a quarter past six."

"And Mr. Redding's been here?"

"Come a few minutes ago. Asked for you. I told him you'd be back any minute and that Colonel Protheroe was waiting in the study, and he said he'd wait too, and went there. He's there now."

"No, he isn't," I said. "I've just met him going down the road."

"Well, I didn't hear him leave. He can't have stayed more than a couple of minutes. The mistress isn't back from town yet."

I nodded absent-mindedly. Mary beat a retreat to the kitchen quarters and I went down the passage and opened the study door.

After the dusk of the passage, the evening sunshine that was pouring into the room made my eyes blink. I took a step or two across the floor and then stopped dead.

For a moment I could hardly take in the meaning of the scene before me.

Colonel Protheroe was lying sprawled across my writing-table in a horrible unnatural position. There was a pool of some dark fluid on the desk by his head, and it was slowly dripping on to the floor with a horrible drip, drip, drip.

I pulled myself together and went across to him. His skin was cold to the touch. The hand that I raised fell back lifeless. The man was dead—shot through the head.

I went to the door and called Mary. When she came I ordered her to run as fast as she could and fetch Dr. Haydock, who lives just at the corner of the road. I told her there had been an accident.

Then I went back and closed the door to await the doctor's coming.

Fortunately, Mary found him at home. Haydock is a good fellow, a big, fine, strapping man with an honest, rugged face.

His eyebrows went up when I pointed silently across the room. But, like a true doctor, he showed no signs of emotion. He bent over the dead man, examining him rapidly. Then he straightened himself and looked across at me.

"Well?" I asked.

"He's dead right enough—been dead half an hour, I should say."

"Suicide?"

"Out of the question, man. Look at the position of the wound. Besides, if he shot himself, where's the weapon?"

True enough, there was no sign of any such thing.

"We'd better not mess around with anything," said Haydock. "I'd better ring up the police."

He picked up the receiver and spoke into it. He gave the facts as curtly as possible and then replaced the telephone and came across to where I was sitting.

"This is a rotten business. How did you come to find him?"

I explained. "Is—is it murder?" I asked rather faintly.

"Looks like it. Mean to say, what else can it be? Extraordinary business. Wonder who had a down on the poor old fellow. Of course I know he wasn't popular, but one isn't often murdered for that reason—worse luck."

"There's one rather curious thing," I said. "I was telephoned for this afternoon to go to a dying parishioner. When I got there everyone was very surprised to see me. The sick man was very much better than he had been for some days, and his wife flatly denied telephoning for me at all."

Haydock drew his brows together.

"That's suggestive—very. You were being got out of the way. Where's your wife?"

"Gone up to London for the day."

"And the maid?"

"In the kitchen—right at the other side of the house."

"Where she wouldn't be likely to hear anything that went on in here. It's a nasty business. Who knew that Protheroe was coming here this evening?"

"He referred to the fact this morning in the village street at the top of his voice as usual."

"Meaning that the whole village knew it? Which they always do in any case. Know of anyone who had a grudge against him?"

The thought of Lawrence Redding's white face and staring eyes came to my mind. I was spared answering by a noise of shuffling feet in the passage outside.

"The police," said my friend, and rose to his feet.

Our police force was represented by Constable Hurst, looking very important but slightly worried.

"Good evening, gentlemen," he greeted us. "The Inspector will be here any minute. In the meantime I'll follow out his instructions. I understand Colonel Protheroe's been found shot—in the Vicarage."

He paused and directed a look of cold suspicion at me, which I tried to meet with a suitable bearing of conscious innocence.

He moved over to the writing-table and announced:

"Nothing to be touched until the Inspector comes."

For the convenience of my readers I append a sketch plan of the room.

He got out his notebook, moistened his pencil and looked expectantly at both of us.

I repeated my story of discovering the body. When he had got it all down, which took some time, he turned to the doctor.

"In your opinion, Dr. Haydock, what was the cause of death?"

"Shot through the head at close quarters."

"And the weapon?"

"I can't say with certainty until we get the bullet out. But I should say in all probability the bullet was fired from a pistol of small caliber—say a Mauser .25."

I started, remembering our conversation of the night before, and Lawrence Redding's admission. The police constable brought his cold, fish-like eye round on me.

"Did you speak, sir?"

I shook my head. Whatever suspicions I might have, they were no more than suspicions, and as such to be kept to myself.

"When, in your opinion, did the tragedy occur?"

The doctor hesitated for a minute before he answered. Then he said:

"The man has been dead just over half an hour, I should say. Certainly not longer."

Hurst turned to me. "Did the girl hear anything?"

"As far as I know she heard nothing," I said. "But you had better ask her."

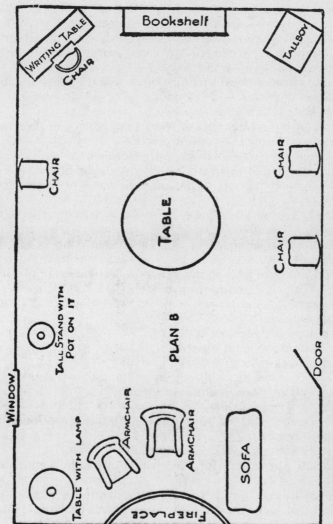

PLAN B

But at this moment Inspector Slack arrived, having come by car from Much Benham, two miles away.

All that I can say of Inspector Slack is that never did a man more determinedly strive to contradict his name. He was a dark man, restless and energetic in manner, with black eyes that snapped ceaselessly. His manner was rude and overbearing in the extreme.

He acknowledged our greetings with a curt nod, seized his subordinate's note-book, perused it, exchanged a few curt words with him in an undertone, then strode over to the body.

"Everything's been messed up and pulled about, I suppose," he said.

"I've touched nothing," said Haydock.

"No more have I," I said.

The Inspector busied himself for some time peering at the things on the table and examining the pool of blood.

"Ah!" he said in a tone of triumph. "Here's what we want. Clock overturned when he fell forward. That'll give us the time of the crime. Twenty-two minutes past six. What time did you say death occurred, doctor?"

"I said about half an hour, but—"

The inspector consulted his watch.

"Five minutes past seven. I got word about ten minutes ago, at five minutes to seven. Discovery of the body was at about a quarter to seven. I understand you were fetched immediately. Say you examined it at ten minutes to—Why, that brings it to the identical second almost!"

"I don't guarantee the time absolutely," said Haydock. "That is an approximate estimate."

"Good enough, sir, good enough."

I had been trying to get a word in.

"About that clock—"

"If you'll excuse me, sir, I'll ask you any questions I want to know. Time's short. What I want is absolute silence."

"Yes, but I'd like to tell you—"

"Absolute silence," said the inspector, glaring at me ferociously. I gave him what he asked for.

He was still peering about the writing-table.

"What was he sitting here for," he grunted. "Did he want to write a note—Hallo—what's this?"

He held up a piece of note-paper triumphantly. So pleased was he with his find that he permitted us to come to his side and examine it with him.

It was a piece of Vicarage note-paper, and it was headed at the top 6:20.

DEAR CLEMENT—it began
    Sorry I cannot wait any longer, but I must . . .

Here the writing tailed off in a scrawl.

"Plain as a pikestaff," said Inspector Slack triumphantly. "He sits down here to write this, an enemy comes softly in through the window and shoots him as he writes. What more do you want?"

"I'd just like to say—" I began.

"Out of the way, if you please, sir. I want to see if there are footprints."

He went down on his hands and knees, moving towards the open window.

"I think you ought to know—" I said obstinately.

The Inspector rose. He spoke without heat, but firmly.

"We'll go into all that later. I'd be obliged if you gentlemen will clear out of here. Right out, if you please."

We permitted ourselves to be shooed out like children.

Hours seemed to have passed—yet it was only a quarter-past seven.

"Well," said Haydock. "That's that. When that conceited ass wants me, you can send him over to the surgery. So long."

"The mistress is back," said Mary, making a brief appearance from the kitchen. Her eyes were round and agog with excitement. "Come in about five minutes ago."

I found Griselda in the drawing-room. She looked frightened, but excited.

I told her everything and she listened attentively.

"The letter is headed 6:20," I ended. "And the clock fell over and has stopped at 6:22."

"Yes," said Griselda. "But that clock, didn't you tell him that it was always kept a quarter of an hour fast?"

"No," I said. "I didn't. He wouldn't let me. I tried my best." Griselda was frowning in a puzzled manner.

"But, Len," she said, "that makes the whole thing perfectly extraordinary. Because when that clock said twenty past six it was really only five minutes past, and at five minutes past I don't suppose Colonel Protheroe had even arrived at the house."

6

WE PUZZLED OVER the business of the clock for some time, but we could make nothing of it. Griselda said I ought to make another effort to tell Inspector Slack about it, but on that point I was feeling what I can only describe as "mulish".

Inspector Slack had been abominably and most unnecessarily rude. I was looking forward to a moment when I could produce my valuable contribution and effect his discomfiture. I would then say in a tone of mild reproach:

"If you had only listened to me, Inspector Slack—"

I expected that he would at least speak to me before he left the house, but to our surprise we learned from Mary that he had departed, having locked up the study door and issued orders that no one was to attempt to enter the room.

Griselda suggested going up to Old Hall.

"It will be so awful for Anne Protheroe—with the police and everything," she said. "Perhaps I might be able to do something for her."

I cordially approved of this plan, and Griselda set off with instructions that she was to telephone to me if she thought that I could be of any use or comfort to either of the ladies.

I now proceeded to ring up the Sunday School teachers, who were coming at 7:45 for their weekly preparation class. I thought that under the circumstances it would be better to put them off.

Dennis was the next person to arrive on the scene, having just returned from a tennis party. The fact that murder had taken place at the Vicarage seemed to afford him acute satisfaction.

"Fancy being right on the spot in a murder case," he exclaimed. "I've always wanted to be right in the midst of one. Why have the police locked up the study? Wouldn't one of the other door keys fit it?"

I refused to allow anything of the sort to be attempted. Dennis gave in with a bad grace. After extracting every possible detail from me he went out into the garden to look for footprints, remarking cheerfully that it was lucky it was only old Protheroe, whom everyone disliked.

His cheerful callousness rather grated on me, but I reflected that I was perhaps being hard on the boy. At Dennis's age a detective story is one of the best things in life, and to find a real detective story, complete with corpse, waiting on one's own front doorstep, so to speak, is bound to send a healthy-minded boy into the seventh heaven of enjoyment. Death means very little to a boy of sixteen.

Griselda came back in about an hour's time. She had seen Anne Protheroe, having arrived just after the Inspector had broken the news to her.

On hearing that Mrs. Protheroe had last seen her husband in the village about a quarter to six, and that she had no light of any kind to throw upon the matter, he had taken his departure, explaining that he would return on the morrow for a fuller interview.

"He was quite decent in his way," said Griselda grudgingly.

"How did Mrs. Protheroe take it?" I asked.

"Well—she was very quiet—but then she always is."

"Yes," I said. "I can't imagine Anne Protheroe going into hysterics."

"Of course it was a great shock. You could see that. She thanked me for coming and said she was very grateful but that there was nothing I could do."

"What about Lettice?"

"She was out playing tennis somewhere. She hadn't got home yet." There was a pause, and then Griselda said:

"You know, Len, she was really very queer—very queer indeed."

"The shock," I suggested.

"Yes—I suppose so. And yet—" Griselda furrowed her brows perplexedly. "It wasn't like that, somehow. She didn't seem so much bowled over as—well—terrified."

"Terrified?"

"Yes—not showing it, you know. At least not meaning to show it. But a queer watchful look in her eyes. I wonder if she has a sort of idea who did kill him. She asked again and again if anyone were suspected."

"Did she?" I said thoughtfully.

"Yes. Of course Anne's got marvelous self-control, but one could see that she was terribly upset. More so than I would have thought, for after all it wasn't as though she were so devoted to him. I should have said she rather disliked him, if anything."

"Death alters one's feelings sometimes," I said.

"Yes, I suppose so."

Dennis came in and was full of excitement over a footprint he had found in one of the flower beds. He was sure that the police had overlooked it and that it would turn out to be the turning point of the mystery.

I spent a troubled night. Dennis was up and about and out of the house long before breakfast to "study the latest developments", as he said.

Nevertheless it was not he, but Mary, who brought us the morning's sensational bit of news.

We had just sat down to breakfast when she burst into the room, her cheeks red and her eyes shining, and addressed us with her customary lack of ceremony.

"Would you believe it? The baker's just told me. They've arrested young Mr. Redding."

"Arrested Lawrence," cried Griselda incredulously. "Impossible. It must be some stupid mistake."

"No mistake about it, mum," said Mary with a kind of gloating exultation. "Mr. Redding, he went there himself and gave himself up. Last night, last thing. Went right in, threw down the pistol on the table, and 'I did it', he says. Just like that."

She looked at us both, nodded her head vigorously, and withdrew, satisfied with the effect she had produced. Griselda and I stared at each other.

"Oh! it isn't true," said Griselda. "It *can't* be true."

She noticed my silence, and said: "Len, *you* don't think it's true?"

I found it hard to answer her. I sat silent, thoughts whirling through my head.

"He must be mad," said Griselda. "Absolutely mad. Or do you think they were looking at the pistol together and it suddenly went off?"

"That doesn't sound at all a likely thing to happen."

"But it must have been an accident of some kind. Because there's not a shadow of a motive. What earthly reason could Lawrence have for killing Colonel Protheroe?"

I could have answered that question very decidedly, but I wished to spare Anne Protheroe as far as possible. There might still be a chance of keeping her name out of it.

"Remember they had had a quarrel," I said.

"About Lettice and her bathing dress. Yes, but that's absurd; and even if he and Lettice were engaged secretly—well, that's not a reason for killing her father."

"We don't know what the true facts of the case may be, Griselda."

"You *do* believe it, Len! Oh! how can you! I tell you, I'm *sure* Lawrence never touched a hair of his head."

"Remember, I met him just outside the gate. He looked like a madman."

"Yes, but—oh! it's impossible."

"There's the clock, too," I said. "This explains the clock. Lawrence must have put it back to 6:20 with the idea of making an alibi for himself. Look how Inspector Slack fell into the trap."

"You're wrong, Len. Lawrence knew about that clock being fast. 'Keeping the vicar up to time!' he used to say. Lawrence would never have made the mistake of putting it back to 6:22. He'd have put the hands somewhere possible—like a quarter to seven."

"He mayn't have known what time Protheroe got here. Or he may have simply forgotten about the clock being fast."

Griselda disagreed.

"No, if you were committing a murder, you'd be awfully careful about things like that."

"You don't know, my dear," I said mildly. "You've never done one."

Before Griselda could reply, a shadow fell across the breakfast table, and a very gentle voice said:

"I hope I am not intruding. You must forgive me. But in the sad circumstances—the very sad circumstances—"

It was our neighbor, Miss Marple. Accepting our polite disclaimers, she stepped in through the window, and I drew up a chair for her. She looked faintly flushed and quite excited.

"Very terrible, is it not? Poor Colonel Protheroe. Not a very pleasant man, perhaps, and not exactly popular, but it's none the less sad for that. And actually shot in the Vicarage study, I understand?"

I said that that had indeed been the case.

"But the dear vicar was not here at the time?" Miss Marple questioned of Griselda. I explained where I had been.

"Mr. Dennis is not with you this morning?" said Miss Marple, glancing round.

"Dennis," said Griselda, "fancies himself as an amateur detective. He is very excited about a footprint he found in one of the flower beds, and I fancy has gone off to tell the police about it."

"Dear, dear," said Miss Marple. "Such a to-do, is it not? And Mr. Dennis thinks he knows who committed the crime. Well, I suppose we all think we know."

"You mean it is obvious?" said Griselda.

"No, dear, I didn't mean that at all. I dare say everyone thinks it is somebody different. That is why it is so important to have *proofs*. I, for instance, am quite *convinced* I know who did it. But I must admit I haven't one shadow of proof. One must, I know, be very careful of what one says at a time like this—criminal libel, don't they call it? I had made up my mind to be *most* careful with Inspector Slack. He sent word he would come and see me this morning, but now he has just phoned up to say it won't be necessary after all."

"I suppose, since the arrest, it isn't necessary," I said.

"The arrest?" Miss Marple leaned forward, her cheeks pink with excitement. "I didn't know there had been an arrest."

It is so seldom that Miss Marple is worse informed than we are that I had taken it for granted that she would know the latest developments.

"It seems we have been talking at cross purposes," I said. "Yes, there has been an arrest—Lawrence Redding."

"Lawrence Redding?" Miss Marple seemed very surprised. "Now I should not have thought—"

Griselda interrupted vehemently.

"I can't believe it even now. No, not though he has actually confessed."

"Confessed?" said Miss Marple. "You say he has confessed? Oh! dear, I see I have been sadly at sea—yes, sadly at sea."

"I can't help feeling it must have been some kind of an accident," said Griselda. "Don't you think so, Len? I mean his coming forward to give himself up looks like that."

Miss Marple leaned forward eagerly.

"He gave himself up, you say?"

"Yes."

"Oh!" said Miss Marple, with a deep sigh. "I am so glad—so very glad."

I looked at her in some surprise.

"It shows a true state of remorse, I suppose," I said.

"Remorse?" Miss Marple looked very surprised. "Oh! but surely, dear, dear vicar, you don't think that he is guilty?"

It was my turn to stare.

"But since he has confessed—"

"Yes, but that just proves it, doesn't it? I mean that he had nothing to do with it."

"No," I said. "I may be dense, but I can't see that it does. If you have not committed a murder, I cannot see the object of pretending you have."

"Oh! of course, there's a reason," said Miss Marple. "Naturally. There's always a reason, isn't there? And young men are so hot-headed and often prone to believe the worst."

She turned to Griselda.

"Don't you agree with me, my dear?"

"I—I don't know," said Griselda. "It's difficult to know what to think. I can't see any reason for Lawrence behaving like a perfect idiot."

"If you had seen his face last night—" I began.

"Tell me," said Miss Marple.

I described my homecoming while she listened attentively.

When I had finished she said:

"I know that I am very often rather foolish and don't take in things as I should, but I really do not see your point.

"It seems to me that if a young man had made up his mind to the great wickedness of taking a fellow creature's life, he would not appear distraught about it afterwards. It would be a premeditated and cold-blooded action and though the murderer might be a little flurried and possibly might make some small mistake, I do not think it likely he would fall into a state of agitation such as you describe. It is difficult to put oneself in such a position, but I cannot imagine getting into a state like that myself."

"We don't know the circumstances," I argued. "If there was a quarrel, the shot may have been fired in a sudden burst of passion, and Lawrence might afterwards have been appalled at what he had done. Indeed, I prefer to think that that is what did actually occur."

"I know, dear Mr. Clement, that there are many ways we prefer to look at things. But one must actually take facts as they are, must one not? And it does not seem to me that the facts bear the interpretation you put upon them. Your maid distinctly stated that Mr. Redding was only in the house a couple of minutes, not long enough, surely, for a quarrel such as you describe. And then again, I understand the colonel was shot through the back of the head while he was writing a letter—at least that is what my maid told me."

"Quite true," said Griselda. "He seems to have been writing a note to say he couldn't wait any longer. The note was dated 6:20, and the clock on the table was overturned and had stopped at 6:22, and that's just what has been puzzling Len and myself so frightfully."

She explained our custom of keeping the clock a quarter of an hour fast.

"Very curious," said Miss Marple. "Very curious indeed. But the note seems to me even more curious still. I mean—"

She stopped and looked round. Lettice Protheroe was standing outside the window. She came in, nodding to us and murmuring "Morning".

She dropped into a chair and said, with rather more animation than usual:

"They've arrested Lawrence, I hear."

"Yes." said Griselda. "It's been a great shock to us."

"I never really thought anyone would murder father," said Lettice. She was obviously taking a pride in letting no hint of distress or emotion escape her. "Lots of people wanted to, I'm sure. There are times when I'd have liked to do it myself."

"Won't you have something to eat or drink, Lettice?" asked Griselda.

"No, thank you. I just drifted round to see if you'd got my beret here—a queer little yellow one. I think I left it in the study the other day."

"If you did, it's there still," said Griselda. "Mary never tidies anything."

"I'll go and see," said Lettice, rising. "Sorry to be such a bother, but I seem to have lost everything else in the hat line."

"I'm afraid you can't get it now," I said. "Inspector Slack has locked the room up."

"Oh! what a bore. Can't we get in through the window?"

"I'm afraid not. It is latched on the inside. Surely, Lettice, a yellow beret won't be much good to you at present?"

"You mean mourning and all that? I shan't bother about mourning. I think it's an awfully archaic idea. It's a nuisance about Lawrence—yes, it's a nuisance."

She got up and stood frowning abstractedly.

"I suppose it's all on account of me and my bathing dress. So silly, the whole thing . . ."

Griselda opened her mouth to say something, but for some unexplained reason shut it again.

A curious smile came to Lettice's lips.

"I think," she said softly, "I'll go home and tell Anne about Lawrence being arrested."

She went out of the window again. Griselda turned to Miss Marple. "Why did you step on my foot?"

The old lady was smiling.

"I thought you were going to say something, my dear. And it is often so much better to let things develop on their own lines. I don't think, you know, that that child is half so vague as she pretends to be. She's got a very definite idea in her head and she's acting upon it."

Mary gave a loud knock on the dining-room door and entered hard upon it.

"What is it?" said Griselda. "And Mary, you must remember not to knock on doors. I've told you about it before."

"Thought you might be busy," said Mary. "Colonel Melchett's here. Wants to see the master."

Colonel Melchett is Chief Constable of the county. I rose at once.

"I thought you wouldn't like my leaving him in the hall, so I put him in the drawing-room," went on Mary. "Shall I clear?"

"Not yet," said Griselda. "I'll ring."

She turned to Miss Marple and I left the room.

7

COLONEL MELCHETT IS a dapper little man with a habit of snorting suddenly and unexpectedly. He has red hair and rather keen bright blue eyes.

"Good morning, vicar," he said. "Nasty business, eh? Poor old Protheroe. Not that I liked him. I didn't. Nobody did, for that matter. Nasty bit of work for you, too. Hope it hasn't upset your missus?"

I said Griselda had taken it very well.

"That's lucky. Rotten thing to happen in one's house. I must say I'm surprised at young Redding—doing it the way he did. No sort of consideration for anyone's feelings."

A wild desire to laugh came over me, but Colonel Melchett evidently saw nothing odd in the idea of a murderer being considerate, so I held my peace.

"I must say I was rather taken aback when I heard the fellow had marched in and given himself up," continued Colonel Melchett, dropping on to a chair.

"How did it happen exactly?"

"Last night. About ten o'clock. Fellow rolls in, throws down a pistol, and says: 'Here I am. I did it.' Just like that."

"What account does he give of the business?'

"Precious little. He was warned, of course, about making a statement. But he merely laughed. Said he came here to see you—found Protheroe here. They had words and he shot him. Won't say what the quarrel was about. Look here, Clement—just between you and me, do you know anything about it? I've heard rumors—about his being forbidden the house and all that. What was it—did he seduce the daughter, or what? We don't want to bring the girl into it more than we can help for everybody's sake. Was that the trouble?"

"No," I said. "You can take it from me that it was something quite different, but I can't say more at the present juncture."

He nodded and rose.

"I'm glad to know. There's a lot of talk. Too many women in this part of the world. Well, I must get along. I've got to see Haydock. He was called out to some case or other, but he ought to be back by now. I don't mind telling you I'm sorry about Redding. He always struck me as a decent young chap. Perhaps they'll think out some kind of defence for him. After-effects of war, shell shock, or something. Especially if no very adequate motive turns up. I must be off. Like to come along?"

I said I would like to very much, and we went out together.

Haydock's house is next door to mine. His servant said the doctor had just come in and showed us into the dining-room, where Haydock was sitting down to a steaming plate of eggs and bacon. He greeted me with an amiable nod.

"Sorry I had to go out. Confinement case. I've been up most of the night, over your business. I've got the bullet for you."

He shoved a little box along the table. Melchett examined it.

"Point two five?"

Haydock nodded.

"I'll keep the technical details for the inquest," he said. "All you want to know is that death was practically instantaneous. Silly young fool, what did he want to do it for? Amazing, by the way, that nobody heard the shot."

"Yes," said Melchett, "that surprises me."

"The kitchen window gives on the other side of the house," I said. "With the study door, the pantry door, and the kitchen door all shut, I doubt if you would hear anything, and there was no one but the maid in the house."

"H'm," said Melchett. "It's odd, all the same. I wonder the old lady—what's her name—Marple, didn't hear it. The study window was open."

"Perhaps she did," said Haydock.

"I don't think she did," said I. "She was over at the Vicarage just now and she didn't mention anything of the kind which I'm certain she would have done if there had been anything to tell."

"May have heard it and paid no attention to it—thought it was a car back-firing."

It struck me that Haydock was looking much more jovial and good-humored this morning. He seemed like a man who was decorously trying to subdue unusually good spirits.

"Or what about a silencer?" he added. "That's quite likely. Nobody would hear anything then."

Melchett shook his head.

"Slack didn't find anything of the kind, and he asked Redding, and Redding didn't seem to know what he was talking about at first and then denied point blank using anything of the kind. And I suppose one can take his word for it."

"Yes, indeed, poor devil."

"Damned young fool," said Colonel Melchett. "Sorry, Clement. But he really is! Somehow one can't get used to thinking of him as a murderer."

"Any motive?" asked Haydock, taking a final draught of coffee and pushing back his chair.

"He says they quarrelled and he lost his temper and shot him."

"Hoping for manslaughter, eh?" The doctor shook his head. "That story doesn't hold water. He stole up behind him as he was writing and shot him through the head. Precious little 'quarrel' about that."

"Anyway, there wouldn't have been time for a quarrel," I said, remembering Miss Marple's words. "To creep up, shoot him, alter the clock hands back to 6:20, and leave again would have taken him all his time. I shall never forget his face when I met him outside the gate, or the way he said, 'You want to see Protheroe—oh! you'll see him all right!' That in itself ought to have made me suspicious of what had just taken place a few minutes before."

Haydock stared at me.

"What do you mean—what had just taken place? When do you think Redding shot him?"

"A few minutes before I got to the house."

The doctor shook his head.

"Impossible. Plumb impossible. He'd been dead much longer than that."

"But, my dear man," cried Colonel Melchett, "you said yourself that half an hour was only an approximate estimate."

"Half an hour, thirty-five minutes, twenty-five minutes, twenty minutes—possibly, but less, no. Why, the body would have been warm when I got to it."

We stared at each other. Haydock's face had changed. It had gone suddenly grey and old. I wondered at the change in him.

"But, look here, Haydock." The colonel found his voice. "If Redding admits shooting him at a quarter to seven—"

Haydock sprang to his feet.

"I tell you it's impossible," he roared. "If Redding says he killed Protheroe at a quarter to seven, then Redding lies. Hang it all, I tell you I'm a doctor, and I know. The blood had begun to congeal."

"If Redding is lying," began Melchett. He stopped, shook his head.

"We'd better go down to the police station and see him," he said.

8

WE WERE RATHER silent on our way down to the police station. Haydock drew behind a little and murmured to me:

"You know I don't like the look of this. I don't like it. There's something here we don't understand."

He looked thoroughly worried and upset.

Inspector Slack was at the police station and presently we found ourselves face to face with Lawrence Redding.

He looked pale and strained but quite composed—marvelously so, I thought, considering the circumstances. Melchett snorted and hummed, obviously nervous.

"Look here, Redding," he said, "I understand you made a statement to Inspector Slack here. You state you went to the Vicarage at approximately a quarter to seven, found Protheroe there, quarrelled with him, shot him, and came away. I'm not reading it over to you, but that's the gist of it."

"Yes."

"I'm going to ask a few questions. You've already been told that you needn't answer them unless you choose. Your solicitor—"

Lawrence interrupted.

"I've nothing to hide. I killed Protheroe."

"Ah! well—" Melchett snorted. "How did you happen to have a pistol with you?"

Lawrence hesitated. "It was in my pocket."

"You took it with you to the Vicarage?"

"Yes."

"Why?"

"I always take it."

He had hesitated again before answering, and I was absolutely sure that he was not speaking the truth.

"Why did you put the clock back?"

"The clock?" He seemed puzzled.

"Yes, the hands pointed to 6:22."

A look of fear sprang up in his face.

"Oh! that—yes. I—I altered it."

Haydock spoke suddenly.

"Where did you shoot Colonel Protheroe?"

"In the study at the Vicarage."

"I mean in what part of the body?"

"Oh!—I—through the head, I think. Yes, through the head."

"Aren't you sure?"

"Since you know, I can't see why it is necessary to ask me."

It was a feeble kind of bluster. There was some commotion outside. A constable without a helmet brought in a note.

"For the vicar. It says very urgent on it."

I tore it open and read:

Please—please—come to me. I don't know what to do. It is all too awful. I want to tell someone. Please come immediately, and bring anyone you like with you—

ANNE PROTHEROE.

I gave Melchett a meaning glance. He took the hint. We all went out together. Glancing over my shoulder, I had a glimpse of Lawrence Redding's face. His eyes were riveted on the paper in my hand, and I have hardly ever seen such a terrible look of anguish and despair in any human being's face.

I remembered Anne Protheroe sitting on my sofa and saying: "I'm a desperate woman," and my heart grew heavy within me. I saw now the possible reason for Lawrence Redding's heroic self-accusation. Melchett was speaking to Slack.

"Have you got any line on Redding's movements earlier in the day? There's some reason to think he shot Protheroe earlier than he says. Get on to it, will you?"

He turned to me and without a word I handed him Anne Protheroe's letter. He read it and pursed up his lips in astonishment. Then he looked at me inquiringly.

"Is this what you were hinting at this morning?"

"Yes. I was not sure then if it was my duty to speak. I am quite sure now." And I told him of what I had seen that night in the studio.

The colonel had a few words with the inspector and then we set off for Old Hall. Dr. Haydock came with us.

A very correct butler opened the door, with just the right amount of gloom in his bearing.

"Good morning," said Melchett. "Will you ask Mrs. Protheroe's maid to tell her we are here and would like to see her, and then return here and answer a few questions."

The butler hurried away and presently returned with the news that he had despatched the message.

"Now let's hear something about yesterday," said Colonel Melchett. "Your master was in to lunch?"

"Yes, sir."

"And in his usual spirits?"

"As far as I could see, yes, sir."

"What happened after that?"

"After luncheon Mrs. Protheroe went to lie down and the colonel went to his study. Miss Lettice went out to a tennis party in the two-seater. Colonel and Mrs. Protheroe had tea at four-thirty, in the drawing-room. The car was ordered for five-thirty to take them to the village. Immediately after they had left Mr. Clement rang up"—he bowed to me—"I told him they had started."

"H'm," said Colonel Melchett. "When was Mr. Redding last here?"

"On Tuesday afternoon, sir."

"I understand that there was a disagreement between them?"

"I believe so, sir. The colonel gave me orders that Mr. Redding was not to be admitted in future."

"Did you overhear the quarrel at all?" asked Colonel Melchett bluntly.

"Colonel Protheroe, sir, had a very loud voice, especially when it was raised in anger. I was unable to help overhearing a few words here and there."

"Enough to tell you the cause of the dispute?"

"I understood, sir, that it had to do with a portrait Mr. Redding had been painting—a portrait of Miss Lettice."

Melchett grunted.

"Did you see Mr. Redding when he left?"

"Yes, sir, I let him out."

"Did he seem angry?"

"No, sir; if I may say so, he seemed rather amused."

"Ah! He didn't come to the house yesterday?"

"No, sir."

"Anyone else come?"

"Not yesterday, sir."

"Well, the day before?"

"Mr. Dennis Clement came in the afternoon. And Dr. Stone was here for some time. And there was a lady in the evening."

"A lady?" Melchett was surprised. "Who was she?"

The butler couldn't remember her name. It was a lady he had not seen before. Yes, she had given her name, and when he told her that the family were at dinner, she had said that she would wait. So he had shown her into the little morning-room.

She had asked for Colonel Protheroe, not Mrs. Protheroe. He had told the colonel and the colonel had gone to the morning-room directly dinner was over.

How long had the lady stayed? He thought about half an hour. The colonel himself had let her out. Ah! yes, he remembered her name now. The lady had been a Mrs. Lestrange.

This was a surprise.

"Curious," said Melchett. "Really very curious."

But we pursued the matter no further, for at that moment a message came that Mrs. Protheroe would see us.

Anne was in bed. Her face was pale and her eyes very bright. There was a look on her face that puzzled me—a kind of grim determination. She spoke to me.

"Thank you for coming so promptly," she said. "I see you've understood what I meant by bringing anyone you liked with you." She paused.

"It's best to get it over quickly, isn't it?" she said. She gave a queer, half-pathetic little smile. "I suppose you're the person I ought to say it to, Colonel Melchett. You see, it was I who killed my husband."

Colonel Melchett said gently:

"My dear Mrs. Protheroe—"

"Oh! it's quite true. I suppose I've said it rather bluntly, but I never can go into hysterics over anything. I've hated him for a long time, and yesterday I shot him."

She lay back on the pillows and closed her eyes.

"That's all. I suppose you'll arrest me and take me away. I'll get up and dress as soon as I can. At the moment I am feeling rather sick."

"Are you aware, Mrs. Protheroe, that Mr. Lawrence Redding has already accused himself of committing the crime?"

Anne opened her eyes and nodded brightly.

"I know. Silly boy. He's very much in love with me, you know. It was frightfully noble of him—but very silly."

"He knew that it was you who had committed the crime?"

"Yes."

"How did he know?"

She hesitated.

"Did you tell him?"

Still she hesitated. Then at last she seemed to make up her mind.

"Yes—I told him . . ."

She twitched her shoulders with a movement of irritation.

"Can't you go away now? I've told you. I don't want to talk about it any more."

"Where did you get the pistol, Mrs. Protheroe?"

"The pistol! Oh! it was my husband's. I got it out of the drawer of his dressing-table."

"I see. And you took it with you to the Vicarage?"

"Yes. I knew he would be there—"

"What time was this?"

"It must have been after six—quarter—twenty past—something like that."

"You took the pistol meaning to shoot your husband?"

"No—I—I meant it for myself."

"I see. But you went to the Vicarage?"

"Yes. I went along to the window. There were no voices. I looked in. I saw my husband. Something came over me—and I fired."

"And then?"

"Then? Oh! then I went away."

"And told Mr. Redding what you had done?"

Again I noticed the hesitation in her voice before she said "Yes."

"Did anybody see you entering or leaving the Vicarage?"

"No—at least, yes. Old Miss Marple. I talked to her a few minutes. She was in her garden."

She moved restlessly on the pillows.

"Isn't that enough? I've told you. Why do you want to go on bothering me?"

Dr. Haydock moved to her side and felt her pulse.

He beckoned to Melchett.

"I'll stay with her," he said in a whisper, "whilst you make the necessary arrangements. She oughtn't to be left. Might do herself a mischief."

Melchett nodded.

We left the room and descended the stairs. I saw a thin, cadaverous-looking man come out of the adjoining room and on impulse I remounted the stairs.

"Are you Colonel Protheroe's valet?"

The man looked surprised. "Yes, sir."

"Do you know whether your late master kept a pistol anywhere?"

"Not that I know of, sir."

"Not in one of the drawers of his dressing-table? Think, man."

The valet shook his head decisively.

"I'm quite sure he didn't, sir. I'd have seen it if so. Bound to."

I hurried down the stairs after the others.

Mrs. Protheroe had lied about the pistol.

Why?

9

AFTER LEAVING A message at the police station, the Chief Constable announced his intention of paying a visit to Miss Marple.

"You'd better come with me, vicar," he said. "I don't want to give a member of your flock hysterics. So lend the weight of your soothing presence."

I smiled. For all her fragile appearance, Miss Marple is capable of holding her own with any policeman or Chief Constable in existence.

"What's she like?" asked the colonel, as we rang the bell. "Anything she says to be depended upon or otherwise?"

I considered the matter.

"I think she is quite dependable," I said cautiously. "That is, in so far as she is talking of what she has actually seen. Beyond that, of course, when you get on to what she thinks—well, that is another matter. She has a powerful imagination and systematically thinks the worst of everyone."

"The typical elderly spinster, in fact," said Melchett, with a laugh. "Well, I ought to know the breed by now. Gad, the tea parties down here!"

We were admitted by a very diminutive maid and shown into a small drawing-room.

"A bit crowded," said Colonel Melchett, looking round. "But plenty of good stuff. A lady's room, eh, Clement?"

I agreed, and at that moment the door opened and Miss Marple made her appearance.

"Very sorry to bother you, Miss Marple," said the colonel, when I had introduced him, putting on his bluff military manner which he had an idea was attractive to elderly ladies. "Got to do my duty, you know."

"Of course, of course," said Miss Marple. "I quite understand. Won't you sit down? And might I offer you a little glass of cherry brandy? My own making. A receipt of my gandmother's."

"Thank you very much, Miss Marple. Very kind of you. But I think I won't. Nothing till lunch time, that's my motto. Now, I want to talk to you about this sad business—very sad business indeed. Upset us all, I'm sure. Well, it seems possible that owing to the position of your house and garden, you may have been able to tell us something we want to know about yesterday evening."

"As a matter of fact I *was* in my little garden from five o'clock onwards yesterday, and, of course, from there—well, one simply cannot help seeing anything that is going on next door."

"I understand, Miss Marple, that Mrs. Protheroe passed this way yesterday evening?"

"Yes, she did. I called out to her, and she admired my roses."

"Could you tell us about what time that was?"

"I should say it was just a minute or two after a quarter past six. Yes, that's right. The church clock had just chimed the quarter."

"Very good. What happened next?"

"Well, Mrs. Protheroe said she was calling for her husband at the Vicarage so that they could go home together. She had come along the lane, you understand, and she went into the Vicarage by the back gate and across the garden."

"She came from the lane?"

"Yes, I'll show you."

Full of eagerness, Miss Marple led us out into the garden and pointed out the lane that ran along by the bottom of the garden.

"The path opposite with the stile leads to the Hall," she explained. "That was the way they were going home together. Mrs. Protheroe came from the village."

"Perfectly, perfectly," said Colonel Melchett. "And she went across to the Vicarage, you say?"

"Yes. I saw her turn the corner of the house. I suppose the colonel wasn't there yet, because she came back almost immediately, and went down the lawn to the studio—that building there. The one the vicar lets Mr. Redding use as a studio."

"I see. And—you didn't happen to hear a shot, Miss Marple?"

"I didn't hear a shot then," said Miss Marple.

"But did you hear one sometime?"

"Yes, I think there was a shot somewhere in the woods. But quite five or ten minutes afterwards—and, as I say, out in the woods. At least, I think so. It couldn't have been—surely it couldn't have been—"

She stopped, pale with excitement.

"Yes, yes, we'll come to all that presently," said Colonel Melchett. "Please go on with your story. Mrs. Protheroe went down to the studio?"

"Yes, she went inside and waited. Presently Mr. Redding came along the lane from the village. He came to the Vicarage gate, looked all round—"

"And saw you, Miss Marple."

"As a matter of fact, he didn't see me," said Miss Marple, flushing slightly. "Because, you see, just at that minute I was bending right over—trying to get up one of those nasty dandelions, you know. So difficult. And then he went through the gate and down to the studio."

"He didn't go near the house?"

"Oh, no! he went straight to the studio. Mrs. Protheroe came to the door to meet him, and then they both went inside."

Here Miss Marple contributed a singularly eloquent pause.

"Perhaps she was sitting to him?" I suggested.

"Perhaps," said Miss Marple.

"And they came out—when?"

"About ten minutes later."

"That was roughly?"

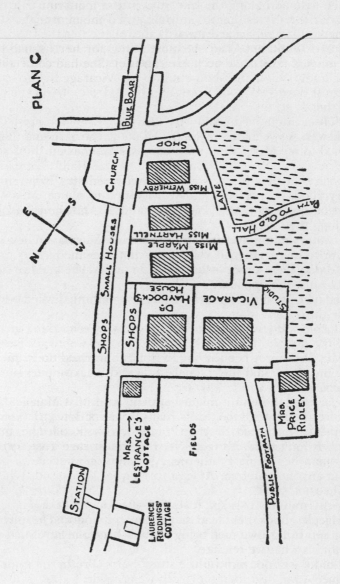

"The church clock had chimed the half-hour. They strolled out through the garden gate and along the lane, and just at that minute, Dr. Stone came down the path leading to the Hall, and climbed over the stile and joined them. They all walked towards the village together. At the end of the lane, I think, but I can't be quite sure, they were joined by Miss Cram. I think it must have been Miss Cram because her skirts were so short."

"You must have very good eyesight, Miss Marple, if you can observe as far as that."

"I was observing a bird," said Miss Marple. "A golden crested wren, I think he was. A sweet little fellow. I had my glasses out, and that's how I happened to see Miss Cram (if it was Miss Cram, and I think so), join them."

"Ah! well, that may be so," said Colonel Melchett. "Now, since you seem very good at observing, did you happen to notice, Miss Marple, what sort of expression Mrs. Protheroe and Mr. Redding had as they passed along the lane?"

"They were smiling and talking," said Miss Marple. "They seemed very happy to be together, if you know what I mean."

"They didn't seem upset or disturbed in any way?"

"Oh, no! Just the opposite."

"Deuced odd," said the colonel. "There's something deuced odd about the whole thing."

Miss Marple suddenly took our breath away by remarking in a placid voice:

"Has Mrs. Protheroe been saying that she committed the crime now?"

"Upon my soul," said the colonel, "how did you come to guess that, Miss Marple?"

"Well, I rather thought it might happen," said Miss Marple. "I think dear Lettice thought so, too. She's really a very sharp girl. Not always very scrupulous, I'm afraid. So Anne Protheroe says she killed her husband. Well, well. I don't think it's true. No, I'm almost sure it isn't true. Not with a woman like Anne Protheroe. Although one never can be quite sure about anyone, can one? At least that's what I've found. When does she say she shot him?"

"At twenty minutes past six. Just after speaking to you."

Miss Marple shook her head slowly and pityingly. The pity was, I think, for two full-grown men being so foolish as to believe such a story. At least that is what we felt like.

"What did she shoot him with?"

"A pistol."

"Where did she find it?"

"She brought it with her."

"Well, that she didn't do," said Miss Marple, with unexpected decision. "I can swear to that. She'd no such thing with her."

"You mightn't have seen it."

"Of course I should have seen it."

"If it had been in her handbag."

"She wasn't carrying a handbag."

"Well it might have been concealed—er—upon her person."

Miss Marple directed a glance of sorrow and scorn upon him.

"My dear Colonel Melchett, you know what young women are nowadays. Not ashamed to show exactly how the Creator made them. She hadn't so much as a handkerchief in the top of her stocking."

Melchett was obstinate.

"You must admit that it all fits in," he said. "The time, the overturned clock pointing to 6:22—"

Miss Marple turned on me.

"Do you mean you haven't told him about that clock yet?"

"What about the clock, Clement?"

I told him. He showed a good deal of annoyance.

"Why on earth didn't you tell Slack this last night?"

"Because," I said, "he wouldn't let me."

"Nonsense, you ought to have inisisted."

"Probably," I said, "Inspector Slack behaves quite differently to you than he does to me. I had no earthly chance of insisting."

"It's an extraordinary business altogether," said Melchett. "If a third person comes along and claims to have done this murder, I shall go into a lunatic asylum."

"If I might be allowed to suggest—" murmured Miss Marple.

"Well?"

"If you were to tell Mr. Redding what Mrs. Protheroe has done and then explain that you don't really believe it is her. And then if you were to go to Mrs. Protheroe and tell her that Mr. Redding is all right—why then, they might each of them tell you the truth. And the truth *is* helpful, though I dare say they don't know very much themselves, poor things."

"It's all very well, but they are the only two people who had a motive for making away with Protheroe."

"Oh, I wouldn't say that, Colonel Melchett," said Miss Marple.

"Why, can you think of anyone else?"

"Oh! yes, indeed. Why," she counted on her fingers, "one, two, three, four, five, six—yes, and a possible seven. I can think of at least seven people who might be very glad to have Colonel Protheroe out of the way."

The colonel looked at her feebly.

"Seven people? In St. Mary Mead?"

Miss Marple nodded brightly.

"Mind you I name no names," she said. "That wouldn't be right. But I'm afraid there's a lot of wickedness in the world. A nice honorable upright soldier like you doesn't know about these things, Colonel Melchett."

I thought the Chief Constable was going to have apoplexy.

10

HIS REMARKS ON the subject of Miss Marple as we left the house were far from complimentary.

"I really believe that wizened-up old maid thinks she knows everything there is to know. And hardly been out of this village all her life. Preposterous. What can she know of life?"

I said mildly that though doubtless Miss Marple knew next to nothing of Life with a capital L, she knew practically everything that went on in St. Mary Mead.

Melchett admitted that grudgingly. She was a valuable witness—particularly valuable from Mrs. Protheroe's point of view.

"I suppose there's no doubt about what she says, eh?"

"If Miss Marple says she had no pistol with her, you can take it for granted that it is so," I said. "If there was the least possibility of such a thing, Miss Marple would have been on to it like a knife."

"That's true enough. We'd better go and have a look at the studio."

The so-called studio was a mere rough shed with a skylight. There were no windows and the door was the only means of entrance or egress. Satisfied on this score, Melchett announced his intention of visiting the Vicarage with the inspector.

"I'm going to the police station now."

As I entered through the front door, a murmur of voices caught my ear. I opened the drawing-room door.

On the sofa beside Griselda, conversing animatedly, sat Miss Gladys Cram. Her legs, which were encased in particularly shiny pink stockings, were crossed, and I had every opportunity of observing that she wore pink striped silk knickers.

"Hullo, Len," said Griselda.

"Good morning, Mr. Clement," said Miss Cram. "Isn't the news about the colonel really too awful? Poor old gentleman."

"Miss Cram," said my wife, "very kindly came in to offer to help us with the Guides. We asked for helpers last Sunday, you remember."

I did remember, and I was convinced, and so, I knew from her tone, was Griselda, that the idea of enrolling herself among them would never have occurred to Miss Cram but for the exciting incident which had taken place at the Vicarage.

"I was only just saying to Mrs. Clement," went on Miss Cram, "you could have struck me all of a heap when I heard the news. A murder? I said. In this quiet one-horse village—for quiet it is, you must admit—not so much as a picture house, and as for Talkies! And then when I heard it was Colonel Protheroe—why, I simply couldn't believe it. He didn't seem the kind, somehow, to get murdered."

"And so," said Griselda, "Miss Cram came round to find out all about it."

I feared this plain speaking might offend the lady, but she merely flung her head back and laughed uproariously, showing every tooth she possessed.

"That's too bad. You're a sharp one, aren't you, Mrs. Clement? But it's only natural, isn't it, to want to hear the ins and outs of a case like this? And I'm sure I'm willing enough to help with the Guides in any way you like. Exciting, that's what it is. I've been stagnating for a bit of fun. I have, really I have. Not that my job isn't a very good one, well paid, and Dr. Stone quite the gentleman in every way. But a girl wants a bit of life out of office hours, and except for you, Mrs. Clement, who is there in the place to talk to except a lot of old cats?"

"There's Lettice Protheroe," I said.

Gladys Cram tossed her head.

"She's too high and mighty for the likes of me. Fancies herself the county, and wouldn't demean herself by noticing a girl who had to work for her living. Not but what I *did* hear her talking of earning her living herself. And who'd employ her, I should like to know? Why, she'd be fired in less than a week. Unless she went as one of those mannequins, all dressed up and sidling about. She could do that, I expect."

"She'd make a very good mannequin," said Griselda. "She's got such a lovely figure." There's nothing of the cat about Griselda. "When was she talking of earning her own living?"

Miss Cram seemed momentarily discomfited, but recovered herself with her usual archness.

"That would be telling, wouldn't it?" she said. "But she did say so. Things not very happy at home, I fancy. Catch me living at home with a stepmother. I wouldn't sit down under it for a minute."

"Ah! but you're so high spirited and independent," said Griselda gravely, and I looked at her with suspicion.

Miss Cram was clearly pleased.

"That's right. That's me all over. Can be led, not driven. A palmist told me that not so very long ago. No. I'm not one to sit down and be bullied. And I've made it clear all along to Dr. Stone that I must have my regular times off. These scientific gentlemen, they think a girl's a kind of machine—half the time they just don't notice her or remember she's there."

"Do you find Dr. Stone pleasant to work with? It must be an interesting job if you are interested in archaeology."

"Of course, I don't know much about it," confessed the girl. "It still seems to me that digging up people that are dead and have been dead for hundreds of years isn't—well, it seems a bit nosey, doesn't it? And there's Dr. Stone so wrapped up in it all that half the time he'd forget his meals if it wasn't for me."

"Is he at the barrow this morning?" asked Griselda.

Miss Cram shook her head.

"A bit under the weather this morning," she explained. "Not up to doing any work. That means a holiday for little Gladys."

"I'm sorry," I said.

"Oh! it's nothing much. There's not going to be a second death. But do tell me, Mr. Clement, I hear you've been with the police all morning. What do they think?"

"Well," I said slowly, "there is still a little—uncertainty."

"Ah!" cried Miss Cram. "Then they don't think it is Mr. Lawrence Redding after all. So handsome, isn't he? Just like a movie star. And such a nice smile when he says good morning to you. I really couldn't believe my ears when I heard the police had arrested him. Still, one has always heard they're very stupid—the county police."

"You can hardly blame them in this instance," I said. "Mr. Redding came in and gave himself up."

"What?" the girl was clearly dumbfounded. "Well—of all the poor fish! If I'd committed a murder, I wouldn't go straight off and give myself up. I should have thought Lawrence Redding would have had more sense. To give in like that! What did he kill Protheroe for? Did he say? Was it just a quarrel?"

"It's not absolutely certain that he did kill him," I said.

"But surely—if he says he has—why really, Mr. Clement, he ought to know."

"He ought to, certainly," I agreed. "But the police are not satisfied with his story."

"But why should he say he'd done it if he hasn't?"

That was a point on which I had no intention of enlightening Miss Cram. Instead I said rather vaguely:

"I believe that in all prominent murder cases, the police receive numerous letters from people accusing themselves of the crime."

Miss Cram's reception of this piece of information was:

"They must be chumps!" in a tone of wonder and scorn.

"Well," she said with a sigh, "I suppose I must be trotting along." She rose. "Mr. Redding accusing himself of the murder will be a bit of news for Dr. Stone."

"Is he interested?" asked Griselda.

Miss Cram furrowed her brows perplexedly.

"He's a queer one. You never can tell with him. All wrapped up in the past. He'd a hundred times rather look at a nasty old bronze knife out of one of those humps of ground than he would see the knife Crippen cut up his wife with, supposing he had a chance to."

"Well," I said, "I must confess I agree with him."

Miss Cram's eyes expressed incomprehension and slight contempt. Then, with reiterated goodbyes, she took her departure.

"Not such a bad sort, really," said Griselda, as the door closed behind her. "Terribly common, of course, but one of those big, bouncing, good-humored girls that you can't dislike. I wonder what really brought her here?"

"Curiosity."

"Yes, I suppose so. Now, Len, tell me all about it. I'm simply dying to hear."

I sat down and recited faithfully all the happenings of the morning, Griselda interpolating the narrative with little exclamations of surprise and interest.

"So it was Anne Lawrence was after all along! Not Lettice. How blind we've all been! That must have been what old Miss Marple was hinting at yesterday. Don't you think so?"

"Yes," I said, averting my eyes.

Mary entered.

"There's a couple of men here—come from a newspaper, so they say. Do you want to see them?"

"No," I said, "certainly not. Refer them to Inspector Slack at the police station."

Mary nodded and turned away.

"And when you've got rid of them," I said, "come back here. There's something I want to ask you."

Mary nodded again.

It was some few minutes before she returned.

"Had a job getting rid of them," she said. "Persistent. You never saw anything like it. Wouldn't take no for an answer."

"I expect we shall be a good deal troubled with them," I said. "Now, Mary, what I want to ask you is this: Are you quite certain you didn't hear the shot yesterday evening?"

"The shot what killed him? No, of course I didn't. If I had of done, I should have gone in to see what had happened."

"Yes, but—" I was remembering Miss Marple's statement that she had heard a shot "in the wood". I changed the form of my question. "Did you hear any other shot—one down in the wood, for instance?"

"Oh! that." The girl paused. "Yes, now I come to think of it, I believe I did. Not a lot of shots, just one. Queer sort of bang it was."

"Exactly," I said. "Now what time was that?"

"Time?"

"Yes, time."

"I couldn't say, I'm sure. Well after tea-time. I do know that."

"Can't you get a little nearer than that?"

"No, I can't. I've got my work to do, haven't I? I can't go on looking at clocks the whole time—and it wouldn't be much good anyway—the alarm loses a good three-quarters every day, and what with putting it on and one thing and another, I'm never exactly sure what time it is."

This perhaps explains why our meals are never punctual. They are sometimes too late and sometimes bewilderingly early.

"Was it long before Mr. Redding came?"

"No, it wasn't long. Ten minutes—a quarter of an hour—not longer than that."

I nodded my head, satisfied.

"Is that all?" said Mary. "Because what I mean to say is, I've got the joint in the oven and the pudding boiling over as likely as not."

"That's all right. You can go."

She left the room, and I turned to Griselda.

"Is it quite out of the question to induce Mary to say sir or ma'am?"

"I have told her. She doesn't remember. She's just a raw girl, remember?"

"I am perfectly aware of that," I said. "But raw things do not necessarily remain raw for ever. I feel a tinge of cooking might be induced in Mary."

"Well, I don't agree with you," said Griselda. "You know how little we can afford to pay a servant. If once we got her smartened up at all, she'd leave. Naturally. And get higher wages. But as long as Mary can't cook and has those awful manners—well, we're safe, nobody else would have her."

I perceived that my wife's methods of housekeeping were not so entirely haphazard as I had imagined. A certain amount of reasoning underlay them. Whether it was worth while having a maid at the price of her not being able to cook, and having a habit of throwing dishes and remarks at one with the same disconcerting abruptness, was a debatable matter.

"And anyway," continued Griselda, "you must make allowances for her manners being worse than usual just now. You can't expect her to feel exactly sympathetic about Colonel Protheroe's death when he jailed her young man."

"Did he jail her young man?"

"Yes, for poaching. You know, that man, Archer. Mary has been walking out with him for two years."

"I didn't know that."

"Darling Len, you never know anything."

"It's queer," I said, "that everyone says the shot came from the wood."

"I don't think it's queer at all," said Griselda. "You see, one so often does hear shots in the wood. So naturally, when you do hear a shot, you just assume as a matter of course that it *is* in the wood. It probably just sounds a bit louder than usual. Of course, if one were in the next room, you'd realize that it was in the house, but from Mary's kitchen with the window right the other side of the house, I don't believe you'd ever think of such a thing."

The door opened again.

"Colonel Melchett's back," said Mary. "And that police inspector with him, and they say they'd be glad if you'd join them. They're in the study."

11

I SAW AT A glance that Colonel Melchett and Inspector Slack had not been seeing eye to eye about the case. Melchett looked flushed and annoyed and the inspector looked sulky.

"I'm sorry to say," said Melchett, "that Inspector Slack doesn't agree with me in considering young Redding innocent."

"If he didn't do it, what does he go and say he did it for?" asked Slack sceptically.

"Mrs. Protheroe acted in an exactly similar fashion, remember, Slack."

"That's different. She's a woman, and women act in that silly way. I'm not saying she did it for a moment. She heard he was accused and she trumped up a story. I'm used to that sort of game. You wouldn't believe the fool things I've known women do. But Redding's different. He's got his head screwed on all right. And if he admits he did it, well, I say he did do it. It's his pistol—you can't get away from that. And thanks to this business of Mrs. Protheroe, we know the motive. That was the weak point before, but now we know it—why, the whole thing's plain sailing."

"You think he can have shot him earlier? At six-thirty, say?"

"He can't have done that."

"You've checked up his movements?"

The inspector nodded.

"He was in the village near the Blue Boar at ten past six. From there he came along the back lane where you say the old lady next door saw him—she doesn't miss much, I should say—and kept his appointment with Mrs. Protheroe in the studio in the garden. They left there together just after six-thirty, and went along the lane to the village, being joined by Dr. Stone. He corroborates that all right—I've seen him. They all stood talking just by the post office for a few minutes, then Mrs. Protheroe went into Miss Hartnell's to borrow a gardening magazine. That's all right too. I've seen Miss Hartnell. Mrs. Protheroe remained there talking to her till just on seven o'clock, when she exclaimed at the lateness of the hour and said she must get home."

"What was her manner?"

"Very easy and pleasant, Miss Hartnell said. She seemed in good spirits—Miss Hartnell is quite sure there was nothing on her mind."

"Well, go on."

"Redding, he went with Dr. Stone to the Blue Boar and they had a drink together. He left there at twenty minutes to seven, went rapidly along the village street and down the road to the Vicarage. Lots of people saw him."

"Not down the back lane this time?" commented the colonel.

"No—he came to the front, asked for the vicar, heard Colonel Protheroe was there, went in—and shot him—just as he said he did! That's the truth of it, and we needn't look further."

Melchett shook his head.

"There's the doctor's evidence. You can't get away from that. Protheroe was shot not later than six-thirty."

"Oh! doctors!" Inspector Slack looked contemptuous. "If you're going to believe doctors. Take out all your teeth—that's what they do nowadays—and then say they're very sorry, but all the time it was appendicitis. Doctors!"

"This isn't a question of diagnosis. Dr. Haydock was absolutely positive on the point. You can't go against the medical evidence, Slack."

"And there's my evidence for what it is worth," I said, suddenly recalling a forgotten incident. "I touched the body and it was cold. That I can swear to."

"You see, Slack?" said Melchett.

"Well, of course, if that's so. But there it was—a beautiful case. Mr. Redding only too anxious to be hanged, so to speak."

"That, in itself, strikes me as a little unnatural," observed Colonel Melchett.

"Well, there's no accounting for tastes," said the inspector. "There's a lot of gentlemen went a bit balmy after the war. Now, I suppose, it means starting again at the beginning." He turned on me. "Why you went out of your way to mislead me about the clock, sir, I can't think. Obstructing the ends of justice, that's what that was."

"I tried to tell you on three separate occasions," I said. "And each time you shut me up and refused to listen."

"That's just a way of speaking, sir. You could have told me perfectly well if you had had a mind to. The clock and the note seemed to tally perfectly. Now, according to you, the clock was all wrong. I never knew such a case. What's the sense of keeping a clock a quarter of an hour fast anyway?"

"It is supposed," I said, "to induce punctuality."

"I don't think we need go further into that now, Inspector," said Colonel Melchett tactfully. "What we want now is the true story from both Mrs. Protheroe and young Redding. I telephoned to Haydock and asked him to bring Mrs. Protheroe over here with him. They ought to be here in about a quarter of an hour. I think it would be as well to have Redding here first."

"I'll get on to the station," said Inspector Slack, and took up the telephone.

"And now," he said, replacing the receiver, "we'll get to work on this room." He looked at me in a meaning fashion.

"Perhaps," I said, "you'd like me out of the way."

The inspector immediately opened the door for me. Melchett called out:

"Come back when young Redding arrives, will you, vicar? You're a friend of his and you may have sufficient influence to persuade him to speak the truth."

I found my wife and Miss Marple with their heads together.

"We've been discussing all sorts of possibilities," said Griselda. "I wish you'd solve the case, Miss Marple, like you did the way Miss Wetherby's gill of picked shrimps disappeared. And all because it reminded you of something quite different about a sack of coals."

"You're laughing, my dear," said Miss Marple, "but after all, that is a very sound way of arriving at the truth. It's really what people call intuition and make such a fuss about. Intuition is like reading a word

without having to spell it out. A child can't do that because it has had
so little experience. But a grown-up person knows the word because
they've seen it often before. You catch my meaning, vicar?"

"Yes," I said slowly, "I think I do. You mean that if a thing reminds
you of something else—well, it's probably the same kind of thing."

"Exactly."

"And what precisely does the murder of Colonel Protheroe remind
you of?"

Miss Marple sighed.

"That is just the difficulty. So many parallels come to the mind. For
instance, there was Major Hargraves, a churchwarden and a man highly
respected in every way. And all the time he was keeping a separate second
establishment—a former housemaid, just think of it! And five children—
actually five children—a terrible shock to his wife and daughter."

I tried hard to visualize Colonel Protheroe in the role of secret sinner
and failed.

"And then there was that laundry business," went on Miss Marple.
"Miss Hartnell's opal pin—left most imprudently in a frilled blouse and
sent to the laundry. And the woman who took it didn't want it in the
least and wasn't by any means a thief. She simply hid it in another
woman's house and told the police she'd seen this other woman take it.
Spite, you know, sheer spite. It's an astonishing motive—spite. A man
in it, of course. There always is."

This time I failed to see any parallel, however remote.

"And then there was poor Elwell's daughter—such a pretty ethereal
girl—tried to stifle her little brother. And there was the money for the
Choirboys' Outing (before your time, vicar) actually taken by the organist.
His wife was sadly in debt. Yes, this case makes one think so many
things—too many. It's very hard to arrive at the truth."

"I wish you would tell me," I said, "who were the seven suspects?"

"The seven suspects?"

"You said you could think of seven people who would—well, be glad
of Colonel Protheroe's death."

"Did I? Yes, I remember I did."

"Was that true?"

"Oh! certainly it was true. But I mustn't mention names. You can think
of them quite easily yourself, I am sure."

"Indeed I can't. There is Lettice Protheroe, I suppose, since she probably
comes into money on her father's death. But it is absurd to think of her
in such a connection, and outside her I can think of nobody."

"And you, my dear?" said Miss Marple, turning to Griselda.

Rather to my surprise Griselda colored up. Something very like tears
started into her eyes. She clenched both her small hands.

"Oh!" she cried indignantly. "People are hateful—hateful. The things
they say! The beastly things they say . . ."

I looked at her curiously. It is very unlike Griselda to be so upset. She noticed my glance and tried to smile.

"Don't look at me as though I were an interesting specimen you didn't understand, Len. Don't let's get heated and wander from the point. I don't believe that it was Lawrence or Anne, and Lettice is out of the question. There must be some clue or other that would help us."

"There is the note, of course," said Miss Marple. "You will remember my saying this morning that that struck me as exceedingly peculiar."

"It seems to fix the time of his death with remarkable accuracy," I said. "And yet, is that possible? Mrs. Protheroe would only have just left the study. She would hardly have had time to reach the studio. The only way in which I can account for it is that he consulted his own watch and that his watch was slow. That seems to me a feasible solution."

"I have another idea," said Griselda. "Suppose, Len, that the clock had already been put back—no, that comes to the same thing—how stupid of me!"

"It hadn't been altered when I left," I said. "I remember comparing it with my watch. Still, as you say, that has no bearing on the present matter."

"What do you think, Miss Marple?" asked Griselda.

"My dear, I confess I wasn't thinking about it from that point of view at all. What strikes me as so curious, and has done from the first, is the subject matter of that letter."

"I don't see that," I said. "Colonel Protheroe merely wrote that he couldn't wait any longer—"

"*At twenty minutes past six?*" said Miss Marple. "Your maid, Mary, had already told him that you wouldn't be in till half-past six at the earliest, and he had appeared to be quite willing to wait until then. And yet at twenty past six he sits down and says he 'can't wait any longer.' "

I stared at the old lady, feeling an increased respect for her mental powers. Her keen wits had seen what we had failed to perceive. It *was* an odd thing—a very odd thing.

"If only," I said, "the letter hadn't been dated—"

Miss Marple nodded her head.

"Exactly," she said. "If it *hadn't* been dated!"

I cast my mind back, trying to recall that sheet of notepaper and the blurred scrawl, and at the top that neatly printed 6:20. Surely these figures were on a different scale to the rest of the letter. I gave a gasp.

"Supposing," I said, "it wasn't dated. Supposing that round about 6:30 Colonel Protheroe got impatient and sat down to say he couldn't wait any longer. And as he was sitting there writing, someone came in through the window—"

"Or through the door," suggested Griselda.

"He'd hear the door and look up."

"Colonel Protheroe was rather deaf, you remember," said Miss Marple.

"Yes, that's true. He wouldn't hear it. Whichever way the murderer came, he stole up behind the colonel and shot him. Then he saw the note and the clock and the idea came to him. He put 6:20 at the top of the letter and he altered the clock to 6:22. It was a clever idea. It gave him, or so he would think, a perfect alibi."

"And what we want to find," said Griselda, "is someone who has a cast-iron alibi for 6:20, but no alibi at all for—well, that isn't so easy. One can't fix the time."

"We can fix it within very narrow limits," I said. "Haydock places 6:30 as the outside limit of time. I suppose one could perhaps shift it to 6:35: from the reasoning we have just been following out, it seems clear that Protheroe would not have got impatient before 6:30. I think we can say we do know pretty well."

"Then that shot I heard—yes, I suppose it is quite possible. And I thought nothing about it—nothing at all. Most vexing. And yet, now I try to recollect, it does seem to me that it was different from the usual sort of shot one hears. Yes, there was a difference."

"Louder?" I suggested.

No, Miss Marple didn't think it had been louder. In fact, she found it hard to say in what way it had been different, but she still insisted that it was.

I thought she was probably persuading herself of the fact rather than actually remembering it, but she had just contributed such a valuable new outlook to the problem that I felt highly respectful towards her.

She rose, murmuring that she must really get back—it had been so tempting just to run over and discuss the case with dear Griselda. I escorted her to the boundary wall and the back gate and returned to find Griselda wrapped in thought.

"Still puzzling over that note?"

"No."

She gave a sudden shiver and shook her shoulders impatiently.

"Len, I've been thinking. How badly someone must have hated Anne Protheroe!"

"Hated her?"

"Yes. Don't you see? There's no real evidence against Lawrence—all the evidence against him is what you might call accidental. He just happens to take it into his head to come here. If he hadn't—well, no one would have thought of connecting him with the crime. But Anne is different. Suppose someone knew that she was here at exactly 6:20—the clock and the time on the letter—everything pointing to her. I don't think it was only because of an alibi it was moved to that exact time—I think there was more in it than that—a direct attempt to fasten the business on her. If it hadn't been for Miss Marple saying she hadn't got the pistol with her and noticing that she was only a moment before going down to the studio—Yes, if it hadn't been for that . . ." She shivered again. "Len, I feel that someone hated Anne Protheroe very much. I—I don't like it."

12

I WAS SUMMONED to the study when Lawrence Redding arrived. He looked haggard, and, I thought, suspicious. Colonel Melchett greeted him with something approaching cordiality.

"We want to ask you a few questions—here, on the spot," he said.

Lawrence sneered slightly.

"Isn't that a French idea? Reconstruction of the crime?"

"My dear boy," said Colonel Melchett, "don't take that tone with us. Are you aware that someone else has also confessed to committing the crime which you pretend to have committed?"

The effect of these words on Lawrence was painful and immediate.

"S-s-omeone else?" he stammered. "Who—who?"

"Mrs. Protheroe," said Colonel Melchett, watching him.

"Absurd. She never did it. She couldn't have. It's impossible."

Melchett interrupted him.

"Strangely enough, we did not believe her story. Neither, I may say, do we believe yours. Dr. Haydock says positively that the murder could not have been committed at the time you say it was."

"Dr. Haydock says that?"

"Yes, so, you see, you are cleared whether you like it or not. And now we want you to help us, to tell us exactly what occurred."

Lawrence still hesitated.

"You're not deceiving me about—about Mrs. Protheroe? You really don't suspect her?"

"On my word of honor," said Colonel Melchett.

Lawrence drew a deep breath.

"I've been a fool," he said. "An absolute fool. How could I have thought for one minute that she did it—"

"Suppose you tell us all about it?" suggested the Chief Constable.

"There's not much to tell. I—I met Mrs. Protheroe that afternoon—" He paused.

"We know all about that," said Melchett. "You may think that your feeling for Mrs. Protheroe and hers for you was a dead secret, but in reality it was known and commented upon. In any case, everything is bound to come out now."

"Very well, then. I expect you are right. I had promised the vicar here" (he glanced at me) "to—to go right away. I met Mrs. Protheroe that evening in the studio at a quarter past six. I told her of what I had decided. She, too, agreed that it was the only thing to do. We—we said goodbye to each other.

"We left the studio, and almost at once Dr. Stone joined us. Anne managed to seem marvelously natural. I couldn't do it. I went off with

Stone to the Blue Boar and had a drink. Then I thought I'd go home, but when I got to the corner of this road, I changed my mind and decided to come along and see the vicar. I felt I wanted someone to talk to about the matter.

"At the door, the maid told me the vicar was out, but would be in shortly, but that Colonel Protheroe was in the study waiting for him. Well, I didn't like to go away again—looked as though I were shirking meeting him. So I said I'd wait too, and I went into the study."

He stopped.

"Well?" said Colonel Melchett.

"Protheroe was sitting at the writing-table—just as you found him. I went up to him—touched him. He was dead. Then I looked down and saw the pistol lying on the floor beside him. I picked it up—*and at once saw that it was my pistol.*

"That gave me a turn. My pistol! And then, straightaway I leaped to one conclusion. Anne must have bagged my pistol some time or other— meaning it for herself if she couldn't bear things any longer. Perhaps she had had it with her today. After we parted in the village she must have come back here and—and—oh! I suppose I was mad to think of it. But that's what I thought. I slipped the pistol in my pocket and came away. Just outside the Vicarage gate, I met the vicar. He said something nice and normal about seeing Protheroe—suddenly I had a wild desire to laugh. His manner was so ordinary and everyday and there was I all strung up. I remember shouting out something absurd and seeing his face change. I was nearly off my head, I believe. I went walking—walking— at last I couldn't bear it any longer. If Anne had done this ghastly thing, I was, at least, morally responsible. I went and gave myself up."

There was a silence when he had finished. Then the colonel said in a businesslike voice:

"I would like to ask just one or two questions. First, did you touch or move the body in any way?"

"No, I didn't touch it at all. One could see he was dead without touching him."

"Did you notice a note lying on the blotter half concealed by his body?"

"No."

"Did you interfere in any way with the clock?"

"I never touched the clock. I seem to remember a clock lying overturned on the table, but I never touched it."

"Now as to this pistol of yours, when did you last see it?"

Lawrence Redding reflected. "It's hard to say exactly."

"Where do you keep it?"

"Oh! in a litter of odds and ends in the sitting-room in my cottage. On one of the shelves of the bookcase."

"You left it lying about carelessly?"

"Yes. I really didn't think about it. It was just there."

"So that anyone who came to your cottage could have seen it?"

"Yes."

"And you don't remember when you last saw it?"

Lawrence drew his brows together in a frown of recollection.

"I'm almost sure it was there the day before yesterday. I remember pushing it aside to get an old pipe. I think it was the day before yesterday—but it may have been the day before that."

"Who has been to your cottage lately?"

"Oh! crowds of people. Someone is always drifting in and out. I had a sort of tea party the day before yesterday. Lettice Protheroe, Dennis, and all their crowd. And then one or other of the old Pussies comes in now and again."

"Do you lock the cottage up when you go out?"

"No; why on earth should I? I've nothing to steal. And no one does lock their houses up round here."

"Who looks after your wants there?"

"An old Mrs. Archer comes in every morning to 'do for me' as it's called."

"Do you think she would remember when the pistol was there last?"

"I don't know. She might. But I don't fancy conscientious dusting is her strong point."

"It comes to this—that almost anyone might have taken that pistol?"

"It seems so—yes."

The door opened and Dr. Haydock came in with Anne Protheroe.

She started at seeing Lawrence. He, on his part, made a tentative step towards her.

"Forgive me, Anne," he said. "It was abominable of me to think what I did."

"I—" She faltered, then looked appealingly at Colonel Melchett. "It is true, what Dr. Haydock told me?"

"That Mr. Redding is cleared of suspicion? Yes. And now what about this story of yours, Mrs. Protheroe? Eh, what about it?"

She smiled rather shamefacedly.

"I suppose you think it dreadful of me?"

"Well, shall we say—very foolish? But that's all over. What I want now, Mrs. Protheroe, is the truth—the absolute truth."

She nodded gravely.

"I will tell you. I suppose you know about—about everything."

"Yes."

"I was to meet Lawrence—Mr. Redding—that evening at the studio. At a quarter past six. My husband and I drove into the village together. I had some shopping to do. As we parted he mentioned casually that he was going to see the vicar. I couldn't get word to Lawrence, and I was rather uneasy. I—well, it was awkward meeting him in the Vicarage garden while my husband was at the Vicarage."

Her cheeks burned as she said this. It was not a pleasant moment for her.

"I reflected that perhaps my husband would not stay very long. To find this out, I came along the back lane and into the garden. I hoped no one would see me, but of course old Miss Marple had to be in her garden! She stopped me and we said a few words, and I explained I was going to call for my husband. I felt I had to say something. I don't know whether she believed me or not. She looked rather—funny.

"When I left her, I went straight across to the Vicarage and round the corner of the house to the study window. I crept up to it very softly, expecting to hear the sound of voices. But to my surprise there were none. I just glanced in, saw the room was empty, and hurried across the lawn and down to the studio where Lawrence joined me almost at once."

"You say the room was empty, Mrs. Protheroe?"

"Yes, my husband was not there."

"Extraordinary."

"You mean, ma'am, that you didn't see him?" said the inspector.

"No, I didn't see him."

Inspector Slack whispered to the Chief Constable, who nodded.

"Do you mind, Mrs. Protheroe just showing us exactly what you did?"

"Not at all."

She rose, Inspector Slack pushed open the window for her, and she stepped out on the terrace and round the house to the left.

Inspector Slack beckoned me imperiously to go and sit at the writing-table.

Somehow I didn't much like doing it. It gave me an uncomfortable feeling. But, of course, I complied.

Presently I heard footsteps outside, they paused for a minute, then retreated. Inspector Slack indicated to me that I could return to the other side of the room. Mrs. Protheroe reentered through the window.

"Is that exactly how it was?" asked Colonel Melchett.

"I think exactly."

"Then can you tell us, Mrs. Protheroe, just exactly where the vicar was in the room when you looked in?" asked Inspector Slack.

"The vicar? I—no, I'm afraid I can't. I didn't see him."

Inspector Slack nodded.

"That's how you didn't see your husband. He was round the corner at the writing-desk."

"Oh!" she paused. Suddenly her eyes grew round with horror. "It wasn't there that—that—"

"Yes, Mrs. Protheroe. It was while he was sitting there."

"Oh!" She quivered.

He went on with his questions.

"Did you know, Mrs. Protheroe, that Mr. Redding had a pistol?"

"Yes. He told me so once."

"Did you ever have that pistol in your possession?"

She shook her head. "No."

"Did you know where he kept it?"

"I'm not sure. I think—yes, I think I've seen it on a shelf in his cottage. Didn't you keep it there, Lawrence?"

"When was the last time you were at the cottage, Mrs. Protheroe?"

"Oh! about three weeks ago. My husband and I had tea there with him."

"And you have not been there since?"

"No. I never went there. You see, it would probably cause a lot of talk in the village."

"Doubtless," said Colonel Melchett dryly. "Where were you in the habit of seeing Mr. Redding, if I may ask?"

"He used to come up to the Hall. He was painting Lettice. We—we often met in the woods afterwards."

Colonel Melchett nodded.

"Isn't that enough?" Her voice was suddenly broken. "It's so awful—having to tell you all these things. And—and there wasn't anything wrong about it. There wasn't—indeed, there wasn't. We were just friends. We—we couldn't help caring for each other."

She looked pleadingly at Dr. Haydock, and that softhearted man stepped forward.

"I really think, Melchett," he said, "that Mrs. Protheroe has had enough. She's had a great shock—in more ways than one."

The Chief Constable nodded.

"There is really nothing more I want to ask you, Mrs. Protheroe," he said. "Thank you for answering my questions so frankly."

"Then—then I may go?"

"Is your wife in?" asked Haydock. "I think Mrs. Protheroe would like to see her."

"Yes," I said, "Griselda is in. You'll find her in the drawing-room."

She and Haydock left the room together and Lawrence Redding with them.

Colonel Melchett had pursed up his lips and was playing with a paper-knife. Slack was looking at the note. It was then that I mentioned Miss Marple's theory. Slack looked closely at it.

"My word," he said, "I believe the old lady's right. Look here, sir, don't you see?—these figures are written in different ink. That date was written with a fountain pen or I'll eat my boots!"

We were all rather excited.

"You've examined the note for fingerprints, of course," said the Chief Constable.

"What do you think, Colonel? No fingerprints on the note at all. Fingerprints on the pistol those of Mr. Lawrence Redding. May have been some others once, before he went fooling round with it and carrying it around in his pocket, but there's nothing clear enough to get hold of now."

"At first the case looked very black against Mrs. Protheroe," said the colonel thoughtfully. "Much blacker than against young Redding. There was that old woman Marple's evidence that she didn't have the pistol with her, but these elderly ladies are often mistaken."

I was silent, but I did not agree with him. I was quite sure that Anne

Protheroe had had no pistol with her since Miss Marple had said so. Miss Marple is not the type of elderly lady who makes mistakes. She has got an uncanny knack of being always right.

"What did get me was that nobody heard the shot. If it was fired then—somebody *must* have heard it—wherever they thought it came from. Slack, you'd better have a word with the maid."

Inspector Slack moved with alacrity towards the door.

"I shouldn't ask her if she heard a shot in the house," I said. "Because if you do, she'll deny it. Call it a shot in the wood. That's the only kind of shot she'll admit to hearing."

"I know how to manage them," said Inspector Slack, and disappeared.

"Miss Marple says she heard a shot later," said Colonel Melchett thoughtfully. "We must see if she can fix the time at all precisely. Of course it may be a stray shot that had nothing to do with the case."

"It may be, of course," I agreed.

The colonel took a turn or two up and down the room.

"Do you know, Clement," he said suddenly, "I've a feeling that this is going to turn out a much more intricate and difficult business than any of us think. Dash it all, there's something behind it." He snorted. "Something we don't know about. We're only beginning, Clement. Mark my words, we're only beginning. All these things, the clock, the note, the pistol—they don't make sense as they stand."

I shook my head. They certainly didn't.

"But I'm going to get to the bottom of it. No calling in of Scotland Yard. Slack's a smart man. He's a very smart man. He's a kind of ferret. He'll nose his way through to the truth. He's done several very good things already, and this case will be his *chef d'oeuvre*. Some men would call in Scotland Yard. I shan't. We'll get to the bottom of this here in Downshire."

"I hope so, I'm sure," I said.

I tried to make my voice enthusiastic, but I had already taken such a dislike to Inspector Slack that the prospect of his success failed to appeal to me. A successful Slack would, I thought, be even more odious than a baffled one.

"Who has the house next door?" asked the colonel suddenly.

"You mean at the end of the road? Mrs. Price Ridley."

"We'll go along to her after Slack has finished with your maid. She might just possibly have heard something. She isn't deaf or anything, is she?"

"I should say her hearing was remarkably keen. I'm going by the amount of scandal she has started by 'just happening to overhear accidentally.' "

"That's the kind of woman we want. Oh! here's Slack."

The inspector had the air of one emerging from a severe tussle.

"Phew!" he said. "That's a tartar you've got, sir."

"Mary is essentially a girl of strong character," I replied.

"Doesn't like the police," he said. "I cautioned her—did what I could to put the fear of the law into her, but no good. She stood right up to me."

"Spirited," I said, feeling more kindly towards Mary.

"But I pinned her down all right. She heard one shot—and one shot only. And it was a good long time after Colonel Protheroe came. I couldn't get her to name a time, but we fixed it at last by means of the fish. The fish was late, and she blew the boy up when he came, and he said it was barely half-past six anyway, and it was just after that she heard the shot. Of course, that's not accurate, so to speak, but it gives us an idea."

"H'm," said Melchett.

"I don't think Mrs. Protheroe's in this after all," said Slack, with a note of regret in his voice. "She wouldn't have had time, to begin with, and then women never like fiddling about with firearms. Arsenic's more in their line. No, I don't think she did it. It's a pity!" He sighed.

Melchett explained that he was going round to Mrs. Price Ridley's, and Slack approved.

"May I come with you?" I asked. "I'm getting interested."

I was given permission, and we set forth. A loud "Hie" greeted us as we emerged from the Vicarage gate, and my nephew, Dennis, came running up the road from the village to join us.

"Look here," he said to the inspector, "what about that footprint I told you about?"

"Gardener's," said Inspector Slack laconically.

"You don't think it might be someone else wearing the gardener's boots?"

"No, I don't!" said Inspector Slack in a discouraging way.

It would take more than that to discourage Dennis, however.

He held out a couple of burnt matches.

"I found these by the Vicarage gate."

"Thank you," said Slack, and put them in his pocket.

Matters appeared now to have reached a deadlock.

"You're not arresting Uncle Len, are you?" inquired Dennis facetiously.

"Why should I?" inquired Slack.

"There's a lot of evidence against him," declared Dennis. "You ask Mary. Only the day before the murder he was wishing Colonel Protheroe out of the world. Weren't you, Uncle Len?"

"Er—" I began.

Inspector Slack turned a slow suspicious stare upon me, and I felt hot all over. Dennis is exceedingly tiresome. He ought to realize that a policeman seldom has a sense of humor.

"Don't be absurd, Dennis," I said irritably.

The innocent child opened his eyes in a stare of surprise.

"I say, it's only a joke," he said. "Uncle Len just said that anyone who murdered Colonel Protheroe would be doing the world a service."

"Ah!" said Inspector Slack, "that explains something the maid said."

Servants very seldom have any sense of humor either. I cursed Dennis heartily in my mind for bringing the matter up. That and the clock together will make the inspector suspicious of me for life.

"Come on, Clement," said Colonel Melchett.

"Where are you going? Can I come, too?" asked Dennis.

"No, you can't," I snapped.

We left him looking after us with a hurt expression. We went up to the neat front door of Mrs. Price Ridley's house and the inspector knocked and rang in what I can only describe as an official manner. A pretty parlormaid answered the bell.

"Mrs. Price Ridley in?" inquired Melchett.

"No, sir." The maid paused and added: "She's just gone down to the police station."

This was a totally unexpected development. As we retraced our steps Melchett caught me by the arm and murmured:

"If she's gone to confess to the crime, too, I really shall go off my head."

13

I HARDLY THOUGHT it likely that Mrs. Price Ridley had anything so dramatic in view, but I did wonder what had taken her to the police station. Had she really got evidence of importance, or that she thought of importance, to offer? At any rate, we should soon know.

We found Mrs. Price Ridley talking at a high rate of speed to a somewhat bewildered-looking police constable. That she was extremely indignant I knew from the way the bow in her hat was trembling. Mrs. Price Ridley wears what, I believe, are known as "Hats for Matrons"—they make a speciality of them in our adjacent town of Much Benham. They perch easily on a superstructure of hair and are somewhat overweighted with large bows of ribbon. Griselda is always threatening to get a matron's hat.

Mrs. Price Ridley paused in her flow of words upon our entrance.

"Mrs. Price Ridley?" inquired Colonel Melchett, lifting his hat.

"Let me introduce Colonel Melchett to you, Mrs. Price Ridley," I said. "Colonel Melchett is our Chief Constable."

Mrs. Price Ridley looked at me coldly, but produced the semblance of a gracious smile for the colonel.

"We've just been round to your house, Mrs. Price Ridley," explained the colonel, "and heard you had come down here."

Mrs. Price Ridley thawed altogether.

"Ah!" she said, "I'm glad *some* notice is being taken of the occurrence. Disgraceful, I call it. Simply disgraceful."

There is no doubt that murder is disgraceful, but it is not the word I should use to describe it myself. It surprised Melchett too, I could see.

"Have you any light to throw upon the matter?" he asked.

"That's your business. It's the business of the police. What do we pay rates and taxes for, I should like to know?"

One wonders how many times that query is uttered in a year!

"We're doing our best, Mrs. Price Ridley," said the Chief Constable.

"But the man here hadn't even heard of it till I told him about it!" cried the lady.

We all looked at the constable.

"Lady been rung up on the telephone," he said. "Annoyed. Matter of obscene language, I understand."

"Oh! I see." The colonel's brow cleared. "We've been talking at cross purposes. You came down here to make a complaint, did you?"

Melchett is a wise man. He knows that when it is a question of an irate middle-aged lady, there is only one thing to be done—to listen to her. When she has said all that she wants to say, there is a chance that she will listen to you.

Mrs. Price Ridley surged into speech.

"Such disgraceful occurrences ought to be prevented. They ought not to occur. To be rung up in one's own house and insulted—yes, insulted. I'm not accustomed to such things happening. Ever since the war there has been a loosening of moral fiber. Nobody minds what they say, and as to the clothes they wear—"

"Quite," said Colonel Melchett hastily. "What happened exactly?"

Mrs. Price Ridley took breath and started again.

"I was rung up—"

"When?"

"Yesterday afternoon—evening to be exact. About half-past six. I went to the telephone, suspecting nothing. Immediately I was foully attacked, threatened—"

"What actually was said?"

Mrs. Price Ridley got slightly pink.

"That I decline to state."

"Obscene language," murmured the constable in a ruminative bass.

"Was bad language used?" asked Colonel Melchett.

"It depends on what you call bad language."

"Could you understand it?" I asked.

"Of course I could understand it."

"Then it couldn't have been bad language," I said.

Mrs. Price Ridley looked at me suspiciously.

"A refined lady," I explained, "is naturally unacquainted with bad language."

"It wasn't that kind of thing," said Mrs. Price Ridley. "At first, I must admit, I was quite taken in. I thought it was a genuine message. Then the—er—person became abusive."

"Abusive?"

"Most abusive. I was quite alarmed."

"Used threatening language, eh?"

"Yes. I am not accustomed to being threatened."

"What did they threaten you with? Bodily damage?"

"Not exactly."

"I'm afraid, Mrs. Price Ridley, you must be more explicit. In what way were you threatened?"

This Mrs. Price Ridley seemed singularly reluctant to answer.

"I can't remember exactly. It was all so upsetting. But right at the end—when I was really *very* upset, this—this—*wretch* laughed."

"Was it a man's voice or a woman's?"

"It was a degenerate voice," said Mrs. Price Ridley, with dignity. "I can only describe it as a kind of perverted voice. Now gruff, now squeaky. Really a very *peculiar* voice."

"Probably a practical joke," said the colonel soothingly.

"A most wicked thing to do, if so. I might have had a heart attack."

"We'll look into it," said the colonel; "eh, inspector? Trace the telephone call. You can't tell me more definitely exactly what was said, Mrs. Price Ridley?"

A struggle began in Mrs. Price Ridley's ample black bosom. The desire for reticence fought against a desire for vengeance. Vengeance triumphed.

"This, of course, will go no further," she began.

"Of course not."

"This creature began by saying—I can hardly bring myself to repeat it—"

"Yes, yes," said Melchett encouragingly.

" '*You are a wicked scandal-mongering old woman!*' Me, Colonel Melchett—a scandal-mongering old woman. '*But this time you've gone too far. Scotland Yard are after you for libel.*' "

"Naturally, you were alarmed," said Melchett, biting his moustache to conceal a smile.

" '*Unless you hold your tongue in the future, it will be the worse for you—in more ways than one.*' I can't describe to you the menacing way *that* was said. I gasped, 'Who are you?' faintly—like that, and the voice answered, '*The Avenger.*' I gave a little shriek. It sounded so awful, and then—the person laughed. Laughed! Distinctly. And that was all. I heard them hang up the receiver. Of course I asked the exchange what number had been ringing me up, but they said they didn't know. You know what exchanges are. Thoroughly rude and unsympathetic."

"Quite," I said.

"I felt quite faint," continued Mrs. Price Ridley. "All on edge and so nervous that when I heard a shot in the woods, I do declare I jumped almost out of my skin. That will show you."

"A shot in the woods?" said Inspector Slack alertly.

"In my excited state, it simply sounded to me like a cannon going off. Oh!' I said, and sank down on the sofa in a state of prostration. Clara had to bring me a glass of damson gin."

"Shocking," said Melchett. "Shocking. All very trying for you. And the shot sounded very loud, you say? As though it were near at hand?"

"That was simply the state of my nerves."

"Of course. Of course. And what time was all this? To help us in tracing the telephone call, you know."

"About half-past six."

"You can't give it us more exactly than that?"

"Well, you see, the little clock on my mantelpiece had just chimed the half-hour, and I said, 'Surely that clock is fast.' (It does gain, that clock.) And I compared it with the watch I was wearing and that only said ten minutes past, but then I put it to my ear and found it had stopped. So I thought: 'Well, if that clock *is* fast, I shall hear the church tower in a moment or two.' And then, of course, the telephone bell rang, and I forgot all about it." She paused breathless.

"Well, that's near enough," said Colonel Melchett. "We'll have it looked into for you, Mrs. Price Ridley."

"Just think of it as a silly joke, and don't worry, Mrs. Price Ridley," I said.

She looked at me coldly. Evidently the incident of the pound note still rankled.

"Very strange things have been happening in this village lately," she said, addressing herself to Melchett. "Very strange things indeed. Colonel Protheroe was going to look into them, and what happened to him, poor man? Perhaps I shall be the next?"

And on that she took her departure, shaking her head with a kind of ominous melancholy. Melchett muttered under his breath: "No such luck." Then his face grew grave, and he looked inquiringly at Inspector Slack.

That worthy nodded his head slowly.

"This about settles it, sir. That's three people who heard the shot. We've got to find out now who fired it. This business of Mr. Redding's has delayed us. But we've got several starting points. Thinking Mr. Redding was guilty, I didn't bother to look into them. But that's all changed now. And now one of the first things to do is to look up that telephone call."

"Mrs. Price Ridley's?"

The inspector grinned.

"No—though I suppose we'd better make a note of that or else we shall have the old girl bothering in here again. No, I meant that fake call that got the vicar out of the way."

"Yes," said Melchett, "that's important."

"And the next thing is to find out what everyone was doing that evening between six and seven. Everyone at Old Hall, I mean, and pretty well everyone in the village as well."

I gave a sigh.

"What wonderful energy you have, Inspector Slack."

"I believe in hard work. We'll begin by just noting down your own movements, Mr. Clement."

"Willingly. The telephone call came through about half-past five."

"A man's voice, or a woman's?"

"A woman's. At least it sounded like a woman's. But of course I took it for granted it was Mrs. Abbott speaking."

"You didn't recognize it as being Mrs. Abbott's?"

"No, I can't say I did. I didn't notice the voice particularly or think about it."

"And you started right away? Walked? Haven't you got a bicycle?"

"No."

"I see. So it took you—how long?"

"It's very nearly two miles, whichever way you go."

"Through Old Hall woods is the shortest way, isn't it?"

"Actually, yes. But it's not particularly good going. I went and came back by the footpath across the fields."

"The one that comes out opposite the Vicarage gate?"

"Yes."

"And Mrs. Clement?"

"My wife was in London. She arrived back by the 6:50 train."

"Right. The maid I've seen. That finishes with the Vicarage. I'll be off to Old Hall next. And then I want an interview with Mrs. Lestrange. Queer, her going to see Protheroe the night before he was killed. A lot of queer things about this case."

I agreed.

Glancing at the clock, I realized that it was nearly lunch time. I invited Melchett to partake of pot luck with us, but he excused himself on the plea of having to go to the Blue Boar. The Blue Boar gives you a first-rate meal of the joint and two-vegetable type. I thought his choice was a wise one. After her interview with the police, Mary would probably be feeling more temperamental than usual.

14

ON MY WAY home, I ran into Miss Hartnell and she detained me at least ten minutes, declaiming in her deep bass voice against the improvidence and ungratefulness of the lower classes. The crux of the matter seemed to be that The Poor did not want Miss Hartnell in their houses. My sympathies were entirely on their side. I am debarred by my social standing from expressing my prejudices in the forceful manner they do.

I soothed her as best I could and made my escape.

Haydock overtook me in his car at the corner of the Vicarage road. "I've just taken Mrs. Protheroe home," he called.

He waited for me at the gate of his house.

"Come in a minute," he said. I complied.

"This is an extraordinary business," he said, as he threw his hat on a chair and opened the door into his surgery.

He sank down on a shabby leather chair and stared across the room. He looked harried and perplexed.

I told him that we had succeeded in fixing the time of the shot. He listened with an almost abstracted air.

"That lets Anne Protheroe out," he said. "Well, well, I'm glad it's neither of those two. I like 'em both."

I believed him, and yet it occurred to me to wonder why, since, as he said, he liked them both, their freedom from complicity seemed to have had the result of plunging him in gloom. This morning he had looked like a man with a weight lifted from his mind, now he looked thoroughly rattled and upset.

And yet I was convinced that he meant what he said. He was fond of both Anne Protheroe and Lawrence Redding. Why, then, this gloomy absorption? He roused himself with an effort.

"I meant to tell you about Hawes. All this business has driven him out of my mind."

"Is he really ill?"

"There's nothing radically wrong with him. You know, of course, that he's had Encephalitis Lethargica, sleepy sickness, as it's commonly called?"

"No," I said, very much surprised. "I didn't know anything of the kind. He never told me anything about it. When did he have it?"

"About a year ago. He recovered all right—as far as one ever recovers. It's a strange disease—has a queer moral effect. The whole character may change after it."

He was silent for a moment or two, and then said:

"We think with horror now of the days when we burnt witches. I believe the day will come when we will shudder to think that we ever hanged criminals."

"You don't believe in capital punishment?"

"It's not so much that." He paused. "You know," he said slowly, "I'd rather have my job than yours."

"Why?"

"Because your job deals very largely with what we call right and wrong— and I'm not at all sure that there's any such thing. Suppose it's all a question of glandular secretion. Too much of one gland, too little of another—and you get your murderer, your thief, your habitual criminal. Clement, I believe the time will come when we'll be horrified to think of the long centuries in which we've indulged in what you may call moral reprobation, to think how we've punished people for disease—which they can't help, poor devils. You don't hang a man for having tuberculosis."

"He isn't dangerous to the community."

"In a sense he is. He infects other people. Or take a man who fancies he's the Emperor of China. You don't say how wicked of him. I take your point about the community. The community must be protected. Shut up these people where they can't do any harm—even put them peacefully out of the way—yes, I'd go as far as that. But don't call it punishment. Don't bring shame on them and their innocent families."

I looked at him curiously.

"I've never heard you speak like this before."

"I don't usually air my theories abroad. Today I'm riding my hobby. You're an intelligent man, Clement, which is more than some parsons are. You won't admit, I dare say, that there's no such thing as what is technically termed 'Sin', but you're broadminded enough to consider the possibility of such a thing."

"It strikes at the root of all accepted ideas," I said.

"Yes, we're a narrow-minded, self-righteous lot, only too keen to judge matters we know nothing about. I honestly believe crime is a case for the doctor, not the policeman and not the parson. In the future, perhaps, there won't be any such thing."

"You'll have cured it?"

"We'll have cured it. Rather a wonderful thought. Have you ever studied the statistics of crime? No—very few people have. I have, though. You'd be amazed at the amount there is of adolescent crime, glands again, you see. Young Neil, the Oxfordshire murderer—killed five little girls before he was suspected. Nice lad—never given any trouble of any kind. Lily Rose, the little Cornish girl—killed her uncle because he docked her of sweets. Hit him when he was asleep with a coal hammer. Went home and a fortnight later killed her elder sister who had annoyed her about some trifling matter. Neither of them hanged, of course. Sent to a home. May be all right later—may not. Doubt if the girl will. The only thing she cares about is seeing the pigs killed. Do you know when suicide is commonest? Fifteen to sixteen years of age. From self-murder to murder of someone else isn't a very long step. But it's not a moral lack—it's a physical one."

"What you say is terrible!"

"No—it's only new to you. New truths have to be faced. One's ideas adjusted. But sometimes—it makes life difficult."

He sat there frowning, yet with a strange look of weariness.

"Haydock," I said, "if you suspected—if you knew—that a certain person was a murderer, would you give that person up to the law, or would you be tempted to shield them?"

I was quite unprepared for the effect of my question. He turned on me angrily and suspiciously.

"What makes you say that, Clement? What's in your mind? Out with it, man."

"Why, nothing particular," I said, rather taken aback. "Only—well, murder is in our minds just now. If by any chance you happened to discover the truth—I wondered how you would feel about it, that was all."

His anger died down. He stared once more straight ahead of him like a man trying to read the answer to a riddle that perplexes him, yet which exists only in his own brain.

"If I suspected—if I knew—I should do my duty, Clement. At least, I hope so."

"The question is—which way would you consider your duty lay?"

He looked at me with inscrutable eyes.

"That question comes to every man some time in his life, I suppose, Clement. And every man has to decide it in his own way."

"You don't know?"

"No, I don't know . . ."

I felt the best thing was to change the subject.

"That nephew of mine is enjoying this case thoroughly," I said. "Spends his entire time looking for footprints and cigarette ash."

Haydock smiled. "What age is he?"

"Just sixteen. You don't take tragedies seriously at that age. It's all Sherlock Holmes and Arsene Lupin to you."

Haydock said thoughtfully:

"He's a fine-looking boy. What are you going to do with him?"

"I can't afford a University education, I'm afraid. The boy himself wants to go into the Merchant Service. He failed for the Navy."

"Well—it's a hard life—but he might do worse. Yes, he might do worse."

"I must be going," I exclaimed, catching sight of the clock. "I'm nearly half an hour late for lunch."

My family were just sitting down when I arrived. They demanded a full account of the morning's activities, which I gave them, feeling, as I did so, that most of it was in the nature of an anticlimax.

Dennis, however, was highly entertained by the history of Mrs. Price Ridley's telephone call, and went into fits of laughter as I enlarged upon the nervous shock her system had sustained and the necessity for reviving her with damson gin.

"Serve the old cat right," he exclaimed. "She's got the worst tongue in the place. I wish I'd thought of ringing her up and giving her a fright. I say, Uncle Len, what about giving her a second dose?"

I hastily begged him to do nothing of the sort. Nothing is more dangerous than the well-meant efforts of the younger generation to assist you and show their sympathy.

Dennis's mood changed suddenly. He frowned and put on his man-of-the-world air.

"I've been with Lettice most of the morning," he said. "You know, Griselda, she's really *very* worried. She doesn't want to show it, but she is. Very worried indeed."

"I should hope so," said Griselda, with a toss of her head.

Griselda is not too fond of Lettice Protheroe.

"I don't think you're ever quite fair to Lettice."

"Don't you?" said Griselda.

"Lot's of people don't wear mourning."

Griselda was silent and so was I. Dennis continued:

"She doesn't talk to most people, but she *does* talk to me. She's awfully worried about the whole thing, and she thinks something ought to be done about it."

"She will find," I said, "that Inspector Slack shares her opinion. He is going up to Old Hall this afternoon, and will probably make the life of everybody there quite unbearable to them in his efforts to get at the truth."

"What do you think *is* the truth, Len?" asked my wife suddenly.

"It's hard to say, my dear. I can't say that at the moment I've any idea at all."

"Did you say that Inspector Slack was going to trace that telephone call—the one that took you to the Abbotts'?"

"Yes."

"But can he do it? Isn't it a very difficult thing to do?"

"I should not imagine so. The exchange will have a record of the calls."

"Oh!" My wife relapsed into thought.

"Uncle Len," said my nephew, "why were you so ratty with me this morning for joking about your wishing Colonel Protheroe to be murdered?"

"Because," I said, "there is a time for everything. Inspector Slack has no sense of humor. He took your words quite seriously, will probably cross-examine Mary, and will get out a warrant for my arrest."

"Doesn't he know when a fellow's ragging?"

"No," I said, "he does not. He has attained to his present position through hard work and zealous attention to duty. That has left him no time for the minor recreations of life."

"Do you like him, Uncle Len?"

"No," I said, "I do not. From the first moment I saw him I disliked him intensely. But I have no doubt that he is a highly successful man in his profession."

"You think he'll find out who shot old Protheroe?"

"If he doesn't," I said, "it will not be for the want of trying."

Mary appeared and said:

"Mr. Hawes wants to see you. I've put him in the drawing-room, and here's a note. Waiting for an answer. Verbal will do." I tore open the note and read it.

DEAR MR. CLEMENT

—I should be so very grateful if you could come and see me this afternoon as early as possible. I am in great trouble and would like your advice.

Sincerely yours,

ESTELLE LESTRANGE.

"Say I will come round in about half an hour," I said to Mary. Then I went into the drawing-room to see Hawes.

15

HAWES'S APPEARANCE DISTRESSED me very much. His hands were shaking and his face kept twitching nervously. In my opinion he should have been in bed, and I told him so. He insisted that he was perfectly well.

"I assure you, sir, I never felt better. Never in my life."

This was obviously so wide of the truth that I hardly knew how to answer. I have a certain admiration for a man who will not give in to illness, but Hawes was carrying the thing rather too far.

"I called to tell you how sorry I was—that such a thing should happen in the Vicarage."

"Yes," I said, "it's not very pleasant."

"It's terrible—quite terrible. It seems they haven't arrested Mr. Redding after all?"

"No. That was a mistake. He made—er—rather a foolish statement."

"And the police are now quite convinced that he is innocent?"

"Perfectly."

"Why is that, may I ask? Is it—I mean, do they suspect anyone else?"

I should never have suspected that Hawes would take such a keen interest in the details of a murder case. Perhaps it is because it happened in the Vicarage. He appeared as eager as a reporter.

"I don't know that I am completely in Inspector Slack's confidence. So far as I know, he does not suspect anyone in particular. He is at present engaged in making inquiries."

"Yes. Yes—of course. But who can one imagine doing such a dreadful thing?"

I shook my head.

"Colonel Protheroe was not a popular man, I know that. But murder! For murder—one would need a very strong motive."

"So I should imagine," I said.

"Who could have such a motive? Have the police any idea?"

"I couldn't say."

"He might have made enemies, you know. The more I think about it, the more I am convinced that he was the kind of man to have enemies. He had a reputation on the Bench for being very severe."

"I suppose he had."

"Why, don't you remember, sir? He was telling you yesterday morning about having been threatened by that man Archer."

"Now I come to think of it, so he did," I said. "Of course, I remember. You were quite near us at the time."

"Yes, I overheard what he was saying. Almost impossible to help it with Colonel Protheroe. He had such a very loud voice, hadn't he? I remember being impressed by your own words. That when his time came, he might have justice meted out to him instead of mercy."

"Did I say that?" I asked, frowning. My remembrance of my own words was slightly different.

"You said it very impressively, sir. I was struck by your words. Justice is a terrible thing. And to think the poor man was struck down shortly afterwards. It's almost as though you had a premonition."

"I had nothing of the sort," I said shortly. I rather dislike Hawes's tendency to mysticism. There is a touch of the visionary about him.

"Have you told the police about this man Archer, sir?"

"I know nothing about him."

"I mean, have you repeated to them what Colonel Protheroe said— about Archer having threatened him?"

"No," I said slowly. "I have not."

"But you are going to do so?"

I was silent. I dislike hounding a man down who has already got the forces of law and order against him. I held no brief for Archer. He is an inveterate poacher—one of those cheerful ne'er-do-wells that are to be found in any parish. Whatever he may have said in the heat of anger when he was sentenced I had no definite knowledge that he felt the same when he came out of prison.

"You heard the conversation," I said at last. "If you feel it your duty to go to the police with it, you must do so."

"It would come better from you, sir."

"Perhaps—but to tell the truth—well, I've no fancy for doing it. I might be helping to put the rope round the neck of an innocent man."

"But if he shot Colonel Protheroe—"

"Oh, if! There's no evidence of any kind that he did."

"His threats."

"Strictly speaking, the threats were not his, but Colonel Protheroe's. Colonel Protheroe was threatening to show Archer what vengeance was worth next time he caught him."

"I don't understand your attitude, sir."

"Don't you," I said wearily. "You're a young man. You're zealous in the cause of right. When you get to my age, you'll find that you like to give people the benefit of the doubt."

"It's not—I mean—"

He paused, and I looked at him in surprise.

"You haven't any—any idea of your own—as to the identity of the murderer, I mean?"

"Good heavens, no."

Hawes persisted. "Or as to the—the motive?"

"No. Have you?"

"I? No, indeed. I just wondered. If Colonel Protheroe had—had confided in you in any way—mentioned anything . . ."

"His confidences, such as they were, were heard by the whole village street yesterday morning," I said dryly.

"Yes. Yes, of course. And you don't think—about Archer?"

"The police will know all about Archer soon enough," I said. "If I'd heard him threaten Colonel Protheroe myself, that would be a different matter. But you may be sure that if he actually has threatened him, half the people in the village will have heard him, and the news will get to the police all right. You, of course, must do as you like about the matter."

But Hawes seemed curiously unwilling to do anything himself.

The man's whole attitude was nervous and queer. I recalled what Haydock had said about his illness. There, I supposed, lay the explanation.

He took his leave unwillingly, as though he had more to say, and didn't know how to say it.

Before he left, I arranged with him to take the service for the Mothers' Union, followed by the meeting of District Visitors. I had several projects of my own for the afternoon.

Dismissing Hawes and his troubles from my mind I started off for Mrs. Lestrange.

On the table in the hall lay the *Guardian* and the *Church Times* unopened.

As I walked, I remembered that Mrs. Lestrange had had an interview with Colonel Protheroe the night before his death. It was possible that something had transpired in that interview which would throw light upon the problem of his murder.

I was shown straight into the little drawing-room, and Mrs. Lestrange rose to meet me. I was struck anew by the marvelous atmosphere that this woman could create. She wore a dress of some dead black material that showed off the extraordinary fairness of her skin. There was something curiously dead about her face. Only the eyes were burningly alive. There was a watchful look in them today. Otherwise she showed no signs of animation.

"It was very good of you to come, Mr. Clement," she said, as she shook hands. "I wanted to speak to you the other day. Then I decided not to do so. I was wrong."

"As I told you then, I shall be glad to do anything that can help you."

"Yes, you said that. And you said it as though you meant it. Very few people, Mr. Clement, in this world have ever sincerely wished to help me."

"I can hardly believe that, Mrs. Lestrange."

"It is true. Most people—most men, at any rate, are out for their own hand." There was a bitterness in her voice.

I did not answer, and she went on:

"Sit down, won't you?"

I obeyed, and she took a chair facing me. She hesitated a moment and then began to speak very slowly and thoughtfully, seeming to weigh each word as she uttered it.

"I am in a very peculiar position, Mr. Clement, and I want to ask your advice. That is, I want to ask your advice as to what I should do next. What is past is past and cannot be undone. You understand?"

Before I could reply, the maid who had admitted me opened the door and said with a scared face:

"Oh! please, ma'am, there is a police inspector here, and he says he must speak to you, please."

There was a pause. Mrs. Lestrange's face did not change. Only her eyes very slowly closed and opened again. She seemed to swallow once or twice, then she said in exactly the same clear, calm voice: "Show him in, Hilda."

I was about to rise, but she motioned me back again with an imperious hand.

"If you do not mind—I should be much obliged if you would stay."

I resumed my seat.

"Certainly, if you wish it," I murmured, as Slack entered with a brisk regulation tread.

"Good afternoon, madam," he began.

"Good afternoon, Inspector."

At this moment, he caught sight of me and scowled. There is no doubt about it, Slack does not like me.

"You have no objection to the vicar's presence, I hope?"

I suppose that Slack could not very well say he had.

"No-o," he said grudgingly. "Though, perhaps, it might be better—"

Mrs. Lestrange paid no attention to the hint.

"What can I do for you, Inspector?" she asked.

"It's this way, madam. Murder of Colonel Protheroe. I'm in charge of the case and making inquiries."

Mrs. Lestrange nodded.

"Just as a matter of form, I'm asking everyone just where they were yesterday evening between the hours of 6 and 7 p.m. Just as a matter of form, you understand."

Mrs. Lestrange did not seem in the least discomposed.

"You want to know where I was yesterday evening between six and seven?"

"If you please, madam."

"Let me see." She reflected a moment. "I was here. In this house."

"Oh!" I saw the inspector's eyes flash. "And your maid—you have only one maid, I think—can confirm that statement?"

"No, it was Hilda's afternoon out."

"I see."

"So, unfortunately, you will have to take my word for it," said Mrs. Lestrange pleasantly.

"You seriously declare that you were at home all the afternoon?"

"You said between six and seven, Inspector. I was out for a walk early in the afternoon. I returned some time before five o'clock."

"Then if a lady—Miss Hartnell, for instance—were to declare that she came here about six o'clock, rang the bell, but could make no one hear and was compelled to go away again—you'd say she was mistaken, eh?"

"Oh! no," Mrs. Lestrange shook her head.

"But—"

"If your maid is in, she can say not at home. If one is alone and does not happen to want to see callers—well, the only thing to do is to let them ring."

Inspector Slack looked slightly baffled.

"Elderly women bore me dreadfully," said Mrs. Lestrange. "And Miss Hartnell is particularly boring. She must have rung at least half a dozen times before she went away."

She smiled sweetly at Inspector Slack.

The inspector shifted his ground.

"Then if anyone were to say they'd seen you out and about then—"

"Oh! but they didn't, did they?" She was quick to sense his weak point. "No one saw me out, because I was in, you see."

"Quite so, madam."

The inspector hitched his chair a little nearer.

"Now I understand, Mrs. Lestrange, that you paid a visit to Colonel Protheroe at Old Hall the night before his death."

Mrs. Lestrange said calmly: "That is so."

"Can you indicate to me the nature of that interview?"

"It concerned a private matter, Inspector."

"I'm afraid I must ask you to tell me the nature of that private matter."

"I shall not tell you anything of the kind. I will only assure you that nothing which was said at that interview could possibly have any bearing upon the crime."

"I don't think you are the best judge of that."

"At any rate, you will have to take my word for it, Inspector."

"In fact, I have to take your word about everything."

"It does seem rather like it," she agreed, still with the same smiling calm.

Inspector Slack grew very red.

"This is a serious matter, Mrs. Lestrange. I want the truth—" He banged his fist down on a table. "And I mean to get it."

Mrs. Lestrange said nothing at all.

"Don't you see, madam, that you're putting yourself in a very fishy position?"

Still Mrs. Lestrange said nothing.

"You'll be required to give evidence at the inquest."

"Yes."

Just the monosyllable. Unemphatic, uninterested. The inspector altered his tactics.

"You were acquainted with Colonel Protheroe?"

"Yes, I was acquainted with him."

"Well acquainted?"

There was a pause before she said:

"I had not seen him for several years."

"You were acquainted with Mrs. Protheroe?"

"No."

"You'll excuse me, but it was a very unusual time to make a call."

"Not from my point of view."

"What do you mean by that?"

"I wanted to see Colonel Protheroe alone. I did not want to see Mrs. Protheroe or Miss Protheroe. I considered this the best way of accomplishing my object."

"Why didn't you want to see Mrs. or Miss Protheroe?"

"That, Inspector, is my business."

"Then you refuse to say more?"

"Absolutely."

Inspector Slack rose.

"You'll be putting yourself in a nasty position, madam, if you're not careful. All this looks bad—it looks very bad."

She laughed. I could have told Inspector Slack that this was not the kind of woman who is easily frightened.

"Well," he said, extricating himself with dignity, "don't say I haven't warned you, that's all. Good afternoon, madam, and mind you we're going to get at the truth."

He departed. Mrs. Lestrange rose and held out her hand.

"I am going to send you away—yes, it is better so. You see, it is too late for advice now. I have chosen my part."

She repeated in a rather forlorn voice:

"I have chosen my part."

16

As I WENT out I ran into Haydock on the doorstep. He glanced sharply after Slack, who was just passing through the gate, and demanded: "Has he been questioning her?"

"Yes."

"He's been civil, I hope?"

Civility, to my mind, is an art which Inspector Slack has never learned, but I presumed that according to his own lights, civil he had been, and anyway, I didn't want to upset Haydock any further. He was looking worried and upset as it was. So I said he had been quite civil.

Haydock nodded and passed on into the house, and I went on down the village street, where I soon caught up the inspector. I fancy that he was walking slowly on purpose. Much as he dislikes me, he is not the man to let dislike stand in the way of acquiring any useful information.

"Do you know anything about the lady?" he asked me point blank.

I said I knew nothing whatever.

"She's never said anything about why she came here to live?"

"No."

"Yet you go and see her?"

"It is one of my duties to call on my parishioners," I replied, evading to remark that I had been sent for.

"H'm, I suppose it is." He was silent for a minute or two and then, unable to resist discussing his recent failure, he went on: "Fishy business, it looks to me."

"You think so?"

"If you ask me, I say 'blackmail'. Seems funny, when you think of what Colonel Protheroe was always supposed to be. But there, you never can tell. He wouldn't be the first churchwarden who'd led a double life."

Faint remembrances of Miss Marple's remarks on the same subject floated through my mind.

"You really think that's likely?"

"Well, it fits the facts, sir. Why did a smart, well-dressed lady come down to this quiet little hole? Why did she go and see him at that funny time of day? Why did she avoid seeing Mrs. and Miss Protheroe? Yes, it all hangs together. Awkward for her to admit—blackmail's a punishable offense. But we'll get the truth out of her. For all we know it may have a very important bearing on the case. If Colonel Protheroe had some guilty secret in his life—something disgraceful—well, you can see for yourself what a field it opens up."

I suppose it did.

"I've been trying to get the butler to talk. He might have overheard some of the conversation between Colonel Protheroe and Lestrange. Butlers do sometimes. But he swears he hasn't the least idea of what the conversation was about. By the way, he got the sack through it. The colonel went for him, being angry at his having let her in. The butler retorted by giving notice. Says he didn't like the place anyway and had been thinking of leaving for some time."

"Really."

"So that gives us another person who had a grudge against the colonel."

"You don't seriously suspect the man—what's his name, by the way?"

"His name's Reeves, and I don't say I do suspect him. What I say is, you never know. I don't like that soapy, oily manner of his."

I wonder what Reeves would say of Inspector Slack's manner.

"I'm going to question the chauffeur now."

"Perhaps, then," I said, "you'll give me a lift in your car. I want a short interview with Mrs. Protheroe."

"What about?"

"The funeral arrangements."

"Oh!" Inspector Slack was slightly taken aback. "The inquest's tomorrow, Saturday."

"Just so. The funeral will probably be arranged for Tuesday."

Inspector Slack seemed to be a little ashamed of himself for his brusqueness. He held out an olive branch in the shape of an invitation to be present at the interview with the chauffeur, Manning.

Manning was a nice lad, not more than twenty-five or -six years of age. He was inclined to be awed by the inspector.

"Now, then, my lad," said Slack, "I want a little information from you."

"Yes, sir," stammered the chauffeur. "Certainly, sir."

If he had committed the murder himself he could not have been more alarmed.

"You took your master to the village yesterday?"

"Yes, sir."

"What time was that?"

"Five-thirty."

"Mrs. Protheroe went too?"

"Yes, sir."

"You went straight to the village?"

"Yes, sir."

"You didn't stop anywhere on the way?"

"No, sir."

"What did you do when you got there?"

"The colonel got out and told me he wouldn't want the car again. He'd walk home. Mrs. Protheroe had some shopping to do. The parcels were put in the car. Then she said that was all, and I drove home."

"Leaving her in the village?"

"Yes, sir."

"What time was that?"

"A quarter past six, sir. A quarter past exactly."

"Where did you leave her?"

"By the church, sir."

"Had the colonel mentioned at all where he was going?"

"He said something about having to see the vet . . . something to do with one of the horses."

"I see. And you drove straight back here?"

"Yes, sir."

"There are two entrances to Old Hall, by the South Lodge and by the North Lodge. I take it that going to the village you would go by the South Lodge?"

"Yes, sir, always."

"And you came back the same way?"

"Yes, sir."

"H'm. I think that's all. Ah! here's Miss Protheroe."

Lettice drifted towards us.

"I want the Fiat, Manning," she said. "Start her for me, will you?"

"Very good, miss."

He went towards a two-seater and lifted the bonnet.

"Just a minute, Miss Protheroe," said Slack. "It's necessary that I should have a record of everybody's movements yesterday afternoon. No offense meant."

Lettice stared at him.

"I never know the time of anything," she said.

"I understand you went out soon after lunch yesterday?"

She nodded.

"Where to, please?"

"To play tennis."

"Who with?"

"The Hartley Napiers."

"At Much Benham?"

"Yes."

"And you returned?"

"I don't know. I tell you I never know these things."

"You returned," I said, "about seven-thirty."

"That's right," said Lettice. "In the middle of the shemozzle. Anne having fits and Griselda supporting her."

"Thank you, miss," said the inspector. "That's all I want to know."

"How queer," said Lettice. "It seems so uninteresting."

She moved towards the Fiat.

The inspector touched his forehead in a surreptitious manner.

"A bit wanting?" he suggested.

"Not in the least," I said. "But she likes to be thought so."

"Well, I'm off to question the maids now."

One cannot really like Slack, but one can admire his energy.

We parted company and I inquired of Reeves if I could see Mrs. Protheroe. "She is lying down, sir, at the moment."

"Then I'd better not disturb her."

"Perhaps if you would wait, sir; I know that Mrs. Protheroe is anxious to see you. She was saying as much at luncheon."

He showed me into the drawing-room, switching on the electric lights since the blinds were down.

"A very sad business all this," I said.

"Yes, sir." His voice was cold and respectful.

I looked at him. What feelings were at work under that impassive demeanor? Were there things that he knew and could have told us? There is nothing so inhuman as the mask of the good servant.

"Is there anything more, sir?"

Was there just a hint of anxiety to be gone behind that correct expression?

"There's nothing more," I said.

I had a very short time to wait before Anne Protheroe came to me. We discussed and settled a few arrangements and then:

"What a wonderfully kind man Dr. Haydock is!" she exclaimed.

"Haydock is the best fellow I know."

"He has been amazingly kind to me. But he looks very sad, doesn't he?"

It had never occurred to me to think of Haydock as sad. I turned the idea over in my mind.

"I don't think I've ever noticed it," I said at last.

"I never have, until today."

"One's own troubles sharpen one's eyes sometimes," I said.

"That's very true." She paused and then said:

"Mr. Clement, there's one thing I absolutely *cannot* make out. If my husband were shot immediately after I left him, how was it that I didn't hear the shot?"

"They have reason to believe that the shot was fired later."

"But the 6:20 on the note?"

"Was possibly added by a different hand—the murderer's."

Her cheek paled.

"How horrible!"

"It didn't strike you that the date was not in his handwriting?"

"None of it looked like his handwriting."

There was some truth in this observation. It was a somewhat illegible scrawl, not so precise as Protheroe's writing usually was.

"You are sure they don't still suspect Lawrence?"

"I think he is definitely cleared."

"But, Mr. Clement, who can it be? Lucius was not popular, I know, but I don't think he had any real enemies. Not—not that kind of enemy."

I shook my head. "It's a mystery."

I thought wonderingly of Miss Marple's seven suspects. Who could they be?

After I took leave of Anne, I proceeded to put a certain plan of mine into action.

I returned from Old Hall by way of the private path. When I reached the stile, I retraced my steps and, choosing a place where I fancied the undergrowth showed signs of being disturbed, I turned aside from the path and forced my way through the bushes. The wood was a thick one, with a good deal of tangled undergrowth. My progress was not very fast, and I suddenly became aware that someone else was moving amongst the bushes not very far from me. As I paused irresolutely, Lawrence Redding came into sight. He was carrying a large stone.

I suppose I must have looked surprised, for he suddenly burst out laughing.

"No," he said, "it's not a clue, it's a peace offering."

"A peace offering?"

"Well, a basis for negotiations, shall we say? I want an excuse for calling on your neighbor, Miss Marple, and I have been told there is nothing she likes so much as a nice bit of rock or stone for the Japanese gardens she makes."

"Quite true," I said. "But what do you want with the old lady?"

"Just this. If there was anything to be seen yesterday evening Miss

Marple saw it. I don't mean anything necessarily connected with the crime—that she would think connected with the crime. I mean some outré or bizarre incident, some simple little happening that might give us a clue to the truth. Something that she wouldn't think worth while mentioning to the police."

"It's possible, I suppose."

"It's worth trying anyhow. Clement, I'm going to get to the bottom of this business. For Anne's sake, if nobody else's. And I haven't any too much confidence in Slack—he's a zealous fellow, but zeal can't really take the place of brains."

"I see," I said, "that you are that favorite character of fiction, the amateur detective. I don't know that they really hold their own with the professional in real life."

He looked at me shrewdly and suddenly laughed.

"What are you doing in the wood, padre?"

I had the grace to blush.

"Just the same as I am doing, I dare swear. We've got the same idea, haven't we? *How did the murderer come to the study?* First way, along the lane and through the gate, second way, by the front door, third way—is there a third way? My idea was to see if there was any signs of the bushes being disturbed or broken anywhere near the wall of the Vicarage garden."

"That was just my idea," I admitted.

"I hadn't really got down to the job, though," continued Lawrence. "Because it occurred to me that I'd like to see Miss Marple first, to make quite sure that no one did pass along the lane yesterday evening whilst we were in the studio."

I shook my head.

"She was quite positive that nobody did."

"Yes, nobody whom she would call anybody—sounds mad, but you see what I mean. But there might have been someone like a postman or a milkman or a butcher's boy—someone whose presence would be so natural that you wouldn't think of mentioning it."

"You've been reading G. K. Chesterton," I said, and Lawrence did not deny it.

"But don't you think there's just possibly something in the idea?"

"Well, I suppose there might be," I admitted.

Without further ado, we made our way to Miss Marple's. She was working in the garden, and called out to us as we climbed over the stile.

"You see," murmured Lawrence, "she sees everybody."

She received us very graciously and was much pleased with Lawrence's immense rock, which he presented with all due solemnity.

"It's very thoughtful of you, Mr. Redding. Very thoughtful indeed."

Emboldened by this, Lawrence embarked on his questions. Miss Marple listened attentively.

"Yes, I see what you mean, and I quite agree, it is the sort of thing no one mentions or bothers to mention. But I can assure you that there was nothing of the kind. Nothing whatever."

"You are sure, Miss Marple?"

"Quite sure."

"Did you see anyone go by the path into the wood that afternoon?" I asked. "Or come from it?"

"Oh! yes, quite a number of people. Dr. Stone and Miss Cram went that way—it's the nearest way to the Barrow for them. That was a little after two o'clock. And Dr. Stone returned that way—as you know, Mr. Redding, since he joined you and Mrs. Protheroe."

"By the way," I said. "That shot—the one you heard, Miss Marple. Mr. Redding and Mrs. Protheroe must have heard it too."

I looked inquiringly at Lawrence.

"Yes," he said, frowning. "I believe I did hear some shots. Weren't there one or two shots?"

"I only heard one," said Miss Marple.

"It's only the vaguest impression in my mind," said Lawrence. "Curse it all, I wish I could remember. If only I'd known. You see, I was so completely taken up with—with—"

He paused, embarrassed.

I gave a tactful cough. Miss Marple, with a touch of prudishness, changed the subject.

"Inspector Slack has been trying to get me to say whether I heard the shot after Mr. Redding and Mrs. Protheroe had left the studio or before. I've had to confess that I really could not say definitely, but I have the impression—which is growing stronger the more I think about it—that it was after."

"Then that lets the celebrated Dr. Stone out anyway," said Lawrence, with a sigh. "Not that there has ever been the slightest reason why he should be suspected of shooting poor old Protheroe."

"Ah!" said Miss Marple. "But I always find it prudent to suspect everybody just a little. What I say is, you really never *know,* do you?"

This was typical of Miss Marple. I asked Lawrence if he agreed with her about the shot.

"I really can't say. You see, it was such an ordinary sound. I should be inclined to think it had been fired when we were in the studio. The sound would have been deadened and—and one would have noticed it less there."

For other reasons than the sound being deadened, I thought to myself!

"I must ask Anne," said Lawrence. "She may remember. By the way, there seems to me to be one curious fact that needs explanation. Mrs. Lestrange, the Mystery Lady of St. Mary Mead, paid a visit to old Protheroe after dinner on Wednesday night. And nobody seems to have any idea what it was all about. Old Protheroe said nothing to either his wife or Lettice."

"Perhaps the vicar knows," said Miss Marple.

Now how did the woman know that I had been to visit Mrs. Lestrange that afternoon? The way she always knows things is uncanny.

I shook my head and said I could throw no light upon the matter.

"What does Inspector Slack think?" asked Miss Marple.

"He's done his best to bully the butler—but apparently the butler wasn't curious enough to listen at the door. So there it is—no one knows."

"I expect someone overheard something, though, don't you?" said Miss Marple. "I mean, somebody always *does*. I think that is where Mr. Redding might find out something."

"But Mrs. Protheroe knows nothing."

"I didn't mean Anne Protheroe," said Miss Marple. "I meant the women servants. They do so hate telling anything to the police. But a nice-looking young man—you'll excuse me, Mr. Redding—and one who has been unjustly suspected—oh! I'm sure they'd tell him at once."

"I'll go and have a try this evening," said Lawrence with vigor. "Thanks for the hint, Miss Marple. I'll go after—well, after a little job the vicar and I are going to do."

It occurred to me that we had better be getting on with it. I said goodbye to Miss Marple and we entered the woods once more.

First we went up the path till we came to a new spot where it certainly looked as though someone had left the path on the right-hand side. Lawrence explained that he had already followed this particular trail and found it led nowhere, but he added that we might as well try again. He might have been wrong.

It was, however, as he had said. After about ten or twelve yards any sign of broken and trampled leaves petered out. It was from this spot that Lawrence had broken back towards the path to meet me earlier in the afternoon.

We emerged on the path again and walked a little farther along it. Again we came to a place where the bushes seemed disturbed. The signs were very slight but, I thought, unmistakable. This time the trail was more promising. By a devious course, it wound steadily nearer to the Vicarage. Presently we arrived at where the bushes grew thickly up to the wall. The wall is a high one and ornamented with fragments of broken bottles on the top. If anyone had placed a ladder against it, we ought to find traces of their passage.

We were working our way slowly along the wall when a sound came to our ears of a breaking twig. I pressed forward, forcing my way through a thick tangle of shrubs—and came face to face with Inspector Slack.

"So it's you," he said. "And Mr. Redding. Now what do you think you two gentlemen are doing?"

Slightly crestfallen, we explained.

"Quite so," said the inspector. "Not being the fools we're usually thought to be, I had the same idea myself. I've been here over an hour. Would you like to know something?"

"Yes," I said meekly.

"Whoever murdered Colonel Protheroe didn't come this way to do it! There's not a sign either on this side of the wall, or the other. Whoever murdered Colonel Protheroe came through the front door. There's no other way he could have come."

"Impossible," I cried.

"Why impossible? Your door stands open. Anyone's only got to walk in. They can't be seen from the kitchen. They know you're safely out of the way, they know Mrs. Clement is in London, they know Mr. Dennis is at a tennis party. Simple as ABC. And they don't need to go or come through the village. Just opposite the Vicarage gate is a public footpath, and from it you can turn into these same woods and come out whichever way you choose. Unless Mrs. Price Ridley were to come out of her front gate at that particular minute, it's all clear sailing. A great deal more so than climbing over walls. The side windows of the upper story of Mrs. Price Ridley's house do overlook most of that wall. No, depend upon it, that's the way he came."

It really seemed as though he must be right.

17

INSPECTOR SLACK CAME round to see me the following morning. He is, I think, thawing towards me. In time, he may forget the incident of the clock.

"Well, sir," he greeted me. "I've traced that telephone call that you received."

"Indeed?" I said eagerly.

"It's rather odd. It was put through from the North Lodge of Old Hall. Now that lodge is empty, the lodge-keepers have been pensioned off and the new lodge-keepers aren't in yet. The place was empty and convenient—a window at the back was open. No fingerprints on the instrument itself—it had been wiped clear. That's suggestive."

"How do you mean?"

"I mean that it shows that call was put through deliberately to get you out of the way. Therefore the murder was carefully planned in advance. If it had been just a harmless practical joke, the fingerprints wouldn't have been wiped off so carefully."

"No. I see that."

"It also shows that the murderer was well acquainted with Old Hall and its surroundings. It wasn't Mrs. Protheroe who put that call through. I've accounted for every moment of her time that afternoon. There are half a dozen servants who can swear that she was at home up till five-thirty. Then the car came round and drove Colonel Protheroe and her to the village. The colonel went to see Quinton, the vet, about one of the horses. Mrs. Protheroe did some ordering at the grocer's and at the fish shop, and from there came straight down the back lane where Miss Marple saw her. All the shops agree she carried no handbag with her. The old lady was right."

"She usually is," I said mildly.

"And Miss Protheroe was over at Much Benham at 5:30."

"Quite so," I said. "My nephew was there too."

"That disposes of her. The maids seem all right—a bit hysterical and upset, but what can you expect? Of course, I've got my eye on the butler—what with giving notice and all. But I don't think he knows anything about it."

"Your inquiries seem to have had rather a negative result, Inspector."

"They do and they do not, sir. There's one very queer thing has turned up—quite unexpectedly, I may say."

"Yes?"

"You remember the fuss that Mrs. Price Ridley, who lives next door to you, was kicking up yesterday morning? About being rung up on the telephone?"

"Yes?" I said.

"Well, we traced the call just to calm her—and where on this earth do you think it was put through from?"

"A call office?" I hazarded.

"No, Mr. Clement. That call was put through from Mr. Lawrence Redding's cottage."

"What?" I exclaimed, surprised.

"Yes. A bit odd, isn't it? Mr. Redding had nothing to do with it. At that time, 6:30, he was on his way to the Blue Boar with Dr. Stone in full view of the village. But there it is. Suggestive, eh? Someone walked into that empty cottage and used the telephone; who was it? That's two queer telephone calls in one day. Makes you think there's some connection between them. I'll eat my hat if they weren't both put through by the same person."

"But with what object?"

"Well, that's what we've got to find out. There seems no particular point in the second one, but there must be a point somewhere. And you see the significance? Mr. Redding's house used to telephone from. Mr. Redding's pistol. All throwing suspicion on Mr. Redding."

"It would be more to the point to have put through the *first* call from his house," I objected.

"Ah! but I've been thinking that out. What did Mr. Redding do most afternoons? He went up to Old Hall and painted Miss Protheroe. And from his cottage he'd go on his motor bicycle, passing through the North Gate. Now you see the point of the call being put through from there. *The murderer is someone who didn't know about the quarrel and that Mr. Redding wasn't going up to Old Hall any more.*"

I reflected a moment to let the inspector's points sink into my brain. They seemed to me logical and unavoidable.

"Were there any fingerprints on the receiver in Mr. Redding's cottage?" I asked.

"There were not," said the inspector bitterly. "That dratted old woman who goes and does for him had been and dusted them off yesterday morning." He reflected wrathfully for a few minutes. "She's a stupid old fool, anyway. Can't remember when she saw the pistol last. It might have been there on the morning of the crime, or it might not. 'She couldn't say, she's sure.' They're all alike!

"Just as a matter of form, I went round and saw Dr Stone," he went on. "I must say he was pleasant as could be about it. He and Miss Cram went up to that mound—or barrow—or whatever you call it, about half-past two yesterday, and stayed there all the afternoon. Dr. Stone came back alone, and she came later. He says he didn't hear any shot, but admits he's absent-minded. But it all bears out what we think."

"Only," I said, "you haven't caught the murderer."

"Hm," said the inspector. "It was a woman's voice you heard through the telephone. It was in all probability a woman's voice Mrs. Price Ridley heard. If only that shot hadn't come hard on the close of the telephone call—well, I'd know where to look."

"Where?"

"Ah! that's just what it's best not to say, sir."

Unblushingly, I suggested a glass of old port. I have some very fine old vintage port. Eleven o'clock in the morning is not the usual time for drinking port, but I did not think that mattered with Inspector Slack. It was, of course, cruel abuse of the vintage port, but one must not be squeamish about such things.

When Inspector Slack had polished off the second glass, he began to unbend and become genial. Such is the effect of that particular port.

"I don't suppose it matters with you, sir," he said. "You'll keep it to yourself? No letting it get round the parish."

I reassured him.

"Seeing as the whole thing happened in your house, it almost seems as though you had a right to know."

"Just what I feel myself," I said.

"Well, then, sir, what about the lady who called on Colonel Protheroe the night before the murder?"

"Mrs. Lestrange," I cried, speaking rather loud in my astonishment.

The inspector threw me a reproachful glance.

"Not so loud, sir. Mrs. Lestrange is the lady I've got my eye on. You remember what I told you—blackmail."

"Hardly a reason for murder. Wouldn't it be a case of killing the goose that laid the golden eggs? That is, assuming that your hypothesis is true, which I don't for a minute admit."

The inspector winked at me in a common manner.

"Ah! she's the kind the gentlemen will always stand up for. Now look here, sir. Suppose she's successfully blackmailed the old gentleman in the past. After a lapse of years, she gets wind of him, comes down here and tries it on again. *But,* in the meantime, things have changed. The law has taken up a very different stand. Every facility is given nowadays to people prosecuting for blackmail—names are not allowed to be reported in the press. Suppose Colonel Protheroe turns round and says he'll have the law on her. She's in a nasty position. They give a very severe sentence for blackmail. The boot's on the other leg. The only thing to do to save herself is to put him out good and quick."

I was silent. I had to admit that the case the inspector had built up was plausible. Only one thing to my mind made it inadmissible—the personality of Mrs. Lestrange.

"I don't agree with you, Inspector," I said. "Mrs. Lestrange doesn't seem to me to be a potential blackmailer. She's—well, it's an old-fashioned word, but she's a—lady."

He threw me a pitying glance.

"Ah! well, sir," he said tolerantly, "you're a clergyman. You don't know half of what goes on. Lady indeed! You'd be surprised if you knew some of the things I know."

"I'm not referring to mere social position. Anyway, I should imagine Mrs. Lestrange to be a *déclassée*. What I mean is a question of—personal refinement."

"You don't see her with the same eyes as I do, sir. I may be a man—but I'm a police officer, too. They can't get over me with their personal refinement. Why, that woman is the kind who could stick a knife into you without turning a hair."

Curiously enough, I could believe Mrs. Lestrange guilty of murder much more easily than I could believe her capable of blackmail.

"But, of course, she can't have been telephoning to the old lady next door and shooting Colonel Protheroe at one and the same time," continued the inspector.

The words were hardly out of his mouth when he slapped his leg ferociously.

"Got it," he exclaimed. "That's the point of the telephone call. Kind of *alibi*. Knew we'd connect it with the first one. I'm going to look into this. She may have bribed some village lad to do the phoning for her. *He'd* never think of connecting it with the murder."

The inspector hurried off.

"Miss Marple wants to see you," said Griselda, putting her head in. "She sent over a very incoherent note—all spidery and underlined. I couldn't read most of it. Apparently she can't leave home herself. Hurry up and go across and see her and find out what it is. I've got my old women coming in two minutes or I'd come myself. I do hate old women—they tell you about their bad legs and sometimes insist on showing them to you. What luck that the inquest is this afternoon! You won't have to go and watch the Boys' Club Cricket Match."

I hurried off, considerably exercised in my mind as to the reason for this summons.

I found Miss Marple in what, I believe, is described as a fluster. She was very pink and slightly incoherent.

"My nephew," she explained. "My nephew, Raymond West, the author.

He is coming down today. Such a to-do. I have to see to everything myself. You cannot trust a maid to air a bed properly, and we must, of course, have a meat meal tonight. Gentlemen require such a lot of meat, do they not? And drink. There certainly should be some drink in the house—and a siphon."

"If I can do anything—" I began.

"Oh! how very kind. But I did not mean that. There is plenty of time really. He brings his own pipe and tobacco, I am glad to say. Glad because it saves me from knowing which kind of cigarettes are right to buy. But rather sorry, too, because it takes so long for the smell to get out of the curtains. Of course, I open the window and shake them well very early every morning. Raymond gets up very late—I think writers often do. He writes very clever books, I believe, though people are not really nearly so unpleasant as he makes out. Clever young men know so little of life, don't you think?"

"Would you like to bring him to dinner at the Vicarage?" I asked, still unable to gather why I had been summoned.

"Oh! no, thank you," said Miss Marple. "It's very kind of you," she added.

"There was—er—something you wanted to see me about, I think," I suggested desperately.

"Oh! of course. In all the excitement it had gone right out of my head." She broke off and called to her maid.

"Emily—Emily. Not those sheets. The frilled ones with the monogram, and don't put them too near the fire."

She closed the door and returned to me on tiptoe.

"It's just rather a curious thing that happened last night," she explained. "I thought you would like to hear about it, though at the moment it doesn't seem to make sense. I felt very wakeful last night—wondering about all this sad business. And I got up and looked out of my window. And what do you think I saw?"

I looked, inquiring.

"Gladys Cram," said Miss Marple, with great emphasis. "As I live, going into the wood with a suitcase."

"A suitcase?"

"Isn't it extraordinary? What should she want with a suitcase in the wood at twelve o'clock at night?"

"You see," said Miss Marple. "I daresay it has nothing to do with the murder. But it is a Peculiar Thing. And just at present we all feel we must take notice of Peculiar Things."

"Perfectly amazing," I said. "Was she going to—er—sleep in the barrow by any chance?"

"She didn't, at any rate," said Miss Marple. "Because quite a short time afterwards she came back, and she hadn't got the suitcase with her."

18

THE INQUEST WAS was held that afternoon (Saturday) at two o'clock at
the Blue Boar. The local excitement was, I need hardly say, tremendous.
There had been no murder in St. Mary Mead for at least fifteen years.
And to have someone like Colonel Protheroe murdered actually in the
Vicarage study is such a feast of sensation as rarely falls to the lot of a
village population.

Various comments floated to my ears which I was probably not meant
to hear.

"There's vicar. Looks pale, don't he? I wonder if he had a hand in it.
'Twas done at Vicarage, after all." "How can you, Mary Adams? And
him visiting Henry Abbott at the time." "Oh! but they do say him and
the colonel had words. There's Mary Hill. Giving herself airs, she is, on
account of being in service there. Hush, here's coroner."

The coroner was Dr. Roberts of our adjoining town of Much Benham.
He cleared his throat, adjusted his eyeglasses, and looked important.

To recapitulate all the evidence would be merely tiresome. Lawrence
Redding gave evidence of finding the body, and identified the pistol as
belonging to him. To the best of his belief he had seen it on the Tuesday,
two days previously. It was kept on a shelf in his cottage, and the door
of the cottage was habitually unlocked.

Mrs. Protheroe gave evidence that she had last seen her husband at
about a quarter to six when they separated in the village street. She
agreed to call for him at the Vicarage later. She had gone to the Vicarage
about a quarter past six, by way of the back lane and the garden gate.
She had heard no voices in the study and had imagined that the room
was empty, but her husband might have been sitting at the writing-table,
in which case she would not have seen him. As far as she knew, he had
been in his usual health and spirits. She knew of no enemy who might
have had a grudge against him.

I gave evidence next, told of my appointment with Protheroe and my
summons to the Abbotts'. I described how I had found the body and
my summoning of Dr. Haydock.

"How many people, Mr. Clement, were aware that Colonel Protheroe
was coming to see you that evening?"

"A good many, I should imagine. My wife knew, and my nephew, and
Colonel Protheroe himself alluded to the fact that morning when I met
him in the village. I should think several people might have overheard
him, as, being slightly deaf, he spoke in a loud voice."

"It was, then, a matter of common knowledge? Anyone might know?"

I agreed.

Haydock followed. He was an important witness. He described carefully
and technically the appearance of the body and the exact injuries. It was

his opinion that deceased had been shot whilst actually in the act of writing. He placed the time of death at approximately 6:20 to 6:30—certainly not later than 6:35. That was the outside limit. He was positive and emphatic on that point. There was no question of suicide, the wound could not have been self-inflicted.

Inspector Slack's evidence was discreet and abridged. He described his summons and the circumstances under which he had found the body. The unfinished letter was produced and the time on it—6:20—noted. Also the clock. It was tacitly assumed that the time of death was 6:22. The police were giving nothing away. Anne Protheroe told me afterwards that she had been told to suggest a slightly earlier period of time than 6:20 for her visit.

Our maid, Mary, was the next witness, and proved a somewhat truculent one. She hadn't heard anything, and didn't want to hear anything. It wasn't as though gentlemen who came to see the vicar usually got shot. They didn't. She'd got her own jobs to look after. Colonel Protheroe had arrived at a quarter past six exactly. No, she didn't look at the clock. She heard the church chime after she had shown him into the study. She didn't hear any shot. If there had been a shot she'd have heard it. Well, of course, she knew there must have been a shot, since the gentleman was found shot—but there it was. She hadn't heard it.

The coroner did not press the point. I realized that he and Colonel Melchett were working in agreement.

Mrs. Lestrange had been subpoenaed to give evidence, but a medical certificate, signed by Dr. Haydock, was produced saying she was too ill to attend.

There was only one other witness, a somewhat doddering old woman. The one who, in Slack's phrase, "did for" Lawrence Redding.

Mrs. Archer was shown the pistol and recognized it as the one she had seen in Mr. Redding's sitting-room "over against the bookcase, he kept it, lying about." She had last seen it on the day of the murder. Yes—in answer to a further question—she was quite sure it was there at lunch time on Thursday—quarter to one when she left.

I remembered what the inspector had told me, and I was mildly surprised. However vague she might have been when he questioned her, she was quite positive about it now.

The coroner summed up in a negative manner, but with a good deal of firmness. The verdict was given almost immediately:

Murder by Person or Persons unknown.

As I left the room I was aware of a small army of young men with bright, alert faces and a kind of superficial resemblance to each other. Several of them were already known to me by sight as having haunted the Vicarage the last few days. Seeking to escape, I plunged back into the Blue Boar and was lucky enough to run straight into the archaeologist, Dr. Stone. I clutched at him without ceremony.

"Journalists," I said briefly and expressively. "If you could deliver me from their clutches?"

"Why, certainly, Mr. Clement. Come upstairs with me."

He led the way up the narrow staircase and into his sitting-room, where Miss Cram was sitting rattling the keys of a typewriter with a practised touch. She greeted me with a broad smile of welcome and seized the opportunity to stop work.

"Awful, isn't it?" she said. "Not knowing who did it, I mean. Not but that I'm disappointed in an inquest. Tame, that's what I call it. Nothing what you might call spicy from beginning to end."

"You were there, then, Miss Cram?"

"I was there all right. Fancy your not seeing me. Didn't you see me? I feel a bit hurt about that. Yes, I do. A gentleman, even if he is a clergyman, ought to have eyes in his head."

"Were you present also?" I asked Dr. Stone, in an effort to escape from this playful badinage. Young women like Miss Cram always make me feel awkward.

"No, I'm afraid I feel very little interest in such things. I am a man very wrapped up in his own hobby."

"It must be a very interesting hobby," I said.

"You know something of it, perhaps?"

I was obliged to confess that I knew next to nothing.

Dr. Stone was not the kind of man whom a confession of ignorance daunts. The result was exactly the same as though I had said that the excavation of barrows was my only relaxation. He surged and eddied into speech. Long barrows, round barrows, stone age, bronze age, paleolithic, neolithic kistvaens and cromlechs—it burst forth in a torrent. I had little to do save nod my head and look intelligent—and that last is perhaps over optimistic. Dr. Stone boomed on. He was a little man. His head was round and bald, his face was round and rosy, and he beamed at you through very strong glasses. I have never known a man so enthusiastic on so little encouragement. He went into every argument for and against his own pet theory—which, by the way, I quite failed to grasp!

He detailed at great length his difference of opinion with Colonel Protheroe.

"An opinionated boor," he said with heat. "Yes, yes, I know he is dead, and one should speak no ill of the dead. But death does not alter facts. An opinionated boor describes him exactly. Because he had read a few books, he set himself up as an authority—against a man who has made a lifelong study of the subject. My whole life, Mr. Clement, has been given up to this work. My whole life—"

He was spluttering with excitement. Gladys Cram brought him back to earth with a terse sentence.

"You'll miss your train if you don't look out," she observed.

"Oh!" The little man stopped in mid speech and dragged a watch from his pocket. "Bless my soul. Quarter to? Impossible."

"Once you start talking you never remember the time. What you'd do without me to look after you, I really don't know."

"Quite right, my dear, quite right." He patted her affectionately on the shoulder. "This is a wonderful girl, Mr. Clement. Never forgets anything. I consider myself extremely lucky to have found her."

"Oh! go on, Dr. Stone," said the lady. "You spoil me, you do."

I could not help feeling that I should be in a material position to add my support to the second school of thought—that which foresees lawful matrimony as the future of Dr. Stone and Miss Cram. I imagined that in her own way Miss Cram was rather a clever young woman.

"You'd better be getting along," said Miss Cram.

"Yes, yes, so I must."

He vanished into the room next door and returned carrying a suitcase.

"You are leaving?" I asked in some surprise.

"Just running up to town for a couple of days," he explained. "My old mother to see tomorrow, some business with my lawyers on Monday. On Tuesday I shall return. By the way, I suppose that Colonel Protheroe's death will make no difference to our arrangements. As regards the barrow, I mean. Mrs. Protheroe will have no objection to our continuing the work?"

"I should not think so."

As he spoke, I wondered who actually would be in authority at Old Hall. It was just possible that Protheroe might have left it to Lettice. I felt that it would be interesting to know the contents of Protheroe's will.

"Causes a lot of trouble in a family, a death does," remarked Miss Cram, with a kind of gloomy relish. "You wouldn't believe what a nasty spirit there sometimes is."

"Well, I must really be going." Dr. Stone made ineffectual attempts to control the suitcase, a large rug and an unwieldy umbrella. I came to his rescue. He protested.

"Don't trouble—don't trouble. I can manage perfectly. Doubtless there will be somebody downstairs."

But down below there was no trace of a boots or anyone else. I suspect that they were being regaled at the expense of the press. Time was getting on, so we set out together to the station, Dr. Stone carrying the suitcase, and I holding the rug and umbrella.

Dr. Stone ejaculated remarks in between panting breaths as we hurried along.

"Really too good of you—didn't mean—to trouble you . . . Hope we shan't miss—the train—Gladys is a good girl—really a wonderful girl—a very sweet nature—not too happy at home, I'm afraid—absolutely—the heart of a child—heart of a child, I do assure you, in spite of—difference in our ages—find a lot in common . . ."

We saw Lawrence Redding's cottage just as we turned off to the station. It stands in an isolated position with no other house near it. I observed two young men of smart appearance standing on the doorstep and a couple more peering in at the windows. It was a busy day for the press.

"Nice fellow, young Redding," I remarked, to see what my companion would say.

He was so out of breath by this time that he found it difficult to say anything, but he puffed out a word which I did not at first quite catch.

"Dangerous," he gasped, when I asked him to repeat his remark.

"Dangerous?"

"Most dangerous. Innocent girls—know no better—taken in by a fellow like that—always hanging round women . . . No good."

From which I deduced that the only young man in the village had not passed unnoticed by the fair Gladys.

"Goodness," ejaculated Dr. Stone. "The train!"

We were close to the station by this time and we broke into a fast sprint. A down train was standing in the station and the up London train was just coming in.

At the door of the booking office we collided with a rather exquisite young man, and I recognized Miss Marple's nephew just arriving. He is, I think, a young man who does not like to be collided with. He prides himself on his poise and general air of detachment, and there is no doubt that vulgar contact is detrimental to poise of any kind. He staggered back. I apologized hastily and we passed in. Dr. Stone climbed on the train and I handed up his baggage just as the train gave an unwilling jerk and started.

I waved to him and then turned away. Raymond West had departed, but our local chemist, who rejoices in the name of Cherubim, was just setting out for the village. I walked beside him.

"Close shave that," he observed. "Well, how did the inquest go, Mr. Clement?"

I gave him the verdict.

"Oh! so that's what happened. I rather thought that would be the verdict. Where's Dr. Stone off to?"

I repeated what he had told me.

"Lucky not to miss the train. Not that you ever know on this line. I tell you, Mr. Clement, it's a crying shame. Disgraceful, that's what I call it. Train I came down by was ten minutes late. And that on a Saturday with no traffic to speak of. And on Wednesday—no, Thursday—yes, Thursday it was—I remember it was the day of the murder because I meant to write a strongly-worded complaint to the company—and the murder put it out of my head—yes, last Thursday. I had been to a meeting of the Pharmaceutical Society. How late do you think the 6:50 was? *Half an hour.* Half an hour exactly! What do you think of that? Ten minutes I don't mind. But if the train doesn't get in till twenty past seven, well, you can't get home before half-past. What I say is, why call it the 6:50?"

"Quite so," I said, and wishing to escape from the monologue I broke away with the excuse that I had something to say to Lawrence Redding whom I saw approaching us on the other side of the road.

19

"VERY GLAD TO have met you," said Lawrence. "Come to my place."

We turned in at the little rustic gate, went up the path, and he drew a key from his pocket and inserted it in the lock.

"You keep the door locked now," I observed.

"Yes." He laughed rather bitterly. "Case of stable door when the steed is gone, eh? It is rather like that. You know, padre," he held the door open and I passed inside, "there's something about all this business that I don't like. It's too much of—how shall I put it—an inside job. Someone knew about that pistol of mine. That means that the murderer, whoever he was, must have actually been in this house—perhaps even had a drink with me."

"Not necessarily," I objected. "The whole village of St. Mary Mead probably knows exactly where you keep your toothbrush and what kind of tooth powder you use."

"But why should it interest them?"

"I don't know," I said, "but it does. If you change your shaving cream it will be a topic of conversation."

"They must be very hard up for news."

"They are. Nothing exciting ever happens here."

"Well, it has now—with a vengeance."

I agreed.

"And who tells them all these things anyway? Shaving cream and things like that?"

"Probably old Mrs. Archer."

"That old crone? She's practically a half-wit, as far as I can make out."

"That's merely the camouflage of the poor," I explained. "They take refuge behind a mask of stupidity. You'll probably find that the old lady has all her wits about her. By the way, she seems very certain now that the pistol was in its proper place midday Thursday. What's made her so positive all of a sudden?"

"I haven't the least idea."

"Do you think she's right?"

"There again I haven't the least idea. I don't go round taking an inventory of my possessions every day."

I looked round the small living-room. Every shelf and table was littered with miscellaneous articles. Lawrence lived in the midst of an artistic disarray that would have driven me quite mad.

"It's a bit of a job finding things sometimes," he said, observing my glance. "On the other hand, everything is handy—not tucked away."

"Nothing is tucked away, certainly," I agreed. "It might perhaps have been better if the pistol had been."

"Do you know I rather expected the coroner to say something of the sort. Coroners are such asses. I expected to be censured or whatever they call it."

"By the way," I asked, "was it loaded?"

Lawrence shook his head.

"I'm not quite so careless as that. It was unloaded, but there was a box of cartridges beside it."

"It was apparently loaded in all six chambers and one shot had been fired."

Lawrence nodded.

"And whose hand fired it? It's all very well, sir, but unless the real murderer is discovered I shall be suspected of the crime to the day of my death."

"Don't say that, my boy."

"But I do say it."

He became silent, frowning to himself. He roused himself at last and said:

"But let me tell you how I got on last night. You know, old Miss Marple knows a thing or two."

"She is, I believe, rather unpopular on that account."

Lawrence proceeded to recount his story.

He had, following Miss Marple's advice, gone up to Old Hall. There, with Anne's assistance, he had had an interview with the parlormaid. Anne had said simply:

"Mr. Redding wants to ask you a few questions, Rose."

Then she had left the room.

Lawrence had felt somewhat nervous. Rose, a pretty girl of twenty-five, gazed at him with a limpid gaze which he found rather disconcerting.

"It's—it's about Colonel Protheroe's death."

"Yes, sir."

"I'm very anxious, you see, to get at the truth."

"Yes, sir."

"I feel that there may be—that someone might—that—that there might be some incident—"

At this point Lawrence felt that he was not covering himself with glory, and heartily cursed Miss Marple and her suggestions.

"I wondered if you could help me?"

"Yes, sir?"

Rose's demeanor was still that of the perfect servant, polite, anxious to assist, and completely uninterested.

"Dash it all," said Lawrence, "haven't you talked the thing over in the servants' hall?"

This method of attack flustered Rose slightly. Her perfect poise was shaken.

"In the servants' hall, sir?"

"Or the housekeeper's room, or the bootboy's dugout, or wherever you do talk? There must be *some* place."

Rose displayed a very faint disposition to giggle, and Lawrence felt encouraged.

"Look here, Rose, you're an awfully nice girl. I'm sure you must understand what I'm feeling like. I don't want to be hanged. I didn't murder your master, but a lot of people think I did. Can't you help me in any way?"

I can imagine at this point that Lawrence must have looked extremely appealing. His handsome head thrown back, his Irish blue eyes appealing. Rose softened and capitulated.

"Oh! sir, I'm sure—if any of us could help in any way. None of us think you did it, sir. Indeed we don't."

"I know, my dear girl, but that's not going to help me with the police."

"The police!" Rose tossed her head. "I can tell you, sir, we don't think much of that inspector. Slack, he calls himself. The police indeed."

"All the same, the police are very powerful. Now, Rose, you say you'll do your best to help me. I can't help feeling that there's a lot we haven't got at yet. The lady, for instance, who called to see Colonel Protheroe the night before he died."

"Mrs. Lestrange?"

"Yes, Mrs. Lestrange. I can't help feeling there's something rather odd about that visit of hers."

"Yes, indeed, sir, that's what we all said."

"You did?"

"Coming the way she did. And asking for the colonel. And of course there's been a lot of talk—nobody knowing anything about her down here. And Mrs. Simmons, she's the housekeeper, sir, she gave it as her opinion that she was a regular bad lot. But after hearing what Gladdie said, well, I didn't know what to think."

"What did Gladdie say?"

"Oh! nothing, sir. It was just—we were talking, you know."

Lawrence looked at her. He had the feeling of something kept back.

"I wonder very much what her interview with Colonel Protheroe was about."

"Yes, sir."

"I believe you know, Rose?"

"Me? Oh! no, sir. Indeed I don't. How could I?"

"Look here, Rose. You said you'd help me. If you overheard anything, anything at all—it mightn't seem important, but anything . . . I'd be so awfully grateful to you. After all, anyone might—might chance—just *chance* to overhear something."

"But I didn't, sir, really I didn't."

"Then somebody else did," said Lawrence acutely.

"Well, sir—"

"Do tell me, Rose."

"I don't know what Gladdie would say, I'm sure."

"She'd want you to tell me. Who *is* Gladdie, by the way?"

"She's the kitchenmaid, sir. And you see, she'd just stepped out to

speak to a friend, and she was passing the window—the study window—
and the master was there with the lady. And of course he did speak very
loud, the master did, always. And naturally, feeling a little curious—I
mean—"

"Awfully natural," said Lawrence, "I mean one would simply have to
listen."

"But of course she didn't tell anyone—except me. And we both thought
it very odd. But Gladdie couldn't say anything, you see, because if it was
known she'd gone out to meet a—a friend—well, it would have meant
a lot of unpleasantness with Mrs. Pratt, that's the cook, sir. But I'm sure
she'd tell you anything, sir, willing."

"Well, can I go to the kitchen and speak to her?"

Rose was horrified by the suggestion.

"Oh! no, sir, that would never do. And Gladdie's a very nervous girl
anyway."

At last the matter was settled, after a lot of discussion over difficult
points. A clandestine meeting was arranged in the shrubbery.

Here, in due course, Lawrence was confronted by the nervous Gladdie
whom he described as more like a shivering rabbit than anything human.
Ten minutes were spent in trying to put the girl at her ease, the shivering
Gladys explaining that she couldn't ever—that she didn't ought, that she
didn't think Rose would have given her away, that anyway she hadn't
meant no harm, indeed she hadn't, and that she'd catch it badly if Mrs.
Pratt ever came to hear of it.

Lawrence reassured, cajoled, persuaded—at last Gladys consented to
speak. "If you'll be sure it'll go no further sir."

"Of course it won't."

"And it won't be brought up against me in a court of law?"

"Never."

"And you won't tell the mistress?"

"Not on any account."

"If it were to get to Mrs. Pratt's ears—"

"It won't. Now tell me, Gladys."

"If you're sure it's all right?"

"Of course it is. You'll be glad some day you've saved me from being
hanged."

Gladys gave a little shriek.

"Oh! indeed, I wouldn't like that, sir. Well, it's very little I heard—
and that entirely by accident as you might say—"

"I quite understand."

"But the master, he was evidently very angry. 'After all these years'—
that's what he was saying—'you dare to come here—It's an outrage—'I
couldn't hear what the lady said—but after a bit he said, 'I utterly refuse—
utterly—' I can't remember everything—seemed as though they were at
it hammer and tongs, she wanting him to do something and he refusing.
'It's a disgrace that you should have come down here,' that's one thing
he said. And 'You shall not see her—I forbid it—' and that made me

prick up my ears. Looked as though the lady wanted to tell Mrs. Protheroe a thing or two, and he was afraid about it. And I thought to myself, 'Well, now, fancy the master. Him so particular. And maybe no beauty himself when all's said and done. Fancy!' I said. And 'Men are all alike,' I said to my friend later. Not that he'd agree. Argued, he did. But he did admit he was surprised at Colonel Protheroe—him being a church-warden and handing round the plate and reading the lessons on Sundays. 'But there,' I said, 'that's very often the worst.' For that's what I've heard my mother say, many a time."

Gladdie paused, out of breath, and Lawrence tried tactfully to get back to where the conversation had started.

"Did you hear anything else?"

"Well, it's difficult to remember exactly, sir. It was all much the same. He said once or twice, 'I don't believe it.' Just like that. 'Whatever Haydock says, I don't believe it.' "

"He said that, did he? 'Whatever Haydock says'?"

"Yes. And he said it was all a plot."

"You didn't hear the lady speak at all?"

"Only just at the end. She must have got up to go and come nearer the window. And I heard what she said. Made my blood run cold, it did. I'll never forget it. *'By this time tomorrow night, you may be dead,'* she said. Wicked the way she said it. As soon as I heard the news, 'There,' I said to Rose. 'There!' "

Lawrence wondered. Principally he wondered how much of Gladys's story was to be depended upon. True in the main, he suspected that it had been embellished and polished since the murder. In especial he doubted the accuracy of the last remark. He thought it highly possible that it owed its being to the fact of the murder.

He thanked Gladys, rewarded her suitably, reassured her as to her misdoings being made known to Mrs. Pratt, and left Old Hall with a good deal to think over.

One thing was clear, Mrs. Lestrange's interview with Colonel Protheroe had certainly not been a peaceful one, and it was one which he was anxious to keep from the knowledge of his wife.

I thought of Miss Marple's churchwarden with his separate establishment. Was this a case resembling that?

I wondered more than ever where Haydock came in? He had saved Mrs. Lestrange from having to give evidence at the inquest. He had done his best to protect her from the police.

How far would he carry that protection?

Supposing he suspected her of crime—would he still try and shield her?

She was a curious woman—a woman of very strong magnetic charm. I myself hated the thought of connecting her with the crime in any way.

Something in me said, "It can't be her!" Why?

And an imp in my brain replied: "Because she's a very beautiful and attractive woman. That's why!"

There is, as Miss Marple would say, a lot of human nature in all of us.

20

WHEN I GOT back to the Vicarage I found that we were in the middle of a domestic crisis.

Griselda met me in the hall and with tears in her eyes dragged me into the drawing-room. "She's going."

"Who's going?"

"Mary. She's given notice."

I really could not take the announcement in a tragic spirit.

"Well," I said, "we'll have to get another servant."

It seemed to me a perfectly reasonable thing to say. When one servant goes, you get another. I was at a loss to understand Griselda's look of reproach.

"Len—you are absolutely heartless. You don't *care*."

I didn't. In fact, I felt almost light-hearted at the prospect of no more burnt puddings and undercooked vegetables.

"I'll have to look for a girl, and find one, and train her," continued Griselda in a voice of acute self-pity.

"Is Mary trained?" I said.

"Of course she is."

"I suppose," I said, "that somebody has heard her address us as sir or ma'am and has immediately wrested her from us as a paragon. All I can say is, they'll be disappointed."

"It isn't that," said Griselda. "Nobody else wants her. I don't see how they could. It's her feelings. They're upset because Lettice Protheroe said she didn't dust properly."

Griselda often comes out with surprising statements, but this seemed to me so surprising that I questioned it. It seemed to me the most unlikely thing in the world that Lettice Protheroe should go out of her way to interfere in our domestic affairs and reprove our maid for slovenly housework. It was completely un-Lettice-like, and I said so.

"I don't see," I said, "what our dust has to do with Lettice Protheroe."

"Nothing at all," said my wife. "That's why it's so unreasonable. I wish you'd go and talk to Mary yourself. She's in the kitchen."

I had no wish to talk to Mary on the subject, but Griselda, who is very energetic and quick, fairly pushed me through the baize door into the kitchen before I had time to rebel.

Mary was peeling potatoes at the sink.

"Er—good afternoon," I said nervously.

Mary looked up and snorted, but made no other response.

"Mrs. Clement tells me that you wish to leave us," I said.

Mary condescended to reply to this.

"There's some things," she said darkly, "as no girl can be asked to put up with."

"Will you tell me exactly what it is that has upset you?"

"Tell you that in two words, I can." (Here, I may say, she vastly underestimated.) "People coming snooping round here when my back's turned. Poking round. And what business of hers is it, how often the study is dusted or turned out? If you and the missus don't complain, it's nobody else's business. If I give satisfaction to you that's all that matters, I say."

Mary has never given satisfaction to me. I confess that I have a hankering after a room thoroughly dusted and tidied every morning. Mary's practice of flicking off the more obvious deposit on the surface of low tables is to my thinking grossly inadequate. However, I realized that at the moment it was no good to go into side issues.

"Had to go to that inquest, didn't I? Standing up before twelve men, a respectable girl like me! And who knows what questions you may be asked. I'll tell you this. I've never before been in a place where they had a murder in the house, and I never want to be again."

"I hope you won't," I said. "On the law of averages, I should say it was very unlikely."

"I don't hold with the law. *He* was a magistrate. Many a poor fellow sent to jail for potting at a rabbit—and him with his pheasants and what not. And then, before he's so much as decently buried, that daughter of his comes round and says I don't do my work properly."

"Do you mean that Miss Protheroe has been here?"

"Found her here when I come back from the Blue Boar. In the study she was. And 'Oh!' she says. 'I'm looking for my little yellow beret—a little yellow hat. I left it here the other day.' 'Well,' I says, 'I haven't seen no hat. It wasn't here when I done the room on Thursday morning,' I says. And 'Oh!' she says, 'but I dare say you wouldn't see it. You don't spend much time doing a room, do you?' And with that she draws her finger along the mantelshelf and looks at it. As though I had time on a morning like this to take off all them ornaments and put them back, with the police only unlocking the room the night before. 'If the vicar and his lady are satisfied that's all that matters, I think, miss,' I said. And she laughs and goes out of the window and says, 'Oh! but are you sure they are?' "

"I see," I said.

"And there it is! A girl has her feelings! I'm sure I'd work my fingers to the bone for you and the missus. And if she wants a new-fangled dish tried, I'm always ready to try it."

"I'm sure you are," I said soothingly.

"But she must have heard something or she wouldn't have said what she did. And if I don't give satisfaction I'd rather go. Not that I take any notice of what Miss Protheroe says. She's not loved up at the Hall,

I can tell you. Never a please or a thank you, and everything scattered right and left. I wouldn't set any store by Miss Lettice Protheroe myself for all that Mr. Dennis is so set upon her. But she's the kind that can always twist a young gentleman round her little finger."

During all this, Mary had been extracting eyes from potatoes with such energy that they had been flying round the kitchen like hailstones. At this moment one hit me in the eye and caused a momentary pause in the conversation.

"Don't you think," I said, as I dabbed my eye with my handkerchief, "that you have been rather too inclined to take offence where none is meant? You know, Mary, your mistress will be very sorry to lose you."

"I've nothing against the mistress—or against you, sir, for that matter."

"Well, then, don't you think you're being rather silly?"

Mary sniffed.

"I was a bit upset like—after the inquest and all. And a girl has her feelings. But I wouldn't like to cause the mistress inconvenience."

"Then that's all right," I said.

I left the kitchen to find Griselda and Dennis waiting for me in the hall. "Well?" exclaimed Griselda.

"She's staying," I said, and sighed.

"Len," said my wife, "you *have* been clever."

I felt rather inclined to disagree with her. I did not think I had been clever. It is my firm opinion that no servant could be a worse one than Mary. Any change, I consider, would have been a change for the better.

But I like to please Griselda. I detailed the heads of Mary's grievance.

"How like Lettice," said Dennis. "She couldn't have left that yellow beret of hers here on Wednesday. She was wearing it for tennis on Thursday."

"That seems to me highly probable," I said.

"She never knows where she's left anything," said Dennis, with a kind of affectionate pride and admiration that I felt was entirely uncalled for. "She loses about a dozen things every day."

"A remarkably attractive trait," I observed.

Any sarcasm missed Dennis.

"She *is* attractive," he said, with a deep sigh. "People are always proposing to her—she told me so."

"They must be illicit proposals if they're made to her down here," I remarked. "We haven't got a bachelor in the place."

"There's Dr. Stone," said Griselda, her eyes dancing.

"He asked her to come and see the barrow the other day," I admitted.

"Of course he did," said Griselda. "She *is* attractive, Len. Even bald-headed archaeologists feel it."

"Lots of S.A.," said Dennis sapiently.

And yet Lawrence Redding is completely untouched by Lettice's charm. Griselda, however, explained that with the air of one who knew she was right.

"Lawrence has got lots of S.A. himself. That kind always likes the—how shall I put it—the Quaker type. Very restrained and diffident. The kind of women whom everybody calls cold. I think Anne is the only woman who could ever hold Lawrence. I don't think they'll ever tire of each other. All the same, I think he's been rather stupid in one way. He's rather made use of Lettice, you know. I don't think he ever dreamed she cared—he's awfully modest in some ways—but I have a feeling she does."

"She can't bear him," said Dennis positively. "She told me so."

I have never seen anything like the pitying silence with which Griselda received this remark.

I went into my study. There was, to my fancy, still a rather eerie feeling in the room. I knew that I must get over this. Once give in to that feeling, and I should probably never use the study again. I walked thoughtfully over to the writing-table. Here Protheroe had sat, red-faced, hearty, self-righteous, and here, in a moment of time, he had been struck down. Here, where I was standing, an enemy had stood . . .

And so—no more Protheroe . . .

Here was the pen his fingers had held.

On the floor was a faint dark stain—the rug had been sent to the cleaners, but the blood had soaked through.

I shivered.

"I can't use this room," I said aloud. "I can't use it."

Then my eye was caught by something—a mere speck of bright blue. I bent down. Between the floor and the desk I saw a small object. I picked it up.

I was standing staring at it in the palm of my hand when Griselda came in.

"I forgot to tell you, Len. Miss Marple wants us to go over tonight after dinner. To amuse the nephew. She's afraid of his being dull. I said we'd go."

"Very well, my dear."

"What are you looking at?"

"Nothing."

I closed my hand, and looking at my wife, observed:

"If you don't amuse Master Raymond West, my dear, he must be very hard to please."

My wife said: "Don't be ridiculous, Len," and turned pink.

She went out again, and I unclosed my hand.

In the palm of my hand was a blue lapis lazuli earring set in seed pearls.

It was rather an unusual jewel, and I knew very well where I had seen it last.

21

I CANNOT SAY that I have at any time a great admiration for Mr. Raymond West. He is, I know, supposed to be a brilliant novelist and has made quite a name as a poet. His poems have no capital letters in them, which is, I believe, the essence of modernity. His books are about unpleasant people leading lives of surpassing dullness.

He has a tolerant affection for "Aunt Jane," whom he alludes to in her presence as a "survival."

She listens to his talk with a flattering interest, and if there is sometimes an amused twinkle in her eye I am sure he never notices it.

He fastened on Griselda at once with flattering abruptness. They discussed modern plays and from there went on to modern schemes of decoration. Griselda affects to laugh at Raymond West, but she is, I think, susceptible to his conversation.

During my (dull) conversation with Miss Marple, I heard at intervals the reiteration "buried as you are down here".

It began at last to irritate me. I said suddenly:

"I suppose you consider us very much out of things down here?"

Raymond West waved his cigarette.

"I regard St. Mary Mead," he said authoritatively, "as a stagnant pool."

He looked at us, prepared for resentment at his statement, but somewhat, I think, to his chagrin, no one displayed annoyance.

"That is really not a very good simile, dear Raymond," said Miss Marple briskly. "Nothing, I believe, is so full of life under the microscope as a drop of water from a stagnant pool."

"Life—of a kind," admitted the novelist.

"It's all much the same kind, really, isn't it?" said Miss Marple.

"You compare yourself to a denizen of a stagnant pond, Aunt Jane?"

"My dear, you said something of the sort in your last book, I remember."

No clever young man likes having his works quoted against himself. Raymond West was no exception.

"That was entirely different," he snapped.

"Life is, after all, very much the same everywhere," said Miss Marple in her placid voice. "Getting born, you know, and growing up—and coming into contact with other people—getting jostled—and then marriage and more babies—"

"And finally death," said Raymond West. "And not death with a death certificate always. Death in life."

"Talking of death," said Griselda, "you know we've had a murder here?"

Raymond West waved murder away with his cigarette.

"Murder is so crude," he said. "I take no interest in it."

That statement did not take me in for a moment. They say all the world loves a lover—apply that saying to murder and you have an even more infallible truth. No one can fail to be interested in a murder. Simple people like Griselda and myself can admit the fact, but anyone like Raymond West has to pretend to be bored—at any rate for the first five minutes.

Miss Marple, however, gave her nephew away by remarking:

"Raymond and I have been discussing nothing else all through dinner."

"I take a great interest in all the local news," said Raymond hastily. He smiled benignly and tolerantly at Miss Marple.

"Have you a theory, Mr. West?" asked Griselda.

"Logically," said Raymond West, again flourishing his cigarette, "only one person could have killed Protheroe."

"Yes?" said Griselda.

We hung upon his words with flattering attention.

"The vicar," said Raymond, and pointed an accusing finger at me.

I gasped.

"Of course," he reassured me, "I know you didn't do it. Life is never what it should be. But think of the drama—the fitness—churchwarden murdered in the vicar's study by the vicar. Delicious!"

"And the motive?" I inquired.

"Oh! that's interesting." He sat up—allowed his cigarette to go out. "Inferiority complex, I think. Possibly too many inhibitions. I should like to write the story of the affair. Amazingly complex. Week after week, year after year, he's seen the man—at vestry meetings—at choirboys' outings—handing round the bag in church—bringing it to the altar. Always he dislikes the man—always he chokes down his dislike. It's unchristian, he won't encourage it. And so it festers underneath, and one day—"

He made a graphic gesture.

Griselda turned to me.

"Have you ever felt like that, Len?"

"Never," I said truthfully.

"Yet I hear you were wishing him out of the world not so long ago," remarked Miss Marple.

(That miserable Dennis! But my fault, of course, for ever making the remark.)

"I'm afraid I was," I said. "It was a stupid remark to make, but really I'd had a very trying morning with him."

"That's disappointing," said Raymond West. "Because, of course, if your subconscious were really planning to do him in, it would never have allowed you to make that remark."

He sighed.

"My theory falls to the ground. This is probably a very ordinary murder— a revengeful poacher or something of that sort."

"Miss Cram came to see me this afternoon," said Miss Marple. "I met her in the village and I asked her if she would like to see my garden."

"Is she fond of gardens?" asked Griselda.

"I don't think so," said Miss Marple, with a faint twinkle. "But it makes a very useful excuse for talk, don't you think?"

"What did you make of her?" asked Griselda. "I don't believe she's really so bad."

"She volunteered a lot of information—really a lot of information," said Miss Marple. "About herself, you know, and her people. They all seem to be dead or in India. Very sad. By the way, she has gone to Old Hall for the weekend."

"What?"

"Yes, it seems Mrs. Protheroe asked her—or she suggested it to Mrs. Protheroe—I don't quite know which way about it was. To do some secretarial work for her—there are so many letters to cope with. It turned out rather fortunately. Dr. Stone being away, she has nothing to do. What an excitement this barrow has been."

"Stone?" said Raymond. "Is that the archaeologist fellow?"

"Yes, he is excavating a barrow. On the Protheroe property."

"He's a good man," said Raymond. "Wonderfully keen on his job. I met him at a dinner not long ago and we had a most interesting talk. I must look him up."

"Unfortunately," I said, "he's just gone to London for the weekend. Why, you actually ran into him at the station this afternoon."

"I ran into you. You had a little fat man with you—with glasses on."

"Yes—Dr. Stone."

"But, my dear fellow—that wasn't Stone."

"Not Stone?"

"Not the archaeologist. I know him quite well. The man wasn't Stone—not the faintest resemblance."

We stared at each other. In particular I stared at Miss Marple.

"Extraordinary," I said.

"The suitcase," said Miss Marple.

"But why?" said Griselda.

"It reminds me of the time the man went round pretending to be the gas inspector," murmured Miss Marple. "Quite a little haul, he got."

"An impostor," said Raymond West. "Now this is really interesting."

"The question is, has it anything to do with the murder?" said Griselda.

"Not necessarily," I said. "But—" I looked at Miss Marple.

"It is," she said, "a Peculiar Thing. Another Peculiar Thing."

"Yes," I said, rising. "I rather feel the inspector ought to be told about this at once."

22

INSPECTOR SLACK'S ORDERS, once I had got him on the telephone, were brief and emphatic. Nothing was to "get about". In particular, Miss Cram was not to be alarmed. In the meantime, a search was to be instituted for the suitcase in the neighborhood of the barrow.

Griselda and I returned home very excited over this new development. We could not say much with Dennis present, as we had faithfully promised Inspector Slack to breathe no word to anybody.

In any case, Dennis was full of his own troubles. He came into my study and began fingering things and shuffling his feet and looking thoroughly embarrassed.

"What is it, Dennis?" I said at last.

"Uncle Len, I don't want to go to sea."

I was astonished. The boy had been so very decided about his career up to now.

"But you were so keen on it."

"Yes, but I've changed my mind."

"What do you want to do?"

"I want to go into finance."

I was even more surprised.

"What do you mean—finance?"

"Just that. I want to go into the city."

"But, my dear boy, I am sure you would not like the life. Even if I obtained a post for you in a bank—"

Dennis said that wasn't what he meant. He didn't want to go into a bank. I asked him what exactly he did mean, and of course, as I suspected, the boy didn't really know.

By "going into finance", he simply meant getting rich quickly, which with the optimism of youth he imagined was a certainty if one "went into the city". I disabused him of this notion as gently as I could.

"What's put it into your head?" I asked. "You were so satisfied with the idea of going to sea."

"I know, Uncle Len, but I've been thinking. I shall want to marry some day—and, I mean, you've got to be rich to marry a girl."

"Facts disprove your theory," I said.

"I know—but a real girl. I mean, a girl who's used to things."

It was very vague, but I thought I knew what he meant.

"You know," I said gently, "all girls aren't like Lettice Protheroe."

He fired up at once.

"You're awfully unfair to her. You don't like her. Griselda doesn't either. She says she's tiresome."

From the feminine point of view Griselda is quite right. Lettice *is* tiresome. I could quite realize, however, that a boy would resent the adjective.

"If only people made a few allowances. Why even the Hartley Napiers are going about grousing about her at a time like this! Just because she left their old tennis party a bit early. Why should she stay if she was bored? Jolly decent of her to go at all, I think."

"Quite a favor," I said, but Dennis suspected no malice. He was full of his own grievance on Lettice's behalf.

"She's awfully unselfish really. Just to show you, she made me stay. Naturally I wanted to go too. But she wouldn't hear of it. Said it was too bad on the Napiers. So, just to please her, I stopped on a quarter of an hour."

The young have very curious views on unselfishness.

"And now I hear Susan Hartley Napier is going about everywhere saying Lettice has rotten manners."

"If I were you," I said, "I shouldn't worry."

"It's all very well, but—"

He broke off.

"I'd—I'd do anything for Lettice."

"Very few of us can do anything for anyone else," I said. "However much we wish it, we are powerless."

"I wish I were dead," said Dennis.

Poor lad. Calf love is a virulent disease. I forebore to say any of the obvious and probably irritating things which come so easily to one's lips. Instead, I said good night, and went up to bed.

I took the eight o'clock service the following morning and when I returned found Griselda sitting at the breakfast table with an open note in her hand. It was from Anne Protheroe.

DEAR GRISELDA

If you and the vicar could come up and lunch here quietly today, I should be so very grateful. Something very strange has occurred, and I should like Mr. Clement's advice.

Please don't mention this when you come, as I have said nothing to anyone.

With love,
Yours affectionately,
ANNE PROTHEROE.

"We must go, of course," said Griselda.

I agreed.

"I wonder what can have happened?"

I wondered too.

"You know," I said to Griselda, "I don't feel we are really at the end of this case yet."

"You mean not till someone has really been arrested?"

"No," I said, "I didn't meant that. I mean that there are ramifications, undercurrents, that we know nothing about. There are a whole lot of things to clear up before we get at the truth."

"You mean things that don't really matter, but that get in the way?"

"Yes, I think that expresses my meaning very well."

"I think we're all making a great fuss," said Dennis, helping himself to marmalade. "It's a jolly good thing old Protheroe is dead. Nobody liked him. Oh! I know the police have got to worry—it's their job. But I rather hope myself they'll never find out. I should hate to see Slack promoted going about swelling with importance over his cleverness."

I am human enough to feel that I agree over the matter of Slack's promotion. A man who goes about systematically rubbing people up the wrong way cannot hope to be popular.

"Dr. Haydock thinks rather like I do," went on Dennis. "He'd never give a murderer up to justice. He said so."

I think that that is the danger of Haydock's views. They may be sound in themselves—it is not for me to say—but they produce an impression on the young, careless mind which I am sure Haydock himself never meant to convey.

Griselda looked out of the window and remarked that there were reporters in the garden.

"I suppose they're photographing the study windows again," she said, with a sigh.

We had suffered a good deal in this way. There was first the idle curiosity of the village—everyone had come to gape and stare. There were next the reporters armed with cameras, and the village again to watch the reporters. In the end we had to have a constable from Much Benham on duty outside the window.

"Well," I said, "the funeral is tomorrow morning. After that, surely, the excitement will die down."

I noticed a few reporters hanging about Old Hall when we arrived there. They accosted me with various queries to which I gave the invariable answer (we had found it the best), that, "I had nothing to say."

We were shown by the butler into the drawing-room, the sole occupant of which turned out to be Miss Cram—apparently in a state of high enjoyment.

"This is a surprise, isn't it?" she said, as she shook hands. "I never should have thought such a thing, but Mrs. Protheroe is kind, isn't she? And, of course, it isn't what you might call nice for a young girl to be staying alone at a place like the Blue Boar, reporters about and all. And, of course, it's not as though I haven't been able to make myself useful— you really need a secretary at a time like this, and Miss Protheroe doesn't do anything to help, does she?"

I was amused to notice that the old animosity against Lettice persisted, but that the girl had apparently become a warm partisan of Anne's. At the same time I wondered if the story of her coming here was strictly accurate. In her account the initiative had come from Anne, but I wondered if that were really so. The first mention of disliking to be at the Blue Boar alone might have easily come from the girl herself. Whilst keeping an open mind on the subject, I did not fancy that Miss Cram was strictly truthful.

At that moment Anne Protheroe entered the room.

She was dressed very quietly in black. She carried in her hand a Sunday paper which she held out to me with a rueful glance.

"I've never had any experience of this sort of thing. It's pretty ghastly, isn't it? I saw a reporter at the inquest. I just said that I was terribly upset and had nothing to say, and then he asked me if I wasn't very anxious to find my husband's murderer, and I said 'Yes'. And then whether I had any suspicions, and I said 'No'. And whether I didn't think the crime showed local knowledge, and I said it seemed to certainly. And that was all. And now look at this!"

In the middle of the page was a photograph, evidently taken at least ten years ago—Heaven knows where they had dug it out. There were large headlines:

WIDOW DECLARES SHE WILL NEVER REST TILL SHE HAS
HUNTED DOWN HUSBAND'S MURDERER.

Mrs. Protheroe, the widow of the murdered man, is certain that the murderer must be looked for locally. She has suspicions, but no certainty. She declared herself prostrate with grief, but reiterated her determination to hunt down the murderer.

"It doesn't sound like me, does it?" said Anne.

"I dare say it might have been worse," I said, handing back the paper.

"Impudent, aren't they?" said Miss Cram. "I'd like to see one of those fellows trying to get something out of me."

By the twinkle in Griselda's eye, I was convinced that she regarded this statement as being more literally true than Miss Cram intended it to appear.

Luncheon was announced, and we went in. Lettice did not come in till half-way through the meal, when she drifted into the empty place with a smile for Griselda and a nod for me. I watched her with some attention, for reasons of my own, but she seemed much the same vague creature as usual. Extremely pretty—that in fairness I had to admit. She was still not wearing mourning, but was dressed in a shade of pale green that brought out all the delicacy of her fair coloring.

After we had had coffee, Anne said quietly:

"I want to have a little talk with the vicar. I will take him up to my sitting-room."

At last I was to learn the reason of our summons. I rose and followed her up the stairs. She paused at the door of the room. As I was about to speak, she stretched out a hand to stop me. She remained listening, looking down towards the hall.

"Good. They are going out into the garden. No—don't go in there. We can go straight up."

Much to my surprise she led the way along the corridor to the extremity of the wing. Here a narrow ladderlike staircase rose to the floor above, and she mounted it, I following. We found ourselves in a dusty boarded passage. Anne opened a door and led me into a large dim attic which was evidently used as a lumber room. There were trunks there, old broken furniture, a few stacked pictures, and the many countless odds and ends which a lumber room collects.

My surprise was so evident that she smiled faintly.

"First of all, I must explain. I am sleeping very lightly just now. Last night—or rather this morning about three o'clock, I was convinced that I heard someone moving about the house. I listened for some time, and at last got up and came out to see. Out on the landing I realized that the sounds came, not from down below, but from up above. I came along to the foot of these stairs. Again I thought I heard a sound. I called up, 'Is anybody there?' But there was no answer, and I heard nothing more, so I assumed that my nerves had been playing tricks on me, and went back to bed.

"However, early this morning, I came up here—simply out of curiosity. And I found *this*!"

She stooped down and turned round a picture that was leaning against the wall with the back of the canvas towards us.

I gave a gasp of surprise. The picture was evidently a portrait in oils, but the face had been hacked and cut in such a savage way as to render it unrecognizable. Moreover, the cuts were clearly quite fresh.

"What an extraordinary thing," I said.

"Isn't it? Tell me, can you think of any explanation?"

I shook my head.

"There's a kind of savagery about it," I said, "that I don't like. It looks as though it had been done in a fit of maniacal rage."

"Yes, that's what I thought."

"What is the portrait?"

"I haven't the least idea. I have never seen it before. All these things were in the attic when I married Lucius and came here to live. I have never been through them or bothered about them."

"Extraordinary," I commented.

I stooped down and examined the other pictures. They were very much what you would expect to find—some very mediocre landscapes, some oleographs and a few cheaply-framed reproductions.

There was nothing else helpful. A large old-fashioned trunk, of the kind that used to be called an "ark", had the initials E.P. upon it. I raised the lid. It was empty. Nothing else in the attic was the least suggestive.

"It really is a most amazing occurrence," I said. "It's so—senseless."

"Yes," said Anne. "That frightens me a little."

There was nothing more to see. I accompanied her down to her sitting-room where she closed the door.

"Do you think I ought to do anything about it? Tell the police?"

I hesitated.

"It's hard to say on the face of it whether—"

"It has anything to do with the murder or not," finished Anne. "I know. That's what is so difficult. On the face of it, there seems no connection whatever."

"No," I said, "but it is another Peculiar Thing."

We both sat silent with puzzled brows.

"What are your plans, if I may ask?" I said presently.

She lifted her head.

"I'm going to live here for at least another six months!" She said it defiantly. "I don't want to. I hate the idea of living here. But I think it's the only thing to be done. Otherwise people will say that I ran away—that I had a guilty conscience."

"Surely not."

"Oh! yes, they will. Especially when—" She paused and then said: "When the six months are up—I am going to marry Lawrence." Her eyes met mine. "We're neither of us going to wait any longer."

"I supposed," I said, "that that would happen."

Suddenly she broke down, burying her head in her hands.

"You don't know how grateful I am to you—you don't know. We'd said goodbye to each other—he was going away. I feel—I feel not so awful about Lucius's death. If we'd been planning to go away together, and he'd died then—it would be so awful now. But you made us both see how wrong it would be. That's why I'm grateful."

"I, too, am thankful," I said gravely.

"All the same, you know," she sat up. "Unless the real murderer is found they'll always think it was Lawrence—oh! yes, they will. And especially when he marries me."

"My dear, Dr. Haydock's evidence made it perfectly clear—"

"What do people care about evidence? They don't even know about it. And medical evidence never means anything to outsiders anyway. That's another reason why I'm staying on here. Mr. Clement, *I'm going to find out the truth.*"

Her eyes flashed as she spoke. She added:

"That's why I asked that girl here."

"Miss Cram?"

"Yes."

"You did ask her, then. I mean, it was your idea?"

"Entirely. Oh! as a matter of fact, she whined a bit. At the inquest—she was there when I arrived. No, I asked her here deliberately."

"But surely," I cried, "you don't think that that silly young woman could have anything to do with the crime?"

"It's awfully easy to appear silly, Mr. Clement. It's one of the easiest things in the world."

"Then you really think—?"

"No, I don't. Honestly, I don't. What I do think is that that girl knows something—or might know something. I wanted to study her at close quarters."

"And the very night she arrives, that picture is slashed," I said thoughtfully.

"You think she did it? But why? It seems so utterly absurd and impossible."

"It seems to me utterly impossible and absurd that your husband should have been murdered in my study," I said bitterly. "But he was."

"I know." She laid her hand on my arm. "It's dreadful for you. I do realize that, though I haven't said very much about it."

I took the blue lapis lazuli earring from my pocket and held it out to her.

"This is yours, I think?"

"Oh! yes." She held out her hand for it with a pleased smile. "Where did you find it?"

But I did not put the jewel into her outstretched hand.

"Would you mind," I said, "if I kept it a little longer?"

"Why, certainly." She looked puzzled and a little inquiring. I did not satisfy her curiosity.

Instead I asked her how she was situated financially.

"It is an impertinent question," I said, "but I really do not mean it as such."

"I don't think it's impertinent at all. You and Griselda are the best friends I have here. And I like that funny old Miss Marple. Lucius was very well off, you know. He left things pretty equally divided between me and Lettice. Old Hall goes to me, but Lettice is to be allowed to choose enough furniture to furnish a small house, and she is left a separate sum for the purpose of buying one, so as to even things up."

"What are her plans, do you know?"

Anne made a comical grimace.

"She doesn't tell them to me. I imagine she will leave here as soon as possible. She doesn't like me—she never has. I dare say it's my fault, though I've really always tried to be decent. But I suppose any girl resents a young stepmother."

"Are you fond of her?" I asked bluntly.

She did not reply at once, which convinced me that Anne Protheroe is a very honest woman.

"I was at first," she said. "She was such a pretty little girl. I don't think I am now. I don't know why. Perhaps it's because she doesn't like me. I like being liked, you know."

"We all do," I said, and Anne Protheroe smiled.

I had one more task to perform. That was to get a word alone with Lettice Protheroe. I managed that easily enough, catching sight of her in the deserted drawing-room. Griselda and Gladys Cram were out in the garden.

I went in and shut the door.

"Lettice," I said, "I want to speak to you about something."

She looked up indifferently.

"Yes?"

I had thought beforehand what to say. I held out the lapis earring and said quietly:

"Why did you drop that in my study?"

I saw her stiffen for a moment—it was almost instantaneous. Her recovery was so quick that I myself could hardly have sworn to the movement. Then she said carelessly:

"I never dropped anything in your study. That's not mine. That's Anne's."

"I know that," I said.

"Well, why ask me, then? Anne must have dropped it."

"Mrs. Protheroe has only been in my study once since the murder, and then she was wearing black and so would not have been likely to have had on a blue earring."

"In that case," said Lettice, "I suppose she must have dropped it before." She added: "That's only logical."

"It's very logical," I said. "I suppose you don't happen to remember when your stepmother was wearing these earrings last?"

"Oh!" She looked at me with a puzzled, trustful gaze. "Is it very important?"

"It might be," I said.

"I'll try and think." She sat there knitting her brows. I have never seen Lettice Protheroe look more charming than she did at that moment. "Oh! yes," she said suddenly. "She had them on—on Thursday. I remember now."

"Thursday," I said slowly, "was the day of the murder. Mrs. Protheroe came to the study in the garden that day, but if you remember, in her evidence, she only came as far as the study window, not inside the room."

"Where did you find this?"

"Rolled underneath the desk."

"Then it looks, doesn't it," said Lettice coolly, "as though she hadn't spoken the truth?"

"You mean that she came right in and stood by the desk?"

"Well, it looks like it, doesn't it?"

Her eyes met mine serenely.

"If you want to know," she said calmly, "I never have thought she was speaking the truth."

"And I *know you* are not, Lettice."

"What do you mean?"

She was startled.

"I mean," I said, "that the last time I saw this earring was on Friday morning when I came up here with Colonel Melchett. It was lying with its fellow on your stepmother's dressing-table. I actually handled them both."

"Oh—!" She wavered, then suddenly flung herself sideways over the arm of her chair and burst into tears. Her short fair hair hung down almost touching the floor. It was a strange attitude—beautiful and unrestrained.

I let her sob for some moments in silence and then I said very gently: "Lettice, why did you do it?"

"What?"

She sprang up, flinging her hair wildly back. She looked wild—almost terrified.

"What do you mean?"

"What made you do it? Was it jealousy? Dislike of Anne?"

"Oh!—oh! yes." She pushed the hair back from her face and seemed suddenly to regain complete self-possession. "Yes, you can call it jealousy. I've always disliked Anne—ever since she came queening it here. I put the damned thing under the desk. I hoped it would get her into trouble. It would have done if you hadn't been such a Nosey Parker, fingering things on dressing-tables. Anyway, it isn't a clergyman's business to go about helping the police."

It was a spiteful, childish outburst. I took no notice of it. Indeed, at that moment, she seemed a very pathetic child indeed.

Her childish attempt at vengeance against Anne seemed hardly to be taken seriously. I told her so, and added that I should return the earring to her and say nothing of the circumstances in which I had found it. She seemed rather touched by that.

"That's nice of you," she said.

She paused a minute and then said, keeping her face averted and evidently choosing her words with care.

"You know, Mr. Clement, I should—I should get Dennis away from here soon, if I were you. I—I think it would be better."

"Dennis?" I raised my eyebrows in slight surprise but with a trace of amusement too.

"I think it would be better." She added, still in the same awkward manner: "I'm sorry about Dennis. I didn't think he—anyway, I'm sorry."

We left it at that.

23

ON THE WAY back, I proposed to Griselda that we should make a detour and go round by the barrow. I was anxious to see if the police were at work and if so, what they had found. Griselda, however, had things to do at home, so I was left to make the expedition on my own.

I found Constable Hurst in charge of operations.

"No sign so far, sir," he reported. "And yet it stands to reason that this is the only place for a *cache.*"

His use of the word cache puzzled me for a moment, as he pronounced it catch, but his real meaning occurred to me almost at once.

"Whatimeantersay is, sir, where else could the young woman be going starting into the wood by that path? It leads to Old Hall, and it leads here, and that's about all."

"I suppose," I said, "that Inspector Slack would disdain such a simple course as asking the young lady straight out."

"Anxious not to put the wind up her," said Hurst. "Anything she writes to Stone or he writes to her may throw light on things—once she knows we're on to her, she'd shut up like *that.*"

Like *what* exactly was left in doubt, but I personally doubted Miss Gladys Cram ever being shut up in the way described. It was impossible to imagine her as other than overflowing with conversation.

"When a man's an h'impostor, you want to know *why* he's an h'impostor," said Constable Hurst didactically.

"Naturally," I said.

"And the answer is to be found in this here barrow—or else why was he for ever messing about with it?"

"A *raison d'être* for prowling about," I suggested, but this bit of French was too much for the constable. He revenged himself for not understanding it by saying coldly:

"That's the h'amateur's point of view."

"Anyway, you haven't found the suitcase," I said.

"We shall do, sir. Not a doubt of it."

"I'm not so sure," I said. "I've been thinking. Miss Marple said it was quite a short time before the girl reappeared empty-handed. In that case, she wouldn't have had time to get up here and back."

"You can't take any notice of what old ladies say. When they've seen something curious, and are waiting all eager like, why, time simply flies for them. And anyway, no lady knows anything about time."

I often wonder why the whole world is so prone to generalize. Generalizations are seldom or never true and are usually utterly inaccurate. I have a poor sense of time myself (hence the keeping of my clock fast) and Miss Marple, I should say, has a very acute one. Her clocks keep time to the minute and she herself is rigidly punctual on every occasion.

However, I had no intention of arguing with Constable Hurst on the point. I wished him good afternoon and good luck and went on my way.

It was just as I was nearing home that the idea came to me. There was nothing to lead up to it. It just flashed into my brain as a possible solution.

You will remember that on my first search of the path, the day after the murder, I had found the bushes disturbed in a certain place. They proved, or so I thought at the time, to have been disturbed by Lawrence, bent on the same errand as myself.

But I remembered that afterwards he and I together had come upon another faintly marked trail which proved to be that of the inspector. On thinking it over, I distinctly remembered that the first trail (Lawrence's) had been much more noticeable than the second, as though more than one person had been passing that way. And I reflected that that was probably what had drawn Lawrence's attention to it in the first instance. Supposing that it had originally been made by either Dr. Stone or else Miss Cram?

I remembered, or else I imagined remembering, that there had been several withered leaves on broken twigs. If so, the trail could not have been made the afternoon of our search.

I was just approaching the spot in question. I recognized it easily enough and once more forced my way through the bushes. This time I noticed fresh twigs broken. Someone *had* passed this way since Lawrence and myself.

I soon came to the place where I had encountered Lawrence. The faint trail, however, persisted farther, and I continued to follow it. Suddenly it widened out into a little clearing which showed signs of recent upheaval. I say a clearing, because the denseness of the undergrowth was thinned out there, but the branches of the trees met overhead and the whole place was not more than a few feet across.

On the other side, the undergrowth grew densely again, and it seemed quite clear that no one had forced a way through it recently. Nevertheless, it seemed to have been disturbed in one place.

I went across and kneeled down, thrusting the bushes aside with both hands. A glint of a shiny brown surface rewarded me. Full of excitement, I thrust my arm in and with a good deal of difficulty I extracted a small brown suitcase.

I uttered an ejaculation of triumph. I had been successful. Coldly snubbed by Constable Hurst, I had yet proved right in my reasoning. Here without doubt was the suitcase carried by Miss Cram. I tried the hasp, but it was locked.

As I rose to my feet I noticed a small brownish crystal lying on the ground. Almost automatically, I picked it up and slipped it into my pocket.

Then grasping my find by the handle, I retraced my steps to the path.

As I climbed over the stile into the lane, an agitated voice near at hand called out:

"Oh! Mr. Clement. You've found it! How clever of you!"

Mentally registering the fact that in the art of seeing without being seen, Miss Marple had no rival, I balanced my find on the palings between us.

"That's the one," said Miss Marple. "I'd know it anywhere."

This, I thought, was a slight exaggeration. There are thousands of cheap shiny suitcases all exactly alike. No one could recognize one particular one seen from such a distance away by moonlight, but I realized that the whole business of the suitcase was Miss Marple's particular triumph and, as such, she was entitled to a little pardonable exaggeration.

"It's locked, I suppose, Mr. Clement?"

"Yes. I'm just going to take it down to the police station."

"You don't think it would be better to telephone?"

Of course unquestionably it would be better to telephone. To stride through the village, suitcase in hand, would be to court a probably undesirable publicity.

So I unlatched Miss Marple's garden gate and entered the house by the French window, and from the sanctity of the drawing-room with the door shut, I telephoned my news.

The result was that Inspector Slack announced he would be up himself in a couple of jiffies.

When he arrived it was in his most cantankerous mood.

"So we've got it, have we?" he said. "You know, sir, you shouldn't keep things to yourself. If you've any reason to believe you know where the article in question was hidden, you ought to have reported it to the proper authorities."

"It was a pure accident," I said. "The idea just happened to occur to me."

"And that's a likely tale. Nearly three-quarters of a mile of woodland, and you go right to the proper spot and lay your hand upon it."

I would have given Inspector Slack the steps in reasoning which led me to this particular spot, but he had achieved his usual result of putting my back up. I said nothing.

"Well?" said Inspector Slack, eyeing the suitcase with dislike and would-be indifference, "I suppose we might as well have a look at what's inside."

He had brought an assortment of keys and wire with him. The lock was a cheap affair. In a couple of seconds the case was open.

I don't know what we had expected to find—something sternly sensational, I imagine. But the first thing that met our eyes was a greasy plaid scarf. The Inspector lifted it out. Next came a faded dark blue overcoat, very much the worse for wear. A checked cap followed.

"A shoddy lot," said the inspector.

A pair of boots very down at heel and battered came next. At the bottom of the suitcase was a parcel done up in newspaper.

"Fancy shirt, I suppose," said the inspector bitterly, as he tore it open.

A moment later he had caught his breath in surprise.

For inside the parcel were some demure little silver objects and a round platter of the same metal.

Miss Marple gave a shrill exclamation of recognition.

"The trencher salts," she exclaimed. "Colonel Protheroe's trencher salts, and the Charles II tazza. Did you ever hear of such a thing!"

The inspector had got very red.

"So that was the game," he muttered. "Robbery. But I can't make it out. There's been no mention of these things being missing."

"Perhaps they haven't discovered the loss," I suggested. "I presume these valuable things would not have been kept out in common use. Colonel Protheroe probably kept them locked away in a safe."

"I must investigate this," said the inspector. "I'll go right up to Old Hall now. So that's why our Dr. Stone made himself scarce. What with the murder and one thing and another, he was afraid we'd get wind of his activities. As likely as not his belongings might have been searched. He got the girl to hide them in the wood with a suitable change of clothing. He meant to come back by a roundabout route and go off with them one night while she stayed here to disarm suspicion. Well, there's one thing to the good. This lets him out over the murder. He'd nothing to do with that. Quite a different game."

He repacked the suitcase and took his departure, refusing Miss Marple's offer of a glass of sherry.

"Well, that's one mystery cleared up," I said with a sigh. "What Slack says is quite true; there are no grounds for suspecting him of the murder. Everything's accounted for quite satisfactorily."

"It really would seem so," said Miss Marple. "Although one never can be quite certain, can one?"

"There's a complete lack of motive," I pointed out. "He'd got what he came for and was clearing out."

"Y—es."

She was clearly not quite satisfied, and I looked at her in some curiosity. She hastened to answer my inquiring gaze with a kind of apologetic eagerness.

"I've no doubt I am *quite* wrong. I'm so stupid about these things. But I just wondered—I mean this silver is very valuable, is it not?"

"A tazza sold the other day for over a thousand pounds, I believe."

"I mean—it's not the value of the metal."

"No, it's what one might call a connoisseur's value."

"That's what I mean. The sale of such things would take a little time to arrange, or even if it was arranged, it couldn't be carried through without secrecy. I mean—if the robbery were reported and a hue and cry were raised, well, the things couldn't be marketed at all."

"I don't quite see what you mean," I said.

"I know I'm putting it badly." She became more flustered and apologetic. "But it seems to me that—that the things couldn't just have been abstracted, so to speak. The only satisfactory thing to do would be to replace these things with copies. Then, perhaps, the robbery wouldn't be discovered for some time."

"That's a very ingenious idea," I said.

"It would be the only way to do it, wouldn't it? And if so, of course, as you say, once the substitution had been accomplished there wouldn't have been any reason for murdering Colonel Protheroe—quite the reverse."

"Exactly," I said. "That's what I said."

"Yes, but I just wondered—I don't know, of course—and Colonel Protheroe always talked a lot about doing things before he actually did do them, and, of course, sometimes never did them at all, but he did say—"

"Yes?"

"That he was going to have all his things valued—a man down from London. For probate—no, that's when you're dead—for insurance. Someone told him that was the thing to do. He talked about it a great deal, and the importance of having it done. Of course, I don't know if he had made any actual arrangements, but if he had . . ."

"I see," I said slowly.

"Of course, the moment the expert saw the silver, he'd know, and then Colonel Protheroe would remember having shown the things to Dr. Stone—I wonder if it was done then—legerdemain, don't they call it? So clever—and then, well, the fat would be in the fire, to use an old-fashioned expression."

"I see your idea," I said. "I think we ought to find out for certain."

I went once more to the telephone. In a few minutes I was through to Old Hall and speaking to Anne Protheroe.

"No, it's nothing very important. Has the inspector arrived yet? Oh! well, he's on his way. Mrs. Protheroe, can you tell me if the contents of Old Hall were ever valued? What's that you say?"

Her answer came clear and prompt. I thanked her, replaced the receiver, and turned to Miss Marple.

"That's very definite. Colonel Protheroe had made arrangements for a man to come down from London on Monday—tomorrow—to make a full valuation. Owing to the colonel's death, the matter has been put off."

"Then there *was* a motive," said Miss Marple softly.

"A motive, yes. But that's all. You forget. When the shot was fired, Dr. Stone had just joined the others, or was climbing over the stile in order to do so."

"Yes," said Miss Marple thoughtfully. "So that rules him out."

24

I RETURNED TO the Vicarage to find Hawes waiting for me in my study. He was pacing up and down nervously, and when I entered the room he started as though he had been shot.

"You must excuse me," he said, wiping his forehead. "My nerves are all to pieces lately."

"My dear fellow," I said, "you positively must get away for a change. We shall have you breaking down altogether, and that will never do."

"I can't desert my post. No, that is a thing I will never do."

"It's not a case of desertion. You are ill. I'm sure Haydock would agree with me."

"Haydock—Haydock. What kind of a doctor is he? An ignorant country practitioner."

"I think you're unfair to him. He has always been considered a very able man in his profession."

"Oh! perhaps. Yes, I dare say. But I don't like him. However, that's not what I came to say. I came to ask you if you would be kind enough to preach tonight instead of me. I—I really do not feel equal to it."

"Why, certainly. I will take the service for you."

"No, no. I wish to take the service. I am perfectly fit. It is only the idea of getting up in the pulpit, of all those eyes staring at me . . ."

He shut his eyes and swallowed convulsively.

It is clear to me that there is something very wrong indeed the matter with Hawes. He seemed aware of my thoughts, for he opened his eyes and said quickly:

"There is nothing really wrong with me. It is just these headaches—these awful racking headaches. I wonder if you could let me have a glass of water."

"Certainly," I said.

I went and fetched it myself from the tap. Ringing bells is a profitless form of exercise in our house.

I brought the water to him and he thanked me. He took from his pocket a small cardboard box, and opening it, extracted a rice-paper capsule, which he swallowed with the aid of the water.

"A headache powder," he explained.

I suddenly wondered whether Hawes might have become addicted to drugs. It would explain a great many of his peculiarities.

"You don't take too many, I hope," I said.

"No—oh, no. Dr. Haydock warned me against that. But it is really wonderful. They bring instant relief."

Indeed he already seemed calmer and more composed.

He stood up.

"Then you will preach tonight? It's very good of you, sir."

"Not at all. And I insist on taking the service too. Get along home and rest. No, I won't have any argument. Not another word."

He thanked me again. Then he said, his eyes sliding past me to the window:

"You—you have been up at Old Hall today, haven't you, sir?"

"Yes."

"Excuse me—but were you sent for?"

I looked at him in surprise, and he flushed.

"I'm sorry, sir. I—I just thought some new development might have arisen and that that was why Mrs. Protheroe had sent for you."

I had not the faintest intention of satisfying Hawes's curiosity.

"She wanted to discuss the funeral arrangements and one or two other small matters with me," I said.

"Oh! that was all. I see."

I did not speak. He fidgeted from foot to foot, and finally said:

"Mr. Redding came to see me last night. I—I can't imagine why."

"Didn't he tell you?"

"He—he just said he thought he'd look me up. Said it was a bit lonely in the evenings. He's never done such a thing before."

"Well, he's supposed to be pleasant company," I said, smiling.

"What does he want to come and see me for? I don't like it." His voice rose shrilly. "He spoke of dropping in again. What does it all mean? What idea do you think he has got into his head?"

"Why should you suppose he has any ulterior motive?" I asked.

"I don't like it," repeated Hawes obstinately. "I've never gone against *him* in any way. I never suggested that *he* was guilty—even when he accused himself I said it seemed most incomprehensible. If I've had suspicions of anybody it's been of Archer—never of him. Archer is a totally different proposition—a godless irreligious ruffian. A drunken blackguard."

"Don't you think you're being a little harsh?" I said. "After all, we really know very little about the man."

"A poacher, in and out of prison, capable of anything."

"Do you really think he shot Colonel Protheroe?" I asked curiously.

Hawes has an inveterate dislike of answering yes or no. I have noticed it several times lately.

"Don't you think yourself, sir, that it's the only possible solution?"

"As far as we know," I said, "there's no evidence of any kind against him."

"His threats," said Hawes eagerly. "You forget about his threats."

I am sick and tired of hearing about Archer's threats. As far as I can make out, there is no direct evidence that he ever made any.

"He was determined to be revenged on Colonel Protheroe. He primed himself with drink and then shot him."

"That's pure supposition."

"But you will admit that it's perfectly probable?"

"No, I don't."

"Possible, then?"

"Possible, yes."

Hawes glanced at me sideways.

"Why don't you think it's probable?"

"Because," I said, "a man like Archer wouldn't think of shooting a man with a pistol. It's the wrong weapon."

Hawes seemed taken aback by my argument. Evidently it wasn't the objection he had expected.

"Do you really think the objection is feasible?" he asked doubtingly.

"To my mind it is a complete stumbling block to Archer's having committed the crime," I said.

In face of my positive assertion, Hawes said no more. He thanked me again and left.

I had gone as far as the front door with him, and on the hall table I saw four notes. They had certain characteristics in common. The handwriting was almost unmistakably feminine, they all bore the words, "By hand, Urgent," and the only difference I could see was that one was noticeably dirtier than the rest.

Their similarity gave me a curious feeling of seeing—not double, but quadruple.

Mary came out of the kitchen and caught me staring at them.

"Come by hand since lunch time," she volunteered. "All but one. I found that in the box."

I nodded, gathered them up, and took them into the study.

The first one ran thus:

DEAR MR. CLEMENT

Something has come to my knowledge which I feel you ought to know. It concerns the death of poor Colonel Protheroe. I should much appreciate your advice on the matter—whether to go to the police or not. Since my dear husband's death, I have such a shrinking from every kind of publicity. Perhaps you could run in and see me for a few minutes this afternoon.

Yours sincerely,
MARTHA PRICE RIDLEY.

I opened the second:

DEAR MR. CLEMENT

I am so troubled—so *exercised* in my mind—to know what I ought to do. Something has come to my ears that I feel may be important. I have such a *horror* of being mixed up with the police in any way. I am so disturbed and distressed. Would it be asking too much of you, dear vicar, to drop in for a few minutes and solve my doubts and perplexities for me in the wonderful way you always do?

Forgive my troubling you,
Yours very sincerely,
CAROLINE WETHERBY.

The third, I felt, I could almost have recited beforehand.

DEAR MR. CLEMENT

Something most important has come to my ears. I feel you should be the first to know about it. Will you call in and see me this afternoon some time. I will wait in for you.

This militant epistle was signed "AMANDA HARTNELL."

I opened the fourth missive. It has been my good fortune to be troubled with very few anonymous letters. An anonymous letter is, I think, the meanest and cruellest weapon there is. This one was no exception. It purported to be written by an illiterate person, but several things inclined me to disbelieve that assumption.

DEAR VICAR

   I think you ought to know what is Going On. Your lady has been seen coming out of Mr. Redding's cottage in a surreptitious manner. You know wot i mean. The two are Carrying On together. i think you ought to know.

                                        A FRIEND.

I made a faint exclamation of disgust and crumpling up the paper tossed it into the open grate just as Griselda entered the room.

"What's that you're throwing down so contemptuously?" she asked.

"Filth," I said.

Taking a match from my pocket, I struck it and bent down. Griselda, however, was too quick for me. She had stooped down and caught up the crumpled ball of paper and smoothed it out before I could stop her.

She read it, gave a little exclamation of disgust, and tossed it back to me, turning away as she did so. I lighted it and watched it burn.

Griselda had moved away. She was standing by the window looking out into the garden.

"Len," she said, without turning round.

"Yes, my dear."

"I'd like to tell you something. Yes, don't stop me. I want to, please. When—when Lawrence Redding came here, I let you think that I had only known him slightly before. That wasn't true. I—had known him rather well. In fact, before I met you, I had been rather in love with him. I think most people are with Lawrence. I was—well, absolutely silly about him at one time. I don't mean I wrote him compromising letters or anything idiotic like they do in books. But I was rather keen on him once."

"Why didn't you tell me?" I asked.

"Oh! because! I don't know exactly except that—well, you're foolish in some ways. Just because you're so much older than I am, you think that I—well, that I'm likely to like other people. I thought you'd be tiresome, perhaps, about me and Lawrence being friends."

"You're very clever at concealing things," I said, remembering what she had told me in that room less than a week ago, and the ingenuous natural way she had talked.

"Yes, I've always been able to hide things. In a way, I like doing it."
Her voice held a childlike ring of pleasure in it.

"But it's quite true what I said. I didn't know about Anne, and I wondered why Lawrence was so different, not—well, really not noticing me. I'm not used to it."

There was a pause.

"You do understand, Len?" said Griselda anxiously.

"Yes," I said, "I understand."

But did I?

25

I FOUND IT hard to shake off the impression left by the anonymous letter. Pitch soils.

However, I gathered up the other three letters, glanced at my watch, and started out.

I wondered very much what this might be that had "come to the knowledge" of three ladies simultaneously. I took it to be the same piece of news. In this, I was to realize that my psychology was at fault.

I cannot pretend that my calls took me past the police station. My feet gravitated there of their own accord. I was anxious to know whether Inspector Slack had returned from Old Hall.

I found that he had, and further, that Miss Cram had returned with him. The fair Gladys was seated in the police station carrying off matters with a high hand. She denied absolutely having taken the suitcase to the woods.

"Just because one of these gossiping old cats has nothing better to do than look out of her window all night you go and pitch upon me. She's been mistaken once, remember, when she said she saw me at the end of the lane on the afternoon of the murder, and if she was mistaken then, in daylight, how can she possibly have recognized me by moonlight?

"Wicked it is, the way these old ladies go on down here. Say anything, they will. And me asleep in my bed as innocent as can be. You ought to be ashamed of yourselves, the lot of you."

"And supposing the landlady of the Blue Boar identifies the suitcase as yours, Miss Cram?"

"If she says anything of the kind, she's wrong. There's no name on it. Nearly everybody's got a suitcase like that. As for poor Dr. Stone, accusing him of being a common burglar! And he has a lot of letters after his name."

"You refuse to give us any explanation, then, Miss Cram?"

"No refusing about it. You've made a mistake, that's all. You and your meddlesome Marples. I won't say a word more—not without my solicitor present. I'm going this minute—unless you're going to arrest me."

For answer, the inspector rose and opened the door for her, and with a toss of the head, Miss Cram walked out.

"That's the line she takes," said Slack, coming back to his chair. "Absolute denial. And, of course, the old lady *may* have been mistaken. No jury would believe you could recognize anyone from that distance on a moonlit night. And, of course, as I say, the old lady may have made a mistake."

"She may," I said, "but I don't think she did. Miss Marple is usually right. That's what makes her unpopular."

The inspector grinned.

"That's what Hurst says. Lord, these villages!"

"What about the silver, Inspector?"

"Seemed to be perfectly in order. Of course, that meant one lot or the other must be a fake. There's a very good man in Much Benham, an authority on old silver. I've phoned over to him and sent a car to fetch him. We'll soon know which is which. Either the burglary was an accomplished fact, or else it was only planned. Doesn't make a frightful lot of difference either way—I mean as far as we're concerned. Robbery's a small business compared with murder. These two aren't concerned with the murder. We'll maybe get a line on him through the girl—that's why I let her go without any more fuss."

"I wondered," I said.

"A pity about Mr. Redding. It's not often you find a man who goes out of his way to oblige you."

"I suppose not," I said, smiling slightly.

"Women cause a lot of trouble," moralized the inspector.

He sighed and then went on, somewhat to my surprise: "Of course there's Archer."

"Oh!" I said. "You've thought of him?"

"Why, naturally, sir, first thing. It didn't need any anonymous letters to put me on his track."

"Anonymous letters," I said sharply. "Did you get one, then?"

"That's nothing new, sir. We get a dozen a day, at least. Oh! yes, we were put wise to Archer. As though the police couldn't look out for themselves! Archer's been under suspicion from the first. The trouble of it is, he's got an alibi. Not that it amounts to anything, but it's awkward to get over."

"What do you mean by its not amounting to anything?" I asked.

"Well, it appears he was with a couple of pals all the afternoon. Not, as I say, that that counts much. Men like Archer and his pals would swear to anything. There's no believing a word they say. *We* know that. But the public doesn't, and the jury's taken from the public, more's the pity. They know nothing, and ten to one believe everything that's said in the witness box, no matter who it is that says it. And of course Archer himself will swear till he's black in the face that he didn't do it."

"Not so obliging as Mr. Redding," I said with a smile.

"Not he," said the inspector, making the remark as a plain statement of fact.

"It is natural, I suppose, to cling to life," I mused.

"You'd be surprised if you knew the murderers that have got off through the soft-heartedness of the jury," said the inspector gloomily.

"But do you really think that Archer did it?" I asked.

It has struck me as curious all along that Inspector Slack never seems to have any personal views of his own on the murder. The easiness or difficulty of getting a conviction are the only points that seem to appeal to him.

"I'd like to be a bit surer," he admitted. "A fingerprint now, or a footprint, or seen in the vicinity about the time of the crime. Can't risk arresting him without something of that kind. He's been seen round Mr. Redding's house once or twice, but he'd say that was to speak to his mother. A decent body, she is. No, on the whole, I'm for the lady. If I could only get definite proof of blackmail—but you can't get definite proof of anything in this crime! It's theory, theory, theory. It's a sad pity that there's not a single spinster lady living along your road, Mr. Clement. I bet she'd have seen something if there had been."

His words reminded me of my calls, and I took leave of him. It was about the solitary instance when I had seen him in a genial mood.

My first call was on Miss Hartnell. She must have been watching for me from the window, for before I had time to ring she had opened the front door, and clasping my hand firmly in hers, had led me over the threshold.

"So good of you to come. In here. More private."

We entered a microscopic room, about the size of a hen-coop. Miss Hartnell shut the door and with an air of deep secrecy waved me to a seat (there were only three). I perceived that she was enjoying herself.

"I'm never one to beat about the bush," she said in her jolly voice, the latter slightly toned down to meet the requirements of the situation. "You know how things go the round in a village like this."

"Unfortunately," I said, "I do."

"I agree with you. Nobody dislikes gossip more than I do. But there it is. I thought it my duty to tell the police inspector that I'd called on Mrs. Lestrange the afternoon of the murder and that she was out. I don't expect to be thanked for doing my duty, I just do it. Ingratitude is what you meet with first and last in this life. Why, only yesterday that impudent Mrs. Baker—"

"Yes, yes," I said, hoping to avert the usual tirade. "Very sad, very sad. But you were saying."

"The lower classes don't know who are their best friends," said Miss Hartnell. "I always say a word in season when I'm visiting. Not that I'm ever thanked for it."

"You were telling the inspector about your call upon Mrs. Lestrange," I prompted.

"Exactly—and by the way, he didn't thank me. Said he'd ask for information when he wanted it—not those words exactly, but that was the spirit. There's a different class of men in the police force nowadays."

"Very probably," I said. "But you were going on to say something?"

"I decided that this time I wouldn't go near any wretched inspector. After all, a clergyman is a gentleman—at least some are," she added.

I gathered that the qualification was intended to include me.

"If I can help you in any way," I began.

"It's a matter of duty," said Miss Hartnell, and closed her mouth with a snap. "I don't want to have to say these things. No one likes it less. But duty is duty."

I waited.

"I've been given to understand," went on Miss Hartnell, turning rather red, "that Mrs. Lestrange gives out that she was at home all the time—that she didn't answer the door because—well, because she didn't choose. Such airs and graces. I only called as a matter of duty, and to be treated like that!"

"She has been ill," I said mildly.

"Ill? Fiddlesticks. You're too unworldly, Mr. Clement. There's nothing the matter with that woman. Too ill to attend the inquest indeed! Medical certificate from Dr. Haydock! She can wind him round her little finger, everyone knows that. Well, where was I?"

I didn't quite know. It is difficult with Miss Hartnell to know where narrative ends and vituperation begins.

"Oh! about calling on her that afternoon. Well, it's fiddlesticks to say she was in the house. She wasn't. I know."

"How can you possibly know?"

Miss Hartnell's face turned a little redder. In someone less truculent, her demeanor might have been called embarrassed.

"I'd knocked and rung," she explained. "Twice. If not three times. And it occurred to me suddenly that the bell might be out of order."

She was, I was glad to note, unable to look me in the face when saying this. The same builder builds all our houses and the bells he installs are always clearly audible when standing on the mat outside the front door. Both Miss Hartnell and I knew this perfectly well, but I suppose decencies have to be preserved.

"Yes?" I murmured.

"I didn't want to push my card through the letter box. That would seem so rude, and whatever I am, I am never rude."

She made this amazing statement without a tremor.

"So I thought I would just go round the house and—and tap on the window pane," she continued unblushingly. "I went all round the house and looked in at all the windows, but there was no one in the house at all."

I understood her perfectly. Taking advantage of the fact that the house was empty, Miss Hartnell had given unbridled rein to her curiosity and had gone round the house, examining the garden and peering in at all the windows to see as much as she could of the interior. She had chosen to tell her story to me, believing that I should be a more sympathetic and lenient audience than the police. The clergy are supposed to give the benefit of the doubt to their parishioners.

I made no comment on the situation. I merely asked a question.

"What time was this, Miss Hartnell?"

"As far as I can remember," said Miss Hartnell, "it must have been close on six o'clock. I went straight home afterwards, and I got in about ten past six, and Mrs. Protheroe came in somewhere round about the half-hour, leaving Dr. Stone and Mr. Redding outside, and we talked about bulbs. And all the time the poor colonel lying murdered. It's a sad world."

"It is sometimes a rather unpleasant one," I said.

I rose.

"And that is all you have to tell me?"

"I just thought it might be important."

"It might," I agreed.

And refusing to be drawn further, much to Miss Hartnell's disappointment, I took my leave.

Miss Wetherby, whom I visited next, received me in a kind of flutter.

"Dear vicar, how truly kind. You've had tea? Really, you won't? A cushion for your back? It is so kind of you to come round so promptly. Always willing to put yourself out for others."

There was a good deal of this before we came to the point, and even then it was approached with a good deal of circumlocution.

"You must understand that I heard this on the best authority."

In St. Mary Mead the best authority is always somebody else's servant.

"You can't tell me who told you?"

"I promised, dear Mr. Clement. And I always think a promise should be a sacred thing."

She looked very solemn.

"Shall we say a little bird told me? That is safe, isn't it?"

I longed to say, "It's damned silly." I rather wish I had. I should have liked to observe the effect on Miss Wetherby.

"Well, this little bird told that she saw a certain lady, who shall be nameless."

"Another kind of bird?" I inquired.

To my great surprise Miss Wetherby went off into paroxysms of laughter and tapped me playfully on the arm, saying:

"Oh! vicar, you must not be so naughty."

When she had recovered, she went on.

"A certain lady, and where do you think this certain lady was going? She turned into the Vicarage road, but before she did so, she looked up and down the road in a most peculiar way—to see if anyone she knew were noticing her, I imagine."

"And the little bird—" I inquired.

"Paying a visit to the fishmonger's—in the room over the shop."

I now know where maids go on their days out. I know there is one place they never go if they can help—anywhere in the open air.

"And the time," continued Miss Wetherby, leaning forward mysteriously, "was just before six o'clock."

"On which day?"

Miss Wetherby gave a little scream.

"The day of the murder, of course, didn't I say so?"

"I inferred it," I replied. "And the name of the lady?"

"Begins with an L," said Miss Wetherby, nodding her head several times.

Feeling that I had got to the end of the information Miss Wetherby had to import, I rose to my feet.

"You won't let the police cross-question me, will you?" said Miss Wetherby, pathetically, as she clasped my hand in both of hers. "I do shrink from publicity. And to stand up in court!"

"In special cases," I said, "they let witnesses sit down."

And I escaped.

There was still Mrs. Price Ridley to see. That lady put me in my place at once.

"I will not be mixed up in any police court business," she said firmly, after shaking my hand coldly. "You understand that, on the other hand, having come across a circumstance which needs explaining, I think it should be brought to the notice of the authorities."

"Does it concern Mrs. Lestrange?" I asked.

"Why should it?" demanded Mrs. Price Ridley coldly.

She had me at a disadvantage there.

"It's a very simple matter," she continued. "My maid, Clara, was standing at the front gate, she went down there for a minute or two—*she* says to get a breath of fresh air. Most unlikely, I should say. Much more probable that she was looking out for the fishmonger's boy—if he calls himself a boy—impudent young jackanapes, thinks because he's seventeen he can joke with all the girls. Anyway, as I say, she was standing at the gate and she heard a sneeze."

"Yes," I said, waiting for more.

"That's all. I tell you she heard a sneeze. And don't start telling me I'm not so young as I once was and may have made a mistake, because it was Clara who heard it and she's only nineteen."

"But," I said, "why shouldn't she have heard a sneeze?"

Mrs. Price Ridley looked at me in obvious pity for my poorness of intellect.

"She heard a sneeze on the day of the murder at a time when there was no one in your house. Doubtless the murderer was concealed in the bushes waiting his opportunity. What you have to look for is a man with a cold in his head."

"Or a sufferer from hay fever," I suggested. "But as a matter of fact, Mrs. Price Ridley, I think that mystery has a very easy solution. Our maid, Mary, has been suffering from a severe cold in the head. In fact, her sniffing has tried us very much lately. It must have been her sneeze your maid heard."

"It was a man's sneeze," said Mrs. Price Ridley firmly. "And you couldn't hear your maid sneeze in your kitchen from our gate."

"You couldn't hear anyone sneezing in the study from your gate," I said. "Or at least, I very much doubt it."

"I said the man might have been concealed in the shrubbery," said Mrs. Price Ridley. "Doubtless when Clara had gone in, he effected an entrance by the front door."

"Well, of course, that's possible," I said.

I tried not to make my voice consciously soothing, but I must have failed, for Mrs. Price Ridley glared at me suddenly.

"I am accustomed not to be listened to, but I might mention also that to leave a tennis racquet carelessly flung down on the grass without a press completely ruins it. And tennis racquets are very expensive nowadays."

There did not seem to be rhyme or reason in this flank attack. It bewildered me utterly.

"But perhaps you don't agree," said Mrs. Price Ridley.

"Oh! I do—certainly."

"I am glad. Well, that is all I have to say. I wash my hands of the whole affair."

She leaned back and closed her eyes like one weary of this world. I thanked her and said goodbye.

On the doorstep, I ventured to ask Clara about her mistress's statement.

"It's quite true, sir, I heard a sneeze. And it wasn't an ordinary sneeze— not by any means."

Nothing about a crime is ever ordinary. The shot was not an ordinary kind of shot. The sneeze was not a usual kind of sneeze. It was, I presume, a special murderer's sneeze. I asked the girl what time this had been, but she was very vague, some time between a quarter and half-past six she thought. Anyway, "it was before the mistress had the telephone call and was took bad."

I asked her if she had heard a shot of any kind. And she said the shots had been something awful. After that, I placed very little credence in her statements.

I was just turning in at my own gate when I decided to pay a friend a visit.

Glancing at my watch, I saw that I had just time for it before taking Evensong. I went down the road to Haydock's house. He came out on the doorstep to meet me.

I noticed afresh how worried and haggard he looked. This business seemed to have aged him out of all knowledge.

"I'm glad to see you," he said. "What's the news?"

I told him the latest Stone development.

"A high-class thief," he commented. "Well, that explains a lot of things.

He'd read up his subject, but he made slips from time to time to me. Protheroe must have caught him out once. You remember the row they had. What do you think about the girl? Is she in it too?"

"Opinion as to that is undecided," I said. "For my own part, I think the girl is all right.

"She's such a prize idiot," I added.

"Oh! I wouldn't say that. She's rather shrewd, is Miss Gladys Cram. A remarkably healthy specimen. Not likely to trouble members of my profession."

I told him that I was worried about Hawes, and that I was anxious that he should get away for a real rest and change.

Something evasive came into his manner when I said this. His answer did not ring quite true.

"Yes," he said slowly. "I suppose that would be the best thing. Poor chap. Poor chap."

"I thought you didn't like him."

"I don't—not much. But I'm sorry for a lot of people I don't like." He added after a minute or two: "I'm even sorry for Protheroe. Poor fellow—nobody ever liked him much. Too full of his own rectitude and too self-assertive. It's an unlovable mixture. He was always the same— even as a young man."

"I didn't know you knew him then?"

"Oh, yes! When he lived in Westmorland, I had a practice not far away. That's a long time ago now. Nearly twenty years."

I sighed. Twenty years ago Griselda was five years old. Time is an odd thing . . .

"Is that all you came to say to me, Clement?"

I looked up with a start. Haydock was watching me with keen eyes.

"There's something else, isn't there?" he said.

I nodded.

I had been uncertain whether to speak or not when I came in but now I decided to do so. I like Haydock as well as any man I know. He is a splendid fellow in every way. I felt that what I had to tell might be useful to him.

I recited my interviews with Miss Hartnell and Miss Wetherby.

He was silent for a long time after I'd spoken.

"It's quite true, Clement," he said at last. "I've been trying to shield Mrs. Lestrange from any inconvenience that I could. As a matter of fact, she's an old friend. But that's not my only reason. That medical certificate of mine isn't the put-up job you all think it was."

He paused, and then said gravely:

"This is between you and me, Clement. Mrs. Lestrange is doomed."

"What?"

"She's a dying woman. I give her a month at longest. Do you wonder that I want to keep her from being badgered and questioned?"

He went on:

"When she turned into this road that evening it was here she came— to this house."

"You haven't said so before."

"I didn't want to create talk. Six to seven isn't my time for seeing patients, and everyone knows that. But you can take my word for it that she was here."

"She wasn't here when I came for you, though. I mean, when we discovered the body."

"No," he seemed perturbed. "She'd left—to keep an appointment."

"In what direction was the appointment? In her own house?"

"I don't know, Clement. On my honor, I don't know."

I believed him, but—

"And supposing an innocent man is hanged?" I said.

He shook his head.

"No," he said. "No one will be hanged for the murder of Colonel Protheroe. You can take my word for that."

But that is just what I could not do. And yet the certainty in his voice was very great.

"No one will be hanged," he repeated.

"This man, Archer—"

He made an impatient movement. "Hasn't got brains enough to wipe his fingerprints off the pistol."

"Perhaps not," I said dubiously.

Then I remembered something, and taking the little brownish crystal I had found in the wood from my pocket, I held it out to him and asked him what it was.

"H'm," he hesitated. "Looks like picric acid. Where did you find it?"

"That," I replied, "is Sherlock Holmes's secret."

He smiled.

"What is picric acid?"

"Well, it's an explosive."

"Yes, I know that, but it's got another use, hasn't it?"

He nodded.

"It's used medically—in solution for burns. Wonderful stuff."

I held out my hand, and rather reluctantly he handed it back to me.

"It's of no consequence probably," I said. "But I found it in rather an unusual place."

"You won't tell me where?"

Rather childishly, I wouldn't.

He had his secrets. Well, I would have mine.

I was a little hurt that he had not confided in me more fully.

26

I WAS IN a strange mood when I mounted the pulpit that night.

The church was unusually full. I cannot believe that it was the prospect of Hawes preaching which had attracted so many. Hawes's sermons are dull and dogmatic. And if the news had got round that I was preaching instead, that would not have attracted them either. For my sermons are dull and scholarly. Neither, I am afraid, can I attribute it to devotion.

Everybody had come, I concluded, to see who else was there, and possibly to exchange a little gossip in the church porch afterwards.

Haydock was in church, which is unusual, and also Lawrence Redding. And to my surprise, beside Lawrence I saw the white, strained face of Hawes. Anne Protheroe was there, but she usually attends Evensong on Sundays, though I had hardly thought she would today. I was far more surprised to see Lettice. Church-going was compulsory on Sunday morning—Colonel Protheroe was adamant on that point, but I had never seen Lettice at evening service before.

Gladys Cram was there, looking rather blatantly young and healthy against a background of wizened spinsters, and I fancied that a dim figure at the end of the church who had slipped in late, was Mrs. Lestrange.

I need hardly say that Mrs. Price Ridley, Miss Hartnell, Miss Wetherby, and Miss Marple were there in full force. All the village people were there, with hardly a single exception. I don't know when we have had such a crowded congregation.

Crowds are queer things. There was a magnetic atmosphere that night, and the first person to feel its influence was myself.

As a rule, I prepare my sermons beforehand. I am careful and conscientious over them, but no one is better aware than myself of their deficiencies.

Tonight I was of necessity preaching *extempore,* and as I looked down on the sea of upturned faces, a sudden madness entered my brain. I ceased to be in any sense a Minister of God. I became an actor. I had an audience before me and I wanted to move that audience—and more, I felt the power to move it.

I am not proud of what I did that night. I am an utter disbeliever in the emotional Revivalist spirit. Yet that night I acted the part of a raving, ranting evangelist.

I gave out my text slowly.

I came not to call the righteous, but sinners to repentance.

I repeated it twice, and I heard my own voice, a resonant, ringing voice unlike the voice of the everyday Leonard Clement.

I saw Griselda from her front pew look up in surprise and Dennis follow her example.

I held my breath for a moment or two, and then I let myself rip.

The congregation in that church were in a state of pent-up emotion, ripe to be played upon. I played upon them. I exhorted sinners to repentance. I lashed myself into a kind of emotional frenzy. Again and again I threw out a denouncing hand and reiterated the phrase.

"I am speaking to *you* . . ."

And each time, from different parts of the church, a kind of sighing gasp went up.

Mass emotion is a strange and terrible thing.

I finished up with those beautiful and poignant words—perhaps the most poignant words in the whole Bible:

"This night thy soul shall be required of thee . . ."

It was a strange, brief possession. When I got back to the Vicarage I was my usual faded, indeterminate self. I found Griselda rather pale. She slipped her arm through mine.

"Len," she said, "you were rather terrible tonight. I—I didn't like it I've never heard you preach like that before."

"I don't suppose you ever will again," I said, sinking down wearily on the sofa. I was tired.

"What made you do it?"

"A sudden madness came over me."

"Oh! it—it wasn't something special?"

"What do you mean—something special?"

"I wondered—that was all. You're very unexpected, Len. I never feel I really know you."

We sat down to cold supper, Mary being out.

"There's a note for you in the hall," said Griselda. "Get it, will you, Dennis?"

Dennis, who had been very silent, obeyed.

I took it and groaned. Across the top left-hand corner was written: *By hand—Urgent.*

"This," I said, "must be from Miss Marple. There's no one else left."

I had been perfectly correct in my assumption.

DEAR MR. CLEMENT

I should so much like to have a little chat with you about one or two things that have occurred to me. I feel we should all try and help in elucidating this sad mystery. I will come over about half-past nine, if I may, and tap on your study window. Perhaps dear Griselda would be so very kind as to run over here and cheer up my nephew. And Mr. Dennis too, of course, if he cares to come. If I do not hear, I will expect them and will come over myself at the time I have stated.

Yours very sincerely,
JANE MARPLE.

I handed the note to Griselda.

"Oh! we'll go," she said cheerfully. "A glass or two of home-made liqueur is just what one needs on Sunday evening. I think it's Mary's blancmange that is so frightfully depressing. It's like something out of a mortuary."

Dennis seemed less charmed at the prospect.

"It's all very well for you," he grumbled. "You can talk all this highbrow stuff about art and books. I always feel a perfect fool sitting and listening to you."

"That's good for you," said Griselda serenely. "It puts you in your place. Anyway, I don't think Mr. Raymond West is so frightfully clever as he pretends to be."

"Very few of us are," I said.

I wondered very much what exactly it was that Miss Marple wished to talk over. Of all the ladies in my congregation, I consider her by far the shrewdest. Not only does she see and hear practically everything that goes on, but she draws amazingly neat and apposite deductions from the facts that come under her notice.

If I were at any time to set out on a career of deceit, it would be of Miss Marple that I should be afraid.

What Griselda called the Nephew Amusing Party started off at a little after nine, and whilst I was waiting for Miss Marple to arrive I amused myself by drawing up a kind of schedule of the facts connected with the crime. I arranged them so far as possible in chronological order. I am not a punctual person, but I am a neat one, and I like things jotted down in a methodical fashion.

At half-past nine punctually, there was a little tap on the window, and I rose and admitted Miss Marple.

She had a very fine Shetland shawl thrown over her head and shoulders and was looking rather old and frail. She came in full of little fluttering remarks.

"So good of you to let me come—and so good of dear Griselda— Raymond admires her so much—the perfect Greuze he always calls her . . . Shall I sit here? I am not taking your chair? Oh! thank you . . . No, I won't have a footstool."

I deposited the Shetland shawl on a chair and returned to take a chair facing my guest. We looked at each other, and a little deprecating smile broke out on her face.

"I feel that you must be wondering why—why I am so interested in all this. You may possibly think it's very unwomanly. No—please—I should like to explain if I may."

She paused a moment, a pink color suffusing her cheeks.

"You see," she began at last, "living alone, as I do, in a rather out-of-the-way part of the world one has to have a hobby. There is, of course, woolwork, and Guides, and Welfare, and sketching, but my hobby is— and always has been—Human Nature. So varied—and so very fascinating. And, of course, in a small village, with nothing to distract one, one has such ample opportunity for becoming what I might call proficient in one's study. One begins to class people, quite definitely, just as though they were birds or flowers, group so-and-so, genus this, species that. Sometimes, of course, one makes mistakes, but less and less as time goes on. And then, too, one tests on oneself. One takes a little problem—for instance, the gill of picked shrimps that amused dear Griselda so much— a quite unimportant mystery but absolutely incomprehensible unless one solves it right. And then there was that matter of the changed cough drops, and the butcher's wife's umbrella—the last absolutely meaningless unless on the assumption that the greengrocer was not behaving at all nicely with the chemist's wife—which, of course, turned out to be the case. It is so fascinating, you know, to apply one's judgement and find that one is right."

"You usually are, I believe," I said, smiling.

"That, I am afraid, is what has made me a little conceited," confessed Miss Marple. "But I have always wondered whether, if some day a really big mystery came along, I should be able to do the same thing. I mean— just solve it correctly. Logically, it ought to be exactly the same thing. After all, a tiny working model of a torpedo is just the same as a real torpedo."

"You mean it's all a question of relativity," I said slowly. "It should be—logically, I admit. But I don't know whether it really is."

"Surely it must be the same," said Miss Marple. "The—what one used to call the factors at school—are the same. There's money, and mutual attraction between people of an—er—opposite sex—and there's queerness, of course—so many people are a little queer, aren't they?—in fact, most people are when you know them well. And normal people do such astonishing things sometimes, and abnormal people are sometimes so very sane and ordinary. In fact, the only way is to compare people with other people you have known or come across. You'd be surprised if you knew how very few distinct types there are in all."

"You frighten me," I said. "I feel I'm being put under the microscope."

"Of course, I wouldn't dream of saying any of this to Colonel Melchett— such an autocratic man, isn't he?—and poor Inspector Slack—well, he's exactly like the young lady in the boot shop who wants to sell you patent leather because she's got it in your size, and doesn't take any notice of the fact that you want brown calf."

That, really, is a very good description of Slack.

"But you, Mr. Clement, know, I'm sure, quite as much about the crime as Inspector Slack. I thought, if we could work together—"

"I wonder," I said. "I think each one of us in his secret heart fancies himself as Sherlock Holmes."

Then I told her of the three summonses I had received that afternoon. I told her of Anne's discovery of the picture with the slashed face. I also told her of Miss Cram's attitude at the police station, and I described Haydock's identification of the crystal I had picked up.

"Having found that myself," I finished up, "I should like it to be important. But it's probably got nothing to do with the case."

"I have been reading a lot of American detective stories from the library lately," said Miss Marple, "hoping to find them helpful."

"Was there anything in them about picric acid?"

"I'm afraid not. I do remember reading a story once, though, in which a man was poisoned by picric acid and lanoline being rubbed on him as an ointment."

"But as nobody has been poisoned here, that doesn't seem to enter into the question," I said.

Then I took up my schedule and handed it to her.

"I've tried," I said, "to recapitulate the facts of the case as clearly as possible."

My schedule

Thursday, 21st inst.

12:30 a.m.—Colonel Protheroe alters his appointment from six to six-fifteen. Overheard by half village very probably.

12:45—Pistol last seen in its proper place. (But this is doubtful, as Mrs. Archer had previously said she could not remember.)

5:30 (approx.)—Colonel and Mrs. Protheroe leave Old Hall for village in car.

5:30—Fake call put through to me from the North Lodge, Old Hall.

6:15 (or a minute or two earlier)—Colonel Protheroe arrives at Vicarage. Is shown into study by Mary.

6:20—Mrs. Protheroe comes along back lane and across garden to study window. Colonel Protheroe not visible.

6:29—Call from Lawrence Redding's cottage put through to Mrs. Price Ridley (according to Exchange).

6:30–6:35—Shot heard. (Accepting telephone call time as correct.) Lawrence Redding, Anne Protheroe and Dr. Stone's evidence seem to point to its being earlier, but Mrs. P. R. probably right.

6:45—Lawrence Redding arrives Vicarage and finds the body.

6:48—I meet Lawrence Redding.

6:49—Body discovered by me.

6:55—Haydock examines body.

NOTE—The only two people who have no kind of alibi for 6:30–6:35 are Miss Cram and Mrs. Lestrange. Miss Cram says she was at the barrow, but no confirmation. It seems reasonable however, to dismiss her from case as there seems nothing to connect her with it. Mrs. Lestrange left Dr. Haydock's house some time after six to keep an appointment. Where was the appointment, and with whom? It could hardly have been with Colonel Protheroe, as he expected to be engaged with me. It is true that Mrs. Lestrange was near the spot at the time the crime was committed, but it seems doubtful what motive she could have had for murdering him. She did not gain by his death, and the inspector's theory of blackmail I cannot accept. Mrs. Lestrange is not that kind of woman. Also it seems unlikely that she should have got hold of Lawrence Redding's pistol.

"Very clear," said Miss Marple, nodding her head in approval. "Very clear indeed. Gentlemen always make such excellent memoranda."

"You agree with what I have written?" I asked.

"Oh, yes—you have put it all beautifully."

I asked her the question then that I had been meaning to put all along.

"Miss Marple," I said. "Who do you suspect? You once said that there were seven people."

"Quite that, I should think," said Miss Marple absently. "I expect every one of us suspects someone different. In fact, one can see they do."

She didn't ask me who I suspected.

"The point is," she said, "that one must provide an explanation for everything. Each thing has got to be explained away satisfactorily. If you have a theory that fits every fact—well, then, it must be the right one. But that's extremely difficult. If it wasn't for that note—"

"The note?" I said, surprised.

"Yes, you remember, I told you. That note has worried me all along. It's wrong, somehow."

"Surely," I said, "that is explained now. It was written at six thirty-five and another hand—the murderer's—put the misleading 6:20 at the top. I think that is clearly established."

"But even then," said Miss Marple, "it's all wrong."

"But why?"

"Listen." Miss Marple leaned forward eagerly. "Mrs. Protheroe passed my garden, as I told you, and she went as far as the study window and she looked in and she didn't see Colonel Protheroe."

"Because he was writing at the desk," I said.

"And that's what's all wrong. That was at twenty past six. We agreed that he wouldn't sit down to say he couldn't wait any longer until after half-past six—so, why was he sitting at the writing-table then?"

"I never thought of that," I said slowly.

"Let us, dear Mr. Clement, just go over it again. Mrs. Protheroe comes to the window and she thinks the room is empty—she must have thought so, because otherwise she would never have gone down to the studio to meet Mr. Redding. It wouldn't have been safe. The room must have been absolutely silent if she thought it was empty. And that leaves us three alternatives, doesn't it?"

"You mean—"

"Well, the first alternative would be that Colonel Protheroe was dead already—but I don't think that's the most likely one. To begin with he'd only been there about five minutes and she or I would have heard the shot, and secondly, the same difficulty remains about his being at the writing-table. The second alternative is, of course, that he was sitting at the writing-table writing a note, but in that case it must have been a different note altogether. It can't have been to say he couldn't wait. And the third—"

"Yes?" I said.

"Well, the third is, of course, that Mrs. Protheroe was right, and that the room was actually empty."

"You mean that, after he had been shown in, he went out again and came back later?"

"Yes."

"But why should he have done that?"

Miss Marple spread out her hands in a little gesture of bewilderment.

"That would mean looking at the case from an entirely different angle," I said.

"One so often has to do that—about everything. Don't you think so?"

I did not reply. I was going over carefully in my mind the three alternatives that Miss Marple had suggested.

With a slight sigh the old lady rose to her feet.

"I must be getting back. I am very glad to have had this little chat— though we haven't got very far, have we?"

"To tell you the truth," I said, as I fetched her shawl, "the whole thing seems to me a bewildering maze."

"Oh! I wouldn't say that. I think, on the whole, one theory fits nearly everything. That is, if you admit one coincidence—and I think one coincidence is allowable. More than one, of course, is unlikely."

"Do you really think that? About the theory, I mean?" I asked, looking at her.

"I admit that there is one flaw in my theory—one fact that I can't get over. Oh! if only that note had been something quite different—"

She sighed and shook her head. She moved towards the window and absent-mindedly reached up her hand and felt the rather depressed-looking plant that stood in a stand.

"You know, dear Mr. Clement, this should be watered oftener. Poor thing, it needs it badly. Your maid should water it every day. I suppose it is she who attends to it?"

"As much," I said, "as she attends to anything."

"A little raw at present," suggested Miss Marple.

"Yes," I said. "And Griselda steadily refuses to attempt to cook. Her idea is that only a thoroughly undesirable maid will remain with us. However, Mary herself gave us notice the other day."

"Indeed. I always imagined she was very fond of you both."

"I haven't noticed it," I said. "But, as a matter of fact, it was Lettice Protheroe who upset her. Mary came back from the inquest in rather a temperamental state and found Lettice here and—well, they had words."

"Oh!" said Miss Marple. She was just about to step through the window when she stopped suddenly, and a bewildering series of changes passed over her face.

"Oh! dear," she muttered to herself. "I *have* been stupid. So that was it. Perfectly possible all the time."

"I beg your pardon?"

She turned a worried face upon me.

"Nothing. An idea that has just occurred to me. I must go home and think things out thoroughly. Do you know, I believe I have been extremely stupid—almost incredibly so."

"I find that hard to believe," I said gallantly.

I escorted her through the window and across the lawn.

"Can you tell me what it is that has occurred to you so suddenly?" I asked.

"I would rather not—just at present. You see, there is still a possibility that I may be mistaken. But I do not think so. Here we are at my garden gate. Thank you so much. Please do not come any further."

"Is the note still a stumbling block?" I asked, as she passed through the gate and latched it behind her.

She looked at me abstractedly.

"The note? Oh! of course that wasn't the real note. I never thought it was. Good night, Mr. Clement."

She went rapidly up the path to the house, leaving me staring after her.

I didn't know what to think.

27

GRISELDA AND DENNIS had not yet returned. I realized that the most natural thing would have been for me to go up to the house with Miss Marple and fetch them home. Both she and I had been so entirely taken up with our preoccupation over the mystery that we had forgotten anybody existed in the world except ourselves.

I was just standing in the hall, wondering whether I would not even now go over and join them, when the door bell rang.

I crossed over to it. I saw there was a letter in the box, and presuming that this was the cause of the ring, I took it out.

As I did so, however, the bell rang again, and I shoved the letter hastily into my pocket and opened the front door.

It was Colonel Melchett.

"Hallo, Clement. I'm on my way home from town in the car. Thought I'd just look in and see if you could give me a drink."

"Delighted," I said. "Come into the study."

He pulled off the leather coat that he was wearing and followed me into the study. I fetched the whisky and soda and two glasses. Melchett was standing in front of the fireplace, legs wide apart, stroking his closely-cropped moustache.

"I've got one bit of news for you, Clement. Most astounding thing you've ever heard. But let that go for the minute. How are things going down here? Any more old ladies hot on the scent?"

"They're not doing so badly," I said. "One of them, at all events, thinks she's got there."

"Our friend, Miss Marple, eh?"

"Our friend, Miss Marple."

"Women like that always think they know everything," said Colonel Melchett.

He sipped his whisky and soda appreciatively.

"It's probably unnecessary interference on my part, asking," I said. "But I suppose somebody has questioned the fish boy. I mean, if the murderer left by the front door, there's a chance the boy may have seen him."

"Slack questioned him right enough," said Melchett. "But the boy says he didn't meet anybody. Hardly likely he would. The murderer wouldn't be exactly courting observation. Lots of cover by your front gate. He would have taken a look to see if the road was clear. The boy had to call at the Vicarage, at Haydock's, and at Mrs. Price Ridley's. Easy enough to dodge him."

"Yes," I said, "I suppose it would be."

"On the other hand," went on Melchett, "if by any chance that rascal Archer did the job, and young Fred Jackson saw him about the place, I doubt very much whether he'd let on. Archer is a cousin of his."

"Do you seriously suspect Archer?"

"Well, you know, old Protheroe had his knife into Archer pretty badly. Lots of bad blood between them. Leniency wasn't Protheroe's strong point."

"No," I said. "He was a very ruthless man."

"What I say is," said Melchett, "Live and let live. Of course, the law's the law, but it never hurts to give a man the benefit of the doubt. That's what Protheroe never did."

"He prided himself on it," I said.

There was a pause, and then I asked:

"What is this 'astounding bit of news' you promised me?"

"Well, it *is* astounding. You know that unfinished letter that Protheroe was writing when he was killed?"

"Yes."

"We got an expert on it—to say whether the 6:20 was added by a different hand. Naturally we sent up samples of Protheroe's handwriting. And do you know the verdict? *That letter was never written by Protheroe at all.*"

"You mean a forgery?"

"It's a forgery. The 6:20 they think is written in a different hand again—but they're not sure about that. The heading is in a different ink, but the letter itself is a forgery. Protheroe never wrote it."

"Are they certain?"

"Well, they're as certain as experts ever are. You know what an expert is! Oh! but they're sure enough."

"Amazing," I said. Then a memory assailed me.

"Why," I said, "I remember at the time Mrs. Protheroe said it wasn't like her husband's handwriting at all, and I took no notice."

"Really?"

"I thought it one of those silly remarks women will make. If there seemed one thing sure on earth it was that Protheroe had written that note."

We looked at each other.

"It's curious," I said slowly. "Miss Marple was saying this evening that that note was all wrong."

"Confound the woman, she couldn't know more about it if she had committed the murder herself."

At that moment the telephone bell rang. There is a queer kind of psychology about a telephone bell. It rang now persistently and with a kind of sinister significance.

I went over and took up the receiver.

"This is the Vicarage," I said. "Who's speaking?"

A strange, high-pitched hysterical voice came over the wire:

"*I want to confess,*" it said. "*My God, I want to confess.*"

"Hallo," I said, "hallo. Look here, you've cut me off. What number was that?"

A languid voice said it didn't know. It added that it was sorry I had been troubled.

I put down the receiver, and turned to Melchett.

"You once said," I remarked, "that you would go mad if anyone else accused themselves of the crime."

"What about it?"

"That was someone who wanted to confess . . . And the exchange has cut us off."

Melchett dashed over and took up the receiver.

"I'll speak to them."

"Do," I said. "You may have some effect. I'll leave you to it. I'm going out. I've a fancy I recognized that voice."

28

I HURRIED DOWN the village street. It was eleven o'clock, and at eleven o'clock on a Sunday night the whole village of St. Mary Mead might be dead. I saw, however, a light in a first floor window as I passed, and, realizing that Hawes was still up, I stopped and rang the door bell.

After what seemed a long time, Hawes's landlady, Mrs. Sadler, laboriously unfastened two bolts, a chain, and turned a key and peered out at me suspiciously.

"Why, it's Vicar!" she exclaimed.

"Good evening," I said. "I want to see Mr. Hawes. I see there's a light in the window, so he's up still."

"That may be. I've not seen him since I took up his supper. He's had a quiet evening—no one to see him, and he's not been out."

I nodded, and passing her, went quickly up the stairs. Hawes has a bedroom and sitting-room on the first floor.

I passed into the latter. Hawes was lying back in a long chair asleep. My entrance did not wake him. An empty cachet box and a glass of water, half-full, stood beside him.

On the floor, by his left foot, was a crumpled sheet of paper with writing on it. I picked it up and straightened it out.

It began: *"My dear Clement—"*

I read it through, uttered an exclamation and shoved it into my pocket. Then I bent over Hawes and studied him attentively.

Next, reaching for the telephone which stood by his elbow, I gave the number of the Vicarage. Melchett must have been still trying to trace the call, for I was told that the number was engaged. Asking them to call me, I put the instrument down again.

I put my hand into my pocket to look at the paper I had picked up once more. With it, I drew out the note that I had found in the letter box and which was still unopened.

Its appearance was horribly familiar. It was the same handwriting as the anonymous letter that had come that afternoon.

I tore it open.

I read it once—twice—unable to realize its contents.

I was beginning to read it a third time when the telephone rang. Like a man in a dream I picked up the receiver and spoke.

"Hallo?"

"Hallo."

"Is that you, Melchett?"

"Yes, where are you? I've traced that call. The number is—"

"I know the number."

"Oh! good. Is that where you are speaking from?"

"Yes."

"What about that confession?"

"I've got the confession all right."

"You mean you've got the murderer?"

I had then the strongest temptation of my life. I looked at Hawes. I looked at the crumpled letter. I looked at the anonymous scrawl. I looked at the empty cachet box with the name of Cherubim on it. I remembered a certain casual conversation.

I made an immense effort.

"I—don't know," I said. "You'd better come round."

And I gave him the address.

Then I sat down in the chair opposite Hawes to think.

I had two clear minutes in which to do so.

In two minutes' time, Melchett would have arrived.

I took up the anonymous letter and read it through again for the third time.

Then I closed my eyes and thought . . .

29

I DON'T KNOW how long I sat there—only a few minutes in reality, I suppose. Yet it seemed as though an eternity had passed when I heard the door open and, turning my head, looked up to see Melchett entering the room.

He stared at Hawes asleep in his chair, then turned to me.

"What's this, Clement? What does it all mean?"

Of the two letters in my hand I selected one and passed it to him. He read it aloud in a low voice.

MY DEAR CLEMENT

It is a peculiarly unpleasant thing that I have to say. After all, I think I prefer writing it. We can discuss it at a later date. It concerns the recent peculations. I am sorry to say that I have satisfied myself beyond any possible doubt as to the identity of the culprit. Painful as it is for me to have to accuse an ordained priest of the church, my duty is only too painfully clear. An example must be made and—

He looked at me questioningly. At this point the writing tailed off in an undistinguishable scrawl where death had overtaken the writer's hand.

Melchett drew a deep breath, then looked at Hawes.

"So that's the solution! The one man we never even considered. And remorse drove him to confess!"

"He's been very queer lately," I said.

Suddenly Melchett strode across to the sleeping man with a sharp exclamation. He seized him by the shoulder and shook him, at first gently, then with increasing violence.

"He's not asleep! He's drugged! What's the meaning of this?"

His eyes went to the empty cachet box. He picked it up.

"Has he—"

"I think so," I said. "He showed me these the other day. Told me he'd been warned against an overdose. It's his way out, poor chap. Perhaps the best way. It's not for us to judge him."

But Melchett was Chief Constable of the County before anything else. The arguments that appealed to me had no weight with him. He had caught a murderer and he wanted his murderer hanged.

In one second he was at the telephone, jerking the receiver up and down impatiently until he got a reply. He asked for Haydock's number.

Then there was a further pause during which he stood, his ear to the telephone and his eyes on the limp figure in the chair.

"Hallo—hallo—hallo—is that Dr. Haydock's? Will the doctor come round at once to High Street? Mr. Hawes's. It's urgent . . . what's that? . . . Well, what number is it then? . . . Oh, sorry."

He rang off, fuming.

"Wrong number, wrong number—always wrong numbers! And a man's life hanging on it. HALLO—you gave me the wrong number . . . Yes— don't waste time—give me three nine—*nine*, not five."

Another period of impatience—shorter this time.

"Hallo—is that you, Haydock? Melchett speaking. Come to 19 High Street at once, will you? Hawes has taken some kind of overdose. At once, man, it's vital."

He rang off, strode impatiently up and down the room.

"Why on earth you didn't get hold of the doctor at once, Clement, I cannot think. Your wits must have all gone wool gathering."

Fortunately it never occurs to Melchett that anyone can possibly have any different ideas on conduct to those he holds himself. I said nothing, and he went on:

"Where did you find this letter?"

"Crumpled on the floor—where it had fallen from his hand."

"Extraordinary business—that old maid was right about its being the wrong note we found. Wonder how she tumbled to that. But what an ass the fellow was not to destroy this one. Fancy keeping it—the most damaging evidence you can imagine!"

"Human nature is full of inconsistencies."

"If it weren't, I doubt if we should ever catch a murderer! Sooner or later they always do some fool thing. You're looking very under the weather, Clement. I suppose this has been the most awful shock to you?"

"It has. As I say, Hawes has been queer in his manner for some time, but I never dreamed—"

"Who would? Hallo, that sounds like a car." He went across to the window, pushing up the sash and leaning out. "Yes, it's Haydock all right."

A moment later the doctor entered the room.

In a few succinct words, Melchett explained the situation.

Haydock is not a man who ever shows his feelings. He merely raised his eyebrows, nodded, and strode across to his patient. He felt his pulse, raised the eyelid and looked intently at the eye.

Then he turned to Melchett.

"Want to save him for the gallows?" he asked. "He's pretty far gone, you know. It will be touch and go, anyway. I doubt if I can bring him round."

"Do everything possible."

"Right."

He busied himself with the case he had brought with him, preparing a hypodermic injection which he injected into Hawes's arm. Then he stood up.

"Best thing is to run him into Much Benham—to the hospital there. Give me a hand to get him down to the car."

We both lent our assistance. As Haydock climbed into the driving seat, he threw a parting remark over his shoulder.

"You won't be able to hang him, you know, Melchett."

"You mean he won't recover?"

"May or may not. I didn't mean that. I meant that even if he does recover—well, the poor devil wasn't responsible for his actions. I shall give evidence to that effect."

"What did he mean by that?" asked Melchett as we went upstairs again.

I explained that Hawes had been a victim of encephalitis lethargica.

"Sleepy sickness, eh? Always some good reason nowadays for every dirty action that's done. Don't you agree?"

"Science is teaching us a lot."

"Science be damned—I beg your pardon, Clement; but all this namby pambyism annoys me. I'm a plain man. Well, I suppose we'd better have a look round here."

But at this moment there was an interruption—and a most amazing one. The door opened and Miss Marple walked into the room.

She was pink and somewhat flustered, and seemed to realize our condition of bewilderment.

"So sorry—so very sorry—to intrude—good-evening, Colonel Melchett. As I say, I am so sorry, but hearing that Mr. Hawes was taken ill, I felt I must come round and see if I couldn't do something."

She paused. Colonel Melchett was regarding her in a somewhat disgusted fashion.

"Very kind of you, Miss Marple," he said dryly. "But no need to trouble. How did you know, by the way?"

It was the question I had been yearning to ask!

"The telephone," explained Miss Marple. "So careless with their wrong numbers, aren't they? You spoke to me first, thinking I was Dr. Haydock. My number is three five."

"So that was it!" I exclaimed.

There is always some perfectly good and reasonable explanation for Miss Marple's omniscience.

"And so," she continued. "I just came round to see if I could be of any use."

"Very kind of you," said Melchett again, even more dryly this time. "But nothing to be done. Haydock's taken him off to hospital."

"Actually to hospital? Oh, that's a great relief! I am so very glad to hear it. He'll be quite safe there. When you say 'nothing to be done', you don't mean that there's nothing to be done for him, do you? You don't mean that he won't recover?"

"It's very doubtful," I said.

Miss Marple's eyes had gone to the cachet box.

"I suppose he took an overdose?" she said.

Melchett, I think, was in favor of being reticent. Perhaps I might have been under other circumstances. But my discussion of the case with Miss

Marple was too fresh in my mind for me to have the same view, though I must admit that her rapid appearance on the scene and eager curiosity repelled me slightly.

"You had better look at this," I said, and handed her Protheroe's unfinished letter.

She took it and read it without any appearance of surprise.

"You had already deduced something of the kind, had you not?" I asked.

"Yes—yes, indeed. May I ask you, Mr. Clement, what made you come here this evening? That is a point which puzzles me. You and Colonel Melchett—not at all what I should have expected."

I explained the telephone call and that I believed I had recognized Hawes's voice. Miss Marple nodded thoughtfully.

"Very interesting. Very providential—if I may use the term. Yes, it brought you here in the nick of time."

"In the nick of time for what?" I said bitterly.

Miss Marple looked surprised.

"To save Mr. Hawes's life, of course."

"Don't you think," I said, "that it might be better if Hawes didn't recover? Better for him—better for everyone. We know the truth now and—"

I stopped—for Miss Marple was nodding her head with such a peculiar vehemence that it made me lose the thread of what I was saying.

"Of course," she said. "Of course! That's what he wants you to think! That you know the truth—and that it's best for everyone as it is. Oh, yes, it all fits in—the letter, and the overdose, and poor Mr. Hawes's state of mind and his confession. It all fits in—*but it's wrong . . .*"

We stared at her.

"That's why I am so glad Mr. Hawes is safe—in hospital—where no one can get at him. If he recovers, he'll tell you the truth."

"The truth?"

"Yes—that he never touched a hair of Colonel Protheroe's head."

"But the telephone call," I said. "The letter—the overdose. It's all so clear."

"That's what he wants you to think. Oh, he's very clever! Keeping the letter and using it this way was very clever indeed."

"Who do you mean," I said, "by 'he'?"

"I mean the murderer," said Miss Marple.

She added very quietly:

"I mean Mr. Lawrence Redding . . ."

30

WE STARED AT her. I really think that for a moment or two we really believed she was out of her mind. The accusation seemed so utterly preposterous.

Colonel Melchett was the first to speak. He spoke kindly and with a kind of pitying tolerance.

"That is absurd, Miss Marple," he said. "Young Redding has been completely cleared."

"Naturally," said Miss Marple. "He saw to that."

"On the contrary," said Colonel Melchett dryly. "He did his best to get himself accused of the murder."

"Yes," said Miss Marple. "He took us all in that way—myself as much as anyone else. You will remember, dear Mr. Clement, that I was quite taken aback when I heard Mr. Redding had confessed to the crime. It upset all my ideas and made me think him innocent—when up to then I had felt convinced that he was guilty."

"Then it was Lawrence Redding you suspected?"

"I know that in books it is always the most unlikely person. But I never find that rule applies in real life. There it is so often the obvious that is true. Much as I have always liked Mrs. Protheroe, I could not avoid coming to the conclusion that she was completely under Mr. Redding's thumb and would do anything he told her, and, of course, he is not the kind of young man who would dream of running away with a penniless woman. From his point of view it was necessary that Colonel Protheroe should be removed—and so he removed him. One of those charming young men who have *no* moral sense."

Colonel Melchett had been snorting impatiently for some time. Now he broke out.

"Absolute nonsense—the whole thing! Redding's time is fully accounted for up to 6:45 and Haydock says positively Protheroe couldn't have been shot then. I suppose you think you know better than a doctor. Or do you suggest that Haydock is deliberately lying—the Lord knows why?"

"I think Dr. Haydock's evidence was absolutely truthful. He is a very upright man. And, of course, it was Mrs. Protheroe who actually shot Colonel Protheroe—not Mr. Redding."

Again we stared at her. Miss Marple arranged her lace fichu, pushed back the fleecy shawl that draped her shoulders, and began to deliver a gentle old-maidish lecture comprising the most astounding statements in the most natural way in the world.

"I have not thought it right to speak until now. One's own belief—even so strong as to amount to knowledge—is not the same as proof. And unless one has an explanation that will fit all the facts (as I was saying to dear Mr. Clement this evening) one cannot advance it with any real conviction. And my own explanation was not quite complete—it lacked just one thing—but suddenly, just as I was leaving Mr. Clement's study, I noticed the palm in the pot by the window—and—well, there the whole thing was! Clear as daylight!"

"Mad—quite mad," muttered Melchett to me.

But Miss Marple beamed on us serenely and went on in her gentle ladylike voice.

"I was very sorry to believe what I did—very sorry. Because I liked them both. But you know what human nature is. And to begin with, when first he and then she both confessed in the most foolish way—well, I was more relieved than I could say. I had been wrong. And I began to think of other people who had a possible motive for wishing Colonel Protheroe out of the way."

"The seven suspects!" I murmured.

She smiled at me.

"Yes, indeed. There was that man Archer—not likely, but primed with drink (so inflaming) you never know. And, of course, there was your Mary. She's been walking out with Archer a long time, and she's a queer-tempered girl. Motive *and* opportunity—why, she was alone in the house! Old Mrs. Archer could easily have got the pistol from Mr. Redding's house for either of those two. And then, of course, there was Lettice—wanting freedom and money to do as she liked. I've known many cases where the most beautiful and ethereal girls have shown next to no moral scruple—though, of course, gentlemen never wish to believe it of them."

I winced.

"And then there was the tennis racquet," continued Miss Marple.

"The tennis racquet?"

"Yes, the one Mrs. Price Ridley's Clara saw lying on the grass by the Vicarage gate. That looked as though Mr. Dennis had got back earlier from his tennis party than he said. Boys of sixteen are so very susceptible and so very unbalanced. Whatever the motive—for Lettice's sake or for yours, it was a possibility. And then, of course, there was poor Mr. Hawes and you—not both of you naturally—but alternatively, as the lawyers say."

"Me?" I exclaimed in lively astonishment.

"Well, yes. I do apologize—and indeed I never really thought—but there was the question of these disappearing sums of money. Either you or Mr. Hawes must be guilty, and Mrs. Price Ridley was going about everywhere hinting that you were the person at fault—principally because you objected so vigorously to any kind of inquiry into the matter. Of course, I myself was always convinced it was Mr. Hawes—he reminded me so much of that unfortunate organist I mentioned; but all the same one couldn't be absolutely *sure*"

"Human nature being what it is," I ended grimly.

"Exactly. And then, of course, there was dear Griselda."

"But Mrs. Clement was completely out of it," interrupted Melchett. "She returned by the 6:50 train."

"That's what she *said*," retorted Miss Marple. "One should never go by what people say. The 6:50 was half an hour late that night. But at a quarter-past seven I saw her with my own eyes starting for Old Hall. So it followed that she must have come by the earlier train. Indeed she was seen; but perhaps you know that?"

She looked at me inquiringly.

Some magnetism in her glance impelled me to hold out the last anonymous letter, the one I had opened so short a time ago. It set out in detail that Griselda had been seen leaving Lawrence Redding's cottage by the back window at twenty past six on the fatal day.

I said nothing then or at any time of the dreadful suspicion that had for one moment assailed my mind. I had seen it in nightmare terms—a past intrigue between Lawrence and Griselda, the knowledge of it coming to Protheroe's ears, his decision to make me acquainted with the facts—and Griselda, desperate, stealing the pistol and silencing Protheroe. As I say—a nightmare only—but invested for a few long minutes with a dreadful appearance of reality.

I don't know whether Miss Marple had any inkling of all this. Very probably she had. Few things are hidden from her.

She handed me back the note with a little nod.

"That's been all over the village," she said. "And it did look rather suspicious, didn't it? Especially with Mrs. Archer swearing at the inquest that the pistol was still in the cottage when she left at midday."

She paused a minute and then went on.

"But I'm wandering terribly from the point. What I want to say—and I believe it my duty—is to put my own explanation of the mystery before you. If you don't believe it—well, I shall have done my best. Even as it is, my wish to be quite sure before I spoke may have cost poor Mr. Hawes his life."

Again she paused, and when she resumed, her voice held a different note. It was less apologetic, more decided.

"That is my own explanation of the facts. By Thursday afternoon the crime had been fully planned down to the smallest detail. Lawrence Redding first called on the vicar, knowing him to be out. He had with him the pistol which he concealed in that pot in the stand by the window. When the vicar came in, Lawrence explained his visit by a statement that he had made up his mind to go away. At five-thirty, Lawrence Redding telephoned from the North Lodge to the vicar, adopting a woman's voice (you remember what a good amateur actor he was).

"Mrs. Protheroe and her husband had just started for the village. And—a very curious thing (though no one happened to think of it that way)—Mrs. Protheroe took no hand-bag with her. Really a *most* unusual thing for a woman to do. Just before twenty past six she passes my garden and stops and speaks, so as to give me every opportunity of noticing that she has no weapon with her and also that she is quite her normal self. They realized, you see, that I am a noticing kind of person. She disappears round the corner of the house to the study window. The poor colonel is sitting at the desk writing his letter to you. He is deaf, as we all know. She takes the pistol from the bowl where it is waiting for her, comes up behind him and shoots him through the head, throws down the pistol and is out again like a flash, and going down the garden to the studio. Nearly anyone would swear that there couldn't have been time!"

"But the shot?" objected the colonel. "You didn't hear the shot?"

"There is, I believe, an invention called a Maxim silencer. So I gather from detective stories. I wonder if, possibly, the sneeze that the maid, Clara, heard might have actually been the shot? But no matter. Mrs. Protheroe is met at the studio by Mr. Redding. They go in together—and, human nature being what it is, I'm afraid they realize that I shan't leave the garden till they come out again!"

I had never liked Miss Marple better than at this moment, with her humorous perception of her own weakness.

"When they do come out, their demeanour is gay and natural. And there, in reality, they made a mistake. Because if they had really said goodbye to each other, as they pretended, they would have looked very different. But you see, that was their weak point. They simply *dare* not appear upset in any way. For the next ten minutes they are careful to provide themselves with what is called an alibi, I believe. Finally Mr. Redding goes to the Vicarage, leaving it as late as he dares. He probably saw you on the footpath from far away and was able to time matters nicely. He picks up the pistol and the silencer, leaves the forged letter with the time on it written in a different ink and apparently in a different handwriting. When the forgery is discovered it will look like a clumsy attempt to incriminate Anne Protheroe.

"But when he leaves the letter, he finds the one actually written by Colonel Protheroe—something quite unexpected. And being a very intelligent young man, and seeing that this letter may come in very useful to him, he takes it away with him. He alters the hands of the clock to the same time as the letter—knowing that it is always kept a quarter of an hour fast. The same idea—attempting to throw suspicion on Mrs. Protheroe. Then he leaves, meeting you outside the gate, and acting the part of someone nearly distraught. As I say, he is really most intelligent. What would a murderer who had committed a crime try to do? Behave naturally, of course. So that is just what Mr. Redding does not do. He gets rid of the silencer, but marches into the police station with the pistol and makes a perfectly ridiculous self-accusation which takes everybody in."

There was something fascinating in Miss Marple's résumé of the case. She spoke with such certainty that we both felt that in this way and in no other could the crime have been committed.

"What about the shot heard in the wood?" I asked. "Was that the coincidence to which you were referring earlier this evening?"

"Oh! dear, no." Miss Marple shook her head briskly.

"*That* wasn't a coincidence—very far from it. It was absolutely necessary that a shot should be heard—otherwise suspicion of Mrs. Protheroe might have continued. How Mr. Redding arranged it, I don't quite know. But I understand that picric acid explodes if you drop a weight on it, and you will remember, dear vicar, that you met Mr. Redding carrying a large stone just in the part of the wood where you picked up that crystal later. Gentlemen are so clever at arranging things—the stone suspended above the crystals and then a time fuse—or do I mean a slow match? Something that would take about twenty minutes to burn through—so that the explosion would come about 6:30 when he and Mrs. Protheroe had come out of the studio and were in full view. A very safe device because what would there be to find afterwards—only a big stone! But even that he tried to remove—when you came upon him."

"I believe you are right," I exclaimed, remembering the start of surprise Lawrence had given on seeing me that day. It had seemed natural enough at the time, but now . . .

Miss Marple seemed to read my thoughts, for she nodded her head shrewdly.

"Yes," she said, "it must have been a very nasty shock for him to come across you just then. But he turned it off very well—pretending he was bringing it to me for my rock gardens. Only—" Miss Marple became suddenly very emphatic—"*It was the wrong sort of stone for my rock gardens!* And that put me on the right track!"

All this time Colonel Melchett had sat like a man in a trance. Now he showed signs of coming to. He snorted once or twice, blew his nose in a bewildered fashion, and said:

"Upon my word! Well, upon my word!"

Beyond that, he did not commit himself. I think that he, like myself, was impressed with the logical certainty of Miss Marple's conclusions. But for the moment he was not willing to admit it.

Instead, he stretched out a hand, picked up the crumpled letter and barked out:

"All very well. But how do you account for this fellow Hawes! Why, he actually rang up and confessed."

"Yes, that was what was so providential. The vicar's sermon, doubtless. You know, dear Mr. Clement, you really preached a most remarkable sermon. It must have affected Mr. Hawes deeply. He could bear it no longer, and felt he must confess—about the misappropriations of the church funds."

"What?"

"Yes—and that, under Providence, is what has saved his life. (For I hope and trust it *is* saved. Dr. Haydock is so clever.) As I see the matter, Mr. Redding kept this letter (a risky thing to do, but I expect he hid it in some safe place) and waited till he found out for certain to whom it referred. He soon made quite sure that it was Mr. Hawes. I understand he came back here with Mr. Hawes last night and spent a long time with him. I suspect that he then substituted a cachet of his own for one of Mr. Hawes's, and slipped this letter in the pocket of Mr. Hawes's dressing-gown. The poor young man would swallow the fatal cachet in all innocence—after his death his things would be gone through and the letter found and everyone would jump to the conclusion that he had shot Colonel Protheroe and taken his own life out of remorse. I rather fancy Mr. Hawes must have found that letter tonight just after taking the fatal cachet. In his disordered state, it must have seemed like something supernatural, and, coming on top of the vicar's sermon, it must have impelled him to confess the whole thing."

"Upon my word," said Colonel Melchett. "Upon my word! *Most* extraordinary! I—I—don't believe a word of it."

He had never made a statement that sounded more unconvincing. It must have sounded so in his own ears, for he went on:

"And can you explain the other telephone call—the one from Mr. Redding's cottage to Mrs. Price Ridley?"

"Ah!" said Miss Marple. "That is what I call the coincidence. Dear Griselda sent that call—she and Mr. Dennis between them, I fancy. They had heard the rumors Mrs. Price Ridley was circulating about the vicar, and they thought of this (perhaps rather childish) way of silencing her. The coincidence lies in the fact that the call should have been put through at exactly the same time as the fake shot from the wood. It led one to believe that the two must be connected."

I suddenly remembered how everyone who spoke of that shot had described it as "different" from the usual shot. They had been right. Yet how hard to explain just in what way the "difference" of the shot consisted.

Colonel Melchett cleared his throat.

"Your solution is a very plausible one, Miss Marple," he said. "But you will allow me to point out that there is not a shadow of proof."

"I know," said Miss Marple. "But you believe it to be true, don't you?"

There was a pause, then the colonel said almost reluctantly:

"Yes, I do. Dash it all, it's the only way the thing could have happened. But there's no proof—not an atom."

Miss Marple coughed.

"That is why I thought perhaps—under the circumstances—"

"Yes?"

"A little trap might be permissible."

31

Colonel Melchett and I both stared at her.

"A trap? What kind of a trap?"

Miss Marple was a little diffident, but it was clear that she had a plan fully outlined.

"Supposing Mr. Redding were to be rung up on the telephone and warned."

Colonel Melchett smiled.

" 'All is discovered. Fly!' That's an old wheeze, Miss Marple. Not that it isn't often successful! But I think in this case young Redding is too downy a bird to be caught that way."

"It would have to be something specific. I quite realize that," said Miss Marple. "I would suggest—this is just a mere suggestion—that the warning should come from somebody who is known to have rather unusual views on these matters. Dr. Haydock's conversation would lead anyone to suppose that he might view such a thing as murder from an unusual angle. If he were to hint that somebody—Mrs. Sadler—or one of her children—had actually happened to see the transposing of the cachets—well, of course, if Mr. Redding is an innocent man, that statement will mean nothing to him, but if he isn't—"

"If he isn't?"

"Well, he might just possibly do something foolish."

"And deliver himself into our hands. It's possible. Very ingenious, Miss Marple. But will Haydock stand for it? As you say, his views—"

Miss Marple interrupted him brightly.

"Oh! but that's theory! So very different from practice, isn't it? But anyway, here he is, so we can ask him."

Haydock was, I think, rather astonished to find Miss Marple with us. He looked tired and haggard.

"It's been a near thing," he said. "A very near thing. But he's going to pull through. It's a doctor's business to save his patient and I saved him, but I'd have been just as glad if I hadn't pulled it off."

"You may think differently," said Melchett, "when you have heard what we have to tell you."

And briefly and succinctly, he put Miss Marple's theory of the crime before the doctor, ending up with her final suggestion.

We were then privileged to see exactly what Miss Marple meant by the difference between theory and practice.

Haydock's views appeared to have undergone complete transformation. He would, I think, have liked Lawrence Redding's head on a charger. It was not, I imagine, the murder of Colonel Protheroe that so stirred his rancor. It was the assault on the unlucky Hawes.

"The damned scoundrel," said Haydock. "The damned scoundrel! That poor devil Hawes. He's got a mother and a sister too. The stigma of being the mother and sister of a murderer would have rested on them for life, and think of their mental anguish. Of all the cowardly dastardly tricks!"

For sheer primitive rage, commend me to a thorough-going humanitarian when you get him well roused.

"If this thing's true," he said, "you can count on me. The fellow's not fit to live. A defenceless chap like Hawes."

A lame dog of any kind can always count on Haydock's sympathy.

He was eagerly arranging details with Melchett when Miss Marple rose and I insisted on seeing her home.

"It is most kind of you, Mr. Clement," said Miss Marple, as we walked down the deserted street. "Dear me, past twelve o'clock. I hope Raymond has gone to bed and not waited up."

"He should have accompanied you," I said.

"I didn't let him know I was going," said Miss Marple.

I smiled suddenly as I remembered Raymond West's subtle psychological analysis of the crime.

"If your theory turns out to be the truth—which I for one do not doubt for a minute," I said, "you will have a very good score over your nephew."

Miss Marple smiled also—an indulgent smile.

"I remember a saying of my Great Aunt Fanny's. I was sixteen at the time and thought it particularly foolish."

"Yes?" I inquired.

"She used to say: 'The young people think the old people are fools; but the old people *know* the young people are fools!' "

32

THERE IS LITTLE more to be told. Miss Marple's plan succeeded. Lawrence Redding was not an innocent man, and the hint of a witness of the change of capsule did indeed cause him to do "something foolish". Such is the power of an evil conscience.

He was, of course, peculiarly placed. His first impulse, I imagine, must have been to cut and run. But there was his accomplice to consider. He could not leave without getting word to her, and he dared not wait till morning. So he went up to Old Hall that night—and two of Colonel Melchett's most efficient officers followed him. He threw gravel at Anne Protheroe's window, aroused her, and an urgent whisper brought her down to speak with him. Doubtless they felt safer outside than in—with the possibility of Lettice waking. But as it happened, the two police officers were able to overhear their conversation in full. It left the matter in no doubt. Miss Marple had been right on every count.

The trial of Lawrence Redding and Anne Protheroe is a matter of public knowledge. I do not propose to go into it. I will only mention that great credit was reflected upon Inspector Slack, whose zeal and intelligence had resulted in the criminals being brought to justice. Naturally, nothing was said of Miss Marple's share in the business. She herself would have been horrified at the thought of such a thing.

Lettice came to see me just before the trial took place. She drifted through my study window, wraith-like as ever. She told me then that she had all along been convinced of her stepmother's complicity. The loss of the yellow beret had been a mere excuse for searching the study. She hoped against hope that she might find something the police had overlooked.

"You see," she said in her dreamy voice, "they didn't hate her like I did. And hate makes things easier for you."

Disappointed in the result of her search, she had deliberately dropped Anne's earring by the desk.

"Since I *knew* she had done it, what did it matter? One way was as good as another. She *had* killed him."

I sighed a little. There are always some things that Lettice will never see. In some respects she is morally color blind.

"What are you going to do, Lettice?" I asked.

"When—when it's all over, I am going abroad." She hesitated and then went on. "I am going abroad with my mother."

I looked up, startled.

She nodded.

"Didn't you ever guess? Mrs. Lestrange is my mother. She is—is dying, you know. She wanted to see me and so she came down here under an assumed name. Dr. Haydock helped her. He's a very old friend of hers— he was keen about her once—you can see that! In a way, he still is. Men always went batty about mother, I believe. She's awfully attractive even now. Anyway, Dr. Haydock did everything he could to help her. She didn't come down here under her own name because of the disgusting way people talk and gossip. She went to see father that night and told him she was dying and had a great longing to see something of me. Father was a beast. He said she'd forfeited all claim, and that I thought she was dead—as though I had ever swallowed that story! Men like father never see an inch before their noses!

"But mother is not the sort to give in. She thought it only decent to go to father first, but when he turned her down so brutally she sent a note to me, and I arranged to leave the tennis party early and meet her at the end of the footpath at a quarter past six. We just had a hurried meeting and arranged when to meet again. We left each other before half-past six. Afterwards I was terrified that she would be suspected of having killed father. After all, she *had* got a grudge against him. That's why I got hold of that old picture of her up in the attic and slashed it about. I was afraid the police might go nosing about and get hold of it and recognize it. Dr. Haydock was frightened too. Sometimes, I believe, he really thought she had done it! Mother is rather a—desperate kind of person. She doesn't count consequences."

She paused.

"It's queer. She and I belong to each other. Father and I didn't. But mother—well, anyway, I'm going abroad with her. I shall be with her till—till the end . . ."

She got up and I took her hand.

"God bless you both," I said. "Some day, I hope, there is a lot of happiness coming to you, Lettice."

"There should be," she said, with an attempt at a laugh. "There hasn't been much so far—has there? Oh, well, I don't suppose it matters. Goodbye, Mr. Clement. You've been frightfully decent to me always—you and Griselda."

Griselda!

I had to own to her how terribly the anonymous letter had upset me, and first she laughed, and then solemnly read me a lecture.

"However," she added, "I'm going to be very sober and godfearing in future—quite like the Pilgrim Fathers."

I did not see Griselda in the role of a Pilgrim Father.

She went on:

"You see, Len, I have a steadying influence coming into my life. It's coming into your life, too, but in your case it will be a kind of—of rejuvenating one—at least, I hope so! You can't call me a dear child half so much when we have a real child of our own. And, Len, I've decided that now I'm going to be a real 'wife and mother' (as they say in books), I must be a housekeeper too. I've bought two books on Household Management and one on Mother Love, and if that doesn't turn me out a pattern I don't know what will! They are all simply screamingly funny— not intentionally, you know. Especially the one about bringing up children."

"You haven't bought a book on How to Treat a Husband, have you?" I asked, with sudden apprehension as I drew her to me.

"I don't need to," said Griselda. "I'm a very good wife. I love you dearly. What more do you want?"

"Nothing," I said.

"Could you say, just for once, that you love me madly?"

"Griselda," I said—"I adore you! I worship you! I am wildly, hopelessly and quite unclerically crazy about you!"

My wife gave a deep and contented sigh.

Then she drew away suddenly.

"Bother! Here's Miss Marple coming. Don't let her suspect, will you? I don't want everyone offering me cushions and urging me to put my feet up. Tell her I've gone down to the golf links. That will put her off the scent—and it's quite true because I left my yellow pullover there and I want it."

Miss Marple came to the window, halted apologetically, and asked for Griselda.

"Griselda," I said, "has gone to the golf links."

An expression of concern leaped into Miss Marple's eyes.

"Oh, but surely," she said, "that is most unwise—just now."

And then in a nice, old-fashioned, ladylike, maiden-lady way, she blushed.

And to cover the moment's confusion, we talked hurriedly of the Protheroe case, and of "Dr. Stone", who had turned out to be a well-known cracksman with several different aliases. Miss Cram, by the way, had been cleared of all complicity. She had at last admitted taking the suitcase to the wood, but had done so in all good faith, Dr. Stone having told her that he feared the rivalry of other archaeologists who would not stick at burglary to gain their object of discrediting his theories. The girl apparently swallowed this not very plausible story. She is now, according to the village, looking out for a more genuine article in the line of an elderly bachelor requiring a secretary.

As we talked, I wondered very much how Miss Marple had discovered our latest secret. But presently, in a discreet fashion, Miss Marple herself supplied me with a clue.

"I hope dear Griselda is not overdoing it," she murmured, and, after a discreet pause, "I was in the bookshop in Much Benham yesterday—"

Poor Griselda—that book on Mother Love has been her undoing!

"I wonder, Miss Marple," I said suddenly, "if you were to commit a murder whether you would ever be found out."

"What a terrible idea," said Miss Marple, shocked. "I hope I could never do such a wicked thing."

"But human nature being what it is," I murmured.

Miss Marple acknowledged the hit with a pretty old-ladyish laugh.

"How naughty of you, Mr. Clement." She rose. "But naturally you are in good spirits."

She paused by the window.

"My love to dear Griselda—and tell her—that any little secret is quite safe with me."

Really Miss Marple is rather a dear . . .

Dead Man's Folly

To Humphrey
and
Peggie Trevelyan

CAST OF CHARACTERS

1

I

IT WAS MISS LEMON, Poirot's efficient secretary, who took the telephone call.

Laying aside her shorthand notebook, she raised the receiver and said without emphasis, "Trafalgar 8137."

Hercule Poirot leaned back in his upright chair and closed his eyes. His fingers beat a meditative soft tattoo on the edge of the table. In his head he continued to compose the polished periods of the letter he had been dictating.

Placing her hand over the receiver, Miss Lemon asked in a low voice, "Will you accept a personal call from Nassecombe, Devon?"

Poirot frowned. The place meant nothing to him.

"The name of the caller?" he demanded cautiously.

Miss Lemon spoke into the mouthpiece.

"*Air raid?*" she asked doubtingly. "Oh, yes—what was the last name again?"

Once more she turned to Hercule Poirot.

"Mrs. Ariadne Oliver."

Hercule Poirot's eyebrows shot up. A memory rose in his mind: wind-swept grey hair . . . an eagle profile . . .

He rose and replaced Miss Lemon at the telephone.

"Hercule Poirot speaks," he announced grandiloquently.

"Is that Mr. Hercules Porrot speaking personally?" the suspicious voice of the telephone operator demanded.

Poirot assured her that that was the case.

"You're through to Mr. Porrot," said the voice.

Its thin reedy accents were replaced by a magnificent booming contralto which caused Poirot hastily to shift the receiver a couple of inches further from his ear.

"M. Poirot, is that really you?" demanded Mrs. Oliver.

"Myself in person, Madame."

"This is Mrs. Oliver. I don't know if you'll remember me—"

"But of course I remember you, Madame. Who could forget you?"

"Well, people do sometimes," said Mrs. Oliver. "Quite often, in fact. I don't think that I've got a very distinctive personality. Or perhaps it's because I'm always doing different things to my hair. But all that's neither here nor there. I hope I'm not interrupting you when you're frightfully busy?"

"No, no, you do not derange me in the least."

"Good gracious—I'm sure I don't want to drive you out of your mind. The fact is, I need you."

"Need me?"

"Yes, at once. Can you take an airplane?"

"I do not take airplanes. They make me sick."

"They do me, too. Anyway I don't suppose it would be any quicker than the train really, because I think the only airport near here is Exeter which is miles away. So come by train. Twelve o'clock from Paddington to Nassecombe. You can do it nicely. You've got three quarters of an hour if my watch is right—though it isn't usually."

"But where are you, Madame? What is all this about?"

"Nasse House, Nassecombe. A car or taxi will meet you at the station at Nassecombe."

"But why do you need me? What is all this about?" Poirot repeated frantically.

"Telephones are in such awkward places," said Mrs. Oliver. "This one's in the hall. . . . People passing through and talking . . . I can't really hear. But I'm expecting you. Everybody will be so thrilled. Goodbye."

There was a sharp click as the receiver was replaced. The line hummed gently.

With a baffled air of bewilderment, Poirot put back the receiver and murmured something under his breath. Miss Lemon sat with her pencil poised, incurious. She repeated in muted tones the final phrase of dictation before the interruption.

"—allow me to assure you, my dear sir, that the hypothesis you have advanced—"

Poirot waved aside the advancement of the hypothesis.

"That was Mrs. Oliver," he said. "Ariadne Oliver, the detective novelist. You may have read—" But he stopped, remembering that Miss Lemon only read improving books and regarded such frivolities as fictional crime with contempt. "She wants me to go down to Devonshire today, at once, in"—he glanced at the clock—"thirty-five minutes."

Miss Lemon raised disapproving eyebrows.

"That will be running it rather fine," she said. "For what reason?"

"You may well ask! She did not tell me."

"How very peculiar. Why not?"

"Because," said Hercule Poirot thoughtfully, "she was afraid of being overheard. Yes, she made that quite clear."

"Well, really," said Miss Lemon, bristling in her employer's defence. "The things people expect! Fancy thinking that you'd go rushing off on some wild goose chase like that! An important man like you! I have always noticed that these artists and writers are very unbalanced—no sense of proportion. Shall I telephone through a telegram, 'Regret unable leave London?' "

Her hand went out to the telephone. Poirot's voice arrested the gesture.

"*Du tout!*" he said. "On the contrary. Be so kind as to summon a taxi immediately." He raised his voice. "Georges! A few necessities of toilet in my small valise. And quickly, very quickly. I have a train to catch."

II

The train, having done one hundred and eighty odd miles of its two hundred and twelve mile journey at top speed, puffed gently and apologetically through the last thirty and drew into Nassecombe station. Only one person alighted, Hercule Poirot. He negotiated with care a yawning gap between the step of the train and the platform and looked round him. At the far end of the train a porter was busy inside a luggage compartment. Poirot picked up his valise and walked back along the platform to the exit. He gave up his ticket and walked out through the booking office.

A large Humber saloon was drawn up outside and a chauffeur in uniform came forward.

"Mr. Hercule Poirot?" he enquired respectfully.

He took Poirot's case from him and opened the door of the car. They drove away from the station over the railway bridge and turned down a country lane which wound between high hedges on either side. Presently the ground fell away on the right and disclosed a very beautiful river view with hills of a misty blue in the distance. The chauffeur drew into the hedge and stopped.

"The River Helm, sir," he said. "With Dartmoor in the distance."

It was clear that admiration was necessary. Poirot made the necessary noises, murmuring. "*Magnifique!*" several times. Actually, Nature appealed to him very little. A well cultivated, neatly arranged kitchen garden was far more likely to bring a murmur of admiration to Poirot's lips. Two girls passed the car, toiling slowly up the hill. They were carrying heavy rucksacks on their backs and wore shorts, with bright coloured scarves tied over their heads.

"There is a Youth Hostel next door to us, sir," explained the chauffeur, who had clearly constituted himself Poirot's guide to Devon. "Hoodown Park. Mr. Fletcher's place it used to be. This Youth Hostel Association bought it and it's fairly crammed in summertime. Take in over a hundred a night they do. They're not allowed to stay longer than a couple of nights—then they've got to move on. Both sexes and mostly foreigners."

Poirot nodded absently. He was reflecting, not for the first time, that seen from the back, shorts were becoming to very few of the female sex. He shut his eyes in pain. Why, oh why, must young women array themselves thus? Those scarlet thighs were singularly unattractive!

"They seem heavily laden," he murmured.

"Yes, sir, and it's a long pull from the station or the bus stop. Best part of two miles to Hoodown Park." He hesitated. "If you don't object, sir, could we give them a lift?"

"By all means, by all means," said Poirot benignantly. There was he in luxury in an almost empty car and here were these two panting and perspiring young women weighed down with heavy rucksacks and without the least idea how to dress themselves so as to appear attractive to the other sex. The chauffeur started the car and came to a slow purring halt beside the two girls. Their flushed and perspiring faces were raised hopefully.

Poirot opened the door and the girls climbed in.

"It is most kind, please," said one of them, a fair girl with a foreign accent. "It is longer way than I think, yes?"

The other girl, who had a sunburnt and deeply flushed face with bronzed chestnut curls peeping out beneath her head scarf, merely nodded her head several times, flashed her teeth and murmured, *"Grazie."* The fair girl continued to talk vivaciously.

"I go to England come for two week holiday. I come from Holland. I like England very much. I have been Stratford Avon, Shakespeare Theatre and Warwick Castle. Then I have been Clovelly, now I have seen Exeter Cathedral and Torquay—very nice— I come to famous beauty spot here and tomorrow I cross river, go to Plymouth where discovery of New World was made from Plymouth Hoe."

"And you, Signorina?" Poirot turned to the other girl. But she only smiled and shook her curls.

"She does not much English speak," said the Dutch girl kindly. "We both a little French speak—so we talk in train. She is coming from near Milan and has relative in England married to gentleman who keeps shop for much groceries. She has come with friend to Exeter yesterday, but friend has eat veal ham pie not good from shop in Exeter and has to stay there sick. It is not good in hot weather, the veal ham pie."

At this point the chauffeur slowed down where the road forked. The girls got out, uttered thanks in two languages and proceeded up the left-hand road. The chauffeur laid aside for a moment his Olympian aloofness and said feelingly to Poirot, "It's not only veal and ham pie—you want to be careful of Cornish pasties too. Put anything in a pasty they will, holiday time!"

He restarted the car and drove down the right-hand road which shortly afterwards passed into thick woods. He proceeded to give a final verdict on the occupants of Hoodown Park Youth Hostel.

"Nice enough young women, some of 'em, at that Hostel," he said, "but it's hard to get them to understand about trespassing. Absolutely shocking the way they trespass. Don't seem to understand that a gentleman's place is private here. Always coming through our woods, they are, and pretending that they don't understand what you say to them." He shook his head darkly.

They went on, down a steep hill through woods, then through big iron gates, and along a drive, winding up finally in front of a big white Georgian house looking out over the river.

The chauffeur opened the door of the car as a tall black-haired butler appeared on the steps.

"Mr. Hercule Poirot?" murmured the latter.

"Yes."

"Mrs. Oliver is expecting you, sir. You will find her down at the Battery. Allow me to show you the way."

Poirot was directed to a winding path that led along the wood with glimpses of the river below. The path descended gradually until it came out at last on an open space, round in shape, with a low battlemented parapet. On the parapet Mrs. Oliver was sitting.

She rose to meet him and several apples fell from her lap and rolled in all directions. Apples seemed to be an inescapable *motif* of meeting Mrs. Oliver.

"I can't think why I always drop things," said Mrs. Oliver somewhat indistinctly, since her mouth was full of apple. "How are you, M. Poirot?"

"Très bien, chère Madame," replied Poirot politely. "And you?"

Mrs. Oliver was looking somewhat different from when Poirot had last seen her, and the reason lay, as she had already hinted over the telephone, in the fact that she had once more experimented with her coiffure. The last time Poirot had seen her, she had been adopting a windswept effect. Today, her hair, richly blued, was piled upward in a multiplicity of rather artificial little curls in a pseudo-Marquise style. The Marquise effect ended at her neck; the rest of her could have been definitely labelled "country practical," consisting of a violent yolk-of-egg rough tweed coat and skirt and a rather bilious-looking mustard colored jumper.

"I knew you'd come," said Mrs. Oliver cheerfully.

"You could not possibly have known," said Poirot severely.

"Oh, yes I did."

"I still ask myself why I am here."

"Well, I know the answer. Curiosity."

Poirot looked at her and his eyes twinkled a little.

"Your famous Woman's Intuition," he said, "has, perhaps, for once not led you too far astray."

"Now, don't laugh at my woman's intuition. Haven't I always spotted the murderer right away?"

Poirot was gallantly silent. Otherwise he might have replied, "At the fifth attempt, perhaps, and not always then!"

Instead he said, looking round him,

"It is indeed a beautiful property that you have here."

"This? But it doesn't belong to me, M. Poirot. Did you think it did? Oh no, it belongs to some people called Stubbs."

"Who are they?"

"Oh, nobody really," said Mrs. Oliver vaguely. "Just rich. No, I'm down here professionally, doing a job."

"Ah, you are getting local color for one of your *chef d'oeuvres?*"

"No, no. Just what I said. I'm doing a job. I've been engaged to arrange a murder."

Poirot stared at her.

"Oh, not a real one," said Mrs. Oliver reassuringly. "There's a big Fête thing on tomorrow, and as a kind of novelty there's going to be a Murder Hunt. Arranged by me. Like a Treasure Hunt, you see; only they've had a Treasure Hunt so often that they thought this would be a novelty. So they offered me a very substantial fee to come down and think it up. Quite fun, really—rather a change from the usual grim routine."

"How does it work?"

"Well, there'll be a Victim, of course. And Clues. And Suspects. All rather conventional—you know, the Vamp and the Blackmailer and the Young Lovers and the Sinister Butler and so on. Half a crown to enter and you get shown the first Clue and you've got to find the Victim and the Weapon and say Whodunit and the Motive. And there are Prizes."

"Remarkable!" said Hercule Poirot.

"Actually," said Mrs. Oliver ruefully, "it's all much harder to arrange than you'd think. Because you've got to allow for real people being quite intelligent, and in my books they needn't be."

"And it is to assist you in arranging this that you have sent for me?"

Poirot did not try very hard to keep an outraged resentment out of his voice.

"Oh no," said Mrs. Oliver. "Of course not! I've done all that. Everything's all set for tomorrow. No, I wanted you for quite another reason."

"What reason?"

Mrs. Oliver's hands strayed upward to her head. She was just about to sweep them frenziedly through her hair in the old familiar gesture when she remembered the intricacy of her hairdo. Instead, she relieved her feelings by tugging at her ear lobes.

"I daresay I'm a fool," she said. "But I think there's something wrong."

2

THERE WAS A moment's silence as Poirot stared at her. Then he asked sharply: "Something wrong? How?"

"I don't know. . . . That's what I want you to find out. But I've felt—more and more—that I was being—oh!—engineered . . . jockeyed along. . . . Call me a fool if you like, but I can only say that if there was to be a real murder tomorrow instead of a fake one, I shouldn't be surprised!"

Poirot stared at her and she looked back at him defiantly.

"Very interesting," said Poirot.

"I suppose you think I'm a complete fool," said Mrs. Oliver defensively.

"I have never thought you a fool," said Poirot.

"And I know what you always say—or look—about intuition."

"One calls things by different names," said Poirot. "I am quite ready to believe that you have noticed something, or heard something, that has definitely aroused in you anxiety. I think it possible that you yourself may not even know just what it is that you have seen or noticed or heard. You are aware only of the result. If I may so put it, you do not know what it is that you know. You may label that intuition if you like."

"It makes one feel such a fool," said Mrs. Oliver, ruefully, "not to be able to be definite."

"We shall arrive," said Poirot encouragingly. "You say that you have had the feeling of being—how did you put it—jockeyed along? Can you explain a little more clearly what you mean by that?"

'Well, it's rather difficult. . . . You see, this is my murder, so to speak. I've thought it out and planned it and it all fits in—dovetails. Well, if you know anything at all about writers, you'll know that they can't stand suggestions. People say 'Splendid, but wouldn't it be better if so and so did so and so?' Or 'wouldn't it be a wonderful idea if the victim was A instead of B? Or the murderer turned out to be D instead of E?' I mean, one wants to say: 'All right then, write it yourself if you want it that way!' "

Poirot nodded. "And that is what has been happening?"

"Not quite. . . . That sort of silly suggestion has been made, and then I've flared up, and they've given in, but have just slipped in some quite minor trivial suggestion and because I've made a stand over the other, I've accepted the triviality without noticing much."

"I see," said Poirot. "Yes—it is a method, that. . . . Something rather crude and preposterous is put forward—but that is not really the point. The small minor alteration is really the objective. Is that what you mean?"

"That's exactly what I mean," said Mrs. Oliver "And, of course, I may be imagining it, but I don't think I am—and none of the things seem to matter anyway. But it's got me worried—that, and a sort of—well—atmosphere."

"Who has made these suggestions of alterations to you?"

"Different people," said Mrs. Oliver. "If it was just one person I'd be more sure of my ground. But it's not just one person—although I think it is really. I mean it's one person working through other quite unsuspecting people."

"Have you an idea as to who that one person is?"

Mrs. Oliver shook her head.

"It's somebody very clever and very careful," she said. "It might be anybody."

"Who is there?" asked Poirot. "The cast of characters must be fairly limited?"

"Well," began Mrs. Oliver. "There's Sir George Stubbs who owns this place. Rich and plebeian and frightfully stupid outside business, I should think, but probably dead sharp in it. And there's Lady Stubbs—Hattie— about twenty years younger than he is, rather beautiful, but dumb as a fish—in fact I think she's definitely half-witted. Married him for his money, of course, and doesn't think about anything but clothes and jewels. Then there's Michael Weyman—he's an architect, quite young, and good-looking in a craggy kind of artistic way. He's designing a tennis pavilion for Sir George and repairing the Folly."

"Folly? What is that—a masquerade?"

"No, it's architectural. One of those little sort of temple things, white, with columns. You've probably seen them at Kew. Then there's Miss Brewis, she's a sort of secretary-housekeeper, who runs things and writes letters—very grim and efficient. And then there are the people roundabout who come in and help. A young married couple who have taken a cottage down by the river. Alec Legge and his wife Peggy—and Captain Warburton, who's the Mastertons' agent. And the Mastertons, of course, and old Mrs. Folliat who lives in what used to be the Lodge. Her husband's people owned Nasse originally. But they've died out, or been killed in wars, and there were lots of death duties so the last heir sold the place."

Poirot considered this list of characters, but at the moment they were only names to him. He returned to the main issue.

"Whose idea was the Murder Hunt?"

"Mrs. Masterton's, I think. She's the local M.P.'s wife, very good at organising. It was she who persuaded Sir George to have the Fête here. You see the place has been empty for so many years that she thinks people will be keen to pay and come in to see it."

"That all seems straightforward enough," said Poirot.

"It all seems straightforward," said Mrs. Oliver obstinately, "but it isn't. I tell you, M. Poirot, there's something wrong."

Poirot looked at Mrs. Oliver and Mrs. Oliver looked back at Poirot.

"How have you accounted for my presence here? For your summons to me?" Poirot asked.

"That was easy," said Mrs. Oliver. "You're to give away the prizes for the Murder Hunt. Everybody's awfully thrilled. I said I knew you, and could probably persuade you to come and that I was sure your name would be a terrific draw—as, of course, it will be," Mrs. Oliver added tactfully.

"And the suggestion was accepted—without demur?"

"I tell you, everybody was thrilled."

Mrs. Oliver thought it unnecessary to mention that amongst the younger generation one or two had asked, "Who is Hercule Poirot?"

"Everybody? Nobody spoke against the idea?"

Mrs. Oliver shook her head.

"That is a pity," said Hercule Poirot.

"You mean it might have given us a line?"

"A would-be criminal could hardly be expected to welcome my presence."

"I suppose you think I've imagined the whole thing," said Mrs. Oliver ruefully. "I must admit that until I started talking to you I hadn't realized how very little I've got to go upon."

"Calm yourself," said Poirot kindly. "I am intrigued and interested. Where do we begin?"

Mrs. Oliver glanced at her watch.

"It's just teatime. We'll go back to the house and then you can meet everybody."

She took a different path from the one by which Poirot had come. This one seemed to lead in the opposite direction.

"We pass by the boathouse this way," Mrs. Oliver explained.

As she spoke the boathouse came into view. It jutted out onto the river and was a picturesque thatched affair.

"That's where the Body's going to be," said Mrs. Oliver. "The body for the Murder Hunt, I mean."

"And who is going to be killed?"

"Oh—a girl hiker, who is really the Yugoslavian first wife of a young Atom Scientist," said Mrs. Oliver glibly.

Poirot blinked.

"Of course it looks as though the Atom Scientist had killed her—but naturally it's not as simple as that."

"Naturally not—since you are concerned—"

Mrs. Oliver accepted the compliment with a wave of the hand.

"Actually," she said, "she's killed by the Country Squire—and the motive is really rather ingenious—I don't believe many people will get it—though there's a perfectly clear pointer in the fifth clue."

Poirot abandoned the subtleties of Mrs. Oliver's plot to ask a practical question.

"But how do you arrange for a suitable body?"

"Girl Guide," said Mrs. Oliver. "Peggy Legge was going to be it—but now they want her to dress up in a turban and do the fortunetelling. So it's a Girl Guide called Marlene Tucker. Rather dumb and sniffs," she added in an explanatory manner. "It's quite easy—just peasant scarves and a rucksack—and all she has to do when she hears someone coming is to flop down on the floor and arrange the cord round her neck. Rather dull for the poor kid—just sticking inside that boathouse until she's found, but I've arranged for her to have a nice bundle of comics—there's a clue to the murderer scribbled on one of them as a matter of fact—so it all works in."

"Your ingenuity leaves me spellbound! The things you think of!"

"It's never difficult to think of things," said Mrs. Oliver. "The trouble is that you think of too many, and then it all becomes too complicated, so you have to relinquish some of them and that is rather agony. We go up this way now."

They started up a steep zigzagging path that led them back along the river at a higher level. At a twist through the trees they came out on a space surmounted by a small white pilastered temple. Standing back and frowning at it was a young man wearing dilapidated flannel trousers and a shirt of rather virulent green. He spun round towards them.

"Mr. Michael Weyman, M. Hercule Poirot," said Mrs. Oliver.

The young man acknowledged the introduction with a careless nod.

"Extraordinary," he said bitterly, "the places people put things! This thing here, for instance. Put up only about a year ago—quite nice of its kind and quite in keeping with the period of the house. But why here? These things were meant to be seen—'situated on an eminence'—that's how they phrased it—with a nice grassy approach and daffodils, et cetera. But here's this poor little devil, stuck away in the midst of trees—not visible from anywhere—you'd have to cut down about twenty trees before you'd even see it from the river."

"Perhaps there wasn't any other place," said Mrs. Oliver.

Michael Weyman snorted.

"Top of that grassy bank by the house—perfect natural setting. But no, these tycoon fellows are all the same—no artistic sense. Has a fancy for a 'Folly' as he calls it, orders one. Looks round for somewhere to put it. Then, I understand, a big oak tree crashes down in a gale. Leaves a nasty scar. 'Oh, we'll tidy the place up by putting a Folly there,' says the silly ass. That's all they ever think about, these rich city fellows, tidying up! I wonder he hasn't put beds of red geraniums and calceolarias all round the house! A man like that shouldn't be allowed to own a place like this!"

He sounded heated.

"This young man," Poirot observed to himself, "assuredly does not like Sir George Stubbs."

"It's bedded down in concrete," said Weyman. "And there's loose soil underneath—so it's subsided. Cracked all up here—it will be dangerous soon— Better pull the whole thing down and re-erect it on the top of the bank near the house. That's my advice, but the obstinate old fool won't hear of it."

"What about the tennis pavilion?" asked Mrs. Oliver.

Gloom settled even more deeply on the young man.

"He wants a kind of Chinese pagoda," he said with a groan. "Dragons if you please! Just because Lady Stubbs fancies herself in Chinese coolie hats! Who'd be an architect? Anyone who wants something decent built hasn't got the money, and those who have the money want something too utterly goddam awful!"

"You have my commiserations," said Poirot gravely.

"George Stubbs," said the architect scornfully. "Who does he think he is? Dug himself in to some cushy Admiralty job in the safe depths of Wales during the War—and grows a beard to suggest he saw active Naval service on convoy duty—or that's what they say. Stinking with money— absolutely stinking!"

"Well, you architects have got to have someone who's got money to spend, or you'd never have a job," Mrs. Oliver pointed out reasonably enough. She moved on towards the house and Poirot and the dispirited architect prepared to follow her.

"These tycoons," said the latter, bitterly, "can't understand first principles." He delivered a final kick to the lopsided Folly. "If the foundations are rotten—everything's rotten."

"It is profound what you say there," said Poirot. "Yes, it is profound."

The path they were following came out from the trees and the house showed white and beautiful before them in its setting of dark trees rising up behind it.

"It is of a veritable beauty, yes," murmured Poirot.

"He wants to build a billiard room on," said Mr. Weyman venomously.

On the bank below them a small elderly lady was busy with pruning shears on a clump of shrubs. She climbed up to greet them, panting slightly.

"Everything neglected for years," she said. "And so difficult nowadays to get a man who understands shrubs. This hillside should be a blaze of color in March and April, but very disappointing this year—all this dead wood ought to have been cut away last autumn—"

"M. Hercule Poirot, Mrs. Folliat," said Mrs. Oliver.

The elderly lady beamed.

"So this is the great M. Poirot! It is kind of you to come and help us tomorrow. This clever lady here has thought out a most puzzling problem—it will be such a novelty."

Poirot was faintly puzzled by the graciousness of the little lady's manner. She might, he thought, have been his hostess.

He said politely, "Mrs. Oliver is an old friend of mine. I was delighted to be able to respond to her request. This is indeed a beautiful spot, and what a superb and noble mansion."

Mrs. Folliat nodded in a matter-of-fact manner.

"Yes. It was built by my husband's great-grandfather in 1790. There was an Elizabethan house previously. It fell into disrepair and burned down in about 1700. Our family has lived here since 1598."

Her voice was calm and matter-of-fact. Poirot looked at her with closer attention. He saw a very small and compact little person, dressed in shabby tweeds. The most noticeable feature about her was her clear china-blue eyes. Her grey hair was closely confined by a hair net. Though obviously careless of her appearance, she had that indefinable air of being someone which is so hard to explain.

As they walked together towards the house, Poirot said diffidently, "It must be hard for you to have strangers living here."

There was a moment's pause before Mrs. Folliat answered. Her voice was clear and precise and curiously devoid of emotion.

"So many things are hard, M. Poirot," she said.

3

IT WAS MRS. FOLLIAT who led the way into the house and Poirot followed her. It was a gracious house, beautifully proportioned. Mrs. Folliat went through a door on the left into a small, daintily furnished sitting room and on into the big drawing room beyond, which was full of people who all seemed, at the moment, to be talking at once.

"George," said Mrs. Folliat. "This is M. Poirot who is so kind as to come and help us. Sir George Stubbs."

Sir George, who had been talking in a loud voice, swung round. He was a big man with a rather florid red face and a slightly unexpected beard. It gave a rather disconcerting effect of an actor who had not quite made up his mind whether he was playing the part of a country squire, or of a "rough diamond" from the Dominions. It certainly did not suggest the Navy, in spite of Michael Weyman's remarks. His manner and voice were jovial, but his eyes were small and shrewd, of a particularly penetrating pale blue.

He greeted Poirot heartily.

"We're so glad that your friend Mrs. Oliver managed to persuade you to come," he said. "Quite a brain wave on her part. You'll be an enormous attraction."

He looked round a little vaguely.

"Hattie?" He repeated the name in a slightly sharper tone. "Hattie!"

Lady Stubbs was reclining in a big armchair a little distance from the others. She seemed to be paying no attention to what was going on round her. Instead she was smiling down at her hand which was stretched out on the arm of the chair. She was turning it from left to right, so that a big solitaire emerald on her third finger caught the light in its green depths.

She looked up now in a slightly startled childlike way and said, "How do you do."

Poirot bowed over her hand.

Sir George continued his introductions.

"Mrs. Masterton."

Mrs. Masterton was a somewhat monumental woman who reminded Poirot faintly of a bloodhound. She had a full underhung jaw and large, mournful, slightly bloodshot eyes.

She bowed and resumed her discourse in a deep voice which again made Poirot think of a bloodhound's baying note.

"This silly dispute about the tea tent has got to be settled, Jim," she said forcefully. "They've got to see sense about it. We can't have the whole show a fiasco because of these idiotic women's local feuds."

"Oh, quite," said the man addressed.

"Captain Warburton," said Sir George.

Captain Warburton, who wore a check sports coat and had a vaguely horsy appearance, showed a lot of white teeth in a somewhat wolfish smile, then continued his conversation.

"Don't you worry, I'll settle it," he said. "I'll go and talk to them like a Dutch uncle. What about the fortunetelling tent? In the space by the magnolia? Or at the far end of the lawn by the rhododendrons?"

Sir George continued his introductions.

"Mr. and Mrs. Legge."

A tall young man with his face peeling badly from sunburn grinned agreeably. His wife, an attractive freckled redhead, nodded in a friendly fashion, then plunged into controversy with Mrs. Masterton, her pleasant high treble making a kind of duet with Mrs. Masterton's deep bay.

"—not by the magolia—a bottleneck—"

"—one wants to disperse things—but if there's a queue—"

"—much cooler. I mean, with the sun full on the house—"

"—and the coconut shy can't be too near the house—the boys are so wild when they throw—"

"And this," said Sir George, "is Miss Brewis—who runs us all."

Miss Brewis was seated behind the large silver tea tray.

She was a spare, efficient-looking woman of forty odd, with a brisk pleasant manner.

"How do you do, M. Poirot," she said. "I do hope you didn't have too crowded a journey. The trains are sometimes too terrible this time of year. Let me give you some tea. Milk? Sugar?"

"Very little milk, Mademoiselle, and four lumps of sugar." He added, as Miss Brewis dealt with his request, "I see that you are all in a great state of activity."

"Yes, indeed. There are always so many last minute things to see to. And people let one down in the most extraordinary way nowadays. Over marquees, and tents and chairs and catering equipment. One has to keep at them. I was on the telephone half the morning."

"What about those pegs, Amanda?" said Sir George. "And the extra putters for the clock golf."

"That's all arranged, Sir George. Mr. Benson at the Golf Club was most kind."

She handed Poirot his cup.

"A sandwich, M. Poirot? Those are tomato and these are pâté. But perhaps," said Miss Brewis, thinking of the four lumps of sugar, "you would rather have a cream cake?"

Poirot would rather have a cream cake, and helped himself to a particularly sweet and squelchy one.

Then, balancing it carefully on his saucer, he went and sat down by his hostess. She was still letting the light play over the jewel on her hand, and she looked up at him with a pleased child's smile.

"Look," she said. "It's pretty, isn't it?"

He had been studying her carefully. She was wearing a big coolie-style hat of vivid magenta straw. Beneath it her face showed its pinky reflection on the dead white surface of her skin. She was heavily made up in an exotic un-English style. Dead white matte skin, vivid cyclamen lips, mascara applied lavishly to the eyes. Her hair showed beneath the hat, black and smooth, fitting like a velvet cap. There was a languorous un-English beauty about the face. She was a creature of the tropical sun, caught, as it were, by chance in an English drawing room. But it was the eyes that startled Poirot. They had a childlike, almost vacant stare.

She had asked her question in a confidential childish way and it was as though to a child that Poirot answered.

"It is a very lovely ring," he said.

She looked pleased.

"George gave it to me yesterday," she said, dropping her voice as though she were sharing a secret with him. "He gives me lots of things. He's very kind."

Poirot looked down at the ring again and the hand outstretched on the side of the chair. The nails were very long and varnished a deep puce.

Into his mind a quotation came: "They toil not, neither do they spin. . . ."

He certainly couldn't imagine Lady Stubbs toiling or spinning. And yet he would hardly have described her as a lily of the field. She was a far more artificial product.

"This is a beautiful room you have here, Madame," he said, looking round appreciatively.

"I suppose it is," said Lady Stubbs vaguely.

Her attention was still on her ring; her head on one side, she watched the green fire in its depths as her hand moved.

She said in a confidential whisper: "D'you see? It's winking at me."

She burst out laughing and Poirot had a sense of sudden shock. It was a loud, uncontrolled laugh.

From across the room Sir George said: "Hattie."

His voice was quite kind but held a faint admonition. Lady Stubbs stopped laughing.

Poirot said in a conventional manner, "Devonshire is a very lovely country. Do you not think so?"

"It's nice in the daytime," said Lady Stubbs. "When it doesn't rain." She added mournfully, "But there aren't any night clubs."

"Ah, I see—you like night clubs?"

"Oh yes," said Lady Stubbs fervently.

"And why do you like night clubs so much?"

"There is music and you dance. And I wear my nicest clothes and bracelets and rings. And all the other women have nice clothes and jewels, but not as nice as mine."

She smiled with enormous satisfaction. Poirot felt a slight pang of pity.

"And all that amuses you very much?"

"Yes. I like the Casino, too. Why are there not any Casinos in England?"

"I have often wondered," said Poirot with a sigh. "I do not think it would accord with the English character."

She looked at him uncomprehendingly. Then she bent slightly towards him.

"I won sixty thousand francs at Monte Carlo once. I put it on number twenty-seven and it came up."

"That must have been very exciting, Madame."

"Oh, it was. George gives me money to play with—but usually I lose it."

She looked disconsolate.

"That is sad."

"Oh, it does not really matter. George is very rich. It is nice to be rich, don't you think so?"

"Very nice," said Poirot gently.

"Perhaps, if I was not rich, I should look like Amanda." Her gaze went to Miss Brewis at the tea table and studied her dispassionately. "She is very ugly, don't you think?"

Miss Brewis looked up at the moment and across to where they were sitting. Lady Stubbs had not spoken loudly, but Poirot wondered whether Amanda Brewis had heard.

As he withdrew his gaze, his eyes met those of Captain Warburton. The Captain's gaze was ironic and amused.

Poirot endeavoured to change the subject.

"Have you been very busy preparing for the Fête?" he asked.

Hattie Stubbs shook her head.

"Oh no, I think it is all very boring—very stupid. There are servants and gardeners. Why should not they make the preparations?"

"Oh, my dear." It was Mrs. Folliat who spoke. She had come to sit on the sofa nearby. "Those are the ideas you were brought up with on your island estates. But life isn't like that in England these days. I wish it were." She sighed. "Nowadays one has to do nearly everything oneself."

Lady Stubbs shrugged her shoulders.

"I think it is stupid. What is the good of being rich if one has to do everything oneself?"

"Some people find it fun," said Mrs. Folliat, smiling at her. "I do really. Not all things, but some. I like gardening myself and I like preparing for a festivity like this one tomorrow."

"It will be like a party?" asked Lady Stubbs hopefully.

"Just like a party—with lots and lots of people."

"Will it be like Ascot? With big hats and everyone very chic?"

"Well—not quite like Ascot," said Mrs. Folliat. She added gently, "But you must try and enjoy country things, Hattie. You should have helped us this morning, instead of staying in bed and not getting up until teatime."

"I had a headache," said Hattie sulkily. Then her mood changed and she smiled affectionately at Mrs. Folliat.

"But I will be good tomorrow. I will do everything you tell me."

"That's very sweet of you, dear."

"I've got a new dress to wear. It came this morning. Come upstairs with me and look at it."

Mrs. Folliat hesitated. Lady Stubbs rose to her feet and said insistently, "You must come. Please. It is a lovely dress. Come now!"

"Oh, very well." Mrs. Folliat gave a half laugh and rose.

As she went out of the room, her small figure following Hattie's tall one, Poirot saw her face and was quite startled at the weariness on it which had replaced her smiling composure. It was as though, relaxed and off her guard for a moment, she no longer bothered to keep up the social mask. And yet—it seemed more than that. Perhaps she was suffering from some disease about which, like many woman do, she never spoke. She was not a person, he thought, who would care to invite pity or sympathy.

Captain Warburton dropped down in the chair Hattie Stubbs had just vacated. He, too, looked at the door through which the two women had just passed, but it was not of the older woman that he spoke. Instead he drawled, with a slight grin,

"Beautiful creature, isn't she?" He observed with the tail of his eye Sir George's exit through a French window with Mrs. Masterton and Mrs. Oliver in tow. "Bowled over old George Stubbs all right. Nothing's too good for her! Jewels, mink, all the rest of it. Whether he realizes she's a bit wanting in the top storey I've never discovered. Probably thinks it doesn't matter. After all, these financial johnnies don't ask for intellectual companionship."

"What nationality is she?" Poirot asked curiously.

"Looks South American, I always think. But I believe she comes from the West Indies. One of those islands with sugar and rum and all that. One of the old families there—a Creole, I don't mean a half-caste. All very intermarried, I believe, on these islands. Accounts for the mental deficiency."

Young Mrs. Legge came over to join them.

"Look here, Jim," she said. "You've got to be on my side. That tent's got to be where we all decided—on the far side of the lawn backing on the rhododendrons. It's the only possible place."

"Ma Masterton doesn't think so."

"Well, you've got to talk her out of it."

He gave her his foxy smile.

"Mrs. Masterton's my boss."

"Wilfrid Masterton's your boss. He's the M.P."

"I daresay, but she should be. She's the one who wears the pants—and don't I know it."

Sir George re-entered the window.

"Oh, there you are, Peggy," he said, "We need you. You wouldn't think everyone could get het up over who butters the buns and who raffles a cake and why the garden produce stall is where the fancy woollens was promised it should be. Where's Amy Folliat? She can deal with these people—about the only person who can."

"She went upstairs with Hattie."

"Oh, did she—"

Sir George looked round in a vaguely helpless manner and Miss Brewis jumped up from where she was writing tickets and said: "I'll fetch her for you, Sir George."

"Thank you, Amanda."

Miss Brewis went out of the room.

"Must get hold of some more wire fencing," murmured Sir George.

"For the Fête?"

"No, no. To put up where we adjoin Hoodown Park in the woods. The old stuff's rotted away, and that's where they get through."

"Who get through?"

"Trespassers!" ejaculated Sir George.

Peggy Legge said amusedly,

"You sound like Betsey Trotwood campaigning against donkeys."

"Betsey Trotwood? Who's she?" asked Sir George simply.

"Dickens."

"Oh, Dickens. I read the *Pickwick Papers* once. Not bad. Not bad at all—surprised me. But, seriously, trespassers are a menace since they've started this Youth Hostel tomfoolery. They come out at you from everywhere wearing the most incredible shirts—boy this morning had one all covered with crawling turtles and things—made me think I'd been hitting the bottle or something. Half of them can't speak English—just gibber at you—" He mimicked: "Oh plees—yes haf you—tell me—iss way to ferry? I say No, it isn't, roar at them, and send them back where they've come from, but half the time they just blink and stare and don't understand. And the girls giggle. All kinds of nationalities, Italian, Yugoslavian, Dutch, Finnish—Esquimaux, I shouldn't be surprised! Half of them Communists, I shouldn't wonder," he ended darkly.

"Come now, George. don't get started on Communists," said Mrs. Legge. "I'll come and help you deal with the rabid women."

She led him out of the window and called over her shoulder: "Come on, Jim. Come and be torn to pieces in a good cause."

"All right, but I want to put M. Poirot in the picture about the Murder Hunt since he's going to present the prizes."

"You can do that presently."

"I will await you here," said Poirot agreeably.

In the ensuing silence, Alec Legge stretched himself out in his chair and sighed.

"Women!" he said. "Like a swarm of bees."

He turned his head to look out of the window.

"And what's it all about? Some silly Garden Fête that doesn't matter to anyone."

"But obviously," Poirot pointed out, "there are those to whom it does matter."

"Why can't people have some *sense*? Why can't they think? Think of the mess the whole world has got itself into. Don't they realise that the inhabitants of the globe are busy committing suicide?"

Poirot judged rightly that he was not intended to reply to this question. He merely shook his head doubtfully.

"Unless we can do something before it's too late—" Alec Legge broke

off. An angry look swept over his face. "Oh yes," he said, "I know what
you're thinking. That I'm nervy, neurotic—all the rest of it. Like those
damned doctors. Advising rest and change and sea air. All right, Peggy
and I came down here and took the Mill Cottage for three months, and
I've followed their prescription. I've fished and bathed and taken long
walks and sunbathed—"

"I noticed that you had sunbathed, yes," said Poirot politely.

"Oh, this?" Alec's hand went to his sore face. "That's the result of a
fine English summer for once in a way. But what's the good of it all?
You can't get away from facing truth just by running away from it."

"No, it is never any good running away."

"And being in a rural atmosphere like this just makes you realise things
more keenly—that and the incredible apathy of the people of this country.
Even Peggy, who's intelligent enough, is just the same. Why bother?
That's what she says. It makes me mad! Why bother!"

"As a matter of interest, why do you?"

"Good God, you too?"

"No, it is not advice. It is just that I would like to know your answer."

"Don't you see, somebody's got to do something."

"And that somebody is you?"

"No, no, not me personally. One can't be personal in times like these."

"I do not see why not. Even in 'these times,' as you call it, one is still
a person."

"But one shouldn't be! In times of stress, when it's a matter of life or
death, one can't think of one's own insignificant ills or preoccupations."

"I assure you, you are quite wrong. In the late war, during a severe
air raid, I was much less preoccupied by the thought of death than by
the pain from a corn on my little toe. It surprised me at the time that
it should be so. 'Think,' I said to myself, 'at any moment now death may
come.' But I was still conscious of my corn—indeed I felt injured that I
should have that to suffer as well as the fear of death. It was because I
might die that every small personal matter in my life acquired increased
importance. I have seen a woman knocked down in a street accident,
with a broken leg, and she has burst out crying because she sees that
there is a run in her stocking."

"Which just shows you what fools women are!"

"It shows you what people are. It is, perhaps, that absorption in one's
personal life that has led the human race to survive."

Alec Legge gave a scornful laugh.

"Sometimes," he said, "I think it's a pity they ever did."

"It is, you know," Poirot persisted, "a form of humility. And humility
is valuable. There was a slogan that was written up in your Underground
railways here, I remember, during the war. 'It all depends on *you*.' It
was composed, I think, by some eminent divine—but in my opinion it
was a dangerous and undesirable doctrine. For it is not true. Everything
does not depend on, say, Mrs. Blank of Little-Blank-in-the-Marsh. And
if she is led to think it does, it will not be good for her character. While

she thinks of the part she can play in world affairs, the baby pulls over the kettle."

"You are rather old-fashioned in your views, I think. Let's hear what your slogan would be."

"I do not need to formulate one of my own. There is an older one in this country which contents me very well."

"What is that?"

"Put your trust in God, and keep your powder dry."

"Well, well—" Alec Legge seemed amused. "Most unexpected coming from you. Do you know what I should like to see done in this country?"

"Something, no doubt, forceful and unpleasant," said Poirot smiling.

Alec Legge remained serious.

"I should like to see every feeble-minded person put out—right out! Don't let them breed. If, for one generation, only the intelligent were allowed to breed, think what the result would be!"

"A very large increase of patients in the psychiatric wards, perhaps," said Poirot drily. "One needs roots as well as flowers on a plant, Mr. Legge. However large and beautiful the flowers, if the earthy roots are destroyed there will be no more flowers." He added in a conversational tone: "Would you consider Lady Stubbs a candidate for the lethal chamber?"

"Yes, indeed. What's the good of a woman like that? What contribution has she ever made to society? Has she ever had an idea in her head that wasn't of clothes or furs or jewels? As I say, what good is she?"

"You and I," said Poirot blandly, "are certainly much more intelligent than Lady Stubbs. But"—he shook his head sadly—"it is true, I fear, that we are not nearly so ornamental."

"Ornamental—" Alec was beginning with a fierce snort, but he was interrupted by the re-entry of Mrs. Oliver and Captain Warburton through the window.

4

"YOU MUST COME and see the clues and things for the Murder Hunt, M. Poirot," said Mrs. Oliver breathlessly.

Poirot rose and followed them obediently.

The three of them went across the hall and into a smalll room furnished plainly as a business office.

"Lethal weapons to your left," observed Captain Warburton, waving his hand towards a small baize-covered card table. On it were laid out a small pistol, a piece of lead piping with a rusty sinister stain on it, a blue bottle labelled Poison, a length of clothesline and a hypodermic syringe.

"Those are the Weapons," explained Mrs. Oliver, "and these are the Suspects."

She handed him a printed card which he read with interest.

SUSPECTS:

Estelle Glynne	—a beautiful and mysterious young woman, the guest of
Colonel Blunt	—the local Squire, whose daughter
Joan	—is married to
Peter Gaye	—a young Atom Scientist.
Miss Willing	—a housekeeper.
Quiett	—a butler.
Maya Stavisky	—a girl hiker.
Esteban Loyola	—an uninvited guest.

Poirot blinked and looked towards Mrs. Oliver in mute incomprehension.

"A magnificent Cast of Characters," he said politely.

"But permit me to ask, Madame, what does the Competitor do?"

"Turn the card over," said Captain Warburton.

Poirot did so.

On the other side was printed:

Name and address

Solution:
    Name of Murderer: _____
    Weapon: _____
    Motive: _____
    Time and Place: _____
    Reasons for arriving at your conclusion: _____
    _____

"Everyone who enters gets one of these," explained Captain Warburton rapidly. "Also a notebook and pencil for copying clues. There will be six clues. You go on from one to the other like a Treasure Hunt, and the weapons are concealed in suspicious places. Here's the first clue. A snapshot. Everyone starts with one of these."

Poirot took the small print from him and studied it with a frown. Then he turned it upside down. He still looked puzzled. Warburton laughed.

"Ingenious bit of trick photography, isn't it?" he said complacently. "Quite simple once you know what it is."

Poirot, who did not know what it was, felt a mounting annoyance.

"Some kind of a barred window?" he suggested.

"Looks a bit like it, I admit. No, it's a section of a tennis net."

"Ah." Poirot looked again at the snapshot. "Yes—it is as you say— quite obvious when you have been told what it is!"

"So much depends on how you look at a thing," laughed Warburton.

"That is a very profound truth."

"The second clue will be found in a box under the centre of the tennis net. In the box are this empty poison bottle—here, and a loose cork."

"Only, you see," said Mrs. Oliver rapidly, "it's a screwtopped bottle, so the cork is really the clue."

"I know, Madame, that you are always full of ingenuity, but I do not quite see—"

Mrs. Oliver interrupted him.

"Oh, but of course," she said, "there's a story! Like in a magazine serial—a synopsis." She turned to Captain Warburton. "Have you got the leaflets?"

"They've not come from the printers yet."

"But they promised!"

"I know. I know. Everyone always promises. They'll be ready this evening at six. I'm going in to fetch them in the car."

"Oh, good."

Mrs. Oliver gave a deep sigh and turned to Poirot.

"Well, I'll have to tell it to you, then. Only I'm not very good at telling things. I mean if I write things, I get them perfectly clear, but if I talk, it always sounds the most frightful muddle; and that's why I never discuss my plots with anyone. I've learnt not to, because if I do, they just look at me blankly and say—'er—yes, but—I don't see what happened—and surely that can't possibly make a book.' So damping. And not true, because when I write it, it does!"

Mrs. Oliver paused for breath, and then went on:

"Well, it's like this. There's Peter Gaye who's a young Atom Scientist and he's suspected of being in the pay of the Communists, and he's married to this girl, Joan Blunt, and his first wife's dead, but she isn't, and she turns up because she's a secret agent, or perhaps not, I mean she may really be a hiker—and the wife's having an affair, and this man Loyola turns up either to meet Maya, or to spy upon her, and there's a blackmailing letter which might be from the housekeeper, or again it might be the butler, and the revolver's missing, and as you don't know who the blackmailing letter's to, and the hypodermic syringe fell out at dinner, and after that it disappeared—"

Mrs. Oliver came to a full stop, estimating correctly Poirot's reaction.

"I know," she said sympathetically. "It sounds just a muddle, but it isn't really—not in my head—and when you see the synopsis leaflet, you'll find it's quite clear.

"And anyway," she ended, "the story doesn't really matter, does it? I mean, not to you. All you've got to do is to present the prizes—very nice prizes, the first's a silver cigarette case shaped like a revolver—and say how remarkably clever the solver has been!"

Poirot thought to himself that the solver would indeed have been clever. In fact he doubted very much that there would be a solver. The whole plot and action of the Murder Hunt seemed to him to be wrapped in impenetrable fog.

"Well," said Captain Warburton cheerfully, glancing at his wrist watch. "I'd better be off to the printers and collect."

Mrs. Oliver groaned.

"If they're not done—"

"Oh, they're done all right. I telephoned. So long."

He left the room.

Mrs. Oliver immediately clutched Poirot by the arm and demanded in a hoarse whisper:

"Well?"

"Well—what?"

"Have you found out anything? Or spotted anybody?"

Poirot replied with mild reproof in his tones:

"Everybody and everything seems to me completely normal."

"Normal?"

"Well, perhaps that is not quite the right word. Lady Stubbs, as you say, is definitely subnormal, and Mr. Legge would appear to be rather abnormal."

"Oh, he's all right." said Mrs. Oliver impatiently. "He's had a nervous breakdown."

Poirot did not question the somewhat doubtful wording of this sentence but accepted it at its face value.

"Everybody appears to be in the expected state of nervous agitation, high excitement, general fatigue, and strong irritation which are characteristic of preparations for this form of entertainment. If you could only indicate—"

"Sh!—" Mrs. Oliver grasped his arm again. "Someone's coming."

It was just like a bad melodrama, Poirot felt, his own irritation mounting.

The pleasant mild face of Miss Brewis appeared round the door.

"Oh, there you are, M. Poirot. I've been looking for you to show you your room."

She led him up the staircase and along a passage to a big airy room looking out over the river.

"There is a bathroom just opposite. Sir George talks of adding more bathrooms, but to do so would sadly impair the proportions of the rooms. I hope you'll find everything quite comfortable?"

"Yes, indeed." Poirot swept an appreciative eye over the small bookstand, the reading lamp and the box labelled "Biscuits" by the bedside. "You seem, in this house, to have everything organised to perfection. Am I to congratulate you, or my charming hostess?"

"Lady Stubbs' time is fully taken up in being charming," said Miss Brewis, a slightly acid note in her voice.

"A very decorative young woman," mused Poirot.

"As you say."

"But in other respects is she not, perhaps—" he broke off. *"Pardon.* I am indiscreet. I comment on something I ought not, perhaps, to mention."

Miss Brewis gave him a steady look. She said drily:

"Lady Stubbs knows perfectly well exactly what she is doing. Besides being, as you said, a very decorative young woman, she is also a very shrewd one."

She had turned away and left the room before Poirot's eyebrows had fully risen in surprise. So that was what the efficient Miss Brewis thought, was it? Or had she merely said so for some reason of her own? And why had she made such a statement to him—to a newcomer? Because he was a newcomer, perhaps? And also because he was a foreigner. As Hercule Poirot had discovered by experience, there were many English people who considered that what one said to foreigners didn't count!

He frowned perplexedly, staring absent-mindedly at the door out of which Miss Brewis had gone. Then he strolled over to the window and stood looking out. As he did so, he saw Lady Stubbs come out of the house with Mrs. Folliat and they stood for a moment or two talking by the big magnolia tree. Then Mrs. Folliat nodded a goodbye, picked up her gardening basket and gloves and trotted off down the drive. Lady Stubbs stood watching her for a moment, then absent-mindedly pulled off a magnolia flower, smelt it and began slowly to walk down the path that led through the trees to the river. She looked just once over her shoulder before she disappeared from sight. From behind the magnolia tree Michael Weyman came quietly into view, paused a moment irresolutely and then followed the tall slim figure down into the trees.

A good-looking and dynamic young man, Poirot thought. With a more attractive personality, no doubt, than that of Sir George Stubbs. . . .

But if so, what of it? Such patterns formed themselves eternally through life. Rich middle-aged unattractive husband, young and beautiful wife with or without sufficient mental development, attractive and susceptible young man. What was there in that to make Mrs. Oliver utter a peremptory summons through the telephone? Mrs. Oliver, no doubt, had a vivid imagination but—

"But after all," murmured Hercule Poirot to himself, "I am not a consultant in adultery—or in incipient adultery."

Could there really be anything in this extraordinary notion of Mrs. Oliver's that something was wrong? Mrs. Oliver was a singularly muddle-headed woman, and how she managed somehow or other to turn out coherent detective stories was beyond him, and yet, for all her muddle-headedness she often surprised him by her sudden perception of truth.

"The time is short—short," he murmured to himself. "Is there something wrong here as Mrs. Oliver believes? I am inclined to think there is. But what? Who is there who could enlighten me? I need to know more, much more, about the people in this house. Who is there who could inform me?"

After a moment's reflection he seized his hat (Poirot never risked going out in the evening air with uncovered head), and hurried out of his room and down the stairs. He heard afar the dictatorial baying of Mrs. Masterton's deep voice. Nearer at hand, Sir George's voice rose with an amorous intonation.

"Damned becoming that yashmak thing. Wish I had you in my harem, Peggy. I shall come and have my fortune told a good deal tomorrow. What'll you tell me, eh?"

There was a slight scuffle and Peggy Legge's voice said breathlessly: "George, you mustn't."

Poirot raised his eyebrows, and slipped out of a conveniently adjacent side door. He set off at top speed down a back drive which his sense of locality enabled him to predict would at some point join the front drive.

His manoeuvre was successful and enabled him (panting very slightly) to come up beside Mrs. Folliat and relieve her in a gallant manner of her gardening basket.

"You permit, Madame?"

"Oh, thank you, M. Poirot, that's very kind of you. But it's not heavy."

"Allow me to carry it for you to your home. You live near here?"

"I actually live in the Lodge by the front gate. Sir George very kindly rents it to me."

The Lodge by the front gate of her former home. . . . How did she really feel about that, Poirot wondered. Her composure was so absolute that he had no clue to her feelings. He changed the subject by observing:

"Lady Stubbs is much younger than her husband, is she not?"

"Twenty-three years younger."

"Physically she is very attractive."

Mrs. Folliat said quietly:

"Hattie is a dear good child."

It was not an answer he had expected. Mrs. Folliat went on:

"I know her very well, you see. For a short time she was under my care."

"I did not know that."

"How should you? It is in a way a sad story. Her people had estates, sugar estates, in the West Indies. As a result of an earthquake, the house there was burned down and her parents and brothers and sisters all lost their lives. Hattie herself was at a convent in Paris and was thus suddenly left without any near relatives. It was considered advisable by the executors that Hattie should be chaperoned and introduced into society after she had spent a certain time abroad. I accepted the charge of her." Mrs. Folliat added with a dry smile: "I can smarten myself up on occasions and naturally I had the necessary connections—in fact, the late Governor had been a close friend of ours."

"Naturally, Madame, I understand all that."

"It suited me very well—I was going through a difficult time. My husband had died just before the outbreak of war. My eldest son, who was in the Navy, went down with his ship; my younger son, who had been out in Kenya, came back, joined the Commandos and was killed in Italy. That meant three lots of death duties and this house had to be put up for sale. I myself was very badly off and I was glad of the distraction of having someone young to look after and travel about with. I became very fond of Hattie, all the more so, perhaps, because I soon realised that she was—shall we say, not fully capable of fending for herself. Understand me, M. Poirot, Hattie is not mentally deficient, but she is what country folk describe as 'simple.' She is easily imposed upon, overdocile, completely open to suggestion. I think myself that it was a blessing that there was practically no money—If she had been an heiress her position might have been one of much greater difficulty. She was attractive to men and being of an affectionate nature was easily attracted and influenced—she had definitely to be looked after. When, after the final winding up of her parents' estate, it was discovered that the plantation was destroyed and there were more debts than assets, I could only be thankful that a man such as Sir George Stubbs had fallen in love with her and wanted to marry her."

"Possibly—yes—it was a solution."

"Sir George," said Mrs. Folliat, "though he is a self-made man and—let us face it—a complete vulgarian, is kindly and fundamentally decent, besides being extremely wealthy. I don't think he would ever ask for mental companionship from a wife, which is just as well. Hattie is everything he wants. She displays clothes and jewels to perfection, is affectionate and willing, and is completely happy with him. I confess that I am very thankful that that is so, for I admit that I deliberately influenced her to accept him. If it had turned out badly"—her voice faltered a little— "it would have been my fault for urging her to marry a man so many years older than herself. You see, as I told you, Hattie is completely suggestible. Anyone she is with at the time can dominate her."

"It seems to me," said Poirot approvingly, "that you made there a most prudent arrangement for her. I am not, like the English, romantic. To arrange a good marriage, one must take more than romance into consideration."

He added:

"And as for this place here, Nasse House, it is a most beautiful spot. Quite, as the saying goes, out of this world."

"Since Nasse had to be sold," said Mrs. Folliat, with a faint tremor in her voice, "I am glad that Sir George bought it. It was requisitioned during the war by the Army and afterwards it might have been bought and made into a Guest House or a school, the rooms cut up and partitioned, distorted out of their natural beauty. Our neighbours, the Fletchers, at Hoodown, had to sell their place and it is now a Youth Hostel. One is glad that young people should enjoy themselves—and fortunately Hoodown is late Victorian, and of no great architectural merit, so that the alterations do not matter. I'm afraid some of the young people trespass on our grounds. It makes Sir George very angry. It's true that they have occasionally damaged the rare shrubs by hacking them about—they come through here trying to get a short cut to the Ferry across the river."

They were standing now by the front gate. The Lodge, a small white one-storeyed building, lay a little back from the drive with a small railed garden round it.

Mrs. Folliat took back her basket from Poirot with a word of thanks.

"I was always very fond of the Lodge," she said, looking at it affectionately. "Merdell, our head gardener for thirty years, used to live here. I much prefer it to the top cottage, though that has been enlarged and modernised by Sir George. It had to be; we've got quite a young man now as head gardener, with a young wife—and these young women must have electric irons and modern cookers and television and all that. One must go with the times—" She sighed. "There is hardly a person left now on the estate from the old days—all new faces."

"I am glad Madame," said Poirot, "that you at least have found a haven."

"You know those lines of Spenser's? 'Sleepe after toyle, port after stormie seas. Ease after warre, death after life does greatly please. . . .' "

She paused and said without any change of tone: "It's a very wicked world, M. Poirot. And there are very wicked people in the world. You probably know that as well as I do. I don't say so before the younger people, it might discourage them, but it's true. . . . Yes, it's a very wicked world. . . ."

She gave him a little nod, then turned and went into the Lodge. Poirot stood still, staring at the shut door.

5

I

IN A MOOD of exploration Poirot went through the front gates and down the steeply twisting road that presently emerged on a small quay. A large bell with a chain had a notice upon it: "Ring for the Ferry." There were various boats moored by the side of the quay. A very old man with rheumy eyes, who had been leaning against a bollard, came shuffling towards Poirot.

"Du ee want the ferry, sir?"

"I thank you, no. I have just come down from Nasse House for a little walk."

"Ah, 'tis up at Nasse yu are? Worked there as a boy I did, and my son, he were head gardener there. But I did use to look after the boats. Old Squire Folliat, he was fair mazed about boats. Sail in all weathers, he would. The Major now, his son, he didn't care for sailing. Horses, that's all he cared about. And a pretty packet went on 'em. That and the bottle—had a hard time with him, his wife did. Yu've seen her, maybe—lives at the Lodge now, she du."

"Yes, I have just left her there now."

"Her be a Folliat, tu, second cousin from over Tiverton way. A great one for the garden, she is, all them there flowering shrubs she had put in. Even when it was took over during the war, and the two young gentlemen was gone to the war, she still looked after they shrubs and kept 'em from being overrun."

"It was hard on her, both her sons being killed."

"Ah, she've had a hard life, she have, what with this and that. Trouble with her husband, and trouble with the young gentleman, tu. Not Mr. Henry. He was as nice a young gentleman as yu could wish, took after his grandfather, fond of sailing and went into the Navy as a matter of course, but Mr. James, he caused her a lot of trouble. Debts and women it were, and then, tu, he were real wild in his temper. Born one of they as can't go straight. But the war suited him, as yu might say—give him his chance. Ah! There's many who can't go straight in peace who dies bravely in war."

"So now," said Poirot, "there are no more Folliats at Nasse."

The old man's flow of talk died abruptly.

"Just as yu say, sir."

Poirot looked curiously at the old man.

"Instead you have Sir George Stubbs. What is thought locally of him?"

"Us understands," said the old man, "that he be powerful rich."

His tone sounded dry and almost amused.

"And his wife?"

"Ah, she's a fine lady from London, she is. No use for gardens, not her. They du say, tu, as her du be wanting up here."

He tapped his temple significantly.

"Not as her isn't always very nice-spoken and friendly. Just over a year they've been here. Bought the place and had it all done up like new. I remember as though 'twere yesterday them arriving. Arrived in the evening, they did, day after the worst gale as I ever remember. Trees down right and left—one down across the drive and us had to get it sawn away in a hurry to get the drive clear for the car. And the big oak up along, that come down and brought a lot of others down with it, made a rare mess, it did."

"Ah yes, where the Folly stands now?"

The old man turned aside and spat disgustedly.

"Folly 'tis called and Folly 'tis—new-fangled nonsense. Never was no Folly in the old Folliats' time. Her ladyship's idea that Folly was. Put up not three weeks after she first come, and I've no doubt she talked Sir George into it. Rare silly it looks stuck up there among the trees, like a heathen temple. A nice summerhouse now, made rustic-like with stained glass—I'd have nothing against that."

Poirot smiled faintly.

"The London ladies," he said, "they must have their fancies. It is sad that the day of the Folliats is over."

"Don't ee never believe that, sir." The old man gave a wheezy chuckle. "Always be Folliats at Nasse."

"But the house belongs to Sir George Stubbs."

"That's as may be—but there's still a Folliat here. Ah! Rare and cunning the Folliats are!"

"What do you mean?"

The old man gave him a sly sideways glance.

"Mrs. Folliat be living up to Lodge, bain't she?" he demanded.

"Yes," said Poirot slowly. "Mrs. Folliat is living at the Lodge and the world is very wicked and all the people in it are very wicked."

The old man stared at him.

"Ah," he said. "Yu've got something there, maybe."

He shuffled away again.

"But what have I got?" Poirot asked himself with irritation as he slowly walked up the hill back to the house.

II

Hercule Poirot made a meticulous toilet, applying a scented pomade to his moustaches and twirling them to a ferocious couple of points. He stood back from the mirror and was satisfied by what he saw.

The sound of a gong resounded through the house, and he descended the stairs.

The butler, having finished a most artistic performance, *crescendo, forte, diminuendo, rallentando,* was just replacing the gong stick on its hook. His dark melancholy face showed pleasure.

Poirot thought to himself: "A blackmailing letter from the housekeeper— or it may be the butler . . ." This butler looked as though blackmailing letters would be well within his scope. Poirot wondered if Mrs. Oliver took her characters from life.

Miss Brewis crossed the hall in an unbecoming flowered chiffon dress and he caught up with her, asking as he did so:

"You have a housekeeper here?"

"Oh no, M. Poirot. I'm afraid one doesn't run to niceties of that kind nowadays, except in a really large establishment, of course. Oh no, I'm the housekeeper—more housekeeper than secretary, sometimes, in this house."

She gave a short acid laugh.

"So you are the housekeeper?" Poirot considered her thoughtfully.

He could not see Miss Brewis writing a blackmailing letter. Now, an anonymous letter—that would be a different thing. He had known anonymous letters written by women not unlike Miss Brewis—solid, dependable women, totally unsuspected by those around them.

"What is your butler's name?" he asked.

"Hendon." Miss Brewis looked a little astonished.

Poirot recollected himself and explained quickly:

"I ask because I had a fancy I had seen him somewhere before."

"Very likely," said Miss Brewis. "None of these people ever seem to stay in any place more than four months. They must soon have done the round of all the available situations in England. After all, it's not many people who can afford butlers and cooks nowadays—"

They came into the drawing room, where Sir George, looking somehow rather unnatural in a dinner jacket, was proffering sherry. Mrs. Oliver, in iron-grey satin, was looking like an obsolete battleship, and Lady Stubbs' smooth black head was bent down as she studied the fashions in *Vogue*.

Alec and Peggy Legge were dining and also Jim Warburton.

"We've a heavy evening ahead of us," he warned them. "No bridge tonight. All hands to the pump. There are any amount of notices to print, and the big card for the Fortunetelling. What name shall we have? Madame Zuleika? Esmeralda? Or Romany Leigh, the Gypsy Queen?"

"The Eastern touch," said Peggy. "Everyone in agricultural districts hates gypsies. Zuleika sounds all right. I brought my paint box over and I thought Michael could do us a curling snake to ornament the notice."

"Cleopatra rather than Zuleika, then?"

Hendon appeared at the door.

"Dinner is served, my lady."

They went in. There were candles on the long table. The room was full of shadows.

Warburton and Alec Legge sat on either side of their hostess. Poirot was between Mrs. Oliver and Miss Brewis. The latter was engaged in brisk general conversation about further details of preparation for tomorrow.

Mrs. Oliver sat in brooding abstraction and hardly spoke.

When she did at last break her silence, it was with a somewhat contradictory explanation.

"Don't bother about me," she said to Poirot. "I'm just remembering if there's anything I've forgotten."

Sir George laughed heartily.

"The fatal flaw, eh?" he remarked.

"That's just it," said Mrs. Oliver. "There always is one. Sometimes one doesn't realize it until a book's actually in print. And then it's agony!" Her face reflected this emotion. She sighed. "The curious thing is that most people never notice it. I say to myself, 'But of course the cook would have been bound to notice that two cutlets hadn't been eaten.' But nobody else thinks of it at all."

"You fascinate me." Michael Weyman leaned across the table. "The Mystery of the Second Cutlet. Please, please never explain. I shall wonder about it in my bath."

Mrs. Oliver gave him an abstracted smile and relapsed into her preoccupations.

Lady Stubbs was also silent. Now and again she yawned. Warburton, Alec Legge and Miss Brewis talked across her.

As they came out of the dining room, Lady Stubbs stopped by the stairs.

"I'm going to bed," she announced. "I'm very sleepy."

"Oh, Lady Stubbs," exclaimed Miss Brewis, "there's so much to be done. We've been counting on you to help us."

"Yes, I know," said Lady Stubbs. "But I'm going to bed."

She spoke with the satisfaction of a small child.

She turned her head as Sir George came out of the dining room.

"I'm tired, George. I'm going to bed. You don't mind?"

He came up to her and patted her on the shoulder affectionately.

"You go and get your beauty sleep, Hattie. Be fresh for tomorrow."

He kissed her lightly and she went up the stairs, waving her hand and calling out:

"Good night, all."

Sir George smiled up at her. Miss Brewis drew in her breath sharply and turned brusquely away.

"Come along, everybody," she said with a forced cheerfulness that did not ring true. "We've got to work."

Presently everyone was set to their tasks. Since Miss Brewis could not be everywhere at once, there were soon some defaulters. Michael Weyman ornamented a placard with a ferociously magnificent Serpent and the words, "MADAME ZULEIKA will tell your Fortune," and then vanished unobtrusively. Alec Legge did a few nondescript chores and then went out avowedly to measure for the Hoopla and did not reappear. The women, as women do, worked energetically and conscientiously. Hercule Poirot followed his hostess' example and went early to bed.

III

Poirot came down to breakfast on the following morning at nine thirty. Breakfast was served in prewar fashion: a row of hot dishes on an electric heater. Sir George was eating a full-sized Englishman's breakfast of scrambled eggs, bacon and kidneys. Mrs. Oliver and Miss Brewis had a modified version of the same. Michael Weyman was eating a plateful of cold ham. Only Lady Stubbs was unheedful of the flesh-pots and was nibbling thin toast and sipping black coffee. She was wearing a large pale pink hat which looked odd at the breakfast table.

The post had just arrived. Miss Brewis had an enormous pile of letters in front of her which she was rapidly sorting into piles. Any of Sir George's marked Personal she passed over to him. The others she opened herself and sorted into categories.

Lady Stubbs had three letters. She opened what were clearly a couple of bills and tossed them aside. Then she opened the third letter and said suddenly and clearly:

"Oh!"

The exclamation was so startled that all heads turned towards her.

"It's from Etienne," she said. "My cousin Etienne. He's coming here in a yacht."

"Let's see, Hattie." Sir George held out his hand. She passed the letter down the table. He smoothed out the sheet and read.

"Who's this Etienne De Sousa? A cousin, you say?"

"I think so. A second cousin. I do not remember him very well—hardly at all. He was—"

"Yes, my dear?"

She shrugged her shoulders.

"It does not matter. It is all a long time ago. I was a little girl."

"I suppose you wouldn't remember him very well. But we must make him welcome, of course," said Sir George heartily. "Pity in a way it's the Fête today, but we'll ask him to dinner. Perhaps we could put him up for a night or two—show him something of the country."

Sir George was being the hearty country squire.

Lady Stubbs said nothing. She stared down into her coffee cup.

Conversation on the inevitable subject of the Fête became general. Only Poirot remained detached, watching the slim exotic figure at the head of the table. He wondered just what was going on in her mind. At that very moment her eyes came up and cast a swift glance along the table to where he sat. It was a look so shrewd and appraising that he was startled. As their eyes met, the shrewd expression vanished—emptiness returned. But that other look had been there, cold, calculating, watchful. . . .

Or had he imagined it? In any case, wasn't it true that people who were slightly mentally deficient very often had a kind of sly native cunning that sometimes surprised even the people who knew them best.

He thought to himself that Lady Stubbs was certainly an enigma. People seemed to hold diametrically opposite ideas concerning her. Miss Brewis had intimated that Lady Stubbs knew very well what she was doing. Yet Mrs. Oliver definitely thought her half-witted, and Mrs. Folliat who had known her long and intimately had spoken of her as someone not quite normal, who needed care and watchfulness.

Miss Brewis was probably prejudiced. She disliked Lady Stubbs for her indolence and her aloofness. Poirot wondered if Miss Brewis had been Sir George's secretary prior to his marriage. If so, she might easily resent the coming of the new regime.

Poirot himself would have agreed wholeheartedly with Mrs. Folliat and Mrs. Oliver—until this morning. And, after all, could he really rely on what had been only a fleeting impression?

Lady Stubbs got up abruptly from the table.

"I have a headache," she said. "I shall go and lie down in my room."
Sir George sprang up anxiously.

"My dear girl. You're all right, aren't you?"

"It's just a headache."

"You'll be fit enough for this afternoon, won't you?"

"Yes—I think so."

"Take some aspirin, Lady Stubbs," said Miss Brewis briskly. "Have you got some or shall I bring it to you?"

"I've got some."

She moved towards the door. As she went she dropped the handkerchief she had been squeezing between her fingers. Poirot, moving quickly forward, picked it up unobtrusively.

Sir George, about to follow his wife, was stopped by Miss Brewis.

"About the parking of cars this afternoon, Sir George. I'm just going to give Mitchell instructions. Do you think that the best plan would be, as you said—?"

Poirot, going out of the room, heard no more.

He caught up with his hostess on the stairs.

"Madame, you dropped this."

He proffered the handkerchief with a bow.

She took it unheedingly.

"Did I? Thank you."

"I am most distressed, Madame, that you should be suffering. Particularly when your cousin is coming."

She answered quickly, almost violently.

"I don't want to see Etienne. I don't like him. He's bad. He was always bad. I'm afraid of him. He does bad things."

The door of the dining room opened and Sir George came across the hall and up the stairs.

"Hattie, my poor darling. Let me come and tuck you in."

They went up the stairs together, his arm round her tenderly, his face worried and absorbed.

Poirot looked up after them, then turned to encounter Miss Brewis moving fast, and clasping papers.

"Lady Stubbs' headache—" he began.

"No more headache than my foot," said Miss Brewis crossly, and disappeared into her office, closing the door behind her.

Poirot sighed and went out through the front door on to the terrace. Mrs. Masterton had just driven up in a small car and was directing the elevation of a tea marquee, baying out orders in rich full-blooded tones.

She turned to greet Poirot.

"Such a nuisance, these affairs," she observed. "And they will always put everything in the wrong place. No—Rogers! More to the left—left—not right! What do you think of the weather, M. Poirot? Looks doubtful to me. Rain, of course, would spoil everything. And we've had such a fine summer this year for a change. Where's Sir George? I want to talk to him about car parking."

"His wife has a headache and has gone to lie down."

"She'll be all right this afternoon," said Mrs. Masterton, confidently. "Likes functions, you know. She'll make a terrific toilet and be as pleased about it as a child. Just fetch me a bundle of those pegs over there, will you? I want to mark the places for the clock golf numbers."

Poirot, thus pressed into service, was worked by Mrs. Masterton relentlessly, as a useful apprentice. She condescended to talk to him in the intervals of hard labor.

"Got to do everything yourself, I find. Only way . . . By the way, you're a friend of the Eliots, I believe?"

Poirot, after his long sojourn in England, comprehended that this was an indication of social recognition. Mrs. Masterton was in fact saying: "Although a foreigner, I understand you are One of Us." She continued to chat in an intimate manner.

"Nice to have Nasse lived in again. We were all so afraid it was going to be a Hotel. You know what it is nowadays; one drives through the country and passes place after place with the board up 'Guest House' or 'Private Hotel' or 'Hotel AA Fully Licensed.' All the houses one stayed in as a girl—or where one went to dances. Very sad. Yes, I'm glad about Nasse and so is poor dear Amy Folliat, of course. She's had such a hard life—but never complains, I will say. Sir George has done wonders for Nasse—and not vulgarized it. Don't know whether it's the result of Amy Folliat's influence—or whether it's his own natural good taste. He has got quite good taste, you know. Very surprising in a man like that."

"He is not, I understand, one of the landed gentry?" said Poirot cautiously.

"He isn't even really Sir George—was christened to it, I understand. Took the idea from Lord George Sanger's Circus, I suspect. Very amusing really. Of course we never let on. Rich men must be allowed their little snobberies, don't you agree? The funny thing is that in spite of his origins George Stubbs would go down perfectly well anywhere. He's a throwback. Pure type of the eighteenth-century country squire. Good blood in him, I'd say. Father a gent and mother a barmaid is my guess."

Mrs. Masterton interrupted herself to yell to a gardener.

"Not by that rhododendron— You must leave room for the skittles over to the right. Right—not left!"

She went on: "Extraordinary how they can't tell their left from their right! The Brewis woman is efficient. Doesn't like poor Hattie, though. Looks at her sometimes as though she'd like to murder her. So many of these good secretaries are in love with their boss. Now where do you think Jim Warburton can have gone to? Silly the way he sticks to calling himself 'Captain.' Not a regular soldier and never within miles of a German. One has to put up, of course, with what one can get these days—and he's a hard worker—but I feel there's something rather fishy about him. Ah! Here are the Legges."

Peggy Legge, dressed in slacks and a yellow pullover, said brightly: "We've come to help."

"Lots to do," boomed Mrs. Masterton. "Now, let me see—"

Poirot, profiting by her inattention, slipped away. As he came round the corner of the house on to the front terrace he became a spectator of a new drama.

Two young women, in shorts, with bright blouses, had come out from the wood and were standing uncertainly looking up at the house. In one of them he thought he recognised the Italian girl of yesterday's lift in the car. From the window of Lady Stubbs' bedroom Sir George leaned out and addressed them wrathfully.

"You're trespassing," he shouted.

"Please?" said the young woman with the green head scarf.

"You can't come through here. Private."

The other young woman, who had a royal blue head scarf, said brightly:

"Please? Nassecombe Quay—" She pronounced it carefully. "It is this way? Please."

"You're trespassing," bellowed Sir George,

"Please?"

"Trespassing! No way through. You've got to go back. *Back!* The way you came."

They stared as he gesticulated. Then they consulted together in a flood of foreign speech. Finally, doubtfully, blue-scarf said:

"Back? To Hostel?"

"That's right. And you take the road—*road*—round that way."

They retreated unwillingly. Sir George mopped his brow and looked down at Poirot.

"Spend my time turning people off," he said. "Used to come through the top gate. I've padlocked that. Now they come through the woods, having got over the fence. Think they can get down to the shore and the quay easily this way. Well, they can, of course, much quicker. But there's no right of way—never has been. And they're practically all foreigners—don't understand what you say, and just jabber back at you in Dutch or something."

"Of these, one is French and the other Italian, I think—I saw the Italian girl on her way from the station yesterday."

"Every kind of language they talk— Yes, Hattie? What did you say?" He drew back into the room.

Poirot turned to find Mrs. Oliver and a well-developed girl of fourteen dressed in Guides' uniform close behind him.

"This is Marlene," said Mrs. Oliver.

Marlene acknowledged the introduction with a pronounced snuffle. Poirot bowed politely.

"She's the Victim," said Mrs. Oliver.

Marlene giggled.

"I'm the horrible Corpse," she said. "But I'm not going to have any blood on me." Her tone expressed disappointment.

"No?"

"No. Just strangled with a cord, that's all. I'd of liked to be stabbed— and have lashings of red paint."

"Captain Warburton thought it might look too realistic," said Mrs. Oliver.

"In a murder I think you ought to have blood," said Marlene sulkily. She looked at Poirot with hungry interest. "Seen lots of murders, haven't you? So she says."

"One or two," said Poirot modestly.

He observed with alarm that Mrs. Oliver was leaving them.

"Any sex maniacs?" asked Marlene with avidity.

"Certainly not."

"I like sex maniacs," said Marlene with relish. "Reading about them, I mean."

"You would probably not like meeting one."

"Oh, I dunno. D'you know what? I believe we've got a sex maniac round here. My granddad saw a body in the woods once. He was scared and ran away, and when he came back it was gone. It was a woman's body. But of course he's batty, my granddad is, so no one listens to what he says."

Poirot managed to escape and regaining the house by a circuitous route took refuge in his bedroom. He felt in need of repose.

6

LUNCH WAS AN early and quickly snatched affair of a cold buffet. At two thirty a minor Film Star was to open the Fête. The weather, after looking ominously like rain, began to improve. By three o'clock the Fête was in full swing. People were paying the admission charge of half-a-crown in large numbers, and cars were lining one side of the long drive. Students from the Youth Hostel arrived in batches conversing loudly in foreign tongues. True to Mrs. Masterton's forecast, Lady Stubbs had emerged from her bedroom just before half past two, dressed in a cyclamen dress with an enormous coolie-shaped hat of black straw. She wore large quantities of diamonds.

Miss Brewis murmured sardonically:

"Thinks it's the Royal Enclosure at Ascot, evidently!"

But Poirot complimented her gravely.

"It is a beautiful creation that you have on, Madame."

"It is nice, isn't it," said Hattie happily. "I wore it for Ascot."

The minor film star was arriving and Hattie moved forward to greet her.

Poirot retreated into the background. He wandered around disconsolately—everything seemed to be proceeding in the normal fashion of fêtes. There was a coconut shy, presided over by Sir George in his heartiest fashion, a skittle alley and a Hoopla. There were various "stalls" displaying local produce of fruit, vegetables, jams and cakes—and others displaying "fancy objects." There were "raffles" of cakes, of baskets of fruit; even, it seemed, of a pig; and a "Lucky Dip" for children at twopence a go.

There was a good crowd of people by now and an Exhibition of Children's Dancing began. Poirot saw no sign of Mrs. Oliver, but Lady Stubbs' cyclamen pink figure showed up amongst the crowd as she drifted rather vaguely about. The focus of attention, however, seemed to be Mrs. Folliat. She was quite transformed in appearance—wearing a hydrangea blue foulard frock and a smart grey hat, she appeared to preside over the proceedings, greeting new arrivals, and directing people to the various side shows.

Poirot lingered near her and listened to some of the conversations.

"Amy, my dear, how are you?"

"Oh Pamela, how nice of you and Edward to come. Such a long way from Tiverton."

"The weather's held for you. Remember the year before the war? Cloudburst came down about four o'clock. Ruined the whole show."

"But it's been a wonderful summer this year. Dorothy! It's ages since I've seen you."

"We felt we had to come and see Nasse in its glory. I see you've cut back the berberis on the bank."

"Yes, it shows the hydrangeas better, don't you think?"

"How wonderful they are. What a blue! But, my dear, you've done wonders in the last year. Nasse is really beginning to look like itself again."

Dorothy's husband boomed in a deep voice:

"Came over to see the Commandant here during the war. Nearly broke my heart."

Mrs. Folliat turned to greet a humbler visitor.

"Mrs. Knapper, I am pleased to see you. Is this Lucy? How she's grown."

"She'll be leaving school next year. Pleased to see you looking so well, Ma'am."

"I'm very well, thank you. You must go and try your luck at Hoopla, Lucy. See you in the tea tent later, Mrs. Knapper. I shall be helping with the teas."

An elderly man, presumably Mr. Knapper, said diffidently:

"Pleased to have you back at Nasse, Ma'am. Seems like old times."

Mrs. Folliat's response was drowned as two women and a big beefy man rushed toward her.

"Amy dear, such ages. This looks the greatest success! Do tell me what you've done about the rose garden. Muriel told me that you're restocking it with all the new Floribundas."

The beefy man chipped in. "Where's Marylin Gale—?"

"Reggie's just dying to meet her. He saw her last picture."

"That her in the big hat? My word, that's some get-up."

"Don't be stupid, darling. That's Hattie Stubbs. You know, Amy, you really shouldn't let her go around quite so like a mannequin."

"Amy?" Another friend claimed attention. "This is Roger, Edward's boy. My dear, so nice to have you back at Nasse."

Poirot moved slowly away and absent-mindedly invested a shilling on a ticket that might win him the pig.

He heard faintly still, the "So good of you to come" refrain from behind him. He wondered whether Mrs. Folliat realized how completely she had slipped into the role of hostess or whether it was entirely unconscious. She was, very definitely this afternoon, Mrs. Folliat of Nasse House.

He was standing by the tent labelled "MADAME ZULEIKA will tell your Fortune for 2/6d." Teas had just begun to be served and there was no longer a queue for the Fortunetelling. Poirot bowed his head, entered the tent and paid over his half crown willingly for the privilege of sinking into a chair and resting his aching feet.

Madame Zuleika was wearing flowing black robes, a gold tinsel scarf wound round her head and a veil across the lower half of her face which slightly muffled her remarks. A gold bracelet hung with lucky charms tinkled as she took Poirot's hand and gave him a rapid reading, agreeably full of money to come, success with a dark beauty and a miraculous escape from an accident.

"It is very agreeable all that you tell me, Madame Legge. I only wish that it could come true."

"Oh!" said Peggy. "So you know me, do you?"

"I had advance information— Mrs. Oliver told me that you were originally to be the Victim, but that you had been snatched from her for the Occult."

"I wish I was being the Body," said Peggy. "Much more peaceful. All Jim Warburton's fault. Is it four o'clock yet? I want my tea. I'm off duty from four to half past."

"Ten minutes to go, still," said Poirot, consulting his large old-fashioned watch. "Shall I bring you a cup of tea here?"

"No, no. I want the break. This tent is stifling. Are there a lot of people waiting still?"

"No—I think they are lining up for tea—"

"Good."

Poirot emerged from the tent and was immediately challenged by a determined woman and made to pay sixpence and guess the weight of a cake.

A Hoopla stall presided over by a fat motherly woman urged him to try his luck and, much to his discomfiture, he immediately won a large kewpie doll. Walking sheepishly along with this he encountered Michael Weyman who was standing gloomily on the outskirts near the top of a path that led down to the quay.

"You seem to have been enjoying yourself, M. Poirot," he said with a sardonic grin.

Poirot contemplated his prize.

"It is truly horrible, is it not?" he said sadly.

A small child near him suddenly burst out crying. Poirot stooped swiftly and tucked the doll into the child's arm.

"*Voilà*, it is for you."

The tears ceased abruptly.

"There, Violet, isn't the gentleman kind? Say Ta, ever so—"

"Children's Fancy Dress," called out Captain Warburton through a megaphone. "The first class—three to five. Form up, please."

Poirot moved towards the house and was cannoned into by a young man who was stepping backwards to take a better aim at a coconut. The young man scowled and Poirot apologized, mechanically, his eye held fascinated by the varied pattern of the young man's shirt. He recognized it as the "turtle" shirt of Sir George's description. Every kind of turtle, tortoise and sea monster appeared to be writhing and crawling over it.

Poirot blinked and was accosted by the Dutch girl to whom he had given a lift the day before.

"So you have come to the Fête," he said. "And your friend?"

"Oh yes, she too comes here this afternoon. I have not seen her yet, but we shall leave together by the bus that goes from the gates at five fifteen. We go to Torquay and there I change to another bus for Plymouth. It is convenient."

This explained what had puzzled Poirot, the fact that the Dutch girl was perspiring under the weight of a rucksack.

He said: "I saw your friend this morning."

"Oh yes, Elsa, a German girl was with her and she told me they had tried to get through woods to the river and quay. And the gentleman who owns the house was very angry and made them go back."

She added, turning her head to where Sir George was urging competitors at the coconut shy,

"But now—this afternoon, he is very polite."

Poirot considered explaining that there was a difference between young women who were trespassers and the same young women when they had paid two shillings entrance fee and were legally entitled to sample the delights of Nasse House and its grounds. But Captain Warburton and his megaphone bore down upon them. The Captain was looking hot and bothered.

"Have you seen Lady Stubbs, Poirot? Anyone seen Lady Stubbs? She's supposed to be judging this Fancy Dress business and I can't find her anywhere."

"I saw her, let me see, oh—about half an hour ago. But then I went to have my fortune told."

"Curse the woman," said Warburton angrily. "Where can she have disappeared to? The children are waiting and we're behind schedule as it is."

He looked round.

"Where's Amanda Brewis?"

Miss Brewis, also, was not in evidence.

"It really is too bad," said Warburton. "One's got to have some co-operation if one's trying to run a show.

He strode off rapidly.

Poirot edged his way towards the roped-off space where teas were being served in a large marquee, but there was a long waiting queue and he decided against it.

He inspected the Fancy Goods stall where a determined old lady very nearly managed to sell him a plastic collar box, and finally made his way round the outskirts to a place where he could contemplate the activity from a safe distance.

He wondered where Mrs. Oliver was.

Footsteps behind him made him turn his head. A young man was coming up the path from the quay; a very dark young man, faultlessly attired in yachting costume. He paused as though disconcerted by the scene before him.

Then he spoke hesitatingly to Poirot.

"You will excuse me. Is this the house of Sir George Stubbs?"

"It is indeed." Poirot paused and then hazarded a guess. "Are you, perhaps, the cousin of Lady Stubbs?"

"I am Etienne De Sousa—"

"My name is Hercule Poirot."

They bowed to each other. Poirot explained the circumstances of the Fête. As he finished Sir George came across the lawn towards them from the coconut shy.

"De Sousa? Delighted to see you. Hattie got your letter this morning. Where's your yacht?"

"It is moored at Helmmouth. I came up the river to the quay here in my launch."

"We must find Hattie. She's somewhere about. . . . You'll dine with us this evening, I hope?"

"You are most kind."

"Can we put you up?"

"That also, is most kind, but I will sleep on my yacht. It is easier so."

"Are you staying here long?"

"Two or three days, perhaps. It depends." De Sousa shrugged elegant shoulders.

"Hattie will be delighted, I'm sure," said Sir George politely. "Where is she? I saw her not long ago."

He looked round in a perplexed manner.

"She ought to be judging the Children's Fancy Dress. I can't understand it. Excuse me a moment. I'll ask Miss Brewis."

He hurried off. De Sousa looked after him. Poirot looked at De Sousa.

"It is some little time since you last saw your cousin?" he asked.

The other shrugged his shoulders.

"I have not seen her since she was fifteen years old. Soon after that she was sent abroad—to school at a convent in France. As a child she promised to have good looks."

He looked enquiringly at Poirot.

"She is a beautiful woman," said Poirot.

"And that is her husband? He seems what they call 'a good fellow,' but not perhaps very polished? Still, for Hattie it might be perhaps a little difficult to find a suitable husband."

Poirot remained with a politely enquiring expression on his face. The other laughed.

"Oh, it is no secret. At fifteen Hattie was mentally undeveloped. Feeble-minded, do you not call it? She is still the same?"

"It would seem so—yes," said Poirot cautiously.

De Sousa shrugged his shoulders.

"Ah well! Why should one ask it of women—that they should be intelligent! It is not necessary."

Sir George was back, fuming, Miss Brewis with him, speaking rather breathlessly.

"I've no idea where she is, Sir George. I saw her over by the fortuneteller's tent last. But that was at least twenty minutes or half an hour ago. She's not in the house."

"Is it not possible," asked Poirot, "that she has gone to observe the progress of Mrs. Oliver's murder hunt?"

Sir George's brow cleared.

"That's probably it. Look here, I can't leave the shows here. I'm in charge. And Amanda's got her hands full. Could you possibly have a look round, Poirot? You know the course."

But Poirot did not know the course. However, an enquiry of Miss Brewis gave him rough guidance. Miss Brewis took brisk charge of De Sousa and Poirot went off murmuring to himself, like an incantation: "Tennis Court, Camellia Garden, the Folly, Upper Nursery Garden, Boathouse . . ."

As he passed the coconut shy he was amused to notice Sir George proffering wooden balls with a dazzling smile of welcome to the same young Italian woman whom he had driven off that morning and who was clearly puzzled at his change of attitude.

He went on his way to the Tennis Court. But there was no one there but an old gentleman of military aspect who was fast asleep on a garden seat with his hat pulled over his eyes. Poirot retraced his steps to the house and went on down to the Camellia Garden.

In the Camellia Garden Poirot found Mrs. Oliver dressed in purple splendor, sitting on a garden seat in a brooding attitude, and looking rather like Mrs. Siddons. She beckoned him to the seat beside her.

"This is only the Second Clue," she hissed. "I think I've made them too difficult. Nobody's come yet."

At this moment a young man in shorts, with a prominent Adam's apple, entered the garden. With a cry of satisfaction he hurried to a tree in one corner and a further satisfied cry announced his discovery of the next clue. Passing them, he felt impelled to communicate his satisfaction.

"Lots of people don't know about cork trees," he said confidentially.

"Clever photograph, the first clue, but I spotted what it was—section of a tennis net. There was a poison bottle, empty, and a cork. Most of 'em will go all out after the bottle clue—I guessed it was a red herring. Very delicate, cork trees, only hardy in this part of the world. I'm interested in rare shrubs and trees. Now where does one go, I wonder?"

He frowned over the entry in the notebook he carried.

"I've copied the next clue but it doesn't seem to make sense." He eyed them suspiciously. "You competing?"

"Oh, no," said Mrs. Oliver. "We're just—looking on."

"Rightyho. . . . 'When lovely woman stoops to folly' . . . I've an idea I've heard that somewhere."

"It is a well-known quotation," said Poirot.

"A Folly can also be a building," said Mrs. Oliver, helpfully. "White—with pillars," she added.

"That's an idea! Thanks a lot. They say Mrs. Ariadne Oliver is down here herself somewhere about. I'd like to get her autograph. You haven't seen her about, have you?"

"No," said Mrs. Oliver firmly.

"I'd like to meet her. Good yarns she writes." He lowered his voice. "But they say she drinks like a fish."

He hurried off and Mrs. Oliver said indignantly:

"Really! That's most unfair when I only like lemonade!"

"And have you not just perpetrated the great unfairness in helping that young man towards the next clue?"

Considering he's the only one who's got here so far, I thought he ought to be encouraged."

"But you wouldn't give him your autograph."

"That's different," said Mrs. Oliver. "Sh! Here come some more."

But these were not clue hunters. They were two women who having paid for admittance were determined to get their money's worth by seeing the grounds thoroughly.

They were hot and dissatisfied.

"You'd think they'd have some nice flower beds," said one to the other. "Nothing but trees and more trees. It's not what I call a garden."

Mrs. Oliver nudged Poirot and they slipped quietly away.

"Supposing," said Mrs. Oliver, distractedly, "that nobody ever finds my body?"

"Patience, Madame, and courage," said Poirot. "The afternoon is still young."

"That's true," said Mrs. Oliver brightening. "And it's half price admission after four thirty, so probably lots of people will flock in. Let's go and see how that Marlene child is getting on. I don't really trust that girl, you know. No sense of responsibility. I wouldn't put it past her to sneak away quietly, instead of being a corpse, and go and have tea. You know what people are like about their teas."

The proceeded amicably along the woodland path and Poirot commented on the geography of the property.

"I find it very confusing," he said. "So many paths, and one is never sure where they lead. And trees, trees everywhere."

"You sound like that disgruntled woman we've just left."

They passed the Folly and zigzagged down the path to the river. The outlines of the boathouse showed beneath them.

Poirot remarked that it would be awkward if the Murder searchers were to light upon the boathouse and find the body by accident.

"A sort of short cut? I thought of that. That's why the last clue is just a key. You can't unlock the door without it. It's a Yale. You can only open it from the inside."

A short steep slope led down to the door of the boathouse which was built out over the river, with a little wharf and a storage place for boats underneath. Mrs. Oliver took a key from a pocket concealed among her purple folds and unlocked the door.

"We've just come to cheer you up, Marlene," she said brightly as she entered.

She felt slightly remorseful at her unjust suspicions of Marlene's loyalty, for Marlene, artistically arranged as the Body, was playing her part nobly, sprawled on the floor by the window.

Marlene made no response. She lay quite motionless. The wind blowing gently through the open window rustled a pile of comics spread out on the table.

"It's all right," said Mrs. Oliver impatiently. "It's only me and M. Poirot. Nobody's got any distance with the clues yet."

Poirot was frowning. Very gently he pushed Mrs. Oliver aside and went and bent over the girl on the floor. A suppressed exclamation came from his lips. He looked up at Mrs. Oliver.

"So—" he said. "That which you expected has happened."

"You don't mean—" Mrs. Oliver's eyes widened in horror. She gasped for one of the basket chairs and sat down. "You can't mean— She isn't dead?"

Poirot nodded.

"Oh, yes," he said. "She is dead. Though not very long dead."

"But how—?"

He lifted the corner of the gay scarf bound round the girl's head, so that Mrs. Oliver could see the ends of the clothesline.

"Just like my murder," said Mrs. Oliver unsteadily. "But who? And why?"

"That is the question," said Poirot.

He forebore to add that those had also been her questions.

And that the answers to them could not be her answers, since the victim was not the Yugoslavian first wife of an atom scientist, but Marlene Tucker, a fourteen-year-old village girl who, as far as was known, had not an enemy in the world.

7

DETECTIVE INSPECTOR BLAND sat behind a table in the study. Sir George had met him on arrival, had taken him down to the boathouse and had now returned with him to the house. Down at the boathouse a photographic unit was now busy and the fingerprint men and the medical officer had just arrived.

"This do for you here all right?" asked Sir George.

"Very nicely, thank you, sir."

"What am I to do about this show that's going on, tell 'em about it, stop it, or what?"

Inspector Bland considered for a moment or two.

"What have you done so far, Sir George?" he asked.

"Haven't said anything. There's a sort of idea floating round that there's been an accident. Nothing more than that. I don't think anyone's suspected yet that it's—er—well, murder."

"Then leave things as they are just for the moment," decided Bland. "The news will get round fast enough, I daresay," he added cynically. He thought again for a moment or two before asking, "How many people do you think there are at this affair?"

"Couple of hundred I should say," answered Sir George, "and more pouring in every moment. People seem to have come from a good long way round. In fact the whole thing's being a roaring success. Damned unfortunate."

Inspector Bland inferred correctly that it was the murder and not the success of the Fête to which Sir George was referring.

"A couple of hundred," he mused, "and any one of them, I suppose, could have done it."

He sighed.

"Tricky," said Sir George sympathetically. "But I don't see what reason any one of them could have had. The whole thing seems quite fantastic— don't see who would want to go murdering a girl like that."

"How much can you tell me about the girl? She was a local girl, I understand?"

"Yes. Her people live in one of the cottages down near the quay. Her father works at one of the local farms—Paterson's I think." He added, "The mother was here at the Fête this afternoon. Miss Brewis—that's my secretary, and she can tell you about everything much better than I can—Miss Brewis winkled the woman out and has got her somewhere, giving her cups of tea."

"Quite so," said the Inspector, approvingly. "I'm not quite clear yet, Sir George, as to the circumstances of all this. What was the girl doing down there in the boathouse? I understand there's some kind of a murder hunt, or treasure hunt, going on."

Sir George nodded.

"Yes. We all thought it rather a bright idea. Doesn't seem quite so bright now. I think Miss Brewis can probably explain it all to you better than I can. I'll send her to you, shall I? Unless there's anything else you want to know about first."

"Not at the moment, Sir George. I may have more questions to ask you later. There are people I shall want to see. You, and Lady Stubbs, and the people who discovered the body. One of them, I gather, is the woman novelist who designed this murder hunt as you call it."

"That's right, Mrs. Oliver. Mrs. Ariadne Oliver."

The Inspector's eyebrows went up slightly.

"Oh—her?" he said. "Quite a best seller. I've read a lot of her books myself."

"She's a bit upset at present," said Sir George, "naturally, I suppose. I'll tell her you'll be wanting her, shall I? I don't know where my wife is. She seems to have disappeared completely from view. Somewhere among the two or three hundred, I suppose—not that she'll be able to tell you much. I mean about the girl or anything like that. Who would you like to see first?"

"I think perhaps your secretary, Miss Brewis, and after that the girl's mother."

Sir George nodded and left the room.

The local police constable, Robert Hoskins, opened the door for him and shut it after he went out. He then volunteered a statement, obviously intended as a commentary on some of Sir George's remarks.

"Lady Stubbs is a bit wanting," he said, "up here." He tapped his forehead. "That's why he said she wouldn't be much help. Scatty, that's what she is."

"Did he marry a local girl?"

"No. Foreigner of some sort. Colored, some say, but I don't think that's so myself."

Bland nodded. He was silent for a moment, doodling with a pencil on a sheet of paper in front of him. Then he asked a question which was clearly off the record.

"Who did it, Hoskins?" he said.

If anyone did have any ideas as to what had been going on, Bland thought, it would be P.C. Hoskins. Hoskins was a man of inquisitive mind with a great interest in everybody and everything. He had a gossiping wife and that, taken with his position as local constable, provided him with vast stores of information of a personal nature.

"Foreigner if you ask me. 'Twouldn't be anyone local. The Tuckers is all right. Nice, respectable family. Nine of 'em all told. Two of the older girls is married, one boy in the Navy, the other one's doing his National Service, another girl's over to a hairdresser's at Torquay. There's three younger ones at home, two boys and a girl." He paused, considering. "None of 'em's what you'd call bright, but Mrs. Tucker keeps her home nice, clean as a pin—youngest of eleven she was. She got her old father living with her."

Bland received this information in silence. Given in Hoskins' particular idiom, it was an outline of the Tuckers' social position and standing.

"That's why I say it was a foreigner," continued Hoskins. "One of those that stop up't the Hostel at Hoodown, likely as not. There's some queer ones among them—and a lot of goings on. Be surprised, you would, at what I've seen 'em doing in the bushes and the woods! Every bit as bad as what goes on in parked cars along the Common."

P.C. Hoskins was by this time an absolute specialist on the subject of sexual "goings on." They formed a large portion of his conversation when off duty and having his pint in the Bull and Bear. Bland said:

"I don't think there was anything—well, of that kind. The doctor will tell us, of course, as soon as he's finished his examination."

"Yes, sir, that'll be up to him, that will. But what I say is you never know with foreigners. Turn nasty they can, all in a moment."

Inspector Bland sighed as he thought to himself that it was not quite as easy as that. It was all very well for Constable Hoskins to put the blame conveniently on "foreigners." The door opened and the doctor walked in.

"Done my bit," he remarked. "Shall they take her away now? The other outfits have packed up."

"Sergeant Cottrill will attend to that," said Bland. "Well, Doc, what's the finding?"

"Simple and straightforward as it can be," said the doctor. "No complications. Garrotted with a piece of clothesline. Nothing could be simpler or easier to do. No struggle of any kind beforehand. I'd say the kid didn't know what was happening to her until it had happened."

"Any signs of assault?"

"None. No assault, signs of rape, or interference of any kind."

"Not presumably a sexual crime, then?"

"I wouldn't say so, no." The doctor added, "I shouldn't say she'd been a particularly attractive girl."

"Was she fond of the boys?"

Bland addressed this question to Constable Hoskins.

"I wouldn't say they'd much use for her," said Constable Hoskins, "though maybe she'd have liked it if they had."

"Maybe," agreed Bland. His mind went back to the pile of comic papers in the boathouse and the idle scrawls on the margin. "Johnny goes with Kate," "Georgie Porgie kisses hikers in the woods." He thought there had been a little wishful thinking there. On the whole, though, it seemed unlikely that there was a sex angle to Marlene Tucker's death. Although, of course, one never knew. . . . There were always those queer criminal individuals, men with a secret lust to kill, who specialized in immature female victims. One of these might be present in this part of the world during this holiday season. He almost believed that it must be so—for otherwise he could really see no reason for so pointless a crime. "However," he thought, "we're only at the beginning. I'd better see what all these people have to tell me."

"What about time of death?" he asked.

The doctor glanced over at the clock and his own watch.

"Just after half past five now," he said. "Say I saw her about twenty past five—she'd been dead about an hour. Roughly, that is to say. Put it between four and twenty to five. Let you know if there's anything more after the autopsy." He added: "You'll get the proper report with the long words in due course. I'll be off now. I've got some patients to see."

He left the room and Inspector Bland asked Hoskins to fetch Miss Brewis. His spirits rose a little when Miss Brewis came into the room. Here, as he recognized at once, was efficiency. He would get clear answers to his questions definite times and no muddle-headedness.

"'Mrs. Tucker's in my sitting room," Miss Brewis said as she sat down. "I've broken the news to her and given her some tea. She's very upset, naturally. She wanted to see the body but I told her it was much better not to. Mr. Tucker gets off work at six o'clock and was coming to join his wife here. I told them to look out for him and bring him along when he arrives. The younger children are at the Fête still, and someone is keeping his eye on them."

"Excellent," said Inspector Bland, with approval. "I think before I see Mrs. Tucker I would like to hear what you and Lady Stubbs can tell me."

"I don't know where Lady Stubbs is," said Miss Brewis acidly. "I rather imagine she got bored with the Fête and has wandered off somewhere, but I don't expect she can tell you anything more than I can. What exactly is it that you want to know?"

"I want to know all the details of this murder hunt first and of how this girl, Marlene Tucker, came to be taking a part in it."

"That's quite easy."

Succinctly and clearly Miss Brewis explained the idea of the murder hunt as an original attraction for the Fête, the engaging of Mrs. Oliver, the well-known novelist, to arrange the matter, and a short outline of the plot.

"Originally," Miss Brewis explained, "Mrs. Alec Legge was to have taken the part of the victim."

"Mrs. Alec Legge?" queried the Inspector.

Constable Hoskins put in an explanatory word.

"She and Mr. Legge have the Lawders' Cottage, the pink one down by Mill Creek. Come here a month ago they did. Two or three months they got it for."

"I see. And Mrs. Legge, you say, was to be the original victim? Why was that changed?"

"Well, one evening Mrs. Legge told all our fortunes and was so good at it that it was decided we'd have a fortuneteller's tent as one of the attractions and that Mrs. Legge should put on Eastern dress and be Madame Zuleika and tell fortunes at half-a-crown a time. I don't think that's really illegal, is it, Inspector? I mean it's usually done at these kind of fêtes."

Inspector Bland smiled faintly.

"Fortunetelling and raffles aren't always taken too seriously, Miss Brewis," he said. "Now and then we have to—er—make an example."

"But usually you're tactful? Well, that's how it was. Mrs. Legge agreed to help us that way and so we had to find somebody else to do the body. The local Guides were helping us at the Fête and I think someone suggested that one of the Guides would do quite well."

"Just who was it who suggested that, Miss Brewis?"

"Really, I don't quite know. . . . I think it may have been Mrs. Masterton, the Member's wife. No, perhaps it was Captain Warburton. . . . Really I can't be sure. But anyway it was suggested."

"Is there any reason why this particular girl should have been chosen?"

"N-no, I don't think so. Her people are tenants on the estate, and her mother, Mrs. Tucker, sometimes comes to help in the kitchen. I don't know quite why we settled on her. Probably her name came to mind first. We asked her and she seemed quite pleased to do it."

"She definitely wanted to do it?"

"Oh, yes, I think she was flattered. She was a very moronic kind of girl," continued Miss Brewis. "She couldn't have acted a part or anything like that. But this was all very simple, and she felt she'd been singled out from the others and was pleased about it."

"What exactly was it that she had to do?"

"She had to stay in the boathouse. When she heard anyone coming to the door she was to lie down on the floor, put the cord round her neck and sham dead." Miss Brewis' tones were calm and businesslike. The fact that the girl who was to sham dead had actually been found dead did not at the moment appear to affect her emotionally.

"Rather a boring way for the girl to spend the afternoon when she might have been at the Fête," suggested Inspector Bland.

"I suppose it was in a way," said Miss Brewis, "but one can't have everything, can one? And Marlene did enjoy the idea of being the body. It made her feel important. She had a pile of papers and things to read to keep her amused."

"And something to eat as well?" said the Inspector. "I noticed there was a tray down there with a plate and glass."

"Oh yes, she had a big plate of sweet cakes, and a raspberry fruit drink. I took them down to her myself."

Bland looked up sharply.

"You took them down to her? When?"

"About the middle of the afternoon."

"What time exactly? Can you remember?"

Miss Brewis considered a moment.

"Let me see. Children's Fancy Dress was judged, there was a little delay—Lady Stubbs couldn't be found, but Mrs. Folliat took her place, so that was all right. . . . Yes, it must have been—I'm almost sure—about five minutes past four that I collected the cakes and the fruit drink."

"And you took them down to her at the boathouse yourself. What time did you reach there?"

"Oh, it takes about five minutes to go down to the boathouse—about quarter past four, I should think."

"And at quarter past four Marlene Tucker was alive and well?"

"Yes, of course," said Miss Brewis, "and very eager to know how people were getting on with the murder hunt, too. I'm afraid I couldn't tell her. I'd been too busy with the side shows on the lawn, but I did know that a lot of people had entered for it. Twenty or thirty to my own knowledge. Probably a good many more."

"How did you find Marlene when you arrived at the boathouse?"

"I've just told you."

"No, no, I don't mean that. I mean, was she lying on the floor shamming dead when you opened the door?"

"Oh, no," said Miss Brewis, "because I called out just before I got there. So she opened the door and I took the tray in and put it on the table."

"At a quarter past four," said Bland, writing it down, "Marlene Tucker was alive and well. You will understand, I'm sure, Miss Brewis, that that is a very important point. You are quite sure of your times?"

"I can't be exactly sure because I didn't look at my watch, but I had looked at it a short time previously and that's as near as I can get." She added, with a sudden dawning realization of the Inspector's point, "Do you mean that it was soon after—"

"It can't have been very long after, Miss Brewis."

"Oh, dear," said Miss Brewis.

It was a rather inadequate expression, but nevertheless it conveyed well enough Miss Brewis' dismay and concern.

"Now, Miss Brewis, on your way down to the boathouse and on your way back again to the house, did you meet anybody or see anyone near the boathouse?"

Miss Brewis considered.

"No," she said, "I didn't meet anyone. I might have, of course, because the grounds are open to everyone this afternoon. But on the whole people tend to stay around the lawn and the side shows and all that. They like to go round the kitchen gardens and the greenhouse, but they don't walk through the woodlands as much as I should have thought they would. People tend to herd together very much at these affairs, don't you think so, Inspector?"

The Inspector said that that was probably so.

"Though I think," said Miss Brewis, with sudden memory, "that there was some one in the Folly."

"The Folly?"

"Yes. A small white temple arrangement. It was put up just a year or two ago. It's to the right of the path as you go down to the boathouse. There was someone in there. A courting couple, I suspect. Someone was laughing and then someone said 'Hush.' "

"You don't know who this courting couple was?"

"I've no idea. You can't see the front of the Folly from the path. The sides and back are enclosed."

The Inspector thought for a moment or two, but it did not seem likely to him that the couple—whoever they were—in the Folly were important. Better find out who they were, perhaps, because they in their turn might have seen someone coming up from or going down to the boathouse.

"And there was no one else on the path? No one at all?" he insisted.

"I see what you're driving at, of course," said Miss Brewis. "I can only assure you that I didn't meet anyone. But then, you see, I needn't have. I mean, if there had been anyone on the path who didn't want me to see them, it's the simplest thing in the world just to slip behind some of the rhododendron bushes. The path's bordered on both sides with shrubs and rhododendron bushes. If anyone who had no business to be there heard someone coming along the path, they could slip out of sight in a moment."

The Inspector shifted on to another tack.

"Is there anything you know about this girl yourself, that could help us?" he asked.

"I really know nothing about her," said Miss Brewis. "I don't think I'd ever spoken to her until this affair. She's one of the girls I've seen about—I know her vaguely by sight, but that's all."

"And you know nothing about her—nothing that could be helpful?"

"I don't know of any reason why anyone should want to murder her," said Miss Brewis. "In fact, it seems to me, if you know what I mean, quite impossible that such a thing should have happened. I can only think that to some unbalanced mind, the fact that she was to be the murdered victim might have induced the wish to make her a real victim. But even that sounds very farfetched and silly."

Bland sighed.

"Oh well," he said, "I suppose I'd better see the mother now."

Mrs. Tucker was a thin, hatchet-faced woman with stringy blond hair and a sharp nose. Her eyes were reddened with crying, but she had herself in hand now, and was ready to answer the Inspector's questions.

"Doesn't seem right that a thing like that should happen," she said. "You read of these things in the papers, but that it should happen to our Marlene—"

"I'm very, very sorry about it," said Inspector Bland gently. "What I want you to do is to think as hard as you can and tell me if there is anyone who could have had any reason to harm the girl?"

"I've been thinking about that already," said Mrs. Tucker, with a sudden sniff. "Thought and thought, I have, but I can't get anywhere. Words with the teacher at school Marlene had now and again, and she'd have her quarrels now and again with one of the girls or boys, but nothing serious in any way. There's no one who had a real down on her, nobody who'd do her a mischief of any kind."

"She never talked to you about anyone who might have been an enemy of any kind?"

"She talked silly often, Marlene did, but nothing of that kind. It was all make-up and hairdos and what she'd like to do to her face and herself. You know what girls are. Far too young she was to put on lipstick and all that muck and her Dad told her so and so did I. But that's what she'd do when she got hold of money. Buy herself scent and lipsticks and hide them away."

Bland nodded. There was nothing here that could help him. An adolescent, rather silly girl, her head full of film stars and glamor—there were hundreds of Marlenes.

"What her Dad'll say, I don't know," said Mrs. Tucker. "Coming here any minute he'll be, expecting to enjoy himself. He's a rare shot at the coconuts, he is."

She broke down suddenly and began to sob.

"If you ask me," she said, "it's one of them nasty foreigners up at the Hostel. You never know where you are with foreigners. Nice-spoken as most of them are, some of the shirts they wear you wouldn't believe. Shirts with girls on them with these bikinis, as they call them. And all of them sunning themselves here and there with no shirts at all on—it all leads to trouble. That's what I say!"

Still weeping, Mrs. Tucker was escorted from the room by Constable Hoskins. Bland reflected that the local verdict seemed to be the comfortable and probably agelong one of attributing every tragic occurrence to unspecified foreigners.

8

"GOT A SHARP tongue, she has," Hoskins said when he returned. "Nags her husband and bullies her old father. I daresay she's spoke sharp to the girl once or twice and now she's feeling bad about it. Not that girls mind what their mothers say to them. Drops off 'em like water off a duck's back."

Inspector Bland cut short these general reflections and told Hoskins to fetch Mrs. Oliver.

The Inspector was slightly startled by the sight of Mrs. Oliver. He had not expected anything so voluminous, so purple and in such a state of emotional disturbance.

"I feel awful," said Mrs. Oliver, sinking down in the chair in front of him like a purple blancmange. "AWFUL," she added in what were clearly capital letters.

The Inspector made a few ambiguous noises, and Mrs. Oliver swept on.

"Because, you see, it's my murder. I did it!"

For a startled moment Inspector Bland thought that Mrs. Oliver was accusing herself of the crime.

"Why I should ever have wanted the Yugoslavian wife of an Atom Scientist to be the victim, I can't imagine," said Mrs. Oliver, sweeping her hands through her elaborate hairdo in a frenzied manner with the result that she looked slightly drunk. "Absolutely asinine of me. It might just as well have been the second gardener who wasn't what he seemed— and that wouldn't have mattered half as much because after all most men can look after themselves. If they can't look after themselves they ought to be able to look after themselves, and in that case I shouldn't have minded so much. Men get killed and nobody minds—I mean nobody except their wives and sweethearts and children and things like that."

At this point the Inspector entertained unworthy suspicions about Mrs. Oliver. This was aided by the faint fragrance of brandy which was wafted towards him. On their return to the house Hercule Poirot had firmly administered to his friend this sovereign remedy for shocks.

"I'm not mad and I'm not drunk," said Mrs. Oliver, intuitively divining his thoughts, "though I daresay with that man about who thinks I drink like a fish and says everybody says so, you probably think so, too."

"What man?" demanded the Inspector, his mind switching from the unexpected introduction of the second gardener into the drama to the further introduction of an unspecified man.

"Freckles and a Yorkshire accent," said Mrs. Oliver, "but, as I say, I'm not drunk and I'm not mad. I'm just upset. Thoroughly UPSET," she repeated, once more resorting to capital letters.

"I'm sure, Madam, it must have been most distressing," said the Inspector.

"The awful thing is," said Mrs. Oliver, "that she wanted to be a sex maniac's victim, and now I suppose she was—is—which should I mean?"

"There's no question of a sex maniac," said the Inspector.

"Isn't there?" said Mrs. Oliver. "Well, thank God for that. Or at least, I don't know. Perhaps she would rather have had it that way. But if he wasn't a sex maniac, why did anybody murder her, Inspector?"

"I was hoping," said the Inspector, "that you could help me there."

Undoubtedly, he thought, Mrs. Oliver had put her finger on the crucial point. Why should anyone murder Marlene?

"I can't help you," said Mrs. Oliver. "I can't imagine who could have done it. At least, of course, I can imagine—I can imagine anything! That's the trouble with me. I can imagine things now—this minute. I could even make them sound all right, but of course none of them would be true. I mean, she could have been murdered by someone who just likes murdering girls (but that's too easy)—and anyway, too much of a coincidence that somebody should be at this Fête who wanted to murder a girl. And how would he know that Marlene was in the boathouse? Or she might have known some secret about somebody's love affairs, or she may have seen someone bury a body at night, or she may have recognized somebody who was concealing his identity—or she may have known a secret about where some treasure was buried during the war. Or the man in the launch may have thrown somebody into the river and she saw it from the window of the boathouse—or she may even have got hold of some very important message in secret code and not known what it was herself."

"Please!" The Inspector held up his hand. His head was whirling.

Mrs. Oliver stopped obediently. It was clear that she could have gone on in this vein for some time, although it seemed to the Inspector that she had already envisaged every possibility, likely or otherwise. Out of the richness of the material presented to him, he seized upon one phrase.

"What did you mean, Mrs. Oliver, by 'the man in the launch'? Are you just imagining a man in a launch?"

"Somebody told me he'd come in a launch," said Mrs. Oliver. "I can't remember who. The one we were talking about at breakfast, I mean," she added.

"Please." The Inspector's tone was now pleading. He had had no idea before what the writers of detective stories were like. He knew that Mrs. Oliver had written forty-odd books. It seemed to him astonishing at the moment that she had not written a hundred and forty. He rapped out a peremptory enquiry. "What is all this about a man at breakfast who came in a launch?"

"He didn't come in the launch at breakfast time," said Mrs. Oliver, "it was a yacht. At least, I don't mean that exactly. It was a letter."

"Well, what was it?" demanded Bland. "A yacht or a letter?"

"It was a letter," said Mrs. Oliver, "to Lady Stubbs. From a cousin in a yacht. And she was frightened," she ended.

"Frightened? What of?"

"Of him, I suppose," said Mrs. Oliver. "Anybody could see it. She was terrified of him and she didn't want him to come, and I think that's why she's hiding now."

"Hiding?" said the Inspector.

"Well, she isn't about anywhere," said Mrs. Oliver. "Everyone's been looking for her. And I think she's hiding because she's afraid of him and doesn't want to meet him."

"Who is this man?" demanded the Inspector.

"You'd better ask M. Poirot," said Mrs. Oliver. "Because he spoke to him and I haven't. His name's Esteban—no, it isn't, that was in my plot. De Sousa, that's what his name is, Etienne De Sousa."

But another name had caught the Inspector's attention.

"Who did you say?" he asked. "M. Poirot?"

"Yes. Hercule Poirot. He was with me when we found the body."

"Hercule Poirot. . . . I wonder now. Can it be the same man? A Belgian, a small man with a very big moustache."

"An enormous moustache," agreed Mrs. Oliver. "Yes. Do you know him?"

"It's a good many years since I met him. I was a young sergeant at the time."

"You met him on a murder case?"

"Yes, I did. What's he doing down here?"

"He was to give away the prizes," said Mrs. Oliver.

There was a momentary hesitation before she gave this answer, but it went unperceived by the Inspector.

"And he was with you when you discovered the body," said Bland. "H'm, I'd like to talk to him."

"Shall I get him for you?" Mrs. Oliver gathered up her purple draperies hopefully.

"There's nothing more that you can add, Madam? Nothing more that you think could help us in any way?"

"I don't think so," said Mrs. Oliver. "I don't know anything. As I say, I could imagine reasons—"

The Inspector cut her short. He had no wish to hear any more of Mrs. Oliver's imagined solutions. They were far too confusing.

"Thank you very much, Madam," he said briskly. "If you'll ask M. Poirot to come and speak to me here I shall be very much obliged to you."

Mrs. Oliver left the room. P.C. Hoskins enquired with interest,

"Who's this Monsieur Poirot, sir?"

"You'd describe him probably as a scream," said Inspector Bland. "Kind of music hall parody of a Frenchman, but actually he's a Belgian. But in spite of his absurdities, he's got brains. He must be a fair age now."

"What about this De Sousa?" asked the Constable. "Think there's anything in that, sir?"

Inspector Bland did not hear the question. He was struck by a fact which, though he had been told it several times, was only now beginning to register.

First it had been Sir George, irritated and alarmed.

"My wife seems to have disappeared. I can't think where she has got to." Then Miss Brewis, contemptuous. "Lady Stubbs was not to be found. She'd got bored with the show." And now Mrs. Oliver with her theory that Lady Stubbs was hiding.

"Eh? What?" he said absently.

Constable Hoskins cleared his throat.

"I was asking you, sir, if you thought there was anything in this business of De Sousa—whoever he is."

Constable Hoskins was clearly delighted at having a specific foreigner, rather than foreigners in the mass, introduced into the case. But Inspector Bland's mind was running on a different course.

"I want Lady Stubbs," he said curtly. "Get hold of her for me. If she isn't about, look for her."

Hoskins looked slightly puzzled but he left the room obediently. In the doorway he paused and fell back a little to allow Hercule Poirot to enter. He looked back over his shoulder with some interest before closing the door behind him.

"I don't suppose," said Bland, rising and holding out his hand, "that you remember me, M. Poirot."

"But assuredly," said Poirot. "It is—now give me a moment, just a little moment. It is the young sergeant—yes, Sergeant Bland whom I met fourteen—no, fifteen years ago."

"Quite right. What a memory!"

"Not at all. Since you remember me, why should I not remember you?"

It would be difficult, Bland thought, to forget Hercule Poirot, and this not entirely for complimentary reasons.

"So here you are, M. Poirot," he said. "Assisting at a murder once again."

"You are right," said Poirot. "I was called down here to assist."

"Called down to assist?" Bland looked puzzled. Poirot said quickly:

"I mean, I was asked down here to give away the prizes of this murder hunt."

"So Mrs. Oliver told me."

"She told you nothing else?" Poirot said it with apparent carelessness. He was anxious to discover whether Mrs. Oliver had given the Inspector any hint of the real motives which had led her to insist on Poirot's journey to Devon.

"Told me nothing else? She never stopped telling me things. Every possible and impossible motive for the girl's murder. She set my head spinning. Phew! What an imagination!"

"She earns her living by her imagination, *mon ami*," said Poirot drily.

"She mentioned a man called De Sousa—did she imagine that?"

"No, that is sober fact."

"There was something about a letter at breakfast and a yacht and coming up the river in a launch. I couldn't make head or tail of it."

Poirot embarked upon an explanation. He told of the scene at the breakfast table, the letter, Lady Stubbs' headache.

"Mrs. Oliver said that Lady Stubbs was frightened. Did you think she was afraid, too?"

"That was the impression she gave me."

"Afraid of this cousin of hers? Why?"

Poirot shrugged his shoulders.

"I have no idea. All she told me was that he was bad—a bad man. She is, you understand, a little simple. Subnormal."

"Yes, that seems to be pretty generally known round here. She didn't say why she was afraid of this De Sousa?"

"No."

"But you think her fear was real?"

"If it was not, then she is a very clever actress," said Poirot drily.

"I'm beginning to have some odd ideas about this case," said Bland.

He got up and walked restlessly to and fro. "It's that cursed woman's fault, I believe."

"Mrs. Oliver's?"

"Yes. She's put a lot of melodramatic ideas into my head."

"And you think they may be true?"

"Not all of them—naturally—but one or two of them mightn't be as wild as they sounded. It all depends—" He broke off as the door opened to readmit P.C. Hoskins.

"Don't seem able to find the lady, sir," he said. "She's not about anywhere."

"I know that already," said Bland irritably. "I told you to find her."

"Sergeant Farrell and P.C. Lorimer are searching the grounds, sir," said Hoskins. "She's not in the house," he added.

"Find out from the man who's taking admission tickets at the gate if she's left the place. Either on foot or in a car."

"Yes, sir."

Hoskins departed.

"And find out when she was last seen and where," Bland shouted after him.

"So that is the way your mind is working," said Poirot.

"It isn't working anywhere yet," said Bland, "but I've just woken up to the fact that a lady who ought to be on the premises isn't on the premises! And I want to know why! Tell me what more you know about what's-his-name De Sousa?"

Poirot described his meeting with the young man who had come up the path from the quay.

"He is probably still here at the Fête," he said. "Shall I tell Sir George that you want to see him?"

"Not for a moment or two," said Bland. "I'd like to find out a little more first. When did you yourself last see Lady Stubbs?"

Poirot cast his mind back. He found it difficult to remember exactly. He recalled vague glimpses of her tall, cyclamen-clad figure with the drooping black hat moving about the lawn talking to people, hovering here and there; occasionally he would hear the strange loud laugh of hers, distinctive among the many other confused sounds.

"I think," he said doubtfully, "it must have been not long before four o'clock."

"And where was she then, and who was she with?"

"She was in the middle of a group of people near the house."

"Was she there when De Sousa arrived?"

"I don't remember. I don't think so; at least I did not see her. Sir George told De Sousa that his wife was somewhere about. He seemed surprised, I remember, that she was not judging the Children's Fancy Dress, as she was supposed to do."

"What time was it when De Sousa arrived?"

"It must have been about half past four, I should think. I did not look at my watch so I cannot tell you exactly."

"And Lady Stubbs had disappeared before he arrived?"

"It seems so."

"Possibly she ran away so as not to meet him," suggested the Inspector.

"Possibly," Poirot agreed.

"Well, she can't have gone far," said Bland. "We ought to be able to find her quite easily, and when we do—" He broke off.

"And supposing you don't?" Poirot put the question with a curious intonation in his voice.

"That's nonsense," said the Inspector vigorously. "Why? What d'you think's happened to her?"

Poirot shrugged his shoulders.

"What indeed! One does not know. All one does know is that she has— disappeared!"

"Dash it all, M. Poirot, you're making it sound quite sinister."

"Perhaps it is sinister."

"It's the murder of Marlene Tucker that we're investigating," said the Inspector, severely.

"But evidently. So—why this interest in De Sousa? Do you think he killed Marlene Tucker?"

Inspector Bland replied irrelevantly,

"It's that woman!"

Poirot smiled faintly.

"Mrs. Oliver, you mean?"

"Yes. You see, M. Poirot, the murder of Marlene Tucker doesn't make sense. It doesn't make sense at all. Here's a nondescript, rather moronic kid found strangled and not a hint of any possible motive."

"And Mrs. Oliver supplied you with a motive?"

"With a dozen at least! Among them she suggested that Marlene might have a knowledge of somebody's secret love affair, or that Marlene might have witnessed somebody being murdered, or that she knew where a buried treasure was hidden, or that she might have seen from the window of the boathouse some action performed by De Sousa in his launch as he was going up the river."

"Ah. And which of those theories appeals to you, *mon cher*?"

"I don't know. But I can't help thinking about them. Listen, M. Poirot. Think back carefully. Would you say from your impression of what Lady Stubbs said to you this morning that she was afraid of her cousin's coming because he might, perhaps, know something about her which she did not want to come to the ears of her husband, or would you say that it was a direct personal fear of the man himself?"

Poirot had no hesitation in his reply.

"I should say it was a direct personal fear of the man himself."

"H'm," said Inspector Bland. "Well, I'd better have a little talk with this young man if he's still about the place."

9

I

ALTHOUGH HE HAD none of Constable Hoskins' ingrained prejudice against foreigners, Inspector Bland took an instant dislike to Etienne De Sousa. The polished elegance of the young man, his sartorial perfection, the rich flowery smell of his brilliantined hair, all combined to annoy the Inspector.

De Sousa was very sure of himself, very much at ease. He also displayed, decorously veiled, a certain aloof amusement.

"One must admit," he said, "that life is full of surprises. I arrive here on a holiday cruise, I admire the beautiful scenery, I come to spend an afternoon with a little cousin that I have not seen for years—and what happens? First I am engulfed in a kind of carnival with coconuts whizzing past my head, and immediately afterwards, passing from comedy to tragedy, I am embroiled in a murder."

He lit a cigarette, inhaled deeply, and said:

"Not that it concerns me in any way, this murder. Indeed, I am at a loss to know why you should want to interview me."

"You arrived here as a stranger, Mr. De Sousa—"

De Sousa interrupted:

"And strangers are necessarily suspicious, is that it?"

"No, no, not at all, sir. No, you don't take my meaning. Your yacht, I understand, is moored in Helmmouth?"

"That is so, yes."

"And you came up the river this afternoon in a motor launch?"

"Again—that is so."

"As you came up the river, did you notice on your right a small boathouse jutting out into the river with a thatched roof and a little mooring quay underneath it?"

De Sousa threw back his handsome, dark head and frowned as he reflected.

"Let me see, there was a creek and a small grey tiled house."

"Further up the river than that, Mr. De Sousa. Set among trees."

"Ah, yes, I remember now. A very picturesque spot. I did not know it was the boathouse attached to this house. If I had done so, I would have moored my boat there and come ashore. When I asked for directions I had been told to come up to the ferry itself and go ashore at the quay there."

"Quite so. And that is what you did?"

"That is what I did."

"You didn't land at, or near, the boathouse?"

De Sousa shook his head.

"Did you see anyone at the boathouse as you passed?"

"See anyone? No. Should I have seen someone?"

"It was just a possibility. You see, Mr. De Sousa, the murdered girl was in the boathouse this afternoon. She was killed there, and she must have been killed at a time not very distant from when you were passing."

Again De Sousa raised his eyebrows.

"You think I might have been a witness to this murder?"

"The murder took place inside the boathouse, but you might have seen the girl—she might have looked out from the window or come out on to the balcony. If you had seen her it would, at any rate, have narrowed the time of death for us. If, when you'd passed, she'd been still alive . . ."

"Ah, I see. Yes, I see. But why ask me particularly? There are plenty of boats going up and down from Helmmouth. Pleasure steamers. They pass the whole time. Why not ask them?"

"We shall ask them," said the Inspector. "Never fear, we shall ask them. I am to take it, then, that you saw nothing unusual at the boathouse?"

"Nothing whatever. There was nothing to show there was anyone there. Of course I did not look at it with any special attention, and I did not pass very near. Somebody might have been looking out of the windows, as you suggest, but if so I should not have seen that person." He added in a polite tone, "I am very sorry that I cannot assist you."

"Oh, well," said Inspector Bland in a friendly manner, "we can't hope for too much. There are just a few other things I would like to know, Mr. De Sousa."

"Yes?"

"Are you alone down here or have you friends with you on this cruise?"

"I have had friends with me until quite recently, but for the last three days I have been on my own—with the crew, of course."

"And the name of your yacht, Mr. De Sousa?"

"The *Esperance*."

"Lady Stubbs is, I understand, a cousin of yours?"

De Sousa shrugged his shoulders.

"A distant cousin. Not very near. In the islands, you must understand, there is much intermarrying. We are all cousins of one another. Hattie is a second or third cousin. I have not seen her since she was practically a little girl, fourteen—fifteen."

"And you thought you would pay her a surprise visit today?"

"Hardly a surprise visit, Inspector. I had already written to her."

"I know that she received a letter from you this morning, but it was a surprise to her to know that you were in this country."

"Oh, but you are wrong there, Inspector. I wrote to my cousin—let me see, three weeks ago. I wrote to her from France just before I came across to this country."

The Inspector was suprised.

"You wrote to her from France telling her you proposed to visit her?"

"Yes. I told her I was going on a yachting cruise and that we should probably arrive at Torquay or Helmmouth round about this date and that I would let her know later exactly when I should arrive."

Inspector Bland stared at him. This statement was at complete variance with what he had been told about the arrival of Etienne De Sousa's letter at the breakfast table. More than one witness had testified to Lady Stubbs' having been alarmed and upset and very clearly startled at the contents of the letter. De Sousa returned his stare calmly. With a little smile he flicked a fragment of dust from his knee.

"Did Lady Stubbs reply to your first letter?" the Inspector asked.

De Sousa hesitated for a moment or two before he answered, then he said,

"It is so difficult to remember. . . . No, I do not think she did. But it was not necessary. I was travelling about, I had no fixed address. And besides, I do not think my cousin, Hattie, is very good at writing letters." He added: "She is not, you know, very intelligent, though I understand that she has grown into a very beautiful woman."

"You have not yet seen her?" Bland put it in the form of a question and De Sousa showed his teeth in an agreeable smile.

"She seems to be most unaccountably missing," he said. "No doubt this *espèce de gala* bores her."

Choosing his words carefully, Inspector Bland said,

"Have you any reason to believe, Mr. De Sousa, that your cousin might have some reason for wishing to avoid you?"

"Hattie wish to avoid me? Really, I do not see why. What reason could she have?"

"That is what I am asking you, Mr. De Sousa."

"You think that Hattie has absented herself from this Fête in order to avoid me? What an absurd idea."

"She has no reason, as far as you know, to be—shall we say, afraid of you in any way?"

"Afraid—of me?" De Sousa's voice was sceptical and amused. "But if I may say so, Inspector, what a fantastic idea!"

"Your relations with her have always been quite amicable?"

"It is as I have told you. I have had no relations with her. I have not seen her since she was a child of fourteen."

"Yet you look her up when you come to England?"

"Oh, as to that, I had seen a paragraph about her in one of your society papers. It mentions her maiden name and that she is married to this rich Englishman, and I think 'I must see what the little Hattie has turned into. Whether her brains now work better than they used to do.' " He shrugged his shoulders again. "It was a mere cousinly politeness. A gentle curiosity—no more."

Again the Inspector stared hard at De Sousa. What, he wondered, was going on behind the mocking, smooth façade? He adopted a more confidential manner.

"I wonder if you can perhaps tell me a little more about your cousin? Her character, her reactions?"

De Sousa appeared politely surprised.

"Really—has this anything to do with the murder of the girl in the boathouse, which I understand is the real matter with which you occupy yourself?"

"It might have a connection," said Inspector Bland.

De Sousa studied him for a moment or two in silence. Then he said with a slight shrug of the shoulders,

"I never knew my cousin at all well. She was a unit in a large family and not particularly interesting to me. But in answer to your question I would say to you that although mentally weak, she was not, as far as I know, ever possessed by any homicidal tendencies."

"Really, Mr. De Sousa, I wasn't suggesting that!"

"Weren't you? I wonder. I can see no other reason for your question. No, unless Hattie has changed very much, she is not homicidal." He rose. "I am sure that you cannot want to ask me anything further, Inspector. I can only wish you every possible success in tracking down the murderer."

"You are not thinking of leaving Helmmouth for a day or two, I hope, Mr. De Sousa?"

"You speak very politely, Inspector. Is that an order?"

"Just a request, sir."

"Thank you. I propose to stay in Helmmouth for two days. Sir George has very kindly asked me to come and stay in the house, but I prefer to remain on the *Esperance*. If you should want to ask me any further questions, that is where you will find me."

He bowed politely.

P.C. Hoskins opened the door for him, and he went out.

"Smarmy sort of fellow," muttered the Inspector to himself.

"Aah," said P.C. Hoskins in complete agreement.

"Say she is homicidal if you like," went on the Inspector, to himself, "why should she attack a nondescript girl? There'd be no sense in it."

"You never know with the barmy ones," said Hoskins.

"The question really is, how barmy is she?"

Hoskins shook his head sapiently.

"Got a low I.Q., I reckon," he said.

The Inspector looked at him with annoyance.

"Don't bring out these newfangled terms like a parrot. I don't care if she's got a high I.Q. or a low I.Q. All I care about is, is she the sort of woman who'd think it funny, or desirable, or necessary, to put a cord round a girl's neck and strangle her? And where the devil is the woman anyway? Go out and see how Frank's getting on."

Hoskins left obediently, and returned a moment or two later with Sergeant Cottrell, a brisk young man with a good opinion of himself, who always managed to annoy his superior officer. Inspector Bland much preferred the rural wisdom of Hoskins to the smart know-all attitude of Frank Cottrell.

"Still searching the grounds, sir," said Cottrell. "The lady hasn't passed out through the gate, we're quite sure of that. It's the second gardener who's there giving out the tickets and taking the admission money. He'll swear she hasn't left."

"There are other ways of leaving than by the main gate, I suppose?"

"Oh, yes, sir. There's the path down to the ferry, but the old boy down there—Merdell his name is—is also quite positive that she hasn't left that way. He's about a hundred, but pretty reliable, I think. He described quite clearly how the foreign gentleman arrived in his launch and asked the way to Nasse House. The old man told him he must go up the road to the gate and pay for admission. But he said the gentleman seemed to know nothing about the Fête and said he was a relation of the family. So the old man set him on the path up from the ferry through the woods. Merdell seems to have been hanging about the quay all the afternoon so he'd be pretty sure to have seen her ladyship if she'd come that way. Then there's the top gate that leads over the fields to Hoodown Park, but that's been wired up because of trespassers, so she didn't go through there. Seems as though she must be still here, doesn't it?"

"That may be so," said the Inspector, "but there's nothing to prevent her, is there, from slipping under a fence and going off across country? Sir George is still complaining of trespassing here from the hostel next door, I understand. If you can get in the way the trespassers get in, you can get out the same way, I suppose."

"Oh, yes, sir, indubitably, sir. But I've talked to her maid, sir. She's wearing"—Cottrell consulted a paper in his hand—"a dress of cyclamen crepe georgette (whatever that is), a large black hat, black court shoes with four-inch French heels. Not the sort of things you'd wear for a cross-country run!"

"She didn't change her clothes?"

"No. I went into that with the maid. There's nothing missing—nothing whatever. She didn't pack a suitcase or anything of that kind. She didn't even change her shoes. Every pair's there and accounted for."

Inspector Bland frowned. Unpleasant possibilities were rising in his mind. He said curtly,

"Get me that secretary woman again—Bruce—whatever her name is."

II

Miss Brewis came in looking rather more ruffled than usual, and a little out of breath.

"Yes, Inspector?" she said, "you wanted me? If it isn't urgent, Sir George is in a terrible state and—"

"What's he in a state about?"

"He's only just realised that Lady Stubbs is—well—really missing. I told him she's probably only gone for a walk in the woods or something, but he's got it into his head that something's happened to her! Quite absurd."

"It might not be so absurd, Miss Brewis. After all, we've had one—murder here this afternoon."

"You surely don't think that Lady Stubbs?—But that's ridiculous! Lady Stubbs can look after herself."

"Can she?"

"Of course she can! She's a grown woman, isn't she?"

"But rather a helpless one by all accounts."

"Nonsense," said Miss Brewis. "It suits Lady Stubbs now and then to play the helpless nitwit if she doesn't want to do anything. It takes her husband in, I daresay, but it doesn't take me in!"

"You don't like her very much, Miss Brewis?" Bland sounded gently interested.

Miss Brewis' lips closed in a thin line.

"It's not my business either to like or dislike her," she said.

The door burst open and Sir George came in.

"Look here," he said violently, "You've got to do something. Where's Hattie? You've got to find Hattie. What the hell's going on round here I don't know! This confounded Fête—some ruddy homicidal maniac's got in here, paying his half crown and looking like everyone else, spending his afternoon going round murdering people. That's what it looks like to me."

"I don't think we need take such an exaggerated view as that, Sir George."

"It's all very well for you sitting there behind the table, writing things down. What I want is my wife."

"I'm having the grounds searched, Sir George."

"Why did nobody tell me she'd disappeared? She's been missing a couple of hours now, it seems. I thought it was odd that she didn't turn up to judge the Children's Fancy Dress stuff, but nobody told me she'd really gone."

"Nobody knew," said the Inspector.

"Well, someone ought to've known. Somebody ought to have noticed."

He turned on Miss Brewis.

"You ought to have known, Amanda, you were keeping an eye on things."

"I can't be everywhere," said Miss Brewis. She sounded suddenly almost tearful. "I've got so much to see to. If Lady Stubbs chose to wander away—"

"Wander away? Why should she wander away? She'd no reason to wander away unless she wanted to avoid that dago fellow."

Bland seized his opportunity.

"There is something I want to ask you," he said. "Did your wife receive a letter from Mr. De Sousa some three weeks ago, telling her he was coming to this country?"

Sir George looked astonished.

"No, of course she didn't."

"You're sure of that?"

"Oh, quite sure. Hattie would have told me. Why, she was thoroughly startled and upset when she got his letter this morning. It more or less knocked her out. She was lying down most of the morning with a headache."

"What did she say to you privately about her cousin's visit? Why did she dread seeing him so much?"

Sir George looked rather embarrassed.

"Blessed if I really know," he said. "She just kept saying that he was wicked."

"Wicked? In what way?"

"She wasn't very articulate about it. Just went on rather like a child saying that he was a wicked man, bad; and that she wished he wasn't coming here. She said he'd done bad things."

"Done bad things? When?"

"Oh, long ago. I should imagine this Etienne De Sousa was the black sheep of the family and that Hattie picked up odds and ends about him during her childhood without understanding them very well. And as a result she's got a sort of horror of him. I thought it was just a childish hangover myself. My wife is rather childish sometimes. Has likes and dislikes, but can't explain them."

"You are sure she did not particularize in any way, Sir George?"

Sir George looked uneasy.

"I wouldn't want you to go by—er—by what she said."

"Then she did say something?"

"All right. I'll let you have it. What she said was—and she said it several times—'He kills people.' "

10

I

"HE KILLS PEOPLE," Inspector Bland repeated.

"I don't think you ought to take it too seriously," said Sir George. "She kept repeating it and saying, 'He kills people,' but she couldn't tell me who he killed or when or why. I thought myself it was just some queer, childlike memory—trouble with the natives—something like that."

"You say she couldn't tell you anything definite—do you mean couldn't, Sir George—or might it have been wouldn't?"

"I don't think"—he broke off—"I don't know. You've muddled me. As I say, I didn't take any of it seriously. I thought perhaps this cousin had teased her a bit when she was a kid—something of that kind. It's difficult to explain to you because you don't know my wife. I am devoted to her, but half the time I don't listen to what she says because it just doesn't make sense. Anyway, this De Sousa fellow couldn't have had anything to do with all this—don't tell me he lands here off a yacht and goes straight away through the woods and kills a wretched Girl Guide in a boathouse! Why should he?"

"I'm not suggesting that anything like that happened," said Inspector Bland, "but you must realize, Sir George, that in looking for the murderer of Marlene Tucker the field is a more restricted one than one might think at first."

"Restricted!" Sir George stared. "You've got the whole ruddy Fête to choose from, haven't you? Two hundred—three hundred—people? Any one of 'em might have done it."

"Yes, I thought so at first, but from what I've learned now that's hardly so. The boathouse door has a Yale lock. Nobody could come in from outside without a key."

"Well, there were three keys."

"Exactly. One key was the final clue in this murder hunt. It is still concealed in the hydrangea walk at the very top of the garden. The second key was in the possession of Mrs. Oliver, the organizer of the murder hunt. Where is the third key, Sir George?"

"It ought to be in the drawer of that desk where you're sitting. No, the right hand one with a lot of the other estate duplicates."

He came over and rummaged in the drawer.

"Yes. Here it is all right."

"Then you see," said Inspector Bland, "what that means? The only people who could have got into the boathouse were first, the person who had completed the murder hunt and found the key (which as far as we know did not happen); second, Mrs. Oliver or some member of the household to whom she may have lent her key, and thirdly someone whom Marlene herself admitted to the room."

"Well, that latter point covers pretty well everyone, doesn't it?"

"Very far from it," said Inspector Bland. "If I understand the arrangement of this murder hunt correctly, when the girl heard anyone approaching the door she was to lie down and enact the part of the Victim, and wait to be discovered by the person who had found the last clue—the key. Therefore, as you must see for yourself, the only people whom she would have admitted, had they called to her from outside and asked her to do so, were the people who had actually arranged the murder hunt. Any inmate, that is, of this house—that is to say, yourself, Lady Stubbs, Miss Brewis, Mrs. Oliver—possibly M. Poirot whom I believe she had met this morning. Who else, Sir George?"

Sir George considered for a moment or two.

"The Legges, of course," he said. "Alec and Peggy Legge. They've been in it from the start. And Michael Weyman, he's an architect staying here in the house to design a tennis pavilion. And Warburton, the Mastertons—oh, and Mrs. Folliat of course."

"That is all—nobody else?"

"That's the lot."

"So you see, Sir George, it is not a very wide field."

George's face went scarlet.

"I think you're talking nonsense—absolute nonsense! Are you suggesting—what are you suggesting?"

"I'm only suggesting," said Inspector Bland, "that there's a great deal we don't know as yet. It's possible, for instance, that Marlene, for some reason, came out of the boathouse. She may even have been strangled somewhere else, and her body brought back and arranged on the floor. But even if so, whoever arranged her was again someone who was thoroughly cognizant with all the details of the murder hunt. We always come back to that." He added in a slightly changed voice, "I can assure you, Sir George, that we're doing all we can to find Lady Stubbs. In the meantime I'd like to have a word with Mr. and Mrs. Alec Legge and Mr. Michael Weyman."

"Amanda."

"I'll see what I can do about it, Inspector," said Miss Brewis. "I expect Mrs. Legge is still telling fortunes in the tent. A lot of people have come in with the half-price admission since five o'clock, and all the side shows are busy. I can probably get hold of Mr. Legge or Mr. Weyman for you—whichever you want to see first."

"It doesn't matter in what order I see them," said Inspector Bland.

Miss Brewis nodded and left the room. Sir George followed her, his voice rising plaintively.

"Look here, Amanda, you've got to—"

Inspector Bland realized that Sir George depended a great deal upon the efficient Miss Brewis. Indeed, at this moment, Bland found the master of the house rather like a small boy.

While waiting, Inpector Bland picked up the telephone, demanded to be put through to the police station at Helmmouth and made certain arrangements with them concerning the yacht *Esperance*.

"You realize, I suppose," he said to Hoskins who was obviously quite incapable of realizing anything of the sort, "that there's just one perfectly possible place where this damn woman might be—and that's on board De Sousa's yacht?"

"How d'you make that out, sir?"

"Well, the woman has not been seen to leave by any of the usual exits, she's togged up in a way that makes it unlikely that she's legging it through the fields or woods, but it is just possible that she met De Sousa by appointment down at the boathouse and that he took her by launch to the yacht, returning to the Fête afterwards."

"And why would he do that, sir?" demanded Hoskins, puzzled.

"I've no idea," said the Inspector, "and it's very unlikely that he did. But it's a possibility. And if she is on the *Esperance,* I'll see to it that she won't get off there without being observed."

"But if her fair hated the sight of him—" Hoskins dropped into the vernacular.

"All we know is that she said she did! Women," said the Inspector sententiously, "tell a lot of lies. Always remember that, Hoskins."

"Aah," said Constable Hoskins appreciatively.

II

Further conversation was brought to an end as the door opened and a tall, vague-looking young man entered. He was wearing a neat grey flannel suit, but his shirt collar was crumpled and his tie askew and his hair stood up on end in an unruly fashion.

"Mr. Alec Legge?" said the Inspector, looking up.

"No," said the young man, "I'm Michael Weyman. You asked for me, I understand."

"Quite true, sir," said Inspector Bland. "Won't you take a chair?" He indicated a chair at the opposite side of the table.

"I don't care for sitting," said Michael Weyman. "I like to stride about. What are all you police doing here anyway? What's happened?"

Inspector Bland looked at him in surprise.

"Didn't Sir George inform you, sir?" he asked.

"Nobody's *informed me*, as you put it, of anything. I don't sit in Sir George's pocket all the time. What *has* happened?"

"You're staying in the house, I understand?"

"Of course I'm staying in the house. What's that got to do with it?"

"Simply that I imagined that all the people staying in the house would by now have been informed of this afternoon's tragedy."

"Tragedy? What tragedy?"

"The girl who was playing the part of the murder victim has been killed."

"No!" Michael Weyman seemed exuberantly surprised. "Do you mean really killed? No fakery-pokery?"

"I don't know what you mean by fakery-pokery. The girl's dead."

"How was she killed?"

"Strangled with a piece of cord."

Michael Weyman gave a whistle.

"Exactly as in the scenario? Well, well, that does give one ideas." He strode over to the window, turned rapidly about and said, "So we're all under suspicion, are we? Or was it one of the local boys?"

"We don't see how it could possibly have been one of the local boys, as you put it," said the Inspector.

"No more do I really," said Michael Weyman. "Well, Inspector, many of my friends call me crazy but I'm not that kind of crazy. I don't roam around the countryside strangling underdeveloped spotty young women."

"You are down here, I understand, Mr. Weyman, designing a tennis pavilion for Sir George?"

"A blameless occupation," said Michael. "Criminally speaking, that is. Architecturally, I'm not so sure. The finished product will probably represent a crime against good taste. But that doesn't interest you, Inspector. What *does* interest you?"

"Well, I should like to know, Mr. Weyman, exactly where you were between quarter past four this afternoon and say five o'clock."

"How do you tape it down to that—medical evidence?"

"Not entirely, sir. A witness saw the girl alive at a quarter past four."

"What witness—or mayn't I ask?"

"Miss Brewis. Lady Stubbs asked her to take down a tray of creamy cakes with some fruit ade to the girl."

"Our Hattie asked her that? I don't believe it for a moment."

"Why don't you believe it, Mr. Weyman?"

"It's not like her. Not the sort of thing she'd think of or bother about. Dear Lady Stubbs' mind revolves entirely round herself."

"I'm still waiting, Mr. Weyman, for your answer to my question."

"Where I was between four fifteen and five o'clock? Well, really Inspector, I can't say offhand. I was about—if you know what I mean."

"About where?"

"Oh, here and there. I mingled a bit on the lawn, watched the locals amusing themselves, had a word or two with the fluttery film star; then when I got sick of it all I went along to the tennis court and mused over the design for the Pavilion. I also wondered how soon someone would identify the photograph that was the first clue for the murder hunt with a section of tennis net."

"Did someone identify it?"

"Yes, I believe someone did come along, but I wasn't really noticing by then. I got a new idea about the Pavilion—a way of making the best of two worlds. My own and Sir George's."

"And after that?"

"After that? Well, I strolled around and came back to the house. I strolled down to the quay and had a crack with old Merdell, then came back. I can't fix any of the times with any accuracy. I was, as I said in the first place, about! That's all there is to it."

"Well, Mr. Weyman," said the Inspector briskly, "I expect we can get some confirmation of all this."

"Merdell can tell you that I talked to him on the quay. But of course that'll be rather later than the time you're interested in. Must have been after five when I got down there. Very unsatisfactory, isn't it, Inspector?"

"We shall be able to narrow it down, I expect, Mr. Weyman."

The Inspector's tone was pleasant but there was a steely ring in it that did not escape the young architect's notice. He sat down on the arm of a chair.

"Seriously," he said, "who can have wanted to murder that girl?"

"You've no ideas yourself, Mr. Weyman?"

"Well, offhand, I'd say it was our prolific authoress, the Purple Peril. Have you seen her Imperial Purple getup? I suggest that she went a bit off her onion and thought how much better the murder hunt would be if there was a *real* body. How's that?"

"Is that a serious suggestion, Mr. Weyman?"

"It's the only probability I can think of."

"There's one other thing I would like to ask you, Mr. Weyman. Did you see Lady Stubbs during the course of the afternoon?"

"Of course I saw her. Who could miss her? Dressed up like a mannequin of Jacques Fath or Christian Dior!"

"When did you see her last?"

"Last? I don't know. Striking an attitude on the lawn about half past three—or a quarter to four perhaps."

"And you didn't see her after that?"

"No. Why?"

"I wondered—because after four o'clock nobody seems to have seen her. Lady Stubbs has—vanished, Mr. Weyman."

"Vanished! Our Hattie?"

"That surprises you?"

"Yes, it does rather. . . . What's she up to, I wonder?"

"D'you know Lady Stubbs well, Mr. Weyman?"

"Never met her till I came down here four or five days ago."

"Have you formed any opinions about her?"

"I should say she knows which side her bread is buttered better than most," said Michael Weyman drily. "A very ornamental young woman and knows how to make the most of it."

"But mentally not very active? Is that right?"

"Depends what you mean by mentally," said Michael Weyman. "I wouldn't describe her as an intellectual. But if you're thinking that she's not all there, you're wrong." A tone of bitterness came into his voice. "I'd say she was very much all there. Nobody more so."

The Inspector's eyebrows rose.

"That's not the generally accepted opinion."

"For some reason she likes playing the dim nitwit. I don't know why. But as I've said before, in my opinion, she's very much all there."

The Inspector studied him for a moment, then he said,

"And you really can't get any nearer to exact times and places between the hours I have mentioned?"

"Sorry." Weyman spoke jerkily. "I'm afraid I can't. Rotten memory, never any good about time." He added, "Finished with me?"

As the Inspector nodded, he left the room quickly.

"And I'd like to know," said the Inspector, half to himself and half to Hoskins, "what there's been between him and her Ladyship. Either he's made a pass at her and she's turned him down, or there's been some kind of a dust up." He went on: "What would you say was the general opinion round these parts about Sir George and his lady?"

"She's daft," said Constable Hoskins.

"I know you think that, Hoskins. Is that the accepted view?"

"I'd say so."

"And Sir George—is he liked?"

"He's liked well enough. He's a good sportsman and he knows a bit about farming. The old lady's done a lot to help."

"What old lady?"

"Mrs. Folliat who lives at the Lodge here."

"Oh, of course. The Folliats used to own this place, didn't they?"

"Yes, and it's owing to the old lady that Sir George and Lady Stubbs have been taken up as well as they have. Got 'em in with the nobs everywhere, she has."

"Paid for doing so, do you think?"

"Oh, no, not Mrs. Folliat." Hoskins sounded shocked. "I understand she knew Lady Stubbs before she was married and it was she who urged on Sir George to buy this place."

"I'll have to talk to Mrs. Folliat," said the Inspector.

"Ah, she's a shrewd old lady, she is. If anything is going on, she'd know about it."

"I must talk to her," said the Inspector. "I wonder where she is now."

11

I

MRS. FOLLIAT WAS at that moment being talked to by Hercule Poirot in the big drawing room. He had found her there leaning back in a chair in a corner of the room. She had started nervously when he came in. Then, sinking back, she had murmured,

"Oh, it's you, M. Poirot."

"I apologise, Madame. I disturbed you."

"No, no—you don't disturb me. I'm just resting, that's all. I'm not as young as I was. The shock—it was too much for me."

"I comprehend," said Poirot. "Indeed, I comprehend."

Mrs. Folliat, a handkerchief clutched in her small hand, was staring up at the ceiling. She said in a voice half stifled with emotion,

"I can hardly bear to think of it. That poor girl. That poor, poor girl. . . ."

"I know," said Poirot, "I know."

"So young," said Mrs. Folliat, "just at the beginning of life." She said again, "I can hardly bear to think of it."

Poirot looked at her curiously. She seemed, he thought, to have aged by about ten years since the time early in the afternoon when he had seen her, the gracious hostess, welcoming her guests. Now her face seemed drawn and haggard with the lines in it clearly marked.

"You said to me only yesterday, Madame, it is a very wicked world."

"Did I say that?" Mrs. Folliat seemed startled. "It's true. . . . Oh, yes, I'm only just beginning to know how true it is." She added in a low voice, "But I never thought anything like this would happen."

Again he looked at her curiously.

"What did you think would happen, then? Something?"

"No, no. I didn't mean that."

Poirot persisted.

"But you did expect something to happen—something out of the usual."

"You misunderstand me, M. Poirot. I only mean that it's the last thing you would expect to happen in the middle of a Fête like this."

"Lady Stubbs this morning also spoke of wickedness."

"Hattie did? Oh, don't speak of her to me—don't speak of her. I don't want to think about her." She was silent for a moment or two and then said, "What did she say—about wickedness?"

"She was speaking of her cousin, Etienne De Sousa. She said that he was wicked, that he was a bad man. She said, too, that she was afraid of him."

He watched, but she merely shook her head incredulously.

"Etienne De Sousa—who is he?"

"Of course, you were not at breakfast. I forgot, Mrs. Folliat. Lady Stubbs received a letter from this cousin of hers whom she had not seen since she was a girl of fifteen. He told her that he proposed to call upon her today, this afternoon."

"And did he come?"

"Yes. He arrived here about half past four."

"Surely—d'you mean that rather handsome, dark young man who came up the ferry path? I wondered who he was at the time."

"Yes, Madame, that was Mr. De Sousa."

Mrs. Folliat said energetically,

"If I were you I should pay no attention to the things Hattie says." She flushed as Poirot looked at her in surprise and went on: "She is like a child—I mean, she uses terms like a child—wicked, good. No half shades. I shouldn't pay any attention to what she tells you about this Etienne De Sousa."

Again Poirot wondered. He said slowly,

"You know Lady Stubbs very well, do you not, Mrs. Folliat?"

"Probably as well as anyone knows her. Possibly even better than her husband knows her. And if I do?"

"What is she really like, Madame?"

"What a very odd question, M. Poirot."

"You know, do you not, Madame, that Lady Stubbs cannot be found anywhere?"

Again her answer surprised him. She expressed no concern or astonishment. She said,

"So she has run away, has she? I see."

"It seems quite natural, that?"

"Natural? Oh, I don't know. Hattie is rather unaccountable."

"Do you think she has run away because she has a guilty conscience?"

"What do you mean, M. Poirot?"

"Her cousin was talking about her this afternoon. He mentioned casually that she had always been mentally subnormal. I think you must know,

Madame, that people who are subnormal mentally are not always accountable for their actions."

"What are you trying to say, M. Poirot?"

"Such people are, as you say, very simple—like children. In a sudden fit of rage they might even kill."

Mrs. Folliat turned on him in sudden anger.

"Hattie was never like that! I won't allow you to say such things. She was a gentle warmhearted girl, even if she was—a little simple mentally. Hattie would never have killed anyone."

She faced him, breathing hard, still indignant.

Poirot wondered. He wondered very much.

II

Breaking into this scene, P.C. Hoskins made his appearance.

He said in an apologetic manner,

"I've been looking for you, Ma'am."

"Good evening, Hoskins." Mrs. Folliat was once more her poised self again, the mistress of Nasse House. "Yes, what is it?"

"The Inspector's compliments, and he'd be glad to have a word with you—if you feels up to it, that is," Hoskins hastened to add; noting, as Hercule Poirot had done, the effects of shock.

"Of course I feel up to it." Mrs. Folliat rose to her feet. She followed Hoskins out of the room. Poirot, having risen politely, sat down again and stared up at the ceiling with a puzzled frown.

The Inspector rose when Mrs. Folliat entered and the Constable held the chair for her to sit down.

"I'm sorry to worry you, Mrs. Folliat," said Bland. "But I imagine that you know all the people in the neighborhood and I think you may be able to help us."

Mrs. Folliat smiled faintly. "I expect," she said, "that I know everyone round here as well as anyone could do. What do you want to know, Inspector?"

"You knew the Tuckers? The family and the girl?"

"Oh yes, of course, they've always been tenants on the estate. Mrs. Tucker was the youngest of a large family. Her eldest brother was our head gardener. She married Alfred Tucker, who is a farm laborer—a stupid man but very nice. Mrs. Tucker is a bit of a shrew. A good housewife, you know, and very clean in the house, but Tucker is never allowed to come anywhere further than the scullery with his muddy boots on. All that sort of thing. She nags the children rather. Most of them have married and gone into jobs now. There was just this poor child, Marlene, left and three younger children. Two boys and a girl still at school."

"Now, knowing the family as you do, Mrs. Folliat, can you think of any reason why Marlene should have been killed today?"

"No, indeed I can't. It's quite, quite flabbergasting, if you know what I mean, Inspector. There was no boy friend or anything of that kind, or I shouldn't think so. Not that I've ever heard of anyway."

"Now what about the people who've been taking part in this murder hunt? Can you tell me anything about them?"

"Well, Mrs. Oliver I'd never met before. She is quite unlike my idea of what a crime novelist would be. She's very upset, poor dear, by what has happened—naturally."

"And what about the other helpers—Captain Warburton, for instance?"

"I don't see any reason why he should murder Marlene Tucker, if that's what you're asking me," said Mrs. Folliat composedly. "I don't like him very much. He's what I call a foxy sort of man, but I suppose one has to be up to all the political tricks and all that kind of thing, if one is a political agent. He's certainly energetic and has worked very hard over this Fête. I don't think he could have killed the girl, anyway, because he was on the lawn the whole time this afternoon."

The Inspector nodded.

"And the Legges. What do you know about the Legges?"

"Well, they seem a very nice young couple. He's inclined to be what I should call—moody. I don't know very much about him. She was a Carstairs before her marriage and I know some relations of hers very well. They took the Mill Cottage for two months and I hope they've enjoyed their holiday here. We've all got very friendly together."

"She's an attractive lady, I understand."

"Oh, yes, very attractive."

"Would you say that at any time Sir George had felt that attraction?"

Mrs. Folliat looked rather astonished.

"Oh no, I'm sure there was nothing of that kind. Sir George is really absorbed by his business, and very fond of his wife. He's not at all a philandering sort of man."

"And there was nothing, you would say, between Lady Stubbs and Mr. Legge?"

Again Mrs. Folliat shook her head.

"Oh, no, positively."

The Inspector persisted.

"There's been no trouble of any kind between Sir George and his wife, that you know of?"

"I'm sure there hasn't," said Mrs. Folliat emphatically. "And I would know if there had been."

"It wouldn't be, then, as a result of any disagreement between husband and wife that Lady Stubbs has gone away?"

"Oh, no." She added lightly, "The silly girl, I understand, didn't want to meet this cousin of hers. Some childish phobia. So she's run away just like a child might do."

"That's your opinion. Nothing more than that?"

"Oh, no. I expect she'll turn up again quite soon. Feeling rather ashamed of herself." She added carelessly, "What's become of this cousin, by the way? Is he still here in the house?"

"I understand he's gone back to his yacht."

"And that's at Helmmouth, is it?"

"Yes, at Helmmouth."

"I see," said Mrs. Folliat. "Well, it's rather unfortunate—Hattie behaving so childishly. However, if he's staying on here for a day or so we can make her see she must behave properly."

It was, the Inspector thought, a question, but although he noticed it he did not answer it.

"You are probably thinking," he said, "that all this is rather beside the point. But you do understand, don't you, Mrs. Folliat, that we have to range over rather a wide field. Miss Brewis, for instance. What do you know about Miss Brewis?"

"Well, she's an excellent secretary. More than a secretary. She practically acts as housekeeper down here. In fact, I don't know what they'd do without her."

"Was she Sir George's secretary before he married his wife?"

"I think so. I'm not quite sure. I've only known her since she came down here with them."

"She doesn't like Lady Stubbs very much, does she?"

"No," said Mrs. Folliat, "I'm afraid she doesn't. I don't think these good secretaries ever do care for wives much, if you know what I mean. Perhaps it's natural."

"Was it you or Lady Stubbs who asked Miss Brewis to take cakes and a fruit drink to the girl in the boathouse?"

Mrs. Folliat looked slightly surprised.

"I remember Miss Brewis collecting some cakes and things and saying she was taking them along to Marlene. I didn't know anyone had particularly asked her to do it, or arranged about it. It certainly wasn't me."

"I see. You say you were in the tea tent from four o'clock on. I believe Mrs. Legge was also having tea in the tent at that time."

"Mrs. Legge? No, I don't think so. At least I don't remember seeing her there. In fact I'm quite sure she wasn't there. We'd had a great influx by the bus from Torquay, and I remember looking round the tent and thinking that they must all be summer visitors; there was hardly a face there that I knew. I think Mrs. Legge must have come in to tea later."

"Oh well," said the Inspector, "it doesn't matter." He added smoothly, "Well, I really think that's all. Thank you, Mrs. Folliat, you've been very kind. We can only hope that Lady Stubbs will return shortly."

"I hope so, too," said Mrs. Folliat. "Very thoughtless of the dear child giving us all so much anxiety." She spoke briskly but the animation in her voice was not very natural. "I'm sure," said Mrs. Folliat, "that she's quite all right. Quite all right."

At that moment the door opened and an attractive young woman with red hair and a freckled face came in and said,

"I hear you've been asking for me?"

"This is Mrs. Legge, Inspector," said Mrs. Folliat. "Peggy dear, I don't know whether you've heard about the terrible thing that has happened?"

"Oh, yes! Ghastly, isn't it?" said Mrs. Legge. She uttered an exhausted sigh, and sank down in the chair as Mrs. Folliat left the room.

"I'm terrible sorry about all this," she said. "It seems really unbelievable, if you know what I mean. I'm afraid I can't help you in any way. You see, I've been telling fortunes all the afternoon, so I haven't seen anything of what was going on."

"I know, Mrs. Legge. But we just have to ask everybody the same routine questions. For instance, just where were you between four fifteen and five o'clock?"

"Well, I went and had tea at four o'clock."

"In the tea tent?"

"Yes."

"It was very crowded, I believe?"

"Oh, frightfully crowded."

"Did you see anyone you knew there?"

"Oh, a few odd people, yes. Nobody to speak to. Goodness, how I wanted that tea! That was four o'clock, as I say. I got back to the fortunetelling tent at half past four and went on with my job. And goodness knows what I was promising the women in the end. Millionaire husbands, film stardom in Hollywood—heaven knows what! Mere journeys across the sea and suspicious dark women seemed too tame."

"What happened during the half hour when you were absent—I meant supposing people wanted to have their fortunes told?"

"Oh, I hung a card up outside the tent. 'Back at four thirty.' "

The Inspector made a note in his pad.

"When did you last see Lady Stubbs?"

"Hattie? I don't really know. She was quite near at hand when I came out of the fortunetelling tent to go to tea, but I didn't speak to her. I don't remember seeing her afterwards. Somebody told me just now that she's missing. Is that true?"

"Yes, it is."

"Oh, well," said Peggy Legge cheerfully, "she's a bit queer in the top story, you know. I dare say having a murder here has frightened her."

"Well, thank you, Mrs. Legge."

Mrs. Legge accepted the dismissal with promptitude. She went out, passing Hercule Poirot in the doorway.

III

Looking at the ceiling, the Inspector spoke.

"Mrs. Legge says she was in the tea tent between four and four thirty. Mrs. Folliat says she was helping in the tea tent from four o'clock on but that Mrs. Legge was not among those present." He paused and then went on, "Miss Brewis says that Lady Stubbs asked her to take a tray of cakes and fruit juice to Marlene Tucker. Michael Weyman says that it's quite impossible Lady Stubbs should have done any such thing—it would be most uncharacteristic of her."

"Ah," said Poirot, "the conflicting statements! Yes, one always has them."

"And what a nuisance they are to clear up, too," said the Inspector. "Sometimes they matter but in nine times out of ten they don't. Well, we've got to do a lot of spade work, that's clear."

"And what do you think now, *mon cher?* What are the latest ideas?"

"I think," said the Inspector gravely, "that Marlene Tucker saw something she was not meant to see. I think that it was because of what Marlene Tucker saw that she had to be killed."

"I will not contradict you," said Poirot. "The point is what did she see?"

"She might have seen a murder," said the Inspector. "Or she might have seen the person who did the murder."

"Murder?" said Poirot, "the murder of whom?"

"What do you think Poirot? Is Lady Stubbs alive or dead?"

Poirot took a moment or two before he replied. Then he said:

"I think, *mon ami,* that Lady Stubbs is dead. And I wlll tell you why I think that. It is because Mrs. Folliat thinks she is dead. Yes, whatever she may say now, or pretend to think, Mrs. Folliat believes that Hattie Stubbs is dead. Mrs. Folliat," he added, "knows a great deal that we do not."

12

HERCULE POIROT CAME down to the breakfast table on the following morning to a depleted table. Mrs. Oliver, still suffering from the shock of yesterday's occurrence, was having her breakfast in bed. Michael Weyman had had a cup of coffee and gone out early. Only Sir George and the faithful Miss Brewis were at the breakfast table. Sir George was giving indubitable proof of his mental condition by being unable to eat any breakfast. His plate lay almost untasted before him. He pushed aside the small pile of letters which, after opening them, Miss Brewis had placed before him. He drank coffee with an air of not knowing what he was doing. He said,

" 'Morning, M. Poirot," perfunctorily and then relapsed into his state of preoccupation. At times a few ejaculatory murmurs came from him.

"So incredible, the whole damn thing. Where can she be?"

"The inquest will be held at the Institute on Thursday," said Miss Brewis. "They rang up to tell us."

Her employer looked at her as if he did not understand.

"Inquest?" he said. "Oh yes, I see." He sounded dazed and uninterested. After another sip or two of coffee he said, "Women are incalculable. What does she think she's doing?"

Miss Brewis pursed her lips. Poirot observed acutely enough that she was in a state of taut nervous tension.

"Hodgson's coming to see you this morning," she remarked, "about the electrification of the milking sheds on the farm. And at twelve o'clock there's the—"

Sir George interrupted.

"I can't see anyone. Put 'em all off! How the devil d'you think a man can attend to business when he's worried half out of his mind about his wife?"

"If you say so, Sir George." Miss Brewis gave the domestic equivalent of a barrister saying "as your lordship pleases." Her dissatisfaction was obvious.

"Never know," said Sir George, "what women get into their heads, or what fool things they're likely to do! You agree, eh?" He shot the last question at Poirot.

"*Les femmes?* They are incalculable," said Poirot, raising his eyebrows and his hands with Gallic fervor. Miss Brewis blew her nose in an annoyed fashion.

"She seemed all right," said Sir George. "Damn pleased about her new ring, dressed herself up to enjoy the Fête. All just the same as usual. Not as though we'd had words or a quarrel of any kind. Going off without a word."

"About those letters, Sir George," began Miss Brewis.

"Damn the bloody letters to hell," said Sir George and pushed aside his coffee cup.

He picked up the letters by his plate and more or less threw them at her.

"Answer them any way you like! I can't be bothered." He went on more or less to himself, in an injured tone, "Doesn't seem to be anything I can do. . . . Don't even know if that police chap's any good. Very soft-spoken and all that."

"The police are, I believe," said Miss Brewis, "very efficient. They have ample facilities for tracing the whereabouts of missing persons."

"They take days sometimes," said Sir George, "to find some miserable kid who's run off and hidden himself in a haystack."

"I don't think Lady Stubbs is likely to be in a haystack, Sir George."

"If only I could do something," repeated the unhappy husband. "I think, you know, I'll put an advertisement in the papers. Take it down, Amanda, will you?" He paused a moment in thought. " 'Hattie. Please come home. Desperate about you. George.' All the papers, Amanda."

Miss Brewis said acidly:

"Lady Stubbs doesn't often read the papers, Sir George. She's no interest at all in current affairs or what's going on in the world." She added, rather cattily, but Sir George was not in the mood to appreciate cattiness, "Of course you could put an advertisement in *Vogue*. That might catch her eye."

Sir George said simply,

"Anywhere you think, but get on with it."

He got up and walked towards the door. With his hand on the handle he paused and came back a few steps. He spoke directly to Poirot.

"Look here, Poirot," he said, "*you* don't think she's dead, do you?"

Poirot fixed his eyes in his coffee cup as he replied,

"I should say it is far too soon, Sir George, to assume anything of that kind. There is no reason as yet to entertain such an idea."

"So you do think so," said Sir George, heavily. "Well," he added defiantly, "I don't! I say she's quite all right." He nodded his head several times with increasing defiance, and went out banging the door behind him.

Poirot buttered a piece of toast thoughtfully. In cases where there was any suspicion of a wife being murdered, he always automatically suspected the husband. (Similarly, with a husband's demise, he suspected the wife.) But in this case he did not suspect Sir George with having done away with Lady Stubbs. From his brief observation of them he was quite convinced that Sir George was devoted to his wife. Moreover, as far as his excellent memory served him (and it served him pretty well), Sir George had been present on the lawn the entire afternoon until he himself had left with Mrs. Oliver to discover the body. He had been there on the lawn when they had returned with the news. No, it was not Sir George who was responsible for Hattie's death. That is, if Hattie were dead. After all, Poirot told himself, there was no reason to believe so as yet. What he had just said to Sir George was true enough. But in his own mind the conviction was unalterable. The pattern, he thought, was the pattern of murder—a double murder.

Miss Brewis interrupted his thought by speaking with almost tearful venom.

"Men are such fools," she said, "such absolute fools! They're quite shrewd in most ways, and then they go marrying entirely the wrong sort of woman."

Poirot was always willing to let people talk. The more people who talked to him, and the more they said, the better. There was nearly always a grain of wheat among the chaff.

"You think it has been an unfortunate marriage?" he demanded.

"Disastrous—quite disastrous."

"You mean—that they were not happy together?"

"She's a thoroughly bad influence over him in every way."

"Now I find that very interesting. What kind of a bad influence?"

"Making him run to and fro at her beck and call, getting expensive presents out of him—far more jewels than one woman could wear. And furs. She's got two mink coats and a Russian ermine. What could any woman want with two mink coats, I'd like to know?"

Poirot shook his head.

"That I would not know," he said.

"Sly," continued Miss Brewis. "Deceitful! Always playing the simpleton—especially when people were here. I suppose because she thought he liked her that way!"

"And did he like her that way?"

"Oh, men!" said Miss Brewis, her voice trembling on the edge of hysteria. "They don't apreciate efficiency or unselfishness, or loyalty or any of those qualities! Now with a clever, capable wife Sir George would have got somewhere."

"Got where?" asked Poirot.

"Well, he could take a prominent part in local affairs. Or stand for Parliament. He's a much more able man then poor Mr. Masterton. I don't know if you've ever heard Mr. Masterton on a platform—a most halting and uninspired speaker. He owes his position entirely to his wife. It's Mrs. Masterton who's the power behind the throne. She's got all the drive and the initiative and the political acumen."

Poirot shuddered inwardly at the thought of being married to Mrs. Masterton, but he agreed quite truthfully with Miss Brewis' words.

"Yes," he said, "she is all that you say. A *femme formidable*," he murmured to himself.

"Sir George doesn't seem ambitious," went on Miss Brewis. "He seems quite content to live here and potter about and play the country squire and just go to London occasionally to attend to all his city directorships and all that, but he could make far more of himself than that with his abilities. He's really a very remarkable man, M. Poirot. That woman never understood him. She just regards him as a kind of machine for tipping out fur coats and jewels and expensive clothes. If he were married to someone who really appreciated his abilities—" She broke off, her voice wavering uncertainly.

Poirot looked at her with a real compassion. Miss Brewis was in love with her employer. She gave him a faithful, loyal and passionate devotion of which he was probably quite unaware and in which he would certainly not be interested. To Sir George, Amanda Brewis was an efficient machine who took the drudgery of daily life off his shoulders, who answered telephone calls, wrote letters, engaged servants, ordered meals and generally made life smooth for him. Poirot doubted if he had ever once thought of her as a woman. And that, he reflected, had its dangers. Women could work themselves up, they could reach an alarming pitch of hysteria unnoticed by the oblivious male who was the object of their devotion.

"A sly, scheming, clever cat, that's what she is," said Miss Brewis tearfully.

"You say is, not was, I observe," said Poirot.

"Of course she isn't dead!" said Miss Brewis, scornfully. "Gone off with a man, that's what she's done! That's her type."

"It is possible. It is always possible," said Poirot. He took another piece of toast, inspected the marmalade pot gloomily and looked down the table to see if there was any kind of jam. There was none, so he resigned himself to butter.

"It's the only explanation," said Miss Brewis. "Of course he wouldn't think of it."

"Has there—been any—trouble with men?" asked Poirot delicately.

"Oh, she's been very clever," said Miss Brewis.

"You mean you have not observed anything of the kind?"

"She'd be careful that I shouldn't," said Miss Brewis.

"But you think that there may have been—what shall I say—surreptitious episodes?"

"She's done her best to make a fool of Michael Weyman," said Miss Brewis. "Taking him down to see the camellia gardens at this time of year! Pretending she's so interested in the tennis pavilion."

"After all, that is his business for being here and I understand Sir George is having it built principally to please his wife."

"She's no good at tennis," said Miss Brewis, "she's no good at any games. Just wants an attractive setting to sit in, while other people run about and get hot. Oh yes, she's done her best to make a fool of Michael Weyman. She'd probably have done it too if he hadn't other fish to fry."

"Ah," said Poirot, helping himself to a very little marmalade, placing it on the corner of a piece of toast and taking a mouthful dubiously. "So he has other fish to fry, Mr. Weyman?"

"It was Mrs. Legge who recommended him to Sir George," said Miss Brewis. "She knew him before she was married. Chelsea, I understand, and all that. She used to paint, you know."

"She seems a very attractive and intelligent young woman," said Poirot tentatively.

"Oh yes, she's very intelligent," said Miss Brewis. "She's had a university education and I daresay could have made a career for herself if she hadn't married."

"Has she been married long?"

"About three years, I believe. I don't think the marriage has turned out very well."

"There is—the incompatibility?"

"He's a queer young man, very moody. Wanders off a lot by himself and I've heard him very bad-tempered with her sometimes."

"Ah, well," said Poirot, "the quarrels, the reconciliations, they are part of early married life. Without them it is possible that life would be drab."

"She's spent a good deal of time with Michael Weyman since he's been down here," said Miss Brewis. "I think he was in love with her before she married Alec Legge. I daresay it's only a flirtation on her side."

"But Mr. Legge was not pleased about it, perhaps?"

"One never knows with him, he's so vague. But I think he's been even moodier than usual lately."

"Did he admire Lady Stubbs, perhaps?"

"I daresay she thought he did. She thinks she only has to hold up a finger for any man to fall in love with her!"

"In any case, if she has gone off with a man, as you suggest, it is not Mr. Weyman, for Mr. Weyman is still here."

"It's somebody she's been meeting on the sly, I've no doubt," said Miss

Brewis. "She often slips out of the house on the quiet and goes off into the woods by herself. She was out the night before last. Yawning and saying she was going up to bed. I caught sight of her not half an hour later slipping out by the side door with a shawl over her head."

Poirot looked thoughtfully at the woman opposite him. He wondered if any reliance at all were to be placed in Miss Brewis' statements where Lady Stubbs was concerned, or whether it was entirely wishful thinking on her part. Mrs. Folliat, he was sure, did not share Miss Brewis' ideas and Mrs. Folliat knew Hattie much better than Miss Brewis knew her. If Lady Stubbs had run away with a lover it would clearly suit Miss Brewis' book very well. She would be left to console the bereaved husband and to arrange for him efficiently the details of divorce. But that did not make it true, or probable, or even likely. If Hattie Stubbs had left with a lover, she had chosen a very curious time to do so, Poirot thought. For his own part he did not believe she had.

Miss Brewis sniffed through her nose and gathered together various scattered correspondence.

"If Sir George really wants those advertisements put in, I suppose I'd better see about it," she said. "Complete nonsense and waste of time. Oh, good morning, Mrs. Masterton."

The door opened with authority and Mrs. Masterton walked in.

"Inquest is set for Thursday, I hear," she boomed. " 'Morning, M. Poirot."

Miss Brewis paused, her hand full of letters.

"Anything I can do for you, Mrs. Masterton?" she asked.

"No thank you, Miss Brewis. I expect you've plenty on your hands this morning, but I do want to thank you for all the excellent work you put in yesterday. You're such a good organizer and such a hard worker. We're all very grateful."

"Thank you, Mrs. Masterton."

"Now don't let me keep you. I'll just sit down and have a word with M. Poirot."

"Enchanted, Madame," said Poirot. He had risen to his feet and he bowed.

Mrs. Masterton pulled out a chair and sat down. Miss Brewis left the room, quite restored to her usual efficient self.

"Marvellous woman, that," said Mrs. Masterton. "Don't know what the Stubbses would do without her. Running a house takes some doing nowadays. Poor Hattie couldn't have coped with it. Extraordinary business, this, M. Poirot. I came to ask you what you thought about it."

"What do you yourself think, Madame?"

"Well, it's an unpleasant thing to face, but I should say we've got some pathological character in this part of the world. Not a native, I hope. Perhaps been let out of an asylum—they're always letting 'em out half cured nowadays. What I mean is no one would ever want to strangle that Tucker girl. There couldn't be any motive, I mean, except some abnormal one. And if this man, whoever he is, *is* abnormal I should say he's probably strangled that poor girl, Hattie Stubbs, as well. She hasn't very much sense you know, poor child. If she met an ordinary-looking man and he asked her to come and look at something in the woods she'd probably go like a lamb, quite unsuspecting and docile."

"You think her body is somewhere on the estate?"

"Yes, M. Poirot, I do. They'll find it once they search around. Mind you, with about sixty-five acres of woodland here, it'll take some finding, if it's been dragged into the bushes or tumbled down a slope into the trees. What they need is bloodhounds," said Mrs. Masterton, looking as she spoke exactly like a bloodhound herself. "Bloodhounds! I shall ring up the Chief Constable myself and say so."

"It is very possible that you are right, Madame," said Poirot. It was clearly the only thing one could say to Mrs. Masterton.

"Of course I'm right," said Mrs. Masterton, "but I must say, you know, it makes me very uneasy because the fellow is somewhere about. I'm calling in at the village when I leave here, telling the mothers to be very careful about their daughters—not let 'em go about alone. It's not a nice thought, Mr. Poirot, to have a killer in our midst."

"A little point, Madame. How could a strange man have obtained admission to the boathouse? That would need a key."

"Oh, that," said Mrs. Masterton, "that's easy enough. She came out, of course."

"Came out of the boathouse?"

"Yes. I expect she got bored, like girls do. Probably wandered out and looked about her. The most likely thing, I think, is that she actually saw Hattie Stubbs murdered. Heard a struggle or something, went to see and the man having disposed of Lady Stubbs naturally had to kill her too. Easy enough for him to take her back to the boathouse, dump her there and come out, pulling the door behind him. It was a Yale lock. It would pull to, and lock."

Poirot nodded gently. It was not his purpose to argue with Mrs. Masterton or to point out to her the interesting fact which she had completely overlooked, that if Marlene Tucker had been killed away from the boathouse, somebody must have known enough about the murder game to put her back in the exact place and position which the victim was supposed to assume. Instead, he said gently,

"Sir George Stubbs is confident that his wife is still alive."

"That's what he says, man, because he wants to believe it. He was very devoted to her, you know." She added, rather unexpectedly, "I like George Stubbs in spite of his origins and his city background and all that, he goes down very well in the country. The worst that can be said about him is that he's a bit of a snob. And after all, social snobbery's harmless enough."

Poirot said somewhat cynically,

"In these days, Madame, surely money has become as acceptable as good birth."

"My dear man, I couldn't agree with you more. There's no need for him to be a snob—only got to buy the place and throw his money about and we'd all come and call! But actually, the man's liked. It's not only his money. Of course Amy Folliat's had something to do with that. She has sponsored them and mind you, she's got a lot of influence in this part of the world. Why, there have been Folliats here since Tudor times."

"There have always been Folliats at Nasse House," Poirot murmured to himself.

"Yes," Mrs. Masterton sighed. "It's sad, the toll taken by the war. Young men killed in battle—death duties and all that. Then whoever comes into a place can't afford to keep it up and has to sell—"

"But Mrs. Folliat, although she has lost her home, still lives on the estate."

"Yes. She's made the Lodge quite charming too. Have you been inside it?"

"No—we parted at the door."

"It wouldn't be everybody's cup of tea," said Mrs. Masterton. "To live at the Lodge of your old home and see strangers in possession. But to do Amy Folliat justice I don't think she feels bitter about that. In fact, she engineered the whole thing. There's no doubt she imbued Hattie with the idea of living down here, and got her to persuade George Stubbs into it. The thing, I think, that Amy Folliat couldn't have borne was to see the place turned into a hotel or institution, or carved up for building." She rose to her feet. "Well, I must be getting along. I'm a busy woman."

"Of course. You have to talk to the Chief Constable about bloodhounds."

Mrs. Masterton gave a sudden deep bray of laughter. "Used to breed 'em at one time," she said. "People tell me I'm a bit like a bloodhound myself."

Poirot was slightly taken aback and she was quick enough to see it.

"I bet you've been thinking so, M. Poirot," she said.

13

AFTER MRS. MASTERTON had left, Poirot went out and strolled through the woods. His nerves were not quite what they should be. He felt an irresistible desire to look behind every bush and to consider every thicket of rhododendron as a possible hiding place for a body. He came at last to the Folly and going inside it he sat down on the stone bench there, to rest his feet which were, as was his custom, enclosed in tight pointed patent leather shoes.

Through the trees he could catch faint glimmers of the river and of the wooded banks on the opposite side. He found himself agreeing with the young architect that this was no place to put an architectural fantasy of this kind. Gaps could be cut in the trees, of course, but even then there would be no proper vista. Whereas, as Michael Weyman had said, on the grassy bank near the house a Folly could have been erected with a delightful vista right down the river to Helmmouth. Poirot's thoughts flew off at a tangent. Helmmouth, the yacht, *Esperance,* and Etienne De Sousa. The whole thing must tie up in some kind of pattern, but what the pattern was he could not visualise. Tempting strands of it showed here and there but that was all.

Something that glittered caught his eye and he bent to pick it up. It had come to rest in a small crack of the concrete base of the temple. He held it in the palm of his hand and looked at it with a faint stirring of recognition. It was a little gold airplane charm. As he frowned at it, a picture came into his mind. A bracelet. A gold bracelet hung over with dangling charms. He was sitting once more in the tent and the voice of Madame Zuleika, alias Peggy Legge, was talking of dark women and journeys across the sea and good fortune in a letter. Yes, she had had on a bracelet from which depended a multiplicity of small gold objects. One of these modern fashions which repeated the fashions of Poirot's early days. Probably that was why it had made an impression on him. Some time or other, presumably, Mrs. Legge had sat here in the Folly and one of the charms had fallen from her bracelet. Perhaps she had not even noticed it. It might have been some days ago—weeks perhaps. Or—it might have been yesterday afternoon. . . .

Poirot considered that latter point. Then he heard footsteps outside and looked up sharply. A figure came round to the front of the Folly and stopped, startled, at the sight of Poirot. Poirot looked with a considering eye on the slim, fair young man wearing a shirt on which a variety of tortoise and turtle was depicted. The shirt was unmistakable. He had observed it closely yesterday when its wearer was throwing coconuts.

He noticed that the young man was almost unusually perturbed. He said quickly in a foreign accent,

"I beg your pardon—I did not know—"

Poirot smiled gently at him but with a reproving air.

"I am afraid," said Poirot gently, "that you are trespassing."

"Yes, I am sorry."

"You come from the Hostel?"

"Yes. Yes, I do. I thought perhaps one could get through the woods this way and so to the quay."

"I am afraid," said Poirot gently, "that you will have to go back the way you came. There is no through road."

The young man said again, showing all his teeth in a would-be agreeable smile,

"I am sorry. I am very sorry."

He bowed and turned away.

Poirot came out of the Folly and back on to the path, watching the boy retreat. When he got to the ending of the path, he looked over his shoulder. Then, seeing Poirot watching him, he quickened his pace and disappeared round the bend.

"*Eh bien,*" said Poirot to himself, "is this a murderer I have seen, or is it not?"

The young man had certainly been at the Fête yesterday and had scowled when he had collided with Poirot, and just as certainly therefore he must know quite well that there was no through path by way of the woods to the ferry. If, indeed, he had been looking for a path to the ferry he would not have taken this path by the Folly but would have kept on the lower level near the river. Moreover, he had arrived at the Folly with the air of one who has reached his rendezvous, and who is badly startled at finding the wrong person at the meeting place.

"So it is like this," said Poirot to himself. "He came here to meet someone. Who did he come to meet?" He added as an afterthought, "And why?"

He strolled down to the bend of the path and looked at it where it wound away into the trees. There was no sign of the young man in the turtle shirt now. Presumably he had deemed it prudent to retreat as rapidly as possible. Poirot retraced his steps, shaking his head.

Lost in thought, he came quietly round the side of the Folly, and stopped on the threshold, startled in his turn. Peggy Legge was there on her knees, her head bent down the cracks in the flooring. She jumped up, startled.

"Oh, M. Poirot, you gave me such a shock. I didn't hear you coming."

"You were looking for something, Madame?"

"I—no, not exactly."

"You had lost something, perhaps," said Poirot. "Dropped something. Or perhaps"—he adopted a roguish, gallant air—"or perhaps, Madame, it is a rendezvous. I am, most unfortunately, not the person you came to meet?"

She had recovered her aplomb by now.

"Does one ever have a rendezvous in the middle of the morning?" she demanded, questioningly.

"Sometimes," said Poirot, "one has to have a rendezvous at the only time one can. Husbands," he added sententiously, "are sometimes jealous."

"I doubt if mine is," said Peggy Legge.

She said the words lightly enough, but behind them Poirot heard an undertone of bitterness.

"He's so completely engrossed in his own affairs."

"All women complain of that in husbands," said Poirot, "especially in English husbands," he added.

"You foreigners are more gallant."

"We know," said Poirot, "that it is necessary to tell a woman at least once a week, and preferably three or four times, that we love her; and that it is also wise to bring her a few flowers, to pay her a few compliments, to tell her that she looks well in her new dress or her new hat."

"Is that what you do?"

"I, Madame, am not a husband," said Hercule Poirot. "Alas!" he added.

"I'm sure there's no alas about it. I'm sure you're quite delighted to be a carefree bachelor."

"No, no, Madame, it is terrible all that I have missed in life."

"I think one's a fool to marry," said Peggy Legge.

"You regret the days when you painted in your studio in Chelsea?"

"You seem to know all about me, M. Poirot."

"I am a gossip," said Hercule Poirot. "I like to hear all about people." He went on: "Do you really regret, Madame?"

"Oh, I don't know." She sat down impatiently on the seat. Poirot sat beside her.

He witnessed once more the phenomenon to which he was becoming accustomed. This attractive, red-haired girl was about to say things to him that she would have thought twice about saying to an Englishman.

"I hoped," she said, "that when we came down here for a holiday away from everything, that things would be the same again. . . . But it hasn't worked out like that."

"No?"

"No. Alec's just as moody and—oh, I don't know—wrapped up in himself. I don't know what's the matter with him. He's so nervy and on edge. People ring him up and leave queer messages for him and he won't tell me anything. That's what makes me mad. He won't tell me anything! I thought at first it was some other woman, but I don't think it is. Not really. . . ."

But her voice held a certain doubt which Poirot was quick to notice.

"Did you enjoy your tea yesterday afternoon, Madame?" he asked.

"Enjoy my tea?" She frowned at him, her thoughts seeming to come back from a long way away. Then she said hastily, "Oh yes. You've no idea how exhausting it was, sitting in that tent muffled up in all those veils. It was stifling."

"The tea tent also must have been somewhat stifling?"

"Oh, yes, it was. However, there's nothing like a cuppa, is there?"

"You were searching for something just now, were you not, Madame? Would it by any possibility be this?" He held out in his hand the little gold charm.

"I—oh, yes. Oh—thank you, M. Poirot. Where did you find it?"

"It was here, on the floor, in that crack over there."

"I must have dropped it some time."

"Yesterday?"

"Oh, no, not yesterday. It was before that."

"But surely, Madame, I remember seeing that particular charm on your wrist when you were telling me my fortune."

Nobody could tell a deliberate lie better than Hercule Poirot. He spoke with complete assurance and before that assurance, Peggy Legge's eyelids dropped.

"I don't really remember," she said. "I only noticed this morning that it was missing."

"Then I am happy," said Poirot gallantly, "to be able to restore it to you."

She was turning the little charm over nervously in her fingers. Now she rose.

"Well, thank you, M. Poirot, thank you very much," she said. Her breath was coming rather unevenly and her eyes were nervous.

She hurried out of the Folly. Poirot leaned back in the seat and nodded his head slowly.

"No," he said to himself, "no, you did not go to the tea tent yesterday afternoon. It was not because you wanted your tea that you were so anxious to know if it was four o'clock. It was here you came yesterday afternoon. Here, to the Folly. Halfway to the boathouse. You came here to meet someone."

Once again he heard footsteps approaching. Rapid, impatient footsteps. "And here perhaps," said Poirot, smiling in anticipation, "comes whoever it was that Mrs. Legge came up here to meet."

But then, as Alec Legge came round the corner of the Folly, Poirot ejaculated:

"Wrong again."

"Eh? What's that?" Alec Legge looked startled.

"I said," explained Poirot, "that I was wrong again. I'm not often wrong," he explained, "and it exasperates me. It was not you I expected to see."

"Whom did you expect to see?" asked Alec Legge.

Poirot replied promptly.

"A young man—a boy almost—in one of those gaily patterned shirts with turtles on it."

He was pleased at the effect of his words. Alec Legge took a step forward. He said rather incoherently,

"How do you know? How did—what d'you mean?"

"I am psychic," said Hercule Poirot, and closed his eyes. Alec Legge took another couple of steps forward. Poirot was conscious that a very angry man was standing in front of him.

"What the devil did you mean?" he demanded.

"Your friend has, I think," said Poirot, "gone back to the Youth Hostel. If you want to see him you will have to go there to find him."

"So that's it," muttered Alec Legge.

He dropped down at the other end of the stone bench.

"So that's why you're down here? It wasn't a question of 'giving away the prizes.' I might have known better." He turned towards Poirot. His face was haggard and unhappy. "I know what it must seem like," he said. "I know what the whole thing looks like. But it isn't as you think it is. I'm being victimized. I tell you that once you get into these people's clutches, it isn't so easy to get out of them. And I want to get out of them. That's the point. I want to get out of them. You get desperate, you know. You feel like taking desperate measures. You feel you're caught like a rat in a trap and there's nothing you can do. Oh, well, what's the good of talking! You know what you want to know now, I suppose. You've got your evidence."

He got up, stumbled a little as though he could hardly see his way, then rushed off energetically without a backward look.

Hercule Poirot remained behind with his eyes very wide open and his eyebrows rising.

"All this is very curious," he murmured. "Curious and interesting. I have the evidence I need, have I? Evidence of what? Murder?"

14

I

INSPECTOR BLAND SAT in Helmmouth Police Station. Superintendent Baldwin, a large, comfortable-looking man, sat on the other side of the table. Between the two men, on the table, was a black sodden mass. Inspector Bland poked at it with a cautious forefinger.

"That's her hat all right," he said. "I'm sure of it, though I don't suppose I could swear to it. She fancied that shape, it seems. So her maid told me. She'd got one or two of them. A pale pink and a sort of puce color but yesterday she was wearing the black one. Yes, this is it. And you fished it out of the river? That makes it look as though it's the way we think it is."

"No certainty yet," said Baldwin. "After all," he added, "anyone could throw a hat into the river."

"Yes," said Bland, "they could throw it in from the boathouse, or they could throw it in off a yacht."

"The yacht's sewed up all right," said Baldwin. "If she's there, alive or dead, she's still there."

"He hasn't been ashore today?"

"Not so far. He's on board. He's been sitting out in a deck chair smoking a cigar."

Inspector Bland glanced at the clock.

"Almost time to go aboard," he said.

"Think you'll find her?" asked Baldwin.

"I wouldn't bank on it," said Bland. "I've got the feeling, you know, that he's a clever devil." He was lost in thought for a moment, poking again at the hat. Then he said, "What about the body—if there was a body? Any ideas about that?"

"Yes," said Baldwin, "I talked to Otterweight this morning. Ex-coast guard man. I always consult him in anything to do with tides and currents. About the time the lady went into the Helm, if she did go into the Helm, the tide was just on the ebb. There is a full moon now and it would be flowing swiftly. Reckon she'd be carried out to sea and the current would take her towards the Cornish coast. There's no certainty where the body would fetch up or if it would fetch up at all. One or two drownings we've had here, we've never recovered the body. It gets broken up, too, on the rocks. Here, by Start Point. On the other hand, it might fetch up any day."

"If it doesn't, it's going to be difficult," said Bland.

"You're certain in your own mind that she did go into the river?"

"I don't see what else it can be," said Inspector Bland sombrely. "We've checked up, you know, on the buses and the trains. This place is a cul-de-sac. She was wearing conspicuous clothes and she didn't take any others with her. So I should say she never left Nasse. Either her body's in the sea or else it's hidden somewhere on the property. What I want now," he went on heavily, "is motive. And the body, of course," he added, as an afterthought. "Can't get anywhere until I find the body."

"What about the other girl?"

"She saw it—or she saw something. We'll get at the facts in the end, but it won't be easy."

Baldwin in his turn looked up at the clock.

"Time to go," he said.

The two police officers were received on board the *Esperance* with all De Sousa's charming courtesy. He offered them drinks which they refused, and went on to express a kindly interest in their activities.

"You are further forward with your enquiries regarding the death of this young girl?"

"We're progressing." Inspecotor Bland told him.

The Superintendent took up the running and expressed very delicately the object of their visit.

"You would like to search the *Esperance*?" De Sousa did not seem annoyed. Instead he seemed rather amused. "But why? You think I conceal the murderer or do you think perhaps that I am the murderer myself?"

"It's necessary, Mr. De Sousa, as I'm sure you'll understand. A search warrant—"

De Sousa raised his hands.

"But I am anxious to co-operate—eager! Let this be all among friends. You are welcome to search where you will in my boat. Ah, perhaps you think that I have here my cousin, Lady Stubbs? You think, perhaps, she has run away from her husband and taken shelter with me? But search, gentlemen, by all means search."

The search was duly undertaken. It was a thorough one. In the end, striving to conceal their chagrin, the two police officers took leave of Mr. De Sousa.

"You have found nothing? How disappointing. But I told you that was so. You will perhaps have some refreshment now. No?"

He accompanied them to where their boat lay alongside.

"And for myself," he asked, "I am free to depart? You understand it becomes a little boring here. The weather is good. I should like very much to proceed to Plymouth."

"If you would be kind enough, sir, to remain here for the inquest—that is tomorrow—in case the Coroner should wish to ask you anything."

"Why, certainly. I want to do all that I can. But after that?"

"After that, sir," said Superintendent Baldwin, his face wooden, "you are of course at liberty to proceed where you will."

The last thing they saw as the launch moved away from the yacht was De Sousa's smiling face looking down on them.

II

The inquest was almost painfully devoid of interest. Apart from the medical evidence and evidence of identity, there was little to feed the curiosity of the spectators. An adjournment was asked for and granted. The whole proceedings had been purely formal.

What followed the inquest, however, was not quite so formal. Inspector Bland spent the afternoon taking a trip in that well-known pleasure steamer, the *Devon Belle*. Leaving Brixwell at about three o'clock, it rounded the headland, proceeded around the coast, entered the mouth of the Helm and went up the river. There were about two hundred and thirty people on board besides Inspector Bland. He sat on the starboard side of the boat, scanning the wooded shore. They came round a bend in the river and passed the isolated gray-tiled boathouse that belonged to Hoodown Park. Inspector Bland looked surreptitiously at his watch. It was just quarter past four. They were coming now close beside the Nasse boathouse. It nestled remote in its trees with its little balcony and its small quay below. There was no sign apparent that there was someone inside. P.C. Hoskins, in accordance with orders, was on duty there.

Not far from the boathouse steps was a small launch. In the launch were a man and girl in holiday kit. They were indulging in what seemed like some rather rough horseplay. The girl was screaming, the man was playfully pretending he was going to duck her overboard. At the same moment a stentorian voice spoke through a megaphone.

"Ladies and gentlemen," it boomed, "you are now approaching the famous village of Gitcham where we shall remain for three quarters of an hour and where you can have a crab or lobster tea, as well as Devonshire cream. On your right are the grounds of Nasse House. You will pass the house itself in two or three minutes; it is just visible through the trees. Originally the home of Sir Gervase Folliat, a contemporary of Sir Francis Drake who sailed with him in his voyage to the new world, it is now the property of Sir George Stubbs. On your left is the famous Gooseacre Rock. There, ladies and gentlemen, it was the habit to deposit scolding wives at low tide and to leave them there until the water came up to their necks."

Everybody on the *Devon Belle* stared with fascinated interest at the

Gooseacre Rock. Jokes were made and there were many shrill giggles and guffaws.

While this was happening, the holidaymaker in the boat, with a final scuffle, did push his lady friend overboard. Leaning over, he held her in the water, laughing and saying, "No, I won't pull you out till you've promised to behave."

Nobody, however, observed this with the exception of Inspector Bland. They had all been listening to the megaphone, staring for the first sight of Nasse House through the trees, and gazing with fascinated interest at the Gooseacre Rock.

The holidaymaker released the girl, she sank under water and a few moments later reappeared on the other side of the boat. She swam to it and got in, heaving herself over the side with practiced skill. Policewoman Alice Jones was an accomplished swimmer.

Inspector Bland came ashore at Gitcham with the other two hundred and thirty passengers and consumed a lobster tea with Devonshire cream and scones. He said to himself as he did so: "So it could be done, and no one would notice!"

III

While Inspector Bland was doing his experiment on the Helm, Hercule Poirot was experimenting with a tent on the lawn at Nasse House. It was in actual fact the same tent where Madame Zuleika had told her fortunes. When the rest of the marquees and stands had been dismantled Poirot had asked for this to remain behind.

He went into it now, closed the flaps and went to the back of it. Deftly he unlaced the flaps there, slipped out, relaced them, and plunged into the hedge of rhododendron that immediately backed the tent. Slipping between a couple of bushes, he soon reached a small rustic arbor. It was a kind of summerhouse with a closed door. Poirot opened the door and went inside.

It was very dim inside because very little light came in through the rhododendrons which had grown up round it since it had been first placed there many years ago. There was a box there with croquet balls in it, and some old rusted hoops. There were one or two broken hockey sticks, a good many earwigs and spiders, and a round irregular mark on the dust on the floor. At this Poirot looked for some time. He knelt down, and taking a little yard measure from his pocket he measured its dimensions carefully. Then he nodded his head in a satisfied fashion.

He slipped out quietly, shutting the door behind him. Then he pursued an oblique course through the rhododendron bushes. He worked his way up the hill in this way and came out a short time after on the path which led to the Folly and down from there to the boathouse.

He did not visit the Folly this time, but went straight down the zigzagging way until he reached the boathouse. He had the key with him and he opened the door and went in.

Except for the removal of the body, and of the tea tray with its glass and plate, it was just as he remembered it. The police had noted and photographed all that it contained. He went over now to the table where the pile of comics lay. He turned them over and his expression was not unlike Inspector Bland's had been as he noted the words Marlene had doodled down there before she died. "Jackie Blake goes with Susan Brown." "Peter pinches girls at the pictures." "Georgie Porgie kisses hikers in the wood." "Biddy Fox likes boys." "Albert goes with Doreen."

He found the remarks pathetic in their young crudity. He remembered Marlene's plain, rather spotty face. He suspected that boys had not pinched Marlene at the pictures. Frustrated. Marlene had got a vicarious thrill by her spying and peering at her young contemporaries. She had spied on people, she had snooped, and she had seen things. Things that she was not meant to have seen—things, usually, of small importance, but on one occasion perhaps something of more importance? Something of whose importance she herself had had no idea?

It was all conjecture. and Poirot shook his head doubtfully. He replaced the pile of comics neatly on the table, his passion for tidiness always in the ascendant. As he did so, he was suddenly assailed with the feeling of something missing. Something—what was it? Something that ought to have been there. . . . Something—he shook his head as the elusive impression faded.

He went slowly out of the boathouse, unhappy and displeased with himself. He, Hercule Poirot, had been summoned to prevent a murder— and he had not prevented it. It had happened. What was even more humiliating was that he had no real ideas, even now, as to what had really happened. It was ignominious. And tomorrow he must return to London defeated. His Ego was seriously deflated—even his moustaches drooped.

15

IT WAS A fortnight later that Inspector Bland had a long and unsatisfying interview with the Chief Constable of the County.

Major Merrall had irritable tufted eyebrows and looked rather like an angry terrier. But his men all liked him and respected his judgment.

"Well, well, well," said Major Merrall. "What have we got? Nothing that we can act on. This fellow De Sousa now? We can't connect him in any way with the Girl Guide. If Lady Stubbs' body had turned up, that would have been different." He brought his eyebrows down towards his nose and glared at Bland. "You think there is a body, don't you?"

"What do you think, sir?"

"Oh, I agree with you. Otherwise, we'd have traced her by now. Unless, of course, she'd made her plans very carefully. And I don't see the least indication of that. She'd no money, you know. We've been into all the financial side of it. Sir George had the money. He made her a very generous allowance, but she's not got a stiver of her own. And there's no trace of a lover. No rumor of one, no gossip—and there would be, mark you, in a country district like that."

He took a turn up and down the floor.

"The plain fact of it is that we don't know. We think De Sousa, for some unknown reason of his own, made away with his cousin. The most probable thing is that he got her to meet him down at the boathouse, took her aboard the launch and pushed her overboard. You've tested that that could happen?"

"Good Lord, sir, you could drown a whole boatful of people during holiday time in the river or on the seashore. Nobody'd think anything of it. Everyone spends their time squealing and pushing each other off things. But the thing De Sousa didn't know about was that that girl was in the boathouse, bored to death with nothing to do and ten to one was looking out of the window."

"Hoskins looked out of the window and watched the performance you put up, and you didn't see him?"

"No, sir. You'd have no idea anyone was in that boathouse unless they came out on the balcony and showed themselves—"

"Perhaps the girl did come out on the balcony. De Sousa realizes she's seen what he's doing, so he comes ashore and deals with her, gets her to let him into the boathouse by asking her what she's doing there. She tells him, pleased with her part in the murder hunt. He puts the cord round her neck in a playful manner—and whoooosh"—Major Merrall made an expressive gesture with his hands—"that's that! Okay, Bland, okay. Let's say that's how it happened. Pure guesswork. We haven't got any evidence. We haven't got a body, and if we attempted to detain De Sousa in this country we'd have a hornet's nest about our ears. We'll have to let him go."

"Is he going, sir?"

"He's laying up his yacht a week from now. Going back to his blasted island."

"So we haven't got much time," said Inspector Bland gloomily.

"There are other possibilities, I suppose?"

"Oh, yes, sir, there are several possibilities. I still hold to it that she must have been murdered by somebody who was in on the facts of the murder hunt. We can clear two people completely. Sir George Stubbs and Captain Warburton. They were running shows on the lawn and taking charge of things the entire afternoon. They are vouched for by dozens of people. The same applies to Mrs. Masterton, if, that is, one can include her at all."

"Include everybody," said Major Merrall. "She's continually ringing me up about bloodhounds. In a detective story," he added wistfully, "she'd be just the woman who had done it. But, dash it, I've known Connie Masterton pretty well all my life. I just can't see her going round strangling Girl Guides or dispensing of mysterious exotic beauties. Now then, who else is there?"

"There's Mrs. Oliver," said Bland. "She devised the murder hunt. She's rather eccentric and she was away on her own for a good part of the afternoon. Then there's Mr. Alec Legge."

"Fellow in the pink cottage, eh?"

"Yes. He left the show fairly early on, or he wasn't seen there. He says he got fed up with it and walked back to his cottage. On the other hand, old Merdell—that's the old boy down at the quay who looks after people's boats for them and helps with the parking—he says Alec Legge passed him going back to the cottage about five o'clock. Not earlier. That leaves about an hour of his time unaccounted for. He says, of course, that Merdell has no idea of time and was quite wrong as to when he saw him. And after all the old man is ninety-two."

"Rather unsatisfactory." said Major Merrall. "No motive or anything of that kind to tie him in?"

"He might have been having an affair with Lady Stubbs," said Bland, doubtfully, "and she might have been threatening to tell his wife, and he might have done her in, and the girl might have seen it happen—"

"And he concealed Lady Stubbs' body somewhere?"

"Yes. But I'm blessed if I know how or where. My men have searched that sixty-five acres and there's no trace anywhere of disturbed earth, and I should say that by now we've rooted under every bush there is! Still, say he did manage to hide the body, he could have thrown her hat into the river as a blind. And Marlene Tucker saw him and so he disposed of her? That part of it's always the same." Inspector Bland paused, then said: "And, of course, there's Mrs. Legge—"

"What have we got on her?"

"She wasn't in the tea tent from four to half past as she says she was," said Inspector Bland slowly. "I spotted that as soon as I'd talked to her and to Mrs. Folliat. Evidence supports Mrs. Folliat's statement. And that's the particular, vital half hour." Again he paused. "Then there's the architect, young Michael Weyman. It's difficult to tie him up with it in any way, but he's what I should call a likely murderer—one of those cocky, nervy young fellows. Would kill anyone, and not turn a hair about it. In with a loose set, I shouldn't wonder."

"You're so damned respectable, Bland," said Major Merrall. "How does he account for his movements?"

"Very vague, sir. Very vague indeed."

"That proves he's a genuine architect," said Major Merrall with feeling.

He had recently built himself a house near the seacoast. "They're so vague, I wonder they're alive at all sometimes."

"Doesn't know where he was or when and there's nobody who seems to have seen him. There is some evidence that Lady Stubbs was keen on him."

"I suppose you're hinting at one of these sex murders?"

"I'm only looking about for what I can find, sir," said Inspector Bland with dignity. "And then there's Miss Brewis—" He paused. It was a long pause.

"That's the secretary, isn't it?"

"Yes, sir. Very efficient woman."

Again there was a pause. Major Merrall eyed his subordinate keenly.

"You've got something on your mind about her, haven't you?" he said.

"Yes, I have, sir. You see, she admits quite openly that she was in the boathouse at about the time the murder must have been committed."

"Would she do that if she was guilty?"

"She might," said Inspector Bland, slowly. "Actually, it's the best thing she could do. You see, if she picks up a tray with a cake and a fruit drink and tells everyone she's taking that for the child down there—well, then, her presence is accounted for. She goes there and comes back and says the girl was alive at that time. We've taken her word for it. But if you remember, sir, and look again at the medical evidence, Dr. Cook's time of death is between four o'clock and quarter to five. We've only Miss Brewis' word for it that Marlene was alive at a quarter past four. And there's one curious point that came up about her testimony. She told me that it was Lady Stubbs who told her to take cakes and a fruit drink to Marlene. But another witness said quite definitely that that wasn't the sort of thing that Lady Stubbs would think about. And I think, you know, that they're right there. It's not like Lady Stubbs. Lady Stubbs was a dumb beauty wrapped up in herself and her own appearance. She never seems to have ordered meals or taken an interest in household management or thought of anybody at all except her own handsome self. The more I think of it, the more it seems most unlikely that she should have told Miss Brewis to take anything to the Girl Guide."

"You know, Bland," said Merrall, "you've got something there. But what's her motive, if so?"

"No motive for killing the girl," said Bland, "but I do think, you know, that she might have a motive for killing Lady Stubbs. According to M. Poirot, whom I told you about, she's head over heels in love with her employer. Supposing she followed Lady Stubbs into the woods and killed her and that Marlene Tucker, bored in the boathouse, came out and happened to see it? Then of course she'd have to kill Marlene, too. What would she do next? Put the girl's body in the boathouse, come back to the house, fetch the tray and go down to the boathouse again. Then she's covered her own absence from the Fête and we've got her testimony, our only reliable testimony on the face of it, that Marlene Tucker was alive at a quarter past four."

"Well," said Major Merrall with a sigh, "keep after it, Bland. Keep after it. What do you think she did with Lady Stubbs' body, if she's the guilty party?"

"Hid it in the woods, buried it, or threw it into the river."

"The last would be rather difficult, wouldn't it?"

"It depends where the murder was committed," said the Inspector. "She's quite a hefty woman. If it was not far from the boathouse, she could have carried her down there and thrown her off the edge of the quay."

"With every pleasure steamer on the Helm looking on?"

"It would be just another piece of horseplay. Risky, but possible. But I think it far more likely that she hid the body somewhere, and just threw the hat into the Helm. It's possible, you see, that she, knowing the house and grounds well, might know some place where you could conceal a body. She may have managed to dispose of it in the river later. Who knows? That is, of course, if she did it," added Inspector Bland as an afterthought. "But actually, sir, I stick to De Sousa—"

Major Merrall had been noting down points on a pad. He looked up now, clearing his throat.

"It comes to this, then. We can summarize it as follows: we've got five or six people who could have killed Marlene Tucker. Some of them are more likely than others, but that's as far as we can go. In a general way, we know why she was killed. She was killed because she saw something. But until we know exactly what it was she saw—we don't know who killed her."

"Put like that, you make it sound a bit difficult, sir."

"Oh, it is difficult. But we shall get there—in the end."

"And meantime that chap will have left England—laughing in his sleeve—having got away with two murders."

"You're fairly sure about him, aren't you? I don't say you're wrong. All the same—"

The Chief Constable was silent for a moment or two, then he said with a shrug of his shoulders,

"Anyway, it's better than having one of these psychopathic murderers. We'd probably be having a third murder on our hands by now."

"They do say things go in threes," said the Inspector gloomily.

He repeated that remark the following morning when he heard that old Merdell, returning home from a visit to his favorite pub across the river at Gitcham, must have exceeded his usual potations and fallen in the river when boarding the quay. His boat was found adrift, and the old man's body was recovered that evening.

The inquest was short and simple. The night had been dark and overcast, old Merdell had had three pints of beer and, after all, he was ninety-two.

The verdict brought in was Accidental Death.

16

I

HERCULE POIROT SAT in a square chair in front of the square fireplace in the square room of his London flat. In front of him were various objects that were not square; that were instead violently and almost impossibly curved. Each of them, studied separately, looked as if they could not have any conceivable function in a sane world. They appeared improbable, irresponsible, and wholly fortuitous. In actual fact, of course, they were nothing of the sort.

Assessed correctly, each had its particular place in a particular universe. Assembled in their proper place in their particular universe, they not only made sense, they made a picture. In other words, Hercule Poirot was doing a jigsaw puzzle.

He looked down at where a rectangle still showed improbably shaped gaps. It was an occupation he found soothing and pleasant. It brought disorder into order. It had, he reflected, a certain resemblance to his own profession. There, too, one was faced with various improbably shaped and unlikely facts which, though seeming to bear no relationship to each other, yet did each have its properly balanced part in assembling the whole. His fingers deftly picked up an improbable piece of dark gray and fitted it into a blue sky. It was, he now perceived, part of an airplane.

"Yes," murmured Poirot to himself, "that is what one must do. The unlikely piece here, the improbable piece there, the oh-so-rational piece that is not what it seems; all of these have their appointed place, and once they are fitted in, *eh bien!* there is an end of the business! All is clear. All is—as they say nowadays—in the picture."

He fitted in, in rapid succession, a small piece of a minaret, another piece that looked as though it was part of a striped awning and was actually the backside of a cat, and a missing piece of sunset that had changed with Turneresque suddenness from orange to pink.

"If one knew what to look for, it would be so easy," said Hercule Poirot to himself. "But one does not know what to look for. And so one looks in the wrong places or for the wrong things." He sighed vexedly. His eyes strayed from the jigsaw puzzle in front of him to the chair on the other side of the fireplace. There, not half an hour ago, Inspector Bland had sat consuming tea and crumpets (square crumpets) and talking sadly. He had had to come to London on police business and that police business having been accomplished, he had come to call upon M. Poirot. He had wondered, he explained, whether Mr. Poirot had any ideas. He had then proceeded to explain his own ideas. On every point he outlined, Poirot had agreed with him. Inspector Bland, so Poirot thought, had made a very fair and unprejudiced survey of the case.

It was now a month, nearly five weeks, since the occurrences at Nasse House. It had been five weeks of stagnation and of negation. Lady Stubbs' body had not been recovered. Lady Stubbs, if living, had not been traced. The odds, Inspector Bland pointed out, were strongly against her being alive. Poirot agreed with him.

"Of course," said Bland, "the body might not have been washed up. There's no telling with a body once it's in the water. It may show up yet, though it will be pretty unrecognizable when it does."

"There is a third possibility," Poirot pointed out.

Bland nodded.

"Yes," he said, "I've thought of that. I keep thinking of that, in fact. You mean the body's there—at Nasse—hidden somewhere where we've never thought of looking. It could be, you know. It just could be. With an old house, and with grounds like that, there are places you'd never think of—that you'd never know were there."

He paused a moment, ruminated, and then said:

"There's a house I was in only the other day. They'd built an air raid shelter, you know, in the war. A flimsy sort of more or less homemade job in the garden, by the wall of the house, and had made a way from it into the house—into the cellar. Well, the war ended, the shelter tumbled down, they heaped it up in irregular mounds and made a kind of rockery of it. Walking through that garden now, you'd never think that the place had once been an air raid shelter and that there was a chamber underneath. Looks as though it was always meant to be a rockery. And all the time, behind a wine bin in the cellar, there's a passage leading into it. That's what I mean. That kind of thing. Some sort of way into some kind of place that no outsider would know about. I don't suppose there's an actual Priest's Hole or anything of that kind?"

"Hardly—not at that period."

"That's what Mr. Weyman says—he says the house was built about 1790 or thereabouts. No reason for priests to hide themselves by that date. All the same, you know, there might be—somewhere, some alteration in the structure—something that one of the family might know about. What do you think, M. Poirot?"

"It is possible, yes," said Poirot. *"Mais oui,* decidedly it is an idea. If one accepts the possibility, then the next thing is—who would know about it? Anyone staying in the house might know, I suppose?"

"Yes. Of course it would let out De Sousa." The Inspector looked dissatisfied. De Sousa was still his preferred suspect. "As you say, anyone who lived in the house, such as a servant or one of the family, might know about it. Someone just staying in the house would be less likely. People who only came in from outside, like the Legges, less likely still."

"The person who would certainly know about such a thing, and who could tell you if you asked her, would be Mrs. Folliat," said Poirot.

Mrs. Folliat, he thought, knew all there was to know about Nasse

House. Mrs. Folliat knew a great deal. . . . Mrs. Folliat had known straight away that Hattie Stubbs was dead. Mrs. Folliat knew, before Marlene and Hattie Stubbs died, that it was a very wicked world and that there were very wicked people in it. Mrs. Folliat, thought Poirot vexedly, was the key to the whole business. But Mrs. Folliat, he reflected, was a key that would not easily turn in the lock.

"I've interviewed the lady several times," said the Inspector. "Very nice, very pleasant she's been about everything, and seems very distressed that she can't suggest anything helpful."

"Can't or won't?" thought Poirot. Bland was perhaps thinking the same.

"There's a type of lady," he said, "that you can't force. You can't frighten them, or persuade them, or diddle them."

"No," Poirot thought, "you couldn't force or persuade or diddle Mrs. Folliat."

The Inspector had finished his tea, and sighed and gone, and Poirot had got out his jigsaw puzzle to alleviate his mounting exasperation. For he was exasperated. Both exasperated and humiliated. Mrs. Oliver had summoned him, Hercule Poirot, to elucidate a mystery! She had felt that there was something wrong, and there had been something wrong. And she had looked confidently to Hercule Poirot, first to prevent it—and he had not prevented it—and secondly to discover the killer, and he had not discovered the killer. He was in a fog, in the type of fog where there are from time to time baffling gleams of light. Every now and then, or so it seemed to him, he had had one of those glimpses. And each time he had failed to penetrate further. He had failed to assess the value of what he seemed, for one brief moment, to have seen.

Poirot got up, crossed to the other side of the hearth, rearranged the second square chair so that it was at a definite geometric angle, and sat down in it. He had passed from the jigsaw of painted wood and cardboard to the jigsaw of a murder problem. He took a notebook from his pocket and wrote in small neat characters:

"Etienne De Sousa, Amanda Brewis, Alec Legge, Peggy Legge, Michael Weyman."

It was physically impossible for Sir George or Jim Warburton to have killed Marlene Tucker. Since it was not physically impossible for Mrs. Oliver to have done so, he added her name after a brief space. He also added the name of Mrs. Masterton since he did not remember of his own knowledge having seen Mrs. Masterton constantly on the lawn between four o'clock and quarter to five. He added the name of Hendon, the butler; more, perhaps, because a sinister butler had figured in Mrs. Oliver's murder hunt than because he had really any suspicions of the dark-haired artist with the gong stick. He also put down "Boy in turtle shirt" with a query mark after it. Then he smiled, shook his head, took a pin from the lapel of his jacket, shut his eyes and stabbed with it. It was as good a way as any other, he thought.

He was justifiably annoyed when the pin proved to have transfixed the last entry.

"I am an imbecile," said Hercule Poirot. "What has a boy in a turtle shirt to do with this?"

But he also realized he must have had some reason for including this enigmatic character in his list. He recalled again the day he had sat in the Folly, and the surprise on the boy's face at seeing him there. Not a very pleasant face, despite the youthful good looks. An arrogant ruthless face. The young man had come there for some purpose. He had come to meet someone, and it followed that that someone was a person whom he could not meet, or did not wish to meet, in the ordinary way. It was a meeting, in fact, to which attention must not be called. A guilty meeting. Something to do with the murder?

Poirot pursued his reflections. A boy who was staying at the Youth Hostel—that is to say, a boy who would be in that neighbourhood for two nights at most. Had he come there casually? One of the many young students visiting Britain? A student on the same pass as the two girls to whom he had given a lift that first day? Or had he come there for a special purpose, to meet some special person? There could have been what seemed a casual encounter on the day of the Fête—possibly there had been?

"I know a good deal," said Hercule Poirot to himself. "I have in my hands many, many pieces of this jigsaw. I have an idea of the kind of crime this was—but it must be that I am not looking at it the right way."

He turned a page of his notebook and wrote: "Did Lady Stubbs ask Miss Brewis to take tea to Marlene? If not, why does Miss Brewis say that she did?"

He considered the point. Miss Brewis might quite easily herself have thought of taking cake and a fruit drink to the girl. But if so why did she not simply say so? Why lie about Lady Stubbs having asked her to do so? Could this be because Miss Brewis went to the boathouse and found Marlene dead? Unless Miss Brewis was herself guilty of the murder, that seemed very unlikely. She was not a nervous woman nor an imaginative one. If she had found the girl dead, she would surely at once have given the alarm.

He stared for some time at the two questions he had written. He could not help feeling that somewhere in those words there was some vital pointer of the truth that had escaped him. After four or five minutes of thought he wrote down something more.

"Etienne De Sousa declares that he wrote to his cousin three weeks before his arrival at Nasse House. Is that statement true or false?"

Poirot felt almost certain that it was false. He recalled the scene at the breakfast table. There seemed no earthly reason why Sir George or Lady Stubbs should pretend to a surprise and, in the latter's case, a dismay, which they did not feel. He could see no purpose to be accomplished by it. Granting, however, that Etienne De Sousa had lied, why did he lie? To give the impression that his visit had been announced and welcomed? It might be so, but it seemed a very doubtful reason. There was certainly no evidence that such a letter had ever been written or received. Was it an attempt on De Sousa's part to establish his *bona fides*—to make his visit appear natural and even expected? Certainly Sir George had received him amicably enough, although he did not know him.

Poirot paused, his thoughts coming to a stop. Sir George did not know De Sousa. His wife, who did know him, had not seen him. Was there perhaps something there? Could it be possible that the Etienne De Sousa who had arrived that day at the Fête was not the real Etienne De Sousa? He went over the idea in his mind, but again he could see no point to it. What had De Sousa to gain by coming and representing himself as De Sousa if he was not De Sousa? In any case De Sousa did not derive any benefit from Hattie's death. Hattie, as the police had ascertained, had no money of her own except that which was allowed her by her husband.

Poirot tried to remember exactly what she had said to him that morning. "He is a bad man. He does wicked things." And, according to Bland, she had said to her husband: "He kills people."

There was something rather significant about that, now that one came to examine all the facts. *He kills people.*

On the day Etienne De Sousa had come to Nasse House one person certainly had been killed, possibly two people. Mrs. Folliat had said that one should pay no attention to these melodramatic remarks of Hattie's. She had said so very insistently. Mrs. Folliat—

Hercule Poirot frowned, then brought his hand down with a bang on the arm of his chair.

"Always, always—I return to Mrs. Folliat. She is the key to the whole business. If I knew what she knows . . . I can no longer sit in an armchair and just think. No, I must take a train and go again to Devon and visit Mrs. Folliat."

II

Hercule Poirot paused for a moment outside the big wrought iron gates of Nasse House. He looked ahead of him along the curving drive. It was no longer summer. Golden brown leaves fluttered gently down from the trees. Near at hand the grassy banks were colored with small mauve cyclamen. Poirot sighed. The beauty of Nasse House appealed to him in spite of himself. He was not a great admirer of nature in the wild; he liked things trim and neat, yet he could not but appreciate the soft wild beauty of massed shrubs and trees.

At his left was the small white porticoed lodge. It was a fine afternoon. Probably Mrs. Folliat would not be at home. She would be out somewhere with her gardening basket or else visiting some friends in the neighborhood. She had many friends. This was her home, and had been for many long years. What was it the old man on the quay had said? "There'll always be Folliats at Nasse House."

Poirot rapped gently upon the door of the Lodge. After a few moments' delay, he heard footsteps inside. They sounded to his ear slow and almost hesitant. Then the door was opened and Mrs. Folliat stood framed in the doorway. He was startled to see how old and frail she looked. She stared at him incredulously for a moment or two, then she said:

"M. Poirot? You!"

He thought for a moment that he had seen fear leap into her eyes. but perhaps that was sheer imagination on his part. He said politely,

"May I come in, Madame?"

"But of course."

She had recovered all her poise now, beckoned him in with a gesture and led the way into her small sitting room. There were some delicate Chelsea figures on the mantel-piece, a couple of chairs covered in exquisite petit point, and a Derby tea service stood on the small table. Mrs. Folliat said:

"I will fetch another cup."

Poirot raised a faintly protesting hand, but she pushed the protest aside.

"Of course you must have some tea."

She went out of the room. He looked round him once more. A piece of needlework, a petit point chair seat, lay on a table with a needle sticking in it. Against the wall was a bookcase with books. There was a little cluster of miniatures on the wall and a faded photograph in a silver frame of a man in uniform with a stiff moustache and a weak chin.

Mrs. Folliat came back into the room with a cup and saucer in her hand.

Poirot said: "Your husband, Madame?"

"Yes."

Noticing that Poirot's eyes swept along the top of the bookcase as though in search of further photographs, she said brusquely:

"I'm not fond of photographs. They make one live in the past too much. One must learn to forget. One must cut away the dead wood."

Poirot remembered how the first time he had seen Mrs. Folliat she had been clipping with secateurs at a shrub on the bank. She had said then, he remembered, something about dead wood. He looked at her thoughtfully, appraising her character. An enigmatical woman, he thought, and a woman who, in spite of the gentleness and fragility of her appearance, had a side to her that could be ruthless. A woman who could cut away dead wood not only from plants but from her own life. . . .

She sat down and poured out a cup of tea, asking:

"Milk? Sugar?"

"Three lumps if you will be so good, Madame."

She handed him his cup and said conversationally,

"I was surprised to see you. Somehow I did not imagine you would be passing through this part of the world again."

"I am not exactly passing through," said Poirot.

"No?" She queried him with slightly uplifted eyebrows.

"My visit to this part of the world is intentional."

She still looked at him in enquiry.

"I came here partly to see you, Madame."

"Really?"

"First of all—there has been no news of the young Lady Stubbs?"

Mrs. Folliat shook her head.

"There was a body washed up the other day in Cornwall," she said. "George went there to see if he could identify it. But it was not her." She added: "I am very sorry for George. The strain has been very great."

"Does he still believe that his wife may be alive?"

Slowly Mrs. Folliat shook her head.

"I think," she said, "that he has given up hope. After all, if Hattie were alive, she couldn't possibly conceal herself successfully with the whole of the Press and the Police looking for her. Even if something like loss of memory had happened to her, well, surely the police would have found her by now?"

"It would seem so, yes," said Poirot. "Do the police still search?"

"I suppose so. I do not really know."

"But Sir George has given up hope."

"He does not say so," said Mrs. Folliat. "Of course I have not seen him lately. He has been mostly in London."

"And the murdered girl? There have been no developments there?"

"Not that I know of." She added: "It seems a senseless crime—absolutely pointless. Poor child. . . ."

"It still upsets you, I see, to think of her, Madame."

Mrs. Folliat did not reply for a moment or two. Then she said:

"I think when one is old, the death of anyone who is young upsets one out of due proportion. We old folks expect to die, but that child had her life before her."

"It might not have been a very interesting life."

"Not from our point of view, perhaps, but it might have been interesting to her."

"And although, as you say, we old folk must expect to die," said Poirot, "we do not really want to. At least I do not want to. I find life very interesting still."

"I don't think that I do."

She spoke more to herself than to him, her shoulders drooped still more.

"I am very tired, M. Poirot. I shall be not only ready, but thankful, when my time comes."

He shot a quick glance at her. He wondered, as he had wondered before, whether it was a sick woman who sat talking to him, a woman who had perhaps the knowledge or even the certainty of approaching death. He could not otherwise account for the intense weariness and lassitude of her manner. That lassitude, he felt, was not really characteristic of the woman. Amy Folliat, he felt, was a woman of character, energy and determination. She had lived through many troubles, loss of her home, loss of wealth, the deaths of her sons. All these, he felt, she had survived. She had cut away the "dead wood" as she herself had expressed it. But there was something now in her life that she could not cut away, that no one could cut away from her. If it was not physical illness he did not see what it could be. She gave a sudden little smile as though she were reading his thoughts.

"Really, you know, I have not very much to live for, M. Poirot," she said. "I have many friends but no near relations, no family."

"You have your home," said Poirot on an impulse.

"You mean Nasse? Yes. . . ."

"It is your home, isn't it, although technically it is the property of Sir George Stubbs? Now Sir George Stubbs has gone to London you rule in his stead."

Again he saw the sharp look of fear in her eyes. When she spoke her voice held an icy edge to it.

"I don't quite know what you mean. M. Poirot. I am grateful to Sir George for renting me this Lodge, but I do rent it. I pay him a yearly sum for it with the right to walk in the grounds."

Poirot spread out his hands.

"I apologize, Madame. I did not mean to offend you."

"No doubt I misunderstood you," said Mrs. Folliat coldly.

"It is a beautiful place," said Poirot. "A beautiful house, beautiful grounds. It has about it great peace, great serenity."

"Yes." Her face lightened. "We have always felt that. I felt it as a child when I first came here."

"But is there the same peace and serenity now, Madame?"

"Why not?"

"Murder unavenged," said Poirot. "The spilling of innocent blood. Until that shadow lifts, there will not be peace." He added: "I think you know that, Madame, as well as I do."

Mrs. Folliat did not answer. She neither moved nor spoke. She sat quite still and Poirot had no idea what she was thinking. He leaned forward a little and spoke again.

"Madame, you know a good deal—perhaps everything—about this murder. You know who killed that girl, you know why. You know who killed Hattie Stubbs, you know, perhaps, where her body lies now."

Mrs. Folliat spoke then. Her voice was loud, almost harsh.

"I know nothing," she said. "Nothing."

"Perhaps I have used the wrong word. You do not know—but I think you guess, Madame. I'm quite sure that you guess."

"Now you are being—excuse me—absurd!"

"It is not absurd—it is something quite different—it is dangerous."

"Dangerous? To whom?"

"To you, Madame. So long as you keep your knowledge to yourself you are in danger. I know murderers better than you do, Madame."

"I have told you already, I have no knowledge."

"Suspicions, then—"

"I have no suspicions."

"That, excuse me, is not true, Madame."

"To speak out of mere suspicion would be wrong—indeed wicked."

Poirot leaned forward. "As wicked as what was done here just over a month ago?"

She shrank back into her chair, huddled into herself. She half whispered: "Don't talk to me of it." And then added, with a long shuddering sigh, "Anyway, it's over now. Done—finished with."

"How can you tell that, Madame? I tell you of my own knowledge that it is never finished with a murderer."

She shook her head.

"No. No, it's the end. And anyway there is nothing I can do. Nothing."

He got up and stood looking down at her. She said almost fretfully, "Why, even the police have given up."

Poirot shook his head.

"Oh, no, Madame, you are wrong there. The police do not give up. And I," he added, "do not give up either. Remember that, Madame. I, Hercule Poirot, do not give up."

It was a very typical exit line.

17

AFTER LEAVING NASSE, Poirot went to the village where, by enquiry, he found the cottage occupied by the Tuckers. His knock at the door went unanswered for some moments, as it was drowned by the high-pitched tones of Mrs. Tucker's voice from inside.

"—And what be yu thinking of, Jim Tucker, bringing them boots of yours on to my nice linoleum? If I've tell ee once I've tell ee a thousand times. Been polishing it all the morning, I have, and now look at it."

A faint rumbling denoted Mr. Tucker's reaction to these remarks. It was on the whole a placatory rumble.

"Yu've no cause to go forgetting. 'Tis all this eagerness to get the sports news on the wireless. Why, 'twouldn't have took ee tu minutes to be off with them boots. And yu, Gary, do ee mind what yu'm doing with that lollipop. Sticky fingers I will not have on my best silver teapot. Marylin, that be someone at the door, that be. Du ee go and see who 'tis."

The door was opened gingerly and a child of about eleven or twelve years old peered out suspiciously at Poirot. One cheek was bulged with a sweet. She was a fat child with small blue eyes and a rather piggy kind of prettiness.

" 'Tis a gentleman, mum," she shouted.

Mrs. Tucker, wisps of hair hanging over her somewhat hot face, came to the door.

"What is it?" she demanded sharply. "We don't need—" She paused, a faint look of recognition came across her face. "Why let me see, now, didn't I see you with the police that day?"

"Alas, Madame, that I have brought back painful memories," said Poirot, stepping firmly inside the door.

Mrs. Tucker cast a swift agonized glance at his feet, but Poirot's pointed patent leather shoes had only trodden the high road. No mud was being deposited on Mrs. Tucker's brightly polished linoleum.

"Come in, won't you, sir," she said, backing before him, and throwing open the door of a room on her right hand.

Poirot was ushered into a devastatingly neat little parlor. It smelled of furniture polish and Brasso and contained a large Jacobean suite, a round table, two potted geraniums and an elaborate brass fender, and a large variety of china ornaments.

"Sit down, sir, do. I can't remember the name. Indeed, I don't think as I ever heard it."

"My name is Hercule Poirot," said Poirot rapidly. "I found myself once more in this part of the world and I called here to offer you my condolences and to ask you if there had been any developments. I trust the murderer of your daughter has been discovered?"

"Not sight or sound of him," said Mrs. Tucker, speaking with some bitterness. "And 'tis a downright wicked shame if you ask me. 'Tis my opinion the police don't disturb themselves when it's only the likes of us. What's the police anyway? If they'm all like Bob Hoskins I wonder the whole country isn't a mass of crime. All that Bob Hoskins does is spend his time looking into parked cars on the Common."

At this point, Mr. Tucker, his boots removed, appeared through the doorway, walking on his stockinged feet. He was a large, red-faced man with a pacific expression.

"Police be all right," he said in a husky voice. "Got their troubles just like anyone else. These here maniacs ar'n't so easy to find. Look the same as you or me, if you take my meaning," he added, speaking directly to Poirot.

The little girl who had opened the door to Poirot appeared behind her father, and a boy of about eight poked his head round her shoulder. They all stared at Poirot with intense interest.

"This is your younger daughter, I suppose," said Poirot.

"That's Marylin, that is," said Mrs. Tucker. "And that's Gary. Come and say how do you do, Gary, and mind your manners."

Gary backed away.

"Shy-like, he is," said his mother.

"Very civil of you, I'm sure, sir," said Mr. Tucker, "to come and ask about Marlene. Ah, that was a terrible business, to be sure."

"I have just called upon Mrs. Folliat," said M. Poirot. "She, too, seems to feel this very deeply."

"She's been poorly-like ever since," said Mrs. Tucker. "She's an old lady and it was a shock to her, happening as it did at her own place."

Poirot noted once more everybody's unconscious assumption that Nasse House still belonged to Mrs. Folliat.

"Makes her feel responsible-like in a way," said Mr. Tucker, "not that 'twere anything to do with her."

"Who was it that actually suggested that Marlene should play the victim?" asked Poirot.

"The lady from London that writes the books," said Mrs. Tucker promptly.

Poirot said mildly,

"But she was a stranger down here. She did not even know Marlene."

" 'Twas Mrs. Masterton what rounded the girls up," said Mrs. Tucker, "and I suppose 'twas Mrs. Masterton said Marlene was to do it. And Marlene, I must say, was pleased enough at the idea."

Once again, Poirot felt he came up against a blank wall. But he knew now what Mrs. Oliver had felt when she first sent for him. Someone had been working in the dark, someone who had pushed forward his own desires through other recognised personalities. Mrs. Oliver, Mrs. Masterton. Those were the figureheads. He said:

"I have been wondering, Mrs. Tucker, whether Marlene was already acquainted with this—er—homicidal maniac."

"She wouldn't know nobody like that," said Mrs. Tucker virtuously.

"Ah," said Poirot, "but as your husband has just observed, these maniacs are very difficult to spot. They look the same as—er—you and me. Someone may have spoken to Marlene at the Fête, or even before it. Made friends with her in a perfectly harmless manner. Given her presents, perhaps."

"Oh, no, sir, nothing of that kind. Marlene wouldn't take presents from a stranger. I brought her up better than that."

"But she might see no harm in it," said Poirot, persisting. "Supposing it had been some nice lady who had offered her things."

"Someone, you mean, like young Mrs. Legge down to the Mill Cottage."

"Yes," said Poirot. "Something like that."

"Give Marlene a lipstick once, she did," said Mrs. Tucker. "Ever so mad, I was. I won't have you putting that muck on your face, Marlene, I said. Think what your father would say. Well, she says, perky as may be, it's the lady down at Lawders' Cottage as give it me. Said as how it would suit me, she did. Well, I said, don't you listen to what no London ladies say. It's all very well for them, painting their faces and blacking their eyelashes and everything else. But you're a decent girl, I said, and you wash your face with soap and water until you're a good deal older than what you are now."

"But she did not agree with you, I expect," said Poirot, smiling.

"When I say a thing I mean it," said Mrs. Tucker.

The fat Marylin suddenly gave an amused giggle. Poirot shot her a keen glance.

"Did Mrs. Legge give Marlene anything else?" he asked.

"Believe she gave her a scarf or summat—one she hadn't no more use for. A showy sort of thing, but not much quality. I know quality when I see it," said Mrs. Tucker, nodding her head. "Used to work at Nasse House as a girl, I did. Proper stuff the ladies wore in those days. No gaudy colors and all this nylon and rayon; real good silk. Why, some of their taffeta dresses would have stood up by themselves."

"Girls like a bit of finery," said Mr. Tucker indulgently. "I don't mind a few bright colors myself, but I won't have this 'ere mucky lipstick."

"A bit sharp I was with her," said Mrs. Tucker, her eyes suddenly misty, "and her gorn in that terrible way. Wished afterwards I hadn't spoken so sharp. Ah, nought but trouble and funerals lately it seems. Troubles never come singly, so they say, and it's true enough."

"You have had other losses?" enquired Poirot politely.

"The wife's father," explained Mr. Tucker. "Come across the ferry in his boat from the Three Dogs late at night, and must have missed his footing getting onto the quay and fallen in the river. Of course he ought to have stayed quiet at home at his age. But there, yu can't do anything with the old 'uns. Always pottering about on the quay he was."

"Father was a great one for the boats always," said Mrs. Tucker. "Used to look after them in the old days for Mr. Folliat, years and years ago that was. Not," she added brightly, "as father's much loss, as you might say. Well over ninety, he was, and trying in many of his ways. Always blabbling some nonsense or other. 'Twas time he went. But of course we had to bury him nice—and two funerals running costs a lot of money."

These economic reflections passed Poirot by—a faint remembrance was stirring.

"An old man—on the quay? I remember talking to him. Was his name—"

"Merdell, sir. That was my name before I married."

"Your father, if I remember rightly, was Head Gardener at Nasse?"

"No—that was my eldest brother. I was the youngest of the family— eleven of us, there were." She added with some pride: "There's been Merdells at Nasse for years, but they're all scattered now. Father was the last of us."

Poirot said softly,

"There'll always be Folliats at Nasse House."

"I beg your pardon, sir?"

"I am repeating what your old father said to me on the quay."

"Ah, talked a lot of nonsense, father did. I had to shut him up pretty sharp now and then."

"So Marlene was Merdell's granddaughter," said Poirot. "Yes—I begin to see—" He was silent for a moment, an immense excitement was surging within him. "Your father was drowned, you say, in the river?"

"Yes, sir. Took a drop too much, he did. And where he got the money from, I don't know. Of course he used to get tips now and again on the quay helping people with boats or with parking their cars. Very cunning he was at hiding his money from me. Yes, I'm afraid as he'd had a drop too much. Missed his footing, I'd say, getting off his boat onto the quay. So he fell in and was drowned. His body was washed up down to Helmmouth the next day. 'Tis a wonder, as you might say, that it never happened before, him being ninety-two and half blinded anyway."

"The fact remains that it did not happen before—"

"Ah well, accidents do happen, sooner or later—"

"Accident," mused Poirot. "I wonder."

He got up. He murmured:

"I should have guessed. Guessed long ago. The child practically told me—"

"I beg your pardon, sir?"

"It is nothing," said Poirot. "Once more I tender you my condolences both on the death of your daughter and on that of your father."

He shook hands with them both and left the cottage. He said to himself:

"I have been foolish—very foolish. I have looked at everything the wrong way round."

"Hi—mister."

It was a cautious whisper. Poirot looked round. The fat child Marylin was standing in the shadow of the cottage wall. She beckoned him to her and spoke in a whisper.

"Mum don't know everything," she said. "Marlene didn't get that scarf off of the lady down at the cottage."

"Where did she get it?"

"Bought it in Torquay. Bought some lipstick, too, and some scent—Newt in Paris—funny name. And a jar of foundation cream, what she'd read about in an advertisement." Marylin giggled. "Mum doesn't know. Hid it at the back of her drawer, Marlene did, under her winter vests. Used to go into the Convenience at the bus stop and do herself up, when she went to the pictures."

Marylin giggled again.

"Mum never knew."

"Didn't your mother find these things after your sister died? "

Marylin shook her fair fluffy head.

"No," she said, "I got 'em now—in my drawer. Mum doesn't know."

Poirot eyed her consideringly and said:

"You seem a very clever girl, Marylin."

Marylin grinned rather sheepishly.

"Miss Bird says it's no good my trying for the grammar school."

"Grammar school is not everything," said Poirot. "Tell me, how did Marlene get the money to buy these things?"

Marylin looked with close attention at a drainpipe.

"Dunno," she muttered.

"I think you do know," said Poirot.

Shamelessly he drew out a half crown from his pocket and added another half crown to it.

"I believe," he said, "there is a new, very attractive shade of lipstick called 'Carmine Kiss.' "

"Sounds smashing," said Marylin, her hand advanced towards the five shillings. She spoke in a rapid whisper. "She used to snoop about a bit, Marlene did. Used to see goings-on—you know what! Marlene would promise not to tell and then they'd give her a present, see?"

Poirot relinquished the five shillings.

"I see," he said.

He nodded to Marylin and walked away. He murmured again under his breath, but this time with intensified meaning:

"I see."

So many things now fell into place. Not all of it. Not clear yet by any means—but he was on the right track. A perfectly clear trail all the way if only he had had the wit to see it. That first conversation with Mrs. Oliver, some casual words of Michael Weyman's, the significant conversation with old Merdell on the quay, an illuminating phrase spoken by Miss Brewis—the arrival of Etienne De Sousa. A public telephone box stood adjacent to the viliage post office. He entered it and rang up a number. A few minutes later he was speaking to Inspector Bland.

"Well, M. Poirot, where are you?"

"I am here, in Nassecombe."

"But you were in London yesterday afternoon."

"It only takes three and a half hours to come here by a good train," Poirot pointed out. "I have a question for you."

"Yes?"

"What kind of a yacht did Etienne De Sousa have?"

"Maybe I can guess what you're thinking, M. Poirot, but I assure you there was nothing of that kind. It wasn't fitted up for smuggling if that's what you mean. There were no fancy hidden partitions or secret cubbyholes. We'd have found them if there had been. There was nowhere on it you could have stowed away a body."

"You are wrong, *mon cher,* that is not what I mean. I only asked what kind of a yacht, big or small?"

"Oh—it was very fancy—must have cost the earth. All very smart, newly painted, luxury fittings."

"Exactly," said Poirot. He sounded so pleased that Inspector Bland felt quite surprised.

"What are you getting at, M. Poirot?" he asked.

"Etienne De Sousa," said Poirot, "was a rich man. That, my friend, is very significant."

"Why?" demanded Inspector Bland.

"It fits in with my latest idea," said Poirot.

"You've got an idea, then?"

"Yes. At last I have an idea. Up to now I have been very stupid."

"You mean we've all been very stupid."

"No," said Poirot, "I mean specially myself. I had the good fortune to have a perfectly clear trail presented to me, and I did not see it."

"But now you're definitely on to something?"

"I think so, yes."

"Look here, M. Poirot—"

But Poirot had rung off. After searching his pockets for available change, he put through a personal call to Mrs. Oliver at her London number.

"But do not," he hastened to add, when he made his demand, "disturb the lady to answer the telephone if she is at work."

He remembered how bitterly Mrs. Oliver had once reproached him for interrupting a train of creative thought and how the world in consequence had been deprived of an intriguing mystery centering round an old-fashioned long-sleeved woollen vest. The Exchange, however, was unable to appreciate his scruples.

"Well," it demanded, "do you want a personal call or don't you?"

"I do," said Poirot, sacrificing Mrs. Oliver's creative genius upon the altar of his own impatience. He was relieved when Mrs. Oliver spoke. She interrupted his apologies.

"It's splendid that you've rung me up," she said. "I was just going out to give a Talk on 'How I Write My Books.' Now I can get my secretary to ring up and say I am unavoidably detained."

"But, Madame, you must not let me prevent—"

"It's not a case of preventing," said Mrs. Oliver joyfully. "I'd have made the most awful fool of myself. I mean, what can you say about how you write books? What I mean is, first you've got to think of something, and when you've thought of it you've got to force yourself to sit down and write it. That's all. It would have taken me just three minutes to explain that, and then the Talk would have been ended and everyone would have been very fed up. I can't imagine why everybody is always so keen for authors to talk about writing. I should have thought it was an author's business to write, not talk."

"And yet it is about how you write that I want to ask you."

"You can ask," said Mrs. Oliver, "but I probably shan't know the answer. I mean one just sits down and writes. Half a minute, I've got a frightfully silly hat on for the Talk—and I must take it off. It scratches my forehead." There was a momentary pause and then the voice of Mrs. Oliver resumed in a relieved voice, "Hats are really only a symbol, nowadays, aren't they? I mean one doesn't wear them for sensible reasons any more; to keep one's head warm, or shield one from the sun, or hide one's face from people one doesn't want to meet. I beg your pardon, M. Poirot, did you say something?"

"It was an ejaculation only. It is extraordinary," said Poirot, and his voice was awed. "Always you give me ideas. So also did my friend Hastings whom I have not seen for many, many years. You have given me now the clue to yet another piece of my problem. But no more of all that. Let me ask you instead my question. Do you know an atom scientist, Madame?"

"Do I know an atom scientist?" said Mrs. Oliver in a surprised voice. "I don't know. I suppose I may. I mean, I know some professors and things. I'm never quite sure what they actually do."

"Yet you made an atom scientist one of the suspects in your Murder Hunt?"

"Oh that! That was just to be up-to-date. I mean, when I went to buy presents for my nephews last Christmas, there was nothing but science fiction and the stratosphere and supersonic toys, and so I thought when I started on the Murder Hunt, 'Better have an Atom Scientist as the chief suspect and be modern.' After all, if I'd needed a little technical jargon for it I could always have got it from Alec Legge."

"Alec Legge—the husband of Peggy Legge? Is he an atom scientist?"

"Yes, he is. Not Harwell. Wales somewhere. Cardiff—or Bristol, is it? It's just a holiday cottage they have on the Helm. Yes, so of course I do know an atom scientist after all!"

"And it was meeting him at Nasse House that probably put the idea of an atom scientist into your head? But his wife is not Yugoslavian."

"Oh, no," said Mrs. Oliver. "Peggy is English as English. Surely you realize that?"

"Then what put the idea of the Yugoslavian wife into your head?"

"I really don't know. . . . Refugees perhaps? Students? All those foreign girls at the Hostel trespassing through the woods and speaking broken English."

"I see. . . . Yes, I see now a lot of things."

"It's about time," said Mrs. Oliver.

"Pardon?"

"I said it was about time," said Mrs. Oliver. "That you did see things, I mean. Up to now you don't seem to have done anything." Her voice held reproach.

"One cannot arrive at things all in a moment," said Poirot, defending himself. "The police," he added, "have been completely baffled."

"Oh, the police," said Mrs. Oliver. "Now if a woman were the head of Scotland Yard . . ."

Recognizing this well-known phrase Poirot hastened to interrupt.

"The matter has been complex," he said. "Extremely complex. But now—I tell you this in confidence—but now I arrive!"

Mrs. Oliver remained unimpressed.

"I daresay," she said, "but in the meantime there have been two murders."

"Three," Poirot corrected her.

"Three murders? Who's the third?"

"An old man called Merdell," said Hercule Poirot.

"I haven't heard of that one," said Mrs. Oliver. "Will it be in the paper?"

"No," said Poirot, "up to now no one has suspected that it was anything but an accident."

"And it wasn't an accident?"

"No," said Poirot, "it was not an accident."

"Well, tell me who did it—did them, I mean—or can't you over the telephone?"

"One does not say these things over the telephone," said Poirot.

"Then I shall ring off," said Mrs. Oliver. "I can't bear it."

"Wait a moment," said Poirot. "There is something eIse I wanted to ask you. Now, what was it?"

"That's a sign of age," said Mrs. Oliver. "I do that, too. Forget things—"

"There was something, some little point—it worried me. I was in the boathouse—"

He cast his mind back. That pile of comics. Marlene's phrases scrawled on the margin. "Albert goes with Doreen." He had had a feeling that there was something lacking—that there was something he must ask Mrs. Oliver.

"Are you still there, M. Poirot?" demanded Mrs. Oliver. At the same time the operator requested more money.

These formalities completed, Poirot spoke once more.

"Are you still there, Madame?"

"I'm still here," said Mrs. Oliver. "Don't let's waste any more money asking each other if we're there. What is it?"

"It is something very important. You remember your Murder Hunt?"

"Well, of course I remember it. It's practically what we've just been talking about, isn't it?"

"I made one grave mistake," said Poirot. "I never read your synopsis for competitors. In the gravity of discovering a murder it did not seem to matter. I was wrong. It did matter. You are a sensitive person, Madame. You are affected by your atmosphere, by the personalities of the people you meet. And these are translated into your work. Not recognizably so, but they are the inspiration from which your fertile brain draws its creations."

"That's very nice flowery language," said Mrs. Oliver, "but what exactly do you mean?"

"That you have always known more about this crime than you have realized yourself. Now for the question I want to ask you—two questions actually, but the first is very important. Did you, when you first began to 'plan' your Murder Hunt, mean the body to be discovered in the boathouse?"

"No, I didn't."

"Where did you intend it to be?"

"In that funny little summerhouse tucked away in the rhododendrons near the house. I thought it was just the place. But then someone, I can't remember who exactly, began insisting that it should be found in the Folly. Well, that, of course, was an absurd idea! I mean, anyone could have strolled in there quite casually and come across it without having followed a single clue! People are so stupid. Of course I couldn't agree to that."

"So, instead, you accepted the boathouse?"

"Yes, that's just how it happened. There was really nothing against the boathouse though I still thought the little summerhouse would have been better."

"Yes, that is the technique you outlined to me the first day. There is one thing more. Do you remember telling me that there was a final clue written on one of the *comics* that Marlene was given to amuse her?"

"Yes, of course."

"Tell me, was it something like"—he forced his memory back to a moment when he had stood reading various scrawled phrases—'Albert goes with Doreen. Georgie Porgie kisses hikers in the woods. Peter pinches girls in the cinema'?"

"Good gracious me, no," said Mrs. Oliver in a slightly shocked voice. "It wasn't anything silly like that. No, mine was a perfectly straightforward clue." She lowered her voice and spoke in mysterious tones: *"Look in the hiker's rucksack."*

"Epatant!" cried Poirot. *"Epatant!* Of course, the *comic* with that on it would have to be taken away. It might have given someone ideas!"

"The rucksack, of course, was on the floor by the body and—"

"Ah, but it is another rucksack of which I am thinking."

"You're confusing me with all these rucksacks," Mrs. Oliver complained. "There was only one in my murder story. Don't you want to know what was in it?"

"Not in the least," said Poirot. "That is to say," he added politely, "I should be enchanted to hear, of course, but—"

Mrs. Oliver swept over the 'but.'

"Very ingenious, I think," she said, the pride of authorship in her voice. "You see, in Marlene's haversack, which was supposed to be the Yugoslavian wife's haversack, if you understand what I mean—"

"Yes, yes," said Poirot, preparing himself to be lost in fog once more.

"Well, in it was the bottle of medicine containing poison with which the country squire poisoned his wife. You see, the Yugoslavian girl had been over here training as a nurse and she'd been in the house when Colonel Blunt poisoned his first wife for her money. And she, the nurse, had got hold of the bottle and taken it away, and then came back to blackmail him. That, of course, is why he killed her! Does that fit in, M. Poirot?"

"Fit in with what?"

"With your ideas," said Mrs. Oliver.

"Not at all," said Poirot, but added hastily, "All the same, my felicitations, Madame. I am sure your Murder Hunt was so ingenious that nobody won the prize."

"But they did," said Mrs. Oliver. "Quite late, about seven o'clock. A very dogged old lady supposed to be quite gaga. She got through all the clues and arrived at the boathouse triumphantly, but of course the police were there. So then she heard about the murder, and she was the last person at the whole Fête to hear about it, I should imagine! Anyway, they gave her the prize." She added with satisfaction, "That horrid young man with the freckles who said I drank like a fish never got further than the hydrangea garden."

"Some day, Madame," said Poirot, "you shall tell me this story of yours."

"Actually," said Mrs. Oliver, "I'm thinking of turning it into a book. It would be a pity to waste it."

And it may here be mentioned that some three years later Hercule Poirot read *The Woman in the Wood,* by Ariadne Oliver, and wondered while he read it why some of the persons and incidents seemed to him vaguely familiar.

18

THE SUN WAS setting when Poirot came to what was called officially Mill Cottage, and known locally as the Pink Cottage down by Lawders' Creek. He knocked on the door and it was flung open with such suddenness that he started back. The angry-looking young man in the doorway stared at him for a moment without recognizing him. Then he gave a short laugh.

"Hullo," he said, "it's the sleuth. Come in, M. Poirot. I'm packing up."

Poirot accepted the invitation and stepped into the cottage. It was plainly, rather badly furnished. And Alec Legge's personal possessions were at the moment taking up a disproportionate amount of room. Books, papers and articles of stray clothing were strewn all around, an open suitcase stood on the floor.

"The final breakup of the *menage,*" said Alec Legge. "Peggy has cleared out. I expect you know that."

"I did not know it, no."

Alec Legge gave a short laugh.

"I'm glad there's something you don't know. Yes, she's had enough of married life. Going to link up her life with that tame architect."

"I am sorry to hear it," said Poirot.

"I don't see why you should be sorry."

"I am sorry," said Poirot, clearing off two books and a shirt and sitting down on the corner of the sofa, "because I do not think she will be as happy with him as she would be with you."

"She hasn't been particularly happy with me this last six months."

"Six months is not a lifetime," said Poirot. "It is a very short space out of what might be a long, happy married life."

"Talking rather like a parson, aren't you?"

"Possibly. May I say, Mr. Legge, that if your wife has not been happy with you it is probably more your fault than hers."

"She certainly thinks so. Everything's my fault, I suppose."

"Not everything, but some things."

"Oh, blame everything on me. I might as well drown myself in the damn river and have done with it."

Poirot looked at him thoughtfully.

"I am glad to observe," he remarked, "that you are now more perturbed with your own troubles than those of the world."

"The world can go hang," said Mr. Legge. He added bitterly, "I seem to have made the most complete fool of myself all along the line."

"Yes," said Poirot, "I would say that you have been more unfortunate than reprehensible in your conduct."

Alec Legge stared at him.

"Who hired you to sleuth me?" he demanded. "Was it Peggy?"

"Why should you think that?"

"Well—nothing's happened officially. So I concluded that you must have come down after me on a private job."

"You are in error," replied Poirot. "I have not at any time been sleuthing you. When I came down here I had no idea that you existed."

"Then how do you know whether I've been unfortunate or made a fool of myself or what?"

"From a result of observation and reflection," said Poirot. "Shall I make a little guess and will you tell me if I am right?"

"You can make as many little guesses as you like," said Alec Legge. "But don't expect me to play."

"I think," said Poirot, "that some years ago you had an interest and sympathy for a certain political party. Like many other young men of a scientific bent. In your profession such sympathies and tendencies are naturally regarded with suspicion. I do not think you were ever seriously compromised, but I do think that pressure was brought upon you to consolidate your position in a way you did not want to consolidate it. You tried to withdraw and you were faced with a threat. You were given a rendezvous with someone. I doubt if I shall ever know that young man's name. He will be for me always the young man in the turtle shirt."

Alec Legge gave a sudden explosion of laughter.

"I suppose that shirt was a bit of a joke. I wasn't seeing that things were funny at the time."

Hercule Poirot continued.

"What with worry over the fate of the world, and the worry over your own predicament, you became, if I may say so, a man almost impossible for any woman to live with happily. You did not confide in your wife. That was unfortunate for you, as I should say that your wife was a woman of loyalty, and that if she had realized how unhappy and desperate you were, she would have been wholeheartedly on your side. Instead of that she merely began to compare you, unfavorably, with a former friend of hers, Michael Weyman."

He rose.

"I should advise you, Mr. Legge, to complete your packing as soon as possible, to follow your wife to London, to ask her to forgive you and to tell her all that you have been through."

"So that's what you advise," said Alec Legge. "And what the hell business is it of yours?"

"None," said Hercule Poirot. He withdrew towards the door. "But I am always right."

There was a moment's silence. Then Alec Legge burst into a wild peal of laughter.

"Do you know," he said, "I think I'll take your advice? Divorce is damned expensive. Anyway, if you've got hold of the woman you want, and are then not able to keep her, it's a bit humiliating, don't you think? I shall go up to her flat in Chelsea, and if I find Michael there I shall take hold of him by that hand-knitted pansy tie he wears and throttle the life out of him! I'd enjoy that. Yes, I'd enjoy it a good deal."

His face suddenly lit up with a most attractive smile.

"Sorry for my filthy temper," he said, "and thanks a lot."

He clapped Poirot on the shoulder. With the force of the blow Poirot staggered and all but fell.

Mr. Legge's friendship was certainly more painful than his animosity.

"And now," said Poirot, leaving Mill Cottage on painful feet and looking up at the darkening sky, "where do I go?"

19

THE CHIEF CONSTABLE and Inspector Bland looked up with keen curiosity as Hercule Poirot was ushered in. The Chief Constable was not in the best of tempers. Only Bland's quiet persistence had caused him to cancel his dinner appointment for that evening.

"I know, Bland, I know," he said fretfully. "Maybe he was a little Belgian wizard in his day—but surely, man, his day's over. He's what age?"

Bland slid tactfully over the answer to this question which, in any case, he did not know. Poirot himself was always reticent on the subject of age.

"The point is, sir, he was there—on the spot. And we're not getting anywhere any other way. Up against a blank wall, that's where we are."

The Chief Constable blew his nose irritably.

"I know. I know. Makes me begin to believe in Mrs. Masterton's homicidal pervert. I'd even use bloodhounds, if there were anywhere to use them."

"Bloodhounds can't follow a scent over water."

"Yes. I know what you've always thought, Bland. And I'm inclined to agree with you. But there's absolutely no motive, you know. Not an iota of motive."

"The motive may be out in the islands."

"Meaning that Hattie Stubbs knew something about De Sousa out there? I suppose that's reasonably possible, given her mentality. She was simple, everyone agrees on that. She might blurt out what she knew to anyone at any time. Is that the way you see it?"

"Something like that."

"If so, he waited a long time before crossing the sea and doing something about it."

"Well, sir, it's possible he didn't know what exactly had become of her. His own story was that he'd seen a piece in some society periodical about Nasse House, and its beautiful *chatelaine* (which I have always thought myself,' added Bland parenthetically, 'to be a silver thing with chains, and bits and pieces hung on it that people's grandmothers used to clip on their waistbands—and a good idea, too. Wouldn't be all these silly women leaving their handbags around.) Seems, though, that in women's jargon *chatelaine* means mistress of a house. As I say, that's his story and maybe it's true enough, and he didn't know where she was or who she'd married until then."

"But once he did know, he came across posthaste in a yacht in order to murder her? It's farfetched, Bland, very farfetched."

"But it could be, sir."

"And what on earth could the woman know?"

"Remember what she said to her husband. 'He kills people.' "

"Murder remembered? From the time she was fifteen? And presumably only her word for it? Surely he'd be able to laugh that off?"

"We don't know the facts," said Bland stubbornly. "You know yourself, sir, how once one knows who did a thing, one can look for the evidence and find it."

"H'm. We've made enquiries about De Sousa—discreetly—through the usual channels—and got nowhere."

"That's just why, sir, this funny old Belgian boy might have stumbled on something. He was in the house—that's the important thing. Lady Stubbs talked to him. Some of the random things she said may have come together in his mind and made sense. However that may be, he's been down in Nassecombe most of today."

"And he rang you up to ask what kind of a yacht Etienne De Sousa had?"

"When he rang up the first time, yes. The second time was to ask me to arrange this meeting."

"Well," the Chief Constable looked at his watch, "if he doesn't come within five minutes—"

But it was at that very moment that Hercule Poirot was shown in.

His appearance was not as immaculate as usual. His moustache was limp, affected by the damp Devon air, his patent leather shoes were heavily coated with mud, he limped, and his hair was ruffled.

"Well, so here you are, M. Poirot." The Chief Constable shook hands. "We're all keyed up, on our toes, waiting to hear what you have to tell us."

The words were faintly ironic, but Hercule Poirot, however damp physically, was in no mood to be damped mentally.

"I cannot imagine," he said, "how it was I did not see the truth before!"

The Chief Constable received this rather coldly.

"Are we to understand that you do see the truth now?"

"Yes—there are details—but the outline is clear."

"We want more than an ouline," said the Chief Constable drily. "We want evidence. Have you got evidence, M. Poirot?"

"I can tell you where to find the evidence."

Inspector Bland spoke. "Such as?"

Poirot turned to him and asked a question.

"Etienne De Sousa has, I suppose, left the country?"

"Two weeks ago." Bland added bitterly: "It won't be easy to get him back."

"He might be persuaded."

"Persuaded? There's not sufficient evidence to warrant an extradition order, then?"

"It is not a question of an extradition order. If the facts are put to him—"

"But what facts, M. Poirot?" The Chief Constable spoke with some irritation. "What are these facts you talk about so glibly?"

"The fact that Etienne De Sousa came here in a lavishly appointed luxury yacht showing that his family is rich; the fact that old Merdell was Marlene Tucker's grandfather (which I did not know until today); the fact that Lady Stubbs was fond of wearing the coolie type of hat; the fact that Mrs. Oliver, in spite of an unbridled and unreliable imagination, is, unrealized by herself, a very shrewd judge of character; the fact that Marlene Tucker had lipsticks and bottles of perfume hidden at the back of her bureau drawer; the fact that Miss Brewis maintains that it was Lady Stubbs who asked her to take a refreshment tray down to Marlene at the boathouse."

"Facts?" The Chief Constable stared. "You call those facts? But there's nothing new there!"

"You prefer evidence—definite evidence—such as— Lady Stubbs' body?"

Now it was Bland who stared.

"You have found Lady Stubbs' body?"

"Not actuallly found it—but I know where it is hidden. You shall go to the spot, and when you have found it, then—then you will have evidence—all the evidence you need! For only one person could have hidden it there."

"And who's that?"

Hercule Poirot smiled—the contented smile of a cat who has lapped up a saucer of cream.

"The person it so often is," he said softly, "the husband. Sir George Stubbs killed his wife."

"But that's impossible, M. Poirot. We know it's impossible."

"Oh, no," said Poirot, "it is not impossible at all! Listen, and I will tell you."

20

HERCULE POIROT PAUSED a moment at the big wrought iron gates. He looked ahead of him along the curving drive. The last of the golden brown leaves fluttered down from the trees. The cyclamen were over.

Poirot sighed. He turned aside and rapped gently on the door of the little white pilastered Lodge.

After a few moments' delay he heard footsteps inside, those slow hesitant footsteps. The door was opened by Mrs. Folliat. He was not startled this time to see how old and frail she looked.

She said: "M. Poirot? You again?"

"May I come in?"

"Of course."

He followed her in.

She offered him tea which he refused. Then she asked in a quiet voice: "Why have you come?"

"I think you can guess, Madame."

Her answer was oblique.

"I am very tired," she said.

"I know." He went on: "There have now been three deaths, Hattie Stubbs, Marlene Tucker, old Merdell."

She said sharply:

"Merdell? That was an accident. He fell from the quay. He was very old, half blind, and he'd been drinking in the pub."

"It was not an accident. Merdell knew too much."

"What did he know?"

"He recognised a face, or a way of walking, or a voice—something like that. I talked to him the day I first came down here. He told me then all about the Folliat family—about your father-in-law and your husband, and your sons who were killed in the war. Only—they were not *both* killed, were they? Your son Henry went down with his ship, but your second son, James, was not killed. He deserted. He was reported at first, perhaps, 'Missing believed killed,' and later you told everyone that he was killed. It was nobody's business to disbelieve that statement. Why should they?"

Poirot paused and then went on.

"Do not imagine I have no sympathy for you, Madame. Life has been hard for you, I know. You can have had no real illusions about your younger son, but he was your son, and you loved him. You did all you could to give him a new life. You had the charge of a young girl, a subnormal but very rich girl. Oh yes, she was rich. You gave out that her parents had lost all their money, that she was poor, and that you had advised her to marry a rich man many years older than herself."

Why should anybody disbelieve your story? Again, it was nobody's business. Her parents and near relatives had been killed. A firm of French lawyers in Paris acted as instructed by lawyers in San Miguel. On her marriage, she assumed control of her own fortune. She was, as you have told me, docile, affectionate, suggestible. Everything her husband asked her to sign, she signed. Securities were probably changed and resold many times, but in the end the desired financial result was reached. Sir George Stubbs, the new personality assumed by your son, became a rich man and his wife became a pauper. It is no legal offense to call yourself 'Sir' unless it is done to obtain money under false pretences. A title creates confidence—it suggests, if not birth, then certainly riches. So the rich Sir George Stubbs, older and changed in appearance and having grown a beard, bought Nasse House and came to live where he belonged, though he had not been there since he was a boy. There was nobody left after the devastations of war who was likely to have recognized him. But old Merdell did. He kept the knowledge to himself, but when he said to me slyly that there would always be Folliats at Nasse House, that was his own private joke.

"So all had turned out well, or so you thought. Your plan, I fully believe, stopped there. Your son had wealth, his ancestral home, and though his wife was subnormal she was a beautiful and docile girl and you hoped he would be kind to her and that she would be happy."

Mrs. Folliat said in a low voice:

"That's how I thought it would be—I would look after Hattie and care for her. I never dreamed—"

"You never dreamed--and your son carefully did not tell you, that at the time of the marriage he was already married. Oh yes—we have searched the records for what we knew must exist. Your son had married a girl in Trieste, a girl of the underground criminal world with whom he concealed himself after his desertion. She had no mind to be parted from him, nor for that matter had he any intention of being parted from her. He accepted the marriage with Hattie as a means to wealth, but in his own mind he knew from the beginning what he intended to do."

"No, no, I do not believe that! I cannot believe it. . . . It was that woman—that wicked creature."

Poirot went on inexorably:

"He meant murder. Hattie had no relations, few friends. Immediately on their return to England, he brought her here. The servants hardly saw her that first evening, and the woman they saw the next morning was not Hattie, but his Italian wife made up as Hattie and behaving roughly much as Hattie behaved. And there again it might have ended. The false Hattie would have lived out her life as the real Hattie though doubtless her mental powers would have unexpectedly improved owing to what would vaguely be called 'new treatment.' The secretary, Miss Brewis, already realized that there was very little wrong with Lady Stubbs' mental processes.

"But then a totally unforeseen thing happened. A cousin of Hattie's wrote that he was coming to England on a yachting trip, and although that cousin had not seen her for many years he would not be likely to be deceived by an impostor.

"It is odd," said Poirot, breaking off his narrative, "that though the thought did cross my mind that De Sousa might not be De Sousa, it never occurred to me that the truth lay the other way round—that is to say, that Hattie was not Hattie."

He went on:

"There might have been several different ways of meeting that situation. Lady Stubbs could have avoided a meeting with a plea of illness, but if De Sousa remained long in England she could hardly have continued to avoid meeting him. But there was already another complication. Old Merdell, garrulous in his old age, used to chatter to his granddaughter. She was probably the only person who bothered to listen to him, and even she dismissed most of what he said because she thought him 'batty.' Nevertheless some of the things he said about having seen 'a woman's body in the woods,' and 'Sir George Stubbs being really Mr. James' made sufficient impression on her to make her hint about them tentatively to Sir George. In doing so, of course, she signed her own death warrant. Sir George and his wife could take no chances of stories like that getting around. I imagine that he handed her out small sums of hush money, and proceeded to make his plans.

"They worked out their scheme very carefully. They already knew the date when De Sousa was due at Helmmouth. It coincided with the date fixed for the Fête. They arranged their plan so that Marlene should be killed and Lady Stubbs 'disappear' in conditions which should throw vague suspicion on De Sousa. Hence the references to his being a 'wicked man' and the accusation: 'He kills people.' Lady Stubbs was to disappear permanently (possibly a conveniently unrecognizable body might be identified at some time by Sir George), and a new personality was to take her place. Actually, 'Hattie' would merely resume her own Italian personality. All that was needed was for her to double the parts over a period of a little more than twenty-four hours. With the connivance of Sir George, this was easy. On the day I arrived, 'Lady Stubbs' was supposed to have remained in her room until just before teatime. Nobody saw her there except Sir George. Actually she slipped out, took a bus or a train to Exeter, and travelled from Exeter in the company of another girl student (several travel every day this time of year) to whom she confided her story of the friend who had eaten bad veal and ham pie. She arrives at the Hostel, books her cubicle, and goes out to 'explore.' By teatime, Lady Stubbs is in the drawing room. After dinner, Lady Stubbs goes early to bed—but Miss Brewis caught a glimpse of her slipping out of the house a short while afterwards. She spends the night in the Hostel, but is out early, and is back at Nasse as Lady Stubbs for breakfast. Again she spends a morning in her room with a 'headache,' and this time manages to stage an appearance as a 'trespasser' rebuffed by Sir George from the window of his wife's room where he pretends to turn and speak to his wife inside that room. The changes of costume were not difficult— shorts and an open shirt under one of the elaborate dresses that Lady Stubbs was fond of wearing. Heavy white make-up for Lady Stubbs with a big coolie hat to shade her face; a gay peasant scarf, sunburned complexion, and bronze red curls for the Italian girl. No one would have dreamed that those two were the same woman.

"And so the final drama was staged. Just before four o'clock Lady Stubbs told Miss Brewis to take a tea tray down to Marlene. That was because she was afraid such an idea might occur to Miss Brewis independently, and it would be fatal if Miss Brewis should inconveniently appear at the wrong moment. Perhaps, too, she had a malicious pleasure in arranging for Miss Brewis to be at the scene of the crime at approximately the time it was committed. Then, choosing her moment, she slipped into the empty fortunetelling tent, out through the back and into the summerhouse in the shrubbery where she kept her hiker's rucksack with its change of costume. She slipped through the woods, called to Marlene to let her in, and strangled the unsuspecting girl then and there. The big coolie hat she threw into the river, then she changed into her hiker dress and make-up, packed up her cyclamen georgette dress and high-heeled shoes in the rucksack—and presently an Italian student from the Youth Hostel joined her Dutch acquaintance at the shows on the lawn, and left with her by the local bus as planned. Where she is now I do not know. I suspect in Soho where she doubtless has underworld affiliations of her own nationality who can provide her with the necessary papers. In any case, it is not for an Italian girl that the police are looking, it is for Hattie Stubbs, simple, subnormal, exotic.

"But poor Hattie Stubbs is dead, as you yourself, Madame, know only too well. You revealed that knowledge when I spoke to you in the drawing room on the day of the Fête. The death of Marlene had been a bad shock to you—you had not had the least idea of what was planned; but you revealed very clearly, though I was dense enough not to see it at the time, that when you talked of 'Hattie,' you were talking of two different people—one a woman you disliked who would be 'better dead,' and against whom you warned me, 'not to believe a word she said'—the other a girl of whom you spoke in the past tense and whom you defended with a warm affection. I think, Madame, that you were very fond of poor Hattie Stubbs. . . ."

There was a long pause.

Mrs. Folliat sat quite still in her chair. At last she roused herself and spoke. Her voice had the coldness of ice.

"Your whole story is quite fantastic, M. Poirot. I really think you must be mad. . . . All this is entirely in your head, you have no evidence whatsoever!"

Poirot went across to one of the windows and opened it.

"Listen, Madame. What do you hear?"

"I am a little deaf. . . . What should I hear?"

"The blows of a pickaxe. . . . They are breaking up the concrete foundation of the Folly. . . . What a good place to bury a body—where a tree has been uprooted and the earth is already disturbed. A little later, to make all safe, concrete over the ground where the body lies, and, on the concrete, erect a Folly. . . ." He added gently: "Sir George's Folly . . . The Folly of the owner of Nasse House."

A long shuddering sigh escaped Mrs. Folliat.

"Such a beautiful place," said Poirot. "Only one thing evil . . . The man who owns it. . . ."

"I know." Her words came hoarsely. "I have always known. . . . Even as a child he frightened me. . . . Ruthless . . . without pity . . . And without conscience . . . But he was my son and I loved him. . . . I should have spoken out after Hattie's death . . . but he was my son—how could I be the one to give him up? And so, because of my silence, that poor silly child was killed. . . . And after her, dear old Merdell . . . Where would it have ended?"

"With a murderer it does not end," said Poirot.

She bowed her head. For a moment or two she stayed so, her hands covering her eyes.

Then Mrs. Folliat of Nasse House, daughter of a long line of brave men, drew herself erect. She looked straight at Poirot and her voice was formal and remote.

"Thank you, M. Poirot," she said, "for coming to tell me yourself of all this. Will you leave me now? There are some things that one has to face quite alone. . . ."

Sad Cypress

Come away, come away, death,
  And in sad cypress let me be laid;
Fly away, fly away, breath;
  I am slain by a fair cruel maid.
My shroud of white, stuck all with yew,
  O prepare it!
My part of death, no one so true
  Did share it.

—SHAKESPEARE

Prologue

"Elinor Katharine Carlisle. You stand charged upon this indictment with the murder of Mary Gerrard upon the 27th of July last. Are you guilty or not guilty?"

Elinor Carlisle stood very straight, her head raised. It was a graceful head, the modeling of the bones sharp and well defined. The eyes were a deep vivid blue, the hair black. The brows had been plucked to a faint thin line.

There was a silence—quite a noticeable silence.

Sir Edwin Bulmer, Counsel for the Defense, felt a thrill of dismay. He thought, *My God, she's going to plead guilty. She's lost her nerve.*

Elinor Carlisle's lips parted. She said, *"Not guilty."*

Counsel for the Defense sank back. He passed a handkerchief over his brow, realizing that it had been a near shave.

Sir Samuel Attenbury was on his feet, outlining the case for the Crown.

"May it please your lordship, gentlemen of the jury, on the 27th of July, at half-past three in the afternoon, Mary Gerrard died at Hunterbury, Maidensford . . ."

His voice ran on, sonorous and pleasing to the ear. It lulled Elinor almost into unconsciousness. From the simple and concise narrative only an occasional phrase seeped through to her conscious mind.

". . . Case a peculiarly simple and straightforward one. . . . It is the duty of the Crown . . . prove motive and opportunity. . . . No one, as far as can be seen, had any motive to kill this unfortunate girl, Mary Gerrard, except the accused. A young girl of a charming disposition—liked by everybody—without, one would have said, an enemy in the world. . . ."

Mary, Mary Gerrard! How far away it all seemed now. Not real any longer. . . .

". . . Your attention will be particularly directed to the following considerations: 1. What opportunities and means had the accused for administering poison? 2. What motive had she for so doing?

"It will be my duty to call before you witnesses who can help you to form a true conclusion on these matters. . . .

". . . As regards the poisoning of Mary Gerrard, I shall endeavor to show you that *no one had any opportunity* to commit this crime except the accused. . . ."

Elinor felt as though imprisoned in a thick mist. Detached words came drifting through the fog.

". . . Sandwiches . . . Fish paste . . . Empty house. . . ."

The words stabbed through the thick enveloping blanket of Elinor's thoughts—pin-pricks through a heavy muffling veil. . . .

The court. Faces. Rows and rows of faces! One particular face with a big black mustache and shrewd eyes. Hercule Poirot, his head a little on one side, his eyes thoughtful, was watching her.

She thought, *He's trying to see just exactly why I did it. He's trying to get inside my head to see what I thought—what I felt. . . .*

Felt? A little blur—a slight sick sense of shock. . . . Roddy's face—his dear, *dear* face with its long nose, its sensitive mouth . . . Roddy! Always Roddy—always, ever since she could remember—since those days at Hunterbury among the raspberries and up in the warren and down by the brook. Roddy—Roddy—Roddy. . . .

Other faces! Nurse O'Brien, her mouth slightly open, her freckled, fresh face thrust forward. Nurse Hopkins looking smug—smug and implacable. Peter Lord's face—Peter Lord—so kind, so sensible, so—so *comforting!* But looking now—what was it—*lost?* Yes—lost! Minding— minding all this frightfully! While she herself, star performer, didn't mind at all!

Here she was, quite calm and cold, standing in the dock, accused of murder. She was in court.

Something stirred; the folds of blanket round her brain lightened— became mere wraiths. *In court!—People. . . .*

People leaning forward, their lips parted a little, their eyes agog, staring at her, Elinor, with a horrible ghoulish enjoyment—listening with a kind of slow, cruel relish to what that tall man was saying about her.

"The facts in this case are extremely easy to follow and are not in dispute. I shall put them before you quite simply. From the very beginning . . ."

Elinor thought, *The beginning. . . . The beginning? The day that horrible anonymous letter came!* THAT *was the beginning of it. . . .*

1

AN ANONYMOUS LETTER! Elinor Carlisle stood looking down at it as it lay open in her hand. She'd never had such a thing before. It gave one an unpleasant sensation. Ill-written, badly spelled, on cheap pink paper.

THIS IS TO WARN YOU,
    I'm naming no Names but there's Someone sucking up to your Aunt and if you're not kareful you'll get Cut Out of Everything.

Girls Are very Artful and Old Ladies is Soft when Young Ones suck up to Them and Flatter them What I say is You'd best come down and see for Yourself whats Going On its not right you and the Young Gentleman should be Done Out of What's yours—and She's very Artful and the Old Lady might Pop off at any time.
WELL-WISHER.

Elinor was still staring at this missive, her plucked brows drawn together in distaste, when the door opened. The maid announced, "Mr. Welman," and Roddy came in.

Roddy! As always when she saw Roddy, Elinor was conscious of a slightly giddy feeling, a throb of sudden pleasure, a feeling that it was incumbent upon her to be very matter-of-fact and unemotional. Because it was so very obvious that Roddy, although he loved her, didn't feel about her the way she felt about him. The first sight of him did something to her, twisted her heart round so that it almost hurt. Absurd that a man—an ordinary, yes, a perfectly ordinary young man—should be able to do that to one! That the mere look of him should set the world spinning, that his voice should make you want—just a little—to cry. Love surely should be a pleasurable emotion—not something that hurt you by its intensity.

One thing was clear: one must be very, very careful to be off-hand and casual about it all. Men didn't like devotion and adoration. Certainly Roddy didn't.

She said lightly, "Hallo, Roddy!"

Roddy said, "Hallo, darling. You're looking very tragic. Is it a bill?"

Elinor shook her head.

Roddy said, "I thought it might be—midsummer, you know—when the fairies dance, and the accounts rendered come tripping along!"

Elinor said, "It's rather horrid. It's an anonymous letter."

Roddy's brows went up. His keen, fastidious face stiffened and changed. He said—a sharp, disgusted exclamation, "No!"

Elinor said again, "It's rather horrid. . . ."

She moved a step toward her desk.

"I'd better tear it up, I suppose."

She could have done that—she almost did—for Roddy and anonymous letters were two things that ought not to come together. She might have thrown it away and thought no more about it. He would not have stopped her. His fastidiousness was far more strongly developed than his curiosity.

But on an impulse Elinor decided differently. She said, "Perhaps, though, you'd better read it first. Then we'll burn it. It's about Aunt Laura."

Roddy's eyebrows rose in surprise. "Aunt Laura?"

He took the letter, read it, gave a frown of distaste, and handed it back. "Yes," he said. "Definitely to be burned! How extraordinary people are!"

Elinor said, "One of the servants, do you think?"

"I suppose so." He hesitated. "I wonder who—who the person is—the one they mention?"

Elinor said thoughtfully, "It must be Mary Gerrard, I think."

Roddy frowned in an effort of remembrance.

"Mary Gerrard? Who is she?"

"The daughter of the people at the lodge. You must remember her as a child? Aunt Laura was always fond of the girl, and took an interest in her. She paid for her schooling and for various extras—piano lessons and French and things."

Roddy said, "Oh, yes, I remember her now; scrawny kid, all legs and arms, with a lot of messy fair hair."

Elinor nodded. "Yes, you probably haven't seen her since those summer holidays when Mum and Dad were abroad. You've not been down at Hunterbury as often as I have, of course, and she's been abroad *au pair* in Germany lately, but we used to rout her out and play with her when we were all kids."

"What's she like now?" asked Roddy.

Elinor said, "She's turned out very nice-looking. Good manners and all that. As a result of her education, you'd never take her for old Gerrard's daughter."

"Gone all lady-like, has she?"

"Yes. I think, as a result of that, she doesn't get on very well at the lodge. Mrs. Gerrard died some years ago, you know, and Mary and her father don't get on. He jeers at her schooling and her 'fine ways.' "

Roddy said irritably, "People never dream what harm they may do by 'educating' someone! Often it's cruelty, not kindness!"

Elinor said, "I suppose she *is* up at the house a good deal. She reads aloud to Aunt Laura, I know, since she had her stroke."

Roddy said, "Why can't the nurse read to her?"

Elinor said with a smile, "Nurse O'Brien's got a brogue you can cut with a knife! I don't wonder Aunt Laura prefers Mary."

Roddy walked rapidly and nervously up and down the room for a minute or two. Then he said, "You know, Elinor, I believe we ought to go down."

Elinor said with a slight recoil, "Because of this—?"

"No, no—not at all. Oh, damn it all, one must be honest, *yes!* Foul as that communication is, there *may* be some truth behind it. I mean, the old girl is pretty ill—"

"Yes, Roddy."

He looked at her with his charming smile—admitting the fallibility of human nature. He said, "And the money does matter—to you and me, Elinor."

She admitted it quickly: "Oh, it does."

He said seriously, "It's not that I'm mercenary. But, after all, Aunt Laura herself has said over and over again that you and I are her only family ties. You're her own niece, her brother's child, and I'm her husband's nephew. She's always given us to understand that at her death all she's got would come to one or the other—or more probably both—of us. And—it's a pretty large sum, Elinor."

"Yes," said Elinor thoughtfully. "It must be."

"It's no joke keeping up Hunterbury." He paused. "Uncle Henry was what you'd call, I suppose, comfortably off when he met your Aunt Laura. But she was an heiress. She and your father were both left very wealthy. Pity your father speculated and lost most of his."

Elinor sighed. "Poor father never had much business sense. He got very worried over things before he died."

"Yes, your Aunt Laura had a much better head than he had. She married Uncle Henry and they bought Hunterbury, and she told me the other day that she'd been exceedingly lucky always in her investments. Practically nothing had slumped."

"Uncle Henry left all he had to her when he died, didn't he?"

Roddy nodded. "Yes, tragic his dying so soon. And she's never married again. Faithful old bean. And she's always been very good to us. She's treated me as if I were her nephew by blood. If I've been in a hole she's helped me out; luckily I haven't done that *too* often!"

"She's been awfully generous to me, too," said Elinor gratefully.

Roddy nodded. "Aunt Laura," he said, "is a brick. But, you know, Elinor, perhaps without meaning to do so, you and I live pretty extravagantly, considering what our means really are!"

She said ruefully, "I suppose we do. Everything costs so much—clothes and one's face—and just silly things like movies and cocktails—and even gramophone records!"

Roddy said, "Darling, you *are* one of the lilies of the field, aren't you? You toil not, neither do you spin!"

Elinor said, "Do you think I ought to, Roddy?"

He shook his head. "I like you as you are: delicate and aloof and ironical. I'd hate you to go all earnest. I'm only saying that if it weren't for Aunt Laura you probably would be working at some grim job."

He went on: "The same with me. I've got a job, of sorts. Being with Lewis & Hume is not too arduous. It suits me. I preserve my self-respect by having a job; but—mark this—but I don't worry about the future because of my expectations—from Aunt Laura."

Elinor said, "We sound rather like human leeches!"

"Nonsense! We've been given to understand that some day we shall have money—that's all. Naturally that fact influences our conduct."

Elinor said thoughtfully, "Aunt Laura has never told us definitely just *how* she has left her money?"

Roddy said, "That doesn't matter! In all probability she's divided it between us; but if that isn't so—if she's left all of it or most of it to you as her own flesh and blood—why, then, darling, I shall still share in it, because *I'm* going to marry *you*—and if the old pet thinks the majority should go to me as the male representative of the Welmans, that's still all right, because *you're* marrying *me*."

He grinned at her affectionately. He said, "Lucky we happen to love each other. You do love me, don't you, Elinor?"

"Yes." She said it coldly, almost primly.

"Yes!" Roddy mimicked her. "You're adorable, Elinor. That little air of yours—aloof—untouchable—*la Princesse Lointaine.* It's that quality of yours that made me love you, I believe."

Elinor caught her breath. She said, "Is it?"

"Yes." He frowned. "Some women are so—oh, I don't know—so damned possessive—so—so dog-like and devoted—their emotions slopping all over the place! I'd hate that. With you I never know—I'm never sure— any minute you might turn around in that cool, detached way of yours and say you'd changed your mind—quite coolly, like that—without batting an eyelash! You're a fascinating creature, Elinor. You're like a work of art, so—so *finished!*"

He went on: "You know, I think ours will be the perfect marriage: We both love each other enough and not too much. We're good friends. We've got a lot of tastes in common. We know each other through and through. We've all the advantages of cousinship without the disadvantages of blood relationship. I shall never get tired of you, because you're such an elusive creature. *You* may get tired of *me*, though. I'm such an ordinary sort of chap—"

Elinor shook her head. She said, "I shan't get tired of you, Roddy— ever."

"My sweet!"

He kissed her.

He said, "Aunt Laura has a pretty shrewd idea of how it is with us, I think, although we haven't been down since we finally fixed it up. It rather gives us an excuse, doesn't it, for going down?"

"Yes. I was thinking the other day—"

Roddy finished the sentence for her: "—that we hadn't been down as often as we might. I thought that, too. When she first had her stroke we went down almost every other week-end. And now it must be almost two months since we were there."

Elinor said, "We'd have gone if she'd asked for us—at once."

"Yes, of course. And we know that she likes Nurse O'Brien and is well looked after. All the same, perhaps, we *have* been a bit slack. I'm talking now not from the money point of view—but the sheer human one."

Elinor nodded. "I know."

"So that filthy letter has done some good, after all! We'll go down to protect our interests *and* because we're fond of the old dear!"

He lit a match and set fire to the letter which he took from Elinor's hand.

"Wonder who wrote it?" he said. "Not that it matters. . . . Someone who was 'on our side,' as we used to say when we were kids. Perhaps they've done us a good turn, too. Jim Partington's mother went out to the Riviera to live, had a handsome young Italian doctor to attend her, became quite crazy about him and left him every penny she had. Jim and his sisters tried to upset the will, but couldn't."

Elinor said, "Aunt Laura likes the new doctor who's taken over Dr. Ransome's practice—but not to that extent! Anyway, that horrid letter mentioned a girl. It must be Mary."

Roddy said, "We'll go down and see for ourselves."

Nurse O'Brien rustled out of Mrs. Welman's bedroom and into the bathroom. She said over her shoulder, "I'll just pop the kettle on. You could do with a cup of tea before you go on, I'm sure, Nurse."

Nurse Hopkins said comfortably, "Well, dear, I can *always* do with a cup of tea. I always say there's nothing like a nice cup of tea—a strong cup!"

Nurse O'Brien said as she filled the kettle and lit the gas-ring, "I've got everything here in this cupboard—teapot and cups and sugar—and Edna brings me up fresh milk twice a day. No need to be forever ringing bells. 'Tis a fine gas-ring, this; boils a kettle in a flash."

Nurse O'Brien was a tall red-haired woman of thirty with flashing white teeth, a freckled face and an engaging smile. Her cheerfulness and vitality made her a favorite with her patients. Nurse Hopkins, the District Nurse who came every morning to assist with the bed-making and toilet of the heavy old lady, was a homely-looking middle-aged woman with a capable air and a brisk manner.

She said now approvingly, "Everything's very well done in this house."

The other nodded. "Yes, old-fashioned, some of it, no central heating, but plenty of fires and all the maids are very obliging girls and Mrs. Bishop looks after them well."

Nurse Hopkins said, "These girls nowadays—I've no patience with 'em—don't know what they want, most of them—and can't do a decent day's work."

"Mary Gerrard's a nice girl," said Nurse O'Brien. "I really don't know what Mrs. Welman would do without her. You saw how she asked for her now? Ah, well, she's a lovely creature, I will say, and she's got a way with her."

Nurse Hopkins said, "I'm sorry for Mary. That old father of hers does his best to spite the girl."

"Not a civil word in his head, the old curmudgeon," said Nurse O'Brien. "There, the kettle's singing. I'll wet the tea as soon as it comes to the boil."

The tea was made and poured, hot and strong. The two nurses sat with it in Nurse O'Brien's room next door to Mrs. Welman's bedroom.

"Mr. Welman and Miss Carlisle are coming down," said Nurse O'Brien. "There was a telegram came this morning."

"There, now, dear," said Nurse Hopkins. "I thought the old lady was looking excited about something. It's some time since they've been down, isn't it?"

"It must be two months and over. Such a nice young gentleman, Mr. Welman. But very proud-looking."

Nurse Hopkins said, "I saw *her* picture in the *Tatler* the other day—with a friend at Newmarket."

Nurse O'Brien said, "She's very well known in society, isn't she? And always has such lovely clothes. Do you think she's really good-looking, Nurse?"

Nurse Hopkins said, "Difficult to tell what these girls really look like under their make-up! In my opinion, she hasn't got anything like the looks Mary Gerrard has!"

Nurse O'Brien pursed her lips and put her head on one side. "You may be right now. But Mary hasn't got the *style!*"

Nurse Hopkins said sententiously, "Fine feathers make fine birds."

"Another cup of tea, Nurse?"

"Thank you, Nurse. I don't mind if I do."

Over their steaming cups the women drew a little closer together. Nurse O'Brien said, "An odd thing happened last night. I went in at two o'clock to settle my dear comfortably, as I always do, and she was lying there awake. But she must have been dreaming, for as soon as I got into the room she said, 'The photograph. I must have the photograph.'

"So I said, 'Why, of course, Mrs. Welman. But wouldn't you rather wait till morning?' And she said, 'No. I want to look at it now.' So I said, 'Well, where *is* this photograph? Is it the one of Mr. Roderick you're meaning?' And she said, 'Roder-ick? No. *Lewis.*' And she began to struggle, and I went to lift her and she got out her keys from the little box beside her bed and told me to unlock the second drawer of the tallboy, and there, sure enough, was a big photograph in a silver frame. *Such* a handsome man. And *'Lewis'* written across the corner. Old-fashioned, of course, must have been taken years ago. I took it to her and she held it there, staring at it a long time. And she just murmured, *'Lewis—Lewis.'* Then she sighed and gave it to me and told me to put it back. And, would you believe it, when I turned round again she'd gone off as sweetly as a child."

Nurse Hopkins said, "Was it her husband, do you think?"

Nurse O'Brien said, "It was not! For this morning I asked Mrs. Bishop, careless-like, what was the late Mr. Welman's first name, and it was Henry, she told me!"

The two women exchanged glances. Nurse Hopkins had a long nose, and the end of it quivered a little with pleasurable emotion. She said thoughtfully, "Lewis—Lewis. I wonder, now. I don't recall the name anywhere round these parts."

"It would be many years ago, dear," the other reminded her.

"Yes, and, of course, I've only been here a couple of years. I wonder, now—"

Nurse O'Brien said, "A *very* handsome man. Looked as though he might be a cavalry officer!"

Nurse Hopkins sipped her tea. She said, "That's very interesting."

Nurse O'Brien said romantically, "Maybe they were boy and girl together and a cruel father separated them."

Nurse Hopkins said with a deep sigh, "Perhaps he was killed in the war."

When Nurse Hopkins, pleasantly stimulated by tea and romantic speculation, finally left the house, Mary Gerrard ran out of the door to overtake her.

"Oh, Nurse, may I walk down to the village with you?"

"Of course you can, Mary, my dear."

Mary Gerrard said breathlessly, "I *must* talk to you. I'm so worried about everything."

The older woman looked at her kindly.

At twenty-one Mary Gerrard was a lovely creature with a kind of wild-rose unreality about her; a long delicate neck, pale golden hair lying close to her exquisitely shaped head in soft natural waves, and eyes of a deep, vivid blue.

Nurse Hopkins said, "What's the trouble?"

"The trouble is that the time is going on and on and I'm not *doing* anything!"

Nurse Hopkins said dryly, "Time enough for that."

"No, but it is so—so unsettling. Mrs. Welman has been wonderfully kind, giving me all that expensive schooling. I do feel now that I ought to be starting to earn my own living. I ought to be training for something."

Nurse Hopkins nodded sympathetically.

"It's such a waste of everything if I don't. I've tried to—to—explain what I feel to Mrs. Welman, but—it's difficult—she doesn't seem to understand. She keeps saying there's plenty of time."

Nurse Hopkins said, "She's a sick woman, remember."

Mary flushed, a contrite flush. "Oh, I know. I suppose I oughtn't to bother her. But it *is* worrying—and Father's so—so *beastly* about it! Keeps jibing me for being a fine lady! But indeed *I* don't want to sit about doing nothing!"

"I know you don't."

"The trouble is that training of any kind is nearly always expensive. I know German pretty well now, and I might do something with that. But I think really I want to be a hospital nurse. I do like nursing and sick people."

Nurse Hopkins said unromantically, "You've got to be as strong as a horse, remember!"

"I am strong! And I really *do* like nursing. Mother's sister, the one in New Zealand, was a nurse. So it's in my blood, you see."

"What about massage?" suggested Nurse Hopkins. "Or Norland? You're fond of children. There's good money to be made in massage."

Mary said doubtfully, "It's expensive to train for it, isn't it? I hoped— but of course that's very greedy of me—she's done so much for me already."

"Mrs. Welman, you mean? Nonsense. In my opinion, she owes you that. She's given you a slap-up education, but not the kind that leads to anything much. You don't want to teach?"

"I'm not clever enough."

Nurse Hopkins said, "There's brains and brains! If you take my advice, Mary, you'll be patient for the present. In my opinion, as I said, Mrs. Welman owes it to you to help you get a start at making your living.

And I've no doubt she means to do it. But the truth of the matter is, she's got fond of you, and she doesn't want to lose you."

Mary said, "Oh!" She drew in her breath with a little gasp. "Do you really think that's it?"

"I haven't the least doubt of it! There she is, poor old lady, more or less helpless, paralyzed one side and nothing and nobody much to amuse her. It means a lot to her to have a fresh, pretty young thing like you about the house. You've a very nice way with you in a sickroom."

Mary said softly, "If you really think so—that makes me feel better. . . . Dear Mrs. Welman, I'm very, *very* fond of her! She's been so good to me always. I'd do *anything* for her!"

Nurse Hopkins said dryly, "Then the best thing you can do is to stay where you are and stop worrying! It won't be for long."

Mary said, "Do you mean—?"

Her eyes looked wide and frightened.

The District Nurse nodded. "She's rallied wonderfully, but it won't be for long. There will be a second stroke and then a third. I know the way of it only too well. You be patient, my dear. If you keep the old lady's last days happy and occupied, that's a better deed than many. The time for the other will come."

Mary said, "You're very kind."

Nurse Hopkins said, "Here's your father coming out from the lodge—and not to pass the time of day pleasantly, I should say!"

They were just nearing the big iron gates. On the steps of the lodge an elderly man with a bent back was painfully hobbling down the two steps.

Nurse Hopkins said cheerfully, "Good morning, Mr. Gerrard."

Ephraim Gerrard said crustily, "Ah!"

"Very nice weather," said Nurse Hopkins.

Old Gerrard said crossly, "Maybe for you. 'Tisn't for me. My lumbago's been at me something cruel."

Nurse Hopkins said cheerfully, "That was the wet spell last week, I expect. This hot dry weather will soon clear *that* away."

Her brisk professional manner appeared to annoy the old man.

He said disagreeably, "Nurses—nurses, you'm all the same. Full of cheerfulness over other people's troubles. Little *you* care! And there's Mary talks about being a nurse, too. Should have thought she'd want to be something better than *that,* with her French and her German and her piano-playing and all the things she's learned at her grand school and her travels abroad."

Mary said sharply, "Being a hospital nurse would be quite good enough for me!"

"Yes, and you'd sooner do nothing at all, wouldn't you? Strutting about with your airs and your graces and your fine-lady-do-nothing ways. Laziness, that's what *you* like, my girl!"

Mary protested, tears springing to her eyes, "It isn't true, Dad. You've no right to say that!"

Nurse Hopkins intervened with a heavy, determinedly humorous air.

"Just a bit under the weather, aren't we, this morning? You don't really mean what you say, Gerrard. Mary's a good girl and a good daughter to you."

Gerrard looked at his daughter with an air of almost active malevolence. "She's no daughter of mine—nowadays—with her French and her history and her mincing talk. Pah!"

He turned and went into the lodge again.

Mary said, the tears still standing in her eyes, "You do see, Nurse, don't you, how difficult it is? He's so unreasonable. He's never really liked me even when I was a little girl. Mum was always standing up for me."

Nurse Hopkins said kindly, "There, there, don't worry. These things are sent to try us! Goodness, I must hurry. Such a round as I've got this morning."

And as she stood watching the brisk retreating figure, Mary Gerrard thought forlornly that nobody was any real good or could really help you. Nurse Hopkins, for all her kindness, was quite content to bring out a little stock of platitudes and offer them with an air of novelty.

Mary thought disconsolately, "*What* SHALL *I do?*"

2

MRS. WELMAN LAY on her carefully built-up pillows. Her breathing was a little heavy, but she was not asleep. Her eyes—eyes still deep and blue like those of her niece Elinor, looked up at the ceiling. She was a big, heavy woman, with a handsome, hawk-like profile. Pride and determination showed in her face.

The eyes dropped and came to rest on the figure sitting by the window. They rested there tenderly—almost wistfully.

She said at last, "Mary—"

The girl turned quickly. "Oh, you're awake, Mrs. Welman."

Laura Welman said, "Yes, I've been awake some time."

"Oh, I didn't know. I'd have—"

Mrs. Welman broke in, "No, that's all right. I was thinking—thinking of many things."

"Yes, Mrs. Welman?"

The sympathetic look, the interested voice, made a tender look come into the older woman's face. She said gently, "I'm very fond of you, my dear. You're very good to me."

"Oh, Mrs. Welman, it's *you* who have been good to *me*. If it hadn't been for you, I don't know what I should have done! You've done *everything* for me."

"I don't know—I don't know, I'm sure." The sick woman moved restlessly, her right arm twitched—the left remaining inert and lifeless. "One means to do the best one can, but it's so difficult to know what is best— what is *right*. I've been too sure of myself always."

Mary Gerrard said, "Oh, no, I'm sure you *always* know what is best and right to do."

But Laura Welman shook her head. "No—no. It worries me. I've had one besetting sin always, Mary: I'm proud. Pride can be the devil. It runs in our family. Elinor has it, too."

Mary said quickly, "It will be nice for you to have Miss Elinor and Mr. Roderick down. It will cheer you up a lot. It's quite a time since they were here."

Mrs. Welman said softly, "They're good children—very good children. And fond of me, both of them. I always know I've only got to send and they'll come at any time. But I don't want to do that too often. They're young and happy—the world in front of them. No need to bring them near decay and suffering before their time."

Mary said, "I'm sure they'd *never* feel like that, Mrs. Welman."

Mrs. Welman went on, talking perhaps more to herself than to the girl: "I always hoped they might marry. But I tried never to suggest anything of the kind. Young people are so contradictory. It would have put them off! I had an idea, long ago, when they were children, that Elinor had set her heart on Roddy. But I wasn't at all sure about *him*. He's a funny creature. Henry was like that—very reserved and fastidious. . . . Yes, Henry. . . ."

She was silent for a little, thinking of her dead husband.

She murmured, "So long ago—so very long ago. . . . We had only been married five years when he died. Double pneumonia . . . We were happy— yes, very happy; but somehow it all seems very *unreal*, that happiness. I was an odd, solemn, undeveloped girl—my head full of ideals and hero-worship. No *reality*."

Mary murmured, "You must have been very lonely—afterward."

"After? Oh, yes—terribly lonely. I was twenty-six—and now I'm over sixty. A long time, my dear—a long, long time." She said with sudden brisk acerbity, "And now *this!*"

"Your illness?"

"Yes. A stroke is the thing I've always dreaded. The indignity of it all! Washed and tended like a baby! Helpless to do anything for myself. It maddens me. The O'Brien creature is good-natured—I will say that for her. She doesn't mind my snapping at her and she's not more idiotic than most of them. But it makes a lot of difference to me to have *you* about, Mary."

"Does it?" The girl flushed. "I—I'm so glad, Mrs. Welman."

Laura Welman said shrewdly, "You've been worrying, haven't you? About the future. You leave it to me, my dear. I'll see to it that you shall have the means to be independent and take up a profession. But be patient for a little—it means too much to me to have you here."

"Oh, Mrs. Welman, of course—of *course!* I wouldn't leave you for the world. Not if you want me—"

"I do want you." The voice was unusually deep and full. "You're—you're quite like a daughter to me, Mary. I've seen you grow up here at Hunterbury from a little toddling thing—have seen you grow into a beautiful girl. I'm proud of you, child. I only hope I've done what was best for you."

Mary said quickly, "If you mean that your having been so good to me and having educated me above—well, above my station—if you think it's made me dissatisfied or—or—given me what Father calls fine-lady ideas, indeed that isn't true. I'm just ever so grateful, that's all. And if I'm anxious to start earning my living, it's only because I feel it's right that I should, and not—and not—well, do nothing after all you've done for me. I—I shouldn't like it to be thought that I was sponging on you."

Laura Welman said, and her voice was suddenly sharp-edged, "So that's what Gerrard's been putting into your head? Pay no attention to your father, Mary; there never has been and never will be any question of your sponging on me! I'm asking you to stay here a little longer solely on my account. Soon it will be over. . . . If they went the proper way about things, my life could be ended here and now—none of this long-drawn-out tomfoolery with nurses and doctors."

"Oh, no, Mrs. Welman, Dr. Lord says you may live for years."

"I'm not at all anxious to, thank you! I told him the other day that in a decently civilized state all there would be to do would be for me to intimate to him that I wished to end it, and he'd finish me off painlessly with some nice drug. 'And if you'd any courage, Doctor,' I said, 'you'd do it anyway!' "

Mary cried, "Oh! What did he say?"

"The disrespectful young man merely grinned at me, my dear, and said he wasn't going to risk being hanged. He said, 'If you'd left me all your money, Mrs. Welman, that would be different, of course!' Impudent young jackanapes! But I like him, His visits do me more good than his medicines."

"Yes, he's very nice," said Mary. "Nurse O'Brien thinks a lot of him and so does Nurse Hopkins."

Mrs. Welman said, "Hopkins ought to have more sense at her age. As for O'Brien, she simpers and says, 'Oh, Doctor,' and tosses those long streamers of hers whenever he comes near her."

"Poor Nurse O'Brien."

Mrs. Welman said indulgently, "She's not a bad sort, really, but all nurses annoy me; they always will think that you'd like 'a nice cup of tea' at five in the morning!" She paused. "What's that? Is it the car?"

Mary looked out of the window.

"Yes, it's the car. Miss Elinor and Mr. Roderick have arrived."

*   *   *

Mrs. Welman said to her niece, "I'm very glad, Elinor, about you and Roddy."

Elinor smiled at her. "I thought you would be, Aunt Laura."

The older woman said, after a moment's hesitation, "You do—care about him, Elinor?"

Elinor's delicate brows lifted. "Of course."

Laura Welman said quickly, "You must forgive me, dear. You know, you're very reserved. It's very difficult to know what you're thinking or feeling. When you were both much younger I thought you were perhaps beginning to care for Roddy—too much."

Again Elinor's delicate brows were raised. "Too much?"

The older woman nodded. "Yes. It's not wise to care too much. Sometimes a very young girl does do just that. . . . I was glad when you went abroad to Germany to finish. Then, when you came back, you seemed quite indifferent to him—and, well, I was sorry for that, too! I'm a tiresome old woman, difficult to satisfy! But I've always fancied that you had, perhaps, rather an intense nature—that kind of temperament runs in our family. It isn't a very happy one for its possessors. . . . But, as I say, when you came back from abroad so indifferent to Roddy, I was sorry about that, because I had always hoped you two would come together. And now you have, and so everything is all right! And you *do* really care for him?"

Elinor said gravely, "I care for Roddy enough and not too much."

Mrs. Welman nodded approval. "I think, then, you'll be happy. Roddy needs love—but he doesn't like violent emotion. He'd shy off from possessiveness."

Elinor said with feeling, "You know Roddy very well!"

Mrs. Welman said, "If Roddy cares for you just a *little* more than you care for him—well, that's all to the good."

Elinor said sharply, "Aunt Agatha's Advice Column. *'Keep your boy friend guessing! Don't let him be too sure of you!'* "

Laura Welman said sharply, "Are you unhappy, child? Is anything wrong?"

"No, no, nothing."

Laura Welman said, "You just thought I was being rather—cheap? My dear, you're young and sensitive. Life, I'm afraid, *is* rather cheap."

Elinor said with some slight bitterness, "I suppose it is."

Laura Welman said, "My child—you *are* unhappy? What is it?"

"Nothing—absolutely nothing." She got up and went to the window. Half turning, she said, "Aunt Laura, tell me, honestly, do you think love is ever a happy thing?"

Mrs. Welman's face became grave. "In the sense you mean, Elinor—no, probably not. To care passionately for another human creature brings always more sorrow than joy; but all the same, Elinor, one would not be without that experience. Anyone who has never really loved has never really lived."

The girl nodded. She said, "Yes—you understand—you've known what it's like—"

She turned suddenly, a questioning look in her eyes. "Aunt Laura—"

The door opened and red-haired Nurse O'Brien came in. She said in a sprightly manner, "Mrs. Welman, here's Doctor come to see you."

Dr. Lord was a young man of thirty-two. He had sandy hair, a pleasantly ugly freckled face and a remarkably square jaw. His eyes were a keen, piercing light blue.

"Good morning, Mrs. Welman," he said.

"Good morning, Dr. Lord. This is my niece, Miss Carlisle."

A very obvious admiration sprang into Dr. Lord's transparent face. He said, "How do you do?" The hand that Elinor extended to him he took rather gingerly as though he thought he might break it.

Mrs. Welman went on: "Elinor and my nephew have come to cheer me up."

"Splendid!" said Dr. Lord, "Just what you need! It will do you a lot of good, I am sure, Mrs. Welman."

He was still looking at Elinor with obvious admiration.

Elinor said, moving toward the door, "Perhaps I shall see you before you go, Dr. Lord?"

"Oh—er—yes, of course."

She went out, shutting the door behind her. Dr. Lord approached the bed, Nurse O'Brien fluttering behind him.

Mrs. Welman said with a twinkle, "Going through the usual bag of tricks, Doctor: pulse, respiration, temperature? What humbugs you doctors are!"

Nurse O'Brien said with a sigh, "Oh, Mrs. Welman. What a thing, now, to be saying to the doctor!"

Dr. Lord said with a twinkle, "Mrs. Welman sees through me, Nurse! All the same, Mrs. Welman, I've got to do my stuff, you know. The trouble with me is I've never learned the right bedside manner."

"Your bedside manner's all right. Actually you're rather proud of it."

Peter Lord chuckled and remarked, "That's what *you* say!"

After a few routine questions had been asked and answered, Dr. Lord leaned back in his chair and smiled at his patient. "Well," he said, "you're going on splendidly."

Laura Welman said, "So I shall be up and walking round the house in a few weeks' time?"

"Not quite so quickly as that."

"No, indeed. You humbug! What's the good of living stretched out like this, and cared for like a baby?"

Dr. Lord said, "What's the good of life, anyway? That's the real question. Ever read about that nice medieval invention, the Little Ease? You couldn't stand, sit, or lie in it. You'd think anyone condemned to that would die in a few weeks. Not at all. One man lived for sixteen years in an iron cage, was released, and lived to a hearty old age."

Laura Welman said, "What's the point of this story?"

Peter Lord said, "The point is that one's got an *instinct* to live. One doesn't live because one's *reason* assents to living. People who, as we say, 'would be better dead' don't want to die! People who apparently have got everything to live for just let themselves fade out of life because they haven't got the energy to fight."

"Go on."

"There's nothing more. You're one of the people who really *want* to live, whatever you say about it! And if your body wants to live, it's no good your brain dishing out the other stuff."

Mrs. Welman said with an abrupt change of subject, "How do you like it down here?"

Peter Lord said, smiling, "It suits me fine."

"Isn't it a bit irksome for a young man like you? Don't you want to specialize? Don't you find a country G.P. practice rather boring?"

Lord shook his sandy head.

"No, I like my job. I like *people,* you know, and I like ordinary everyday diseases. I don't really want to pin down the rare bacillus of an obscure disease. I like measles and chicken pox and all the rest of it. I like seeing how different bodies react to them. I like seeing if I can't improve on recognized treatment. The trouble with me is I've got absolutely no ambition. I shall stay here till I grow side-whiskers and people begin saying, 'Of course, we've always had Dr. Lord, and he's a nice old man; but he *is* very old-fashioned in his methods and perhaps we'd better call in young so-and-so, who's very up to date.' "

"H'm," said Mrs. Welman. "You seem to have got it all taped out!"

Peter Lord got up. "Well," he said, "I must be off."

Mrs. Welman said, "My niece will want to speak to you, I expect. By the way, what do you think of her? You haven't seen her before."

Dr. Lord went suddenly scarlet. His very eyebrows blushed. He said, "I—oh! she's very good-looking, isn't she? And—er—clever and all that, I should think."

Mrs. Welman was diverted. She thought to herself, *How very young he is, really.* Aloud she said, "You ought to get married."

Roddy had wandered into the garden. He had crossed the broad sweep of lawn and gone along a paved walk and had then entered the walled kitchen-garden. It was well-kept and well-stocked. He wondered if he and Elinor would live at Hunterbury one day. He supposed that they would. He himself would like that. He preferred country life. He was a little doubtful about Elinor. Perhaps she'd like living in London better.

A little difficult to know where you were with Elinor. She didn't reveal much of what she thought and felt about things. He liked that about her. He hated people who reeled off their thoughts and feelings to you, who took it for granted that you wanted to know all their inner mechanism. Reserve was always more interesting.

Elinor, he thought judicially, was really quite perfect. Nothing about her ever jarred or offended. She was delightful to look at, witty to talk to—altogether the most charming of companions.

He thought complacently to himself, *I'm damned lucky to have got her. Can't think what she sees in a chap like me.*

For Roderick Welman, in spite of his fastidiousness, was not conceited.
It did honestly strike him as strange that Elinor should have consented
to marry him.

Life stretched ahead of him pleasantly enough. One knew pretty well
where one was; that was always a blessing. He supposed that Elinor and
he would be married quite soon—that is, if Elinor wanted to; perhaps
she'd rather put it off for a bit. He mustn't rush her. They'd be a bit
hard-up at first. Nothing to worry about, though. He hoped sincerely
that Aunt Laura wouldn't die for a long time to come. She was a dear
and had always been nice to him, having him there for holidays, always
interested in what he was doing.

His mind shied away from the thought of her actual death (his mind
usually did shy away from any concrete unpleasantness). He didn't like
to visualize anything unpleasant too clearly. But—er—afterward—well,
it would be very pleasant to live here, especially as there would be plenty
of money to keep it up. He wondered exactly how his aunt had left it.
Not that it really mattered. With some women it would matter a good
deal whether husband or wife had the money. But not with Elinor. She
had plenty of tact and she didn't care enough about money to make too
much of it.

He thought, *No, there's nothing to worry about—whatever happens!*

He went out of the walled garden by the gate at the far end. From
there he wandered into the little wood where the daffodils were in spring.
They were over now, of course. But the green light was very lovely
where the sunlight came filtering through the trees.

Just for a moment an odd restlessness came to him—a rippling of his
previous placidity. He felt, *There's something—something I haven't got—
something I want—I want—I want. . . .*

The golden green light, the softness in the air—with them came a
quickened pulse, a stirring of the blood, a sudden impatience.

A girl came through the trees toward him—a girl with pale, gleaming
hair and a rose-flushed skin.

He thought, *How beautiful—how unutterably beautiful.*

Something gripped him; he stood quite still, as though frozen into
immobility. The world, he felt, was spinning, was topsy-turvy, was suddenly
and impossibly and gloriously crazy!

The girl stopped suddenly, then she came on. She came up to him
where he stood, dumb and absurdly fish-like, his mouth open.

She said, with a little hesitation, "Don't you remember me, Mr. Roderick?
It's a long time, of course. I'm Mary Gerrard, from the lodge."

Roddy said, "Oh—oh—you're Mary Gerrard?"

She said, "Yes."

Then she went on rather shyly: "I've changed, of course, since you
saw me."

He said, "Yes, you've changed. I—I wouldn't have recognized you."

He stood staring at her. He did not hear footsteps behind him. Mary
did and turned.

Elinor stood motionless a minute. Then she said, "Hallo, Mary."

Mary said, "How do you do, Miss Elinor? It's nice to see you. Mrs. Welman has been looking forward to you coming down."

Elinor said, "Yes—it's a long time. I—Nurse O'Brien sent me to look for you. She wants to lift Mrs. Welman up, and she says you usually do it with her."

Mary said, "I'll go at once."

She moved off, breaking into a run. Elinor stood looking after her. Mary ran well, grace in every movement.

Roddy said softly, "Atalanta."

Elinor did not answer. She stood quite still for a minute or two. Then she said, "It's nearly lunch-time. We'd better go back."

They walked side by side toward the house.

"Oh! Come on, Mary. It's a grand film—all about Paris. And a story by a tiptop author. There was an opera of it once."

"It's frightfully nice of you, Ted, but I really won't."

Ted Bigland said angrily, "I can't make you out nowadays, Mary. You're different—altogether different."

"No, I'm not, Ted."

"You are! I suppose because you've been away to that grand school and to Germany. You're too good for us now."

"It's not true, Ted. I'm not like that." She spoke vehemently.

The young man, a fine, sturdy specimen, looked at her appraisingly in spite of his anger. "Yes, you are. You're almost a lady, Mary."

Mary said with sudden bitterness, "Almost isn't much good, is it?"

He said with sudden understanding, "No, I reckon it isn't."

Mary said quickly, "Anyway, who cares about that sort of thing nowadays? Ladies and gentlemen, and all that!"

"It doesn't matter like it did—no," Ted assented, but thoughtfully. "All the same, there's a *feeling*. Lord, Mary, you *look* like a countess or something."

Mary said, "That's not saying much. I've seen countesses looking like old-clothes women!"

"Well, you know what I mean."

A stately figure of ample proportions, handsomely dressed in black, bore down upon them. Her eyes gave them a sharp glance.

Ted moved aside a step or two. He said, "Afternoon, Mrs. Bishop."

Mrs. Bishop inclined her head graciously. "Good afternoon, Ted Bigland. Good afternoon, Mary." She passed on, a ship in full sail.

Ted looked respectfully after her.

Mary murmured, "Now, she really is like a duchess!"

"Yes—she's got a manner. Always makes me feel hot inside my collar."

Mary said slowly, "She doesn't like me."

"Nonsense, my girl."

"It's true. She doesn't. She's always saying sharp things to me."

"Jealous," said Ted, nodding his head sapiently. "That's all it is."

Mary said doubtfully, "I suppose it might be that."

"That's it, depend upon it. She's been housekeeper at Hunterbury for years, ruling the roost and ordering everyone about, and now old Mrs. Welman takes a fancy to you, and it puts her out! That's all it is."

Mary said, a shade of trouble on her forehead, "It's silly of me, but I can't bear it when anyone doesn't like me. I want people to like me."

"Sure to be women who don't like you, Mary! Jealous cats who think you're too good-looking!"

Mary said, "I think jealousy's horrible."

Ted said slowly, "Maybe—*but it exists all right*. Say, I saw a lovely film over at Alledore last week. Clark Gable. All about one of these millionaire blokes who neglected his wife, and then she pretended she'd done the dirty on him. And there was another fellow—"

Mary moved away. She said, "Sorry, Ted, I must go. I'm late."

"Where are you going?"

"I'm going to have tea with Nurse Hopkins."

Ted made a face. "Funny taste. That woman's the biggest gossip in the village! Pokes that long nose of hers into everything."

Mary said, "She's been very kind to me always."

"Oh, I'm not saying there's any harm in her. But she talks."

Mary said, "Good-by, Ted."

She hurried off, leaving him standing gazing resentfully after her.

Nurse Hopkins occupied a small cottage at the end of the village. She herself had just come in and was untying her bonnet strings when Mary entered.

"Ah, there you are. I'm a bit late. Old Mrs. Caldecott was bad again. Made me late with my round of dressings. I saw you with Ted Bigland at the end of the street."

Mary said rather dispiritedly, "Yes."

Nurse Hopkins looked up alertly from where she was stooping to light the gas-ring under the kettle.

Her long nose twitched. "Was he saying something particular to you, my dear?"

"No. He just asked me to go to the movies."

"*I* see," said Nurse Hopkins promptly. "Well, of course, he's a nice young fellow and doesn't do too badly at the garage, and his father does rather better than most of the farmers round here. All the same, my dear, you don't seem to me cut out for Ted Bigland's wife. Not with your education and all. As I was saying, if I was you I'd go in for massage when the time comes. You get about a bit and see people that way, and your time's more or less your own."

Mary said, "I'll think it over. Mrs. Welman spoke to me the other day. She was very sweet about it. It was just exactly as you said it was. She doesn't want me to go away just now. She'd miss me, she said. But she told me not to worry about the future, that she meant to help me."

Nurse Hopkins said dubiously, "Let's hope she's put that down in black and white! Sick people are odd."

Mary asked, "Do you think Mrs. Bishop really dislikes me—or is it only my fancy?"

Nurse Hopkins considered a minute. "She puts on a sour face, I must say. She's one of those who don't like seeing young people having a good time or anything done for them. Thinks, perhaps, Mrs. Welman is a bit too fond of you, and resents it."

She laughed cheerfully.

"I shouldn't worry if I was you, Mary, my dear. Just open that paper bag, will you? There's a couple of doughnuts in it."

3

YOUR AUNT HAD SECOND STROKE LAST NIGHT NO CAUSE IMMEDIATE ANXIETY BUT SUGGEST YOU SHOULD COME DOWN IF POSSIBLE LORD.

Immediately on receipt of the telegram Elinor had rung up Roddy, and now they were in the train together bound for Hunterbury.

Elinor had not seen much of Roddy in the week that had elapsed since their visit. On the two brief occasions when they had met, there had been an odd kind of constraint between them. Roddy had sent her flowers—a great sheaf of long-stemmed roses. It was unusual on his part. At a dinner they had had together he had seemed more attentive than usual, consulting her preferences in food and drink, being unusually assiduous in helping her on and off with her coat. A little, Elinor thought, as though he were playing a part in a play—the part of the devoted fiancé.

Then she had said to herself, *Don't be an idiot. Nothing's wrong. You imagine things! It's that beastly, brooding, possessive mind of yours.*

Her manner to him had been perhaps a shade more detached, more aloof than usual.

Now, in this sudden emergency, the constraint passed, they talked together naturally enough.

Roddy said, "Poor old dear, and she was so well when we saw her the other day."

Elinor said, "I do mind so terribly for *her*. I know how she hated being ill, anyway, and now I suppose she'll be more helpless still, and she'll simply loathe that! One does feel, Roddy, that people ought to be set free—if they themselves really want it."

Roddy said, "I agree. It's the only civilized thing to do. You put animals out of their pain. I suppose you don't do it with human beings simply because, human nature being what it is, people would get shoved off for their money by their fond relations—perhaps when they weren't really bad at all."

Elinor said thoughtfully, "It would be in the doctors' hands, of course."

"A doctor might be a crook."

"You could trust a man like Dr. Lord."

Roddy said carelessly, "Yes, he seems straightforward enough. Nice fellow."

Dr. Lord was leaning over the bed. Nurse O'Brien hovered behind him. He was trying, his forehead puckered, to understand the slurred sounds coming from his patient's mouth.

He said, "Yes, yes. . . . Now, don't get excited. Take plenty of time. Just raise this right hand a little when you mean *yes*. There's something you're worried about?"

He received the affirmatory sign.

"Something urgent? Yes. Something you want *done*? Someone sent for? Miss Carlisle? And Mr. Welman? They're on their way."

Again Mrs. Welman tried incoherently to speak. Dr. Lord listened attentively.

"You wanted them to come, but it's not that? Someone else? A relation? No? Some business matter? I see. Something to do with money? *Lawyer?* That's right, isn't it? You want to see your lawyer? Want to give him instructions about something?

"Now, now—that's all right. Keep calm. Plenty of time. What's that you're saying—Elinor?" He caught the garbled name. "She knows what lawyer? And she will arrange with him? Good. She'll be here in about half an hour. I'll tell her what you want and I'll come up with her and we'll get it all straight. Now, don't worry any more. Leave it all to me. I'll see that things are arranged the way you want them to be."

He stood a moment watching her relax, then he moved quietly away and went out on the landing. Nurse O'Brien followed him. Nurse Hopkins was just coming up the stairs. He nodded to her.

She said breathlessly, "Good evening, Doctor."

"Good evening, Nurse."

He went with the two of them into Nurse O'Brien's room next door and gave them their instructions. Nurse Hopkins would remain on overnight and take charge with Nurse O'Brien.

"Tomorrow I'll have to get hold of a second resident nurse. Awkward, this diphtheria epidemic over at Stamford. The nursing homes there are working shorthanded as it is."

Then, having given his orders, which were listened to with reverent attention (which sometimes tickled him), Dr. Lord went downstairs, ready to receive the niece and nephew who, his watch told him, were due to arrive any minute now.

In the hall he encountered Mary Gerrard. Her face was pale and anxious. She asked, "Is she better?"

Dr. Lord said, "I can ensure her a peaceful night—that's about all that can be done."

Mary said brokenly, "It seems so cruel—so unfair—"

He nodded sympathetically enough. "Yes, it does seem like that sometimes. I believe—"

He broke off. "That's the car."

He went out into the hall. Mary ran upstairs.

Elinor exclaimed as she came into the drawing-room, "Is she very bad?"

Roddy was looking pale and apprehensive.

The doctor said gravely, "I'm afraid it will be rather a shock to you. She's badly paralyzed. Her speech is almost unrecognizable. By the way, she's definitely worried about something. It's to do with sending for her lawyer. You know who he is, Miss Carlisle?"

Elinor said quickly, "Mr. Seddon—of Bloomsbury Square. But he wouldn't be there at this time of the evening, and I don't know his home address."

Dr. Lord said reassuringly, "Tomorrow will be in plenty of time. I'm anxious to set Mrs. Welman's mind at rest as soon as possible. If you will come up with me now, Miss Carlisle, I think together we shall be able to reassure her."

"Of course. I will come up at once."

Roddy said hopefully, "You don't want me?"

He felt faintly ashamed of himself, but he had a nervous dread of going up to the sickroom, of seeing Aunt Laura lying there inarticulate and helpless.

Dr. Lord reassured him promptly. "Not the least need, Mr. Welman. Better not to have too many people in the room."

Roddy's relief showed plainly.

Dr. Lord and Elinor went upstairs. Nurse O'Brien was with the patient.

Laura Welman, breathing deeply and stertorously, lay as though in a stupor. Elinor stood looking down on her, shocked by the drawn, twisted face.

Suddenly Mrs. Welman's right eyelid quivered and opened. A faint change came over her face as she recognized Elinor. She tried to speak.

"*Elinor* . . ." The word would have been meaningless to anyone who had not guessed at what she wanted to say.

Elinor said quickly, "I'm here, Aunt Laura. You're worried about something? You want me to send for Mr. Seddon?"

Another of those hoarse, raucous sounds. Elinor guessed at the meaning. She said, "Mary Gerrard?"

Slowly the right hand moved shakily in assent.

A long burble of sound came from the sick woman's lips. Dr. Lord and Elinor frowned helplessly. Again and again it came. Then Elinor got a word.

"*Provision*? You want to make *provision* for her in your will? You want her to have some money? I see, dear Aunt Laura. That will be quite simple. Mr. Seddon will come down tomorrow and everything shall be arranged exactly as you wish."

The sufferer seemed relieved. The look of distress faded from that appealing eye. Elinor took her hand in hers and felt a feeble pressure from her fingers.

Mrs. Welman said with a great effort, *"You—all—you . . ."*

Elinor said, "Yes, yes, leave it all to me. I will see that everything you want is done!"

She felt the pressure of the fingers again. Then it relaxed. The eyelids drooped and closed.

Dr. Lord laid a hand on Elinor's arm and drew her gently away out of the room. Nurse O'Brien resumed her seat near the bed.

Outside on the landing Mary Gerrard was talking to Nurse Hopkins. She started forward.

"Oh, Dr. Lord, can I go in to her, please?"

He nodded. "Keep quite quiet, though, and don't disturb her."

Mary went into the sickroom.

Dr. Lord said, "Your train was late. You—" He stopped.

Elinor had turned her head to look after Mary. Suddenly she became aware of his abrupt silence. She turned her head and looked at him inquiringly. He was staring at her, a startled look in his face. The color rose in Elinor's cheeks.

She said hurriedly, "I beg your pardon. What did you say?"

Peter Lord said slowly, "What was I saying? I don't remember. Miss Carlisle, you were splendid in there!" He spoke warmly. "Quick to understand, reassuring, everything you should have been."

The very faintest of sniffs came from Nurse Hopkins.

Elinor said, "Poor darling. It upset me terribly seeing her like that."

"Of course. But you didn't show it. You must have great self-control."

Elinor said, her lips set very straight, "I've learned not—to show my feelings."

The doctor said slowly, "All the same, the mask's bound to slip once in a while."

Nurse Hopkins had bustled into the bathroom. Elinor said, raising her delicate eyebrows and looking full at him, "The mask?"

Dr. Lord said, "The human face is, after all, nothing more nor less than a mask."

"And underneath?"

"Underneath is the primitive man or woman."

She turned away quickly and led the way downstairs. Peter Lord followed, puzzled and unwontedly serious.

Roddy came out into the hall to meet them. "Well?" he asked anxiously.

Elinor said, "Poor darling. It's very sad to see her. I shouldn't go, Roddy—till—till—she asks for you."

Roddy asked, "Did she want anything—special?"

Peter Lord said to Elinor, "I must be off now. There's nothing more I can do for the moment. I'll look in early tomorrow. Good-by, Miss Carlisle. Don't—don't worry too much."

He held her hand in his for a moment or two. He had a strangely reassuring and comforting clasp. He looked at her, Elinor thought, rather oddly as though—as though he was sorry for her.

As the door shut behind the doctor, Roddy repeated his question.

Elinor said, "Aunt Laura is worried about—about certain business matters. I managed to pacify her and told her Mr. Seddon would certainly come down tomorrow. We must telephone him first thing."

Roddy asked, "Does she want to make a new will?"

Elinor answered, "She didn't say so."

"What did she—?"

He stopped in the middle of the question.

Mary Gerrard was running down the stairs. She crossed the hall and disappeared through the door to the kitchen quarters.

Elinor said in a harsh voice, "Yes? What is it you wanted to ask?"

Roddy said vaguely, "I—what? I've forgotten what it was."

He was staring at the door through which Mary Gerrard had gone.

Elinor's hands closed. She could feel her long, pointed nails biting into the flesh of her palms. She thought, *I can't bear it—I can't bear it. It's not imagination—it's true. Roddy—Roddy, I* CAN'T *lose you.*

And she thought, *What did that man—the doctor—what did he see in my face upstairs? He saw something. . . . Oh, God, how awful life is—to feel as I feel now. Say something, fool. Pull yourself together!*

Aloud she said, in her calm voice, "About meals, Roddy. I'm not very hungry. I'll sit with Aunt Laura and the nurses can both come down."

Roddy said in alarm, "And have dinner with *me?*"

Elinor said coldly, "They won't bite you!"

"But what about you? You must have something. Why don't *we* dine first, and let them come down afterward?"

Elinor said, "No, the other way's better." She added wildly, "They're so touchy, you know."

She thought, *I can't sit through a meal with him—alone—talking—behaving as usual.*

She said impatiently, "Oh, do let me arrange things my own way!"

4

IT WAS NO mere housemaid who wakened Elinor the following morning. It was Mrs. Bishop in person, rustling in her old-fashioned black, and weeping unashamedly.

"Oh, Miss Elinor, she's gone."

"What?"

Elinor sat up in bed.

"Your dear aunt. Mrs. Welman. My dear mistress. Passed away in her sleep."

"Aunt Laura? Dead?"

Elinor stared. She seemed unable to take it in.

Mrs. Bishop was weeping now with more abandon. "To think of it," she sobbed. "After all these years! Eighteen years I've been here. But indeed it doesn't seem like it."

Elinor said slowly, "So Aunt Laura died in her sleep—quite peacefully. What a blessing for her!"

Mrs. Bishop wept.

"So *sudden*. The doctor saying he'd call again this morning and everything just as usual."

Elinor said rather sharply, "It wasn't exactly *sudden*. After all, she'd been ill for some time. I'm just so thankful she's been spared more suffering."

Mrs. Bishop said tearfully that there was indeed that to be thankful for. She added, "Who'll tell Mr. Roderick?"

Elinor said, "I will."

She threw on a dressing-gown and went along to his door and tapped. His voice answered, saying, "Come in."

She entered. "Aunt Laura's dead, Roddy. She died in her sleep."

Roddy, sitting up in bed, drew a deep sigh. "Poor dear Aunt Laura! Thank God for it, I say. I couldn't have borne to see her go on lingering in the state she was yesterday."

Elinor said mechanically, "I didn't know you'd seen her?"

He nodded rather shamefacedly. "The truth is, Elinor, I felt the most awful coward, because I'd funked it! I went along there yesterday evening. The nurse, the fat one, left the room for something—went down with a hot-water bottle, I think—and I slipped in. She didn't know I was there, of course. I just stood a bit and looked at her. Then, when I heard Mrs. Gamp stumping up the stairs again, I slipped away. But it was—pretty terrible!"

Elinor nodded. "Yes, it was."

Roddy said, "She'd have hated it like hell—every minute of it!"

"I know."

Roddy said, "It's marvelous the way you and I always see alike over things."

Elinor said in a low voice, "Yes, it is."

He said, "We're both feeling the same thing at this minute: *just utter thankfulness that she's out of it all.*"

Nurse O'Brien said, "What is it, Nurse? Can't you find something?"

Nurse Hopkins, her face rather red, was hunting through the little attaché case that she had laid down in the hall the preceding evening.

She grunted, "Most annoying. How I came to do such a thing I can't imagine!"

"What is it?"

Nurse Hopkins replied not very intelligibly: "It's Eliza Rykin—that sarcoma, you know. She's got to have double injections—night and morning—morphine. Gave her the last tablet in the old tube last night on my way here, and I could swear I had the new tube in here, too."

"Look again. Those tubes are so small."

Nurse Hopkins gave a final stir to the contents of the attaché case.

"No, it's not here! I must have left it in my cupboard after all! Really, I did think I could trust my memory better than *that*. I could have sworn I took it out with me!"

"You didn't leave the case anywhere, did you, on the way here?"

"Of course not!" said Nurse Hopkins sharply.

"Oh, well, dear," said Nurse O'Brien, "it must be all *right*?"

"Oh, yes! The only place I've laid my case down was here in this hall, and nobody *here* would pinch anything! Just my memory, I suppose. But it vexes me, if you understand, Nurse. Besides, I shall have to go right home first to the other end of the village and back again."

Nurse O'Brien said, "Hope you won't have too tiring a day, dear, after last night. Poor old lady. I didn't think she would last long."

"No, nor I. I dare say Doctor will be surprised!"

Nurse O'Brien said with a tinge of disapproval, "He's always so *hopeful* about his cases."

Nurse Hopkins, as she prepared to depart, said, "Ah, he's young! He hasn't our experience."

On which gloomy pronouncement she departed.

Dr. Lord raised himself up on his toes. His sandy eyebrows climbed right up his forehead till they nearly got merged in his hair.

He said in surprise, "So she's conked out—eh?"

"Yes, Doctor."

On Nurse O'Brien's tongue exact details were tingling to be uttered, but with stern discipline she waited.

Peter Lord said thoughtfully, "Conked out?"

He stood for a moment thinking, then he said sharply, "Get me some boiling water."

Nurse O'Brien was surprised and mystified, but true to the spirit of hospital training, hers not to reason why. If a doctor had told her to go and get the skin of an alligator she would have murmured automatically, "Yes, Doctor," and glided obediently from the room to tackle the problem.

Roderick Welman said, "Do you mean to say that my aunt died *intestate*— that she never made a will *at all*?"

Mr. Seddon polished his eyeglasses. He said, "That seems to be the case."

Roddy said, "But how extraordinary!"

Mr. Seddon gave a deprecating cough. "Not so extraordinary as you might imagine. It happens oftener than you would think. There's a kind of superstition about it. People *will* think they've got plenty of time. The mere fact of making a will seems to bring the possibility of death nearer to them. Very odd—but there it is!"

Roddy said, "Didn't you ever—er—expostulate with her on the subject?"

Mr. Seddon replied dryly, "Frequently."

"And what did she say?"

Mr. Seddon sighed. "The usual things. That there was plenty of time! That she didn't intend to die just yet! That she hadn't made up her mind definitely, exactly how she wished to dispose of her money!"

Elinor said, "But surely, after her first stroke—?"

Mr. Seddon shook his head. "Oh, no, it was worse then. She wouldn't hear the subject mentioned!"

Roddy said, "Surely that's very odd?"

Mr. Seddon said again, "Oh, no. Naturally, her illness made her much more nervous."

Elinor said in a puzzled voice, "But she wanted to die."

Polishing his eyeglasses, Mr. Seddon said, "Ah, my dear Miss Elinor, the human mind is a very curious piece of mechanism. Mrs. Welman may have *thought* she wanted to die, but side by side with that feeling there ran the hope that she would recover absolutely. And because of that hope, I think she felt that to make a will would be unlucky. It isn't so much that she didn't mean to make one, as that she was eternally putting it off.

"You know," went on Mr. Seddon, suddenly addressing Roddy in an almost personal manner, "how one puts off and avoids a thing that is distasteful—that you don't want to face?"

Roddy flushed. He muttered, "Yes, I—I—yes, of course. I know what you mean."

"Exactly," said Mr. Seddon. "Mrs. Welman *always* meant to make a will, but tomorrow was always a better day to make it than today! She kept telling herself that there was plenty of time."

Elinor said slowly, "So that's why she was so upset last night—and in such a panic that you should be sent for."

Mr. Seddon replied, "Undoubtedly!"

Roddy said in a bewildered voice, "But what happens now?"

"To Mrs. Welman's estate?" The lawyer coughed. "Since Mrs. Welman died intestate, all her property goes to her next of kin—that is, to Miss Elinor Carlisle."

Elinor said slowly, "All to *me?*"

"The Crown takes a certain percentage," Mr. Seddon explained. He went into details.

He ended, "There are no settlements or trusts. Mrs. Welman's money was hers absolutely to do with as she chose. It passes, therefore, straight to Miss Carlisle. Er—the death duties, I am afraid, will be somewhat heavy, but even after their payment, the fortune will still be a considerable one, and it is very well invested in sound, gilt-edged securities."

Elinor said, "But Roderick—"

Mr. Seddon said with a little apologetic cough, "Mr. Welman is only Mrs. Welman's *husband's* nephew. There is no blood relationship."

"Quite," said Roddy.

Elinor said slowly, "Of course, it doesn't much matter which of us gets it, as we're going to be married."

But she did not look at Roddy.

It was Mr. Seddon's turn to say, "Quite!"

He said it rather quickly.

"But it doesn't matter, does it?" Elinor said. She spoke almost pleadingly. Mr. Seddon had departed.

Roddy's face twitched nervously. He said, "You ought to have it. It's quite right you should. For heaven's sake, Elinor, don't get it into your head that I grudge it to you. *I* don't want the damned money!"

Elinor said, her voice slightly unsteady, "We did agree, Roddy, in London that it wouldn't matter which of us it was, as—as we were going to be married?"

He didn't answer.

She persisted, "Don't you remember saying that, Roddy?"

He said, "Yes."

He looked down at his feet. His face was white and sullen; there was pain in the taut lines of his sensitive mouth.

Elinor said with a sudden gallant lift of the head, "It doesn't matter— *if we're going to be married. . . . But are we, Roddy?*"

He said, "Are we what?"

"Are we going to marry each other?"

"I understood that was the idea." His tone was indifferent, with a slight edge to it. He went on: "Of course, Elinor, if you've other ideas now—"

Elinor cried out, "Oh, Roddy, can't you be *honest?*"

He winced. Then he said in a low, bewildered voice, "I don't know what's happened to me."

Elinor said in a stifled voice, "I do."

He said quickly, "Perhaps it's true that I don't, after all, quite like the idea of living on my wife's money."

Elinor, her face white, said, "It's not that. It's something else." She paused, then she said, "It's—Mary, isn't it?"

Roddy muttered unhappily, "I suppose so. How did you know?"

Elinor said, her mouth twisting sideways in a crooked smile, "It wasn't difficult. Every time you look at her—it's there in your face for anyone to read."

Suddenly his composure broke. "Oh, Elinor—I don't know what's the matter! I think I'm going mad! It happened when I saw her—that first day—in the wood . . . just her face—it—it's turned everything upside down. *You* can't understand that."

Elinor said, "Yes, I can. Go on."

Roddy said helplessly, "I didn't want to fall in love with her—I was quite happy with you. Oh, Elinor, what a cad I am, talking like this to you—"

Elinor said, "Nonsense. Go on. Tell me."

He said brokenly, "You're wonderful. Talking to you helps frightfully. I'm so terribly fond of you, Elinor! You must believe that. This other thing is like an enchantment! It's upset everything: my conception of life—and my enjoyment of things—and—all the decent, ordered, reasonable things."

Elinor said gently, "Love—isn't very reasonable."

Roddy said miserably. "No."

Elinor said, and her voice trembled a little, "Have you said anything to her?"

Roddy said, "This morning—like a fool—I lost my head—"

Elinor said, "Yes?"

Roddy said, "Of course she—shut me up at once! She was shocked. Because of Aunt Laura and—of *you*—"

Elinor drew the diamond ring off her finger. She said, "You'd better take it back, Roddy."

Taking it, he murmured without looking at her, "Elinor, you've no idea what a beast I feel."

Elinor said in her calm voice, "Do you think she'll marry you?"

He shook his head. "I've no idea. Not—not for a long time. I don't think she cares for me now; but she might come to care."

Elinor said, "I think you're right. You must give her time. Not see her for a bit, and then—start afresh."

"Darling Elinor! You're the best friend anyone ever had." He took her hand suddenly and kissed it. "You know, Elinor, I *do* love you—just as much as ever! Sometimes Mary seems just like a dream. I might wake up from it—and find she wasn't there."

Elinor said, "If Mary wasn't there—"

Roddy said with sudden feeling, "Sometimes I wish she wasn't. . . . You and I, Elinor, *belong*. We do belong, don't we?"

Slowly she bent her head.

She said. "Oh, yes—we belong."

She thought, *If Mary wasn't there* . . .

5

Nurse Hopkins said with emotion, "It was a beautiful funeral!"

Nurse O'Brien responded, "It was, indeed. And the flowers! Did you ever see such beautiful flowers? A harp of white lilies there was, and a cross of yellow roses. Beautiful!"

Nurse Hopkins sighed and helped herself to buttered teacake. The two nurses were sitting in the Blue Tit Café.

Nurse Hopkins went on: "Miss Carlisle is a generous girl. She gave me a nice present, though she'd no call to do so."

"She's a fine, generous girl," agreed Nurse O'Brien warmly. "I do detest stinginess."

Nurse Hopkins said, "Well, it's a grand fortune she's inherited."

Nurse O'Brien said, "I wonder—" and stopped.

Nurse Hopkins said, "Yes?" encouragingly.

" 'Twas strange the way the old lady made no will."

"It was wicked," Nurse Hopkins said sharply. "People ought to be forced to make wills! It only leads to unpleasantness when they don't."

"I'm wondering," said Nurse O'Brien "if she *had* made a will, how she'd have left her money?"

Nurse Hopkins said firmly, "I know *one* thing."

"What's that?"

"She'd have left a sum of money to Mary—Mary Gerrard."

"Yes, indeed, and that's true," agreed the other. She added excitedly, "Wasn't I after telling you that night of the state she was in, poor dear, and the doctor doing his best to calm her down. Miss Elinor was there holding her auntie's hand and swearing by God Almighty," said Nurse O'Brien, her Irish imagination suddenly running away with her, "that the lawyer should be sent for and everything done accordingly. 'Mary! Mary!' the poor old lady said. 'Is it Mary Gerrard you're meaning?' says Miss Elinor, and straightaway she swore that Mary should have her rights!"

Nurse Hopkins said rather doubtfully, "Was it like that?"

Nurse O'Brien replied firmly, "That was the way of it, and I'll tell you this, Nurse Hopkins: In my opinion, if Mrs. Welman had lived to make that will, it's likely there might have been surprises for all! Who knows she mightn't have left every penny she possessed to Mary Gerrard!"

Nurse Hopkins said dubiously, "I don't think she'd do that. I don't hold with leaving your money away from your own flesh and blood."

Nurse O'Brien said oracularly, "There's flesh and blood and flesh and blood."

Nurse Hopkins responded instantly, "Now, what might you mean by *that?*"

Nurse O'Brien said with dignity, "I'm not one to gossip! And I wouldn't be blackening anyone's name that's dead."

Nurse Hopkins nodded her head slowly and said, "That's right. I agree with you. Least said soonest mended."

She filled up the teapot.

Nurse O'Brien said, "By the way, now, did you find that tube of morphine all right when you got home?"

Nurse Hopkins frowned. She said, "No. It beats me to know what can have become of it, but I think it may have been this way: I *might* have set it down on the edge of the mantelpiece as I often do while I lock the cupboard, and it *might* have rolled and fallen into the waste-paper basket that was all full of rubbish and that was emptied out into the dustbin just as I left the house." She paused. "It *must* be that way, for I don't see what else could have become of it."

"I see," said Nurse O'Brien. "Well, dear, that must have been it. It's not as though you'd left your case about anywhere else—only just in the hall at Hunterbury—so it seems to me that what you suggested just now must be so. It's gone into the rubbish bin."

"That's right," said Nurse Hopkins eagerly. "It couldn't be any other way, could it?"

She helped herself to a pink sugar cake. She said, "It's not as though—" and stopped.

The other agreed quickly—perhaps a little too quickly.

"I'd not be worrying about it any more if I was you," she said comfortably.

Nurse Hopkins said, "I'm *not* worrying."

Young and severe in her black dress, Elinor sat in front of Mrs. Welman's massive writing table in the library. Various papers were spread out in front of her. She had finished interviewing the servants and Mrs. Bishop. Now it was Mary Gerrard who entered the room and hesitated a minute by the doorway.

"You wanted to see me, Miss Elinor," she said.

Elinor looked up. "Oh, yes, Mary. Come here and sit down, will you?"

Mary came and sat in the chair Elinor indicated. It was turned a little toward the window, and the light from it fell on her face, showing the dazzling purity of the skin and bringing out the pale gold of the girl's hair.

Elinor held one hand shielding her face a little. Between the fingers she could watch the other girl's face.

She thought, *Is it possible to hate anyone so much and not show it?*

Aloud she said in a pleasant, businesslike voice, "I think you know, Mary, that my aunt always took a great interest in you and would have been concerned about your future."

Mary murmured in her soft voice, "Mrs. Welman was very good to me always."

Elinor went on, her voice cold and detached: "My aunt, if she had had time to make a will, would have wished, I know, to leave several legacies. Since she died without making a will, the responsibility of carrying out her wishes rests on me. I have consulted with Mr. Seddon, and by his advice we have drawn up a schedule of sums for the servants according to their length of service, etc." She paused. "You, of course, don't come quite into that class."

She half hoped, perhaps, that those words might hold a sting, but the face she was looking at showed no change. Mary accepted the words at their face value and listened to what more was to come.

Elinor said, "Though it was difficult for my aunt to speak coherently, she was able to make her meaning understood that last evening. She definitely wanted to make some provision for your future."

Mary said quietly, "That was very good of her."

Elinor said brusquely, "As soon as probate is granted, I am arranging that two thousand pounds should be made over to you—that sum to be yours to do with absolutely as you please."

Mary's color rose. "Two thousand pounds? Oh, Miss Elinor, that *is* good of you! I don't know what to say."

Elinor said sharply, "It isn't particularly good of me, and please don't say anything."

Mary flushed. "You don't know what a difference it will make to me," she murmured.

Elinor said, "I'm glad."

She hesitated. She looked away from Mary to the other side of the room. She said with a slight effort, "I wonder—have you any plans?"

Mary said quickly, "Oh, yes. I shall train for something. Massage, perhaps. That's what Nurse Hopkins advises."

Elinor said, "That sounds a very good idea. I will try and arrange with Mr. Seddon that some money shall be advanced to you as soon as possible— at once, if that is feasible."

"You're very, *very* good, Miss Elinor," said Mary gratefully.

Elinor said curtly, "It was Aunt Laura's wish." She hesitated, then said, "Well, that's all, I think."

This time the definite dismissal in the words pierced Mary's sensitive skin. She got up, said quietly, "Thank you very much, Miss Elinor," and left the room.

Elinor sat quite still, staring ahead of her. Her face was quite impassive. There was no clue in it as to what was going on in her mind. But she sat there, motionless, for a long time.

Elinor went at last in search of Roddy. She found him in the morning-room. He was standing staring out of the window. He turned sharply as Elinor came in.

She said, "I've got through it all! Five hundred for Mrs. Bishop—she's been here such years. A hundred for the cook and fifty each for Milly and Olive. Five pounds each to the others. Twenty-five for Stephens, the head gardener; and there's old Gerrard, of course, at the lodge. I haven't done anything about him yet. It's awkward. He'll have to be pensioned off, I suppose?"

She paused and then went on rather hurriedly: "I'm settling two thousand on Mary Gerrard. Do you think that's what Aunt Laura would have wished? It seemed to me about the right sum."

Roddy said without looking at her, "Yes, exactly right. You've always got excellent judgment, Elinor."

He turned to look out of the window again.

Elinor held her breath for a minute, then she began to speak with nervous haste, the words tumbling out incoherently: "There's something more. I want to—it's only right—I mean, *you've* got to have your proper share, Roddy."

As he wheeled round, anger on his face, she hurried on: "No, *listen*,

Roddy. This is just bare justice! The money that was your uncle's—that he left to his wife—naturally he always assumed it would come to you. Aunt Laura meant it to, too. I know she did, from lots of things she said. If *I* have *her* money, *you* should have the amount that was *his*—it's only right. I—I can't bear to feel that I've robbed you—just because Aunt Laura funked making a will. You must—you *must* see sense about this!"

Roderick's long, sensitive face had gone dead white. He said, "My God, Elinor, do you want to make me feel an utter cad? Do you think for one moment I could—could take this money from you?"

"I'm not *giving* it to you. It's just—fair."

Roddy cried out, "I don't want your money!"

"It isn't mine!"

"It's yours by law—and that's all that matters! For God's sake, don't let's be anything but strictly businesslike! I won't take a penny from you. You're not going to do the Lady Bountiful to me!"

Elinor cried out, "Roddy!"

He made a quick gesture. "Oh, my dear, I'm sorry. I don't know what I'm saying. I feel so bewildered—so utterly lost."

Elinor said gently, "Poor Roddy."

He had turned away again and was playing with the tassel of the window blind. He said in a different tone, a detached one, "Do you know what—Mary Gerrard proposes doing?"

"She's going to train as a masseuse, so she says."

He said, "I see."

There was a silence. Elinor drew herself up; she flung back her head. Her voice when she spoke was suddenly compelling: "Roddy, I want you to listen to me carefully!"

He turned to her, slightly surprised. "Of course, Elinor."

"I want you, if you will, to follow my advice."

"And what is your advice?"

Elinor said calmly, "You are not particularly tied? You can always get a holiday, can't you?"

"Oh, yes."

"Then do—just that. Go abroad somewhere for—say, three months. Go by yourself. Make new friends and see new places. Let's speak quite frankly. At this moment you think you're in love with Mary Gerrard. Perhaps you are. But it isn't a moment for approaching her—you know that only too well. Our engagement is definitely broken off. Go abroad, then, as a free man, and at the end of the three months, as a free man, make up your mind. You'll know then whether you—really love Mary or whether it was only a temporary infatuation. And if you are quite sure you *do* love her—well, then, come back and go to her and tell her so, and that you're quite sure about it, and perhaps then she'll listen."

Roddy came to her. He caught her hand in his.

"Elinor, you're wonderful! So clear-headed! So marvelously impersonal! There's no trace of pettiness or meanness about you. I admire you more than I can ever say. I'll do exactly what you suggest. Go away, cut free from everything—and find out whether I've got the genuine disease or if I've just been making the most ghastly fool of myself. Oh, Elinor, my dear, you don't know how truly fond I am of you. I do realize you were always a thousand times too good for me. Bless you, dear, for all your goodness."

Quickly, impulsively, he kissed her and went out.

It was as well, perhaps, that he did not look back and see her face.

It was a couple of days later that Mary acquainted Nurse Hopkins with her improved prospects.

That practical woman was warmly congratulatory. "That's a great piece of luck for you, Mary," she said. "The old lady may have meant well by you, but unless a thing's down in black and white, intentions don't go for much! You might easily have got nothing at all."

"Miss Elinor said that the night Mrs. Welman died she told her to do something for me."

Nurse Hopkins snorted. "Maybe she did. But there's many would have forgotten conveniently afterward. Relations are like that. I've seen a few things, *I* can tell you! People dying and saying they know they can leave it to their dear son or their dear daughter to carry out their wishes. Nine times out of ten, dear son and dear daughter find some very good reason to do nothing of the kind. Human nature's human nature, and nobody likes parting with money if they're not legally compelled to! I tell you, Mary, my girl, you've been lucky. Miss Carlisle's straighter than most."

Mary said slowly, "And yet—somehow—I feel she doesn't like me."

"With good reason, I should say," said Nurse Hopkins bluntly. "Now don't look so innocent, Mary! Mr. Roderick's been making sheep's eyes at you for some time now."

Mary went red.

Nurse Hopkins went on: "He's got it badly, in my opinion. Fell for you all of a sudden. What about you, my girl? Got any feeling for him?"

Mary said hesitatingly, "I—I don't know. I don't think so. But, of course, he's very nice."

"H'm," said Nurse Hopkins. "He wouldn't be *my* fancy! One of those men who are finicky and a bundle of nerves. Fussy about their food, too, as likely as not. Men aren't much at the best of times. Don't be in too much of a hurry, Mary, my dear. With your looks you can afford to pick and choose. Nurse O'Brien passed the remark to me the other day that you ought to go on the films. They like blondes, I've always heard."

Mary said, with a slight frown creasing her forehead, "Nurse, what do you think I ought to do about Father? He thinks I ought to give some of this money to him."

"Don't do anything of the kind," said Nurse Hopkins wrathfully. "Mrs. Welman never meant that money for him. It's my opinion he'd have lost his job years ago if it hadn't been for you. A lazier man never stepped!"

Mary said, "It seems funny when she'd all that money that she never made a will to say how it was to go."

Nurse Hopkins shook her head. "People are like that. You'd be surprised. Always putting it off."

Mary said, "It seems downright silly to me."

Nurse Hopkins said with a faint twinkle, "Made a will yourself, Mary?"

Mary stared at her. "Oh, no."

"And yet you're over twenty-one."

"But I—I haven't got anything to leave—at least I suppose I have now."

Nurse Hopkins said sharply, "Of course you have. And a nice tidy little sum, too."

Mary said, "Oh, well, there's no hurry."

"There you go," said Nurse Hopkins dryly. "Just like everyone else. Because you're a healthy young girl isn't a reason why you shouldn't be smashed up in a charabanc or a bus, or run over in the street, any minute."

Mary laughed. She said, "I don't even know how to make a will."

"Easy enough. You can get a form at the post office. Let's go and get one right away."

In Nurse Hopkins's cottage the form was spread out and the important matter discussed. Nurse Hopkins was enjoying herself thoroughly. A will, as she said, was next best to a death, in her opinion.

Mary said, "Who'd get the money if I didn't make a will?"

Nurse Hopkins said rather doubtfully, "Your father, I suppose."

Mary said sharply, "He shan't have it. I'd rather leave it to my auntie in New Zealand."

"It wouldn't be much use leaving it to your father, anyway—*he's* not long for this world, I should say."

Mary had heard Nurse Hopkins make this kind of pronouncement too often to be impressed by it.

"I can't remember my auntie's address. We've not heard from her for years."

"I don't suppose that matters," said Nurse Hopkins. "You know her Christian name?"

"Mary. Mary Riley."

"That's all right. Put down you leaving everything to Mary Riley, sister of the late Eliza Gerrard of Hunterbury, Maidensford."

Mary bent over the form, writing. As she came to the end she shivered suddenly. A shadow had come between her and the sun. She looked up to see Elinor Carlisle standing outside the window looking in.

Elinor said, "What are you doing so busily?"

Nurse Hopkins said with a laugh, "She's making her will, that's what she's doing."

"Making her will?" Suddenly Elinor laughed—a strange laugh—almost hysterical.

She said, "So you're making your will, Mary. *That's funny. That's very funny.*"

Still laughing, she turned away and walked rapidly along the street. Nurse Hopkins stared.

"Did you ever? What's come to her?"

Elinor had not taken more than half a dozen steps—she was still laughing—when a hand fell on her arm from behind. She stopped abruptly and turned.

Dr. Lord looked straight at her, his brow creased into a frown. He said peremptorily, "What were you laughing at?"

Elinor said, "Really—I don't know."

Peter Lord said, "That's rather a silly answer!"

Elinor flushed. She said, "I think I must be nervous—or something. I looked in at the District Nurse's cottage and—and Mary Gerrard was writing out her will. It made me laugh; I don't know why!"

Lord said abruptly, *"Don't you?"*

Elinor said, "It was silly of me—I tell you—I'm nervous."

Peter Lord said, "I'll write you out a tonic."

Elinor said incisively, "How useful!"

He grinned disarmingly. "Quite useless, I agree. But's the only thing one can do when people won't tell one what is the matter with them!"

Elinor said, "There's nothing the matter with me."

Peter Lord said calmly, "There's quite a lot the matter with you."

Elinor said, "I've had a certain amount of nervous strain, I suppose."

He said, "I expect you've had quite a lot. But that's not what I'm talking about." He paused. "Are you—are you staying down here much longer?"

"I'm leaving tomorrow."

"You won't—live down here?"

Elinor shook her head. "No—never. I think—I think—I shall sell the place if I can get a good offer."

Dr. Lord said rather flatly, "I see."

Elinor said, "I must be getting home now."

She held out her hand very firmly. Peter Lord took it. He held it. He said very earnestly, "Miss Carlisle, will you please tell me what was in your mind when you laughed just now?"

She wrenched her hand away quickly. "What should there be in my mind?"

"That's what I'd like to know."

His face was grave and a little unhappy.

Elinor said impatiently, "It just struck me as funny, that was all!"

"That Mary Gerrard was making a will? Why? Making a will is a perfectly sensible procedure. Saves a lot of trouble. Sometimes, of course, it *makes* trouble!"

Elinor said impatiently, "Of course—everyone should make a will. I didn't mean that."

Dr. Lord said, "Mrs. Welman ought to have made a will."

Elinor said with feeling, "Yes, indeed."

The color rose in her face.

Dr. Lord said unexpectedly, "What about you?"

"*Me?*"

"Yes, you said just now everyone should make a will! Have *you?*"

Elinor stared at him for a minute, then she laughed. "How extraordinary!" she said. "No, I haven't. I hadn't thought of it! I'm just like Aunt Laura. Do you know, Dr. Lord, I shall go home and write to Mr. Seddon about it at once."

Peter Lord said, "Very sensible."

In the library Elinor had just finished a letter:

DEAR MR. SEDDON,

Will you draft a will for me to sign? Quite a simple one. I want to leave everything to Roderick Welman absolutely.

Yours sincerely,

ELINOR CARLISLE.

She glanced at the clock. The post would be going in a few minutes.

She opened the drawer of the desk, then remembered she had used the last stamp that morning.

There were some in her bedroom she was sure.

She went upstairs. When she re-entered the library with the stamp in her hand, Roddy was standing by the window.

He said, "So we leave here tomorrow. Good old Hunterbury. We've had some good times here."

Elinor said, "Do you mind its being sold?"

"Oh, no, no! I quite see it's the best thing to be done."

There was a silence. Elinor picked up her letter, glanced through it to see if it was all right. Then she sealed and stamped it.

6

LETTER FROM NURSE O'Brien to Nurse Hopkins, July 14th:

Laborough Court.

DEAR HOPKINS,

Have been meaning to write to you for some days now. This is a lovely house and the pictures, I believe, quite famous. But I can't say it's as comfortable as Hunterbury was, if you know what I mean.

Being in the dead country it's difficult to get maids, and the girls they have got are a raw lot, and some of them not too obliging, and though I'm sure I'm never one to give trouble, meals sent up on a tray should at least be hot, and no facilities for boiling a kettle and the tea *not* always made with boiling water! Still, all that's neither here nor there. The patient's a nice quiet gentleman—double pneumonia, but the crisis is past.

What I've got to tell you that will really interest you is the very queerest coincidence you ever knew. In the drawing-room, on the grand piano, there's a photograph in a big silver frame, and would you believe it, it's the same photograph that I told you about—the one signed *Lewis* that old Mrs. Welman asked for. Well, of course I *was* intrigued—and who wouldn't be? And I asked the butler who it was, which he answered at once saying it was Lady Rattery's brother—Sir Lewis Rycroft. He lived not far from here, and he was killed in the War. Very sad, wasn't it? I asked casual-like was he married, and the butler said yes, but that Lady Rycroft went into an asylum, poor thing, soon after the marriage. She was still alive, he said. Now, isn't that interesting? And we were quite wrong, you see, in all our ideas. They must have been very fond of each other, he and Mrs. W., and unable to marry because of the wife being in an asylum. Just like the pictures, isn't it? And her remembering all those years and looking at his photograph just before she died. He was killed in 1917, the butler said. Quite a romance, that's what I feel.

No movies anywhere near here! Oh, it's awful to be buried in the country. No wonder they can't get decent maids!

Well, good-by for the present, dear, write and tell me all the news.

Yours sincerely,
EILEEN O'BRIEN.

Letter from Nurse Hopkins to Nurse O'Brien, July 14th:

Rose Cottage.

DEAR O'BRIEN,

Everything goes on here much as usual. Hunterbury is deserted—all the servants gone and a board up: *For Sale*. I saw Mrs. Bishop the other day, she is staying with her sister who lives about a mile away. She was very upset, as you can imagine, at the place being sold. It seems she made sure Miss Carlisle would marry Mr. Welman and live there. Mrs. B. says that the engagement is off! Miss Carlisle went to London soon after you left. She was *very* peculiar in her manner once or twice. I really didn't know what to make of her! Mary Gerrard has gone to London and is starting to train for a masseuse. Very sensible of her, I think. Miss Carlisle's going to settle two thousand pounds on her, which I call very handsome and more than what many would do.

By the way, it's funny how things come about. Do you remember telling me something about a photograph signed *Lewis* that Mrs. Welman showed you? I was having a chat the other day with Mrs. Slattery (she was housekeeper to old Dr. Ransome who had the practice before Dr. Lord), and of course she's lived here all her life and knows a lot about the gentry round about. I just brought the subject up in a casual manner, speaking of Christian names and saying that the name of Lewis was uncommon and among others she mentioned Sir Lewis Rycroft over at Forbes Park. He served in the War in the 17th Lancers and was killed toward the end of the War. So I said, *he was a great friend of Mrs. Welman's at Hunterbury, wasn't he?* And at once she gave me a *look* and said, *Yes, very* close friends they'd been, and *some said more than friends,* but that she herself wasn't one to *talk*—and why shouldn't they be friends? So I said but surely Mrs. Welman was a *widow* at the time, and she said, Oh, yes, *she* was a widow. So, dear, I saw *at once* she meant something by *that,* so I said it was odd then, that they'd never married, and she said at once, "They couldn't marry. He'd got a *wife* in an asylum!" So now, you see, we know *all* about it! Curious the way things come about, isn't it? Considering the easy way you get divorces nowadays, it does seem a shame that insanity shouldn't have been a ground for it then.

Do you remember a good-looking young chap, Ted Bigland, who used to hang around after Mary Gerrard a lot? He's been at me for her address in London, but I haven't given it to him. In my opinion, Mary's a cut above Ted Bigland. I don't know if you realized it, dear, but Mr. R—— W—— was taken with her. A pity, because it's made trouble. Mark my words, that's the reason for the engagement between him and Miss Carlisle being off. And, if you ask me, it's hit *her* badly. I don't know what she saw in *him,* I'm sure—he wouldn't have been my cup of tea, but I hear from reliable sources that she's always been *madly* in love with him. It does seem a mix-up, doesn't it? And she's got all that money, too. I believe he was always led to expect his aunt would leave him something substantial.

Old Gerrard at the lodge is failing rapidly—has had several nasty dizzy spells. He's just as rude and cross-grained as ever. He actually said the other day that Mary wasn't his daughter. "Well," I said, "I'd be *ashamed* to say a thing like that about your wife if I were you." He just looked at me and said, "You're nothing but a fool. You don't understand." Polite, wasn't it? I took him up pretty sharply, I can tell you. His wife was lady's maid to Mrs. Welman before her marriage, I believe.

Yours ever,
JESSIE HOPKINS.

Post card from Nurse Hopkins to Nurse O'Brien:

Fancy our letters just crossing! Isn't this weather awful?

Post card from Nurse O'Brien to Nurse Hopkins:

Got your letter this morning. What a *coincidence!*

Letter from Roderick Welman to Elinor Carlisle, July 15th:

DEAR ELINOR,
   Just got your letter. No, really, I have no feelings about Hunterbury being sold. Nice of you to consult me. I think you're doing the wisest thing if you don't fancy living there, which you obviously don't. You may have some difficulty in getting rid of it, though. It's a biggish place for present-day needs, though, of course, it's been modernized and is up to date, with good servants' quarters, and gas and electric light and all that. Anyway, I hope you'll have luck!
   The heat here is glorious. I spend hours in the sea. Rather a funny crowd of people, but I don't mix much. You told me once that I wasn't a good mixer I'm afraid it's true. I find most of the human race extraordinarily repulsive. They probably reciprocate this feeling.
   I have long felt that you are one of the only really satisfactory representatives of humanity. Am thinking of wandering on to the Dalmatian coast in a week or two. Address c/o Thomas Cook, Dubrovnik, from the 22nd onward. If there's anything I can do, let me know.

                              Yours, with admiration and gratitude,
                              RODDY.

Letter from Mr. Seddon of Messrs. Seddon, Blatherwick & Seddon to Miss Elinor Carlisle, July 20th:

                                        104 Bloomsbury Square.
DEAR MISS CARLISLE,
   I certainly think you should accept Major Somervell's offer of twelve thousand five hundred (£12,500) for Hunterbury. Large properties are extremely difficult to sell at the moment, and the

price offered seems to be most advantageous. The offer depends, however, on immediate possession, and I know Major Somervell has been seeing other properties in the neighborhood, so I would advise immediate acceptance.

Major Somervell is willing, I understand, to take the place furnished for three months, by which time the legal formalities should be accomplished and the sale can go through.

As regards the lodgekeeper, Gerrard, and the question of pensioning him off, I hear from Dr. Lord that the old man is seriously ill and not expected to live.

Probate has not yet been granted, but I have advanced one hundred pounds to Miss Mary Gerrard pending the settlement.

Yours sincerely,
EDMUND SEDDON.

Letter from Dr. Lord to Miss Elinor Carlisle, July 24th:

DEAR MISS CARLISLE,
Old Gerrard passed away today. Is there anything I can do for you? I hear you have sold the house to our new M.P., Major Somervell.

Yours sincerely,
PETER LORD.

Letter from Elinor Carlisle to Mary Gerrard, July 25th:

DEAR MARY,
I am so sorry to hear of your father's death.

I have had an offer for Hunterbury—from a Major Somervell. He is anxious to get in as soon as possible. I am going down there to go through my aunt's papers and clear up generally. Would it be possible for you to get your father's things moved out of the lodge as quickly as possible? I hope you are doing well and not finding your massage training too strenuous.

Yours very sincerely,
ELINOR CARLISLE.

Letter from Mary Gerrard to Nurse Hopkins, July 25th:

DEAR NURSE HOPKINS,

Thank you so much for writing to me about Father. I'm glad he didn't suffer. Miss Elinor writes me that the house is sold and that she would like the lodge cleared out as soon as possible. Could you put me up if I came down tomorrow for the funeral? Don't bother to answer if that's all right.

Yours affectionately,
MARY GERRARD.

7

ELINOR CARLISLE CAME out of the King's Arms on the morning of Thursday, July 27th, and stood for a minute or two looking up and down the main street of Maidensford. Suddenly, with an exclamation of pleasure, she crossed the road.

There was no mistaking that large, dignified presence, that serene gait as of a galleon in full sail.

"Mrs. Bishop!"

"Why, Miss Elinor! This *is* a surprise! I'd no notion you were in these parts! If I'd known you were coming to Hunterbury I'd have been there myself! Who's doing for you there? Have you brought someone down from London?"

Elinor shook her head. "I'm not staying at the house. I am staying at the King's Arms."

Mrs. Bishop looked across the road and sniffed dubiously.

"It is *possible* to stay there, I've heard," she allowed. "It's clean, I know. And the cooking, they say, is fair, but it's hardly what *you're* accustomed to, Miss Elinor."

Elinor said, smiling, "I'm really quite comfortable. It's only for a day or two. I have to sort out things at the house. All my aunt's personal things, and then there are a few pieces of furniture I should like to have in London."

"The house is really sold, then?"

"Yes. To a Major Somervell. Our new Member. Sir George Kerr died, you know, and there's been a bye-election."

"Returned unopposed," said Mrs. Bishop grandly. "We've never had anyone but a Conservative for Maidensford."

Elinor said, "I'm glad someone has bought the house who really wants to live in it. I should have been sorry if it had been turned into a hotel or built upon."

Mrs. Bishop shut her eyes and shivered all over her plump, aristocratic person.

"Yes, indeed, that would have been dreadful—quite dreadful. It's bad enough as it is to think of Hunterbury passing into the hands of strangers."

Elinor said, "Yes, but, you see, it would have been a very large house for me to live in—alone."

Mrs. Bishop sniffed.

Elinor said quickly, "I meant to ask you: Is there any especial piece of furniture that you might care to have? I should be very glad for you to have it, if so."

Mrs. Bishop beamed. She said graciously, "Well, Miss Elinor, that is very thoughtful of you—very kind, I'm sure. If it's not taking a liberty—"

She paused and Elinor said, "Oh, no."

"I have always had a great admiration for the secretaire in the drawing-room. Such a *handsome* piece."

Elinor remembered it, a somewhat flamboyant piece of inlaid marquetry. She said quickly, "Of course you shall have it, Mrs. Bishop. Anything else?"

"No, indeed, Miss Elinor. You have already been extremely generous."

Elinor said, "There are some chairs in the same style as the secretaire. Would you care for those?"

Mrs. Bishop accepted the chairs with becoming thanks. She explained, "I am staying at the moment with my sister. Is there anything I can do for you up at the house, Miss Elinor? I could come up there with you, if you like."

"No, thank you."

Elinor spoke quickly, rather abruptly.

Mrs. Bishop said, "It would be no trouble, I assure you—a pleasure. Such a melancholy task going through all dear Mrs. Welman's things."

Elinor said, "Thank you, Mrs. Bishop, but I would rather tackle it alone. One can do some things better alone—"

Mrs. Bishop said stiffly, "As you please, of course."

She went on: "That daughter of Gerrard's is down here. The funeral was yesterday. She's staying with Nurse Hopkins. I did hear *they* were going up to the lodge this morning."

Elinor nodded. She said, "Yes, I asked Mary to come down and see to that. Major Somervell wants to get in as soon as possible."

"I see."

Elinor said, "Well, I must be getting on now. So glad to have seen you, Mrs. Bishop. I'll remember about the secretaire and the chairs."

She shook hands and passed on.

She went into the baker's and bought a loaf of bread. Then she went into the dairy and bought half a pound of butter and some milk. Finally she went into the grocer's.

"I want some paste for sandwiches, please."

"Certainly, Miss Carlisle." Mr. Abbott himself bustled forward, elbowing aside his junior apprentice. "What would you like? Salmon and shrimp? Turkey and tongue? Salmon and sardine? Ham and tongue?"

He whipped down pot after pot and arrayed them on the counter.

Elinor said with a faint smile, "In spite of their names, I always think they taste much alike."

Mr. Abbott agreed instantly. "Well, perhaps they do in a way. Yes, in a way. But, of course, they're very tasty—very tasty."

Elinor said, "One used to be rather afraid of eating fish pastes. There have been cases of ptomaine poisoning from them, haven't there?"

Mr. Abbott put on a horrified expression. "I can assure you this is an excellent brand—*most* reliable—we never have any complaints."

Elinor said, "I'll have one of salmon and anchovy and one of salmon and shrimp. Thank you."

Elinor Carlisle entered the grounds of Hunterbury by the back gate. It was a hot, clear summer's day. There were sweet peas in flower. Elinor passed by a row of them. The undergardener, Horlick, who was remaining on to keep the place in order, greeted her respectfully.

"Good morning, miss. I got your letter. You'll find the side door open, miss. I've unfastened the shutters and opened most of the windows."

Elinor said, "Thank you, Horlick."

As she moved on, the young man said nervously, his Adam's apple jerking up and down in spasmodic fashion, "Excuse me, miss—"

Elinor turned back. "Yes?"

"Is it true that the house is sold? I mean, is it really settled?"

"Oh, yes!"

Horlick said nervously, "I was wondering, miss, if you would say a word for me—to Major Somervell, I mean. He'll be wanting gardeners. Maybe he'll think I'm too young for head gardener, but I've worked under Mr. Stephens for four years now, and I reckon I know a tidyish bit, and I've kept things going fairly well since I've been here, single-handed."

Elinor said quickly, "Of course I will do all I can for you, Horlick. As a matter of fact, I intended to mention you to Major Somervell and tell him what a good gardener you are."

Horlick's face grew dusky red. "Thank you, miss. That's very kind of you. You can understand it's been a bit of a blow, like—Mrs. Welman dying, and then the place being sold off so quick—and I—well, the fact of the matter is I was going to get married this autumn, only one's got to be sure—"

He stopped.

Elinor said kindly, "I hope Major Somervell will take you on. You can rely on me to do all I can."

Horlick said again, "Thank you, miss. We all hoped, you see, as how the place would be kept on by the family. Thank you, miss."

Elinor walked on.

Suddenly, rushing over her like the stream from a broken dam, a wave of wild resentment swept over her.

"We all hoped the place would be kept on by the family. . . ."

She and Roddy could have lived here! *She and Roddy. . . .* Roddy would have wanted that. It was what she herself would have wanted. They had always loved Hunterbury, both of them. Dear Hunterbury. . . . In the years before her parents had died, when they had been in India, she had come here for holidays. She had played in the woods, rambled by the stream, picked sweet peas in great flowering armloads, eaten fat green gooseberries and dark red luscious raspberries. Later, there had been apples. There had been places, secret lairs, where she had curled up with a book and read for hours.

She had loved Hunterbury. Always, at the back of her mind, she had felt sure of living there permanently some day. Aunt Laura had fostered that idea. Little words and phrases: "Some day, Elinor, you may like to cut down those yews. They are a little gloomy, perhaps!" "One might have a water garden here. Some day, perhaps, *you* will."

And Roddy? Roddy, too, had looked forward to Hunterbury being his home. It had lain, perhaps, behind his feeling for her, Elinor. He had felt, subconsciously, that it was fitting and right that they two should be together at Hunterbury.

And they *would* have been together there. They would have been together *here—now*—not packing up the house for selling, but redecorating it, planning new beauties in house and garden, walking side by side in gentle proprietary pleasure, happy—yes, *happy* together—but for the fatal accident of a girl's wild-rose beauty.

What did Roddy know of Mary Gerrard? Nothing—less than nothing! What did he care for her—for the real Mary? She had, quite possibly, admirable qualities, but did Roddy know anything about them? It was the old story—Nature's hoary old joke!

Hadn't Roddy himself said it was an "enchantment"?

Didn't Roddy himself—*really*—want to be free of it?

If Mary Gerrard were to—die, for instance, wouldn't Roddy some day acknowledge, "It was all for the best. I see that now. We had nothing in common."

He would add, perhaps, with gentle melancholy, "She was a lovely creature."

Let her be that to him—yes—an exquisite memory—a thing of beauty and a joy forever.

If anything were to happen to Mary Gerrard, Roddy would come back to her—Elinor. She was quite sure of that!

If anything were to happen to Mary Gerrard. . . .

Elinor turned the handle of the side door. She passed from the warm sunlight into the shadow of the house. She shivered

It felt cold in here, dark, sinister. It was as though Something was there, waiting for her, in the house. . . .

She walked along the hall and pushed the baize door that led into the butler's pantry.

It smelled slightly musty. She pushed up the window, opening it wide.

She put down her parcels—the butter, the loaf, the little glass bottle of milk. She thought, *Stupid! I meant to get coffee.*

She looked in the canisters on a shelf. There was a little tea in one of them, but no coffee.

She thought, *Oh, well, it doesn't matter*.

She unwrapped the two glass jars of fish paste.

She stood staring at them for a minute. Then she left the pantry and went upstairs. She went straight to Mrs. Welman's room. She began on the big tallboy, opening drawers, sorting, arranging, folding clothes in little piles.

In the lodge Mary Gerrard was looking round rather helplessly. She hadn't realized, somehow, how cramped it all was.

Her past life rushed back over her in a flood. Mum making clothes for her dolls. Dad always cross and surly. Disliking her. Yes, disliking her. . . .

She said suddenly to Nurse Hopkins, "Dad didn't say anything—send me any message before he died, did he?"

Nurse Hopkins said cheerfully and callously, "Oh, dear me, no. He was unconscious for an hour before he passed away."

Mary said slowly, "I feel perhaps I ought to have come down and looked after him. After all, he *was* my father."

Nurse Hopkins said with a trace of embarrassment, "Now, just you listen to me, Mary: whether he was your father or not doesn't enter into it. Children don't care much about their parents in these days, from what I can see, and a good many parents don't care for their children, either. That's as may be but, anyway, it's a waste of breath to go back over the past and sentimentalize. We've got to go on living—that's our job—and not too easy, either, sometimes!"

Mary said slowly, "I expect you're right. But I feel perhaps it was my fault we didn't get *on* better."

Nurse Hopkins said robustly, "Nonsense!"

The word exploded like a bomb. It quelled Mary.

Nurse Hopkins turned to more practical matters. "What are you going to do with the furniture? Store it? Or sell it?"

Mary said doubtfully, "I don't know. What do you think?"

Running a practical eye over it, Nurse Hopkins said, "Some of it's quite good and solid. You might store it and furnish a little flat of your own in London some day. Get rid of the rubbish. The chairs are good—so's the table. And that's a nice bureau—it's the kind that's out of fashion, but it's solid mahogany, and they say Victorian stuff will come in again one day. I'd get rid of that great wardrobe, if I were you. Too big to fit in anywhere. Takes up half the bedroom as it is."

They made a list between them of pieces to be kept or let go.

Mary said, "The lawyer's been very kind—Mr. Seddon, I mean. He advanced me some money, so that I could get started with my training fees and other expenses. It will be a month or so before the money can be definitely made over to me, so he said."

Nurse Hopkins said, "How do you like your work?"

"I think I shall like it very much. It's rather strenuous at first. I come home tired to death."

Nurse Hopkins said grimly, "I thought I was going to die when I was a probationer at St. Luke's. I felt I could never stick it for three years. But I did."

They had sorted through the old man's clothes. Now they came to a tin box full of papers.

Mary said, "We must go through these, I suppose."

They sat down one on each side of the table.

Nurse Hopkins grumbled as she started with a handful. "Extraordinary what rubbish people keep! Newspaper cuttings! Old letters. All sorts of things!"

Mary said, unfolding a document, "Here's Dad's and Mum's marriage certificate. At St. Albans, 1919."

Nurse Hopkins said, "Marriage lines, that's the old-fashioned term. Lots of the people in this village use that term yet."

Mary said in a stifled voice, "But, Nurse—"

The other looked up sharply. She saw the distress in the girl's eyes. She said sharply, "What's the matter?"

Mary Gerrard said in a shaky voice, "Don't you see? This is 1939. And I'm twenty-one. In 1919 I was a year old. That means—that means—that my father and mother weren't married till—till—*afterward.*"

Nurse Hopkins frowned. She said robustly, "Well, after all, what of it? Don't go worrying about that, at *this* time of day!"

"But, Nurse, I can't help it."

Nurse Hopkins spoke with authority, "There's many couples that don't go to church till a bit after they should do so. But so long as they do it in the end, what's the odds? That's what I say!"

Mary said in a low voice, "Is that why—do you think—my father never liked me? Because, perhaps, my mother *made* him marry her?"

Nurse Hopkins hesitated. She bit her lip, then she said, "It wasn't quite like that, I imagine." She paused. "Oh, well, if you're going to worry about it, you may as well know the truth. You aren't Gerrard's daughter at all."

Mary said, "Then *that* was why!"

Nurse Hopkins said, "Maybe."

Mary said, a red spot suddenly burning in each cheek, "I suppose it's wrong of me, but I'm glad! I've always felt uncomfortable because I didn't care for my father, but if he *wasn't* my father, well that makes it all right! How did you know about it?"

Nurse Hopkins said, "Gerrard talked about it a good deal before he died. I shut him up pretty sharply, but he didn't care. Naturally, *I* shouldn't have said anything to you about it if this hadn't cropped up."

Mary said slowly, "I wonder who my real father was."

Nurse Hopkins hesitated. She opened her mouth, then shut it again. She appeared to be finding it hard to make up her mind on some point.

Then a shadow fell across the room, and the two women looked round to see Elinor Carlisle standing at the window.

Elinor said, "Good morning."

Nurse Hopkins said, "Good morning, Miss Carlisle. Lovely day, isn't it?"

Mary said, "Oh—good morning, Miss Elinor."

Elinor said, "I've been making some sandwiches. Won't you come up and have some? It's just on one o'clock, and it's such a bother to have to go home for lunch. I got enough for three on purpose."

Nurse Hopkins said in pleased surprise, "Well, I must say, Miss Carlisle, that's extremely thoughtful of you. It *is* a nuisance to have to break off what you're doing and come all the way back from the village. I hoped we might finish this morning. I went round and saw my cases early. But, there, turning out takes you longer than you think."

Mary said gratefully, "Thank you, Miss Elinor, it's very kind of you."

The three of them walked up the drive to the house. Elinor had left the front door open. They passed inside into the cool of the hall. Mary shivered a little. Elinor looked at her sharply.

She said, "What is it?"

Mary said, "Oh, nothing—just a shiver. It was coming in—out of the sun."

Elinor said in a low voice, "That's queer. That's what I felt this morning."

Nurse Hopkins said in a loud, cheerful voice and with a laugh, "Come, now, you'll be pretending there are ghosts in the house next. *I* didn't feel anything!"

Elinor smiled. She led the way into the morning-room on the right of the front door. The blinds were up and the windows open. It looked cheerful.

Elinor went across the hall and brought back from the pantry a big plate of sandwiches. She handed it to Mary, saying, "Have one?"

Mary took one. Elinor stood watching her for a moment as the girl's even white teeth bit into the sandwich. She held her breath for a minute, then expelled it in a little sigh. Absent-mindedly she stood for a minute with the plate held to her waist, then at sight of Nurse Hopkins's slightly parted lips and hungry expression she flushed and quickly proffered the plate to the older woman.

Elinor took a sandwich herself. She said apologetically, "I meant to make some coffee, but I forgot to get any. There's some beer on that table, though, if anyone likes that?"

Nurse Hopkins said sadly, "If only I'd thought to bring along some tea now."

Elinor said absently, "There's a little tea still in the canister in the pantry."

Nurse Hopkins's face brightened. "Then I'll just pop out and put the kettle on. No milk, I suppose?"

Elinor said, "Yes, I brought some."

"Well, then, that's all right," said Nurse Hopkins and hurried out.

Elinor and Mary were alone together. A queer tension crept into the atmosphere. Elinor, with an obvious effort, tried to make conversation. Her lips were dry. She passed her tongue over them. She said, rather stiffly, "You—like your work in London?"

"Yes, thank you. I—I'm very grateful to you—"

A sudden harsh sound broke from Elinor. A laugh so discordant, so unlike her, that Mary stared at her in surprise. Elinor said, "You needn't be so grateful!"

Mary, rather embarrassed, said, "I didn't mean—that is—" She stopped.

Elinor was staring at her—a glance so searching, so, yes, strange that Mary flinched under it.

She said, "Is—is anything wrong?"

Elinor got up quickly. She said, turning away, "What should be wrong?"

Mary murmured, "You—you looked—"

Elinor said with a little laugh, "Was I staring? I'm so sorry. I do sometimes—when I'm thinking of something else."

Nurse Hopkins looked in at the door and remarked brightly, "I've put the kettle on," and went out again.

Elinor was taken with a sudden fit of laughter. "Polly put the kettle on, Polly put the kettle on, Polly put the kettle on—we'll all have tea! Do you remember playing that, Mary, when we were children?"

"Yes, indeed I do."

Elinor said, *"When we were children.* It's a pity, Mary, isn't it, that one can never go back?"

Mary said, "Would you like to go back?"

Elinor said with force, "Yes—*yes.*"

Silence fell between them for a little while.

Then Mary said, her face flushing, "Miss Elinor, you mustn't think—"

She stopped, warned by the sudden stiffening of Elinor's slender figure, the uplifted line of her chin.

Elinor said in a cold, steel-like voice, "What mustn't I think?"

Mary murmured, "I—I've forgotten what I was going to say."

Elinor's body relaxed—as at a danger past.

Nurse Hopkins came in with a tray. On it was a brown teapot, and milk and three cups.

She said, quite unconscious of anticlimax, "Here's the tea!"

She put the tray in front of Elinor. Elinor shook her head. "I won't have any."

She pushed the tray along toward Mary. Mary poured out two cups. Nurse Hopkins sighed with satisfaction. "It's nice and strong."

Elinor got up and moved over to the window. Nurse Hopkins said persuasively, "Are you sure you won't have a cup, Miss Carlisle? Do you good."

Elinor murmured, "No, thank you."

Nurse Hopkins drained her cup, replaced it in the saucer, and murmured, "I'll just turn off the kettle. I put it on in case we needed to fill up the pot again."

She bustled out.

Elinor wheeled round from the window. She said, and her voice was suddenly charged with a desperate appeal, "Mary—"

Mary Gerrard answered quickly, "Yes?"

Slowly the light died out of Elinor's face. The lips closed. The desperate pleading faded and left a mere mask—frozen and still.

She said, "Nothing."

The silence came down heavily on the room.

Mary thought, *How queer everything is today. As though—as though we were waiting for something.*

Elinor moved at last.

She came from the window and picked up the tea-tray, placing on it the empty sandwich plate.

Mary jumped up. "Oh, Miss Elinor, let me."

Elinor said sharply, "No, you stay here. I'll do this."

She carried the tray out of the room. She looked back once over her shoulder at Mary Gerrard by the window, young and alive and beautiful. . . .

Nurse Hopkins was in the pantry. She was wiping her face with a handkerchief. She looked up sharply as Elinor entered. She said, "My word, it's hot in here!"

Elinor answered mechanically, "Yes, the pantry faces south."

Nurse Hopkins relieved her of the tray.

"You let me wash up, Miss Carlisle. You're not looking quite the thing."

Elinor said, "Oh, I'm all right."

She picked up a dish-cloth. "I'll dry."

Nurse Hopkins slipped off her cuffs. She poured hot water from the kettle into the basin.

Elinor said idly, looking at her wrist, "You've pricked yourself."

Nurse Hopkins laughed. "On the rose trellis at the lodge—a thorn. I'll get it out presently."

The rose trellis at the lodge. Memory poured in waves over Elinor. She and Roddy quarreling—the Wars of the Roses. She and Roddy quarreling—and making it up. Lovely, laughing, happy days. A sick wave of revulsion passed over her. What had she come to now? What black abyss of hate—of evil? She swayed a little as she stood.

She thought, *I've been mad—quite mad.*

Nurse Hopkins was staring at her curiously.

"Downright odd, she seemed," so ran Nurse Hopkins's narrative later. "Talking as if she didn't know what she was saying, and her eyes so bright and queer."

The cups and saucers rattled in the basin. Elinor picked up an empty fish-paste pot from the table and put it into the basin. As she did so she said, and marveled at the steadiness of her voice, "I've sorted out some clothes upstairs, Aunt Laura's things. I thought, perhaps, Nurse, you could advise me where they would be useful in the village."

Nurse Hopkins said briskly, "I will indeed. There's Mrs. Parkinson, and old Nellie, and that poor creature who's not quite all there at Ivy Cottage. Be a godsend to them."

She and Elinor cleared up the pantry. Then they went upstairs together.

In Mrs. Welman's room clothes were folded in neat bundles: underclothing, dresses, and certain articles of handsome clothing, velvet teagowns, a musquash coat. The latter, Elinor explained, she thought of giving to Mrs. Bishop.

Nurse Hopkins nodded assent. She noticed that Mrs. Welman's sables were laid on the chest of drawers. *Going to have them remodeled for herself,* she thought.

She cast a look at the big tallboys. She wondered if Elinor had found that photograph signed *Lewis,* and what she had made of it, if so.

Funny, she thought to herself, *the way O'Brien's letter crossed mine. I never dreamed a thing like that could happen. Her hitting on that photo just the day I wrote to her about Mrs. Slattery.*

She helped Elinor sort through the clothing and volunteered to tie them up in separate bundles for the different families and see to their distribution herself.

She said, "I can be getting on with that while Mary goes down to the lodge and finishes up there. She's only got a box of papers to go through. Where is the girl, by the way? Did she go down to the lodge?"

Elinor said, "I left her in the morning-room."

Nurse Hopkins said, "She'd not be there all this time." She glanced at her watch. "Why, it's nearly an hour we've been up here!"

She bustled down the stairs. Elinor followed her.

They went into the morning-room.

Nurse Hopkins exclaimed, "Well, I never, she's fallen asleep."

Mary Gerrard was sitting in a big armchair by the window. She had dropped down a little in it. There was a queer sound in the room: stertorous, labored breathing.

Nurse Hopkins went across and shook the girl. "Wake up, my dear—"

She broke off. She bent lower, pulled down an eyelid. Then she started shaking the girl in grim earnest.

She turned on Elinor. There was something menacing in her voice as she said, "What's all this?"

Elinor said, "I don't know what you mean. Is she ill?"

Nurse Hopkins said, "Where's the phone? Get hold of Dr. Lord as soon as you can."

Elinor said, "What's the matter?"

"The matter? The girl's ill. She's dying."

Elinor recoiled a step. She said, *"Dying?"*

Nurse Hopkins said, "She's been poisoned."

Her eyes, hard with suspicion, glared at Elinor.

8

HERCULE POIROT, HIS egg-shaped head gently tilted to one side, his eyebrows raised inquiringly, his finger tips joined together, watched the young man who was striding so savagely up and down the room, his pleasant freckled face puckered and drawn.

Hercule Poirot said, *"Eh bien,* my friend, what *is* all this?"

Peter Lord stopped dead in his pacing.

He said, "Monsieur Poirot, you're the only man in the world who can help me. I've heard Stillingfleet talk about you; he's told me what you did in that Benedict Farley case. How every mortal soul thought it was suicide and you showed that it was murder."

Hercule Poirot said, "Have you, then, a case of suicide among your patients about which you are not satisfied?"

Peter Lord shook his head. He sat down opposite Poirot.

He said, "There's a young woman. She's been arrested and she's going to be tried for murder! I want you to find evidence that will prove that she didn't do it!"

Poirot's eyebrows rose a little higher. Then he assumed a discreet and confidential manner.

He said, "You and this young lady—you are affianced—yes? You are in love with each other?"

Peter Lord laughed—a sharp, bitter laugh.

He said, "No, it's not like that! She has the bad taste to prefer a long-nosed, supercilious ass with a face like a melancholy horse! Stupid of her, but there it is!"

Poirot said, "I see."

Lord said bitterly, "Oh, yes, you see all right! No need to be so tactful about it. I fell for her straightaway. And because of that I don't want her hanged. See?"

Poirot said, "What is the charge against her?"

"She's accused of murdering a girl called Mary Gerrard, by poisoning her with morphine hydrochloride. You've probably read the account of the inquest in the papers."

Poirot said, "And the motive?"

"Jealousy!"

"And in your opinion she didn't do it?"

"No, of course not."

Hercule Poirot looked at him thoughtfully for a moment or two, then said, "What is it exactly that you want me to do? To investigate this matter?"

"I want you to get her off."

"I am not a defending counsel, *mon cher.*"

"I'll put it more clearly: *I want you to find evidence that will enable her counsel to get her off.*"

Hercule Poirot said, "You put this a little curiously."

Peter Lord said, "Because I don't wrap it up, you mean? It seems simple enough to me. *I want this girl acquitted.* I think *you* are the only man who can do it!"

"You wish me to look into the facts? To find out the truth? To discover what really happened?"

"I want you to find any facts that will tell in her favor."

Hercule Poirot, with care and precision, lighted a very tiny cigarette. He said, "But is it not a little unethical what you say there? To arrive at the truth, yes, that always interests me. But the truth is a two-edged weapon. Supposing that I find facts *against* the lady? Do you demand that I suppress them?"

Peter Lord stood up. He was very white. He said, "That's impossible! Nothing that you could find could be more against her than the facts are already! They're utterly and completely damning! There's any amount of evidence against her black and plain for all the world to see! You couldn't find anything that would damn her more completely than she is already! I'm asking you to use all your ingenuity—Stillingfleet says you're damned ingenious—to ferret out a loophole, a possible alternative."

Hercule Poirot said, "Surely her lawyers will do that?"

"Will they?" The young man laughed scornfully. "They're licked before they start! Think it's hopeless! They've briefed Bulmer, K.C., the forlorn hope man; that's a give-away in itself! Big orator—sob stuff—stressing the prisoner's youth—all that! But the judge won't let him get away with it. Not a hope!"

Hercule Poirot said, "Supposing she is guilty—do you still want to get her acquitted?"

Peter Lord said quietly, "Yes."

Hercule Poirot moved in his chair. He said, "You interest me."

After a minute or two he said, "You had better, I think, tell me the exact facts of the case."

"Haven't you read anything about it in the papers?"

Hercule Poirot waved a hand. "A mention of it—yes. But the newspapers, they are so inaccurate, I never go by what they say."

Peter Lord said, "It's quite simple. Horribly simple. This girl, Elinor Carlisle, had just come into a place near here—Hunterbury Hall—and a fortune from her aunt, who died intestate. Aunt's name was Welman. Aunt had a nephew by marriage—Roderick Welman. He was engaged to Elinor Carlisle—long-standing business, known each other since children. There was a girl down at Hunterbury: Mary Gerrard, daughter of the lodgekeeper. Old Mrs. Welman had made a lot of fuss about her, paid for her education, etc. Consequence is, girl was to outward seeming a lady. Roderick Welman, it seems, fell for her. In consequence, engagement is broken off.

"Now we come to the doings. Elinor Carlisle put up the place for sale and a man called Somervell bought it. Elinor came down to clear out her aunt's personal possessions and so on. Mary Gerrard, whose father had just died, was clearing out the lodge. That brings us to the morning of July 27th.

"Elinor Carlisle was staying at the local pub. In the street she met the former housekeeper, Mrs. Bishop. Mrs. Bishop suggested coming up to the house to help her. Elinor refused—rather overvehemently. Then she went to the grocer's shop and bought some fish paste, and there she made a remark about food poisoning. You see? Perfectly innocent thing to do; but, of course, it tells against her! She went up to the house, and about one o'clock she went down to the lodge, where Mary Gerrard was busy with the District Nurse, a Nosey Parker of a woman called Hopkins, helping her, and told them that she had made some sandwiches ready up at the house. They came up to the house with her, ate sandwiches, and about an hour or so later I was sent for and found Mary Gerrard unconscious. Did all I could, but it was no good. Autopsy revealed large dose of morphine had been taken a short time previously. And the police found a scrap of a label with *morphia hydrochlor* on it just where Elinor Carlisle had been spreading the sandwiches."

"What else did Mary Gerrard eat or drink?"

"She and the District Nurse drank tea with the sandwiches. Nurse made it and Mary poured it out. Couldn't have been anything there. Of course, I understand Counsel will make a song and dance about sandwiches, too, saying all three ate them, therefore *impossible* to ensure that only one person should be poisoned. They said that in the Hearne case, you remember."

Poirot nodded. He said, "But actually it is very simple. You make your pile of sandwiches. *In one of them is the poison.* You hand the plate. In our state of civilization it is a foregone conclusion that the person to whom the plate is offered will take *the sandwich that is nearest to them.* I presume that Elinor Carlisle handed the plate to Mary Gerrard first?"

"Exactly."

"Although the nurse, who was an older woman, was in the room."

"Yes."

"That does not look very good."

"It doesn't mean a thing, really. You don't stand on ceremony at a picnic lunch."

"Who cut the sandwiches?"

"Elinor Carlisle."

"Was there anyone else in the house?"

"No one."

Poirot shook his head. "It is bad, that. And the girl had *nothing* but the tea and the sandwiches?"

"Nothing. Stomach contents tell us that."

Poirot said, "It is suggested that Elinor Carlisle hoped the girl's death would be taken for food poisoning? How did she propose to explain the fact that only *one* member of the party was affected?"

Peter Lord said, "It does happen that way sometimes. Also, there were two pots of paste—both much alike in appearance. The idea would be that one pot was all right and that by a coincidence all the bad paste was eaten by Mary."

"An interesting study in the laws of probability," said Poirot. "The mathematical chances against that happening would be high, I fancy. But another point, if food poisoning was to be suggested: *Why not choose a different poison?* The symptoms of morphine are not in the least like those of food poisoning. Atropine, surely, would have been a better choice!"

Peter Lord said slowly, "Yes, that's true. But there's something more. That damned District Nurse swears she lost a tube of morphine!"

"When?"

"Oh, weeks earlier, the night old Mrs. Welman died. The nurse says she left her case in the hall and found a tube of morphine missing in the morning. All buncombe, I believe. Probably smashed it at home some time before and forgot about it."

"She has only remembered it *since* the death of Mary Gerrard?"

Peter Lord said reluctantly, "As a matter of fact, she *did* mention it at the time—to the nurse on duty."

Hercule Poirot was looking at Peter Lord with some interest. He said gently, "I think, *mon cher,* there is something else—something that you have not yet told me."

Peter Lord said, "Oh, well, I suppose you'd better have it all. They're applying for an exhumation order and going to dig up old Mrs. Welman."

Poirot said, *"Eh bien?"*

Peter Lord said, "When they do, *they'll probably find what they're looking for—morphine!"*

"You knew that?"

Peter Lord, his face white under the freckles, muttered, "I suspected it."

Hercule Poirot beat with his hand on the arm of his chair. He cried out, *"Mon Dieu,* I do not understand you! You *knew* when she died that she had been murdered?"

Peter Lord shouted, "Good Lord, no! I never dreamed of such a thing! I thought she'd taken it herself."

Poirot sank back in his chair. "Ah! You thought *that.*"

"Of course I did! She'd talked to me about it. Asked me more than once if I couldn't 'finish her off.' She hated illness, the helplessness of it—the—what she called the *indignity* of lying there tended like a baby. And she was a very determined woman."

He was silent a moment, then he went on: "I was surprised at her death. I hadn't expected it. I sent the nurse out of the room and made as thorough an investigation as I could. Of course, it was impossible to be sure without an autopsy. Well, what was the good of that? *If* she'd taken a short-cut, why make a song and dance about it and create a scandal? Better sign the certificate and let her be buried in peace. After all, I couldn't be sure. I decided wrong, I suppose. But I never dreamed for one moment of foul play! I was quite sure she'd done it herself."

Poirot asked, "How did you think she had got hold of the morphine?"

"I hadn't the least idea. But, as I tell you, she was a clever, resourceful woman, with plenty of ingenuity and remarkable determination."

"Would she have got it from the nurses?"

Peter Lord shook his head. "Never on your life! You don't know nurses!"

"From her family?"

"Possibly. Might have worked on their feelings."

Hercule Poirot said, "You have told me that Mrs. Welman died intestate. If she had lived, would she have made a will?"

Peter Lord grinned suddenly. "Putting your finger with fiendish accuracy on all the vital spots, aren't you? Yes, she was going to make a will; very agitated about it. Couldn't speak intelligently, but made her wishes clear. Elinor Carlisle was to have telephoned the lawyer first thing in the morning."

"So Elinor Carlisle knew that her aunt wanted to make a will? And if her aunt died without making one, Elinor Carlisle inherited everything?"

Peter Lord said quickly, "She didn't know that. She'd no idea her aunt had never made a will."

"That, my friend, is what she *says*. She *may* have known."

"Look here, Poirot, are you the Prosecuting Counsel?"

"At the moment, yes. I must know the full strength of the case against her. Could Elinor Carlisle have taken the morphine from the attaché case?"

"Yes. So could anyone else. Roderick Welman. Nurse O'Brien. Any of the servants."

"Or Dr. Lord?"

Peter Lord's eyes opened wide. He said, "Certainly. But what would be the idea?"

"Mercy, perhaps."

Peter Lord shook his head. "Nothing doing there! You'll have to believe me!"

Hercule Poirot leaned back in his chair. He said, "Let us entertain a supposition. Let us say that Elinor Carlisle did take that morphine from the attaché case and did administer it to her aunt. Was anything said about the loss of the morphine?"

"Not to the household. The two nurses kept it to themselves."

Poirot said, "What, in your opinion, will be the action of the Crown?"

"You mean if they find morphine in Mrs. Welman's body?"

"Yes."

Peter Lord said grimly, "It's possible that if Elinor is acquitted of the present charge she will be rearrested and charged with the murder of her aunt."

Poirot said thoughtfully, "The motives are different; that is to say, in the case of Mrs. Welman the motive would have been *gain,* whereas in the case of Mary Gerrard the motive is supposed to be *jealousy.*"

"That's right."

Poirot said, "What line does the defense propose to take?"

Peter Lord said, "Bulmer proposes to take the line that there was no motive. He'll put forward the theory that the engagement between Elinor and Roderick was a family business, entered into for family reasons, to please Mrs. Welman, and that the moment the old lady was dead Elinor broke it off of her own accord. Roderick Welman will give evidence to that effect. I think he almost believes it!"

"Believes that Elinor did not care for him to any great extent?"

"Yes."

"In which case," said Poirot, "she would have no reason for murdering Mary Gerrard."

"Exactly."

"But in that case, who *did* murder Mary Gerrard?"

"As you say."

Poirot shook his head. *"C'est difficile."*

Peter Lord said vehemently, "That's just it! If *she* didn't, *who did?* There's the tea; but both Nurse Hopkins and Mary drank that. The defense will try to suggest that Mary Gerrard took the morphine herself after the other two had left the room—that she committed suicide, in fact."

"Had she any reason for committing suicide?"

"None whatever."

"Was she of a suicidal type?"

"No."

Poirot said, "What was she like, this Mary Gerrard?"

Peter Lord considered, "She was—well, she was a nice kid. Yes, definitely a nice kid."

Poirot sighed. He murmured, "This Roderick Welman, did he fall in love with her because she was a nice kid?"

Peter Lord smiled. "Oh, I get what you mean. She was beautiful, all right."

"And you yourself? You had no feeling for her?"

Peter Lord stared. "Good Lord, no."

Hercule Poirot reflected for a moment or two, then he said, "Roderick Welman says that there was affection between him and Elinor Carlisle, but nothing stronger. Do you agree to that?"

"How the hell should I know?"

Poirot shook his head. "You told me when you came into this room that Elinor Carlisle had the bad taste to be in love with a long-nosed, supercilious ass. That, I presume, is a description of Roderick Welman. So, according to you, she *does* care for him."

Peter Lord said in a low, exasperated voice, "She cares for him all right! Cares like hell!"

Poirot said, "Then there *was* a motive."

Peter Lord swerved round on him, his face alight with anger. "Does it matter? She might have done it, yes! *I don't care if she did.*"

Poirot said, "Aha!"

"But I don't want her hanged, I tell you! Supposing she *was* driven desperate? Love's a desperate and twisting business. It can turn a worm into a fine fellow—and it can bring a decent, straight man down to the dregs! Suppose she *did* do it. Haven't you got any pity?"

Hercule Poirot said, "I do not approve of murder."

Peter Lord stared at him, looked away, stared again, and finally burst out laughing.

"Of all the things to say—so prim and smug, too! Who's asking you to approve? I'm not asking you to tell lies! Truth's truth, isn't it? If you find something that tells in an accused person's favor, you wouldn't be inclined to suppress it because she's guilty, would you?"

"Certainly not."

"Then why the hell can't you do what I ask you?"

Hercule Poirot said, "My friend, I am perfectly prepared to do so."

9

PETER LORD STARED at him, took out a handkerchief, wiped his face, and threw himself down in a chair.

"Whoof!" he said. "You got me all worked up! I didn't see in the least what you were getting at!"

Poirot said, "I was examining the case against Elinor Carlisle. Now I know it. Morphine was administered to Mary Gerrard; and, as far as I can see, it *must* have been given in the sandwiches. Nobody touched those sandwiches *except Elinor Carlisle*. Elinor Carlisle had a *motive* for killing Mary Gerrard, and she is, in your opinion, *capable* of killing Mary Gerrard, and in all probability she *did* kill Mary Gerrard. I see no reason for believing otherwise.

"That, *mon ami,* is one side of the question. Now we will dismiss all those considerations from our mind and we will approach the matter from the opposite angle: *If Elinor Carlisle did not kill Mary Gerrard, who did?* Or did Mary Gerrard commit suicide?"

Peter Lord sat up. A frown creased his forehead. He said, "You weren't quite accurate just now."

"*I? Not accurate?*" Poirot sounded affronted.

Peter Lord pursued relentlessly, "No. You said nobody but Elinor Carlisle touched those sandwiches. You don't know that."

"There was no one else in the house."

"*As far as we know.* But you are excluding a short period of time. *There was a time during which Elinor Carlisle left the house to go down to the lodge.* During that period of time the sandwiches were on a plate in the pantry, and somebody *could* have tampered with them."

Poirot drew a deep breath. He said, "You are right, my friend. I admit it. There *was* a time during which somebody could have had access to the plate of sandwiches. We must try to form some idea *who that somebody could be;* that is to say, *what kind of person.*"

He paused.

"Let us consider this Mary Gerrard. *Someone,* not Elinor Carlisle, desired her death. *Why?* Did anyone stand to gain by her death? Had she money to leave?"

Peter Lord shook his head. "Not now. In another month she would have had two thousand pounds. Elinor Carlisle was making that sum over to her because she believed her aunt would have wished it. But the old lady's estate isn't wound up yet."

Poirot said, "Then we can wash out the money angle. Mary Gerrard was beautiful, you say. With that there are always complications. She had admirers?"

"Probably. I don't know much about it."

"Who would know?"

Peter Lord grinned. "I'd better put you on to Nurse Hopkins. She's the town crier. She knows everything that goes on in Maidensford."

"I was going to ask you to give me your impressions of the two nurses."

"Well, O'Brien's Irish, good nurse, competent, a bit silly, could be spiteful, a bit of a liar—the imaginative kind that's not so much deceitful, but just has to make a good story out of everything."

Poirot nodded.

"Hopkins is a sensible, shrewd, middle-aged woman, quite kindly and competent, but a sight too much interested in other people's business!"

"If there had been trouble over some young man in the village, would Nurse Hopkins know about it?"

"You bet!"

He added slowly, "All the same, I don't believe there can be anything very obvious in that line. Mary hadn't been home long. She'd been away in Germany for two years."

"She was twenty-one?"

"Yes."

"There may be some German complication."

Peter Lord's face brightened. He said eagerly, "You mean that some German fellow may have had it in for her? He may have followed her over here, waited his time, and finally achieved his object?"

"It sounds a little melodramatic," said Hercule Poirot doubtfully.

"But it's *possible?*"

"Not very probable, though."

Peter Lord said, "I don't agree. Someone *might* get all het up about the girl, and see red when she turned him down. He may have fancied she treated him badly. It's an idea."

"It is an idea, yes," said Hercule Poirot, but his tone was not encouraging.

Peter Lord said pleadingly, "Go on, Poirot."

"You want me, I see, to be the conjurer. To take out of the empty hat rabbit after rabbit."

"You can put it that way if you like."

"There *is* another possibility," said Hercule Poirot.

"Go on."

"*Someone* abstracted a tube of morphine from Nurse Hopkins's case that evening in June. *Suppose Mary Gerrard saw the person who did it?*"

"She would have said so."

"No, no, *mon cher.* Be reasonable. If Elinor Carlisle, or Roderick Welman, or Nurse O'Brien, or even any of the servants, were to open that case and abstract a little glass tube, what would anyone think? Simply that the person in question had been sent by the nurse to fetch something from it. The matter would pass straight out of Mary Gerrard's mind again, but it is possible that, later, she *might* recollect the fact and might mention it casually to the person in question—oh, without the least suspicion in the world. But to the person guilty of the murder of Mrs. Welman, imagine the effect of that remark! Mary had seen; Mary must be silenced at all costs! I can assure you, my friend, that anyone who has once committed a murder finds it only too easy to commit another!"

Peter Lord said with a frown, "I've believed all along that Mrs. Welman took the stuff herself."

"But she was paralyzed—helpless—she had just had a second stroke."

"Oh, I know. My idea was that, having got hold of morphine somehow or other, she kept it by her in a receptacle close at hand."

"But in that case she must have got hold of the morphine *before* her second attack, and the nurse missed it afterward."

"Hopkins may only have missed the morphine that morning. It might have been *taken* a couple of days before, and she hadn't noticed it."

"How would the old lady have got hold of it?"

"I don't know. Bribed a servant, perhaps. If so, that servant's never going to tell."

"You don't think either of the nurses were bribable?"

Lord shook his head. "Not on your life! To begin with, they're both very strict about their professional ethics—and in addition they'd be scared to death to do such a thing. They'd know the danger to themselves."

Poirot said, "That is so."

He added thoughtfully, "It looks, does it not, as though we return to our muttons? Who is the most likely person to have taken that morphine tube? *Elinor Carlisle.* We may say that she wished to make sure of inheriting a large fortune. We may be more generous and say that she was actuated by pity, that she took the morphine and administered it in compliance with her aunt's often-repeated request; but *she* took it—*and Mary Gerrard saw her do it.* And so we are back at the sandwiches and the empty house, and we have Elinor Carlisle once more—but this time with a different motive to save her neck."

Peter Lord cried out, "That's fantastic. I tell you, she isn't that kind of person! Money doesn't really mean anything to her—or to Roderick Welman, either, I'm bound to admit. I've heard them both say as much!"

"You have? That is very interesting. That is the kind of statement I always look upon with a good deal of suspicion myself."

Peter Lord said, "Damn you, Poirot, must you always twist everything round so that it comes back to that girl?"

"It is not I that twist things round; they come round of themselves. It is like the pointer at the fair. It swings round, and when it comes to rest it points always at the same name—*Elinor Carlisle.*"

Peter Lord said, "No!"

Hercule Poirot shook his head sadly. Then he said, "Has she relations, this Elinor Carlisle? Sisters, cousins? A father or mother?"

"No. She's an orphan—alone in the world."

"How pathetic it sounds! Bulmer, I am sure, will make great play with that! Who, then, inherits her money if she dies?"

"I don't know. I haven't thought."

Poirot said reprovingly, "One should always think of these things. Has she made a will, for instance?"

Peter Lord flushed. He said uncertainly, "I—I don't know."

Hercule Poirot looked at the ceiling and joined his finger tips. He remarked, "It would be well, you know, to tell me."

"Tell you what?"

"Exactly what is in your mind—no matter how damaging it may happen to be to Elinor Carlisle."

"How do you know—"

"Yes, yes, I know. There is *something*—some incident in your mind! It will be as well to tell me, otherwise I shall imagine it is something worse than it is!"

"It's nothing, really—"

"We will agree it is nothing. But let me hear what it is."

Slowly, unwillingly, Peter Lord allowed the story to be dragged from him—that scene of Elinor leaning in at the window of Nurse Hopkins's cottage, and of her laughter.

Poirot said thoughtfully, "She said that, did she, '*So you're making your will, Mary? That's funny—that's very funny.*' And it was very clear to you what was in her mind. She had been thinking, perhaps, *that Mary Gerrard was not going to live long.*"

Peter Lord said, "I only imagined that. I don't know."

Poirot said, "No, you did not only imagine it."

10

HERCULE POIROT SAT in Nurse Hopkins's cottage.

Dr. Lord had brought him there, had introduced him, and had then, at a glance from Poirot, left him to a tête-à-tête.

Having, to begin with, eyed his foreign appearance somewhat askance, Nurse Hopkins was now thawing rapidly.

She said with a faintly gloomy relish, "Yes, it's a terrible thing. One of the most terrible things I've ever known. Mary was one of the most beautiful girls you've ever seen. Might have gone on the films any time! And a nice steady girl, too, and not stuck-up, as she might have been with all the notice taken of her."

Poirot, inserting a question adroitly, said, "You mean the notice taken of her by Mrs. Welman?"

"That's what I mean. The old lady had taken a tremendous fancy to her—really, a tremendous fancy."

Hercule Poirot murmured, "Surprising, perhaps?"

"That depends. It might be quite natural, really. I mean—" Nurse Hopkins bit her lip and looked confused. "What I mean is, Mary had a very pretty way with her; nice soft voice and pleasant manners. And it's my opinion it does an elderly person good to have a young face about."

Hercule Poirot said, "Miss Carlisle came down occasionally, I suppose, to see her aunt!"

Nurse Hopkins said sharply, "Miss Carlisle came down when it suited her."

Poirot murmured, "You do not like Miss Carlisle."

Nurse Hopkins cried out, "I should hope not, indeed! A poisoner! A cold-blooded poisoner!"

"Ah," said Hercule Poirot, "I see you have made up your mind."

Nurse Hopkins said suspiciously, "What do you mean? Made up my mind?"

"You are quite sure that it was she who administered morphine to Mary Gerrard?"

"Who else could have done it, I should like to know? You're not suggesting that *I* did?"

"Not for a moment. But her guilt has not yet been proved, remember."

Nurse Hopkins said with calm assurance, "She did it, all right. Apart from anything else, you could see it in her face. Queer she was, all the time. And taking me away upstairs and keeping me there—delaying as long as possible. And then when I turned on her, after finding Mary like that, it was there in her face as plain as anything. She knew I knew!"

Hercule Poirot said thoughtfully, "It is certainly difficult to see who else could have done it. Unless, of course, she did it herself."

"What do you mean, *did it herself*? Do you mean that Mary committed suicide? I never heard such nonsense!"

Hercule Poirot said, "One can never tell. The heart of a young girl, it is very sensitive, very tender." He paused. "It would have been possible, I suppose? She could have slipped something into her tea without your noticing her?"

"Slipped it into her cup, you mean?"

"Yes. You weren't watching her all the time."

"I wasn't watching her—no. Yes, I suppose she *could* have done that. . . .

But it's all nonsense! What would she want to do a thing like that for?"

Hercule Poirot shook his head with a resumption of his former manner. "A young girl's heart—as I say, so sensitive. An unhappy love affair, perhaps—"

Nurse Hopkins gave a snort. "Girls don't kill themselves for love affairs—not unless they're in the family way—and Mary wasn't *that*, let me tell you!" She glared at him belligerently.

"And she was not in love?"

"Not she. Quite fancy free. Keen on her job and enjoying life."

"But she must have had admirers, since she was such an attractive girl."

Nurse Hopkins said, "She wasn't one of these girls who are all sex appeal. She was a quiet girl!"

"But there were young men, no doubt, in the village who admired her."

"There was Ted Bigland, of course," said Nurse Hopkins.

Poirot extracted various details as to Ted Bigland.

"Very gone on Mary, he was," said Nurse Hopkins. "But as I told her, she was a cut above him."

Poirot said, "He must have been angry when she would not have anything to do with him?"

"He was sore about it, yes," admitted Nurse Hopkins. "Blamed *me* for it, too."

"He thought it was your fault?"

"That's what he said. I'd a perfect right to advise the girl. After all, I know something of the world. I didn't want the girl to throw herself away."

Poirot said gently, "What made you take so much interest in the girl?"

"Well, I don't know." Nurse Hopkins hesitated. She looked shy and a little ashamed of herself. "There was something—well—romantic about Mary."

Poirot murmured, "About *her*, perhaps, but not about her circumstances. She was the lodgekeeper's daughter, wasn't she?"

Nurse Hopkins said, "Yes—yes, of course. At least—"

She hesitated, looked at Poirot, who was gazing at her in the most sympathetic manner.

"As a matter of fact," said Nurse Hopkins, in a burst of confidence, "she wasn't old Gerrard's daughter at all. He told me so. Her father was a gentleman."

Poirot murmured, "I see. . . . And her mother?"

Nurse Hopkins hesitated, bit her lip, and then went on: "Her mother had been lady's maid to old Mrs. Welman. She married Gerrard after Mary was born."

"As you say, quite a romance—a mystery romance."

Nurse Hopkins's face lit up. "Wasn't it? One can't help taking an interest in people when one knows something that nobody else does about them. Just by chance I happened to find out a good deal. As a matter of fact, it was Nurse O'Brien who set me on the track; but that's another story. But, as you say, it's interesting knowing past history. There's many a tragedy that goes unguessed at. It's a sad world."

Poirot sighed and shook his head.

Nurse Hopkins said with sudden alarm, "But I oughtn't to have gone talking like this. I wouldn't have a word of this get out for anything! After all, it's nothing to do with the case. As far as the world is concerned, Mary was Gerrard's daughter, and there mustn't be a hint of anything else. Damaging her in the eyes of the world after she's dead! He married her mother, and that's enough."

Poirot murmured, "But you know, perhaps, who her real father was?"

Nurse Hopkins said reluctantly, "Well, perhaps I do; but, then again, perhaps I don't. That is, I don't *know* anything. I could make a guess. Old sins have long shadows, as they say! But I'm not one to talk, and I shan't say another word."

Poirot tactfully retired from the fray and attacked another subject. "There is something else—a delicate matter. But I am sure I can rely on your discretion."

Nurse Hopkins bridled. A broad smile appeared on her homely face.

Poirot continued, "I speak of Mr. Roderick Welman. He was, so I hear, attracted by Mary Gerrard."

Nurse Hopkins said, "Bowled over by her!"

"Although at the time he was engaged to Miss Carlisle?"

"If you ask me," said Nurse Hopkins, "he was never really sweet on Miss Carlisle. Not what I'd call *sweet* on her."

Poirot asked, using an old-fashioned term, "Did Mary Gerrard—er—encourage his advances?"

Nurse Hopkins said sharply, "She behaved very well. Nobody could say she led him on!"

Poirot said, "Was she in love with him?"

Nurse Hopkins said sharply, "No, she wasn't."

"But she liked him?"

"Oh, yes, she *liked* him well enough."

"And I suppose, in time, something might have come of it?"

"That may be. But Mary wouldn't have done anything in a hurry. She told him down here he had no business to speak like that to her when he was engaged to Miss Elinor. And when he came to see her in London she said the same."

Poirot asked with an air of engaging candor, "What do you yourself think of Mr. Roderick Welman?"

Nurse Hopkins said, "He's a nice enough young fellow. Nervy, though. Looks as though he might be dyspeptic later on. Those nervy ones often are."

"Was he very fond of his aunt?"

"I believe so."

"Did he sit with her much when she was so ill?"

"You mean when she had that second stroke? The night before she died when they came down? I don't believe he even went into her room!"

"Really."

Nurse Hopkins said quickly, "She didn't ask for him. And, of course, we'd no idea the end was so near. There are a lot of men like that, you know; fight shy of a sick-room. They can't help it. And it's not heartlessness. They just don't want to be upset in their feelings."

Poirot nodded comprehendingly. He said, "Are you *sure* Mr. Welman did not go into his aunt's room before she died?"

"Well, not while *I* was on duty! Nurse O'Brien relieved me at three a.m., and she may have fetched him before the end; but, if so, she didn't mention it to me."

Poirot suggested, "He may have gone into her room when you were absent?"

Nurse Hopkins snapped, "I don't leave my patients unattended, Mr. Poirot."

"A thousand apologies. I did not mean that. I thought perhaps you might have had to boil water, or to run downstairs for some necessary stimulant."

Mollified, Nurse Hopkins said, "I did go down to change the bottles and get them refilled. I knew there'd be a kettle on the boil down in the kitchen."

"You were away long?"

"Five minutes, perhaps."

"Ah, yes, then Mr. Welman *may* have just looked in on her then?"

"He must have been very quick about it if he did."

Poirot sighed. He said, "As you say, men fight shy of illness. It is the women who are the ministering angels. What should we do without them? Especially women of your profession—a truly noble calling."

Nurse Hopkins, slightly red in the face, said, "It's very kind of you to say that. I've never thought of it that way myself. Too much hard work in nursing to think about the noble side of it."

Poirot said, "And there is nothing else you can tell me about Mary Gerrard?"

There was an appreciable pause before Nurse Hopkins answered, "I don't know of anything."

"Are you quite sure?"

Nurse Hopkins said rather incoherently, "You don't understand. I was *fond* of Mary."

"And there's nothing more you can tell me?"

"No, there is not! And that's flat."

11

IN THE AWESOME majesty of Mrs. Bishop's black-clad presence Hercule Poirot sat humbly insignificant.

The thawing of Mrs. Bishop was no easy matter. For Mrs. Bishop, a lady of conservative habits and views, strongly disapproved of foreigners. And a foreigner most indubitably Hercule Poirot was. Her responses were frosty and she eyed him with disfavor and suspicion.

Dr. Lord's introduction of him had done little to soften the situation. "I am sure," said Mrs. Bishop when Dr. Lord had gone, "Dr. Lord is a very clever doctor and means well. Dr. Ransome, his predecessor, had been here *many* years!"

Dr. Ransome, that is to say, could be trusted to behave in a manner suitable to the county. Dr. Lord, a mere irresponsible youngster, an upstart who had taken Dr. Ransome's place, had only one recommendation: "cleverness" in his profession.

Cleverness, the whole demeanor of Mrs. Bishop seemed to say, is not enough!

Hercule Poirot was persuasive. He was adroit. But charm he ever so wisely, Mrs. Bishop remained aloof and implacable.

The death of Mrs. Welman had been very sad. She had been much respected in the neighborhood. The arrest of Miss Carlisle was "Disgraceful!" and believed to be the result of "these new-fangled police methods." The views of Mrs. Bishop upon the death of Mary Gerrard were vague in the extreme, "I couldn't say, I'm sure," being the most she could be brought to say.

Hercule Poirot played his last card. He recounted with naïve pride a recent visit of his to Sandringham. He spoke with admiration of the graciousness and delightful simplicity and kindness of Royalty.

Mrs. Bishop, who followed daily in the court circular the exact movements of Royalty, was overborne. After all, if They had sent for Mr. Poirot— Well, naturally, that made All the Difference. Foreigner or no foreigner, who was she, Emma Bishop, to hold back where Royalty had led the way?

Presently she and M. Poirot were engaged in pleasant conversation on a really interesting theme—no less than the selection of a suitable future husband for the Princess.

Having finally exhausted all possible candidates as Not Good Enough, the talk reverted to less exalted circles.

Poirot observed sententiously, "Marriage, alas, is fraught with dangers and pitfalls!"

Mrs. Bishop said, "Yes, indeed—with this nasty divorce," rather as though she were speaking of a contagious disease such as chicken pox.

"I suspect," said Poirot, "that Mrs. Welman, before her death, must have been anxious to see her niece suitably settled for life?"

Mrs. Bishop bowed her head. "Yes, indeed. The engagement between Miss Elinor and Mr. Roderick was a great relief to her. It was a thing she had always hoped for."

Poirot ventured, "The engagement was perhaps entered into partly from a wish to please her?"

"Oh, no, I wouldn't say *that*, Mr. Poirot. Miss Elinor has always been devoted to Mr. Roddy—always was, as a tiny tot—quite beautiful to see. Miss Elinor has a very loyal and devoted nature!"

Poirot murmured, "And he?"

Mrs. Bishop said austerely, "Mr. Roderick was devoted to Miss Elinor."

Poirot said, "Yet the engagement, I think, was broken off?"

The color rose in Mrs. Bishop's face. She said, "Owing, Mr. Poirot, to the machinations of a snake in the grass."

Poirot said, appearing suitably impressed, "Indeed?"

Mrs. Bishop, her face becoming redder still, explained, "In this country, Mr. Poirot, there is a certain Decency to be observed when mentioning the Dead. But that young woman, Mr. Poirot, was Underhand in her Dealings."

Poirot looked at her thoughtfully for a moment. Then he said with an apparent lack of guile, "You surprise me. I had been given the impression that she was a very simple and unassuming girl."

Mrs. Bishop's chin trembled a little. "She was Artful, Mr. Poirot. People were Taken In by her. That Nurse Hopkins, for instance! Yes, and my poor dear mistress, too!"

Poirot shook his head sympathetically and made a clacking noise with his tongue.

"Yes, indeed," said Mrs. Bishop, stimulated by these encouraging noises. "She was failing, poor dear, and that young woman Wormed her way into her Confidence. *She* knew which side of her bread was buttered. Always hovering about, reading to her, bringing her little nosegays of flowers. It was Mary this and Mary that and 'Where's Mary?' all the time! The money she spent on the girl, too! Expensive schools and finishing places abroad—and the girl nothing but old Gerrard's daughter! *He* didn't like it, I can tell you! Used to complain of her Fine Lady ways. Above Herself, that's what *She* was."

This time Poirot shook his head and said commiseratingly, "Dear, dear."

"And then Making Up to Mr. Roddy the way she did! He was too simple to See Through her. And Miss Elinor, a nice-minded young lady as she is, of course she wouldn't realize what was Going On. But Men, they are all alike: easily caught by flattery and a pretty face!"

Poirot sighed. "She had, I suppose, admirers of her own class?" he asked.

"Of course she had. There was Rufus Bigland's son Ted—as nice a boy as you could find. But, oh, no, my fine lady was too good for *him!* I'd no patience with such airs and graces!"

Poirot said, "Was he not angry about her treatment of him?"

"Yes, indeed. He accused her of carrying on with Mr. Roddy. I know *that* for a *fact*. I don't blame the boy for feeling sore!"

"Nor I," said Poirot. "You interest me extremely, Mrs. Bishop. Some people have the knack of presenting a character clearly and vigorously in a few words. It is a great gift. I have at last a clear picture of Mary Gerrard."

"Mind you," said Mrs. Bishop, "I'm not saying a word *against* the girl! I wouldn't do such a thing—and she in her grave. But there's no doubt that she caused a lot of trouble!"

Poirot murmured, "Where would it have ended, I wonder?"

"That's what *I* say!" said Mrs. Bishop. "You can take it from me, Mr. Poirot, that if my dear mistress hadn't died when she did—awful as the shock was at the time, I see now that it was a Mercy in Disguise—I don't know what might have been the end of it!"

Poirot said invitingly, "You mean?"

Mrs. Bishop said solemnly, "I've come across it time and again. My own sister was in service where it happened. Once when old Colonel Randolph died and left every penny away from his poor wife to a hussy living at Eastbourne—and once old Mrs. Dacres—left it to the organist of the church—one of those long-haired young men—and she with married sons and daughters."

Poirot said, "You mean, I take it, that Mrs. Welman might have left all her money to Mary Gerrard?"

"It wouldn't have surprised me!" said Mrs. Bishop. "That's what the young woman was working up to, I've no doubt. And if I ventured to say a word, Mrs. Welman was ready to bite my head off, though I'd been with her nearly twenty years. It's an ungrateful world, Mr. Poirot. You try to do your duty and it is not appreciated."

"Alas," sighed Poirot, "how true that is!"

"But Wickedness doesn't always flourish," said Mrs. Bishop.

Poirot said, "True. Mary Gerrard is dead."

Mrs. Bishop said comfortably, "She's gone to her reckoning, and we mustn't judge her."

Poirot mused, "The circumstances of her death seem quite inexplicable."

"These police and their new-fangled ideas," said Mrs. Bishop. "Is it likely that a well-bred, nicely brought-up young lady like Miss Elinor would go about poisoning anyone? Trying to drag *me* into it, too, saying *I* said her manner was peculiar!"

"But was it not peculiar?"

"And why shouldn't it be?" Mrs. Bishop's bust heaved with a flash of jet. "Miss Elinor's a young lady of feelings. She was going to turn out her aunt's things—and that's always a painful business."

Poirot nodded sympathetically. He said, "It would have made it much easier for her if you had accompanied her."

"I wanted to, Mr. Poirot, but she took me up quite sharp. Oh, well, Miss Elinor was always a very proud and reserved young lady. I wish, though, that I *had* gone with her."

Poirot murmured, "You did not think of following her up to the house?"

Mrs. Bishop reared her head majestically. "I don't go where I'm not wanted, Mr. Poirot."

Poirot looked abashed. He murmured, "Besides, you had doubtless matters of importance to attend to that morning?"

"It was a very warm day, I remember. Very sultry." She sighed. "I walked to the cemetery to place a few flowers on Mrs. Welman's grave, a token of respect, and I had to rest there quite a long time. Quite overcome by the heat, I was. I got home late for lunch, and my sister was quite upset when she saw the State of Heat I was in! Said I never should have done it on a day like that."

Poirot looked at her with admiration. He said, "I envy you, Mrs. Bishop. It is pleasant indeed to have nothing with which to reproach oneself after a death. Mr. Roderick Welman, I fancy, must blame himself for not going in to see his aunt that night, though naturally he could not know she was going to pass away so soon."

"Oh, but you're quite wrong, Mr. Poirot. I can tell you that for a fact. Mr. Roddy *did* go into his aunt's room. I was just outside on the landing myself. I'd heard that nurse go off downstairs, and I thought maybe I'd better make sure the mistress wasn't needing anything, for you know what nurses are—always staying downstairs to gossip with the maids, or else worrying them to death by asking them for things. Not that Nurse Hopkins was as bad as that red-haired Irish nurse. Always chattering and making trouble, *she* was! But, as I say, I thought I'd just see everything was all right, and it was then that I saw Mr. Roddy slip into his aunt's room. I don't know whether she knew him or not; but anyway he hasn't got anything to *reproach* himself with!"

Poirot said, "I am glad. He is of a somewhat nervous disposition."

"Just a trifle cranky. He always has been."

Poirot said, "Mrs. Bishop, you are evidently a woman of great understanding. I have formed a high regard for your judgment. What do you think is the truth about the death of Mary Gerrard?"

Mrs. Bishop snorted. "Clear enough, I should think! One of those nasty pots of paste of Abbott's. Keeps them on those shelves for months! My second cousin was took ill and nearly died once, with tinned crab!"

Poirot objected, "But what about the morphine found in the body?"

Mrs. Bishop said grandly, "*I* don't know anything about morphine! I know what *doctors* are. Tell them to look for something, and they'll find it! Tainted fish paste isn't *good* enough for *them!*"

Poirot said, "You do not think it possible that she committed suicide?"

"She?" Mrs. Bishop snorted. "No, indeed. Hadn't she made up her mind to marry Mr. Roddy? Catch *her* committing suicide!"

12

SINCE IT WAS Sunday, Hercule Poirot found Ted Bigland at his father's farm.

There was little difficulty in getting Ted Bigland to talk. He seemed
to welcome the opportunity—as though it was a relief.

He said thoughtfully, "So you're trying to find out who killed Mary?
It's a black mystery, that."

Poirot said, "You do not believe that Miss Carlisle killed her, then?"

Ted Bigland frowned—a puzzled, almost childlike frown it was.

He said slowly, "Miss Elinor's a lady. She's the kind—well, you couldn't
imagine her doing anything like that—anything *violent,* if you know what
I mean. After all, 'tisn't likely, is it, sir, that a nice young lady would go
and do a thing of that kind?"

Hercule Poirot nodded in a contemplative manner. He said, "No, it
is not likely. But when it comes to jealousy—"

He paused, watching the good-looking, fair young giant before him.

Ted Bigland said, "Jealousy? I know things happen that way, but it's
usually drink and getting worked up that makes a fellow see red and
run amuck. Miss Elinor—a nice quiet young lady like that—"

Poirot said, *"But Mary Gerrard died*—and she did not die a natural
death. Have you any idea—is there anything you can tell me to help me
find out—who killed Mary Gerrard?"

Slowly the boy shook his head. He said, "It doesn't seem right. It
doesn't seem *possible,* if you take my meaning, that anyone could have
killed Mary. She was—she was like a flower."

And suddenly, for a vivid minute, Hercule Poirot had a new conception
of the dead girl. In that halting rustic voice the girl Mary lived and
bloomed again. *"She was like a flower."*

There was suddenly a poignant sense of loss, of something exquisite
destroyed.

In his mind phrase after phrase succeeded each other. Peter Lord's
"She was a nice kid." Nurse Hopkins's *"She could have gone on the films any
time."* Mrs. Bishop's venomous *"No patience with her airs and graces."* And
now last, putting to shame, laying aside those other views, the quiet,
wondering, *"She was like a flower."*

Hercule Poirot said, "But then—?" He spread out his hands in a wide,
appealing foreign gesture.

Ted Bigland nodded his head. His eyes had still the dumb, glazed
look of an animal in pain. He said, "I know, sir. I know what you say's
true. She didn't die natural. But I've been wondering—"

He paused.

Poirot said, "Yes?"

Ted Bigland said slowly, "I've been wondering if in some way it couldn't
have been an *accident?*"

"An accident? But what kind of an accident?"

"I know, sir. I know. It doesn't sound like sense. But I keep thinking
and thinking, and it seems to me it must have been that way. Something
that wasn't meant to happen or something that was all a mistake. Just—
well, just an *accident!*"

He looked pleadingly at Poirot, embarrassed by his own lack of eloquence.

Poirot was silent a moment or two. He seemed to be considering. He said at last, "It is interesting that you feel that."

Ted Bigland said deprecatingly, "I dare say it doesn't make sense to you, sir. I can't figure out *how* and *why* about it. It's just a *feeling* I've got."

Hercule Poirot said, "Feeling is sometimes an important guide. You will pardon me, I hope, if I seem to tread on painful gound, but you cared very much for Mary Gerrard, did you not?"

A little dark color came up in the tanned face. Ted said simply, "Everyone knows that around here, I reckon."

"You wanted to marry her?"

"Yes."

"But she—was not willing?"

Ted's face darkened a little. He said, with a hint of suppressed anger, "Mean well, people do, but they shouldn't muck up people's lives by interfering. All this schooling and going abroad! It changed Mary. I don't mean it spoiled her, or that she was stuck-up—she wasn't. But it— oh, it bewildered her! She didn't know where she was any more. She was—well, put it crudely—she was too good for *me*, but she still wasn't good enough for a real gentleman like Mr. Welman."

Hercule Poirot said, watching him, "You don't like Mr. Welman?"

Ted Bigland said with simple violence, "Why the hell should I? Mr. Welman's all right. I've nothing against him. He's not what I call much of a *man!* I could pick him up and break him in two. He's got brains, I suppose. . . . But that's not much help to you if your car breaks down, for instance. You may know the principle that makes a car run, but it doesn't stop you from being as helpless as a baby when all that's needed is to take the mag out and give it a wipe."

Poirot said, "Of course, you work in a garage?"

Ted Bigland nodded. "Henderson's, down the road."

"You were there on the morning when—this thing happened?"

Ted Bigland said, "Yes, testing out a car for a gentleman. A choke somewhere, and I couldn't locate it. Ran it round for a bit. Seems odd to think of now. It was a lovely day, some honeysuckle still in the hedges. . . . Mary used to like honeysuckle. We used to go picking it together before she went away abroad."

Again there was that puzzled, child-like wonder on his face. Hercule Poirot was silent. With a start Ted Bigland came out of his trance.

He said, "Sorry, sir. Forget what I said about Mr. Welman. I was sore— because of his hanging round after Mary. He ought to have let her alone. She wasn't his sort—not really."

Poirot said, "Do you think she cared for him?"

Again Ted Bigland frowned. "I don't—not really. But she might have. I couldn't say."

Poirot asked, "Was there any other man in Mary's life? Anyone, for instance, she had met abroad?"

"I couldn't say, sir. She never mentioned anybody."

"Any enemies—here in Maidensford?"

"You mean anyone who had it in for her?" He shook his head. "Nobody knew her very well. But they all liked her."

Poirot said, "Did Mrs. Bishop, the housekeeper at Hunterbury, like her?"

Ted gave a sudden grin. He said, "Oh, that was just spite! The old dame didn't like Mrs. Welman taking such a fancy to Mary."

Poirot asked, "Was Mary Gerrard happy when she was down here? Was she fond of old Mrs. Welman?"

Ted Bigland said, "She'd have been happy enough, I dare say, if Nurse had let her alone. Nurse Hopkins, I mean. Putting ideas into her head of earning her living and going off to do massage."

"She was fond of Mary, though?"

"Oh, yes, she was *fond* enough of her; but she's the kind who always knows what's best for everyone!"

Poirot said slowly, "Supposing that Nurse Hopkins knows something— something, let us say, that would throw a discreditable light on Mary— do you think she would keep it to herself?"

Ted Bigland looked at him curiously.

"I don't quite get your meaning, sir."

"Do you think that if Nurse Hopkins knew something against Mary Gerrard she would hold her tongue about it?"

Ted Bigland said, "I doubt if that woman could hold her tongue about anything! She's the greatest gossip in the village. But if she'd hold her tongue about *anybody,* it would probably be about Mary." He added, his curiosity getting the better of him, "I'd like to know *why* you ask that?"

Hercule Poirot said, "One has, in talking to people, a certain impression. Nurse Hopkins was, to all seeming, perfectly frank and outspoken, but I formed the impression—and very strongly—that she was keeping *something* back. It is not necessarily an *important* thing. It may have no bearing on the crime. *But there is something that she knows which she has not told.* I also formed the impression that this something—whatever it is—is something definitely damaging or detrimental to the character of Mary Gerrard."

Ted shook his head helplessly.

Hercule Poirot sighed. "Ah, well. I shall learn what it is in time."

13

POIROT LOOKED WITH interest at the long, sensitive face of Roderick Welman.

Roddy's nerves were in a pitiable condition. His hands twitched, his eyes were bloodshot, his voice was husky and irritable.

He said, looking down at the card, "Of course, I know your name, Monsieur Poirot. But I don't see what Dr. Lord thinks you can do in this matter! And, anyway, what business is it of *his?* He attended my aunt, but otherwise he's a complete stranger. Elinor and I had not even met him until we went down there this June. Surely it is Seddon's business to attend to all this sort of thing?"

Hercule Poirot said, "Technically that is correct."

Roddy went on unhappily, "Not that Seddon gives me much confidence. He's so confoundedly gloomy."

"It is a habit, that, of lawyers."

"Still," said Roddy, cheering up a little, "we've briefed Bulmer. He's supposed to be pretty well at the top of the tree, isn't he?"

Hercule Poirot said, "He has a reputation for leading forlorn hopes."

Roddy winced palpably.

Poirot said, "It does not displease you, I hope, that I should endeavor to be of assistance to Miss Carlisle?"

"No, no, of course not. But—"

"But what can I do? It is that, that you would ask?"

A quick smile flashed across Roddy's worried face—a smile so suddenly charming that Hercule Poirot understood the subtle attraction of the man.

Roddy said apologetically, "It sounds a little rude, put like that. But, really, of course, that *is* the point. I won't beat about the bush. What *can* you do, Monsieur Poirot?"

Poirot said, "I can search for the truth."

"Yes." Roddy sounded a little doubtful.

Poirot said, "I might discover facts that would be helpful to the accused."

Roddy sighed. "If you only could!"

Hercule Poirot went on: "It is my earnest desire to be helpful. Will you assist me by telling me just what you think of the whole business?"

Roddy got up and walked restlessly up and down.

"What can I say? The whole thing's so absurd—so fantastic! The mere idea of Elinor—Elinor, whom I've known since she was a child—actually doing such a melodramatic thing as poisoning someone. It's quite laughable, of course! But how on earth explain that to a jury?"

Poirot said stolidly, "You consider it quite impossible that Miss Carlisle should have done such a thing?"

"Oh, quite! That goes without saying! Elinor's an exquisite creature—beautifully poised and balanced—no violence in her nature. She's intellectual, sensitive, and altogether devoid of animal passions. But get twelve fatheaded fools in a jury box, and God knows what they can be made to believe! After all, let's be reasonable: they're not there to judge character; they're there to sift evidence. Facts—facts—*facts!* And the facts are unfortunate!"

Hercule Poirot nodded thoughtfully. He said, "You are a person, Mr. Welman, of sensibility and intelligence. The facts condemn Miss Carlisle. Your knowledge of her acquits her. *What, then, really happened?* What *can* have happened?"

Roddy spread out his hands in exasperation. "That's the devil of it all! I suppose the nurse couldn't have done it?"

"She was never near the sandwiches—oh, I have made the inquiries very minutely—and she could not have poisoned the tea without poisoning herself as well. I have made quite sure of that. Moreover, *why* should she wish to kill Mary Gerrard?"

Roddy cried out, "Why should *anyone* wish to kill Mary Gerrard?"

"That," said Poirot, "seems to be the unanswerable question in this case. No *one* wished to kill Mary Gerrard." (He added in his own mind, *Except Elinor Carlisle.*) "Therefore, the next step logically would seem to be: Mary Gerrard was not killed! But that, alas, is not so. She *was* killed!"

He added, slightly melodramatically, *"But she is in her grave, and oh, the difference to me!"*

"I beg your pardon," said Roddy.

Hercule Poirot explained, "Wordsworth. I read him much. Those lines express, perhaps, what you feel?"

"I?"

Roddy looked stiff and unapproachable.

Poirot said, "I apologize—I apologize deeply! It is so hard—to be a detective and also a *pukka sahib*. As it is so well expressed in your language, there are things that one does not say. But, alas, a detective is forced to say them! He must ask questions: about people's private affairs, about their feelings!"

Roddy said, "Surely all this is quite unnecessary?"

Poirot said quickly and humbly, "If I might just understand the position? Then we will pass from the unpleasant subject and not refer to it again. It is fairly widely known, Mr. Welman, that you—admired Mary Gerrard? That is, I think, true?"

Roddy got up and stood by the window. He played with the shade tassel. He said, "Yes."

"You fell in love with her?"

"I suppose so."

"Ah, and you are now heart-broken by her death—"

"I—I suppose—I mean—well, really, M. Poirot—"

He turned—a nervous, irritable, sensitive creature at bay.

Hercule Poirot said, "If you could just tell me—just show me clearly—then it would be finished with."

Roddy Welman sat down in a chair. He did not look at the other man. He spoke in a series of jerks.

"It's very difficult to explain. Must we go into it?"

Poirot said, "One cannot always turn aside and pass by from the unpleasantnesses of life, Mr. Welman! You say you *suppose* you cared for this girl. You are not sure, then?"

Roddy said, "I don't know. . . . She was so lovely. Like a dream. That's what it seems like now. A dream! Not real! All that—my seeing her first—my—well, my infatuation for her! A kind of madness! And now everything is finished—gone—as though—as though it had never happened."

Poirot nodded his head. He said, "Yes, I understand."

He added, "You were not in England yourself at the time of her death?"

"No, I went abroad on July 9th and returned on August 1st. Elinor's telegram followed me about from place to place. I hurried home as soon as I got the news."

Poirot said, "It must have been a great shock to you. You had cared for the girl very much."

Roddy said, and there was bitterness and exasperation in his voice, "Why should these things happen to one? It's not as though one *wished* them to happen! It is contrary to all—to all one's ordered expectation of life!"

Hercule Poirot said, "Ah, but life is like that! It does not permit you to arrange and order it as you will. It will not permit you to escape emotion, to live by the intellect and by reason! You cannot say, 'I will feel so much and no more.' Life, Mr. Welman, whatever else it is, is not *reasonable!*"

Roderick Welman murmured, "So it seems."

Poirot said, "A spring morning, a girl's face—and the well-ordered sequence of existence is routed."

Roddy winced and Poirot went on: "Sometimes it is little more than that—a *face*. What did you really know of Mary Gerrard, Mr. Welman?"

Roddy said heavily, "What did I know? So little; I see that now. She was sweet, I think, and gentle; but really, I know nothing—nothing at all. . . . That's why, I suppose, I don't miss her."

His antagonism and resentment were gone now. He spoke naturally and simply. Hercule Poirot, as he had a knack of doing, had penetrated the other's defenses. Roddy seemed to feel a certain relief in unburdening himself.

He said, "Sweet—gentle—not very clever. Sensitive, I think, and kind. She had a refinement that you would not expect to find in a girl of her class."

"Was she the kind of girl who would make enemies unconsciously?"

Roddy shook his head vigorously. "No, no, I can't imagine anyone disliking her—really disliking her, I mean. Spite is different."

Poirot said quickly, "Spite? So there was spite, you think?"

Roddy said absently, "Must have been—to account for that letter."

Poirot said sharply, "What letter?"

Roddy flushed and looked annoyed. He said, "Oh, nothing important."

Poirot repeated, "What letter?"

"An anonymous letter." He spoke reluctantly.

"When did it come? To whom was it written?"

Rather unwillingly Roddy explained.

Hercule Poirot murmured, "It is interesting, that. Can I see it, this letter?"

"Afraid you can't. As a matter of fact, I burned it."

"Now, why did you do that, Mr. Welman?"

Roddy said rather stiffly, "It seemed the natural thing to do at the time."

Poirot said, "And in consequence of this letter, you and Miss Carlisle went hurriedly down to Hunterbury?"

"We went down, yes. I don't know about *hurriedly.*"

"But you were a little uneasy, were you not? Perhaps, even, a little alarmed?"

Roddy said even more stiffly, "I won't admit that."

Hercule Poirot cried, "But surely that was only natural! Your inheritance—that which was promised you—was in jeopardy! Surely it is natural that you should be unquiet about the matter! Money, it is very important!"

"Not as important as you make out."

Poirot said, "Such unworldliness is indeed remarkable!"

Roddy flushed. He said, "Oh, of course, the money *did* matter to us. We weren't completely indifferent to it. But our main object was to—to see my aunt and make sure she was all right."

Poirot said, "You went down there with Miss Carlisle. At that time your aunt had not made a will. Shortly afterward she had another attack of her illness. She then wishes to make a will, but, conveniently for Miss Carlisle, perhaps, she dies that night before that will can be made."

"Look here, what are you hinting at?" Roddy's face was wrathful.

Poirot answered him like a flash: "You have told me, Mr. Welman, as regards the death of Mary Gerrard, that the motive attributed to Elinor Carlisle is absurd—that she was, emphatically, not that kind of a person. But there is now another interpretation. Elinor Carlisle had reason to fear that she might be disinherited in favor of an outsider. The letter has warned her—her aunt's broken murmurings confirm that fear. In the hall below is an attaché case with various drugs and medical supplies. It is easy to abstract a tube of morphine. And afterward, so I have learned, *she sits in the sickroom alone with her aunt while you and the nurses are at dinner.*"

Roddy cried, "Good God, Monsieur Poirot, what are you suggesting now? That Elinor killed Aunt Laura? Of all the ridiculous ideas!"

Poirot said, "But you know, do you not, that an order to exhume Mrs. Welman's body has been applied for?"

"Yes, I know. But they won't find anything!"

"Suppose they do?"

"They won't!" Roddy spoke positively.

Poirot shook his head. "I am not so sure. And there was only *one* person, you realize, who would benefit by Mrs. Welman's dying at that moment."

Roddy sat down. His face was white, and he was shaking a little. He stared at Poirot. Then he said, "I thought—you were on *her* side."

Hercule Poirot said, "Whatever side one is on, one must face *facts!* I think, Mr. Welman, that you have so far preferred in life to avoid facing an awkward truth whenever it is possible."

Roddy said, "Why harrow oneself by looking on the worst side?"

Hercule Poirot replied gravely, "Because it is sometimes necessary."

He paused a minute and then said, "Let us face the possibility that your aunt's death may be found to be due to the administration of morphine. What then?"

Roddy shook his head helplessly. "I don't know."

"But you must try to *think*. Who could have given it to her? You must admit that Elinor Carlisle had the best opportunity to do so?"

"What about the nurses?"

"Either of them could have done so, certainly. But Nurse Hopkins was concerned about the disappearance of the tube at the time and mentioned it openly. There was no need for her to do so. The death certificate had been signed. Why call attention to the missing morphine if she was guilty? It will probably bring her censure for carelessness as it is, and if she poisoned Mrs. Welman it was surely idiotic to draw attention to the morphine. Besides, what could she gain by Mrs. Welman's death? Nothing. The same applies to Nurse O'Brien. She could have administered morphine, could have taken it from Nurse Hopkins's case; but, again—*why should she?*"

Roddy shook his head. "All that's true enough."

Poirot said, "Then there is *yourself*."

Roddy started like a nervous horse. "Me?"

"Certainly. *You* could have abstracted the morphine. *You* could have given it to Mrs. Welman! You were alone with her for a short period that night. But, again, *why should you?* If she lived to make a will, it is at least probable that you would have been mentioned in it. So again, you see, there is no motive. Only two people had a motive."

Roddy's eyes brightened. "*Two* people?"

"Yes. One was Elinor Carlisle."

"And the other?"

Poirot said slowly, "The other was the writer of that anonymous letter."

Roddy looked incredulous.

Poirot said, "*Somebody* wrote that letter—somebody who hated Mary Gerrard or at least disliked her—somebody who was, as they say, 'on your side.' Somebody, that is, *who did not want Mary Gerrard to benefit at Mrs. Welman's death.* Now, have you any idea, Mr. Welman, who the writer of that letter could be?"

Roddy shook his head. "I've no idea at all. It was an illiterate letter, misspelled, cheap-looking."

Poirot waved a hand. "There is nothing much to that! It might easily have been written by an educated person who chose to disguise the fact. That is why I wish you had the letter still. People who try to write in an uneducated manner usually give themselves away."

Roddy said doubtfully, "Elinor and I thought it might be one of the servants."

"Had you any idea which of them?"

"No—no idea whatsoever."

"Could it, do you think, have been Mrs. Bishop, the housekeeper?"

Roddy looked shocked. "Oh, no, she's a most respectable, high-and-mighty creature. Writes beautifully involved and ornate letters with long words in them. Besides, I'm sure she would never—"

As he hesitated, Poirot cut in, "She did not like Mary Gerrard!"

"I suppose she didn't. I never noticed anything, though."

"But perhaps, Mr. Welman, you do not notice very much?"

Roddy said slowly, "You don't think, Poirot, that my aunt could have taken that morphine herself?"

Poirot said, "It is an idea, yes."

Roddy said, "She hated her—her helplessness, you know. Often said she wished she could die."

Poirot said, "But, then, she could not have risen from her bed, gone downstairs, and helped herself to the tube of morphine from the nurse's case."

Roddy said slowly, "No, but somebody could have got it for her."

"Who?"

"Well, one of the nurses."

"No, neither of the nurses. They would understand the danger to themselves far too well! The nurses are the last people to suspect."

"Then—somebody else—"

He started, opened his mouth, shut it again.

Poirot said quietly, "You have remembered something, have you not?"

Roddy said doubtfully, "Yes—but—"

"You wonder if you ought to tell me?"

"Well, yes."

Poirot said, a curious smile tilting the corners of his mouth, "When did Miss Carlisle say it?"

Roddy drew a deep breath.

"By Jove, you are a wizard! It was in the train coming down. We'd had the telegram, you know, saying Aunt Laura had had another stroke. Elinor said how terribly sorry she was for her, how the poor dear hated being ill, and that now she would be more helpless still and that it would be absolute hell for her. Elinor said, 'One does feel that people *ought* to be set free if they themselves really want it.'"

"And you said—what?"

"I agreed."

Poirot spoke very gravely, "Just now, Mr. Welman, you scouted the possibility of Miss Carlisle having killed your aunt for monetary gain. Do you also scout the possibility that she may have killed Mrs. Welman *out of compassion?*"

Roddy said, "I—I—no, I can't."

Hercule Poirot bowed his head. He said, "Yes, I thought—I was sure—that you would say that."

14

IN THE OFFICES of Messrs. Seddon, Blatherwick & Seddon, Hercule Poirot was received with extreme caution, not to say distrust.

Mr. Seddon, a forefinger stroking his closely shaven chin, was noncommittal and his shrewd gray eyes appraised the detective thoughtfully.

"Your name is familiar to me, Monsieur Poirot, of course. But I am at a loss to understand your position in this case."

Hercule Poirot said, "I am acting, Monsieur, in the interests of your client."

"Ah—indeed? And who—er—engaged you in that capacity?"

"I am here at the request of Dr. Lord."

Mr. Seddon's eyebrows rose very high. "Indeed! That seems to me very irregular—very irregular. Dr. Lord, I understand, has been subpoenaed as a witness for the prosecution."

Hercule Poirot shrugged his shoulders. "Does that matter?"

Mr. Seddon said, "The arrangements for Miss Carlisle's defense are entirely in our hands. I really do not think we need any outside assistance in this case."

Poirot asked, "Is that because your client's innocence will be so easily proved?"

Mr. Seddon winced. Then he became wrathful in a dry legal fashion. "That," he said, "is a most improper question. Most improper."

Hercule Poirot said, "The case against your client is a very strong one."

"I really fail to see, Poirot, how you know anything about it."

Poirot said, "Although I am actually retained by Dr. Lord, I have here a note from Mr. Roderick Welman."

He handed it over with a bow.

Mr. Seddon perused the few lines it contained and remarked grudgingly, "That, of course, throws a new complexion on the matter. Mr. Welman has made himself responsible for Miss Carlisle's defense. We are acting at his request."

He added with visible distaste, "Our firm does very little in—er—criminal procedure, but I felt it my duty to my—er—late client—to undertake the defense of her niece. I may say we have already briefed Sir Edwin Bulmer, K.C."

Poirot said, and his smile was suddenly ironic, "No expense will be spared. Very right and proper!"

Looking over his glasses, Mr. Seddon said, "Really, Monsieur Poirot—"

Poirot cut into his protest. "Eloquence and emotional appeal will not save your client. It will need more than that."

Mr. Seddon said dryly, "What do you advise?"

"There is always the truth."

"Quite so."

"But in this case will truth help us?"

Mr. Seddon said sharply, "That, again, is a most improper remark."

Poirot said, "There are certain questions to which I should like answers."

Mr. Seddon said cautiously, "I cannot, of course, guarantee to answer without the consent of my client."

"Naturally I understand that." He paused and then said, "Has Elinor Carlisle any enemies?"

Mr. Seddon showed a faint surprise. "As far as I know, none."

"Did the late Mrs. Welman, at any period of her life, make a will?"

"Never. She always put it off."

"Has Elinor Carlisle made a will?"

"Yes."

"Recently? Since her aunt's death?"

"Yes."

"To whom has she left her property?"

"That, Poirot, is confidential. I cannot tell you without authorization from my client."

Poirot said, "Then I shall have to interview your client!"

Mr. Seddon said with a cold smile, "That, I fear, will not be easy."

Poirot rose and made a gesture. "Everything," he said, "is easy to Hercule Poirot."

15

CHIEF INSPECTOR MARSDEN was affable. "Well, Monsieur Poirot," he said. "Come to set me right about one of my cases?"

Poirot murmured deprecatingly, "No, no. A little curiosity on my part, that is all."

"Only too happy to satisfy it. Which case is it?"

"Elinor Carlisle."

"Oh, yes, girl who poisoned Mary Gerrard. Coming up for trial in two weeks' time. Interesting case. She did in the old woman too, by the way. Final report isn't in yet, but it seems there's no doubt of it. Morphia. Cold-blooded bit of goods. Never turned a hair at the time of her arrest or after. Giving nothing away. But we've got the goods on her all right. She's for it."

"You think she did it?"

Marsden, an experienced, kindly looking man, nodded his head affirmatively. "Not a doubt of it. Put the stuff in the top sandwich. She's a cool customer."

"You have no doubts? No doubts at all?"

"Oh, no. I'm quite sure. It's a pleasant feeling when you *are* sure! We don't like making mistakes any more than anyone else would. We're not just out to get a conviction, as some people think. This time I can go ahead with a clear conscience."

Poirot said slowly, "I see."

The Scotland Yard man looked at him curiously. "Is there anything on the other side?"

Slowly Poirot shook his head. "As yet, no. So far everything I have found out about the case points to Elinor Carlisle's being guilty."

Inspector Marsden said with cheerful certainty, "She's guilty, all right."

Poirot said, "I should like to see her."

Inspector Marsden smiled indulgently. He said, "Got the present Home Secretary in your pocket, haven't you? That will be easy enough."

16

PETER LORD SAID, "Well?"

Hercule Poirot said, "No, it is not very well."

Peter Lord said heavily, "You haven't got hold of anything?"

Poirot said slowly, "Elinor Carlisle killed Mary Gerrard out of jealousy—Elinor Carlisle killed her aunt so as to inherit her money—Elinor Carlisle killed her aunt out of compassion. My friend, you may make your choice !"

Peter Lord said, "You're talking nonsense!"

Hercule Poirot said, "Am I?"

Lord's freckled face looked angry. He said, "What *is* all this?"

Hercule Poirot said, "Do you think it is possible, that?"

"Do I think what is possible?"

"That Elinor Carlisle was unable to bear the sight of her aunt's misery and helped her out of existence?"

"Nonsense!"

"Is it nonsense? You have told me yourself that the old lady asked *you* to help her."

"She didn't mean it seriously. She knew I wouldn't do anything of the sort."

"Still, the idea was in her mind. Elinor Carlisle *might* have helped her."

Peter Lord strolled up and down. He said at last, "One can't deny that that sort of thing is possible. But Elinor Carlisle is a level-headed, clear-thinking kind of young woman. I don't think she'd be so carried away by pity as to lose sight of the risk. And she'd realize exactly what the risk was. She'd be liable to stand accused of murder."

"So you don't think she would do it?"

Peter Lord said slowly, "I think a woman might do such a thing for her husband, or for her child, or for her mother, perhaps. I don't think she'd do it for an aunt, though she might be fond of that aunt. And I think in any case she'd only do it if the person in question was actually suffering unbearable pain."

Poirot said thoughtfully, "Perhaps you are right."

Then he added, "Do you think Roderick Welman's feelings could have been sufficiently worked upon to induce *him* to do such a thing?"

Peter Lord replied scornfully, "He wouldn't have the guts!"

Poirot murmured, "I wonder. In some ways, *mon cher,* you underestimate that young man."

"Oh, he's clever and intellectual and all that, I dare say."

"Exactly," said Poirot. "And he has charm, too. Yes, I felt that."

"Did you? I never have!"

Then Peter Lord said earnestly, "Look here, Poirot, isn't there *anything?*"

Poirot said, "They are not fortunate so far, my investigations! They lead always back to the same place. No one stood to gain by Mary Gerrard's death. No one hated Mary Gerrard—*except Elinor Carlisle.* There is only one question that we might perhaps ask ourselves. We might say, perhaps, *Did anyone hate Elinor Carlisle?"*

Slowly Dr. Lord shook his head. "Not that I know of. . . . You mean— that someone might have framed her for the crime?"

Poirot nodded. He said, "It is a very far-fetched speculation, that, and there is nothing to support it—except, perhaps, the very completeness of the case against her."

He told the other of the anonymous letter.

"You see," he said, "that makes it possible to outline a very strong case against her. She was warned that she might be completely cut out of her aunt's will—that this girl, a stranger, might get all the money. So, when her aunt in her halting speech was asking for a lawyer, Elinor took no chances, and saw to it that the old lady should die that night!"

Peter Lord cried, "What about Roderick Welman? He stood to lose, too!"

Poirot shook his head. "No, it was to his advantage that the old lady should make a will. If she died intestate, he got nothing, remember. Elinor was the next of kin."

Lord said, "But he was going to marry Elinor!"

Poirot said, "True. But remember that immediately afterward the engagement was broken off—that he showed her clearly that he wished to be released from it."

Peter Lord groaned and held his head. He said, "It comes back to her, then. Every time!"

"Yes. Unless—"

He was silent for a minute. Then he said, "There is *something—*"

"Yes?"

"Something—some little piece of the puzzle that is missing. It is something—of that I am certain—that concerns Mary Gerrard. My friend, you hear a certain amount of gossip, of scandal, down here. Have you ever heard anything against her?"

"Against Mary Gerrard? Her character, you mean?"

"Anything. Some bygone story about her. Some indiscretion on her part. A hint of scandal. A doubt of her honesty. A malicious rumor concerning her. Anything—anything at all—but something that definitely is *damaging to her.*"

Peter Lord said slowly, "I hope you're not going to suggest that line. Trying to rake up things about a harmless young woman who's dead and can't defend herself. And, anyway, I don't believe you can do it!"

"She was like the female Sir Galahad—a blameless life?"

"As far as I know, she was. I never heard anything else."

Poirot said gently, "You must not think, my friend, that I would stir the mud where no mud is. No, no, it is not like that at all. But the good Nurse Hopkins is not adept at hiding her feelings. She was fond of Mary, and there is something about Mary she does not want known; that is to say, there is something against Mary that she is afraid I will find out. She does not think that it has any bearing on the crime. But, then, she is convinced that the crime was committed by Elinor Carlisle, and clearly this fact, whatever it is, has nothing to do with Elinor. But, you see, my friend, it is imperative that I should know *everything.* For it may be that there is a wrong done by Mary to some third person, and in that case, that third person might have a motive for desiring her death."

Peter Lord said, "But surely, in that case, Nurse Hopkins would realize that, too."

Poirot said, "Nurse Hopkins is quite an intelligent woman within her limitations, but her intellect is hardly the equal of *mine.* She might not see, but Hercule Poirot would!"

Peter Lord said, shaking his head, "I'm sorry. I don't know anything."

Poirot said thoughtfully, "No more does Ted Bigland—and he has lived here all his life and Mary's. No more does Mrs. Bishop, for if she knew anything unpleasant about the girl, she would not have been able to keep it to herself! *Eh bien,* there is one more hope."

"Yes?"

"I am seeing the other nurse, Nurse O'Brien, today."

Peter Lord said, shaking his head, "She doesn't know much about this part of the world. She was only here for a month or two."

Poirot said, "I am aware of that. But, my friend, Nurse Hopkins, we have been told, has the long tongue. She has not gossiped in the village, where such talk might have done Mary Gerrard harm. But I doubt if she could refrain from giving at least a hint about something that was occupying her mind to a stranger and a colleague! Nurse O'Brien *may* know something."

17

NURSE O'BRIEN TOSSED her red head and smiled widely across the tea-table at the little man opposite her.

She thought to herself, *It's the funny little fellow he is—and his eyes green like any cat's, and with all that Dr. Lord saying he's the clever one!*

Hercule Poirot said, "It is a pleasure to meet someone so full of health and vitality. Your patients, I am sure, must all recover."

Nurse O'Brien said, "I'm not one for pulling a long face, and not many of my patients die on me, I'm thankful to say."

Poirot said, "Of course, in Mrs. Welman's case, it was a merciful release."

"Ah! it was that, the poor dear." Her eyes were shrewd as she looked at Poirot and asked, "Is it about that you want to talk to me? I was after hearing that they're digging her up."

Poirot said, "You yourself had no suspicion at the time?"

"Not the least in the world, though indeed I might have had, with the face Dr. Lord had on him that morning, and him sending me here, there, and everywhere for things he didn't need! But he signed the certificate, for all that."

Poirot began, "He had his reasons—" but she took the words out of his mouth.

"Indeed and he was right. It does a doctor no good to think things and offend the family, and then if he's wrong it's the end of him, and no one would be wishing to call him in any more. A doctor's got to be *sure!*"

Poirot said, "There is a suggestion that Mrs. Welman might have committed suicide."

"She? And her lying there helpless? Just lift one hand, that was all *she* could do!"

"Someone might have helped her?"

"Ah! I see now what you're meaning. Miss Carlisle, or Mr. Welman, or maybe Mary Gerrard?"

"It would be possible, would it not?"

Nurse O'Brien shook her head. She said, "They'd not dare—any of them!"

Poirot said slowly, "Perhaps not."

Then he said, "When was it Nurse Hopkins missed the tube of morphine?"

"It was that very morning. 'I'm sure I had it here,' she said. Very sure she was at first, but you know how it is; after a while your mind gets confused, and in the end she made sure she'd left it at home."

Poirot murmured, "And even then you had no suspicion?"

"Not the least in the world! Sure, it never entered my head for a moment that things weren't as they should be. And even now 'tis only a suspicion they have."

"The thought of that missing tube never caused either you or Nurse Hopkins an uneasy moment?"

"Well, I wouldn't say that. I do remember that it came into my head— and into Nurse Hopkins's head, too, I believe—in the Blue Tit Café we were at the time. And I saw the thought pass into her mind from mine. 'It couldn't be any other way than that I left it on the mantelpiece and it fell into the dustbin, could it?' she says. And 'No, indeed, that was the way of it,' I said to her, and neither of us saying what was in our minds and the fear that was on us."

Hercule Poirot asked, "And what do you think now?"

Nurse O'Brien said, "If they find morphine in her there'll be little doubt who took the tube, nor what it was used for—though I'll not be believing she sent the old lady the same road till it's proved there's morphine in her."

Poirot said, "You have no doubt at all that Elinor Carlisle killed Mary Gerrard?"

"There's no question of it at all, in my opinion! Who else had the reason or the wish to do it?"

"That is the question," said Poirot.

Nurse O'Brien went on dramatically: "Wasn't I there that night when the old lady was trying to speak, and Miss Elinor promising her that everything should be done decently and according to her wishes? And didn't I see her face looking after Mary as she went down the stairs one day, and the black hate that was on it? 'Twas murder she had in her heart that minute."

Poirot said, "If Elinor Carlisle killed Mrs. Welman, why did she do it?"

"Why? For the money, of course. Two hundred thousand pounds, no less. That's what she got by it, and that's why she did it—if she did it. She's a bold, clever young lady, with no fear in her, and plenty of brains."

Hercule Poirot said, "If Mrs. Welman had lived to make a will, how do you think she'd have left her money?"

"Ah, it's not for me to be saying that," said Nurse O'Brien, betraying, however, every symptom of being about to do so. "But it's my opinion that every penny the old lady had would have gone to Mary Gerrard."

"Why?" said Hercule Poirot.

The simple monosyllable seemed to upset Nurse O'Brien. "Why? Is it *why* you're asking? Well—I'd say that that would be the way of it."

Poirot murmured, "Some people might say that Mary Gerrard had played her cards very cleverly, that she had managed so to ingratiate herself with the old woman as to make her forget the ties of blood and affection."

"They might that," said Nurse O'Brien slowly.

Poirot asked, "*Was* Mary Gerrard a clever, scheming girl?"

Nurse O'Brien said, still rather slowly, "I'll not think that of her. All she did was natural enough, with no thought of scheming. She wasn't that kind. And there's reasons often for these things that never get made public."

Hercule Poirot said softly, "You are, I think, a very discreet woman, Nurse O'Brien."

"I'm not one to be talking of what doesn't concern me."

Watching her very closely, Poirot went on: "You and Nurse Hopkins, you have agreed together, have you not, that there are some things which are best not brought out into the light of day?"

Nurse O'Brien said, "What would you be meaning by that?"

Poirot said quickly, "Nothing to do with the crime—or crimes. I mean—the other matter."

Nurse O'Brien said, nodding her head, "What would be the use of raking up mud and an old story, and she a decent elderly woman with never a breath of scandal about her, and dying respected and looked up to by everybody."

Hercule Poirot nodded in assent. He said cautiously, "As you say, Mrs. Welman was much respected in Maidensford."

The conversation had taken an unexpected turn, but his face expressed no surprise or puzzlement.

Nurse O'Brien went on: "It's so long ago, too. All dead and forgotten. I've a soft heart for a romance myself, and I do say and I always have said that it's hard for a man who's got a wife in an asylum to be tied all his life with nothing but death that can free him."

Poirot murmured, still in bewilderment, "Yes, it is hard."

Nurse O'Brien said, "Did Nurse Hopkins tell you how her letter crossed mine?"

Poirot said truthfully, "She did not tell me *that*."

" 'Twas an odd coincidence. But there, that's always the way of it! Once you hear a name, maybe, and a day or two later you'll come across it again, and so on and so on. That I should be seeing the self-same photograph on the piano and at the same minute Nurse Hopkins was hearing all about it from the doctor's housekeeper."

"That," said Poirot, "is very interesting."

He murmured tentatively, "Did Mary Gerrard know—about this?"

"Who'd be telling her?" said Nurse O'Brien. "Not I—and not Hopkins. After all, what good would it be to her?"

She flung up her red head and gazed at him steadily.

Poirot said with a sigh, "What, indeed?"

18

ELINOR CARLISLE. Across the width of the table that separated them Poirot looked at her searchingly.

They were alone together. Through a glass wall a warder watched them.

Poirot noted the sensitive, intelligent face with the square, white forehead, and the delicate modeling of the ears and nose. Fine lines; a proud, sensitive creature, showing breeding, self-restraint and—something else— a capacity for passion.

He said, "I am Hercule Poirot. I have been sent to you by Dr. Peter Lord. He thinks that I can help you."

Elinor Carlisle said, "Peter Lord. . . ."

Her tone was reminiscent. For a moment she smiled a little wistfully. She went on formally: "It was kind of him, but I do not think there is anything you can do."

Hercule Poirot said, "Will you answer my questions?"

She sighed. She said, "Believe me—really—it would be better not to ask them. I am in good hands. Mr. Seddon has been most kind. I am to have a very famous counsel."

Poirot said, "He is not so famous as I am!"

Elinor Carlisle said with a touch of weariness, "He has a great reputation."

"Yes, for defending criminals. I have a great reputation—for demonstrating innocence."

She lifted her eyes at last—eyes of a vivid, beautiful blue. They looked straight into Poirot's. She said, "Do you believe I am innocent?"

Hercule Poirot said, "Are you?"

Elinor smiled, an ironic little smile. She said, "Is that a sample of your questions? It is very easy, isn't it, to answer Yes?"

He said unexpectedly, "You are very tired, are you not?"

Her eyes widened a little. She answered, "Why, yes—that more than anything. How did you know?"

Hercule Poirot said, "I knew."

Elinor said, "I shall be glad when it is—over."

Poirot looked at her for a minute in silence. Then he said, "I have seen your—cousin, shall I call him for convenience?—Mr. Roderick Welman."

Into the white, proud face the color crept slowly. He knew then that one question of his was answered without his asking it.

She said, and her voice shook very slightly, "You've seen Roddy?"

Poirot said, "He is doing all he can for you."

"I know."

Her voice was quick and soft.

Poirot said, "Is he poor or rich?"

"Roddy? He has not very much money of his own."

"And he is extravagant?"

She said, almost absently, "Neither of us ever thought it mattered. We knew that some day—"

She stopped.

Poirot said quickly, "You counted on your inheritance? That is understandable."

He went on: "You have heard, perhaps, the result of the autopsy on your aunt's body. She died of morphine poisoning."

Elinor Carlisle said coldly, "I did not kill her."

"Did you help her to kill herself?"

"Did I help—? Oh, I see. No, I did not."

"Did you know that your aunt had not made a will?"

"No, I had no idea of that."

Her voice was flat now—dull. The answer was mechanical, uninterested.

Poirot said, "And you yourself, have you made a will?"

"Yes."

"Did you make it the day Dr. Lord spoke to you about it?"

"Yes." Again that swift wave of color.

Poirot said, "How have you left your fortune, Miss Carlisle?"

Elinor said quietly, "I have left everything to Roddy—to Roderick Welman."

Poirot said, "Does he know that?"

She said quickly, "Certainly not."

"You didn't discuss it with him?"

"Of course not. He would have been horribly embarrassed and would have disliked what I was doing very much."

"Who else knows the contents of your will?"

"Only Mr. Seddon—and his clerks, I suppose."

"Did Mr. Seddon draw up the will for you?"

"Yes. I wrote to him that same evening—I mean the evening of the day Dr. Lord spoke to me about it."

"Did you post your letter yourself?"

"No. It went in the box from the house with the other letters."

"You wrote it, put it in an envelope, sealed it, stamped it, and put it in the box—*comme ça?* You did not pause to reflect? To read it over?"

Elinor said, staring at him, "I read it over—yes. I had gone to look for some stamps. When I came back with them, I just re-read the letter to be sure I had put it clearly."

"Was anyone in the room with you?"

"Only Roddy."

"Did he know what you were doing?"

"I told you—no."

"Could anyone have read that letter when you were out of the room?"

"I don't know. One of the servants, you mean? I suppose they could have if they had chanced to come in while I was out of the room."

"And before Mr. Roderick Welman entered it?"

"Yes."

Poirot said, "And he could have read it, too?"

Elinor's voice was clear and scornful. She said, "I can assure you, Monsieur Poirot, that my 'cousin,' as you call him, does not read other people's letters."

Poirot said, "That is the accepted idea, I know. You would be surprised how many people do the things that 'are not done.' "

Elinor shrugged her shoulders.

Poirot said in a casual voice, "Was it on that day that the idea of killing Mary Gerrard first came to you?"

For the third time color swept over Elinor Carlisle's face. This time it was a burning tide. She said, "Did Peter Lord tell you that?"

Poirot said gently, "It *was* then, wasn't it? When you looked through the window and saw her making her will. It was then, was it not, that it struck you how funny it would be—and how convenient—if Mary Gerrard should happen to die?"

Elinor said in a low, suffocated voice, "He knew—he looked at me and he knew—"

Poirot said, "Dr. Lord knows a good deal. He is no fool, that young man with the freckled face and the sandy hair."

Elinor said in a low voice, "Is it true that he sent you to—help me?"

"It is true, Mademoiselle."

She sighed and said, "I don't understand. No, I don't understand."

Poirot said, "Listen, Miss Carlisle. It is necessary that you tell me just what happened that day when Mary Gerrard died—where you went, what you did. More than that, I want to know even what you thought."

She stared at him. Then slowly a queer little smile came to her lips. She said, "You must be an incredibly simple man. Don't you realize how easy it is for me to lie to you?"

Hercule Poirot said placidly, "It does not matter."

She was puzzled. "Not matter?"

"No. For lies, Mademoiselle, tell a listener just as much as truth can. Sometimes they tell more. Come, now, commence. You met your housekeeper, the good Mrs. Bishop. She wanted to come and help you. You would not let her. Why?"

"I wanted to be alone."

"Why?"

"*Why? Why?* Because I wanted to—to think."

"You wanted to imagine—yes. And then what did you do next?"

Elinor, her chin raised defiantly, said, "I bought some paste for sandwiches."

"Two pots?"

"Two."

"And you went to Hunterbury. What did you do there?"

"I went up to my aunt's room and began to go through her things."

"What did you find?"

"Find?" She frowned. "Clothes—old letters—photographs—jewelry."

Poirot said, "No secrets?"

"Secrets? I don't understand you."

"Then let us proceed. What next?"

Elinor said, "I came down to the pantry and I cut sandwiches."

Poirot said softly, "And you thought—what?"

Her blue eyes flashed suddenly. She said, "I thought of my namesake, Eleanor of Aquitaine."

Poirot said, "I understand perfectly."

"Do you?"

"Oh, yes. I know the story. She offered Fair Rosamond, did she not, the choice of a dagger *or a cup of poison.* Rosamond chose the poison."

Elinor said nothing. She was white now.

Poirot said, "But perhaps, this time, *there was to be no choice.* Go on, Mademoiselle, what next?"

Elinor said, "I put the sandwiches ready on a plate and I went down to the lodge. Nurse Hopkins was there as well as Mary. I told them I had some sandwiches up at the house."

Poirot was watching her. He said softly, "Yes, and you all came up to the house together, did you not?"

"Yes. We—ate the sandwiches in the morning-room."

Poirot said in the same soft tone, "Yes, yes—*still in the dream.* And then—"

"Then?" She stared. "I left her—standing by the window. I went out into the pantry. It was still like you say—*in a dream.* Nurse was there washing up. I gave her the paste-pot."

"Yes—yes. And what happened then? What did you think of next?"

Elinor said dreamily, "There was a mark on Nurse's wrist. I mentioned it and she said it was a thorn from the rose trellis by the lodge. *The roses by the lodge.* . . . Roddy and I had a quarrel once—long ago—about the Wars of the Roses. I was Lancaster and he was York. He liked white roses. I said they weren't real—they didn't even smell! I liked red roses, big and dark and velvety and smelling of summer. We quarreled in the most idiotic way. You see, it all came back to me—there in the pantry— and something—something broke—the black hate I'd had in my heart— it went away—with remembering how we were together as children. I didn't hate Mary any more. I didn't want her to die."

She stopped.

"But later, when we went back into the morning-room, she was dying."

She stopped. Poirot was staring at her very intently. She flushed and said, "Will you ask me—again—*did I kill Mary Gerrard?*"

Poirot rose to his feet. He said quickly, "I shall ask you—nothing. There are things I do not want to know."

19

DR. LORD MET the train at the station as requested.

Hercule Poirot alighted from it. He looked very Londonified and was wearing pointed patent-leather shoes.

Peter Lord scrutinized his face anxiously, but Hercule Poirot was giving nothing away.

Peter Lord said, "I've done my best to get answers to your questions. First, Mary Gerrard left here for London on July 10th. Second, I haven't got a housekeeper—a couple of giggling girls run my house. I think you must mean Mrs. Slattery, who was Ransome's (my predecessor's) housekeeper. I can take you to her this morning if you like. I've arranged that she shall be in."

Poirot said, "Yes, I think it would be as well if I saw her first."

"Then you said you wanted to go to Hunterbury. I could come with you there. It beats me why you haven't been there already. I can't think why you wouldn't go when you were down here before. I should have thought the first thing to be done in a case like this was to visit the place where the crime took place."

Holding his head a little on one side, Hercule Poirot inquired, "Why?"

"Why?" Peter Lord was rather disconcerted by the question. "Isn't it the usual thing to do?"

Hercule Poirot said, "One does not practice detection with a textbook! One uses one's natural intelligence."

Peter Lord said, "You might find a clue of some sort there."

Poirot sighed. "You read too much detective fiction. Your police force in this country is quite admirable. I have no doubt that they searched the house and grounds most carefully."

"For evidence *against* Elinor Carlisle—not for evidence in her favor."

Poirot sighed. "My dear friend, it is not a monster—this police force! Elinor Carlisle was arrested because sufficient evidence was found to make out a case against her—a very strong case, I may say. It was useless for me to go over ground when the police had gone over it already."

"But you do want to go there now?" objected Peter.

Hercule Poirot nodded his head. He said, "Yes—now it is necessary. Because now I know *exactly what I am looking for*. One must understand with the cells of one's brain before one uses one's eyes."

"Then you *do* think there might be—something—there still?"

Poirot said gently, "I have a little idea we shall find something—yes."

"Something to prove Elinor's innocence?"

"Ah, I did not say that."

Peter Lord stopped dead. "You don't mean you *still* think she's guilty?"

Poirot said gravely, "You must wait, my friend, before you get an answer to that question."

Poirot lunched with the doctor in a pleasant square room with a window open on to the garden.

Lord said, "Did you get what you wanted out of old Slattery?"

"Yes."

"What *did* you want with her?"

"Gossip! Talk about old days. Some crimes have their roots in the past. I think this one had."

Peter Lord said irritably, "I don't understand a word you are talking about."

Poirot smiled. He said, "This fish is deliciously fresh."

Lord said impatiently, "I dare say. I caught it myself before breakfast this morning. Look here, Poirot, am I to have any idea what you're driving at? Why keep me in the dark?"

The other shook his head. "Because as yet there is no light. I am always brought up short by the fact that there was no one who had any reason to kill Mary Gerrard—except Elinor Carlisle."

Peter Lord said, "You can't be sure of that. She'd been abroad for some time, remember."

"Yes, yes, I have made the inquiries."

"You've been to Germany yourself?"

"Myself, no." With a slight chuckle he added, "I have my spies!"

"Can you depend on other people?"

"Certainly. It is not for me to run here and there, doing amateurishly the things that for a small sum someone else can do with professional skill. I can assure you, *mon cher,* I have several irons on the fire. I have some useful assistants—one of them a former burglar."

"What do you use him for?"

"The last thing I have used him for was a very thorough search of Mr. Welman's flat."

"What was he looking for?"

Poirot said, "One always likes to know exactly what lies have been told one."

"Did Welman tell you a lie?"

"Definitely."

"Who else has lied to you?"

"Everybody, I think: Nurse O'Brien romantically; Nurse Hopkins stubbornly; Mrs. Bishop venomously. You yourself—"

"Good God!" Peter Lord interrupted him unceremoniously. "You don't think I've lied to you, do you?"

"Not yet," Poirot admitted.

Dr. Lord sank back in his chair. He said, "You're a disbelieving sort of fellow, Poirot."

Then he said, "If you've finished, shall we set off for Hunterbury? I've got some patients to see later, and then there's the surgery."

"I am at your disposal, my friend."

They set off on foot, entering the grounds by the back gate. Halfway to the house they met a tall, good-looking young fellow wheeling a barrow. He touched his cap respectfully to Dr. Lord.

"Good morning, Horlick. This is Horlick, the gardener, Poirot. He was working here that morning."

Horlick said, "Yes, sir, I was. I saw Miss Elinor that morning and talked to her."

Poirot asked, "What did she say to you?"

"She told me the house was as good as sold, and that rather took me aback, sir; but Miss Elinor said as how she'd speak for me to Major Somervell, and that maybe he'd keep me on—if he didn't think me too young, perhaps, as head—seeing as how I'd had good training under Mr. Stephens, here."

Dr. Lord said, "Did she seem much the same as usual, Horlick?"

"Why, yes, sir, except that she looked a bit excited like—and as though she had something on her mind."

Hercule Poirot said, "Did you know Mary Gerrard?"

"Oh, yes, sir. But not very well."

Poirot said, "What was she like?"

Horlick looked puzzled. "Like, sir? Do you mean to look at?"

"Not exactly. I mean, what kind of a girl was she?"

"Oh, well, sir, she was a very superior sort of a girl. Nice spoken and all that. Thought a lot of herself, I should say. You see, old Mrs. Welman had made a lot of fuss over her. Made her father wild, that did. He was like a bear with a sore head about it."

Poirot said, "By all that I've heard, he had not the best of tempers, that old one?"

"No, indeed, he hadn't. Always grumbling, and crusty as they make them. Seldom had a civil word for you."

Poirot said, "You were here on that morning. Whereabouts were you working?"

"Mostly in the kitchen garden, sir."

"You cannot see the house from there?"

"No, sir."

Peter Lord said, "If anybody had come up to the house—up to the pantry window—you wouldn't have seen them?"

"No, I wouldn't, sir."

Peter Lord said, "When did you go to your dinner?"

"One o'clock, sir."

"And you didn't see anything—any man hanging about—or a car outside—anything like that?"

The man's eyebrows rose in slight surprise. "Outside the back gate, sir? There was your car there—nobody else's."

Peter Lord cried, "*My* car? It wasn't my car! I was over Withenbury direction that morning. Didn't get back till after two."

Horlick looked puzzled. "I made sure it was your car, sir," he said doubtfully.

Peter Lord said quickly, "Oh, well, it doesn't matter. Good morning, Horlick."

He and Poirot moved on. Horlick stared after them for a minute or two, then slowly resumed his progress with the wheelbarrow.

Peter Lord said softly—but with great excitement, "Something—at last. Whose car was it standing in the lane that morning?"

Poirot said, "What make is your car, my friend?"

"A Ford ten—sea-green. They're pretty common, of course."

"And you are sure that it was not yours? You haven't mistaken the day?"

"Absolutely certain. I was over at Withenbury, came back late, snatched a bit of lunch, and then the call came through about Mary Gerrard and I rushed over."

Poirot said softly, "Then it would seem, my friend, that we have come upon something tangible at last."

Peter Lord said, *"Someone was here that morning*—someone who was not Elinor Carlisle, nor Mary Gerrard, nor Nurse Hopkins."

Poirot said, "This is very interesting. Come, let us make our investigations. Let us see, for instance, supposing a man (or woman) were to wish to approach the house unseen, how they would set about it."

Halfway along the drive a path branched off through some shrubbery. They took this and at a certain turn in it Peter Lord clutched Poirot's arm, pointing to a window.

He said, "That's the window of the pantry where Elinor Carlisle was cutting the sandwiches."

Poirot murmured, "And from here, *anyone could see her cutting them.* The window was open, if I remember rightly?"

Peter Lord said, "It was wide open. It was a hot day, remember."

Hercule Poirot said musingly, "Then if anyone wished to watch unseen what was going on, somewhere about here would be a good spot."

The two men cast about. Peter Lord said, "There's a place here— behind these bushes. Some stuff's been trampled down here. It's grown up again now, but you can see plainly enough."

Poirot joined him. He said thoughtfully, "Yes, this is a good place. It is concealed from the path, and that opening in the shrubs gives one a good view of the window. Now, what did he do, our friend who stood here? Did he perhaps smoke?"

They bent down, examining the ground and pushing aside the leaves and branches. Suddenly Hercule Poirot uttered a grunt.

Peter Lord straightened up from his own search. "What is it?"

"A match box, my friend. An empty match box, trodden heavily into the ground, sodden and decayed."

With care and delicacy he salvaged the object. He displayed it at last on a sheet of notepaper taken from his pocket.

Peter Lord said. "It's foreign. My God! *German matches!*"

Hercule Poirot said, "And Mary Gerrard had recently come from Germany!"

Peter Lord said exultingly, "We've got something now! You can't deny it."

Hercule Poirot said slowly, "Perhaps."

"But, damn it all, man. Who on earth round here would have had foreign matches?"

Hercule Poirot said, "I know—I know."

His eyes, perplexed eyes, went to the gap in the bushes and the view of the window. He said, "It is not quite so simple as you think. There is one great difficulty. Do you not see it yourself?"

"What? Tell me."

Poirot sighed. "If you do not see for yourself— But come, let us go on."

They went on to the house. Peter Lord unlocked the back door with a key.

He led the way through the scullery to the kitchen, through that, along a passage where there was a cloakroom on one side and the butler's pantry on the other. The two men looked round the pantry.

It had the usual cupboards with sliding glass doors for glass and china. There was a gas ring and two kettles and canisters marked *Tea* and *Coffee* on a shelf above. There was a sink and draining-board and a washing-up bowl. In front of the window was a table.

Peter Lord said, "It was on this table that Elinor Carlisle cut the sandwiches. The fragment of the morphine label was found in this crack in the floor under the sink."

Poirot said thoughtfully, "The police are careful searchers. They do not miss much."

Peter Lord said violently, "There's no evidence that Elinor ever handled that tube! I tell you, someone was watching her from the shrubbery outside. She went down to the lodge and he saw his chance and slipped in, uncorked the tube, crushed some tablets of morphine to powder, and put them into the top sandwich. He never noticed that he'd torn a bit off the label of the tube, and that it had fluttered down the crack. He hurried away, started up his car, and went off again."

Poirot sighed. "And still you do not see! It is extraordinary how dense an intelligent man can be."

Peter Lord demanded angrily, "Do you mean to say that you don't believe someone stood in those bushes watching this window?"

Poirot said, "Yes, I believe that."

"Then we've got to find whoever it was!"

Poirot murmured, "We shall not have to look far, I fancy."

"Do you mean you *know?*"

"I have a very shrewd idea."

Peter Lord said slowly, "Then your minions who made inquiries in Germany *did* bring you something."

Hercule Poirot said, tapping his forehead, "My friend, it is all here, in my head. Come, let us look over the house."

They stood at last in the room where Mary Gerrard had died.

The house had a strange atmosphere in it; it seemed alive with memories and forebodings.

Peter Lord flung up one of the windows. He said with a slight shiver, "This place feels like a tomb."

Poirot said, "If walls could speak. It is all here, is it not, here in the house—the beginning of the whole story."

He paused and then said softly, "It was in this room that Mary Gerrard died?"

Peter Lord said, "They found her sitting in that chair by the window."

Hercule Poirot said thoughtfully, "A young girl—beautiful—romantic. Did she scheme and intrigue? Was she a superior person who gave herself airs? Was she gentle and sweet, with no thought of intrigue—just a young thing beginning life—a girl like a flower?"

"Whatever she was," said Peter Lord, "someone wished her dead."

Hercule Poirot murmured, "I wonder—"

Lord stared at him. "What do you mean?"

Poirot shook his head. "Not yet."

He turned about. "We have been all through the house. We have seen all that there is to be seen here. Let us go down to the lodge."

Here again all was in order, the rooms dusty, but neat and emptied of personal possessions. The two men stayed only a few minutes. As they came out into the sun, Poirot touched the leaves of a pillar rose growing up a trellis. It was pink and sweet-scented. He murmured, "Do you know the name of this rose? It is Zephyrine Droughin, my friend."

Peter Lord said irritably, "What of it?"

Hercule Poirot said, "When I saw Elinor Carlisle, she spoke to me of roses. It was then that I began to see—not daylight, but the little glimpse of light that one gets in a train when one is about to come out of a tunnel. It is not so much daylight, but the promise of daylight."

Peter Lord said harshly, "What did she tell you?"

"She told me of her childhood, of playing here in this garden, and of how she and Roderick Welman were on different sides. They were enemies, for he preferred the white rose of York—cold and austere—and she, so she told me, loved red roses, the red rose of Lancaster. Red roses that have scent and color and passion and warmth. And that, my friend, is the difference between Elinor Carlisle and Roderick Welman."

Peter Lord said, "Does that explain—anything?"

Poirot said, "It explains Elinor Carlisle—who is passionate and proud and who loved desperately a man who was incapable of loving her."

Peter Lord said, "I don't understand you."

Poirot said, "But I understand *her*. I understand both of them. Now, my friend, we will go back once more to that little clearing in the shrubbery."

They went there in silence. Peter Lord's freckled face was troubled and angry.

When they came to the spot, Poirot stood motionless for some time, and Peter Lord watched him.

Then suddenly the little detective gave a vexed sigh. He said, "It is so simple, really. Do you not see, my friend, the fatal fallacy in your reasoning? According to your theory, someone, a man, presumably, who had known Mary Gerrard in Germany came here intent on killing her. But *look*, my friend, *look!* Use the two eyes of your body, since the eyes of the mind do not seem to serve you. What do you see from here? A window, is it not? And at that window—a girl. A girl cutting sandwiches. That is to say, Elinor Carlisle. But think for a minute of this: *What on earth was to tell the watching man that those sandwiches were going to be offered to Mary Gerrard?* No one knew that *but Elinor Carlisle herself—nobody!* Not even Mary Gerrard, nor Nurse Hopkins.

"So what follows—if a man stood here watching, and if he afterward went to that window and climbed in and tampered with the sandwiches? What did he think and believe? He thought, he must have thought, *that the sandwiches were to be eaten by Elinor Carlisle herself.*"

20

POIROT KNOCKED AT the door of Nurse Hopkins's cottage. She opened it to him with her mouth full of Bath bun.

She said sharply, "Well, Mr. Poirot, what do you want *now?*"

"I may enter?"

Somewhat grudgingly Nurse Hopkins drew back and Poirot was permitted to cross the threshold. Nurse Hopkins was hospitable with the teapot, and a minute later Poirot was regarding with some dismay a cup of inky beverage.

"Just made—nice and strong!" said Nurse Hopkins.

Poirot stirred his tea cautiously and took one heroic sip. He said, "Have you any idea why I have come here?"

"I couldn't say, I'm sure, until you tell me. I don't profess to be a mind-reader."

"I have come to ask you for the truth."

Nurse Hopkins uprose in wrath. "And what's the meaning of that, I should like to know? A truthful woman I've always been. Not one to shield myself in any way. I spoke up about that missing tube of morphine at the inquest when many a one in my place would have sat tight and said nothing. For well enough did I know that I should get censured for carelessness in leaving my case about, and, after all, it's a thing might happen to anybody! I was blamed for that—and it won't do me any good in my profession, I can tell you. But that didn't make any difference to me! I knew something that had a bearing on the case, and so I spoke out. And I'll thank you, Mr. Poirot, to keep any nasty insinuation to yourself! There's not a thing about Mary Gerrard's death that I haven't been open and aboveboard as daylight about, and if *you* think differently, I'd be obliged if you'd give chapter and verse for it! I've concealed nothing—nothing at all! And I'm prepared to take the oath and stand up in court and say so."

Poirot did not attempt to interrupt. He knew only too well the technique of dealing with an angry woman. He allowed Nurse Hopkins to flare up and simmer down. Then he spoke—quietly and mildly.

He said, "I did not suggest that there is anything about the crime which you have not told."

"Then what did you suggest, I'd like to know?"

"I asked you to tell the truth—not about the death, but about the *life* of Mary Gerrard."

"Oh!" Nurse Hopkins seemed momentarily taken aback. She said, "So that's what you're getting at? But it's got nothing to do with the murder."

"I did not say that it had. I said that you were withholding knowledge concerning her."

"Why shouldn't I—if it's nothing to do with the crime?"

Poirot shrugged his shoulders. "Why should you?"

Nurse Hopkins, very red in the face, said, "Because it's common decency! They're all dead now—everyone concerned. And it's no business of anyone else's!"

"If it is only surmise—perhaps not. But if you have *actual knowledge,* that's different."

Nurse Hopkins said slowly, "I don't know exactly what you mean."

Poirot said, "I will help you. I have had hints from Nurse O'Brien and I have had a long conversation with Mrs. Slattery, who has a very good memory for events that happened over twenty years ago. I will tell you exactly what I have learned. Well, over twenty years ago there was a love affair between two people. One of them was Mrs. Welman, who had been a widow for some years and who was a woman capable of a deep and passionate love. The other party was Sir Lewis Rycroft, who had the great misfortune to have a wife who was hopelessly insane. The law in those days gave no promise of relief by divorce, and Lady Rycroft, whose physical health was excellent, might live to be ninety. The liaison between those two people was, I think, guessed at, but they were both discreet and careful to keep up appearances. Then Sir Lewis Rycroft was killed in action."

"Well?" said Nurse Hopkins.

"I suggest," said Poirot, "that there was a child born after his death, and that that child was Mary Gerrard."

Nurse Hopkins said, "You seem to know all about it!"

Poirot said, "That is what I *think.* But it is possible that you have got definite proof that that is so."

Nurse Hopkins sat silent a minute or two, frowning, then abruptly she rose, went across the room, opened a drawer, and took out an envelope. She brought it across to Poirot.

She said, "I'll tell you how this came into my hands. Mind, I'd had my suspicions. The way Mrs. Welman looked at the girl, for one thing, and then hearing the gossip on top of it. And old Gerrard told me when he was ill that Mary wasn't his daughter.

"Well, after Mary died I finished clearing up the lodge, and in a drawer among some of the old man's things I came across this letter. You see what's written on it."

Poirot read the superscription written in faded ink: *For Mary—to be sent to her after my death.*

Poirot said, "This writing is not recent?"

"It wasn't Gerrard who wrote that," explained Nurse Hopkins. "It was Mary's mother, who died fourteen years ago. She meant this for the girl, but the old man kept it among his things and so she never saw it—and I'm thankful she didn't! She was able to hold up her head to the end, and she'd no cause to feel ashamed."

She paused and then said, "Well, it was sealed up, but when I found it I'll admit to you that I opened it and read it then and there, which I dare say I should not have done. But Mary was dead, and I guessed more or less at what was inside it and I didn't see that it was any concern of anyone else's. All the same, I haven't liked to destroy it, because I didn't feel somehow it would be right to do that. But, there, you'd better read it yourself."

Poirot drew out the sheet of paper covered in small, angular writing:

> *This is the truth I've written down here in case it should ever be needed. I was lady's maid to Mrs. Welman at Hunterbury, and very kind to me she was. I got into trouble, and she stood by me and took me back into her service when it was all over; but the baby died. My mistress and Sir Lewis Rycroft were fond of each other, but they couldn't marry, because he had a wife already and she was in a madhouse, poor lady. He was a fine gentleman and devoted to Mrs. Welman. He was killed, and she told me soon after that she was going to have a child. After that she went up to Scotland and took me with her. The child was born there—at Ardlochrie. Bob Gerrard, who had washed his hands of me and flung me off when I had my trouble, had been writing to me again. The arrangement was that we should marry and live at the lodge and he should think that the baby was mine. If we lived on the place it would seem natural that Mrs. Welman should be interested in the child and she'd see to educating her and giving her a place in the world. She thought it would be better for Mary never to know the truth. Mrs. Welman gave us both a handsome sum of money; but I would have helped her without that. I've been quite happy with Bob, but he never took to Mary. I've held my tongue and never said anything to anybody, but I think it's right in case I die that I should put this down in black and white.*
>
> ELIZA GERRARD (*born* ELIZA RILEY).

Hercule Poirot drew a deep breath and folded up the letter again.

Nurse Hopkins said anxiously, "What are you going to do about it? They're all dead now! It's no good raking up these things. Everyone looked up to Mrs. Welman in these parts; there's never been anything said against her. All this old scandal—it would be cruel. The same with Mary. She was a sweet girl. Why should anyone have to know she was a bastard? Let the dead rest in peace in their graves, that's what I say."

Poirot said, "One has to consider the living."

Nurse Hopkins said, "But this has got nothing to do with the murder."

Hercule Poirot said gravely, "It may have a great deal to do with it."

He went out of the cottage, leaving Nurse Hopkins with her mouth open, staring after him.

He had walked some way when he became aware of hesitating footsteps just behind him. He stopped and turned round.

It was Horlick, the young gardener from Hunterbury. He was looking the picture of embarrassment and twisting his cap round and round in his hands.

"Excuse me, sir. Could I have a word with you?"

Horlick spoke with a kind of gulp.

"Certainly. What is it?"

Horlick twisted the cap even more fiercely. He said, averting his eyes and looking the picture of misery and embarrassment, "It's about that car."

"The car that was outside the back gate that morning?"

"Yes, sir. Dr. Lord said this morning that it wasn't his car—*but it was, sir.*"

"You know that for a fact?"

"Yes, sir. Because of the number, sir. It was MSS 2022. I noticed it particular—MSS 2022. You see, we know it in the village, and always call it Miss Tou-Tou! I'm quite sure of it, sir."

Poirot said with a faint smile, "But Dr. Lord says he was over at Withenbury that morning."

Horlick said miserably, "Yes, sir. I heard him. But it *was* his car, sir. I'll take my oath on that."

Poirot said gently, "Thank you, Horlick, that's just exactly what you may have to do."

21

WAS IT VERY hot in the court? Or very cold? Elinor Carlisle could not be quite sure. Sometimes she felt burning and immediately after she shivered.

She had not heard the end of the Prosecuting Counsel's speech. She had gone back to the past—gone slowly through the whole business again, from the day when that miserable letter came to the moment when that smooth-faced police officer had said with horrible fluency:

"You are Elinor Katharine Carlisle. I have here a warrant for your arrest upon the charge of murdering Mary Gerrard by administering poison to her on the 27th of July last, and I must warn you that anything you say will be taken down in writing and may be used as evidence at your trial."

Horrible, frightening fluency. She felt caught up in a smooth-running, well-oiled machine—inhuman, passionless.

And now here she was, standing in the dock in the open glare of publicity, with hundreds of eyes that were neither impersonal nor inhuman, feasting upon her and gloating.

Only the jury did not look at her. Embarrassed, they kept their eyes studiously turned away. She thought, *It's because—soon—they know what they're going to say.*

Dr. Lord was giving evidence. Was this Peter Lord—that freckled, cheery young doctor who had been so kind and so friendly at Hunterbury? He was very stiff now. Sternly professional. His answers came monotonously. He had been summoned by telephone to Hunterbury Hall; too late for anything to be done; Mary Gerrard had died a few minutes after his arrival; death consistent, in his opinion, with morphia poisoning in one of its less common forms—the "foudroyante" variety.

Sir Edwin Bulmer rose to cross-examine.

"You were the late Mrs. Welman's regular medical attendant?"

"I was."

"During your visits to Hunterbury in June last, you had occasion to see the accused and Mary Gerrard together?"

"Several times."

"What should you say was the manner of the accused to Mary Gerrard?"

"Perfectly pleasant and natural."

Sir Edwin Bulmer said with a slight, disdainful smile, "You never saw any signs of this 'jealous hatred' we have heard so much about?"

Peter Lord, his jaw set, said firmly, "No."

Elinor thought, *But he did—he did. He told a lie for me there. He knew.*

Peter Lord was succeeded by the police surgeon. His evidence was longer, more detailed. Death was due to morphia poisoning of the "foudroyante" variety. Would he kindly explain the term? With some enjoyment he did so. Death from morphine poisoning might result in several different ways. The most common was a period of intense excitement followed by drowsiness and narcosis, pupils of eyes contracted. Another not so common form had been named by the French "foudroyante." In these cases deep sleep supervened in a very short time—about ten minutes; the pupils of the eyes were usually dilated.

The court had adjourned and sat again. There had been some hours of expert medical testimony.

Dr. Alan Garcia, the distinguished analyst, full of learned terms, spoke with gusto of the stomach contents. Bread, fish paste, tea, presence of morphia—more learned terms and various decimal points. Amount taken by the deceased estimated to be about four grains. Fatal dose could be as low as one grain.

Sir Edwin rose, still bland. "I should like to get it quite clear. You found in the stomach nothing but bread, butter, fish paste, tea, and morphia. There were no other foodstuffs?"

"None."

"That is to say, the deceased had eaten nothing but sandwiches and tea for some considerable time?"

"That is so."

"Was there anything to show in what particular vehicle the morphia had been administered?"

"I don't quite understand."

"I will simplify that question. The morphia could have been taken in the fish paste, or in the bread, or in the butter on the bread, or in the tea, or in the milk that had been added to the tea?"

"Certainly."

"There was no special evidence that the morphia was in the fish paste rather than in the other mediums?"

"No."

"And, in fact, the morphia *might* have been taken separately—that is to say, not in any vehicle at all? It could have been simply swallowed in its tablet form?"

"That is so, of course."

Sir Edwin sat down.

Sir Samuel Attenbury re-examined.

"Nevertheless, you are of the opinion that, however the morphia was taken, it was taken at the same time as the other food and drink?"

"Yes."

"Thank you."

Inspector Brill had taken the oath with mechanical fluency. He stood there, soldierly and stolid, reeling off his evidence with practiced ease.

"Summoned to the house. . . . The accused said, 'It must have been bad fish paste' . . . search of the premises . . . one jar of fish paste washed out was standing on the draining-board in the pantry, another half full . . . further search of pantry kitchen. . . ."

"What did you find?"

"In a crack behind the table, between the floorboards, I found a tiny scrap of paper."

The exhibit went to the jury.

"What did you take it to be?"

"A fragment off a printed label—such as are used on glass tubes of morphia."

Counsel for the Defense arose with leisurely ease.

He said, "You found this scrap in a crack in the flooring?"

"Yes."

"Part of a label?"

"Yes."

"Did you find the rest of that label?"

"No."

"You did not find any glass tube or any bottle to which that label might have been affixed?"

"No."

"What was the state of that scrap of paper when you found it? Was it clean or dirty?"

"It was quite fresh."

"What do you mean, quite fresh?"

"There was surface dust on it from the flooring, but it was quite clean otherwise."

"It could not have been there for any length of time?"

"No, it had found its way there quite recently."

"You would say, then, that it had come there on the actual day you found it—not earlier?"

"Yes."

With a grunt Sir Edwin sat down.

Nurse Hopkins in the box, her face red and self-righteous.

All the same, Elinor thought, Nurse Hopkins was not so frightening as Inspector Brill. It was the inhumanity of Inspector Brill that was so paralyzing. He was so definitely part of a great machine. Nurse Hopkins had human passions, prejudices.

"Your name is Jessie Hopkins?"

"Yes."

"You are a certified District Nurse and you reside at Rose Cottage, Hunterbury?"

"Yes."

"Where were you on the 28th of June last?"

"I was at Hunterbury Hall."

"You had been sent for?"

"Yes. Mrs. Welman had had a stroke—the second. I went to assist Nurse O'Brien until a second nurse could be found."

"Did you take a small attaché case with you?"

"Yes."

"Tell the jury what was in it."

"Bandages, dressings, a hypodermic syringe, and certain drugs, including a tube of morphine hydrochloride."

"For what purpose was the morphine there?"

"One of the cases in the village had to have hypodermic injections of morphia morning and evening."

"What were the contents of the tube?"

"There were twenty tablets, each containing half-grain Morphine Hydrochloride."

"What did you do with your attaché case?"

"I laid it down in the hall."

"That was on the evening of the 28th. When did you next have occasion to look in the case?"

"The following morning about nine o'clock, just as I was preparing to leave the house."

"Was anything missing?"

"The tube of morphine was missing."

"Did you mention this loss?"

"I spoke of it to Nurse O'Brien, the nurse in charge of the patient."

"This case was lying in the hall, where people were in the habit of passing to and fro?"

"Yes."

Sir Samuel paused. Then he said, "You knew the dead girl, Mary Gerrard, intimately?"

"Yes."

"What was your opinion of her?"

"She was a very sweet girl—and a good girl."

"Was she of a happy disposition?"

"Very happy."

"She had no troubles that you know of?"

"No."

"At the time of her death was there anything whatever to worry her or make her unhappy about the future?"

"Nothing."

"She would have had no reason to have taken her own life?"

"No reason at all."

It went on and on—the damning story. How Nurse Hopkins had accompanied Mary to the lodge, the appearance of Elinor, her excitable manner, the invitation to sandwiches, the plate being handed first to Mary, Elinor's suggestion that everything be washed up, and her further suggestion that Nurse Hopkins should come upstairs with her and assist in sorting out clothes.

There were frequent interruptions and objections from Sir Edwin Bulmer.

Elinor thought, *Yes, it's all true—and she believes it. She's certain I did it. And every word she says is the truth—that's what's so horrible. It's all true.*

Once more, as she looked across the court, she saw the face of Hercule Poirot regarding her thoughtfully—almost kindly. *Seeing her with too much knowledge.*

The piece of cardboard with the scrap of label pasted on it was handed to the witness.

"Do you know what this is?"

"It's a bit of a label."

"Can you tell the jury what label?"

"Yes—it's a part of a label off a tube of hypodermic tablets. Morphine tablets half-grain—like the one I lost."

"You are sure of that?"

"Of course I'm sure. It's off my tube."

The judge said, "Is there any special mark on it by which you can identify it as the label of the tube you lost?"

"No, my lord, but it must be the same."

"Actually, all you can say is that it is exactly similar?"

"Well, yes, that's what I mean."

The court adjourned.

22

IT WAS ANOTHER day. Sir Edwin Bulmer was on his feet cross-examining. He was not at all bland now. He said sharply, "This attaché case we've heard so much about. On June 28th it was left in the main hall of Hunterbury all night?"

Nurse Hopkins agreed: "Yes."

"Rather a careless thing to do, wasn't it?"

Nurse Hopkins flushed. "Yes, I suppose it was."

"Are you in the habit of leaving dangerous drugs lying about where anyone could get at 'em?"

"No, of course not."

"Oh! You're not? But you did it on this occasion?"

"Yes."

"And it's a fact, isn't it, that *anybody in the house* could have got at that morphia if they'd wanted to?"

"I suppose so."

"No suppose about it. It is so, isn't it?"

"Well—yes."

"It wasn't only Miss Carlisle who could have got it? Any of the servants could? Or Dr. Lord? Or Mr. Roderick Welman? Or Nurse O'Brien? Or Mary Gerrard herself?"

"I suppose so—yes."

"It is so, isn't it?"

"Yes."

"Was anyone aware you'd got morphia in that case?"

"I don't know."

"Well, did you talk about it to anyone?"

"No."

"So, as a matter of fact, Miss Carlisle couldn't have known that there was any morphia there?"

"She might have looked to see."

"That's very unlikely, isn't it?"

"I don't know, I'm sure."

"There were people who'd be more likely to know about the morphia than Miss Carlisle. Dr. Lord, for instance. He'd know. You were administering this morphia under his orders, weren't you?"

"Of course."

"Mary Gerrard knew you had it there, too?"

"No, she didn't."

"She was often in your cottage, wasn't she?"

"Not very often."

"I suggest to you that she was there very frequently, and that she, of all the people in the house, would be the most likely to guess that there was morphia in your case."

"I don't agree."

Sir Edwin paused a minute. "You told Nurse O'Brien in the morning that the morphia was missing?"

"Yes."

"I put it to you that what you really said was, 'I have left the morphia at home. I shall have to go back for it.' "

"No, I didn't."

"You didn't suggest that the morphia had been left on the mantel-piece in your cottage?"

"Well, when I couldn't find it I thought that must have been what had happened."

"In fact, you didn't really know what you'd done with it!"

"Yes, I did. I put it in the case."

"Then why did you suggest on the morning of June 29th that you had left it at home?"

"Because I thought I might have."

"I put it to you that you're a very careless woman."

"That's not true."

"You make rather inaccurate statements sometimes, don't you?"

"No, I don't. I'm very careful what I say."

"Did you make a remark about a prick from a rose tree on July 27th— the day of Mary Gerrard's death?"

"I don't see what that's got to do with it!"

The judge said, "Is that relevant, Sir Edwin?"

"Yes, my lord, it is an essential part of the defense, and I intend to call witnesses to prove that that statement was a lie."

He resumed. "Do you still say you pricked your wrist on a rose tree on July 27th?"

"Yes, I did." Nurse Hopkins looked defiant.

"When did you do that?"

"Just before leaving the lodge and coming up to the house on the morning of July 27th."

Sir Edwin said skeptically, "And what rose tree was this?"

"A climbing one just outside the lodge, with pink flowers."

"You're sure of that?"

"I'm quite sure."

Sir Edwin paused and then asked, "You persist in saying the morphia was in the attaché case when you came to Hunterbury on June 28th?"

"I do. I had it with me."

"Supposing that presently Nurse O'Brien goes into the box and swears that you said you had probably left it at home?"

"It was in my case. I'm sure of it."

Sir Edwin sighed. "You didn't feel at all uneasy about the disappearance of the morphia?"

"Not—uneasy—no."

"Oh, so you were quite at ease, notwithstanding the fact that a large quantity of a dangerous drug had disappeared?"

"I didn't think at the time anyone had taken it."

"I see. You just couldn't remember for the moment what you had done with it?"

"Not at all. It was in the case."

"Twenty half-grain tablets—that is, ten grains of morphia. Enough to kill several people, isn't it?"

"Yes."

"But you are not uneasy—and you don't even report the loss officially?"

"I thought it was all right."

"I put it to you that if the morphia had really disappeared the way it did you would have been bound, as a conscientious person, to report the loss officially."

Nurse Hopkins, very red in the face, said, "Well, I didn't."

"That was surely a piece of criminal carelessness on your part. You don't seem to take your responsibilities very seriously. Did you often mislay these dangerous drugs?"

"It never happened before."

It went on for some minutes. Nurse Hopkins, flustered, red in the face, contradicting herself—an easy prey to Sir Edwin's skill.

"Is it a fact that on Thursday, July 6th, the dead girl, Mary Gerrard, made a will?"

"She did."

"Why did she do that?"

"Because she thought it was the proper thing to do. And so it was."

"Are you sure it wasn't because she was depressed and uncertain about her future?"

"Nonsense."

"It showed, though, that the idea of death was present in her mind— that she was brooding on the subject."

"Not at all. She just thought it was the proper thing to do."

"Is this the will? Signed by Mary Gerrard, witnessed by Emily Biggs and Roger Wade, confectioners' assistants, and leaving everything of which she died possessed to Mary Riley, sister of Eliza Riley?"

"That's right."

It was handed to the jury.

"To your knowledge, had Mary Gerrard any property to leave?"

"Not then, she hadn't."

"But she was shortly going to have?"

"Yes."

"Is it not a fact that a considerable sum of money—two thousand pounds—was being given to Mary by Miss Carlisle?"

"Yes."

"There was no compulsion on Miss Carlisle to do this? It was entirely a generous impulse on her part?"

"She did it of her own free will, yes."

"But surely, if she had hated Mary Gerrard, as is suggested, she would not of her own free will have handed over to her a large sum of money."

"That's as may be."

"What do you mean by that answer?"

"I don't mean anything."

"Exactly. Now, had you heard any local gossip about Mary Gerrard and Mr. Roderick Welman?"

"He was sweet on her."

"Have you any evidence of that?"

"I just knew it, that's all."

"Oh—you 'just knew it.' That's not very convincing to the jury, I'm afraid. Did you say on one occasion Mary would have nothing to do with him because he was engaged to Miss Elinor and she said the same to him in London?"

"That's what she told me."

Sir Samuel Attenbury re-examined: "When Mary Gerrard was discussing with you the wording of this will, did the accused look in through the window?"

"Yes, she did."

"What did she say?"

"She said, 'So you're making your will, Mary. That's funny.' And she laughed. Laughed and laughed. And it's my opinion," said the witness viciously, "that it was at that moment the idea came into her head. The idea of making away with the girl! She'd murder in her heart that very minute."

The judge spoke sharply: "Confine yourself to answering the questions that are asked you. The last part of that answer is to be struck out."

Elinor thought, *How queer. When anyone says what's true, they strike it out.* She wanted to laugh hysterically.

Nurse O'Brien was in the box.

"On the morning of June 29th did Nurse Hopkins make a statement to you?"

"Yes. She said she had a tube of morphine hydrochloride missing from her case."

"What did you do?"

"I helped her to hunt for it."

"But you could not find it?"

"No."

"To your knowledge, was the case left overnight in the hall?"

"It was."

"Mr. Welman and the accused were both staying in the house at the time of Mrs. Welman's death—that is, on June 28th to 29th?"

"Yes."

"Will you tell us of an incident that occurred on June 29th—the day after Mrs. Welman's death?"

"I saw Mr. Roderick Welman with Mary Gerrard. He was telling her he loved her, and he tried to kiss her."

"He was at the time engaged to the accused?"

"Yes."

"What happened next?"

"Mary told him to think shame of himself, and him engaged to Miss Elinor!"

"In your opinion, what was the feeling of the accused toward Mary Gerrard?"

"She hated her. She would look after her as though she'd like to destroy her."

Sir Edwin jumped up.

Elinor thought, *Why do they wrangle about it? What does it matter?*

Sir Edwin Bulmer cross-examined: "Is it not a fact that Nurse Hopkins said she thought she had left the morphia at home?"

"Well, you see, it was this way. After—"

"Kindly answer my question. Did she not say that she had probably left the morphia at home?"

"Yes."

"She was not really worried at the time about it?"

"No, not then."

"Because she thought she had left it at home. So naturally she was not uneasy."

"She couldn't imagine anyone taking it."

"Exactly. It wasn't till after Mary Gerrard's death from morphia that her imagination got to work."

The judge interrupted: "I think, Sir Edwin, that you have already been over that point with the former witness."

"As your lordship pleases."

"Now, regarding the attitude of the accused to Mary Gerrard, there was no quarrel between them at any time?"

"No quarrel, no."

"Miss Carlisle was always quite pleasant to the girl?"

"Yes. 'Twas the way she looked at her."

"Yes—yes—yes. But we can't go by that sort of thing. You're Irish, I think?"

"I am that."

"And the Irish have rather a vivid imagination, haven't they?"

Nurse O'Brien cried excitedly, "Every word I've told you is the truth."

Mr. Abbott, the grocer, in the box. Flustered—unsure of himself (slightly thrilled, though, at his importance). His evidence was short. The purchase of two pots of fish paste. The accused had said, "There's a lot of food poisoning with fish paste." She had seemed excited and queer.

No cross-examination.

23

OPENING SPEECH FOR the Defense:

"Gentlemen of the jury, I might, if I like, submit to you that there is no case against the accused. The onus of proof is on the Prosecution, and so far, in my opinion—and, I have no doubt, yours—they have proved exactly nothing at all! The Prosecution avers that Elinor Carlisle, having obtained possession of morphine (which everyone else in the house had had equal opportunity of purloining, and as to which there exists considerable doubt whether it was ever in the house at all), proceeds to poison Mary Gerrard. Here the Prosecution has relied solely on opportunity. It has sought to prove motive, but I submit that that is just what it has not been able to do. For, members of the jury, there is no motive! The Prosecution has spoken of a broken engagement. I ask you—a broken engagement! If a broken engagement is a cause for murder, why are we not having murders committed every day? And this engagement, mark you, was not an affair of desperate passion, it was an engagement entered into mainly for family reasons. Miss Carlisle and Mr. Welman had grown up together; they had always been fond of each other, and gradually they drifted into a warmer attachment; but I intend to prove to you it was at best a very lukewarm affair."

(Oh, Roddy—Roddy. A lukewarm affair?)

"Moreover, this engagement was broken off, not by Mr. Welman—but by the prisoner. I submit to you that the engagement between Elinor Carlisle and Roderick Welman was entered into mainly to please old Mrs. Welman. When she died, both parties realized that their feelings were not strong enough to justify them in entering upon matrimony. They remained, however, good friends. Moreover, Elinor Carlisle, who had inherited her aunt's fortune, in the kindliness of her nature, was planning to settle a considerable sum of money on Mary Gerrard. And this is the girl she is accused of poisoning! The thing is farcical.

"The only thing that there is against Elinor Carlisle is the circumstances under which the poisoning took place.

"The Prosecution has said in effect:

" 'No one but Elinor Carlisle could have killed Mary Gerrard.' Therefore they have had to search about for a possible motive. But, as I have said to you, they have been unable to find any motive, because there was none.

Now, is it true that no one but Elinor Carlisle could have killed Mary Gerrard? No, it is not. There is the possibility that Mary Gerrard committed suicide. There is the possibility that someone tampered with the sandwiches while Elinor Carlisle was out of the house at the lodge. There is a third possibility. It is a fundamental law of evidence that if it can be shown that there is an alternative theory which is possible and consistent with the evidence, the accused must be acquitted. I propose to show you that there was another person who had not only an equal opportunity to poison Mary Gerrard, but who had a far better motive for doing so. I propose to call evidence to show you that there was another person who had access to the morphine, and who had a very good motive for killing Mary Gerrard, and I can show that that person had an equally good opportunity of doing so. I submit to you that no jury in the world will convict this woman of murder when there is no evidence against her except that of opportunity, and when it can be shown that there is not only evidence of opportunity against another person, but an overwhelming motive. I shall also call witnesses to prove that there has been deliberate perjury on the part of one of the witnesses for the Crown. But first I will call the prisoner, that she may tell you her own story, and that you may see for yourself how entirely unfounded the charges against her are."

She had taken the oath. She was answering Sir Edwin's questions in a low voice. The judge leaned forward. He told her to speak louder.

Sir Edwin was talking gently and encouragingly—all the questions to which she had rehearsed the answers.

"You were fond of Roderick Welman?"

"Very fond. He was like a brother to me—or a cousin. I always thought of him as a cousin."

The engagement . . . drifted into it . . . very pleasant to marry someone you had known all your life. . . .

"Not, perhaps, what might be called a passionate affair?"

(*Passionate? Oh, Roddy.*)

"Well, no . . . you see, we knew each other so well . . ."

"After the death of Mrs. Welman, was there a slightly strained feeling between you?"

"Yes, there was."

"How did you account for this?"

"I think it was partly the money."

"The money?"

"Yes. Roderick felt uncomfortable. He thought people might think he was marrying me for that."

"The engagement was not broken off on account of Mary Gerrard?"

"I did think Roderick was rather taken with her, but I didn't believe it was anything serious."

"Would you have been upset if it had been?"

"Oh, no. I should have thought it rather unsuitable, that is all."

"Now, Miss Carlisle. Did you or did you not take a tube of morphine from Nurse Hopkins's attaché case on June 28th?"

"I did not."

"Have you at any time had morphine in your possession?"

"Never."

"Were you aware that your aunt had not made a will?"

"No. It came as a great surprise to me."

"Did you think she was trying to convey to you a message on the night of June 28th when she died?"

"I understood that she had made no provision for Mary Gerrard, and was anxious to do so."

"And in order to carry out her wishes, you yourself were prepared to settle a sum of money on the girl?"

"Yes. I wanted to carry out Aunt Laura's wishes. And I was grateful for the kindness Mary had shown to my aunt."

"On July 26th did you come down from London to Maidensford and stay at the King's Arms?"

"Yes."

"What was your purpose in coming down?"

"I had an offer for the house, and the man who had bought it wanted possession as quickly as possible. I had to look through my aunt's personal things and settle things up generally."

"Did you buy various provisions on your way to Hunterbury Hall on July 27th?"

"Yes. I thought it would be easier to have a picnic lunch there than to come back to the village."

"Did you then go on to the house, and did you sort through your aunt's personal effects?"

"I did."

"And after that?"

"I came down to the pantry and cut some sandwiches. I then went down to the lodge and invited the District Nurse and Mary Gerrard to come up to the house."

"Why did you do this?"

"I wished to save them a hot walk back to the village and back again to the lodge."

"It was, in fact, a natural and kindly action on your part. Did they accept the invitation?"

"Yes. They walked up to the house with me."

"Where were the sandwiches you had cut?"

"I left them in the pantry on a plate."

"Was the window open?"

"Yes."

"Anyone could have got into the pantry while you were absent?"

"Certainly."

"If anybody had observed you from outside while you were cutting the sandwiches, what would they have thought?"

"I suppose that I was preparing to have a picnic lunch."

"They could not know, could they, that anyone was to share the lunch?"

"No. The idea of inviting the other two only came to me when I saw what a quantity of food I had."

"So that if anyone had entered the house during your absence and placed morphine in one of those sandwiches, it would be *you* they were attempting to poison?"

"Well, yes, it would."

"What happened when you had all arrived back at the house?"

"We went into the morning-room. I fetched the sandwiches and handed them to the other two."

"Did you drink anything with them?"

"I drank water. There was beer on a table, but Nurse Hopkins and Mary preferred tea. Nurse Hopkins went into the pantry and made it. She brought it in on a tray and Mary poured it out."

"Did you have any?"

"No."

"But Mary Gerrard and Nurse Hopkins both drank tea?"

"Yes."

"What happened next?"

"Nurse Hopkins went and turned the gas-ring off."

"Leaving you alone with Mary Gerrard?"

"Yes."

"What happened next?"

"After a few minutes I picked up the tray and the sandwich plate and carried them into the pantry. Nurse Hopkins was there, and we washed them together."

"Did Nurse Hopkins have her cuffs off at the time?"

"Yes. She was washing the things, while I dried them."

"Did you make a certain remark to her about a scratch on her wrist?"

"I asked her if she had pricked herself."

"What did she reply?"

"She said, 'It was a thorn from the rose tree outside the lodge. I'll get it out presently.' "

"What was her manner at the time?"

"I think she was feeling the heat. She was perspiring and her face was a queer color."

"What happened after that?"

"We went upstairs, and she helped me with my aunt's things."

"What time was it when you went downstairs again?"

"It must have been an hour later."

"Where was Mary Gerrard?"

"She was sitting in the morning-room. She was breathing very queerly and was in a coma. I rang up the doctor on Nurse Hopkins's instructions. He arrived just before she died."

Sir Edwin squared his shoulders dramatically.

"Miss Carlisle, did you kill Mary Gerrard?"

(That's your cue. Head up, eyes straight.)

"No!"

Sir Samuel Attenbury. A sick beating at one's heart. Now—now she was at the mercy of an enemy! No more gentleness, no more questions to which she knew the answers!

But he began quite mildly.

"You were engaged to be married, you have told us, to Mr. Roderick Welman?"

"Yes."

"You were fond of him?"

"Very fond."

"I put it to you that you were deeply in love with Roderick Welman and that you were wildly jealous of his love for Mary Gerrard?"

"No." *(Did it sound properly indignant, that "no"?)*

Sir Samuel said menacingly, "I put it to you that you deliberately planned to put this girl out of the way, in the hope that Roderick Welman would return to you."

"Certainly not." *(Disdainful—a little weary. That was better.)*

The questions went on. It was just like a dream—a bad dream—a nightmare . . .

Question after question—horrible, hurting questions. Some of them she was prepared for, some took her unawares.

Always trying to remember her part. Never once to let go, to say, "Yes, I did hate her. . . . Yes, I did want her dead. . . . Yes, all the time I was cutting the sandwiches I was thinking of her dying. . . ."

To remain calm and cool and answer as briefly and passionlessly as possible. . . .

Fighting. . . .

Fighting every inch of the way. . . .

Over now. . . . The horrible man was sitting down. And the kindly, unctuous voice of Sir Edwin Bulmer was asking a few more questions. Easy, pleasant questions, designed to remove any bad impression she might have made under cross-examination.

She was back again in the dock. Looking at the jury, wondering. . . .

(Roddy. Roddy standing there, blinking a little, hating it all. Roddy—looking somehow—not quite real.)

(But nothing's real any more. Everything is whirling round in a devilish way. Black's white, and top is bottom and east is west. . . . And I'm not Elinor Carlisle;

I'm "the accused." And, whether they hang me or whether they let me go, nothing will ever be the same again. If there were just something—just one sane thing to hold to. . . .)

(Peter Lord's face, perhaps, with its freckles and its extraordinary air of being just the same as usual. . . .)

Where had Sir Edwin got to now?

"Will you tell us what was the state of Miss Carlisle's feelings toward you?"

Roddy answered in his precise voice, "I should say she was deeply attached to me, but certainly not passionately in love with me."

"You considered your engagement satisfactory?"

"Oh, quite. We had a good deal in common."

"Will you tell the jury, Mr. Welman, exactly why that engagement was broken off?"

"Well, after Mrs. Welman died it pulled us up, I think, with a bit of a shock. I didn't like the idea of marrying a rich woman when I myself was penniless. Actually the engagement was dissolved by mutual consent. We were both rather relieved."

"Now, will you tell us just what your relations were with Mary Gerrard?"

(Oh, Roddy, poor Roddy, how you must hate all this!)

"I thought her very lovely."

"Were you in love with her?"

"Just a little."

"When was the last time you saw her?"

"Let me see. It must have been the 5th or 6th of July."

Sir Edwin said, a touch of steel in his voice, "You saw her after that, I think."

"No, I went abroad—to Venice and Dalmatia."

"You returned to England—when?"

"When I received a telegram—let me see—on the 1st of August, it must have been."

"But you were actually in England on July 27th, I think."

"No."

"Come, now, Mr. Welman. You are on oath, remember. Is it not a fact that your passport shows that you returned to England on July 25th and left it again on the night of the 27th?"

Sir Edwin's voice held a subtly menacing note. Elinor frowned, suddenly jerked back to reality. Why was Counsel bullying his own witness?

Roderick had turned rather pale. He was silent for a minute or two, then he said with an effort, "Well—yes, that is so."

"Did you go to see this girl Mary Gerrard in London on the 25th at her lodgings?"

"Yes, I did."

"Did you ask her to marry you?"

"Er—er—yes."

"What was her answer?"

"She refused."

"You are not a rich man, Mr. Welman?"

"No."

"And you are rather heavily in debt?"

"What business is that of yours?"

"Were you not aware of the fact that Miss Carlisle had left all her money to you in the event of her death?"

"This is the first I have heard of it."

"Were you in Maidensford on the morning of July 27th?"

"I was not."

Sir Edwin sat down.

Counsel for the Prosecution said: "You say that in your opinion the accused was not deeply in love with you."

"That is what I said."

"Are you a chivalrous man, Mr. Welman?"

"I don't know what you mean."

"If a lady were deeply in love with you and you were not in love with her, would you feel it incumbent upon you to conceal the fact?"

"Certainly not."

"Where did you go to school, Mr. Welman?"

"Eton."

Sir Samuel said with a quiet smile, "That is all."

Alfred James Wargrave.

"You are a rose-grower and live at Emsworth, Berks?"

"Yes."

"Did you on October 20th go to Maidensford and examine a rose tree growing at the lodge at Hunterbury Hall?"

"I did."

"Will you describe this tree?"

"It was a climbing rose—Zephyrine Droughin. It bears a sweetly scented pink flower. It has no thorns."

"It would be impossible to prick oneself on a rose tree of this description?"

"It would be quite impossible. It is a thornless tree."

No cross-examination.

"You are James Arthur Littledale. You are a qualified chemist and employed by the wholesale chemists, Jenkins & Hale?"

"I am."

"Will you tell me what this scrap of paper is?"

The exhibit was handed to him.

"It is a fragment of one of our labels."

"What kind of a label?"

"The label we attach to tubes of hypodermic tablets."

"Is there enough here for you to say definitely what drug was in the tube to which this label was attached?"

"Yes. I should say quite definitely that the tube in question contained hypodermic tablets of apomorphine hydrochloride 1/20 grain."

"Not morphine hydrochloride?"

"No, it could not be that."

"Why not?"

"On such a tube the word morphine is spelled with a capital *M*. The end of the line of the *m* here, seen under my magnifying glass, shows plainly that it is part of a small *m*, not a capital *M*."

"Please let the jury examine it with the glass. Have you labels here to show what you mean?"

The labels were handed to the jury.

Sir Edwin resumed:

"You say this is from a tube of apomorphine hydrochloride? What exactly is apomorphine hydrochloride?"

"The formula is $C_{17}H_{17}NO_2$. It is a derivative of morphine prepared by saponifying morphine by heating it with dilute hydrochloric acid in sealed tubes. The morphine loses one molecule of water."

"What are the special properties of apomorphine?"

Mr. Littledale said quietly, "Apomorphine is the quickest and most powerful emetic known. It acts within a few minutes."

"So if anybody had swallowed a lethal dose of morphine and were *to inject a dose of apomorphine hypodermically within a few minutes,* what would result?"

"Vomiting would take place almost immediately and the morphine would be expelled from the system."

"Therefore, if two people were to share the same sandwich *or drink from the same pot of tea,* and one of them were then to inject a dose of apomorphine hypodermically, what would be the result, supposing the shared food or drink to have contained morphine?"

"The food or drink together with the morphine would be vomited by the person who injected the apomorphine."

"And that person would suffer no ill results?"

"No."

There was suddenly a stir of excitement in court and order for silence from the judge.

"You are Amelia Mary Sedley and you reside ordinarily at 17 Charles Street, Boonamba, Auckland?"

"Yes."

"Do you know a Mrs. Draper?"

"Yes. I have known her for over twenty years."

"Do you know her maiden name?"

"Yes. I was at her marriage. Her name was Mary Riley."

"Is she a native of New Zealand?"

"No, she came out from England."

"You have been in court since the beginning of these proceedings?"

"Yes, I have."

"Have you seen this Mary Riley—or Draper—in court?"

"Yes."

"Where did you see her?"

"Giving evidence in this box."

"Under what name?"

"Jessie Hopkins."

"And you are quite sure that this Jessie Hopkins is the woman you know as Mary Riley or Draper?"

"Not a doubt of it."

A slight commotion at the back of the court.

"When did you last see Mary Draper—until today?"

"Five years ago. She went to England."

Sir Edwin said with a bow, "Your witness."

Sir Samuel, rising with a highly perplexed face, began: "I suggest to you, Mrs.—Sedley, that you may be mistaken."

"I'm not mistaken."

"You may have been misled by a chance resemblance."

"I know Mary Draper well enough."

"Nurse Hopkins is a certified District Nurse."

"Mary Draper was a hospital nurse before her marriage."

"You understand, do you not, that you are accusing a Crown witness of perjury?"

"I understand what I'm saying."

"Edward John Marshall, you lived for some years in Auckland, New Zealand, and now reside at 14 Wren Street, Deptford?"

"That's right."

"Do you know Mary Draper?"

"I've known her for years in New Zealand."

"Have you seen her today in court?"

"I have. She called herself Hopkins, but it was Mrs. Draper all right."

The judge lifted his head. He spoke in a small, clear, penetrating voice, "It is desirable, I think, that the witness Jessie Hopkins should be recalled."

A pause, a murmur.

"Your lordship, Jessie Hopkins left the court a few minutes ago."

"Hercule Poirot."

Hercule Poirot entered the box, took the oath, twirled his mustache, and waited, with his head a little on one side. He gave his name and address and calling.

"Poirot, do you recognize this document?"

"Certainly."

"How did it originally come into your possession?"

"It was given me by the District Nurse, Nurse Hopkins."

Sir Edwin said, "With your permission, my lord, I will read this aloud, and it can then go to the jury."

24

CLOSING SPEECH FOR the Defense:

"Gentlemen of the jury, the responsibility now rests with you. It is for you to say if Elinor Carlisle is to go forth free from the court. If, after the evidence you have heard, you are satisfied that Elinor Carlisle poisoned Mary Gerrard, then it is your duty to pronounce her guilty.

"But if it should seem to you that there is equally strong evidence, and perhaps far stronger evidence, against another person, then it is your duty to free the accused without more ado.

"You will have realized by now that the facts of the case are very different from what they originally appeared to be.

"Yesterday, after the dramatic evidence given by Monsieur Hercule Poirot, I called other witnesses to prove beyond any reasonable doubt that the girl Mary Gerrard was the illegitimate daughter of Laura Welman. That being true, it follows, as his lordship will doubtless instruct you, that Mrs. Welman's next of kin was not her niece, Elinor Carlisle, but her illegitimate daughter who went by the name of Mary Gerrard. And therefore Mary Gerrard at Mrs. Welman's death inherited a vast fortune. That, gentlemen, is the crux of the situation. A sum in the neighborhood of two hundred thousand pounds was inherited by Mary Gerrard. But she herself was unaware of the fact. She was also unaware of the true identity of the woman Hopkins. You may think, gentlemen, that Mary Riley or Draper may have had some perfectly legitimate reason for changing her name to Hopkins. If so, why has she not come forward to state what the reason was?

"All that we do know is this: That at Nurse Hopkins's instigation, Mary Gerrard made a will leaving everything she had to 'Mary Riley, sister of Eliza Riley.' We know that Nurse Hopkins, by reason of her profession, had access to morphine and to apomorphine and was well acquainted with their properties. Furthermore, it has been proved that Nurse Hopkins was not speaking the truth when she said that her wrist had been pricked by a thorn from a thornless rose tree. Why did she lie, if it were not that she wanted hurriedly to *account for the mark just made by the hypodermic needle*? Remember, too, that the accused has stated on oath that Nurse Hopkins, when she joined her in the pantry, was looking ill, and her face was of a greenish color—comprehensible enough if she had just been violently sick.

"I will underline yet another point: *If* Mrs. Welman had lived twenty-four hours longer, she would have made a will; and in all probability that will would have made a suitable provision for Mary Gerrard, but would not have left her the bulk of her fortune, since it was Mrs. Welman's belief that her unacknowledged daughter would be happier if she remained in another sphere of life.

"It is not for me to pronounce on the evidence against another person, except to show that this other person had equal opportunities and a far stronger motive for the murder.

"Looked at from that point of view, gentlemen of the jury, I submit to you that the case against Elinor Carlisle falls to the ground."

From Mr. Justice Beddingfeld's summing-up:

". . . You must be perfectly satisfied that this woman did, in fact, administer a dangerous dose of morphia to Mary Gerrard on July 27th. If you are not satisfied, you must acquit the prisoner.

"The Prosecution has stated that the only person who had the opportunity to administer poison to Mary Gerrard was the accused. The Defense has sought to prove that there were other alternatives. There is the theory that Mary Gerrard committed suicide, but the only evidence in support of that theory is the fact that Mary Gerrard made a will shortly before she died. There is not the slightest proof that she was depressed or unhappy or in a state of mind likely to lead her to take her own life. It has also been suggested that the morphine might have been introduced into the sandwiches by someone entering the pantry during the time that Elinor Carlisle was at the lodge. In that case, the poison was intended for Elinor Carlisle, and Mary Gerrard's death was a mistake. The third alternative suggested by the Defense is that another person had an equal opportunity to administer morphine, and that in the latter case the poison was introduced into the tea and not into the sandwiches. In support of that theory the Defense has called the witness Littledale, who has sworn that the scrap of paper found in the pantry was part of a label on a tube containing tablets of apomorphine hydrochloride, a very powerful emetic. You have had an example of both types of labels submitted to you. In my view, the police were guilty of gross carelessness in not checking the original fragment more closely and in jumping to the conclusion that it was a morphine label.

"The witness Hopkins has stated that she pricked her wrist on a rose tree at the lodge. The witness Wargrave has examined that tree, and it has no thorns on it. You have to decide what caused the mark on Nurse Hopkins's wrist and why she should tell a lie about it. . . .

"If the Prosecution has convinced you that the accused and no other committed the crime, then you must find the accused guilty.

"If the alternative theory suggested by the Defense is possible and consistent with the evidence, the accused must be acquitted.

"I will ask you to consider the verdict with courage and diligence, weighing only the evidence that has been put before you."

Elinor was brought back into the court.

The jury filed in.

"Gentlemen of the jury, are you agreed upon your verdict?"

"Yes."

"Look upon the prisoner at the bar, and say whether she is guilty or not guilty."

"*Not guilty.*"

25

THEY HAD BROUGHT her out by a side door.

She had been aware of faces welcoming her—Roddy—the detective with the big mustache.

But it was to Peter Lord she had turned.

"I want to get away."

She was with him now in the smooth Daimler, driving rapidly out of London.

He had said nothing to her. She had sat in the blessed silence.

Every minute taking her farther and farther away.

A new life. . . .

That was what she wanted. . . .

A new life.

She said suddenly, "I—I want to go somewhere quiet—where there won't be any *faces.*"

Peter Lord said quietly, "That's all arranged. You're going to a sanatorium. Quiet place. Lovely gardens. No one will bother you—or get at you."

She said with a sigh, "Yes—that's what I want."

It was being a doctor, she supposed, that made him understand. He knew—and didn't bother her. So blessedly peaceful to be here with him, going away from it all, out of London—to a place that was *safe.*

She wanted to forget—forget everything. None of it was real any longer. It was all gone, vanished, finished with—the old life and the old emotions. She was a new, strange, defenseless creature, very crude and raw, beginning all over again. Very strange and very afraid.

But it was comforting to be with Peter Lord.

They were out of London now, passing through suburbs. She said at last, "It was all you—all you."

Peter Lord said, "It was Hercule Poirot. The fellow's a kind of magician!"

But Elinor shook her head. She said obstinately, "It was *you.* *You* got hold of him and made him do it!"

Peter grinned. "I made him do it, all right."

Elinor said, "Did you know I hadn't done it, or weren't you sure?"

Peter said simply, "I was never quite sure."

Elinor said, "That's why I nearly said 'guilty' right at the beginning—

because, you see, I *had* thought of it. . . . I thought of it that day when I laughed outside the cottage."

Peter said, "Yes, I knew."

She said wonderingly, "It seems so queer now—like a kind of possession. That day I bought the paste and cut the sandwiches I was pretending to myself, I was thinking, 'I've mixed poison with this, and when she eats she will die—and then Roddy will come back to me.' "

Peter Lord said, "It helps some people to pretend that sort of thing to themselves. It isn't a bad thing, really. You take it out of yourself in a fantasy. Like sweating a thing out of your system."

Elinor said, "Yes, that's true. Because it went—suddenly! The blackness, I mean! When that woman mentioned the rose tree outside the lodge— it all swung back into—into being normal again."

Then with a shiver she said, "Afterward when we went into the morning-room and she was dead—dying, at least—I felt then: Is there much difference between *thinking* and *doing* murder?"

Peter Lord said, "All the difference in the world!"

"Yes, but is there?"

"Of course there is! Thinking murder doesn't really do any harm. People have silly ideas about that; they think it's the same as *planning* murder! It isn't. If you think murder long enough, you suddenly come through the blackness and feel that it's all rather silly!"

Elinor cried, "Oh! you *are* a comforting person."

Peter Lord said rather incoherently, "Not at all. Just common sense."

Elinor said, and there were suddenly tears in her eyes, "Every now and then—in court—I looked at you. It gave me courage. You looked so—so *ordinary*."

Then she laughed. "That's rude!"

He said, "I understand. When you're in the middle of a nightmare something ordinary is the only hope. Anyway, ordinary things are the best. I've always thought so."

For the first time since she had entered the car she turned her head and looked at him.

The sight of his face didn't hurt her as Roddy's face always hurt her; it gave her no sharp pang of pain and pleasure mixed; instead, it made her feel warm and comforted.

She thought, *How nice his face is—nice and funny—and, yes, comforting.*

They drove on. They came at last to a gateway and a drive that wound upward till it reached a quiet white house on the side of a hill.

He said, "You'll be quite safe here. No one will bother you."

Impulsively she laid her hand on his arm. She said, "You—you'll come and see me?"

"Of course."

"Often?"

Peter Lord said, "As often as you want me."

She said, "Please come—*very often*."

26

HERCULE POIROT SAID, "So you see, my friend, the lies people tell me are just as useful as the truth."

Peter Lord said, "Did everyone tell you lies?"

Hercule Poirot nodded. "Oh, yes! For one reason or another, you comprehend. The one person to whom truth was an obligation and who was sensitive and scrupulous concerning it—that person was the one who puzzled me most!"

Peter Lord murmured, "Elinor herself!"

"Precisely. The evidence pointed to her as the guilty party. And she herself, with her sensitive and fastidious conscience, did nothing to dispel that assumption. Accusing herself of the will, if not the deed, she came very near to abandoning a distasteful and sordid fight and pleading guilty in court to a crime she had not committed."

Peter Lord breathed a sigh of exasperation. "Incredible."

Poirot shook his head. "Not at all. She condemned herself—because she judged herself by a more exacting standard than ordinary humanity applies!"

Peter Lord said thoughtfully, "Yes, she's like that."

Hercule Poirot went on: "From the moment that I started my investigations there was always the strong possibility that Elinor Carlisle was guilty of the crime of which she was accused. But I fulfilled my obligations toward you and I discovered that a fairly strong case could be made out against another person."

"Nurse Hopkins?"

"Not to begin with. Roderick Welman was the first person to attract my attention. In his case, again, we start with a lie. He told me that he left England on July 9th and returned on August 1st. But Nurse Hopkins had mentioned casually that Mary Gerrard had rebuffed Roderick Welman's advances both in Maidensford 'and again when she saw him in London.' Mary Gerrard, you informed me, went to London on July 10th—*a day after* Roderick Welman had left England. When did Mary Gerrard have an interview with Roderick Welman in London? I set my burglarious friend to work, and by an examination of Welman's passport I discovered that he had been in England from July 25th to the 27th. *And he had deliberately lied about it.*

"There had always been that period of time in my mind when the sandwiches were on a plate in the pantry and Elinor Carlisle was down at the lodge. But all along I realized that in that case Elinor must have been the intended victim, not Mary. Had Roderick Welman any motive for killing Elinor Carlisle? Yes, a very good one. She had made a will leaving him her entire fortune, and by adroit questioning I discovered that Roderick Welman could have made himself acquainted with that fact."

Peter Lord said, "And why did you decide that he was innocent?"

"Because of one more lie. Such a silly, stupid, negligible little lie, too. Nurse Hopkins said that she had scratched her wrist on a rose tree, that she had got a thorn in it. And I went and saw the rose tree, and *it had no thorns*. So clearly Nurse Hopkins had told a lie—and the lie was so silly and so seemingly pointless that it focused my attention upon her.

"I began to wonder about Nurse Hopkins. Up till then she had struck me as a perfectly credible witness, consistent throughout, with a strong bias against the accused arising naturally enough out of her affection for the dead girl. But now, with that silly, pointless lie in my mind, I considered Nurse Hopkins and her evidence very carefully, and I realized something that I had not been clever enough to see before. Nurse Hopkins knew something about Mary Gerrard which she was very anxious should come out."

Peter Lord said in surprise, "I thought it was the other way round?"

"Ostensibly, yes. She gave a very fine performance of someone who knows something and isn't going to tell! But when I thought it over carefully I realized that every word she had said on the subject had been uttered with diametrically the opposite end in view. My conversation with Nurse O'Brien confirmed that belief. Hopkins had used her very cleverly without Nurse O'Brien being conscious of the fact.

"It was clear then that Nurse Hopkins had a game of her own to play. I contrasted the two lies, hers and Roderick Welman's. Was either of them capable of an innocent explanation?

"In Roderick's case, I answered immediately. Yes. Roderick Welman is a very sensitive creature. To admit that he had been unable to keep to his plan of staying abroad, and had been compelled to slink back and hang around the girl, who would have nothing to do with him, would have been most hurtful to his pride. Since there was no question of his having been near the scene of the murder or of knowing anything about it, he took the line of least resistance and avoided unpleasantness (a most characteristic trait!) by ignoring that hurried visit to England and simply stating that he returned on August 1st when the news of the murder reached him.

"Now as to Nurse Hopkins, could there be an innocent explanation of her lie? The more I thought of it, the more extraordinary it seemed to me. *Why* should Nurse Hopkins find it necessary to lie because she had a mark on her wrist? What was the significance of that mark?

"I began to ask myself certain questions. Who did the morphine that was stolen belong to? Nurse Hopkins. Who could have administered that morphine to old Mrs. Welman? Nurse Hopkins. Yes, but why call attention to its disappearance? There could be only one answer to that if Nurse Hopkins was guilty: because the other murder, the murder of Mary Gerrard, was already planned, and a scapegoat had been selected, but that scapegoat must be shown to *have had a chance of obtaining morphine*.

"Certain other things fitted in. The anonymous letter written to Elinor. That was to create bad feeling between Elinor and Mary. The idea doubtless was that Elinor would come down and object to Mary's influence over Mrs. Welman. The fact that Roderick Welman fell violently in love with Mary was, of course, a totally unforeseen circumstance—but one that Nurse Hopkins was quick to appreciate. Here was a perfect motive for the scapegoat, Elinor.

"But what was the *reason* for the two crimes? What motive could there be for Nurse Hopkins to do away with Mary Gerrard? I began to see a light—oh, very dim as yet. Nurse Hopkins had a good deal of influence over Mary, and one of the ways she had used that influence was to induce the girl *to make a will.* But the will did not benefit Nurse Hopkins. It benefited an aunt of Mary's who lived in New Zealand. And then I remembered a chance remark that someone in the village had made to me. That aunt had been a hospital nurse.

"The light was not quite so dim now. The pattern—the design of the crime—was becoming apparent. The next step was easy. I visited Nurse Hopkins once more. We both played the comedy very prettily. In the end she allowed herself to be persuaded to tell what she had been aiming to tell all along! Only she tells it, perhaps, just a little sooner than she meant to do! But the opportunity is so good that she cannot resist. And, after all, the truth has got to be known sometime. So, with well-feigned reluctance, she produces the letter. And then, my friend, it is no longer conjecture. I *know!* The letter gives her away."

Peter Lord frowned and said, "How?"

"Mon cher! The superscription on that letter was as follows: *For Mary, to be sent to her after my death.* But the gist of the contents made it perfectly plain that Mary *Gerrard* was not to know the truth. Also, the word *sent* (not given) on the envelope was illuminating. It was not Mary Gerrard to whom that letter was written, but another Mary. It was to her sister, Mary *Riley,* in New Zealand that Eliza Riley wrote the truth.

"Nurse Hopkins did not find that letter at the lodge after Mary Gerrard's death. She had had it in her possession for many years. She received it in New Zealand, where it was sent to her after her sister's death."

He paused. "Once one had seen the truth with the eyes of the mind the rest was easy. The quickness of air travel made it possible for a witness who knew Mary Draper well in New Zealand to be present in court."

Peter Lord said, "Supposing you had been wrong and Nurse Hopkins and Mary Draper had been two entirely different people?"

Poirot said coldly, "I am never wrong!"

Peter Lord laughed.

Hercule Poirot went on: "My friend, we know something now of this woman Mary Riley or Draper. The police of New Zealand were unable to get sufficient evidence for a conviction, but they had been watching her for some time when she suddenly left the country. There was a patient of hers, an old lady, who left her 'dear Nurse Riley' a very snug little legacy, and whose death was somewhat of a puzzle to the doctor attending her. Mary Draper's husband insured his life in her favor for a considerable sum, and his death was sudden and unaccountable. Unfortunately for her, though he had made out a check to the insurance company, he had forgotten to post it. Other deaths may lie at her door. It is certain she is a remorseless and unscrupulous woman.

"One can imagine that her sister's letter suggested possibilities to her resourceful mind. When New Zealand became too hot, as you say, to hold her, and she came to this country and resumed her profession in the name of Hopkins (a former colleague of hers in hospital who died abroad), Maidensford was her objective. She may perhaps have contemplated some form of blackmail. But old Mrs. Welman was not the kind of woman to allow herself to be blackmailed, and Nurse Riley, or Hopkins, very wisely, did not attempt anything of the sort. Doubtless she made inquiries and discovered that Mrs. Welman was a very wealthy woman, and some chance word of Mrs. Welman's may have revealed the fact that the old lady had not made a will.

"So, on that June evening, when Nurse O'Brien retailed to her colleague that Mrs. Welman was asking for her lawyer, Hopkins did not hesitate. Mrs. Welman must die intestate so that her illegitimate daughter would inherit her money. Hopkins had already made friends with Mary Gerrard and acquired a good deal of influence over the girl. All that she had to do now was to persuade the girl to make a will leaving her money to her mother's sister, and she inspired the wording of that will very carefully. There was no mention of the relationship, just 'Mary Riley, sister of the late Eliza Riley.' Once that was signed, Mary Gerrard was doomed. The woman only had to wait for a suitable opportunity. She had, I fancy, already planned the method of the crime, with the use of the apomorphine to secure her own alibi. She may have meant to get Elinor to her cottage, but when Elinor came down to the lodge and asked them both to come up and have sandwiches she realized at once that a perfect opportunity had arisen. The circumstances were such that Elinor was practically certain to be convicted."

Peter Lord said slowly, "If it hadn't been for you—she would have been convicted."

Hercule Poirot said quickly, "No, it is you, my friend, she has to thank for her life."

"I? I didn't do anything. I tried—"

He broke off. Hercule Poirot smiled a little. *"Mais oui,* you tried very hard, did you not? You were impatient because I did not seem to you to be getting anywhere. And you were afraid, too, that she might, after all, be guilty. And so, with great impertinence, you also told me the lies! But, *mon cher,* you were not very clever about it. In future I advise you to stick to the measles and the whooping cough and leave crime detection alone."

Peter Lord blushed. He said, "Did you know—all the time?"

Poirot said severely, "You lead me by the hand to a clearing in the shrubs, and you assist me to find a German matchbox that you have just put there! *C'est l'enfantillage!"*

Peter Lord winced. He groaned. "Rub it in!"

Poirot went on: "You converse with the gardener and lead him to say that he saw your car in the road, and then you give a start and pretend that it was *not* your car. And you look hard at me to make sure that I realize that someone, a stranger, must have been there that morning."

"I was a damned fool," said Peter Lord.

"What were you doing at Hunterbury that morning?"

Peter Lord blushed. "It was just sheer idiocy. I—I'd heard she was down. I went up to the house on the chance of seeing her. I didn't mean to speak to her. I—I just wanted to—well—see her. From the path in the shrubbery I saw her in the pantry cutting bread and butter—"

"Charlotte and the poet Werther. Continue, my friend."

"Oh, there's nothing to tell. I just slipped into the bushes and stayed there watching her till she went away."

Poirot said gently, "Did you fall in love with Elinor Carlisle the first time you saw her?"

"I suppose so."

There was a long silence.

Then Peter Lord said, "Oh, well, I suppose she and Roderick Welman will live happy ever afterward."

Hercule Poirot said, "My dear friend, you suppose nothing of the sort!"

"Why not? She'll forgive him the Mary Gerrard business. It was only a wild infatuation on his part, anyway."

Hercule Poirot said, "It goes deeper than that. There is, sometimes, a deep chasm between the past and the future. When one has walked in the valley of the shadow of death, and come out of it into the sunshine—then, *mon cher*, it is a new life that begins. The past will not serve."

He waited a minute and then went on: "A new life—that is what Elinor Carlisle is beginning now—and it is you who have given her that life."

"No."

"Yes. It was your determination, your arrogant insistence, that compelled me to do as you asked. Admit now, it is to you she turns in gratitude, is it not?"

Peter Lord said slowly, "Yes, she's very grateful—now. She asked me to go and see her—often."

"Yes, she needs you."

Peter Lord said violently, "Not as she needs—him!"

Hercule Poirot shook his head. "She never *needed* Roderick Welman. She loved him, yes, unhappily—even desperately."

Peter Lord, his face set and grim, said harshly, "She will never love me like that."

Hercule Poirot said softly, "Perhaps not. But she needs you, my friend, because it is only with you that she can begin the world again."

Peter Lord said nothing.

Hercule Poirot's voice was very gentle as he said, "Can you not accept *facts*? She loved Roderick Welman. What of it? With you, *she can be happy*."

Towards Zero

To Robert Graves

Dear Robert,

Since you are kind enough to say you like my stories, I venture to dedicate this book to you. All I ask is that you should sternly restrain your critical faculties (doubtless sharpened by your recent excesses in that line!) when reading it.

This is a story for your pleasure and *not* a candidate for Mr. Graves's literary pillory!

Your friend,
AGATHA CHRISTIE

CONTENTS

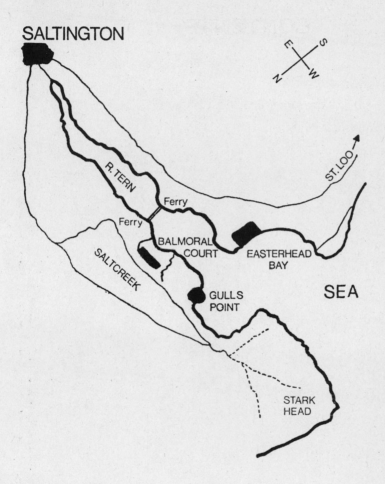

SALTINGTON

R. TERN

Ferry

Ferry

SALTCREEK

BALMORAL
COURT

EASTERHEAD
BAY

GULLS
POINT

SEA

STARK
HEAD

ST. LOO

Prologue: November 19th

THE GROUP ROUND the fireplace was nearly all composed of lawyers or those who had an interest in the law. There was Martindale the solicitor, Rufus Lord, KC, young Daniels who had made a name for himself in the Carstairs case, a sprinkling of other barristers, Mr. Justice Cleaver, Lewis of Lewis and Trench and old Mr. Treves. Mr. Treves was close on eighty, a very ripe and experienced eighty. He was a member of a famous firm of solicitors, and the most famous member of that firm, he was said to know more of backstairs history than any man in England and he was a specialist on criminology.

Unthinking people said Mr. Treves ought to write his memoirs. Mr. Treves knew better. He knew that he knew too much.

Though he had long retired from active practice, there was no man in England whose opinion was so respected by the members of his own fraternity. Whenever his thin precise little voice was raised there was always a respectful silence.

The conversation now was on the subject of a much talked of case which had finished that day at the Old Bailey. It was a murder case and the prisoner had been acquitted. The present company was busy trying the case over again and making technical criticisms.

The prosecution had made a mistake in relying on one of its witnesses— old Depleach ought to have realized what an opening he was giving to the defence. Young Arthur had made the most of that servant girl's evidence. Bentmore, in his summing up, had very rightly put the matter in its correct perspective, but the mischief was done by then—the jury had believed the girl. Juries were funny—you never knew what they'd swallow and what they wouldn't. But let them once get a thing into their heads and no one was ever going to get it out again. They believed that the girl was speaking the truth about the crowbar and that was that. The medical evidence had been a bit above their heads. All those long terms and scientific jargon—damned bad witnesses, those scientific johnnies— always hemmed and hawed and couldn't say yes or no to a plain question— always "in certain circumstances that might take place"—and so on!

They talked themselves out, little by little, and as the remarks became more spasmodic and disjointed, a general feeling grew of something lacking. One head after another turned in the direction of Mr. Treves. For Mr. Treves had as yet contributed nothing to the discussion. Gradually it became apparent that the company was waiting for a final word from its most respected colleague.

Mr. Treves, leaning back in his chair, was absent-mindedly polishing his glasses. Something in the silence made him look up sharply.

"Eh?" he said. "What was that? You asked me something?"

Young Lewis spoke.

"We were talking, sir, about the Lamorne case."

He paused expectantly.

"Yes, yes," said Mr. Treves. "I was thinking of that."

There was a respectful hush.

"But I'm afraid," said Mr. Treves, still polishing, "that I was being fanciful. Yes, fanciful. Result of getting on in years, I suppose. At my age one can claim the privilege of being fanciful, if one likes."

"Yes, indeed, sir," said young Lewis, but he looked puzzled.

"I was thinking," said Mr. Treves, "not so much of the various points of law raised—though they were interesting—very interesting—if the verdict had gone the other way there would have been good grounds for appeal. I rather think—but I won't go into that now. I was thinking, as I say, not of the points of law but of the—well, of the *people* in the case."

Everybody looked rather astonished. They had considered the people in the case only as regarding their credibility or otherwise as witnesses. No one had even hazarded a speculation as to whether the prisoner had been guilty or as innocent as the court had pronounced him to be.

"Human beings, you know," said Mr. Treves thoughtfully. "Human beings. All kinds and sorts and sizes and shapes of 'em. Some with brains and a good many more without. They'd come from all over the place, Lancashire, Scotland—that restaurant proprietor from Italy and that school teacher woman from somewhere out Middle West. All caught up and enmeshed in the thing and finally all brought together in a court of law in London on a grey November day. Each one contributing his little part. The whole thing culminating in a trial for murder."

He paused and gently beat a delicate tattoo on his knee.

"I like a good detective story," he said. "But, you know, they begin in the wrong place! They begin with the murder. But the murder is the *end*. The story begins long before that—years before sometimes—with all the causes and events that bring certain people to a certain place at a certain time on a certain day. Take that little maid servant's evidence— if the kitchenmaid hadn't pinched her young man she wouldn't have thrown up her situation in a huff and gone to the Lamornes and been the principal witness for the defence. That Guiseppe Antonelli—coming over to exchange with his brother for a month. The brother is as blind as a bat. He wouldn't have seen what Guiseppe's sharp eyes saw. If the constable hadn't been sweet on the cook at No. 48, *he* wouldn't have been late on his beat . . ."

He nodded his head gently:

"All converging towards a given spot . . . And then, when the time comes—over the top! *Zero Hour.* Yes, all of them converging towards zero . . ."

He repeated: "Towards zero . . ."

Then gave a quick little shudder.

"You're cold, sir, come nearer the fire."

"No, no," said Mr. Treves. "Just someone walking over my grave, as they say. Well, well, I must be making my way homewards."

He gave an affable little nod and went slowly and precisely out of the room.

There was a moment of dubious silence and then Rufus Lord, KC, remarked that poor old Treves was getting on.

Sir William Cleaver said:

"An acute brain—a very acute brain—but Anno Domini tells in the end."

"Got a groggy heart, too," said Lord. "May drop down any minute, I believe."

"He takes pretty good care of himself," said young Lewis.

At that moment Mr. Treves was carefully stepping into his smooth-running Daimler. It deposited him at a house in a quiet square. A solicitous butler valet helped him off with his coat. Mr. Treves walked into his library where a coal fire was burning. His bedroom lay beyond, for out of consideration for his heart he never went upstairs.

He sat down in front of the fire and drew his letters towards.

His mind was still dwelling on the fancy he had outlined at the Club.

"Even now," thought Mr. Treves to himself, "some drama—some murder to be—is in course of preparation. If I were writing one of these amusing stories of blood and crime, I should begin now with an elderly gentleman sitting in front of the fire opening his letters—going, unbeknownst to himself—towards zero . . ."

He slit open an envelope and gazed down absently at the sheet he abstracted from it.

Suddenly his expression changed. He came back from romance to reality.

"Dear me," said Mr. Treves. "How extremly annoying! Really, how very vexing. After all these years! This will alter all my plans."

"Open the Door and Here are the People"

January 11th.

The man in the hospital bed shifted his body slightly and stifled a groan.

The nurse in charge of the ward got up from her table and came down to him. She shifted his pillows and moved him into a more comfortable position.

Angus MacWhirter only gave a grunt by way of thanks.

He was in a state of seething rebellion and bitterness.

By this time it ought to have been over. He ought to have been out of it all! Curse that damned ridiculous tree growing out of the cliff! Curse those officious sweethearts who braved the cold of a winter's night to keep a tryst on the cliff edge.

But for them (and the tree!) it would have been over—a plunge into the deep icy water, a brief struggle perhaps, and then oblivion—the end of a misused, useless, unprofitable life.

And now where was he? Lying ridiculously in a hospital bed with a broken shoulder and with the prospect of being hauled up in a police court for the crime of trying to take his own life.

Curse it, it was his *own* life, wasn't it?

And if he had succeeded in the job, they would have buried him piously as of unsound mind!

Unsound mind, indeed! He'd never been saner! And to commit suicide was the most logical and sensible thing that could be done by a man in his position.

Completely down and out, with his health permanently affected, with a wife who had left him for another man. Without a job, without affection, without money, health or hope, surely to end it all was the only possible solution?

And now here he was in this ridiculous plight. He would shortly be admonished by a sanctimonious magistrate for doing the common-sense thing with a commodity which belonged to him and to him only—his life.

He snorted with anger. A wave of fever passed over him.

The nurse was beside him again.

She was young, red-haired, with a kindly, rather vacant face.

"Are you in much pain?"

"No, I'm not."

"I'll give you something to make you sleep."

"You'll do nothing of the sort."

"But—"

"Do you think I can't bear a bit of pain and sleeplessness?"

She smiled in a gentle, slightly superior way.

"Doctor said you could have something."

"I don't care what doctor said."

She straightened the covers and set a glass of lemonade a little nearer to him. He said, slightly ashamed of himself:

"Sorry if I was rude."

"Oh, that's all right."

It annoyed him that she was so completely undisturbed by his bad temper. Nothing like that could penetrate her nurse's armour of indulgent indifference. He was a patient—not a man.

He said:

"Damned interference—all this damned interference . . ."

She said reprovingly:

"Now, now, that isn't very nice."

"Nice?" he demanded. "*Nice*? My God."

She said calmly: "You'll feel better in the morning."

He swallowed.

"You nurses. You *nurses*! You're inhuman, that's what you are!"

"We know what's best for you, you see."

"That's what's so infuriating! About you. About a hospital. About the world. Continual interference! Knowing what's best for other people. I tried to kill myself. You know that, don't you?"

She nodded.

"Nobody's business but mine whether I threw myself off a bloody cliff or not. I'd finished with life. I was down and out!"

She made a little clicking noise with her tongue. It indicated abstract sympathy. He was a patient. She was soothing him by letting him blow off steam.

"Why shouldn't I kill myself if I want to?" he demanded.

She replied to that quite seriously.

"Because it's wrong."

"Why is it wrong?"

She looked at him doubtfully. She was not disturbed in her own belief, but she was much too inarticulate to explain her reaction.

"Well—I mean—it's wicked to kill yourself. You've got to go on living whether you like it or not."

"Why have you?"

"Well, there are other people to consider, aren't there?"

"Not in my case. There's not a soul in the world who'd be the worse for my passing on."

"Haven't you got any relations? No mother or sisters or anything?"

"No. I had a wife once but she left me—quite right too! She saw I was no good."

"But you've got friends, surely?"

"No, I haven't. I'm not a friendly sort of man. Look here, nurse, I'll tell you something. I was a happy sort of chap once. Had a good job and a good-looking wife. There was a car accident. My boss was driving the car and I was in it. He wanted me to say he was driving under thirty at the time of the accident. He wasn't. He was driving nearer fifty. Nobody was killed, nothing like that, he just wanted to be in the right for the insurance people. Well, I wouldn't say what he wanted. It was a lie. I don't tell lies."

The nurse said:

"Well, I think you were quite right. Quite right."

"You do, do you? That pigheadedness of mine cost me my job. My boss was sore. He saw to it that I didn't get another. My wife got fed up seeing me mooch about unable to get anything to do. She went off with a man who had been my friend. He was doing well and going up in the world. I drifted along, going steadily down. I took to drinking a bit. That didn't help me to hold down jobs. Finally I came down to hauling—strained my inside—the doctor told me I'd never be strong again. Well, there wasn't much to live for then. Easiest way, and the cleanest way, was to go right out. My life was no good to myself or anyone else."

The little nurse murmured:

"You don't know that."

He laughed. He was better tempered already. Her naïve obstinacy amused him.

"My dear girl, what use am I to anybody?"

She said confusedly:

"You don't know. You may be—someday—"

"Someday? There won't be any someday. Next time I shall make sure."

She shook her head decidedly.

"Oh, no," she said. "You won't kill yourself now."

"Why not?"

"They never do."

He stared at her. *"They never do."* He was one of a class of would-be suicides. Opening his mouth to protest energetically, his innate honesty suddenly stopped him.

Would he do it again? Did he really mean to do it?

He knew suddenly that he didn't. For no reason. Perhaps the right reason was the one she had given out of her specialized knowledge. Suicides didn't do it again.

All the more he felt determined to force an admission from her on the ethical side.

"At any rate I've got a right to do what I like with my own life."

"No—no, you haven't."

"But why not, my dear girl, why?"

She flushed. She said, her fingers playing with the little gold cross that hung round her neck:

"You don't understand. God may need you."

He stared—taken aback. He did not want to upset her childlike faith. He said mockingly:

"I suppose that one day I may stop a runaway horse and save a golden-haired child from death—eh? Is that it?"

She shook her head. She said with vehemence and trying to express what was so vivid in her mind and so halting on her tongue:

"It may be just by *being* somewhere—not doing anything—just by being at a certain place at a certain time—oh, I can't say what I mean, but you might just—just walk along a street some day and just by doing that accomplish something terribly important—perhaps even without knowing what it was."

The red-haired little nurse came from the west coast of Scotland and some of her family had "the sight."

Perhaps, dimly, she saw a picture of a man walking up a road on a night in September and thereby saving a human being from a terrible death . . .

February 14*th.*
There was only one person in the room and the only sound to be heard was the scratching of that person's pen as it traced line after line across the paper.

There was no one to read the words that were being traced. If there had been, they would hardly have believed their eyes. For what was being written was a clear, carefully detailed project for murder.

There are times when a body is conscious of a mind controlling it—when it bows obedient to that alien something that controls its actions. There are other times when a mind is conscious of owning and controlling a body and accomplishing its purpose by using that body.

The figure sitting writing was in the last-named state. It was a mind, a cool, controlled intelligence. This mind had only one thought and one purpose—the destruction of another human being. To the end that this purpose might be accomplished, the scheme was being worked out meticulously on paper. Every eventuality, every possibility was being taken into account. The thing had got to be absolutely foolproof. The scheme, like all good schemes, was not absolutely cut and dried. There were certain alternative actions at certain points. Moreover, since the mind was intelligent, it realized that there must be intelligent provision left for the unforeseen. But the main lines were clear and had been closely tested. The time, the place, the method, the victim! . . .

The figure raised its head. With its hand, it picked up the sheets of paper and read them carefully through. Yes, the thing was crystal clear.

Across the serious face a smile came. It was a smile that was not quite sane. The figure drew a deep breath.

As man was made in the image of his Maker, so there was now a terrible travesty of a creator's joy.

Yes, everything planned—everyone's reaction foretold and allowed for, the good and evil in everybody played upon and brought into harmony with one evil design.

There was one thing lacking still . . .

With a smile the writer traced a date—a date in September.

Then, with a laugh, the paper was torn in pieces and the pieces carried across the room and put into the heart of the glowing fire. There was no carelessness. Every single piece was consumed and destroyed. The plan was now only existent in the brain of its creator.

March 8*th.*
Superintendent Battle was sitting at the breakfast table. His jaw was set in a truculent fashion and he was reading, slowly and carefully, a letter that his wife had just tearfully handed to him. There was no expression visible on his face, for his face never did register any expression. It had the aspect of a face carved out of wood. It was solid and durable and,

in some way, impressive. Superintendent Battle had never suggested brilliance; he was, definitely, not a brilliant man, but he had some other quality, difficult to define, that was nevertheless forceful.

"I can't believe it," said Mrs. Battle, sobbing. "Sylvia!"

Sylvia was the youngest of Superintendent and Mrs. Battle's five children. She was sixteen and at school near Maidstone.

The letter was from Miss Amphrey, headmistress of the school in question. It was a clear, kindly and extremely tactful letter. It set out, in black and white, that various small thefts had been puzzling the school authorities for some time, that the matter had at last been cleared up, that Sylvia Battle had confessed, and that Miss Amphrey would like to see Mr. and Mrs. Battle at the earliest opportunity "to discuss the position."

Superintendent Battle folded up the letter, put it in his pocket, and said: "You leave this to me, Mary."

He got up, walked round the table, patted her on the cheek and said, "Don't worry, dear, it will be all right."

He went from the room, leaving comfort and reassurance behind him.

That afternoon, in Miss Amphrey's modern and individualistic drawing-room, Superintendent Battle sat very squarely on his chair, his large wooden hands on his knees, confronting Miss Amphrey and managing to look, far more than usual, every inch a policeman.

Miss Amphrey was a very successful headmistress. She had personality— a great deal of personality, she was enlightened and up to date, and she combined discipline with modern ideas of self-determination.

Her room was representative of the spirit of Meadway. Everything was of a cool oatmeal color—there were big jars of daffodils and bowls of tulips and hyacinths. One or two good copies of the antique Greek, two pieces of advanced modern sculpture, two Italian primitives on the walls. In the midst of all this, Miss Amphrey herself, dressed in a deep shade of blue, with an eager face suggestive of a conscientious greyhound, and clear blue eyes looking serious through thick lenses.

"The important thing," she was saying in her clear well-modulated voice, "is that this should be taken the right way. It is the girl herself we have to think of, Mr. Battle. Sylvia herself! It is most important—*most* important, that her life should not be crippled in any way. She must not be made to assume a burden of *guilt*—blame must be very very sparingly meted out, if at all. We must arrive at the reason *behind* these quite trivial pilferings. A sense of inferiority, perhaps? She is not good at games you know—an obscure wish to shine in a different sphere—the desire to assert her ego? We must be very very careful. That is why I wanted to see you alone first—impress upon you to be very very careful with Sylvia. I repeat again, it's very important to get at what is *behind* this."

"That, Miss Amphrey," said Superintendent Battle, "is why I have come down."

His voice was quiet, his face unemotional, his eyes surveyed the school mistress appraisingly.

"I have been very gentle with her," said Miss Amphrey.

Battle said laconically:

"Good of you, Ma'am."

"You see, I really love and understand these young things."

Battle did not reply directly. He said:

"I'd like to see my girl now, if you don't mind, Miss Amphrey."

With renewed emphasis Miss Amphrey admonished him to be careful—to go slow—not to antagonize a child just budding into womanhood.

Superintendent Battle showed no signs of impatience. He just looked blank.

She took him at last to her study. They passed one or two girls in the passages. They stood politely to attention but their eyes were full of curiosity. Having ushered Battle into a small room, not quite so redolent of personality as the one downstairs, Miss Amphrey withdrew and said she would send Sylvia to him.

Just as she was leaving the room, Battle stopped her.

"One minute, Ma'am, how did you come to pitch upon Sylvia as the one responsible for these—er—leakages?"

"My methods, Mr. Battle, were psychological."

Miss Amphrey spoke with dignity.

"Psychological? H'm. What about the evidence, Miss Amphrey?"

"Yes, yes, I quite understand, Mr. Battle—you would feel that way. Your—er—profession steps in. But psychology is beginning to be recognized in criminology. I can assure you that there is no mistake—Sylvia freely admits the whole thing."

Battle nodded.

"Yes, yes—I know that. I was just asking how you came to pitch upon her to begin with."

"Well, Mr. Battle, this business of things being taken out of the girls' lockers was on the increase. I called the school together and told them the facts. At the same time, I studied their faces unobtrusively. Sylvia's expression struck me at once. It was guilty—confused. I knew at that moment who was responsible. I wanted, not to *confront* her with her guilt, but to get her to admit it *herself*. I set a little test for her—a word association."

Battle nodded to show he understood.

"And finally the child admitted it all."

Her father said:

"I see."

Miss Amphrey hesitated a minute, then went out.

Battle was standing looking out of the window when the door opened again.

He turned round slowly and looked at his daughter.

Sylvia stood just inside the door, which she had closed behind her. She was tall, dark, angular. Her face was sullen and bore marks of tears. She said timidly rather than defiantly:

"Well, here I am."

Battle looked at her thoughtfully for a minute or two. He sighed.

"I should never have sent you to this place," he said. "That woman's a fool."

Sylvia lost sight of her own problems in sheer amazement.

"Miss Amphrey? Oh, but she's *wonderful*. We all think so."

"H'm," said Battle. "Can't be quite a fool, then, if she sells the idea of herself as well as that. All the same, Meadway wasn't the place for you—although I don't know—this might have happened anywhere."

Sylvia twisted her hands together. She looked down. She said:

"I'm—I'm sorry, Father. I really am."

"So you should be," said Battle shortly. "Come here."

She came slowly and unwillingly across the room to him. He took her chin in his great square hand and looked closely into her face.

"Been through a good deal, haven't you?" he said gently.

Tears started into her eyes.

Battle said slowly:

"You see, Sylvia, I've known all along with you, that there was *something*. Most people have got a weakness of some kind or another. Usually it's plain enough. You can see when a child's greedy, or bad tempered, or got a streak of the bully in him. You were a good child, very quiet—very sweet tempered—no trouble in any way—and sometimes I've worried. Because if there's a flaw you don't see, sometimes it wrecks the whole show when the article is tried out."

"Like me!" said Sylvia.

"Yes, like you. You've cracked under strain—and in a damned queer way too. It's a way, oddly enough, I've never come across before."

The girl said suddenly and scornfully:

"I should think you'd come across thieves often enough!"

"Oh yes—I know all about them. And that's why, my dear—not because I'm your father (fathers don't know much about their children) but because I'm a *policeman* I know well enough you're not a thief. *You* never took a thing in this place. Thieves are of two kinds, the kind that yields to sudden and overwhelming temptation—(and that happens damned seldom—it's amazing what temptation the ordinary normal honest human being can withstand) and there's the kind that just takes what doesn't belong to them almost as a matter of course. You don't belong to either type. You're not a thief. You're a very unusual type of liar."

Sylvia began, "But—"

He swept on.

"You've admitted it all? Oh yes, I know *that*. There was a saint once—went out with bread for the poor. Husband didn't like it. Met her and asked what there was in her basket. She lost her nerve and said it was roses—He tore open her basket and roses it was—a miracle! Now if you'd been Saint Elizabeth and were out with a basket of roses, and your husband had come along and asked what you'd got, you'd have lost your nerve and said 'Bread'."

He paused and then said gently:

"That's how it happened, isn't it?"

There was a longer pause and then the girl suddenly bent her head. Battle said:

"Tell me, child. What happened exactly?"

"She had us all up. Made a speech. And I saw her eyes on me and I knew she thought it was me! I felt myself getting red—and I saw some of the girls looking at me and whispering in corners. I could see they all thought so. And then the Amp had me up here with some of the others one evening and we played a sort of word game—she said words and we gave answers—"

Battle gave a disgusted grunt.

"And I could see what it meant—and—and I sort of got paralysed. I tried not to give the wrong word—I tried to think of things quite outside—like squirrels or flowers—and the Amp was there watching me with eyes like gimlets—you know, sort of boring inside one. And after that—oh, it got worse and worse, and one day the Amp talked to me quite kindly and so—so *understandingly*—and—and I broke down and said I *had* done it—and oh! Daddy, the relief!"

Battle was stroking his chin.

"I see."

"You do understand?"

"No, Sylvia, I don't understand, because I'm not made that way. If anyone tried to make me say I'd done something I hadn't I'd feel more like giving them a sock on the jaw. But I see how it came about in your case—and that gimlet-eyed Amp of yours has had as pretty an example of unusual psychology shoved under her nose as any half-baked exponent of misunderstood theories could ask for. The thing to do now is clear up this mess. Where's Miss Amphrey?"

Miss Amphrey was hovering tactfully near at hand. Her sympathetic smile froze on her face as Superintendent Battle said bluntly:

"In justice to my daughter, I must ask that you call in your local police over this."

"But, Mr. Battle, Sylvia herself—"

"Sylvia has never touched a thing that didn't belong to her in this place."

"I quite understand that, as a father—"

"I'm not talking as a father, but as a policeman. Get the police to give you a hand over this. They'll be discreet. You'll find the things hidden away somewhere and the right set of fingerprints on them, I expect. Petty pilferers don't think of wearing gloves. I'm taking my daughter away with me now. If the police find evidence—*real* evidence—to connect her with the thefts, I'm prepared for her to appear in court and take what's coming to her, but I'm not afraid."

As he drove out of the gate with Sylvia beside him some five minutes later, he asked:

"Who's a girl with fair hair, rather fuzzy, very pink cheeks and a spot on her chin, blue eyes far apart. I passed her in the passage."

"That sounds like Olive Parsons."

"Ah, well, I shouldn't be surprised if she were the one."

"Did she look frightened?"

"No, looked smug! Calm smug look I've seen in the police court hundreds of times! I'd bet good money she's the thief—but you won't find her confessing—not much!"

Sylvia said with a sigh:

"It's like coming out of a bad dream. Oh Daddy, I am sorry! Oh, I *am* sorry! How could I be such a fool, such an utter fool? I do feel awful about it."

"Ah, well," said Superintendent Battle, patting her on the arm with a hand he disengaged from the wheel, and uttering one of his pet forms of trite consolation. "Don't you worry. These things are sent to try us. Yes, these things are sent to try us. At least, I suppose so. I don't see what else they can be sent for . . ."

April 19*th*.

The sun was pouring down on Nevile Strange's house at Hindhead.

It was an April day such as usually occurs at least once in a month, hotter than most of the June days to follow.

Nevile Strange was coming down the stairs. He was dressed in white flannels and held four tennis racquets under his arm.

If a man could have been selected from amongst other Englishman as an example of a lucky man with nothing to wish for, a Selection Committee might have chosen Nevile Strange. He was a man well known to the British public, a first-class tennis player and all-round sportsman. Though he had never reached the finals at Wimbledon, he had lasted several of the opening rounds and in the mixed doubles had twice reached the semi-finals. He was, perhaps, too much of an all-round athlete to be a Champion tennis player. He was scratch at golf, a fine swimmer, and had done some good climbs in the Alps. He was thirty-three, had magnificent health, good looks, plenty of money, an extremely beautiful wife whom he had recently married and, to all appearances, no cares or worries.

Nevertheless as Nevile Strange went downstairs this fine morning a shadow went with him. A shadow perceptible, perhaps, to no eyes but his. But he was aware of it, the thought of it furrowed his brow and made his expression troubled and indecisive.

He crossed the hall, squared his shoulders as though definitely throwing off some burden, passed through the living-room and out on to a glass-enclosed veranda where his wife, Kay, was curled up amongst cushions drinking orange juice.

Kay Strange was twenty-three and unusually beautiful. She had a slender but subtly voluptuous figure, dark red hair, such a perfect skin that she used only the slightest make-up to enhance it, and those dark eyes and brows which so seldom go with red hair and which are so devastating when they do.

Her husband said lightly:

"Hullo, Gorgeous, what's for breakfast?"

Kay replied: "Horribly bloody looking kidneys for you—and mushrooms—and rolls of bacon."

"Sounds all right," said Nevile.

He helped himself to the aforementioned viands and poured out a cup of coffee. There was a companionable silence for some minutes.

"Oo," said Kay voluptuously, wriggling bare toes with scarlet manicured nails. "Isn't the sun lovely? England's not so bad after all."

They had just come back from the South of France.

Nevile, after a bare glance at the newspaper headlines, had turned to the Sports page and merely said "Um . . ."

Then, proceeding to toast and marmalade, he put the paper aside and opened his letters.

There were a good many of these, but most of them he tore across and chucked away. Circulars, advertisements, printed matter.

Kay said: "I don't like my color scheme in the living-room. Can I have it done over, Nevile?"

"Anything you like, beautiful."

"Peacock blue," said Kay dreamily, "and ivory satin cushions."

"You'll have to throw in an ape," said Nevile.

"You can be the ape," said Kay.

Nevile opened another letter.

"Oh, by the way," said Kay. "Shirty has asked us to go to Norway on the yacht at the end of June. Rather sickening we can't."

She looked cautiously sideways at Nevile and added wistfully: "I would love it so."

Something, some cloud, some uncertainty, seemed hovering on Nevile's face.

Kay said rebelliously:

"Have we got to go to dreary old Camilla's?"

Nevile frowned.

"Of course we have. Look here, Kay, we've had this out before. Sir Matthew was my guardian. He and Camilla looked after me. Gull's Point is my home, as far as any place is home to me."

"Oh all right, all right," said Kay. "If we must, we must. After all, we get all that money when she dies, so I suppose we have to suck up a bit."

Nevile said angrily:

"It's not a question of sucking up! She's no control over the money. Sir Matthew left it in trust for her during her lifetime and to come to me and my wife afterwards. It's a question of *affection*. Why can't you understand that?"

Kay said, after a moment's pause:

"I do understand really. I'm just putting on an act because—well because I know I'm only allowed there on sufferance as it were. They hate me! Yes, they do! Lady Tressilian looks down that long nose of hers at me and Mary Aldin looks over my shoulder when she talks to me. It's all very well for *you*. You don't see what goes on."

"They always seem to be very polite to you. You know quite well I wouldn't stand for it if they weren't."

Kay gave him a curious look from under her dark lashes.

"They're polite enough. But they know how to get under my skin all right. I'm the interloper, that's what they feel."

"Well," said Nevile, "after all, I suppose—that's natural enough, isn't it?"

His voice had changed slightly. He got up and stood looking out at the view with his back to Kay.

"Oh yes, I daresay, it's natural. They were devoted to Audrey, weren't they?" Her voice shook a little. "Dear, well-bred, cool, colorless Audrey! Camilla's not forgiven me for taking her place."

Nevile did not turn. His voice was lifeless, dull. He said: "After all, Camilla's old—past seventy. Her generation doesn't really like divorce, you know. On the whole I think she's accepted the position very well considering how fond she was of—of Audrey."

His voice changed just a little as he spoke her name.

"They think you treated her badly."

"So I did," said Nevile under his breath, but his wife heard.

"Oh Nevile—don't be so stupid. Just because she chose to make such a frightful fuss."

"She didn't make a fuss. Audrey never made fusses."

"Well, you know what I mean. Because she went away and was ill, and went about everywhere looking broken-hearted. That's what I call a fuss! Audrey's not what I call a good loser. From my point of view if a wife can't hold her husband she ought to give him up gracefully! You two had nothing in common. She never played a game and was as anaemic and washed up as—as a dish rag. No life or go in her! If she really cared about you, she ought to have thought about your happiness first and been glad you were going to be happy with someone more suited to you."

Nevile turned. A faintly sardonic smile played round his lips.

"What a little sportsman! How to play the game in love and matrimony!"

Kay laughed and reddened.

"Well, perhaps I was going a bit too far. But at any rate once the thing had happened, there it was. You've got to accept these things!"

Nevile said quietly:

"Audrey accepted it. She divorced me so that you and I could marry."

"Yes, I know—" Kay hesitated.

Nevile said: "You've never understood Audrey."

"No, I haven't. In a way, Audrey gives me the creeps. I don't know what it is about her. You never know what she's thinking . . . She's—she's a little frightening."

"Oh! nonsense, Kay."

"Well, she frightens *me*. Perhaps it's because she's got brains."

"My lovely nitwit!"

Kay laughed.

"You always call me that!"

"Because it's what you are!"

They smiled at each other. Nevile came over to her and, bending down, kissed the back of her neck.

"Lovely, lovely Kay," he murmured.

"Very good Kay," said Kay. "Giving up a lovely yachting trip to go and be snubbed by her husband's prim Victorian relations."

Nevile went back and sat down by the table.

"You know," he said, "I don't see why we shouldn't go on that trip with Shirty if you really want to so much."

Kay sat up in astonishment.

"And what about Saltcreek and Gull's Point?"

Nevile said in a rather unnatural voice:

"I don't see why we shouldn't go there early in September."

"Oh, but Nevile, surely—" She stopped.

"We can't go in July and August because of the Tournaments," said Nevile. "But we'd finish up at St. Loo the last week in August, and it would fit in very well if we went on to Saltcreek from there."

"Oh, it would fit in all right—beautifully. But I thought—well, *she* always goes there for September, doesn't she?"

"Audrey, you mean?"

"Yes. I suppose they could put her off, but—"

"Why should they put her off?"

Kay stared at him dubiously.

"You mean, we'd be there at the same time? What an extraordinary idea."

Nevile said irritably:

"I don't think it's at all an extraordinary idea. Lots of people do it nowadays. Why shouldn't we all be friends together? It makes things so much *simpler*. Why, you said so yourself only the other day."

"*I* did?"

"Yes, don't you remember? We were talking about the Howes, and you said it was the sensible civilized way to look at things, and that Leonard's new wife and his Ex were the best of friends."

"Oh, *I* wouldn't mind. I *do* think it's sensible. But—well, I don't think Audrey would feel like that about it."

"Nonsense."

"It isn't nonsense. You know, Nevile, Audrey really was terribly fond of you . . . I don't think she'd stand for it for a moment."

"You're quite wrong, Kay. Audrey thinks it would be quite a good thing."

"Audrey—what do you mean, Audrey thinks. How do you know what Audrey thinks?"

Nevile looked slightly embarrassed. He cleared his throat a little self-consciously.

"As a matter of fact, I happened to run into her yesterday when I was up in London."

"You never told me."

Nevile said irritably:

"I'm telling you now. It was absolute chance. I was walking across the Park and there she was coming towards me. You wouldn't want me to run away from her, would you?"

"No, of course not," said Kay, staring. "Go on."

"I—we—well, we stopped, of course, and then I turned round and walked with her. I—I felt it was the least I could do."

"Go on," said Kay.

"And then we sat down on a couple of chairs and talked. She was very nice—very nice indeed."

"Delightful for you," said Kay.

"And we got talking, you know, about one thing and another. She was quite natural and normal—and—and all that."

"Remarkable!" said Kay.

"And she asked how you were—"

"Very kind of her!"

"And we talked about you for a bit. Really, Kay, she couldn't have been nicer."

"Darling Audrey!"

"And then it sort of came to me—you know—how nice it would be if—if you two could be friends—if we could all get together. And it occurred to me that perhaps we might manage it at Gull's Point this summer. Sort of place it could happen quite naturally."

"*You* thought of that?"

"I—well—yes, of course. It was all my idea."

"You've never said anything to me about having any such idea."

"Well, I only happened to think of it just then."

"I see. Anyway, you suggested it and Audrey thought it was a marvelous brainwave?"

For the first time, something in Kay's manner seemed to penetrate to Nevile's consciousness.

He said:

"Is anything the matter, Gorgeous?"

"Oh no, nothing! Nothing at all! It didn't occur to you or Audrey whether *I* should think it a marvelous idea?"

Nevile stared at her.

"But, Kay, why on earth should *you* mind?"

Kay bit her lip.

Nevile went on:

"You said yourself only the other day—"

"Oh, don't go into all that again! I was talking about other people—not *us*."

"But that's partly what made me think of it."

"More fool me. Not that I believe that."

Nevile was looking at her with dismay.

"But, Kay, why should you mind? I mean, there's nothing for you to mind about!"

"Isn't there?"

"Well, I mean—any jealousy or that—would be on the other side." He paused, his voice changed. "You see, Kay, you and I treated Audrey damned badly. No, I don't mean that. It was nothing to do with you. I treated her very badly. It's no good just saying that I couldn't help myself. I feel that if this could come off I'd feel better about the whole thing. It would make me a lot happier."

Kay said slowly: "So you haven't been happy?"

"Darling idiot, what do you mean? Of course I've been happy, radiantly happy. But—"

Kay cut in.

"*But*—that's it! There's always been a '*but*' in this house. Some damned creeping shadow about the place. Audrey's shadow."

Nevile stared at her.

"You mean to say you're jealous of Audrey?" he asked.

"I'm not jealous of her. I'm afraid of her . . . Nevile, you don't know what Audrey's like."

"Not know what she's like when I've been married to her for over eight years?"

"You don't know," Kay repeated, "what Audrey is like."

April 30th.

"Preposterous!" said Lady Tressilian. She drew herself up on her pillow and glared fiercely round the room. "Absolutely preposterous! Nevile must be mad."

"It does seem rather odd," said Mary Aldin.

Lady Tressilian had a striking looking profile with a slender bridged nose down which, when so inclined, she could look with telling effect. Though now over seventy and in frail health her native vigor of mind was in no way impaired. She had, it is true, long periods of retreat from life and its emotions when she would lie with half-closed eyes, but from these semi-comas she would emerge with all her faculties sharpened to the uttermost, and with an incisive tongue. Propped up by pillows in a large bed set across one corner of her room, she held her court like some French Queen. Mary Aldin, a distant cousin, lived with her and looked after her. The two women got on together excellently. Mary was thirty-six, but had one of these smooth ageless faces that change little with passing years. She might have been thirty or forty-five. She had a good figure, an air of breeding, and dark hair to which one lock of white across the front gave a touch of individuality. It was at one time a fashion, but Mary's white lock of hair was natural and she had had it since her girlhood.

She looked down now reflectively at Nevile Strange's letter which Lady Tressilian had handed to her.

"Yes," she said. "It does seem rather odd."

"You can't tell me," said Lady Tressilian, "that this is Nevile's own idea! Somebody's put it into his head. Probably that new wife of his."

"Kay. You think it was Kay's idea?"

"It would be quite like her. New and vulgar! If husbands and wives *have* to advertise their difficulties in public and have recourse to divorce, then they might at least part decently. The new wife and the old wife making friends is quite disgusting in my mind. Nobody has any *standards* nowadays!"

"I suppose it is just the modern way," said Mary.

"It won't happen in my house," said Lady Tressilian. "I consider I've done all that could be asked of me having that scarlet-toed creature here at all."

"She is Nevile's wife."

"Exactly. Therefore I felt that Matthew would have wished it. He was devoted to the boy and always wanted him to look on this as his home. Since to refuse to receive his wife would have made an open breach, I gave way and asked her here. I do *not* like her—she's quite the wrong wife for Nevile—no background, no roots!"

"She's quite well born," said Mary placatingly.

"Bad stock!" said Lady Tressilian. "Her father, as I've told you, had to resign from all his clubs after that card business. Luckily he died shortly after. And her mother was notorious on the Riviera. What a bringing up for the girl. Nothing but Hotel life—and that mother! Then she meets Nevile on the tennis courts, makes a dead set at him and never rests until she gets him to leave his wife—of whom he was extremely fond—and go off with her! I blame her entirely for the whole thing!"

Mary smiled faintly. Lady Tressilian had the old-fashioned characteristic of always blaming the woman and being indulgent towards the man in the case.

"I suppose, strictly speaking, Nevile was equally to blame," she suggested.

"Nevile was very much to blame," agreed Lady Tressilian. "He had a charming wife who had always been devoted—perhaps too devoted—to him. Nevertheless, if it hadn't been for that girl's persistence, I am convinced he would have come to his senses. But she was determined to marry him! Yes, my sympathies are entirely with Audrey. I am very fond of Audrey."

Mary sighed. "It has all been very difficult," she said.

"Yes, indeed. One is at a loss to know how to act in such difficult circumstances. Matthew was fond of Audrey, and so am I, and one cannot deny that she was a very good wife to Nevile though perhaps it is a pity that she could not have shared his amusements more. She was never an athletic girl. The whole business was very distressing. When I was a girl these things simply did not happen. Men had their affairs, naturally, but they were never allowed to break up married life."

"Well, they happen now," said Mary bluntly.

"Exactly. You have so much common sense, dear. It is of no use recalling bygone days. These things happen, and girls like Kay Mortimer steal other women's husbands and nobody thinks the worse of them!"

"Except people like you, Camilla!"

"I don't count. That Kay creature doesn't worry whether I approve

of her or not. She's too busy having a good time. Nevile can bring her
here when he comes and I'm even willing to receive her friends—though
I do not much care for that very theatrical-looking young man who is
alway's hanging round her—what is his name?"

"Ted Latimer?"

"That is it. A friend of her Riviera days—and I should very much like
to know how he manages to live as he does."

"By his wits," suggested Mary.

"One might pardon that. I rather fancy he lives by his looks. *Not* a
pleasant friend for Nevile's wife! I disliked the way he came down last
summer and stayed at the Easterhead Bay Hotel while they were here."

Mary looked out of the open window. Lady Tressilian's house was
situated on a steep cliff overlooking the river Tern. On the other side
of the river was the newly created summer resort of Easterhead Bay,
consisting of a big sandy bathing beach, a cluster of modern bungalows
and a large Hotel on the headland looking out to sea. Saltcreek itself
was a straggling picturesque fishing village set on the side of a hill. It
was old-fashioned, conservative and deeply contemptuous of Easterhead
Bay and its summer visitors.

The Easterhead Bay Hotel was nearly exactly opposite Lady Tressilian's
house, and Mary looked across the narrow strip of water at it now where
it stood in its blatant newness.

"I am glad," said Lady Tressilian, closing her eyes, "that Matthew never
saw that vulgar building. The coastline was *quite* unspoilt in his time."

Sir Matthew and Lady Tressilian had come to Gull's Point thirty years
ago. It was nine years since Sir Matthew, an enthusiastic sailing man,
had capsized his dinghy and been drowned almost in front of his wife's
eyes.

Everybody had expected her to sell Gull's Point and leave Saltcreek,
but Lady Tressilian had not done so. She had lived on in the house, and
her only visible reaction had been to dispose of all the boats and do away
with the boathouse. There were no boats available for guests at Gull's
Point. They had to walk along to the ferry and hire a boat from one of
the river boatmen there.

Mary said, hesitating a little:

"Shall I write, then, to Nevile and tell him that what he proposes does
not fit in with our plans?"

"I certainly shall not dream of interfering with Audrey's visit. She has
always come to us in September and I shall not ask her to change her
plans."

Mary said, looking down at the letter:

"You did see that Nevile says Audrey—er—approves of the idea—that
she is quite willing to meet Kay?"

"I simply don't believe it," said Lady Tressilian. "Nevile, like all men,
believes what he wants to believe!"

Mary persisted:

"He says he has actually spoken to her about it."

"What a very odd thing to do! No—perhaps, after all, it isn't!"

Mary looked at her inquiringly.

"Like Henry the Eighth," said Lady Tressilian.

Mary looked puzzled.

Lady Tressilian elaborated her last remark.

"Conscience, you know! Henry was always trying to get Catherine to agree that the divorce was the right thing. Nevile knows that he has behaved badly—he wants to feel *comfortable* about it all. So he has been trying to bully Audrey into saying everything is all right and that she'll come and meet Kay and that she doesn't mind at all."

"I wonder," said Mary slowly.

Lady Tressilian looked at her sharply.

"What's in your mind, my dear?"

"I was wondering—" She stopped, then went on: "It—it seems so *unlike* Nevile—this letter! You don't think that, for some reason, Audrey *wants* this—this meeting?"

"Why should she?" said Lady Tressilian sharply. "After Nevile left her she went to her aunt, Mrs. Royde, at the Rectory, and had a complete breakdown. She was absolutely like a ghost of her former self. Obviously it hit her terribly hard. She's one of those quiet self-contained people who feel things intensely."

Mary moved uneasily.

"Yes, she is intense. A queer girl in many ways . . ."

"She suffered a lot . . . Then the divorce went through and Nevile married the girl, and little by little Audrey began to get over it. Now she's almost back to her old self. You can't tell me she wants to rake up old memories again?"

Mary said with gentle obstinacy: "Nevile says she does."

The old lady looked at her curiously.

"You're extraordinarily obstinate about this, Mary. Why? Do you *want* to have them here together?"

Mary Aldin flushed. "No, of course not."

Lady Tressilian said sharply:

"It's not *you* who have been suggesting all this to Nevile?"

"How can you be so absurd?"

"Well, I don't believe for a minute it's really his idea. It's not *like* Nevile." She paused a minute, then her face cleared. "It's the 1st of May tomorrow, isn't it? Well, on the 3rd Audrey is coming to stay with the Darlingtons at Esbank. It's only twenty miles away. Write and ask her to come over and lunch here."

May 5th.

"Mrs. Strange, m'lady."

Audrey Strange came into the big bedroom, crossed the room to the big bed, stooped down and kissed the old lady and sat down in the chair placed ready for her.

"Nice to see you, my dear," said Lady Tressilian.

"And nice to see you," said Audrey.

There was a quality of intangibility about Audrey Strange. She was of medium height with very small hands and feet. Her hair was ash blonde and there was very little color in her face. Her eyes were set wide apart and were a clear pale grey. Her features were small and regular, a straight little nose set in a small oval face. With such coloring, with a face that was pretty but not beautiful, she had nevertheless a quality about her that could not be denied nor ignored and that drew your eyes to her again and again. She was a little like a ghost, but you felt at the same time that a ghost might be possessed of more reality than a live human being . . .

She had a singularly lovely voice: soft and clear, like a small silver bell.

For some minutes she and the old lady talked of mutual friends and current events. Then Lady Tressilian said:

"Besides the pleasure of seeing you, my dear, I asked you to come because I've had rather a curious letter from Nevile."

Audrey looked up. Her eyes were wide, tranquil and calm. She said: "Oh yes?"

"He suggests—a preposterous suggestion, *I* call it!—that he and—and Kay should come here in September. He says he wants you and Kay to be friends and that you yourself think it a good idea?"

She waited. Presently Audrey said in her gentle placid voice:

"Is it—so preposterous?"

"My dear—do you really want this to happen?"

Audrey was silent again for a minute or two, then she said gently:

"I think, you know, it might be rather a good thing."

"You really want to meet this—you want to meet Kay?"

"I do think, Camilla, that it might—simplify things."

"Simplify things!" Lady Tressilian repeated the words helplessly.

Audrey spoke very softly.

"Dear Camilla. You have been so good. If Nevile wants this—"

"A fig for what Nevile wants!" said Lady Tressilian robustly. "Do *you* want it, that's the question?"

A little color came in Audrey's cheeks. It was the soft delicate glow of a sea shell.

"Yes," she said. "I do want it."

"Well," said Lady Tressilian. "Well—"

She stopped.

"But, of course," said Audrey. "It is entirely your choice. It is your house and—"

Lady Tressilian shut her eyes.

"I'm an old woman," she said. "Nothing makes sense any more."

"But of course—I'll come some other time. Any time will suit me."

"You'll come in September as you always do," snapped Lady Tressilian. "And Nevile and Kay shall come too. I may be old but I can adapt myself, I suppose, as well as anyone else to the changing phases of modern life. Not another word, that's settled."

She closed her eyes again. After a minute or two she said, peering through half-shut lids at the young woman sitting beside her:

"Well, got what you want?"

Audrey started.

"Oh, yes, yes. Thank you."

"My dear," said Lady Tressilian, and her voice was deep and concerned, "are you sure this isn't going to hurt you? You were very fond of Nevile, you know. This may reopen old wounds."

Audrey was looking down at her small gloved hands. One of them, Lady Tressilian noticed, was clenched on the side of the bed.

Audrey lifted her head. Her eyes were calm and untroubled.

She said:

"All that is quite over now. *Quite* over."

Lady Tressilian leaned more heavily back on her pillows. "Well, you should know. I'm tired—you must leave me now, dear. Mary is waiting for you downstairs. Tell them to send Barrett to me."

Barrett was Lady Tressilian's elderly and devoted maid.

She came in to find her mistress lying back with closed eyes.

"The sooner I'm out of this world the better, Barrett," said Lady Tressilian. "I don't understand anything or anyone in it."

"Ah! don't say that, my lady, you're tired."

"Yes, I'm tired. Take that eiderdown off my feet and give me a dose of my tonic."

"It's Mrs. Strange coming that's upset you. A nice lady, but *she* could do with a tonic, I'd say. Not healthy. Always looks as though she's seeing things other people don't see. But she's got a lot of character. She makes herself *felt,* as you might say."

"That's very true, Barrett," said Lady Tressilian. "Yes, that's very true."

"And she's not the kind you forget easily, either. I've often wondered if Mr. Nevile thinks about her sometimes. The new Mrs. Strange is very handsome—very handsome indeed—but Miss Audrey is the kind you remember when she isn't there."

Lady Tressilian said with a sudden chuckle:

"Nevile's a fool to want to bring those two women together. *He's* the one who'll be sorry for it!"

May 29th.

Thomas Royde, pipe in mouth, was surveying the progress of his packing with which the deft fingered Malayan No. 1 boy was busy. Occasionally his glance shifted to the view over the plantations. For some six months he would not see that view which had been so familiar for the past seven years.

It would be queer to be in England again.

Allen Drake, his partner, looked in.

"Hullo, Thomas, how goes it?"

"All set now."

"Come and have a drink, you lucky devil. I'm consumed with envy."

Thomas Royde moved slowly out of the bedroom and joined his friend. He did not speak, for Thomas Royde was a man singularly economical of words. His friends had learned to gauge his reactions correctly from the quality of his silences.

A rather thickset figure, with a straight solemn face and observant thoughtful eyes, he walked a little sideways, crab-like. This, the result of being jammed in a door during an earthquake, had contributed towards his nickname of the Hermit Crab. It had left his right arm and shoulder partially helpless which, added to an artificial stiffness of gait, often led people to think he was feeling shy and awkward when in reality he seldom felt anything of the kind.

Allen Drake mixed the drinks.

"Well," he said. "Good hunting!"

Royde said something that sounded like "Ah hum."

Drake looked at him curiously.

"Phlegmatic as ever," he remarked. "Don't know how you manage it. How long is it since you went home?"

"Seven years—nearer eight."

"It's a long time. Wonder you haven't gone completely native."

"Perhaps I have."

"You always did belong to Our Dumb Friends rather than to the human race! Planned out your leave?"

"Well—yes—partly."

The bronze impassive face took a sudden and a deeper brick red tinge.

Allen Drake said with lively astonishment:

"I believe there's a girl! Damn it all, you *are* blushing!"

Thomas Royde said rather huskily: "Don't be a fool!"

And he drew very hard on his ancient pipe.

He broke all previous records by continuing the conversation himself.

"Dare say," he said, "I shall find things a bit changed."

Allen Drake said curiously:

"I've always wondered why you chucked going home last time. Right at the last minute, too."

Royde shrugged his shoulders.

"Thought that shooting trip might be interesting. Bad news from home about then."

"Of course. I forgot. Your brother was killed—in that motoring accident."

Thomas Royde nodded.

Drake reflected that, all the same, it seemed a curious reason for putting off a journey home. There was a mother—he believed a sister also. Surely at such a time—then he remembered something. Thomas had cancelled his passage *before* the news of his brother's death arrived.

Allen looked at his friend curiously. Dark horse, old Thomas!

After a lapse of three years he could ask:

"You and your brother great pals?"

"Adrian and I? Not particularly. Each of us always went his own way. He was a barrister."

"Yes," thought Drake, "a very different life. Chambers in London, parties—a living earned by the shrewd use of the tongue." He reflected that Adrian Royde must have been a very different chap from old Silent Thomas.

"Your mother's alive, isn't she?"

"The mater? Yes."

"And you've got a sister, too."

Thomas shook his head.

"Oh, I thought you had. In that snapshot—"

Royde mumbled. "Not a sister. Sort of distant cousin or something. Brought up with us because she was an orphan."

Once more a slow tide of color suffused the bronzed skin.

Drake thought, "Hallo—o—?"

He said: "Is she married?"

"She was. Married that fellow Nevile Strange."

"Fellow who plays tennis and racquets and all that?"

"Yes. She divorced him."

"And you're going home to try your luck with her?" thought Drake. Mercifully he changed the subject of the conversation.

"Going to get any fishing or shooting?"

"Shall go home first. Then I thought of doing a bit of sailing down at Saltcreek."

"I know it. Attractive little place. Rather a decent old-fashioned Hotel there."

"Yes. The Balmoral Court. May stay there, or may put up with friends who've got a house there."

"Sounds all right to me."

"Ah hum. Nice peaceful place, Saltcreek. Nobody to hustle you."

"I know," said Drake. "The kind of place where nothing ever happens."

May 29th.

"It is really *most annoying*," said old Mr. Treves. "For twenty-five years now I have been to the Marine Hotel at Leahead—and now, would you believe it, the whole place is being pulled down. Widening the front or some nonsense of that kind. Why they can't let these seaside places alone—Leahead always had a peculiar charm of its own—Regency— pure Regency."

Rufus Lord said consolingly:

"Still, there are other places to stay there, I suppose?"

"I really don't feel I can go to Leahead at all. At the Marine, Mrs. Mackay understood my requirements perfectly. I had the same rooms every year—and there was hardly ever a change in the service. And the cooking was excellent—quite excellent."

"What about trying Saltcreek? There's rather a nice old-fashioned Hotel there. The Balmoral Court. Tell you who keeps it. Couple of the name of Rogers. She used to be cook to old Lord Mounthead—he had the best dinners in London. She married the butler and they run this hotel now. It sounds to me just your kind of place. Quiet—none of these jazz bands—and first-class cooking and service."

"It's an idea—it's certainly an idea. Is there a sheltered terrace?"

"Yes—a covered-in veranda and a terrace beyond. You can get sun or shade as you prefer. I can give you some introductions in the neighborhood, too, if you like. There's old Lady Tressilian—she lives almost next door. A charming house and she herself is a delightful woman in spite of being very much of an invalid."

"The judge's widow, do you mean?"

"That's it."

"I used to know Matthew Tressilian, and I think I've met her. A charming woman—though, of course, that's a long time ago. Saltcreek is near St. Loo, isn't it? I've several friends in that part of the world. Do you know, I really think Saltcreek is a very good idea. I shall write and get particulars. The middle of August is when I wish to go there—the middle of August to the middle of September. There is a garage for the car, I suppose? And my chauffeur?"

"Oh yes. It's thoroughly up-to-date."

"Because, as you know, I have to be careful about walking uphill. I should prefer rooms on the ground floor, though I suppose there is a lift."

"Oh yes, all that sort of thing."

"It sounds," said Mr. Treves, "as though it would solve my problem perfectly. And I should enjoy renewing my acquaintance with Lady Tressilian."

July 28th.

Kay Strange, dressed in shorts and a canary-colored woolly, was leaning forward watching the tennis players. It was the semi-final of the St. Loo tournament, men's singles, and Nevile was playing young Merrick, who was regarded as the coming star in the tennis firmament. His brilliance was undeniable—some of his serves quite unreturnable—but he occasionally struck a wild patch when the older man's experience and court craft won the day.

The score was Three All in the final set.

Slipping on to a seat next to Kay, Ted Latimer observed in a lazy ironic voice:

"Devoted wife watches her husband slash his way to victory!"

Kay started.

"How you startled me. I didn't know you were there."

"I am always there. You should know that by this time."

Ted Latimer was twenty-five and extremely good-looking—even though unsympathetic old colonels were wont to say of him:

"Touch of the Dago!"

He was dark and beautifully sunburnt and a wonderful dancer.

His dark eyes could be very eloquent, and he managed his voice with the assurance of an actor. Kay had known him since she was fifteen.

They had oiled and sunned themselves at Juan les Pins, had danced together and played tennis together. They had been not only friends but allies.

Young Merrick was serving from the left-hand court. Nevile's return was unplayable, a superb shot to the extreme corner.

"Nevile's backhand is good," said Ted. "It's better than his forehand. Merrick's weak on the backhand and Nevile knows it. He's going to pound at it all he knows how."

The game ended. *"Four three—Strange leads."*

He took the next game on his service. Young Merrick was hitting out wildly.

"Five three."

"Good for Nevile," said Latimer.

And then the boy pulled himself together. His play became cautious. He varied the pace of his shots.

"He's got a head on him," said Ted. "And his footwork is first class. It's going to be a fight."

Slowly the boy pulled up to five all. They went to seven all, and Merrick finally won the match at nine seven.

Nevile came up to the net, grinning and shaking his head ruefully, to shake hands.

"Youth tells," said Ted Latimer. "Nineteen against thirty-three. But I can tell you the reason, Kay, why Nevile has never been actual championship class. He's too good a loser."

"Nonsense."

"It isn't. Nevile, blast him, is always the complete good sportsman. I've never seen him lose his temper over losing a match."

"Of course not," said Kay. "People don't."

"Oh yes, they do! We've all seen them. Tennis stars who give way to nerves—and who damn' well snatch every advantage. But old Nevile— he's always ready to take the count and grin. Let the best man win and all that. God, how I hate the public school spirit! Thank the lord I never went to one."

Kay turned her head.

"Being rather spiteful, aren't you?"

"Positively feline!"

"I wish you wouldn't make it so clear you don't like Nevile."

"Why should I like him? He pinched my girl."

His eyes lingered on her.

"I wasn't your girl. Circumstances forbade."

"Quite so. Not even the proverbial tuppence a year between us."

"Shut up. I fell in love with Nevile and married him—"

"And he's a jolly good fellow—and so say all of us!"

"Are you trying to annoy me?"

She turned her head as she asked the question. He smiled—and presently she returned his smile.

"How's the summer going, Kay?"

"So, so. Lovely yachting trip. I'm rather tired of all this tennis business."

"How long have you got of it? Another month?"

"Yes. Then in September we go to Gull's Point for a fortnight."

"I shall be at the Easterhead Bay Hotel," said Ted. "I've booked my room."

"It's going to be a lovely party!" said Kay. "Nevile and I, and Nevile's Ex, and some Malayan planter who's home on leave."

"That does sound hilarious!"

"And the dowdy cousin, of course. Slaving away round that unpleasant old woman—and she won't get anything for it, either, since the money comes to me and Nevile."

"Perhaps," said Ted, "she doesn't know that?"

"That would be rather funny," said Kay.

But she spoke absently. She stared down at the racquet she was twiddling in her hands. She caught her breath suddenly.

"Oh Ted!"

"What's the matter, sugar?"

"I don't know. It's just sometimes I get—I get cold feet! I get scared and feel queer."

"That doesn't sound like you, Kay."

"It doesn't, does it? Anyway," she smiled rather uncertainly, "you'll be at the Easterhead Bay Hotel."

"All according to plan."

When Kay met Nevile outside the changing rooms, he said:

"I see the boy friend's arrived."

"Ted?"

"Yes, the faithful dog—or faithful lizard might be more apt."

"You don't like him, do you?"

"Oh, I don't mind him. If it amuses you to pull him around on a string—"

He shrugged his shoulders.

Kay said:

"I believe you're jealous."

"Of Latimer?" His surprise was genuine.

Kay said:

"Ted's supposed to be very attractive."

"I'm sure he is. He has that lithe South American charm."

"You *are* jealous."

Nevile gave her arm a friendly squeeze.

"No, I'm not, Gorgeous. You can have your tame adorers—a whole court of them if you like. I'm the man in possession, and possession is nine points of the law."

"You're very sure of yourself," said Kay, with a slight pout.

"Of course. You and I are Fate. Fate let us meet. Fate brought us together. Do you remember when we met at Cannes and I was going on to Estoril and suddenly, when I got there, the first person I met was lovely Kay! I knew then that it was Fate—and that I couldn't escape."

"It wasn't exactly Fate," Kay said. "It was me!"

"What do you mean by 'it was me'?"

"Because it was! You see, I heard you say at Cannes you were going to Estoril, so I set to work on Mums and got her all worked up—and that's why the first person you saw when you got there was Kay."

Nevile looked at her with a rather curious expression. He said slowly: "You never told me that before."

"No, because it wouldn't have been good for you. It might have made you conceited! But I always *have* been good at planning. Things don't happen unless you make them! You call me a nitwit sometimes—but in my own way I'm quite clever. I make things happen. Sometimes I have to plan a long way beforehand."

"The brainwork must be intense."

"It's all very well to laugh."

Nevile said with a sudden curious bitterness:

"Am I just beginning to understand the woman I've married? For Fate—read Kay!"

Kay said:

"You're not cross, are you, Nevile?"

He said rather absently:

"No—no, of course not. I was just—thinking . . ."

August 10*th.*

Lord Cornelly, that rich and eccentric peer, was sitting at the monumental desk which was his especial pride and pleasure. It had heen designed for him at immense expense and the whole furnishing of the room was subordinated to it. The effect was terrific and only slightly marred by the unavoidable addition of Lord Cornelly himself, an insignificant and rotund litle man completely dwarfed by the desk's magnificence.

Into this scene of City splendor there entered a blonde secretary, also in harmony with the luxury furnishings.

Gliding silently across the floor, she laid a slip of paper before the great man.

Lord Cornelly peered down at it.

"MacWhirter? MacWhirter? Who's he? Never heard of him. Has he got an appointment?"

The blonde secretary indicated that such was the case.

"MacWhirter, eh? Oh! *MacWhirter!*! That fellow! Of course! Send him in. Send him in at once."

Lord Cornelly chuckled gleefully. He was in high good-humor.

Throwing himself back in his chair, he stared up into the dour unsmiling face of the man he had summoned to an interview.

"You're MacWhirter, eh? Angus MacWhirter?"

"That's my name."

MacWhirter spoke stiffly, standing erect and unsmiling.

"You were with Herbert Clay? That's right, isn't it?"

"Yes."

Lord Cornelly began to chuckle again.

"I know all about you. Clay got his driving-licence endorsed, all because you wouldn't back him up and swear he was going at twenty miles an hour! Livid about it he was!" The chuckle increased. "Told us all about it in the Savoy Grill. 'That damned pig-headed Scot!' That's what he said! Went on and on. D'you know what *I* was thinking?"

"I've not the least idea."

MacWhirter's tone was repressive. Lord Cornelly took no notice. He was enjoying his remembrance of his own reactions.

"I thought to myself: 'That's the kind of chap I could do with! Man who can't be bribed to tell lies.' You won't have to tell lies for *me*. I don't do my business that way. I go about the world looking for honest men— and there are damned few of them!"

The little peer cackled with shrill laughter, his shrewd monkey-like face wrinkled with mirth. MacWhirter stood solidly, not amused.

Lord Cornelly stopped laughing. His face became shrewd, alert.

"If you want a job, MacWhirter, I've got one for you."

"I could do with a job," said MacWhirter.

"It's an important job. It's a job that can only be given to a man with good qualifications—you've got those all right—I've been into that—and to a man who can be trusted—absolutely."

Lord Cornelly waited. MacWhirter did not speak.

"Well, man, can I depend upon you absolutely?"

MacWhirter said drily:

"You'll not know that from hearing me answer that of course you can."

Lord Cornelly laughed.

"You'll do. You're the man I've been looking for. Do you know South America at all?"

He went into details. Half an hour later MacWhirter stood on the pavement, a man who had landed an interesting and extremely well-paid job—and a job that promised a future.

Fate, after having frowned, had chosen to smile upon him. But he was in no mood to smile back. There was no exultation in him, though his sense of humor was grimly tickled when he thought back over the interview. There was a stern poetic justice in the fact that it was his former employer's diatribes against him that had actually got him his present advancement!

He was a fortunate man, he supposed. Not that he cared! He was willing to address himself to the task of living, not with enthusiasm, not even with pleasure, but in a methodical day after day spirit. Seven months ago, he had attempted to take his own life; chance, and nothing but chance, had intervened, but he was not particularly grateful. True, he felt no present disposition to do away with himself. That phase was over for good. You could not, he admitted, take your life in cold blood. There had to be some extra fillip of despair, of grief, of desperation or of passion. You could not commit suicide merely because you felt that life was a dreary round of uninteresting happenings.

On the whole he was glad that his work would take him out of England. He was to sail for South America at the end of September. The next few weeks would be busy getting together certain equipment and being put in touch with the somewhat complicated ramifications of the business.

But there would be a week's leisure before he left the country. He wondered what he should do with that week? Stay in London? Go away?

An idea stirred nebulously in his brain.

Saltcreek?

"I've a damned good mind to go down there," said MacWhirter to himself.

It would be, he thought, grimly amusing.

August 19th.

"And bang goes my holiday," said Superintendent Battle disgustedly.

Mrs. Battle was disappointed, but long years as the wife of a police officer had prepared her to take disappointments philosophically.

"Oh well," she said, "it can't be helped. And I suppose it *is* an interesting case?"

"Not so that you'd notice it," said Superintendent Battle. "It's got the Foreign Office in a twitter—all those tall thin young men rushing about and saying Hush Hush here, there and everywhere. It'll straighten out easy enough—and we shall save everybody's face. But it's not the kind of case I'd put in my Memoirs, supposing I was ever foolish enough to write any."

"We could put our holiday off, I suppose—" began Mrs. Battle doubtfully, but her husband interrupted her decisively.

"Not a bit of it. You and the girls go off to Britlington—the rooms have been booked since March—pity to waste them. I tell you what I'll do—go down and spend a week with Jim when this blows over."

Jim was Superintendent Battle's nephew, Inspector James Leach.

"Saltington's quite close to Easterhead Bay and Saltcreek," he went on. "I can get a bit of sea air and a dip in the briny."

Mrs. Battle sniffed.

"More likely he'll rope you in to help him over a case!"

"They don't have any cases this time of the year unless it's a woman who pinches a few sixpennyworths from Woolworth's. And anyway Jim's all right—he does't need his wits sharpening for him."

"Oh well," said Mrs. Battle. "I suppose it will work out all right, but it is disappointing."

"These things are sent to try us," Superintendent Battle assured her.

Snow White and Red Rose

I

THOMAS ROYDE FOUND Mary Aldin waiting for him on the platform at Saltington when he got out of the train. He had only a dim recollection of her, and now that he saw her again he was rather surprisedly aware of pleasure in her brisk capable way of dealing with things.

She called him by his Christian name.

"How nice to see you, Thomas. After all these years."

"Nice of you to put me up. Hope it isn't a bother."

"Not at all. On the contrary. You'll be particularly welcome. Is that your porter? Tell him to bring the things out this way. I've got the car right at the end."

The bags were stowed in the Ford. Mary took the wheel and Royde got in beside her. They drove off and Thomas noticed that she was a good driver, deft and careful in traffic and with a nice judgment of distance and spaces.

Saltington was seven miles from Saltcreek. Once they were out of the small market town and on the open road, Mary Aldin reopened the subject of his visit.

"Really, Thomas, your visit just now is going to be a godsend. Things are rather difficult—and a stranger—or partial stranger is just what is needed."

"What's the trouble?"

His manner, as always, was incurious—almost lazy. He asked the question, it seemed, more from politeness than because he had any desire for the information. It was a manner particularly soothing to Mary Aldin. She wanted badly to talk to someone—but she much preferred to talk to someone who was not too much interested.

She said:

"Well—we've got rather a difficult situation. Audrey is here, as you probably know?"

She paused questioningly and Thomas Royde nodded.

"And Nevile and his wife also."

Thomas Royde's eyebrows went up. He said after a minute or two: "Bit awkward—what?"

"Yes it is. It was Nevile's idea."

She paused. Royde did not speak, but as though aware of some current of disbelief issuing from him, she repeated assertively: "It was Nevile's idea."

"Why?"

She raised her hands for a moment from the steering-wheel.

"Oh, some modern reaction! All sensible and friends together. That idea. But I don't think, you know, it's working very well."

"Possibly it mightn't." He added, "What's the new wife like?"

"Kay? Good-looking, of course. Really very good-looking. And quite young."

"And Nevile's keen on her?"

"Oh yes. Of course they've only been married a year."

Thomas Royde turned his head slowly to look at her. His mouth smiled a little. Mary said hastily:

"I didn't mean that exactly."

"Come now, Mary. I think you did."

"Well, one can't help seeing that they've really got very little in common. Their friends, for instance—" She came to a stop.

Royde asked:

"He met her, didn't he, on the Riviera? I don't know much about it. Only just the bare facts that the mater wrote."

"Yes they met first at Cannes. Nevile was attracted, but I should imagine he'd been attracted before—in a harmless sort of way. I still think myself that if he'd been left to himself nothing would have come of it. He *was* fond of Audrey, you know."

Thomas nodded.

Mary went on:

"I don't think he wanted to break up his marriage—I'm sure he didn't. But the girl was absolutely determined. She wouldn't rest until she'd got him to leave his wife—and what's a man to do in those circumstances? It flatters him, of course."

"Head over heels in love with him, was she?"

"I suppose it may have been that."

Mary's tone sounded doubtful. She met his inquiring glance with a flush.

"What a cat I am! There's a young man always hanging about—good-looking in a gigolo kind of way—an old friend of hers—and I can't help wondering sometimes whether the fact that Nevile is very well off and distinguished and all that didn't have something to do with it. The girl hadn't a penny of her own, I gather."

She paused, looking rather ashamed. Thomas Royde merely said: "Uh hum," in a speculative voice.

"However," said Mary, "that's probably plain cat! The girl is what one would call glamorous—and that probably rouses the feline instincts of middle-aged spinsters."

Royde looked thoughtfully at her, but his poker face showed no recognizable reaction. He said, after a minute or two:

"But what, exactly, is the present trouble about?"

"Really, you know, I haven't the least idea! That's what's so odd. Naturally we consulted Audrey first—and she seemed to have no feeling against meeting Kay—she was charming about it all. She *has* been charming. No one could have been nicer. Audrey, of course, in everything she does is always just right. Her manner to them both is perfect. She's very reserved, as you know, and one never has any idea of what she is really thinking or feeling—but honestly I don't believe she *minds at all.*"

"No reason why she should," said Thomas Royde. He added, rather belatedly, "After all, it's three years ago."

"Do people like Audrey forget? She was very fond of Nevile."

Thomas Royde shifted in his seat.

"She's only thirty-two. Got her life in front of her."

"Oh, I know. But she *did* take it hard. She had quite a bad nervous breakdown, you know."

"I know. The mater wrote me."

"In a way," said Mary, "I think it was good for your mother to have Audrey to look after. It took her mind off her own grief—about your brother's death. We were so sorry about that."

"Yes. Poor old Adrian. Always did drive too fast."

There was a pause. Mary stretched out her hand as a sign she was taking the turn that led down the hill to Saltcreek.

Presently, as they were slipping down the narrow twisting road, she said:

"Thomas—you know Audrey very well?"

"So so. Haven't seen much of her for the last ten years."

"No, but you knew her as a child. She was like a sister to you and Adrian?"

He nodded.

"Was she—was she at all unbalanced in any way? Oh I don't mean that quite the way it sounds. But I've a feeling that there is something very wrong with her now. She's so completely detached, her poise is so unnaturally perfect—but I wonder sometimes what is going on behind the façade. I've a feeling, now and then, of some really powerful emotion. And I don't quite know what it is! But I do feel that she isn't *normal.* There's *something*! It worries me. I do know that there's an atmosphere in the house that affects everybody. We're all nervous and jumpy. But I don't know what it is. And sometimes, Thomas, it frightens me."

"Frightens you?" His slow wondering tone made her pull herself together with a little nervous laugh.

"It sounds absurd . . . But that's what I meant just now—your arrival will be good for us—create a diversion. Ah, here we are."

They had slipped round the last corner. Gull's Point was built on a plateau of rock overlooking the river. On two sides it had sheer cliff going down to the water. The gardens and tennis court were on the left of the house. The garage—a modern after-thought—was actually farther along the road, on the other side of it.

Mary said:

"I'll put the car away now and come back. Hurstall will look after you."

Hurstall, the aged butler, was greeting Thomas with the pleasure of an old friend.

"Very glad to see you, Mr. Royde, after all these years. And so will her ladyship be. You're in the east room, sir. I think you'll find everyone in the garden, unless you want to go to your room first."

Thomas shook his head. He went through the drawing-room to the window which opened on to the terrace. He stood there a moment, watching, unobserved himself.

Two women were the only occupants of the terrace. One was sitting on the corner of the balustrade looking out over the water. The other woman was watching her.

The first was Audrey—the other, he knew, must be Kay Strange. Kay did not know she was being overlooked and she took no pains to disguise her expression. Thomas Royde was not, perhaps, a very observant man where women were concerned, but he could not fail to notice that Kay Strange disliked Audrey Strange very much.

As for Audrey, she was looking out across the river and seemed unconscious of, or indifferent to, the other's presence.

It was seven years since Thomas had seen Audrey Strange. He studied her now very carefully. Had she changed, and, if so, in what way?

There was a change, he decided. She was thinner, paler, altogether more ethereal-looking—but there was something else, something he could not quite define. It was as though she were holding herself tightly in leash, watchful over every movement—and yet all the time intensely aware of everything going on round her. She was like a person, he thought, who had a secret to hide. But what secret? He knew a little of the events that had befallen her in the last few years. He had been prepared for lines of sorrow and loss—but this was something else. She was like a child who, by a tightly clenched hand over a treasure—calls attention to what it wants to hide.

And then his eyes went to the other woman—the girl who was now Nevile Strange's wife. Beautiful, yes. Mary Aldin had been right. He rather fancied dangerous, too. He thought: I wouldn't like to trust her near Audrey if she had a knife in her hand . . .

And yet, why should she hate Nevile's first wife? All that was over and done with. Audrey had no part or parcel in their lives nowadays. Footsteps rang out on the terrace as Nevile came round the corner of the house. He looked warm and was carrying a picture paper.

"Here's the *Illustrated Review*," he said. "Couldn't get the other—"

Then two things happened at precisely the same minute.

Kay said: "Oh good, give it to me," and Audrey, without moving her head, held out her hand almost absent-mindedly.

Nevile had stopped half-way between the two women. A dawn of embarrassment showed in his face. Before he could speak, Kay said, her voice rising with a slight note of hysteria, "I want it. Give it me! Give it me, Nevile!"

Audrey Strange started, turned her head, withdrew her hand and murmured with just the slightest air of confusion:

"Oh sorry. I thought you were speaking to me, Nevile."

Thomas Royde saw the color come up brick-red in Nevile Strange's neck. He took three quick steps forward and held out the picture paper to Audrey.

She said, hesitating, her air of embarrassment growing.

"Oh, but—"

Kay pushed back her chair with a rough movement. She stood up, then, turning, she made for the drawing-room window. Royde had no time to move before she had charged into him blindly.

The shock made her recoil; she looked at him as he apologized. He saw then why she had not seen him, her eyes were brimming with tears— tears, he fancied, of anger.

"Hallo," she said. "Who are you? Oh! of course, the man from Malay!"

"Yes," said Thomas. "I'm the man from Malay."

"I wish to God I was in Malay," said Kay. "Anywhere but here! I loathe this beastly lousy house! I loathe everyone in it."

Emotional scenes always alarmed Thomas. He regarded Kay warily and murmured nervously:

"Ah—hum."

"Unless they're very careful," said Kay, "I shall kill someone! Either Nevile or that whey-faced cat out there!"

She brushed past him and went out of the room, banging the door.

Thomas Royde stood stock still. He was not quite sure what to do next, but he was glad that young Mrs. Strange had gone. He stood and looked at the door that she had slammed so vigorously. Something of a tiger cat, the new Mrs. Strange.

The window was darkened as Nevile Strange paused in the space between the french doors. He was breathing rather fast.

He greeted Thomas vaguely.

"Oh—er—hullo, Royde, didn't know you'd arrived. I say, have you seen my wife?"

"She passed through about a minute ago," said the other.

Nevile in his turn went out through the drawing-room door. He was looking annoyed.

Thomas Royde went slowly through the open window. He was not a heavy walker. Not until he was a couple of yards away did Audrey turn her head.

Then he saw those wide apart eyes open wider, saw her lips part. She slipped down from the wall and came towards him, hands outstretched.

"Oh Thomas," she said. "Dear Thomas! How glad I am you've come."

As he took the two small white hands in his and bent down to her, Mary Aldin in her turn arrived at the french windows. Seeing the two on the terrace she checked herself, watched them for a moment or two, then slowly turned away and went back into the house.

II

Upstairs Nevile had found Kay in her bedroom. The only large double bedroom in the house was Lady Tressilian's. A married couple was always given the two rooms with the communicating door and a small bathroom beyond on the west side of the house. It was a small isolated suite.

Nevile passed through his own room and on into his wife's. Kay had flung herself down on her bed. Raising a tear-stained face, she cried angrily:

"So you've come! About time, too!"

"What *is* all this fuss about? Have you gone quite crazy, Kay?"

Nevile spoke quietly, but there was a dent at the corner of his nostril that registered restrained anger.

"Why did you give that *Illustrated Review* to her and not to me?"

"Really, Kay, you are a child! All this fuss about a wretched little picture paper."

"You gave it to her and not to me," repeated Kay obstinately.

"Well, why not? What does it matter?"

"It matters to me."

"I don't know what's wrong with you. You can't behave in this hysterical fashion when you're staying in other people's houses. Don't you know how to behave in public?"

"Why did you give it to Audrey?"

"Because she wanted it."

"So did I, and I'm your wife."

"All the more reason, in that case, for giving it to an older woman and one who, technically, is no relation."

"She scored off me! She wanted to and she did. You were on her side!"

"You're talking like an idiotic jealous child. For goodness' sake, control yourself, and try to behave properly in public!"

"Like she does, I suppose?"

Nevile said coldly: "At any rate Audrey can behave like a lady. She doesn't make an exhibition of herself."

"She's turning you against me! She hates me and she's getting her revenge."

"Look here, Kay, will you stop being melodramatic and completely foolish? I'm fed up!"

"Then let's go away from here! Let's go tomorrow. I hate this place!"

"We've only been here four days."

"It's quite enough! Do let's go, Nevile."

"Now look here, Kay, I've had enough of this. We came here for a fortnight and I'm going to stay for a fortnight."

"If you do," said Kay, "you'll be sorry. You and your Audrey! You think she's wonderful!"

"I don't think Audrey is wonderful. I think she's an extremely nice and kindly person whom I've treated very badly and who has been most generous and forgiving."

"That's where you're wrong," said Kay. She got up from the bed. Her fury had died down. She spoke seriously—almost soberly.

"Audrey hasn't forgiven you, Nevile. Once or twice I've seen her looking at you . . . I don't know what is going on in her mind but something is— She's the kind that doesn't let anyone know what they're thinking."

"It's a pity," said Nevile, "that there aren't more people like that."

Kay's face went very white.

"Do you mean that for me?" There was a dangerous edge to her voice.

"Well—you haven't shown much reticence, have you? Every bit of ill temper and spite that comes into your mind you blurt straight out. You make a fool of yourself and you make a fool of me!"

"Anything more to say?"

Her voice was icy.

He said in an equally cold tone:

"I'm sorry if you think that was unfair. But it's the plain truth. You've no more self-control than a child."

"You never lose your temper, do you? Always the self-controlled charming-mannered little pukka sahib! I don't believe you've got any feelings. You're just a *fish*—a damned cold-blooded *fish*! Why don't you let yourself go now and then? Why don't you shout at me, swear at me, tell me to go to Hell?"

Nevile shrugged. His shoulders sagged.

"Oh lord," he said.

Turning on his heel he left the room.

III

"You look exactly as you did at seventeen, Thomas Royde," said Lady Tressilian. "Just the same owlish look. And no more conversation now than you had then. Why not?"

Thomas said vaguely,

"I dunno. Never had the gift of the gab."

"Not like Adrian. Adrian was a very clever and witty talker."

"Perhaps that's why. Always left the talking to him."

"Poor Adrian. So much promise."

Thomas nodded.

Lady Tressilian changed the subject. She was granting an audience to Thomas. She usually preferred her visitors one at a time. It did not tire her and she was able to concentrate her attention on them.

"You've been here twenty-four hours," she said. "What do you think of our Situation?"

"Situation?"

"Don't look stupid. You do that deliberately. You know quite well what I mean. The eternal triangle which has established itself under my roof."

Thomas said cautiously: "Seems a bit of friction."

Lady Tressilian smiled rather diabolically.

"I will confess to you, Thomas, I am rather enjoying myself. This came about through no wish of mine—indeed I did my utmost to prevent it. Nevile was obstinate. He would insist on bringing these two together— and now he is reaping what he has sown!"

Thomas Royde shifted a little in his chair.

"Seems funny," he said.

"Elucidate," snapped Lady Tressilian.

"Shouldn't have thought Strange was that kind of chap."

"It's interesting your saying that. Because it is what I felt. It was uncharacteristic of Nevile. Nevile, like most men, is usually anxious to avoid any kind of embarrassment or possible unpleasantness. I suspected that it wasn't originally Nevile's idea—but, if not, I don't see whose idea it can have been." She paused and said with only the slightest upward inflection, "It wouldn't be Audrey's?"

Thomas said promptly, "No, not Audrey."

"And I can hardly believe it was that unfortunate young woman, Kay's, idea. Not unless she is a really remarkable actress. You know, I have almost felt sorry for her lately."

"You don't like her much, do you?"

"No. She seems to me empty-headed and lacking in any kind of poise. But, as I say, I do begin to feel sorry for her. She is blundering about like a daddy-long-legs in lamp-light. She has no idea of what weapons to use. Bad temper, bad manners, childish rudeness—all things which have a most unfortunate effect upon a man like Nevile."

Thomas said quietly:

"I think Audrey is the one who is in a difficult position."

Lady Tressilian gave him a sharp glance.

"You've always been in love with Audrey, haven't you, Thomas?"

His reply was quite imperturbable. "Suppose I have."

"Practically from the time you were children together?"

He nodded.

"And then Nevile came along and carried her off from under your nose?"

He moved uneasily in his chair.

"Oh well—I always knew I hadn't a chance."

"Defeatist," said Lady Tressilian.

"I always have been a dull dog."

"Dobbin!"

"Good old Thomas!—that's what Audrey feels about me."

" 'True Thomas,' " said Lady Tressilian. "That was your nickname, wasn't it?"

He smiled as the words brought back memories of childish days. "Funny! I haven't heard that for years."

"It might stand you in good stead now," said Lady Tressilian.

She met his glance clearly and deliberately.

"Fidelity," she said, "is a quality that anyone who has been through Audrey's experience might appreciate. The dog-like devotion of a lifetime, Thomas, does sometimes get its reward."

Thomas Royde looked down, his fingers fumbling with a pipe.

"That," he said, "is what I came home hoping."

IV

"So here we all are," said Mary Aldin.

Hurstall, the old butler, wiped his forehead. When he went into the kitchen, Mrs. Spicer, the cook, remarked upon his expression.

"I don't think I can be well, and that's the truth," said Hurstall. "If I can so express myself, everything that's said and done in this house lately seems to me to mean something that's different from what it sounds like—if you know what I mean?"

Mrs. Spicer did not seem to know what he meant, so Hurstall went on:

"Miss Aldin, now, as they all sat down to dinner—she says *"So here we all are"*—and just that gave me a turn! Made me think of a trainer who's got a lot of wild animals into a cage, and then the cage door shuts. I felt, all of a sudden, as though we were all caught in a trap."

"Law, Mr. Hurstall," said Mrs. Spicer, "you must have eaten something that's disagreed."

"It's not my digestion. It's the way everyone's strung up. The front door banged just now and Mrs. Strange—our Mrs. Strange, Miss Audrey—she jumped as though she had been shot. And there's the silences, too. Very queer they are. It's as though, all of a sudden, everybody's afraid to speak. And then they all break out at once just saying the things that first come into their heads."

"Enough to make anyone embarrassed," said Mrs. Spicer.

"Two Mrs. Stranges in the house. What I feel is, it isn't *decent.*"

In the dining-room, one of those silences that Hurstall had described was proceeding.

It was with quite an effort that Mary Aldin turned to Kay and said:

"I asked your friend, Mr. Latimer, to dine tomorrow night!"

"Oh good," said Kay.

Nevile said:

"Latimer? Is he down here?"

"He's staying at the Easterhead Bay Hotel," said Kay.

Nevile said:

"We might go over and dine there one night. How late does the ferry go?"

"Until half-past one," said Mary.

"I suppose they dance there in the evenings?"

"Most of the people are about a hundred," said Kay.

"Not very amusing for your friend," said Nevile to Kay.

Mary said quickly:

"We might go over and bathe one day at Easterhead Bay. It's quite warm still and it's a lovely sandy beach."

Thomas Royde said in a low voice to Audrey:

"I thought of going out sailing tomorrow. Will you come?"

"I'd like to."

"We might all go sailing," said Nevile.

"I thought you said you were going to play golf," said Kay.

"I did think of going over to the links. I was right off my wooden shots the other day."

"What a tragedy!" said Kay.

Nevile said good-humoredly: "Golf's a tragic game."

Mary asked Kay if she played.

"Yes—after a fashion."

Nevile said:

"Kay would be very good if she took a little trouble. She's got a natural swing."

Kay said to Audrey:

"You don't play any games, do you?"

"Not really. I play tennis after a fashion—but I'm a complete rabbit."

"Do you still play the piano, Audrey?" asked Thomas.

She shook her head.

"Not nowadays."

"You used to play rather well," said Nevile.

"I thought you didn't like music, Nevile," said Kay.

"I don't know much about it," said Nevile vaguely. "I always wondered how Audrey managed to stretch an octave, her hands are so small."

He was looking at them as she laid down her dessert knife and fork.

She flushed a little and said quickly:

"I've got a very long little finger. I expect that helps."

"You must be selfish then," said Kay. "If you're unselfish you have a short little finger."

"Is that true?" asked Mary Aldin. "Then I must be unselfish. Look, my little fingers are quite short."

"I think you are very unselfish," said Thomas Royde, eyeing her thoughtfully.

She went red—and continued, quickly.

"Who's the most unselfish of us? Let's compare little fingers. Mine are shorter than yours, Kay. But Thomas, I think, beats me."

"I beat you both," said Nevile. "Look," he stretched out a hand.

"Only one hand, though," said Kay. "Your left hand little finger is short but your right hand one is much longer. And your left hand is what you are born with and the right hand is what you make of your life. So that means that you were born unselfish but have become more selfish as time goes on."

"Can you tell fortunes, Kay?" asked Mary Aldin. She stretched out her hand, palm upward. "A fortune-teller told me I should have two husbands and three children. I shall have to hurry up!"

Kay said:

"Those little crosses aren't children, they're journeys. That means you'll take three journeys across water."

"That seems unlikely too," said Mary Aldin.

Thomas Royde asked her: "Have you travelled much?"

"No, hardly at all."

He heard an undercurrent of regret in her voice.

"You would like to?"

"Above everything."

He thought in his slow reflective way of her life. Always in attendance on an old woman. Calm, tactful, an excellent manager. He asked curiously:

"Have you lived with Lady Tressilian long?"

"For nearly fifteen years. I came to be with her after my father died. He had been a helpless invalid for some years before his death."

And then, answering the question she felt to be in his mind:

"I'm thirty-six. That's what you wanted to know, wasn't it?"

"I did wonder," he admitted. "You might be—any age, you see."

"That's rather a two-edged remark!"

"I suppose it is. I didn't mean it that way."

That somber thoughtful gaze of his did not leave her face. She did not find it embarrassing. It was too free from self-consciousness for that—a genuine thoughtful interest. Seeing his eyes on her hair, she put up her hand to the one white lock.

"I've had that," she said, "since I was very young."

"I like it," said Thomas Royde simply.

He went on looking at her. She said at last, in a slightly amused tone of voice:

"Well, what is the verdict?"

He reddened under his tan.

"Oh, I suppose it is rude of me to stare. I was wondering about you— what you are really like."

"Please," she said hurriedly, and rose from the table. She said as she went into the drawing-room with her arm through Audrey's:

"Old Mr. Treves is coming to dinner tomorrow, too."

"Who's he?" asked Nevile.

"He brought an introduction from the Rufus Lords. A delightful old gentleman. He's staying at the Balmoral Court. He's got a weak heart and looks very frail, but his faculties are perfect and he has known a lot of interesting people. He was a solicitor or a barrister—I forget which."

"Everybody down here is terribly old," said Kay discontentedly.

She was standing just under a tall lamp. Thomas was looking that way, and he gave her that same slow interested attention that he gave to anything that was immediately occupying his line of vision.

He was struck suddenly with her intense and passionate beauty. A beauty of vivid coloring, of abundant and triumphant vitality. He looked across from her to Audrey, pale and moth-like in a silvery gray dress.

He smiled to himself and murmured:

"Red Rose and Snow White."

"What?" It was Mary Aldin at his elbow.

He repeated the words. "Like the old fairy story, you know—"

Mary Aldin said: "It's a very good description . . ."

V

Mr. Treves sipped his glass of port appreciatively. A very nice wine. And an excellently cooked and served dinner. Clearly Lady Tressilian had no difficulties with her servants.

The house was well managed, too, in spite of the mistress of it being an invalid.

A pity, perhaps, that the ladies did not leave the dining-room when the port went round. He preferred the old-fashioned routine. But these young people had their own ways.

His eyes rested thoughtfully on that brilliant and beautiful young woman who was the wife of Nevile Strange.

It was Kay's night tonight. Her vivid beauty glowed and shone in the candle-lit room. Beside her, Ted Latimer's sleek dark head bent to hers. He was playing up to her. She felt triumphant and sure of herself.

The mere sight of such radiant vitality warmed Mr. Treves' old bones.

Youth—there was really nothing like youth!

No wonder the husband had lost his head and left his first wife. Audrey was sitting next to him. A charming creature and a lady—but then that was the kind of woman who invariably did get left, in Mr. Treves' experience.

He glanced at her. Her head had been down and she was staring at her plate. Something in the complete immobility of her attitude struck Mr. Treves. He looked at her more keenly. He wondered what she was thinking about. Charming the way the hair sprang up from that small shell-like ear . . .

With a little start, Mr. Treves came to himself as he realized that a move was being made. He got hurriedly to his feet.

In the drawing-room, Kay Strange went straight to the gramophone and put on a record of dance music.

Mary Aldin said apologetically to Mr. Treves:

"I'm sure you hate jazz."

"Not at all," said Mr. Treves, untruly but politely.

"Later, perhaps, we might have some bridge?" she suggested. "But it is no good starting a rubber now, as I know Lady Tressilian is looking forward to having a chat with you."

"That will be delightful. Lady Tressilian never joins you down here?"

"No, she used to come down in an invalid chair. That is why we had the lift put in. But nowadays she prefers her own room. There she can talk to whomsoever she likes, summoning them by a kind of Royal Command."

"Very aptly put, Miss Aldin. I am always sensible of the Royal touch in Lady Tressilian's manner."

In the middle of the room Kay was moving in a slow dance step.

She said: "Just take that table out of the way, Nevile."

Her voice was autocratic, assured. Her eyes were shining, her lips parted.

Nevile obediently moved the table. Then he took a step towards her, but she turned deliberately towards Ted Latimer.

"Come on, Ted, let's dance."

Ted's arm went round her immediately. They danced, swaying, bending, their steps perfectly together. It was a lovely performance to watch.

Mr. Treves murmured:

"Er—quite professional."

Mary Aldin winced slightly at the word—yet surely Mr. Treves had spoken in simple admiration. She looked at his little wise nut-cracker face. It bore, she thought, an absent-minded look as though he were following some train of thought of his own.

Nevile stood hesitating a moment, then he walked to where Audrey was standing by the window.

"Dance, Audrey?"

His tone was formal, almost cold. Mere politeness, you might have said, inspired his request. Audrey Strange hesitated a minute before nodding her head and taking a step towards him.

Mary Aldin made some commonplace remarks to which Mr. Treves did not reply. He had so far shown no signs of deafness and his courtesy was punctilious—she realized that it was absorption that held him aloof. She could not quite make out if he was watching the dancers, or was staring across the room at Thomas Royde, standing alone at the other end.

With a little start Mr. Treves said:

"Excuse me, my dear lady, you were saying?"

"Nothing. Only that it was an unusually fine September."

"Yes, indeed—rain is badly needed locally, so they tell me at my hotel."

"You are comfortable there, I hope?"

"Oh yes, though I must say I was vexed when I arrived to find—" Mr. Treves broke off.

Audrey had disengaged herself from Nevile. She said with an apologetic little laugh:

"It's really too hot to dance."

She went towards the open window and out on to the terrace.

"Oh! go after her, you fool," murmured Mary. She meant the remark to be under her breath, but it was loud enough for Mr. Treves to turn and stare at her in astonishment.

She reddened and gave an embarrassed laugh.

"I'm speaking my thoughts aloud," she said ruefully. "But really he does irritate me. He's so *slow.*"

"Mr. Strange?"

"Oh no, not Nevile. Thomas Royde."

Thomas Royde was just preparing to move forward, but by now Nevile, after a moment's pause, had followed Audrey out of the window.

For a moment Mr. Treves' eye, interestedly speculative, rested on the window, then his attention returned to the dancers.

"A beautiful dancer, young Mr.—Latimer, did you say the name was?"

"Yes. Edward Latimer."

"Ah yes, Edward Latimer. An old friend, I gather, of Mrs. Strange?"

"Yes."

"And what does this very—er—decorative young gentleman do for a living?"

"Well, really, I don't quite know."

"In-deed," said Mr. Treves, managing to put a good deal of comprehension into one harmless word.

Mary went on:

"He is staying at the Easterhead Bay Hotel."

"A very pleasant situation," said Mr. Treves.

He added dreamily after a moment or two: "Rather an interesting shaped head—a curious angle from the crown to the neck—rendered less noticeable by the way he has his hair cut, but distinctly unusual." After another pause, he went on still more dreamily: "The last man I saw with a head like that got ten years' penal servitude for a brutal assault on an elderly jeweler."

"Surely," exclaimed Mary, "you don't mean—?"

"Not at all, not at all," said Mr. Treves. "You mistake me entirely. I am suggesting no disparagement of a guest of yours. I was merely pointing out that a hardened and brutal criminal can be in appearance a most charming and personable young man. Odd, but so it is."

He smiled gently at her. Mary said: "You know, Mr. Treves, I think I am a little frightened of you."

"Nonsense, dear lady."

"But I am. You are—such a very shrewd observer."

"My eyes," said Mr. Treves complacently, "are as good as ever they were." He paused and added: "Whether that is fortunate or unfortunate, I cannot at the moment decide."

"How could it be unfortunate?"

Mr. Treves shook his head doubtfully.

"One is sometimes placed in a position of responsibility. The right course of action is not always easy to determine."

Hurstall entered bearing the coffee tray.

After talking to Mary and the old lawyer, he went down the room to Thomas Royde. Then, by Mary's directions, he put the tray down on a low table and left the room.

Kay called over Ted's shoulder. "We'll finish out this tune."

Mary said: "I'll take Audrey's out to her."

She went to the french windows, cup in hand. Mr. Treves accompanied her. As she paused on the threshold he looked out over her shoulder.

Audrey was sitting on the corner of the balustrade. In the bright moonlight her beauty came to life—a beauty born of line rather than color. The exquisite line from the jaw to the ear, the tender modeling of chin and mouth, and the really lovely bones of the head and the small straight nose. That beauty would be there when Audrey Strange was an old woman—it had nothing to do with the covering flesh—it was the bones themselves that were beautiful. The sequined dress she wore accentuated the effect of the moonlight. She sat very still and Nevile Strange stood and looked at her.

Nevile took a step towards her.

"Audrey," he said, "you—"

She shifted her position, then sprang lightly to her feet and clapped a hand to her ear:

"Oh! my earring—I must have dropped it."

"Where? Let me look—"

They both bent down, awkward and embarrassed—and collided in doing so. Audrey sprang away, Nevile exclaimed:

"Wait a sec—my cuff button—it's caught in your hair. Stand still."

She stood quite still as he fumbled with the button.

"Oo—you're pulling it out by the roots—how clumsy you are, Nevile, do be quick."

"Sorry I—I seem to be all thumbs."

The moonlight was bright enough for the two onlookers to see what Audrey could not see, the trembling of Nevile's hands as he strove to free the strand of fair silvery hair.

But Audrey herself was trembling too—as though suddenly cold.

Mary Aldin jumped as a quiet voice said behind her:

"Excuse me—"

Thomas Royde passed between them and out.

"Shall I do that, Strange?" he asked.

Nevile straightened up and he and Audrey moved apart.

"It's all right. I've done it."

Nevile's face was rather white.

"You're cold," said Thomas to Audrey. "Come in and have coffee."

She came back with him and Nevile turned away staring out to sea.

"I was bringing it out to you," said Mary. "But perhaps you'd better come in."

"Yes," said Audrey, "I think I'd better come in."

They all went back into the drawing-room. Ted and Kay had stopped dancing.

The door opened and a tall gaunt woman dressed in black came in. She said respectfully:

"Her ladyship's compliments and she would be glad to see Mr. Treves up in her room."

VI

Lady Tressilian received Mr. Treves with evident pleasure.

He and she were soon deep in an agreeable flood of reminiscences and a recalling of mutual acquaintances.

At the end of half an hour Lady Tressilian gave a deep sigh of satisfaction.

"Ah," she said, "I've enjoyed myself! There's nothing like exchanging gossip and remembering old scandals."

"A little malice," agreed Mr. Treves, "adds a certain savor to life."

"By the way," said Lady Tressilian, "what do you think of our example of the eternal triangle?"

Mr. Treves looked discreetly blank. "Er—what triangle?"

"Don't tell me you haven't noticed it! Nevile and his wives."

"Oh that! The present Mrs. Strange is a singularly attractive young woman."

"So is Audrey," said Lady Tressilian.

Mr. Treves admitted: "She has charm—yes."

Lady Tressilian exclaimed:

"Do you mean to tell me you can understand a man leaving Audrey, who is a—a person of rare quality—for—for a *Kay?*"

Mr. Treves replied calmly:

"Perfectly. It happens frequently."

"Disgusting. I should soon grow tired of Kay if I were a man and wish I had never made such a fool of myself!"

"That also happens frequently. These sudden passionate infatuations," said Mr. Treves, looking very passionless and precise himself, "are seldom of long duration."

"And then what happens?" demanded Lady Tressilian.

"Usually," said Mr. Treves, "the—er—parties adjust themselves. Quite often there is a second divorce. The man then marries a third party— someone of a sympathetic nature."

"Nonsense! Nevile isn't a Mormon—whatever some of your clients may be!"

"The remarriage of the original parties occasionally takes place."

Lady Tressilian shook her head.

"That *no*! Audrey has too much pride."

"You think so?"

"I am sure of it. Do not shake your head in that aggravating fashion!"

"It has been my experience," said Mr. Treves, "that women possess little or no pride where love affairs are concerned. Pride is a quality often on their lips, but not apparently in their actions."

"You don't understand Audrey. She was violently in love with Nevile. Too much so, perhaps. After he left her for this girl (though I don't blame him entirely—the girl pursued him everywhere, and you know what men are!) she never wanted to see him again."

Mr. Treves coughed gently.

"And yet," he said, "she is here!"

"Oh well," said Lady Tressilian, annoyed. "I don't profess to understand these modern ideas. I imagine that Audrey is here just to show that she doesn't care, and that it doesn't matter!"

"Very likely," Mr. Treves stroked his jaw. "She can put it to herself that way, certainly."

"You mean," said Lady Tressilian, "that you think she is still hankering after Nevile and that—oh *no*! I won't believe such a thing!"

"It could be," said Mr. Treves.

"I won't have it," said Lady Tressilian. "I won't have it in my house."

"You are already disturbed, are you not?" asked Mr. Treves shrewdly. "There is tension. I have felt it in the atmosphere."

"So you feel it too?" said Lady Tressilian sharply.

"Yes, I am puzzled, I must confess. The true feelings of the parties remain obscure, but in my opinion, there is gunpowder about. The explosion may come any minute."

"Stop talking like Guy Fawkes and tell me what to do," said Lady Tressilian.

Mr. Treves held up his hands.

"Really, I am at a loss to know what to suggest. There is, I feel sure, a focal point. If we could isolate that—but there is so much that remains obscure."

"I have no intention of asking Audrey to leave," said Lady Tressilian. "As far as my observation goes, she has behaved perfectly in a very difficult situation. She has been courteous, but aloof. I consider her conduct irreproachable. '

"Oh quite," said Mr. Treves. "Quite. But it's having a most marked effect on young Nevile Strange all the same."

"Nevile," said Lady Tressilian, "is *not* behaving well. I shall speak to him about it. But I couldn't turn him out of the house for a moment. Matthew regarded him as practically his adopted son."

"I know."

Lady Tressilian sighed. She said in a lowered voice:

"You know that Matthew was drowned here?"

"Yes."

"So many people have been surprised at my remaining here. Stupid of them. I have always felt Matthew near to me here. The whole house is full of him. I should feel lonely and strange anywhere else." She paused, and went on, "I hoped at first that it might not be very long before I joined him. Especially when my health began to fail. But it seems I am one of these creaking gates—these perpetual invalids who never die." She thumped her pillow angrily.

"It doesn't please me, I can tell you! I always hoped that when my time came, it would come quickly—that I should meet Death face to face—not feel him creeping along behind me, always at my shoulder—gradually forcing me to sink to one indignity after another of illness. Increased helplessness—increasing dependence on other people!"

"But very devoted people, I am sure. You have a faithful maid?"

"Barrett? The one who brought you up. The comfort of my life! A grim old battleaxe, absolutely devoted. She's been with me for years."

"And you are lucky, I should say, in having Miss Aldin."

"You are right. I am lucky in having Mary."

"She is a relation?"

"A distant cousin. One of those selfless creatures whose lives are continually being sacrificed to those of other people. She looked after her father—a clever man—but terribly exacting. When he died I begged her to make her home with me, and I have blessed the day she came to me. You've no idea what horrors most companions are. Futile boring creatures. Driving one mad with their inanity. They are companions because they are fit for nothing better. To have Mary, who is a well-read intelligent woman, is marvellous. She has really a first-class brain—a man's brain. She has read widely and deeply and there is nothing she cannot discuss. And she is as clever domestically as she is intellectually. She runs the house perfectly and keeps the servants happy—she eliminates all quarrels and jealousies—I don't know how she does it—just tact, I suppose."

"She has been with you long?"

"Twelve years—no, more than that. Thirteen—fourteen—something like that. She has been a great comfort."

Mr. Treves nodded.

Lady Tressilian, watching him through half-closed lids, said suddenly: "What's the matter? You're worried about something?"

"A trifle," said Mr. Treves. "A mere trifle. Your eyes are sharp."

"I like studying people," said Lady Tressilian. "I always knew at once if there was anything on Matthew's mind." She sighed and leaned back on her pillows. "I must say good-night to you now"—it was a Queen's dismissal, nothing discourteous about it—"I am very tired. But it has been a great, great pleasure. Come and see me again soon."

"You may depend upon my taking advantage of those kind words. I only hope I have not talked too long."

"Oh no. I always tire very suddenly. Ring my bell for me, will you, before you go."

Mr. Treves pulled gingerly at a large old-fashioned bell-pull that ended in a huge tassel.

"Quite a survival," he remarked.

"My bell? Yes. No new-fangled electric bells for me. Half the time they're out of order and you go on pressing away! This thing never fails. It rings in Barrett's room upstairs—the bell hangs over her bed. So there's never any delay in answering it. If there is I pull it again pretty quickly."

As Mr. Treves went out of the room he heard the bell pulled a second time and heard the tinkle of it somewhere above his head. He looked up and noticed the wires that ran along the ceiling. Barrett came hurriedly down a flight of stairs and passed him, going to her mistress.

Mr. Treves went slowly downstairs, not troubling with the little lift on the downward journey. His face was drawn into a frown of uncertainty.

He found the whole party assembled in the drawing-room, and Mary Aldin at once suggested bridge, but Mr. Treves refused politely on the plea that he must very shortly be starting home.

"My Hotel," he said, "is old-fashioned. They do not expect anyone to be out after midnight."

"It's a long time from that—only half-past ten," said Nevile. "They don't lock you out, I hope?"

"Oh no. In fact I doubt if the door is locked at all at night. It is shut at nine o'clock but one has only to turn the handle and walk in. People seem very haphazard down here, but I suppose they are justified in trusting to the honesty of the local people."

"Certainly no one locks their door in the day-time here," said Mary. "Ours stands wide open all day long—but we do lock it up at night."

"What's the Balmoral Court like?" asked Ted Latimer. "It looks a queer high Victorian atrocity of a building."

"It lives up to its name," said Mr. Treves. "And has good solid Victorian comfort. Good beds, good cooking—roomy, Victorian wardrobes. Immense baths, with mahogany surrounds."

"Weren't you saying you were annoyed about something at first?" asked Mary.

"Ah yes. I had carefully reserved by letter two rooms on the ground floor. I have a weak heart, you know, and stairs are forbidden me. When I arrived I was vexed to find the rooms were not available. Instead I was allotted two rooms (very pleasant rooms, I must admit) on the top floor. I protested, but it seems that an old resident who had been going to Scotland this month was ill and had been unable to vacate the rooms."

"Mr. Lucan, I expect?" said Mary.

"I believe that is the name. Under the circumstances, I had to make the best of things. Fortunately there is a good automatic lift—so that I have really suffered no inconvenience."

Kay said: "Ted, why don't you come and stay at the Balmoral Court? You'd be much more accessible."

"Oh, I don't think it looks my kind of place."

"Quite right, Mr. Latimer," said Mr. Treves. "It would not be at all in your line of country."

For some reason or other Ted Latimer flushed.

"I don't know what you mean by that," he said.

Mary Aldin, sensing constraint, hurriedly made a remark about a newspaper sensation of the moment.

"I see they've detained a man in the Kentish Town trunk case—" she said.

"It's the second man they've detained," said Nevile. "I hope they've got the right one this time."

"They may not be able to hold him even if he is," said Mr. Treves.

"Insufficient evidence?" asked Royde.

"Yes."

"Still," said Kay, "I suppose they always get the evidence in the end."

"Not always, Mrs. Strange. You'd be surprised if you knew how many of the people who have committed crimes are walking about the country free and unmolested."

"Because they've never been found out, you mean?"

"Not only that. There is a man"—he mentioned a celebrated case of two years back—"the police know who committed those child murders—know it without a shadow of doubt—but they are powerless. That man has been given an alibi by two people, and though that alibi is false there is no proving it to be so. Therefore the murderer goes free."

"How dreadful," said Mary.

Thomas Royde knocked out his pipe and said in his quiet reflective voice:

"That confirms what I have always thought—that there are times when one is justified in taking the law into one's own hands."

"What do you mean, Mr. Royde?"

Thomas began to refill his pipe. He looked thoughtfully down at his hands as he spoke in jerky disconnected sentences.

"Suppose you knew—of a dirty piece of work—knew that the man who did it isn't accountable to existing laws—that he's immune from punishment. Then I hold—that one is justified in executing sentence oneself."

Mr. Treves said warmly:

"A most pernicious doctrine, Mr. Royde! Such an action would be quite unjustifiable!"

"Don't see it. I'm assuming, you know, that the *facts* are proved—it's just that the *law* is powerless!"

"Private action is still not to be excused."

Thomas smiled—a very gentle smile:

"I don't agree," he said. "If a man ought to have his neck wrung, I wouldn't mind taking the responsibility of wringing it for him!"

"And in turn would render yourself liable to the law's penalties!"

Still smiling, Thomas said: "I'd have to be careful, of course . . . In fact one would have to go in for a certain amount of low cunning . . ."

Audrey said in her clear voice:

"You'd be found out, Thomas."

"Matter of fact," said Thomas, "I don't think I should."

"I knew a case once," began Mr. Treves, and stopped. He said apologetically: "Criminology is rather a hobby of mine, you know."

"Please go on," said Kay.

"I have had a fairly wide experience of criminal cases," said Mr. Treves. "Only a few of them have held any real interest. Most murderers have been lamentably uninteresting and very short-sighted. However! I could tell you of one interesting example."

"Oh do," said Kay. "I like murders."

Mr. Treves spoke slowly, apparently choosing his words with great deliberation and care.

"The case concerned a child. I will not mention the child's age or sex. The facts were as follows: Two children were playing with bows and arrows. One child sent an arrow through the other child in a vital spot and death resulted. There was an inquest, the surviving child was completely distraught and the accident was commiserated and sympathy expressed for the unhappy author of the deed." He paused.

"Was that all?" asked Ted Latimer.

"That was all. A regrettable accident. But there is, you see, another side to the story. A farmer, some time previously, happened to have passed up a certain path in a wood nearby. There, in a little clearing, he had noticed a child practicing with a bow and arrow."

He paused—to let his meaning sink in.

"You mean," said Mary Aldin incredulously, "that it was *not* an accident—that it was intentional?"

"I don't know," said Mr. Treves. "I have never known. But it was stated at the inquest that the children were unused to bows and arrows and in consequence shot wildly and ignorantly."

"And that was not so?"

"That, in the case of *one* of the children, was certainly not so."

"What did the farmer do?" said Audrey breathlessly.

"He did nothing. Whether he acted rightly or not, I have never been sure. It was the future of a child that was at stake. A child, he felt, ought to be given the benefit of a doubt."

Audrey said:

"But you yourself have no doubt about what really happened?"

Mr. Treves said gravely:

"Personally, I am of the opinion that it was a particularly ingenious murder—a murder committed by a child and planned down to every detail beforehand."

Ted Latimer asked:

"Was there a reason?"

"Oh yes, there was a motive. Childish teasings, unkind words—enough to foment hatred. Children hate easily—"

Mary exclaimed: "But the deliberation of it."

Mr. Treves nodded.

"Yes, the deliberation of it was bad. A child, keeping that murderous intention in its heart, quietly practicing day after day and then the final piece of acting—the awkward shooting—the catastrophe, the pretence of grief and despair. It was all incredible—so incredible that probably it would not have been believed in court."

"What happened to—to the child?" asked Kay curiously.

"Its name was changed, I believe," said Mr. Treves. "After the publicity of the inquest that was deemed advisable. That child is a grown-up person today—somewhere in the world. The question is, has it still got a murderer's heart?"

He added thoughtfully:

"It was a long time ago, but I would recognize my little murderer anywhere."

"Surely not," objected Royde.

"Oh, yes, there was a certain physical peculiarity—well, I will not dwell on the subject. It is not a very pleasant one. I must really be on my way home."

He rose.

Mary said, "You will have a drink first?"

The drinks were on a table at the other end of the room. Thomas Royde, who was near them, stepped forward and took the stopper out of the whisky decanter.

"A whisky and soda, Mr. Treves? Latimer, what about you?"

Nevile said to Audrey in a low voice:

"It's a lovely evening. Come out for a little."

She had been standing by the window looking out at the moonlit terrace. He stepped past her and stood outside, waiting. She turned back into the room, shaking her head quickly.

"No, I'm tired. I—I think I'll go to bed."

She crossed the room and went out. Kay gave a wide yawn.

"I'm sleepy too. What about you, Mary?"

"Yes, I think so. Good-night, Mr. Treves. Look after Mr. Treves, Thomas."

"Good-night, Miss Aldin. Good-night, Mrs. Strange."

"We'll be over for lunch tomorrow, Ted," said Kay. "We could bathe if it's still like this."

"Right. I'll be looking for you. Good-night, Miss Aldin."

The two women left the room.

Ted Latimer said agreeably to Mr. Treves:

"I'm coming your way, sir. Down to the ferry, so I pass the Hotel."

"Thank you, Mr. Latimer. I shall be glad of your escort."

Mr. Treves, although he had declared his intention of departing, seemed in no hurry. He sipped his drink with pleasant deliberation and devoted himself to the task of extracting information from Thomas Royde as to the condition of life in Malaya.

Royde was monosyllabic in his answers. The everyday details of existence might have been secrets of National importance from the difficulty with which they were dragged from him. He seemed to be lost in some abstraction of his own, out of which he roused himself with difficulty to reply to his questioner.

Ted Latimer fidgeted. He looked bored, impatient, anxious to be gone. Suddenly interrupting, he exclaimed:

"I nearly forgot. I brought Kay over some gramophone records she wanted. They're in the hall. I'll get them. Will you tell her about them tomorrow, Royde?"

The other man nodded. Ted left the room.

"That young man has a restless nature," murmured Mr. Treves.

Royde grunted without replying.

"A friend, I think, of Mrs. Strange's?" pursued the old lawyer.

"Of Kay Strange's," said Thomas.

Mr. Treves smiled.

"Yes," he said. "I meant that. He would hardly be a friend of the first Mrs. Strange."

Royde said emphatically:

"No, he wouldn't."

Then, catching the other's quizzical eye, he said, flushing a little, "What I mean is—"

"Oh, I quite understand what you meant, Mr. Royde. You yourself are a friend of Mrs. Audrey Strange, are you not?"

Thomas Royde slowly filled his pipe from his tobacco pouch. His eyes bent to his task, he said or rather mumbled:

"M—yes. More or less brought up together."

"She must have been a very charming young girl?"

Thomas Royde said something that sounded like "Um—yum."

"A little awkward having two Mrs. Stranges in the house?"

"Oh yes—yes, rather."

"A difficult position for the original Mrs. Strange."

Thomas Royde's face flushed.

"Extremely difficult."

Mr. Treves leaned forward. His question popped out sharply:

"Why did she come, Mr. Royde?"

"Well—I suppose—" The other's voice was indistinct. "She—didn't like to refuse."

"To refuse whom?"

Royde shifted awkwardly.

"Well, as a matter of fact, I believe she always comes this time of year— beginning of September."

"And Lady Tressilian asked Nevile Strange and his new wife at the same time?" The old gentleman's voice held a nice note of polite incredulity.

"As to that, I believe Nevile asked himself."

"He was anxious, then, for this—reunion?"

Royde shifted uneasily. He replied, avoiding the other's eye:

"I suppose so."

"Curious," said Mr. Treves.

"Stupid sort of thing to do," said Thomas Royde, goaded into longer speech.

"Somewhat embarrassing one would have thought," said Mr. Treves.

"Oh, well—people do that sort of thing nowadays," said Thomas Royde vaguely.

"I wondered," said Mr. Treves, "if it had been anybody else's idea?"

Royde stared.

"Whose else's could it have been?"

Mr. Treves sighed.

"There are so many kind friends about in the world—always anxious to arrange other people's lives for them—to suggest courses of action that are not in harmony—" He broke off as Nevile Strange strolled back through the french windows. At the same moment Ted Latimer entered by the door from the hall.

"Hullo, Ted, what have you got there?" asked Nevile.

"Gramophone records for Kay. She asked me to bring them over."

"Oh did she? She didn't tell me." There was just a moment of constraint between the two, then Nevile strolled over to the drink tray and helped himself to a whisky and soda. His face looked excited and unhappy and he was breathing deeply.

Someone in Mr. Treves' hearing had referred to Nevile as "that lucky beggar Strange—got everything in the world he could wish for." Yet he did not look, at this moment, at all a happy man.

Thomas Royde with Nevile's re-entry, seemed to feel that his duties as host were over. He left the room without attempting to say good-night, and his walk was slightly more hurried than usual. It was almost an escape.

"A delightful evening," said Mr. Treves politely as he set down his glass. "Most—er—instructive."

"Instructive?" Nevile raised his eyebrows slightly.

"Information re the Malay States," suggested Ted, smiling broadly. "Hard work dragging answers out of Taciturn Thomas."

"Extraordinary fellow, Royde," said Nevile. "I believe he's always been the same. Just smokes that awful old pipe of his and listens and says Um and Ah occasionally and looks wise like an owl."

"Perhaps he thinks the more," said Mr. Treves. "And now I really must take my leave."

"Come and see Lady Tressilian again soon," said Nevile as he accompanied the two men to the hall. "You cheer her up enormously. She has so few contacts now with the outside world. She's wonderful, isn't she?"

"Yes, indeed. A most stimulating conversationalist."

Mr. Treves dressed himself carefully with overcoat and muffler, and after renewed good-nights he and Ted Latimer set out together.

The Balmoral Court was actually only about a hundred yards away, around one curve of the road. It loomed up prim and forbidding, the first outpost of the straggling country street.

The ferry, where Ted Latimer was bound, was two or three hundred yards farther down, at a point where the river was at its narrowest.

Mr. Treves stopped at the door of the Balmoral Court and held out his hand.

"Good-night, Mr. Latimer. You are staying down here much longer?"

Ted smiled with a flash of white teeth. "That depends, Mr. Treves. I haven't had time to be bored—yet."

"No—no, so I should imagine. I suppose like most young people nowadays, boredom is what you dread most in the world, and yet, I can assure you, there are worse things."

"Such as?"

Ted Latimer's voice was soft and pleasant, but it held an undercurrent of something else—something not quite so easy to define.

"Oh, I leave it to your imagination, Mr. Latimer. I would not presume to give you advice, you know. The advice of such elderly fogeys as myself is invariably treated with scorn. Rightly so, perhaps, who knows? But we old buffers like to think that experience has taught us something. We have noticed a good deal, you know, in the course of a lifetime."

A cloud had come over the face of the moon. The street was very dark. Out of the darkness a man's figure came towards them walking up the hill.

It was Thomas Royde.

"Just been down to the ferry for a bit of a walk," he said indistinctly because of the pipe clenched between his teeth.

"This your pub?" he asked Mr. Treves. "Looks as though you were locked out."

"Oh, I don't think so," said Mr. Treves.

He turned the big brass door knob and the door swung back.

"We'll see you safely in," said Royde.

The three of them entered the hall. It was dimly lit with only one electric light. There was no one to be seen, and an odor of bygone dinner, rather dusty velvet, and good furniture polish met their nostrils.

Suddenly Mr. Treves gave an exclamation of annoyance.

On the lift in front of them hung a notice:

LIFT OUT OF ORDER

"Dear me," said Mr. Treves. "How extremely vexing. I shall have to walk up all those stairs."

"Too bad," said Royde. "Isn't there a service lift—luggage—all that?"

"I'm afraid not. This one is used for all purposes. Well I must take it slowly, that is all. Good-night to you both."

He started slowly up the wide staircase. Royde and Latimer wished him good-night, then let themselves out into the dark street.

There was a moment's pause, then Royde said abruptly:

"Well, good-night."

"Good-night. See you tomorrow."

"Yes."

Ted Latimer strode lightly down the hill towards the ferry. Thomas Royde stood looking after him for a moment, then he walked slowly in the opposite direction towards Gull's Point.

The moon came out from behind the cloud and Saltcreek was once more bathed in silvery radiance.

VII

"Just like summer," murmured Mary Aldin.

She and Audrey were sitting on the beach just below the imposing edifice of the Easterhead Bay Hotel. Audrey wore a white swim suit and looked like a delicate ivory figure. Mary had not bathed. A little way along from them Kay lay on her face exposing her bronzed limbs and back to the sun.

"Ugh," she sat up. "The water's horribly cold," she said accusingly.

"Oh well, it *is* September," said Mary.

"It's always cold in England," said Kay discontentedly. "How I wish we were in the South of France. That really is hot."

Ted Latimer from beyond her murmured:

"The sun here isn't a real sun."

"Aren't you going in at all, Mr. Latimer?" asked Mary.

Kay laughed.

"Ted never goes in the water. Just suns himself like a lizard."

She stretched out a toe and prodded him. He sprang up.

"Come and walk, Kay, I'm cold."

They went off together along the beach.

"Like a lizard? Rather an unfortunate comparison," murmured Mary Aldin, looking after them.

"Is that what you think of him?" asked Audrey.

Mary Aldin frowned.

"Not quite. A lizard suggests something quite tame. I don't think he is tame."

"No," said Audrey thoughtfully. "I don't think so either."

"How well they look together," said Mary, watching the retreating pair. "They match somehow, don't they?"

"I suppose they do."

"They like the same things," went on Mary. "And have the same opinions—and use the same language. What a thousand pities it is that—"

She stopped.

Audrey said sharply:

"That what?"

Mary said slowly:

"I suppose I was going to say what a pity it was that Nevile and she ever met."

Audrey sat up stiffly. What Mary called to herself "Audrey's frozen look" had come over her face. Mary said quickly:

"I'm sorry, Audrey. I shouldn't have said that."

"I'd so much rather—not talk about it if you don't mind."

"Of course, of course. It was very stupid of me. I—I hoped you'd got over it, I suppose."

Audrey turned her head slowly. With a calm expressionless face she said:

"I assure you there is nothing to get over. I—I have no feeling of any kind in the matter. I hope—I hope with all my heart that Kay and Nevile will always be very happy together."

"Well, that's very nice of you, Audrey."

"It isn't nice. It is—just true. But I do think it is—well—unprofitable to keep on going back over the past. 'It's a pity this happened—that!' It's all over now. Why take it up? We've got to go on living our lives in the present."

"I suppose," said Mary simply, "that people like Kay and Ted are exciting to me because—well, they are so different from anything or anyone that I have ever come across."

"Yes, I suppose they are."

"Even you," said Mary with sudden bitterness, "have lived and had experiences that I shall probably never have. I know you've been unhappy—very unhappy—but I can't help feeling that even that is better than—well—nothing. Emptiness!"

She said the last word with a fierce emphasis.

Audrey's wide eyes looked a little startled.

"I never dreamt you ever felt like that."

"Didn't you?" Mary Aldin laughed apologetically. "Oh just a momentary fit of discontent, my dear. I didn't really mean it."

"It can't be very gay for you," said Audrey slowly. "Just living here with Camilla—dear thing though she is. Reading to her, managing the servants, never going away."

"I'm well fed and housed," said Mary. "Thousands of women aren't even that. And really, Audrey, I am quite contented. I have," a smile played for a moment round her lips, "my private distractions."

"Secret vices?" asked Audrey, smiling also.

"Oh, I plan things," said Mary vaguely. "In my mind, you know. And I like experimenting sometimes—upon people. Just seeing, you know, if I can make them react to what I say in the way I mean."

"You sound almost sadistic, Mary. How little I really know you!"

"Oh it's all quite harmless. Just a childish little amusement."

Audrey asked curiously:

"Have you experimented on me?"

"No. You're the only person I have always found quite incalculable. I never know, you see, what you are thinking."

"Perhaps," said Audrey gravely, "that is just as well."

She shivered and Mary exclaimed:

"You're cold."

"Yes. I think I will go and dress. After all, it is September."

Mary Aldin remained alone, staring at the reflection on the water.
The tide was going out. She stretched herself out on the sand, closing
her eyes.

They had had a good lunch at the Hotel. It was still quite full although
it was past the height of the season. A queer mixed looking lot of people.
Oh well, it had been a day out. Something to break the monotony of
day following day. It had been a relief, too, to get away from that sense
of tension, that strung-up atmosphere that there had been lately at Gull's
Point. It hadn't been Audrey's fault, but Nevile—

Her thoughts broke up abruptly as Ted Latimer plumped himself
down on the beach beside her.

"What have you done with Kay?" Mary asked.

Ted replied briefly:

"She's been claimed by her legal owner."

Something in his tone made Mary Aldin sit up. She glanced across
the stretch of shining golden sands to where Nevile and Kay were walking
by the water's edge. Then she glanced quickly at the man beside her.

She had thought of him as nerveless, as queer, as dangerous, even.
Now for the first time she got a glimpse of someone young and hurt.
She thought:

"He was in love with Kay—really in love with her—and then Nevile
came and took her away . . ."

She said gently:

"I hope you are enjoying yourself down here."

They were conventional words. Mary Aldin seldom used any words
but conventional ones—that was her language. But her tone was an
offer—for the first time—of friendliness. Ted Latimer responded to it.

"As much, probably, as I should enjoy myself anywhere."

Mary said:

"I'm sorry."

"But you don't care a damn, really! I'm an outsider—and what does
it matter what outsiders feel and think."

She turned her head to look at this bitter and handsome young man.
He returned her look with one of defiance.

She said slowly as one who makes a discovery:

"I see. You don't like us."

He laughed shortly.

"Did you expect me to?"

She said thoughtfully:

"I suppose, you know, that I did expect just that. One takes, of course,
too much for granted. One should be more humble. Yes, it would not
have occurred to me that you would not like us. We have tried to make
you welcome—as Kay's friend."

"Yes—as Kay's friend!"

The interruption came with a quick venom.

Mary said with disarming sincerity:

"I wish you would tell me—really I wish it—just why you dislike us? What have we done? What is wrong with us?"

Ted Latimer said, with a blistering emphasis on the one word: "Smug!"

"Smug?" Mary queried it without rancor, examining the charge with judicial appraisement.

"Yes," she admitted. "I see that we could seem like that."

"You are like that. You take all the good things of life for granted. You're happy and superior in your little roped-off enclosure shut off from the common herd. You look at people like me as though I were one of the animals outside!"

"I'm sorry," said Mary.

"It's true, isn't it?"

"No, not quite. We are stupid, perhaps, and unimaginative—but not malicious. I myself am conventional and, superficially, I dare say, what you call smug. But really, you know, I'm quite human inside. I'm very sorry, this minute, because you are unhappy, and I wish I could do something about it."

"Well—if that's so—it's nice of you."

There was a pause, then Mary said gently:

"Have you always been in love with Kay?"

"Pretty well."

"And she?"

"I thought so—until Strange came along."

Mary said gently:

"And you're still in love with her?"

"I should think that was obvious."

After a moment or two, Mary said quietly:

"Hadn't you better go away from here?"

"Why should I?"

"Because you are only letting yourself in for more unhappiness."

He looked at her and laughed.

"You're a nice creature," he said. "But you don't know much about the animals prowling about outside your litte enclosure. Quite a lot of things may happen in the near future."

"What sort of things?" said Mary sharply.

He laughed.

"Wait and see."

VIII

When Audrey had dressed she went along the beach and out along a jutting point of rocks, joining Thomas Royde, who was sitting there smoking a pipe exactly opposite to Gull's Point, which stood white and serene on the opposite side of the river.

Thomas turned his head at Audrey's approach, but he did not move. She sat down beside him without speaking. They were silent with the comfortable silence of two people who know each other very well indeed.

"How near it looks," said Audrey at last, breaking the silence.

Thomas looked across at Gull's Point.

"Yes, we could swim home."

"Not at this tide. There was a housemaid Camilla had once. She was an enthusiastic bather, used to swim across and back whenever the tide was right. It has to be low or high—but when it's running out it sweeps you right down to the mouth of the river. It did that to her one day— only luckily she kept her head and came ashore all right on Easter Point— only very exhausted."

"It doesn't say anything about its being dangerous here."

"It isn't this side. The current is the other side. It's deep there under the cliffs. There was a would-be suicide last year—threw himself off Stark Head—but he was caught by a tree half-way down the cliff and the coast-guards got to him all right."

"Poor devil," said Thomas. "I bet he didn't thank them. Must be sickening to have made up your mind to get out of it all and then be saved. Makes a fellow feel a fool."

"Perhaps he's glad now," suggested Audrey dreamily.

She wondered vaguely where the man was now and what he was doing.

Thomas puffed away at his pipe. By turning his head very slightly he could look at Audrey. He noted her grave absorbed face as she stared across the water. The long brown lashes that rested on the pure line of the cheek, the small shell-like ear.

That reminded him of something.

"Oh by the way, I've got your earring—the one you lost last night."

His fingers delved into his pocket. Audrey stretched out a hand.

"Oh good, where did you find it? On the terrace?"

"No. It was near the stairs. You must have lost it as you came down to dinner. I noticed you hadn't got it at dinner."

"I'm glad to have it back."

She took it. Thomas reflected that it was rather a large barbaric earring for so small an ear. The ones she had on today were large, too.

He remarked:

"You wear your earrings even when you bathe. Aren't you afraid of losing them?"

"Oh, these are very cheap things. I hate being without earrings because of this."

She touched her left ear. Thomas remembered.

"Oh yes, that time old Bouncer bit you."

Audrey nodded.

They were silent, re-living a childish memory. Audrey Standish (as she then was), a long spindle-legged child, putting her face down on old

Bouncer who had had a sore paw. A nasty bite, he had given her. She had had to have a stitch put in it. Not that there was much to show now—just the tiniest little scar.

"My dear girl," he said, "you can hardly see the mark. Why do you mind?"

Audrey paused before answering with evident sincerity:

"It's because—because I just can't bear a *blemish*."

Thomas nodded. It fitted in with his knowledge of Audrey—of her instinct for perfection. She was in herself so perfectly finished an article.

He said suddenly:

"You're far more beautiful than Kay."

She turned quickly.

"Oh no, Thomas. Kay—Kay is really lovely."

"On the outside. Not underneath."

"Are you referring," said Audrey with faint amusement, "to my beautiful soul?"

Thomas knocked out the ashes of his pipe.

"No," he said. "I think I mean your bones."

Audrey laughed.

Thomas packed a new pipeful of tobacco. They were silent for quite five minutes, but Thomas glanced at Audrey more than once though he did it so unobtrusively that she was unaware of it.

He said at last quietly:

"What's wrong, Audrey?"

"Wrong? What do you mean by wrong?"

"Wrong with you. There's something."

"No, there's nothing. Nothing at all."

"But there is."

She shook her head.

"Won't you tell me?"

"There's nothing to tell."

"I suppose I'm being a chump—but I've got to say it—" He paused. "Audrey—can't you forget about it? Can't you let it all go?"

She dug her small hands convulsively into the rock.

"You don't understand—you can't begin to understand."

"But Audrey, my dear, I do. That's just it. I *know*."

She turned a small doubtful face to him.

"I know exactly what you've been through. And—and what it must have meant to you."

She was very white now, white to the lips.

"I see," she said. "I didn't think—anyone knew."

"Well, I do. I—I'm not going to talk about it. But what I want to impress upon you is that it's all over—it's past and done with."

She said in a low voice:

"Some things don't pass."

"Look here, Audrey, it's no good brooding and remembering. Granted you've been through Hell. It does no good to go over and over a thing in your mind. Look foreward—not back. You're quite young. You've got your life to live and most of that is in front of you now. Think of tomorrow, not of yesterday."

She looked at him with a steady wide-eyed gaze that was singularly unrevealing of her real thoughts.

"And supposing," she said, "that I can't do that."

"But you must."

Audrey said gently:

"I thought you didn't understand. I'm—I'm not quite normal about—some things, I suppose."

He broke in roughly:

"Rubbish. You—" He stopped.

"I—what?"

"I was thinking of you as you were when you were a girl—before you married Nevile. Why did you marry Nevile?"

Audrey smiled.

"Because I fell in love with him."

"Yes, yes, I know that. But why did you fall in love with him? What attracted you to him so much?"

She crinkled her eyes as though trying to see through the eyes of a girl now dead.

"I think," she said, "it was because he was so 'positive.' He was always so much the opposite of what I was, myself. I always felt shadowy—not quite real. Nevile was very real. And so happy and sure of himself and so—everything that I was not." She added with a smile: "And very good-looking."

Thomas Royde said bitterly:

"Yes, the ideal Englishman—good at sport, modest, good-looking, always the little pukka sahib—getting everything he wanted all along the line."

Audrey sat very upright and stared at him.

"You hate him," she said slowly. "You hate him very much, don't you?"

He avoided her eyes, turning away to cup a match in his hands as he relit the pipe, that had gone out.

"Wouldn't be surprising if I did, would it?" he said indistinctly. "He's got everything that I haven't. He can play games, and swim and dance, and talk. And I'm a tongue-tied oaf with a crippled arm. He's always been brilliant and successful and I've always been a dull dog. And he married the only girl I ever cared for."

She made a faint sound. He said savagely:

"You've always known that, haven't you? You knew I cared about you ever since you were fifteen. You know that I still care—"

She stopped him.

"No. Not now."

"What do you mean—not now?"

Audrey got up. She said in a quiet reflective voice:

"Because—now—I am different."

"Different in what way?"

He got up too and stood facing her.

Audrey said in a quick rather breathless voice:

"If you don't know, I can't tell you . . . I'm not always sure myself. I only know—"

She broke off, and turning abruptly away she walked quickly back over the rocks towards the Hotel.

Turning a corner of the cliff she came across Nevile. He was lying full length peering into a rock pool. He looked up and grinned.

"Hullo, Audrey."

"Hullo, Nevile."

"I'm watching a crab. Awfully active little beggar. Look, there he is."

She knelt down and stared where he pointed.

"See him?"

"Yes."

"Have a cigarette?"

She accepted one and he lighted it for her. After a moment or two, during which she did not look at him, he said, nervously:

"I say, Audrey?"

"Yes?"

"It's all right, isn't it? I mean—between us."

"Yes. Yes, of course."

"I mean—we're friends and all that."

"Oh yes—yes, of course."

"I do want us to be friends."

He looked at her anxiously. She gave him a nervous smile.

He said conversationally:

"It's been a jolly day, hasn't it? Weather good and all that?"

"Oh yes—yes."

"Quite hot really for September."

There was a pause.

"Audrey—"

She got up.

"Your wife wants you. She's waving to you."

"Who—oh, Kay."

"I said your wife."

He scrambled to his feet and stood looking at her.

He said in a very low voice:

"You're my wife, Audrey . . ."

She turned away. Nevile ran down on to the beach and across the sand to join Kay.

IX

On their arrival back at Gull's Point, Hurstall came out into the hall and spoke to Mary.

"Would you go up at once to her ladyship, Miss? She is feeling very upset and wanted to see you as soon as you got in."

Mary hurried up the stairs. She found Lady Tressilian looking white and shaken.

"Dear Mary, I'm so glad you have come. I am feeling most distressed. Poor Mr. Treves is dead."

"Dead?"

"Yes, isn't it terrible? So sudden. Apparently he didn't even get undressed last night. He must have collapsed as soon as he got home."

"Oh dear, I am sorry."

"One knows, of course, that he was delicate. A weak heart. I hope nothing happened while he was here to overstrain it? There was nothing indigestible for dinner?"

"I don't think so—no, I am sure there wasn't. He seemed quite well and in good spirits."

"I am really very distressed. I wish, Mary, that you would go to the Balmoral Court and make a few inquiries of Mrs. Rogers. Ask her if there is anything we can do. And then the funeral. For Matthew's sake I would like to do anything we could. These things are so awkward at a Hotel."

Mary spoke firmly:

"Dear Camilla, you really must not worry. This has been a shock to you."

"Indeed it has."

"I will go to the Balmoral Court at once and then come back and tell you all about things."

"Thank you, Mary dear, you are always so practical and understanding."

"Please try and rest now. A shock of this kind is so bad for you."

Mary Aldin left the room and came downstairs. Entering the drawing-room she exclaimed: "Old Mr. Treves is dead. He died last night after returning home."

"Poor old boy," exclaimed Nevile. "What was it?"

"Heart apparently. He collapsed as soon as he got in."

Thomas Royde said thoughtfully: "I wonder if the stairs did him in."

"Stairs?" Mary looked at him inquiringly.

"Yes. When Latimer and I left him he was just starting up. We told him to take it slow."

Mary exclaimed:

"But how very foolish of him not to take the lift."

"The lift was out of order."

"Oh, I see. How very unfortunate. Poor old man."

She added: "I'm going round there now. Camilla wants to know if there is anything we can do."

Thomas said: "I'll come with you."

They walked together down the road and round the corner to the Balmoral Court. Mary remarked:

"I wonder if he has any relatives who ought to be notified?"

"He didn't mention anyone."

"No, and people usually do. They say 'my niece,' or 'my cousin.' "

"Was he married?"

"I believe not."

They entered the open door of the Balmoral Court.

Mrs. Rogers, the proprietress, was talking to a tall middle-aged man, who raised a friendly hand in greeting to Mary.

"Good-afternoon, Miss Aldin."

"Good-afternoon, Dr. Lazenby. This is Mr. Royde. We came round with a message from Lady Tressilian to know if there is anything we can do."

"That's very kind of you, Miss Aldin," said the Hotel proprietress. "Come into my room, won't you?"

They all went into the small comfortable sitting-room and Dr. Lazenby said:

"Mr. Treves was dining at your place last night, wasn't he?"

"Yes."

"How did he seem? Did he show any signs of distress?"

"No, he seemed very well and cheerful."

The doctor nodded.

"Yes, that's the worst of these heart cases. The end is nearly always sudden. I had a look at his prescriptions upstairs and it seems quite clear that he was in a very precarious state of health. I shall communicate with his London doctor, of course."

"He was very careful of himself always," said Mrs. Rogers. "And I'm sure he had every care here we could give him."

"I'm sure of that, Mrs. Rogers," said the doctor tactfully. "It was just some tiny additional strain, no doubt."

"Such as walking upstairs," suggested Mary.

"Yes, that might do it. In fact almost certainly would—that is, if he ever walked up those three flights—but surely he never did anything of that kind?"

"Oh no," said Mrs. Rogers. "He always used the lift. Always. He was most particular."

"I mean," said Mary, "that with the lift being out of order last night—"

Mrs. Rogers was staring at her in surprise.

"But the lift wasn't out of order at all yesterday, Miss Aldin."

Thomas Royde coughed.

"Excuse me," he said. "I came home with Mr. Treves last night. There was a placard on the lift saying 'Out of order.' "

Mrs. Rogers stared.

"Well, that's an odd thing. I'd have declared there was nothing wrong with the lift—in fact I'm sure there wasn't. I'd have heard about it if there was. We haven't had anything go wrong with the lift (touching wood) since—oh, not for a good eighteen months. Very reliable it is."

"Perhaps," suggsted the doctor, "some porter or hall boy put that notice up when he was off duty?"

"It's an automatic lift, Doctor, it doesn't need anyone to work it."

"Ah yes, so it is. I was forgetting."

"I'll have a word with Joe," said Mrs. Rogers. She bustled out of the room calling, "Joe—Joe."

Dr. Lazenby looked curiously at Thomas.

"Excuse me, you're quite sure, Mr.—er—"

"Royde," put in Mary.

"Quite sure," said Thomas.

Mrs. Rogers came back with the porter. Joe was emphatic that nothing whatever had been wrong with the lift on the preceding night. There was such a placard as Thomas had described—but it was tucked away under the desk and hadn't been used for over a year.

They all looked at each other and agreed it was a most mysterious thing. The doctor suggested some practical joke on the part of one of the Hotel visitors, and perforce they left it at that.

In reply to Mary's inquiries, Doctor Lazenby explained that Mr. Treves' chauffeur had given him the address of Mr. Treves' solicitors, and he was communicating with them and that he would come round and see Lady Tressilian and tell her what was going to be done about the funeral.

Then the busy cheerful doctor hurried off and Mary and Thomas walked slowly back to Gull's Point.

Mary said:

"You're quite sure you saw that notice, Thomas?"

"Both Latimer and I saw it."

"What an extraordinary thing!" said Mary.

X

It was the 12th of September. "Only two more days," said Mary Aldin. Then she bit her lip and flushed.

Thomas Royde looked at her thoughtfully.

"Is that how you feel about it?"

"I don't know what's the matter with me," said Mary. "Never in all my life have I been so anxious for a visit to come to an end. And usually we enjoy having Nevile so much. And Audrey too."

Thomas nodded.

"But this time," went on Mary, "one feels as though one were sitting on dynamite. At any minute the whole thing may explode. That's why I said to myself first thing this morning: 'Only two days more.' Audrey goes on Wednesday and Nevile and Kay on Thursday."

"And I go on Friday," said Thomas.

"Oh, I'm not counting you. You've been a tower of strength. I don't know what I should have done without you."

"The human buffer?"

"More than that. You've been so kind and so—so calm. That sounds rather ridiculous but it really does express what I mean."

Thomas looked pleased though slightly embarrassed.

"I don't know why we've all been so het up," said Mary reflectively. "After all, if there were an—an outburst—it would be awkward and embarrassing, but nothing more."

"But there's been more to your feeling than that."

"Oh yes, there has. A definite feeling of apprehension. Even the servants feel it. The kitchenmaid burst into tears and gave notice this morning— for no reason at all. The cook's jumpy—Hurstall is all on edge—even Barrett, who is usually as calm as a—a battleship—has shown signs of nerves. And all because Nevile had this ridiculous idea of wanting his former and his present wife to make friends and so soothe his own conscience."

"In which ingenious idea he has singularly failed," remarked Thomas.

"Yes. Kay is—is getting quite beside herself. And really, Thomas, I can't help sympathizing with her." She paused. "Did you notice the way Nevile looked after Audrey as she went up the stairs last night? He still cares about her, Thomas. The whole thing has been the most tragic mistake."

Thomas started filling his pipe.

"He should have thought of that before," he said in a hard voice.

"Oh I know. That's what one says. But it doesn't alter the fact that the whole thing is a tragedy. I can't help feeling sorry for Nevile."

"People like Nevile—" began Thomas and then stopped.

"Yes."

"People like Nevile think they can always have everything their own way—and have everything they want, too. I don't suppose Nevile has ever had a setback over anything in his life till he came up against this business of Audrey. Well, he's got it now. He can't have Audrey. She's out of his reach. No good his making a song and dance about it. He's just got to lump it."

"I suppose you're quite right. But you do sound hard. Audrey was so much in love with Nevile when she married him—and they always got on together so well."

"Well, she's out of love with him now."

"I wonder," murmured Mary under her breath.

Thomas was going on:

"And I'll tell you something else. Nevile had better look out for Kay. She's a dangerous kind of young woman—really dangerous. If she got her temper up she'd stop at nothing."

"Oh dear," Mary sighed and, returning to her original remarks, said hopefully: "Well, it's only two days more."

Things had been very difficult for the last four or five days. The death of Mr. Treves had given Lady Tressilian a shock which had told adversely on her health. The funeral had taken place in London, for which Mary was thankful, since it enabled the old lady to take her mind off the sad event more quickly than she might have been able to do otherwise. The domestic side of the household had been very nervy and difficult and Mary really felt tired and dispirited this morning.

"It's partly the weather," she said aloud. "It's unnatural."

It had indeed been an unusually hot and fine spell for September. On several days the thermometer had registered 70 in the shade.

Nevile strode out of the house and joined them as she spoke.

"Blaming the weather?" he asked, with a glance up at the sky. "It is rather incredible. Hotter than ever today. And no wind. Makes one feel jumpy somehow. However, I think we'll get rain before very long. Today is just a bit too tropical to last."

Thomas Royde had moved very gently and aimlessly away and now disappeared round the corner of the house.

"Departure of gloomy Thomas," said Nevile. "Nobody could say he shows any enjoyment of my company."

"He's rather a dear," said Mary.

"I disagree. Narrow-minded prejudiced sort of chap."

"He always hoped to marry Audrey, I think. And then you came along and cut him out."

"It would have taken him about seven years to make up his mind to ask her to marry him. Did he expect the poor girl to wait while he made up his mind?"

"Perhaps," said Mary deliberately, "it will all come right now."

Nevile looked at her and raised an eyebrow.

"True love rewarded? Audrey marry that wet fish? She's a lot too good for that. No, I don't see Audrey marrying gloomy Thomas."

"I believe she is really very fond of him, Nevile."

"What matchmakers you women always are! Can't you let Audrey enjoy her freedom for a bit?"

"If she does enjoy it, certainly."

Nevile said quickly:

"You think she's not happy?"

"I really haven't the least idea."

"No more have I," said Nevile slowly. "One never does know what Audrey is feeling." He paused and then added, "But Audrey is one hundred per cent thoroughbred. She's white all through."

Then he said, more to himself than to Mary:

"God, what a damned fool I've been!"

Mary went into the house a little worried. For the third time she repeated to herself the comforting words, "Only two days more."

Nevile wandered restlessly about the garden and terraces.

Right at the end of the garden he found Audrey sitting on the low wall looking down at the water below. It was high tide and the river was full.

She got up at once and came towards him.

"I was just coming back to the house. It must be nearly tea-time."

She spoke quickly and nervously without looking at him.

He walked beside her without speaking.

Only when they reached the terrace again did he say:

"Can I talk to you, Audrey?"

She said at once, her fingers gripping the edge of the balustrade: "I think you'd better not."

"That means you know what I want to say."

She did not answer.

"What about it, Audrey? Can't we go back to where we were? Forget everything that has happened?"

"Including Kay?"

"Kay," said Nevile, "will be sensible."

"What do you mean by sensible?"

"Simply this. I shall go to her and tell her the truth. Fling myself on her generosity. Tell her, what is true, that you are the only woman I ever loved."

"You loved Kay when you married her."

"My marriage to Kay was the biggest mistake I ever made. I—"

He stopped. Kay had come out of the drawing-room window. She walked towards them, and before the fury in her eyes even Nevile shrank a little.

"Sorry to interrupt this touching scene," said Kay. "But I think it's about time I did."

Audrey moved away. "I'll leave you alone," she said.

Her face and voice were colorless.

"That's right," said Kay. "You've done all the mischief you wanted to do, haven't you? I'll deal with you later. Just now I'd rather have it out with Nevile."

"Look here, Kay, Audrey has absolutely nothing to do with this. It's not her fault. Blame me if you like—"

"And I do like," said Kay. Her eyes blazed at Nevile. "What sort of man do you think you are?"

"A pretty poor sort of man," said Nevile bitterly.

"You leave your wife, come bull-headed after me, get your wife to give you a divorce. Crazy about me one minute, tired of me the next. Now I suppose you want to go back to that whey-faced, mewling, double-crossing little cat—"

"Stop that, Kay!"

"Well, what do you want?"

Nevile was very white. He said:

"I'm every kind of a worm you like to call me. But it's no good, Kay. *I can't go on.* I think—really—I must have loved Audrey all the time. My love for you was—was a kind of madness. But it's no good, my dear— you and I don't belong. I shouldn't be able to make you happy in the long run. Believe me, Kay, it's better to cut our losses. Let's try and part friends. Be generous."

Kay said in a deceptively quiet voice:

"What exactly are you suggesting?"

Nevile did not look at her. His chin took on a dogged angle.

"We can get a divorce. You can divorce me for desertion."

"Not for some time. You'll have to wait for it."

"I'll wait," said Nevile.

"And then, after three years or whatever it is, you'll ask dear sweet Audrey to marry you all over again?"

"If she'll have me."

"She'll have you all right!" said Kay viciously. "And where do I come in?"

"You'll be free to find a better man than I am. Naturally I shall see you're well provided for—"

"Cut the bribes!" Her voice rose, as she lost control of herself. "Listen to me, Nevile. You can't do this thing to me! I'll not divorce you. I married you because I loved you. I know when you started turning against me. It was after I let you know I followed you to Estoril. You wanted to think it was all Fate. It's upset your vanity to think it was *me*. Well, I'm not ashamed of what I did. You fell in love with me and married me and I'm not going to let you go back to that sly little cat who's got her hooks into you again. She meant this to happen—but she's not going to bring it off! I'll kill you first. Do you hear? I'll kill you. I'll kill her too. I'll see you both dead. I'll—"

Nevile took a step forward and caught her by the arm.

"Shut up, Kay. For goodness' sake. You can't make this kind of scene here."

"Can't I? You'll see. I'll—"

Hurstall stepped out on the terrace. His face was quite impassive.

"Tea is served in the drawing-room," he announced.

Kay and Nevile walked slowly towards the drawing-room window. Hurstall stood aside to let them pass in.

Up in the sky the clouds were gathering.

XI

The rain started falling at a quarter to seven. Nevile watched it from the window of his bedroom. He had no further conversation with Kay. They had avoided each other after tea.

Dinner that evening was a stilted difficult meal. Nevile was sunk in abstraction. Kay's face had an unusual amount of make-up for her. Audrey sat like a frozen ghost. Mary Aldin did her best to keep some kind of a conversation going and was slightly annoyed with Thomas Royde for not playing up to her better.

Hurstall was nervous and his hands trembled as he handed the vegetables.

As the meal drew to a close, Nevile said with elaborate casualness: "Think I shall go over to Easterhead after dinner and look up Latimer. We might have a game of billiards."

"Take the latch key," said Mary. "In case you're back late."

"Thanks, I will."

They went into the drawing-room, where coffee was served.

The turning on of the wireless and the news was a welcome diversion.

Kay, who had been yawning ostentatiously ever since dinner, said she would go up to bed. She had a headache, she said.

"Have you got any aspirin?" asked Mary

"Yes, thank you."

Kay left the room.

Nevile tuned the wireless on to a program with music. He sat silent on the sofa for some time. He did not look once at Audrey, but sat huddled up looking like an unhappy little boy. Against her will, Mary felt quite sorry for him.

"Well," he said, at last rousing himself, "better be off if I'm going."

"Are you taking your car or going by ferry?"

"Oh, ferry. No sense in going a round of fifteen miles. I shall enjoy a bit of a walk."

"It's raining, you know."

"I know. I've got a Burberry." He went towards the door.

"Good-night."

In the hall, Hurstall came to him.

"If you please, sir, will you go up to Lady Tressilian? She wants to see you specially."

Nevile glanced at the clock. It was already ten o'clock.

He shrugged his shoulders and went upstairs and along the corridor to Lady Tressilian's room and tapped on the door. While he waited for her to say Come in, he heard the voices of the others in the hall down below. Everybody was going to bed early tonight, it seemed.

"Come in," said Lady Tressilian's clear voice.

Nevile went in, shutting the door behind him.

Lady Tressilian was all ready for the night. All the lights were extinguished except one reading lamp by her bed. She had been reading, but she now laid down the book. She looked at Nevile over the top of her spectacles. It was, somehow, a formidable glance.

"I want to speak to you, Nevile," she said.

In spite of himself, Nevile smiled faintly.

"Yes, Headmaster," he said.

Lady Tressilian did not smile.

"There are certain things, Nevile, that I will not permit in my house. I have no wish to listen to anybody's private conversations, but if you and your wife insist on shouting at each other exactly under my bedroom windows, I can hardly fail to hear what you say. I gather that you were outlining a plan whereby Kay was to divorce you and in due course you would remarry Audrey. That, Nevile, is a thing you simply cannot do and I will not hear of it for a moment."

Nevile seemed to be making an effort to control his temper.

"I apologize for the scene," he said, shortly. "As for the rest of what you say, surely that is my business!"

"No, it is not. You have used my house in order to get into touch with Audrey—or else Audrey has used it—"

"She has done nothing of the sort. She—"

Lady Tressilian stopped him with upraised hand.

"Anyway, you can't do this thing, Nevile. Kay is your wife. She has certain rights of which you cannot deprive her. In this matter I am entirely on Kay's side. You have made your bed and must lie upon it. Your duty now is to Kay and I'm telling you so plainly—"

Nevile took a step forward. His voice rose:

"This is nothing whatever to do with you—"

"What is more," Lady Tressilian swept on, regardless of his protest, "Audrey leaves this house tomorrow—"

"You can't do that! I won't stand for it—"

"Don't shout at me, Nevile."

"I tell you I won't have it—"

Somewhere along the passage a door shut . . .

XII

Alice Bentham, the gooseberry-eyed housemaid, came to Mrs. Spicer, the cook, in some perturbation.

"Oh, Mrs. Spicer, I don't rightly know what I ought to do."

"What's the matter, Alice?"

"It's Miss Barrett. I took her in her cup of tea over an hour ago. Fast asleep she was and never woke up, but I didn't like to do much. And then, five minutes ago, I went in again because she hadn't come down and her ladyship's tea all ready and waiting for her to take in. So I went in again and she's sleeping ever so—I can't stir her."

"Have you shaken her?"

"Yes, Mrs. Spicer. I shook her hard—but she just goes on lying there and she's ever such a horrid color."

"Goodness, she's not dead, is she?"

"Oh no, Mrs. Spicer, because I can hear her breathing, but it's funny breathing. I think she's ill or something."

"Well, I'll go up and see myself. You take in her ladyship's tea. Better make a fresh pot. She'll be wondering what's happened."

Alice obediently did as she was told whilst Mrs. Spicer went up to the second floor.

Taking the tray along the corridor, Alice knocked at Lady Tressilian's door. After knocking twice and getting no answer she went in. A moment later, there was a crash of broken crockery and a series of wild screams, and Alice came rushing out of the room and down the stairs to where Hurstall was crossing the hall to the dining-room.

"Oh, Mr. Hurstall—there've been burglars and her ladyship's dead—killed—with a great hole in her head and blood everywhere . . ."

A Fine Italian Hand . . .

I

SUPERINTENDENT BATTLE HAD enjoyed his holiday. There were still three days of it to run and he was a little disappointed when the weather changed and the rain fell. Still, what else could you expect in England? And he'd been extremely lucky up to now.

He was breakfasting with Inspector James Leach, his nephew, when the telephone rang.

"I'll come right along, sir." Jim put the receiver back.

"Serious?" asked Superintendent Battle. He noted the expression on his nephew's face.

"We've got a murder. Lady Tressilian. An old lady, very well known down here, an invalid. Has that house at Saltcreek that hangs right over the cliff."

Battle nodded.

"I'm going along to see the old man" (thus disrespectfully did Leach speak of his Chief Constable). "He's a friend of hers. We're going along together."

As he went to the door he said pleadingly:

"You'll give me a hand, won't you, Uncle, over this? First case of this kind I've had."

"As long as I'm here, I will. Case of robbery and housebreaking, is it?"

"I don't know yet."

II

Half an hour later, Major Robert Mitchell, the Chief Constable, was speaking gravely to uncle and nephew.

"It's early to say as yet," he said, "but one thing seems clear. This wasn't an outside job. Nothing taken, no signs of breaking in. All the windows and doors found shut this morning."

He looked directly at Battle.

"If I were to ask Scotland Yard, do you think they'd put you on the job? You're on the spot, you see. And then there's your relationship with Leach here. That is, if you're willing. It means cutting the end of your holiday."

"That's all right," said Battle. "As for the other, sir, you'll have to put it up to Sir Edgar (Sir Edgar Cotton was Assistant Commissioner) "but I believe he's a friend of yours?"

Mitchell nodded.

"Yes, I think I can manage Edgar all right. That's settled, then! I'll get through right away."

He spoke into the telephone. "Get me the Yard."

"You think it's going to be an important case, sir?" asked Battle.

Mitchell said gravely:

"It's going to be a case where we don't want the possibility of making a mistake. We want to be absolutely sure of our man—or woman, of course."

Battle nodded. He understood quite well that there was something behind the words.

"Thinks he knows who did it," he said to himself. "And doesn't relish the prospect. Somebody well known and popular or I'll eat my boots!"

III

Battle and Leach stood in the doorway of the well-furnished handsome bedroom. On the floor in front of them a police officer was carefully testing for fingerprints the handle of a golf club—a heavy niblick. The head of the club was blood-stained and had one or two white hairs sticking to it.

By the bed, Dr. Lazenby, who was police surgeon for the district, was bending over the body of Lady Tressilian.

He straightened up with a sigh.

"Perfectly straightforward. She was hit from in front with terrific force. First blow smashed in the bone and killed her, but the murderer struck again to make sure. I won't give you fancy terms—just the plain horse sense of it."

"How long has she been dead?" asked Leach.

"I'd put it between ten o'clock and midnight."

"You can't go nearer than that?"

"I'd rather not. All sorts of factors to take into account. We don't hang people on *rigor mortis* nowadays. *Not earlier than ten, not later than midnight.*"

"And she was hit with this niblick?"

The doctor glanced over at it.

"Presumably. Luck, though, that the murderer left it behind. I couldn't have deduced a niblick from the wound. As it happens the sharp edge of the club didn't touch the head—it was the angled back of the club that must have hit her."

"Wouldn't that have been rather difficult to do?" asked Leach.

"If it had been done on purpose, yes," agreed the doctor. "I can only suppose, that by a rather odd chance, it just happened that way."

Leach was raising his hands, instinctively trying to reconstruct the blow.

"Awkward," he commented.

"Yes," said the doctor thoughtfully. "The whole thing was awkward. She was struck, you see, on the right temple—but whoever did it must have stood on the right-hand side of the bed—facing the head of the bed—there's no room on the left, the angle from the wall is too small."

Leach pricked up his ears.

"Left-handed?" he queried.

"You won't get me to commit myself on that point," said Lazenby. "Far too many snags. I'll say, if you like, that the easiest explanation is that the murderer was left-handed—but there are other ways of accounting for it. Suppose, for instance, the old lady had turned her head slightly to the left just as the man hit. Or he may have previously moved the bed out, stood on the left of it and afterwards moved the bed back."

"Not very likely—that last."

"Perhaps not, but it *might* have happened. I've had some experience in these things, and I can tell you, my boy, deducing that a murderous blow was struck left-handed is full of pitfalls."

Detective Sergeant Jones, from the door, remarked, "This golf club is the ordinary right-handed kind."

Leach nodded. "Still, it mayn't have belonged to the man who used it. It *was* a man, I suppose, Doctor?"

"Not necessarily. If the weapon was that heavy niblick a woman could have landed a terrible swipe with it."

Superintendent Battle said in his quiet voice:

"But you couldn't swear that that was the weapon, could you, Doctor?"

Lazenby gave him a quick interested glance.

"No. I can only swear that it *might* have been the weapon, and that presumably it *was* the weapon. I'll analyze the blood on it, make sure that it's the same blood group—also the hairs."

"Yes," said Battle, approvingly, "It's always as well to be thorough."

Lazenby asked curiously:

"Got any doubts about that golf club yourself, Superintendent?"

Battle shook his head.

"Oh no, no. I'm a simple man. Like to believe the things I see with my eyes. She was hit with something heavy—that's heavy. It has blood and hair on it, therefore presumably her blood and hair. Ergo—that was the weapon used."

Leach asked: "Was she awake or asleep when she was hit?"

"In my opinion, awake. There's astonishment on her face. I'd say— this is just a private personal opinion—that she didn't expect what was going to happen. There's no sign of any attempt to fight—and no horror or fear. I'd say offhand that either she had just woken up from sleep and was hazy and didn't take things in—or else she recognized her assailant as someone who could not possibly wish to harm her."

"The bedside lamp was on and nothing else," said Leach thoughtfully.

"Yes, that cuts either way. She may have turned it on when she was suddenly woken up by someone entering her room. Or it may have been on already."

Detective Sergeant Jones rose to his feet. He was smiling appreciatively.

"Lovely set of prints on that club," he said. "Clear as anything!"

Leach gave a deep sigh.

"That ought to simplify things."

"Obliging chap," said Dr. Lazenby. "Left the weapon—left his finger- prints on it—wonder he didn't leave his visiting card!"

"It might be," said Superintendent Battle, "that he just lost his head. Some do."

The doctor nodded.

"True enough. Well, I must go and look after my other patient."

"What patient?" Battle sounded suddenly interested.

"I was sent for by the butler before this was discovered. Lady Tressilian's maid was found in a coma this morning."

"What was wrong with her?"

"Heavily doped with one of the barbiturates. She's pretty bad, but she'll pull round."

"The maid?" said Battle. His rather ox-like eyes went heavily to the big bell-pull, the tassel of which rested on the pillow near the dead woman's hand.

Lazenby nodded.

"Exactly. That's the first thing Lady Tressilian would have done if she'd cause to feel alarm—pull that bell and summon the maid. Well, she could have pulled it till all was blue. The maid wouldn't have heard."

"That was taken care of, was it?" said Battle. "You're sure of that? She wasn't in the habit of taking sleeping draughts?'

"I'm positive she wasn't. There's not a sign of such a thing in her room. And I've found out how it was given to her. Senna pods. She drank a brew of senna pods every night. The stuff was in that."

Superintendent Battle scratched his chin.

"H'm," he said. "Somebody knew all about this house. You know, Doctor, this is a very odd sort of murder."

"Well," said Lazenby, "that's *your* business."

"He's a good man, our doctor," said Leach when Lazenby had left the room.

The two men were alone now. The photographs had been taken, and measurements recorded. The two police officers knew every fact that was to be known about the room where the crime had been committed.

Battle nodded in answer to his nephew's remark. He seemed to be puzzling over something.

"Do you think anyone could have handled that club—with gloves on, say—after those fingerprints were made?"

Leach shook his head.

"I don't and no more do you. You couldn't grasp that club—not *use* it, I mean, without smearing those prints. They weren't smeared. They were as clear as clear. You saw for yourself."

Battle agreed.

"And now we ask very nicely and politely if everyone will allow us to take their fingerprints—no compulsion, of course. And everyone will say yes—and then one of two things will happen. Either none of these fingerprints will agree, or else—"

"Or else we'll have got our man?"

"I suppose so. Or our woman, perhaps."

Leach shook his head.

"No, not a woman. Those prints on the clubs were a man's. Too big for a woman's. Besides this isn't a woman's crime."

"No," agreed Battle. "Quite a man's crime. Brutal, masculine, rather athletic and slightly stupid. Know anybody in the house like that?"

"I don't know anyone in the house yet. They're all together in the dining-room."

Battle moved towards the door.

"We'll go and have a look at them." He glanced over his shoulder at the bed, shook his head and remarked:

"I don't like that bell-pull."

"What about it?"

"It doesn't fit."

He added as he opened the door:

"Who wanted to kill her, I wonder? A lot of cantankerous old ladies about just asking for a tap on the skull. She doesn't look that sort. I should think she was *liked*." He paused a minute and then asked:

"Well off, wasn't she? Who gets her money?"

Leach answered the implication of the words.

"You've hit it! That will be the answer. It's one of the first things to find out."

As they went downstairs together, Battle glanced at the list in his hand. He read out.

"Miss Aldin, Mr. Royde, Mr. Strange, Mrs. Strange, Mrs. Audrey Strange. H'm, seem a lot of the Strange family."

"Those are his two wives, I understand."

Battle's eyebrows rose and he murmured:

"Bluebeard, is he?"

The family were assembled round the dining-room table, where they had made a pretence of eating.

Superintendent Battle glanced keenly at the faces turned to him. He was sizing them up after his own peculiar methods. His view of them might have surprised them had they known it. It was a sternly biased view. No matter what the law pretends as to regarding people as innocent until they are proved guilty, Superintendent Battle always regarded everyone connected with a murder case as a potential murderer.

He glanced from Mary Aldin, sitting upright and pale at the head of the table, to Thomas Royde, filling a pipe beside her, to Audrey sitting with her chair pushed back, a coffee cup and saucer in her right hand, a cigarette in her left, to Nevile looking dazed and bewildered, trying with a shaking hand to light a cigarette, to Kay with her elbows on the table and the pallor of her face showing through her make-up.

These were Superintendent Battle's thoughts:

Suppose that's Miss Aldin. Cool customer—competent woman, I should say. Won't catch her off her guard easily. Man next to her is a dark horse—got a groggy arm—poker face—got an inferiority complex as likely as not. That's one of these wives, I suppose—she's scared to death— yes, she's scared all right. Funny about that coffee cup. That's Strange, I've seen him before somewhere. He's got the jitters all right—nerves shot to pieces. Red-headed girl's a tartar—devil of a temper. Brains as well as temper, though.

Whilst he was thus sizing them up, Inspector Leach was making a stiff little speech. Mary Aldin mentioned everyone present by name.

She ended up:

"It has been a terrible shock to us, of course, but we are anxious to help you in any way we can."

"To begin with," said Leach, holding it up, "does anybody know anything about this golf club?"

With a little cry, Kay said, "How horrible. Is that what—" and stopped.

Nevile Strange got up and came round the table.

"Looks like one of mine. Can I just see?"

"It's quite all right *now*," said Inspector Leach. "You can handle it."

That little significant "now" did not seem to produce any reaction in the onlookers. Nevile examined the club.

"I think it's one of the niblicks out of my bag," he said. "I can tell you for sure in a minute or two. If you will just come with me." They followed him to a big cupboard under the stairs. He flung open the door of it and to Battle's confused eyes it seemed literally crowded with tennis racquets. At the same time, he remembered where he had seen Nevile Strange before. He said quickly:

"I've seen you play at Wimbledon, sir."

Nevile half turned his head. "Oh yes, have you?"

He was throwing aside some of the racquets. There were two golf bags in the cupboard leaning up against fishing tackle.

"Only my wife and I play golf," explained Nevile. "And that's a man's club. Yes, that's right— it's mine."

He had taken out his bag, which contained at least fourteen clubs.

Inpector Leach thought to himself:

"These athletic chaps certainly take themselves seriously. Wouldn't like to be his caddy."

Nevile was saying:

"It's one of Walter Hudson's niblicks from St. Esbert's."

"Thank you, Mr. Strange. That settles one question."

Nevile said: "What beats me is that nothing was taken. And the house doesn't seem to have been broken into?" His voice was bewildered—but it was also frightened.

Battle said to himself:

"They've been thinking it out, all of them . . ."

"The servants," said Nevile, "are so absolutely harmless."

"I shall talk to Miss Aldin about the servants," said Inspector Leach smoothly. "In the meantime I wonder if you could give me any idea who Lady Tressilian's solicitors are?"

"Askwith & Trelawny," replied Nevile promptly. "St. Loo."

"Thank you, Mr. Strange. We shall have to find out from them all about Lady Tressilian's property."

"Do you mean," asked Nevile, "who inherits her money?"

"That's right, sir. Her will, and all that."

"I don't know about her will," said Nevile. "She had not very much of her own to leave so far as I know. I can tell you about the bulk of her property."

"Yes, Mr. Strange?"

"It comes to me and my wife under the will of the late Sir Matthew Tressilian. Lady Tressilian only had a life interest in it."

"Indeed, is that so?" Inspector Leach looked at Nevile with the interested attention of someone who spots a possibly valuable addition to his pet collection. The look made Nevile wince nervously. Inspector Leach went on and his voice was impossibly genial.

"You've no idea of the amount, Mr. Strange?"

"I couldn't tell you offhand. In the neighborhood of a hundred thousand pounds, I believe."

"Indeed. To each of you?"

"No. Divided between us."

"I see. A very considerable sum."

Nevile smiled. He said quietly: "I've got plenty to live on of my own, you know, without hankering to step into dead people's shoes."

Inspector Leach looked shocked at having such ideas attributed to him.

They went back into the dining-room and Leach said his neat little piece. This was on the subject of fingerprints—a matter of routine—elimination of those of the household in the dead woman's bedroom.

Everyone expressed willingness—almost eagerness—to have their fingerprints taken. They were shepherded into the library for that purpose, where Detective Sergeant Jones was waiting for them with his little roller.

Battle and Leach began on the servants.

Nothing very much was to be got from them. Hurstall explained his system of locking up the house and swore that he had found it untouched in the morning. There were no signs of any entry by an intruder. The front door, he explained, had been left on the latch. That is to say, it was not bolted, but could be opened from outside with a key. It was left like that because Mr. Nevile had gone over to Easterhead Bay and would be back late.

"Do you know what time he came in?"

"Yes, sir, I think it was about half-past two. Someone came back with him, I think. I heard voices and then a car drive away and then I heard the door close and Mr. Nevile come upstairs."

"What time did he leave here last night for Easterhead Bay?"

"About twenty past ten. I heard the door close."

Leach nodded. There did not seem to be much more to be got from Hurstall at the moment. He interviewed the others. They were all disposed to be nervous and frightened, but no more so than was natural under the circumstances.

Leach looked questioningly at his uncle as the door closed behind the slightly hysterical kitchenmaid, who had tailed the procession.

Battle said: "Have the housemaid back—not the popeyed one—the tall thin bit of vinegar. She knows something."

Emma Wales was clearly uneasy. It alarmed her that this time it was the big square elderly man who took upon himself the task of questioning her.

"I'm just going to give you a bit of advice, Miss Wales," he said pleasantly. "It doesn't do, you know, to hold anything back from the police. Makes them look at you unfavorably, if you understand what I mean—"

Emma Wales protested indignantly but uneasily:

"I'm sure I never—"

"Now, now." Battle held up a large square hand. "You saw something or else you heard something—what was it?"

"I didn't exactly hear it—I mean I couldn't help hearing it—Mr. Hurstall, he heard it too. And I don't think, not for a moment I don't, that it had anything to do with the murder."

"Probably not, probably not. Just tell us what it was."

"Well, I was going up to bed. Just after ten it was—and I'd slipped along first to put Miss Aldin's hot water bottle in her bed. Summer or winter she always has one, and so of course I had to pass right by her ladyship's door."

"Go on," said Battle.

"And I heard her and Mr. Nevile going at it hammer and tongs. Voices right up. Shouting, he was. Oh, it was a proper quarrel!"

"Remember exactly what was said?"

"Well, I wasn't really listening as you might say."

"No. But still you must have heard some of the words."

"Her ladyship was saying as she wouldn't have something or other going on in her house and Mr. Nevile was saying, 'Don't you dare say anything against her.' All worked up he was."

Battle, with an expressionless face, tried once more, but he could get no more out of her. In the end he dismissed the woman.

He and Jim looked at each other. Leach said, after a minute or two: "Jones ought to be able to tell us something about those prints by now." Battle asked:

"Who's doing the rooms?"

"Williams. He's a good man. He won't miss anything."

"You're keeping the occupants out of them?"

"Yes, until Williams has finished."

The door opened at that minute and young Williams put his head in. "There's something I'd like you to see. In Mr. Nevile Strange's room."

They got up and followed him to the suite on the west side of the house.

Williams pointed to a heap on the floor. A dark blue coat, trousers and waistcoat.

Leach said sharply:

"Where did you find this?"

"Bundled down into the bottom of the wardrobe. Just look at *this*, sir."

He picked up the coat and showed the edges of the dark blue cuffs.

"See those dark stains? That's blood, sir, or I'm a Dutchman. And see here, it's spattered all up the sleeve."

"H'm." Battle avoided the other's eager eyes. "Looks bad for young Nevile, I must say. Any other suit in the room?"

"Dark gray pinstripe hanging over a chair. Lots of water on the floor here by the wash basin."

"Looking as though he washed the blood off himself in the devil of a hurry? Yes. It's near the open window, though, and the rain has come in a good deal."

"Not enough to make those pools on the floor, sir. They're not dried up yet."

Battle was silent. A picture was forming itself before his eyes. A man with blood on his hands and sleeves, flinging off his clothes, bundling the bloodstained garments into the cupboard, sluicing water furiously over his hands and bare arms.

He looked across at a door in the other wall.

Williams answered the look.

"Mrs. Strange's room, sir. The door is locked."

"Locked? On this side?"

"No. On the other."

"On her side, eh?"

Battle was reflective for a minute or two. He said at last:

"Let's see that old butler again."

Hurstall was nervous. Leach said crisply:

"Why didn't you tell us, Hurstall, that you overheard a quarrel between Mr. Strange and Lady Tressilian last night?"

The old man blinked.

"I really didn't think twice about it, sir. I don't imagine it was what you'd call a quarrel—just an amicable difference of opinion."

Resisting the temptation to say, "Amicable difference of opinion my foot!" Leach went on:

"What suit was Mr. Strange wearing last night at dinner?"

Hurstall hesitated. Battle said quietly:

"Dark blue suit or gray pinstripe? I daresay someone else can tell us if you don't remember."

Hurstall broke his silence.

"I remember now, sir. It was his dark blue. The family," he added, anxious not to lose prestige, "have not been in the habit of changing into evening dress during the summer months. They frequently go out after dinner—sometimes in the garden, sometimes down to the quay."

Battle nodded. Hurstall left the room. He passed Jones in the doorway. Jones looked excited.

He said:

"It's a cinch, sir. I've got all their prints. There's only one lot fills the bill. Of course I've only been able to make a rough comparison as yet, but I'll bet they're the right ones."

"Well?" said Battle.

"The prints on that niblick, sir, *were made by Mr. Nevile Strange.*"

Battle leaned back in his chair.

"Well," he said, "that seems to settle it, doesn't it?"

IV

They were in the Chief Constable's office—three men with grave worried faces.

Major Mitchell said with a sigh:

"Well, I suppose there's nothing to be done but arrest him?"

Leach said quietly:

"Looks like it, sir."

Mitchell looked across at Superintendent Battle.

"Cheer up, Battle," he said kindly. "Your best friend isn't dead."

Superintendent Battle sighed.

"I don't like it," he said.

"I don't think any of us like it," said Mitchell. "But we've ample evidence, I think, to apply for a warrant."

"More than ample," said Battle.

"In fact if we don't apply for one, anybody might ask why the dickens not?"

Battle nodded an unhappy head.

"Let's go over it," said the Chief Constable. "You've got motive—Strange and his wife come into a considerable sum of money at the old lady's death. He's the last person known to have seen her alive—he was heard quarrelling with her. The suit he wore that night had bloodstains on it, of course, most damning of all, his fingerprints were found on the actual weapon—*and no one else's.*"

"And yet sir," said Battle, "*you* don't like it either."

"I'm damned if I do."

"What is it exactly you don't like about it, sir?"

Major Mitchell rubbed his nose. "Makes the fellow out a bit too much of a fool, perhaps?" he suggested.

"And yet, sir, they do behave like fools sometimes."

"Oh I know—I know. Where would we be if they didn't?"

Battle said to Leach:

"What don't *you* like about it, Jim?"

Leach stirred unhappily.

"I've always liked Mr. Strange. Seen him on and off down here for years. He's a nice gentleman—and he's a sportsman."

"I don't see," said Battle slowly, "why a good tennis player shouldn't be a murderer as well. There's nothing against it." He paused. "What *I* don't like is the niblick."

"The niblick?" asked Mitchell, slightly puzzled.

"Yes, sir, or alternatively, the bell. The bell or the niblick—not both."

He went on in his slow careful voice.

"What do we think actually happened? Did Mr. Strange go to her room, have a quarrel, lose his temper, and hit her over the head with a niblick? If so, and it was unpremeditated, how did he happen to have a niblick with him? It's not the sort of thing you carry about with you in the evenings."

"He might have been practicing swings—something like that."

"He might—but nobody says so. Nobody saw him doing it. The last time anybody saw him with a niblick in his hand was about a week previously when he was practicing sand shots down on the sands. As I look at it, you see, you can't have it both ways. Either there was a quarrel and he lost his temper—and, mind you, I've seen him on the courts, and in one of these tournament matches these tennis stars are all het up and a mass of nerves, and if their tempers fray easily it's going to show. I've never seen Mr. Strange ruffled. I should say he'd got an excellent control over his temper—better than most—and yet we're suggesting that he goes berserk and hits a frail old lady over the head."

"There's another alternative, Battle," said the Chief Constable.

"I know, sir. The theory that it was premeditated. He wanted the old lady's money. That fits in with the bell—which entailed the doping of the maid—but it *doesn't* fit in with the niblick and the quarrel! If he'd made up his mind to do her in, he'd be very careful *not* to quarrel with her. He could dope the maid, creep into her room in the night—crack her over the head and stage a nice little robbery, wiping the niblick and putting it carefully back where it belonged! It's all wrong, sir—it's a mixture of cold premeditation and unpremeditated violence—and the two don't mix!"

"There's something in what you say, Battle—but—what's the alternative?"

"It's the niblick that takes my fancy, sir."

"Nobody could have hit her over the head with that niblick without disturbing Nevile's prints—that's quite certain."

"In that case," said Superintendent Battle, "she was hit over the head with something else."

Major Mitchell drew a deep breath.

"That's rather a wild assumption, isn't it?"

"I think it's common sense, sir. Either Strange hit her with that niblick or nobody did. I plump for nobody. In that case that niblick was put there deliberately and blood and hair smeared on it. Dr. Lazenby doesn't like the niblick much—had to accept it because it was the obvious thing and because he couldn't say definitely that it *hadn't* been used."

Major Mitchell leaned back in his chair.

"Go on, Battle," he said. "I'm giving you a free hand. What's the next step?"

"Take away the niblick," said Battle, "and what is left? First, motive. Had Nevile Strange really got a motive for doing away with Lady Tressilian? He inherited money—a lot depends to my mind on whether he needed that money. He says not. I suggest we verify that. Find out the state of his finances. If he's in a hole financially, and needs money, then the case against him is very much strengthened. If, on the other hand, he was speaking the truth and his finances are in a good state, why then—"

"Well, what then?"

"Why then, we might have a look at the motives of the *other* people in the house."

"You think, then, that Nevile Strange was framed?"

Superintendent Battle screwed up his eyes.

"There's a phrase I read somewhere that tickled my fancy. Something about a fine Italian hand. That's what I seem to see in this business. Ostensibly it's a blunt brutal straightforward crime, but it seems to me I catch glimpses of something else—of a fine Italian hand at work behind the scenes . . ."

There was a long pause while the Chief Constable looked at Battle. "You may be right," he said at last. "Dash it all, there's *something* funny about this business. What's your idea now, of our plan of campaign?"

Battle stroked his square jaw.

"Well, sir," he said, "I'm always in favor of going about things the obvious way. Everything's been set to make us suspicious of Mr. Nevile Strange. Let's go on being suspicious of him. Needn't go so far as actually to arrest him, but hint at it, question him, put the wind up him—and observe everybody's reactions generally. Verify his statements, go over his movements that night with a toothcomb. In fact, show our hand as plainly as may be."

"Quite Machiavellian," said Major Mitchell with a twinkle. "Imitation of a heavy-handed policeman by star actor Battle."

The Superintendent smiled.

"I always like doing what's expected of me, sir. This time I mean to be a bit slow about it—take my time. I want to do some nosing about. Being suspicious of Mr. Nevile Strange is a very good excuse for nosing about. I've an idea, you know, that something rather odd has been going on in that house."

"Looking for the sex angle?"

"If you like to put it that way, sir."

"Handle it your own way, Battle. You and Leach carry on between you."

"Thank you, sir." Battle stood up. "Nothing suggestive from the solicitors?"

"No. I rang them up. I know Trelawny fairly well. He's sending me a copy of Sir Matthew's will and also of Lady Tressilian's. She had about five hundred a year of her own—invested in gilt-edged securities. She left a legacy to Barrett and a small one to Hurstall, the rest to Mary Aldin."

"That's three we might keep an eye on," said Battle.

Mitchell looked amused.

"Suspicious fellow, aren't you?"

"No use letting oneself be hypnotized by fifty thousand pounds," said Battle stolidly. "Many a murder has been done for less than fifty pounds. It depends on how much you want the money. Barrett got a legacy— and maybe she took the precaution to dope herself so as to avert suspicion."

"She very nearly passed out. Lazenby hasn't let us question her yet."

"Overdid it out of ignorance, perhaps. Then Hurstall may have been in bad need of cash for all we know. And Miss Aldin, if she's no money of her own, might have fancied a bit of life on a nice little income before she's too old to enjoy it."

The Chief Constable looked doubtful.

"Well," he said, "it's up to you two. Get on with the job."

V

Back at Gull's Point, the two police officers received Williams' and Jones' reports.

Nothing of a suspicious or suggestive nature had been found in any of the bedrooms. The servants were clamoring to be allowed to get on with the housework. Should he give them the word?

"Might as well, I suppose," said Battle. "I'll just have a stroll myself first through the two upper floors. Rooms that haven't been done very often tell you something about their occupants that's useful to know."

Sergeant Jones put down a small cardboard box on the table.

"From Mr. Nevile Strange's dark blue coat," he announced. "The red hairs were on the cuff, blonde hairs on the inside of the collar and the right shoulder."

Battle took out the two long red hairs and the half-dozen blonde ones and looked at them. He said, with a faint twinkle in his eye:

"Convenient. One blonde, one red head and one brunette in this house. So we know where we are at once. Red hair on the cuff, blonde on the collar? Mr. Nevile Strange does seem to be a bit of a Bluebeard. His arm round one wife and the other one's head on his shoulder."

"The blood on the sleeve has gone for analysis, sir. They'll ring us up as soon as they get the result."

Leach nodded.

"What about the servants?"

"I followed your instructions, sir. None of them is under notice to leave, or seems likely to have borne a grudge against the old lady. She was strict, but well liked. In any case the management of the servants lay with Miss Aldin. She seems to have been popular with them."

"Thought she was an efficient woman the moment I laid eyes on her," said Battle. "If she's our murderess, she won't be easy to hang."

Jones looked startled.

"But those prints on that niblick, sir, were—"

"I know—I know," said Battle. "The singularly obliging Mr. Strange's. There's a general belief that athletes aren't overburdened with brains (not at all true, by the way) but I can't believe Nevile Strange is a complete moron. What about those senna pods of the maid's?"

"They were always on the shelf in the servants' bathroom on the second floor. She used to put 'em in to soak midday, and they stood there until the evening when she went to bed."

"So that absolutely anybody could get at them! Anybody inside the house, that is to say."

Leach said with conviction:

"It's an inside job all right!"

"Yes, I think so. Not that this is one of those closed circle crimes. It isn't. Anyone who had a key could have opened the front door and walked in. Nevile Strange had that key last night—but it would probably be a simple matter to have got one cut, or an old hand could do it with a bit of wire. But I don't see any outsider knowing about the bell and that Barrett took senna at night! That's local inside knowledge!

"Come along, Jim, my boy. Let's go up and see this bathroom and all the rest of it."

They started on the top floor. First came a boxroom full of old broken furniture and junk of all kinds.

"I haven't looked through this, sir," said Jones. "I didn't know—"

"What you were looking for? Quite right. Only waste of time. From the dust on the floor nobody has been in here for at least six months."

The servants' rooms were all on this floor, also two unoccupied bedrooms with a bathroom, and Battle looked into each room and gave it a cursory glance, noticing that Alice, the pop-eyed housemaid, slept with her window shut; that Emma, the thin one, had a great many relations, photographs of whom were crowded on her chest of drawers, and that Hurstall had one or two pieces of good, though cracked, Dresden and Crown Derby porcelain.

The cook's room was severely neat and the kitchen-maid's chaotically untidy. Battle passed on into the bathroom which was the room nearest to the head of the stairs. Williams pointed out the long shelf over the wash basin, on which stood tooth glass and brushes, various unguents and bottles of salts and hair lotion. A packet of senna pods stood open at one end.

"No prints on the glass or packet?"

"Only the maid's own. I got hers from her room."

"He didn't need to handle the glass," said Leach. "He'd only have to drop the stuff in."

Battle went down the stairs followed by Leach. Halfway down this top flight was a rather awkwardly placed window. A pole with a hook on the end stood in a corner.

"You draw down the top sash with that," explained Leach. "But there's a burglar screw. The window can be drawn down, only so far. Too narrow for anyone to get in that way."

"I wasn't thinking of anyone getting in," said Battle. His eyes were thoughtful.

He went in the first bedroom on the next floor, which was Audrey Strange's. It was neat and fresh, ivory brushes on the dressing table—no clothes lying about. Battle looked into the wardrobe. Two plain coats and skirts, a couple of evening dresses, one or two summer frocks. The dresses were cheap, the tailormades well cut and expensive, but not new.

Battle nodded. He stood at the writing table a minute or two, fiddling with the pen tray on the left of the blotter.

Williams said: "Nothing of any interest on the blotting paper or in the waste paper basket."

"Your word's good enough," said Battle. "Nothing to be seen here."

They went on to the other rooms.

Thomas Royde's was untidy, with clothes lying about. Pipes and pipe ash on the tables and beside the bed, where a copy of Kipling's *Kim* lay half open.

"Used to native servants clearing up after him," said Battle. "Likes reading old favorites. Conservative type."

Mary Aldin's room was small but comfortable. Battle looked at the travel books on the shelves and the old-fashioned dented silver brushes. The furnishings and coloring in the room were more modern than the rest of the house.

"She's not so conservative," said Battle. "No photographs either. Not one who lives in the past."

There were three or four empty rooms, all well kept and dusted ready for occupation, and a couple of bathrooms. Then came Lady Tressilian's big double room. After that, reached by going down three little steps, came the two rooms and bathroom occupied by the Stranges.

Battle did not waste much time in Nevile's room. He glanced out of the open casement window below which the rocks fell sheer to the sea. The view was to the west, towards Stark Head, which rose wild and forbidding out of the water.

"Gets the afternoon sun," he murmured. "But rather a grim morning outlook. Nasty smell of seaweed at low tide, too. And that headland has got a grim look. Don't wonder it attracts suicides!"

He passed into the larger room, the door of which had been unlocked.

Here everything was in wild confusion. Clothes lay about in heaps— filmy underwear, stockings, jumpers tried on and discarded—a patterned summer frock thrown sprawling over the back of a chair. Battle looked inside the wardrobe. It was full of furs, evening dresses, shorts, tennis frocks, play-suits.

Battle shut the doors again almost reverently.

"Expensive tastes," he remarked. "She must cost her husband a lot of money."

Leach said darkly:

"Perhaps that's why—"

He left the sentence unfinished.

"Why he needed a hundred—or rather fifty thousand pounds? Maybe. We'd better see, I think, what he has to say about it."

They went down to the library. Williams was dispatched to tell the servants they could get on with the housework. The family were free to return to their rooms if they wished. They were to be informed of that fact and also that Inspector Leach would like an interview with each of them separately, starting with Mr. Nevile Strange.

When Williams had gone out of the room, Battle and Leach established themselves behind a massive Victorian table. A young policeman with notebook sat in the corner of the room, his pencil poised.

Battle said:

"You carry on for a start, Jim. Make it impressive." As the other nodded his head, Battle rubbed his chin and frowned.

"I wish I knew what keeps putting Hercule Poirot into my head."

"You mean that old chap—the Belgian—comic little guy?"

"Comic my foot," said Superintendent Battle. "About as dangerous as a black mamba and a she-leopard—that's what *he* is when he starts making a mountebank of himself! I wish he was here—this sort of thing would be right up his street."

"In what way?"

"Psychology," said Battle. "Real psychology—not the half-baked stuff people hand out who know nothing about it." His memory dwelt resentfully on Miss Amphrey and his daughter Sylvia. "No—the real genuine article— knowing just what makes the wheels go round. Keep a murderer talking— that's one of his lines. Says everyone is bound to speak what's true sooner or later—because in the end it's easier than telling lies. And so they make some little slip they don't think matters—and that's when you get them."

"So you're going to give Nevile Strange plenty of rope?"

Battle gave an absent-minded assent. Then he added, in some annoyance and perplexity:

"But what's really worrying me is—what put Hercule Poirot into my head? Upstairs—that's where it was. Now what did I see that reminded me of that little guy?"

The conversation was put to an end by the arrival of Nevile Strange.

He looked pale and worried, but much less nervous than he had done at the breakfast table. Battle eyed him keenly. Incredible that a man who knew—and he must know if he were capable of any thought processes at all—that he had left his fingerprints on the instrument of the crime— and who had since had his fingerprints taken by the police—should show neither intense nervousness nor elaborate brazening of it out.

Nevile Strange looked quite natural—shocked, worried, grieved—and just slightly and healthily nervous.

Jim Leach was speaking in his pleasant west country voice.

"We would like you to answer certain questions, Mr. Strange. Both as to your movements last night, and in reference to particular facts. At the same time I must caution you that you are not bound to answer these questions unless you like and that if you prefer to do so you may have your solicitor present."

He leaned back to observe the effect of this.

Nevile Strange looked, quite plainly, bewildered.

"He hasn't the least idea what we're getting at, or else he's a damned good actor," Leach thought to himself. Aloud he said, as Nevile did not answer, "Well, Mr. Strange?"

Nevile said: "Of course, ask me anything you like."

"You realize," said Battle pleasantly, "that anything you say will be taken down in writing and may subsequently be used in a court of law in evidence."

A flash of temper showed on Strange's face. He said sharply:

"Are you threatening me?"

"No, no, Mr. Strange. Warning you."

Nevile shrugged his shoulders.

"I suppose all this is part of your routine. Go ahead."

"You are ready to make a statement?"

"If that's what you call it."

"Then will you tell us exactly what you did last night? From dinner onwards, shall we say?"

"Certainly. After dinner we went into the drawing-room. We had coffee. We listened to the wireless—the news and so on. Then I decided to go across to Easterhead Bay Hotel and look up a chap who is staying there—a friend of mine."

"That friend's name is?"

"Latimer. Edward Latimer."

"An intimate friend?"

"Oh, so-so. We've seen a good deal of him since he's been down here. He's been over to lunch and dinner and we've been over there."

Battle said:

"Rather late, wasn't it, to go off to Easterhead Bay?"

"Oh, it's a gay spot—they keep it up till all hours."

"But this is rather an early-to-bed household, isn't it?"

"Yes, on the whole. However, I took the latchkey with me. Nobody had to sit up."

"Your wife didn't think of going with you?"

There was a slight change, a stiffening in Nevile's tone as he said:

"No, she had a headache. She'd already gone up to bed."

"Please go on, Mr. Strange."

"I was just going up to change—"

Leach interrupted.

"Excuse me, Mr. Strange. Change into what? Into evening dress, or out of evening dress?"

"Neither. I was wearing a blue suit—my best, as it happened, and as it was raining a bit and I proposed to take the ferry and walk the other side—it's about half a mile, as you know—I changed into an older suit— a grey pinstripe, if you want me to go into every detail."

"We do like to get things clear," said Leach humbly. "Please go on."

"I was going upstairs, as I say, when Barrett came and told me Lady Tressilian wanted to see me, so I went along and had a jaw with her for a bit."

Battle said gently:

"You were the last person to see her alive, I think, Mr. Strange?"

Nevile flushed.

"Yes—yes—I suppose I was. She was quite all right then."

"How long were you with her?"

"About twenty minutes to half an hour, I should think, then I went to my room, changed my suit and hurried off. I took the latchkey with me."

"What time was that?"

"About half-past ten, I should think. I hurried down the hill, just caught the ferry starting and went across to the Easterhead side. I found Latimer at the Hotel, we had a drink or two and a game of billiards. The time passed so quickly that I found I'd lost the last ferry back. It goes at one-thirty. So Latimer very decently got out his car and drove me back. That, as you know, means going all the way round by Saltington— sixteen miles. We left the Hotel at two o'clock and got back here somewhere around half past, I should say. I thanked Ted Latimer, asked him in for a drink, but he said he'd rather get straight back, so I let myself in and went straight to bed. I didn't see or hear anything amiss. The house seemed all asleep and peaceful. Then this morning I heard that girl screaming and—".

Leach stopped him.

"Quite, quite. Now to go back a little—to your conversation with Lady Tressilian—she was quite normal in her manner?"

"Oh, absolutely."

"What did you talk about?"

"Oh, one thing and another."

"Amicably?"

Nevile flushed.

"Certainly."

"You didn't, for instance," went on Leach smoothly, "have a violent quarrel?"

Nevile did not answer at once. Leach said:

"You had better tell the truth, you know. I'll tell you frankly some of your conversation was overheard."

Nevile said shortly:

"We had a bit of a disagreement. It was nothing."

"What was the subject of the disagreement?"

With an effort Nevile recovered his temper. He smiled.

"Frankly," he said, "she ticked me off. That often happened. If she disapproved of anyone she let them have it straight from the shoulder. She was old-fashioned, you see, and she was inclined to be down on modern ways and modern lines of thought—divorce—all that. We had an argument and I may have got a bit heated, but we parted on perfectly friendly terms—agreeing to differ." He added, with some heat, "I certainly didn't bash her over the head because I lost my temper over an argument—if that's what you think!"

Leach glanced at Battle. Battle leaned forward ponderously across the table. He said:

"You recognized that niblick as your property this morning. Have you any explanation for the fact that your fingerprints were found upon it?"

Nevile stared. He said sharply:

"I—but of course they would be—it's my club—I've often handled it."

"Any explanation, I mean, for the fact that your fingerprints show that *you were the last person to have handled it*?"

Nevile sat quite still. The color had gone out of his face.

"That's not true," he said at last. "It can't be. Somebody could have handled it after me—someone wearing gloves."

"No, Mr. Strange—nobody could have handled it *in the sense you mean*—by raising it to strike—without blurring your own marks."

There was a pause—a very long pause.

"Oh, God," said Nevile convulsively, and gave a long shudder. He put his hands over his eyes. The two policemen watched him.

Then he took away his hands. He sat up straight.

"It isn't true," he said quietly. "It simply isn't true. You think I killed her, but I didn't. I swear I didn't. There's some horrible mistake."

"You've no explanation to offer about these fingerprints?"

"How can I have? I'm dumbfounded."

"Have you any explanation for the fact that the sleeves and cuffs of your dark blue suit are stained with blood?"

"Blood?" It was a horror-struck whisper. "It couldn't be!"

"You didn't, for instance, cut yourself—"

"No. No, of course I didn't!"

They waited a little while.

Nevile Strange, his forehead creased, seemed to be thinking. He looked up at them at last with frightened horror-stricken eyes.

"It's fantastic!" he said. "Simply fantastic. It's none of it *true*."

"Facts are true enough," said Superintendent Battle.

"But why should I do such a thing? It's unthinkable—unbelievable! I've known Camilla all my life."

Leach coughed.

"I believe you told us yourself, Mr. Strange, that you come into a good deal of money upon Lady Tressilian's death?"

"You think that's why— But I don't want money! I don't *need* it!"

"That," said Leach, with his little cough, "is what you *say*, Mr. Strange."

Nevile sprang up.

"Look here, that's something I *can* prove. That I didn't need money. Let me ring up my bank manager—you can talk to him yourself."

The call was put through. The line was clear and in a very few minutes they were through to London. Nevile spoke:

"That you, Ronaldson? Nevile Strange speaking. You know my voice. Look here, will you give the police—they're here now—all the information they want about my affairs—yes—yes, please."

Leach took the phone. He spoke quietly. It went on, question and answer.

He replaced the phone at last.

"Well?" said Nevile eagerly.

Leach said impassively:

"You have a substantial credit balance, and the bank have charge of all your investments and report them to be in a favorable condition."

"So you see it's true what I said!"

"It seems so—but again, Mr. Strange, you may have commitments, debts—payment of blackmail—reasons for requiring money of which we do not know."

"But I haven't! I assure you I haven't. You won't find anything of that kind."

Superintendent Battle shifted his heavy shoulders. He spoke in a kind, fatherly voice.

"We've sufficient evidence, as I'm sure you'll agree, Mr. Strange, to ask for a warrant for your arrest. We haven't done so—*as yet*. We're giving you the benefit of the doubt, you see."

Nevile said bitterly: "You mean, don't you, that you've made up your minds I did it, but you want to get at the motive so as to clinch the case against me?"

Battle was silent. Leach looked at the ceiling.

Nevile said desperately:

"It's like some awful dream. There's nothing I can say or do. It's like—like being in a trap and you can't get out."

Superintendent Battle stirred. An intelligent gleam showed between his half-closed lids.

"That's very nicely put," he said. "Very nicely put indeed. It gives me an idea . . ."

VI

Sergeant Jones adroitly got rid of Nevile through the hall and then brought Kay in by the french window so that husband and wife did not meet.

"He'll see all the others, though," Leach remarked.

"All the better," said Battle. "It's only this one I want to deal with whilst she's still in the dark."

The day was overcast with a sharp wind. Kay was dressed in a tweed skirt and a purple sweater, above which her hair looked like a burnished copper bowl. She looked half frightened, half excited. Her beauty and vitality bloomed against the dark Victorian background of books and saddleback chairs.

Leach led her easily enough over her account of the previous evening.

She had had a headache and gone to bed early—about quarter past nine, she thought. She had slept heavily and heard nothing until the next morning, when she was wakened by hearing someone screaming.

Battle took up the questioning.

"Your husband didn't come in to see how you were before he went off for the evening?"

"No."

"You didn't see him from the time you left the drawing-room until the following morning. Is that right?"

Kay nodded.

Battle stroked his jaw.

"Mrs. Strange, the door between your room and that of your husband was locked. Who locked it?"

Kay said shortly: "I did."

Battle said nothing—but he waited—waited like an elderly father cat—for a mouse to come out of the hole he was watching.

His silence did what questions might not have accomplished. Kay bust out impetuously:

"Oh, I suppose you've got to have it all! That old doddering Hurstall must have heard us before tea and he'll tell you if I don't. He's probably told you already. Nevile and I had had a row—a flaming row! I was furious with him! I went up to bed and locked the door, because I was still in a flaming rage with him!"

"I see—I see," said Battle, at his most sympathetic. "And what was the trouble all about?"

"Does it matter? Oh, I don't mind telling you. Nevile has been behaving like a perfect idiot. It's all that woman's fault, though."

"What woman?"

"His first wife. She got him to come here in the first place."

"You mean—to meet you?"

"Yes. Nevile thinks it was all his own idea—poor innocent! But it wasn't. He never thought of such a thing until he met her in the Park one day and she got the idea into his head and made him believe he'd thought of it himself. He quite honestly thinks it was his idea, but I've seen Audrey's fine Italian hand behind it from the first."

"Why should she do such a thing?" asked Battle.

"Because she wanted to get hold of him again," said Kay. She spoke quickly and her breath came fast. "She's never forgiven him for going off with me. This is her revenge. She got him to fix up that we'd all be here together and then she got to work on him. She's been doing it ever since we arrived. She's clever, you know. Knows just how to look pathetic and elusive—yes, and how to play up another man, too. She got Thomas Royde, a faithful old dog who's always adored her, to be here at the same time, and she drove Nevile mad by pretending she was going to marry him."

She stopped, breathing angrily.

Battle said mildly:

"I should have thought he'd be glad for her to—er—find happiness with an old friend."

"Glad? He's as jealous as Hell!"

"Then he must be very fond of her."

"Oh, he is," said Kay bitterly. "*She's* seen to that!"

Battle's finger still ran dubiously over his jaw.

"You might have objected to this arrangement of coming here," he suggested.

"How could I? It would have looked as though I were jealous!"

"Well," said Batttle, "after all, you were, weren't you?"

Kay flushed.

"Always! I've always been jealous of Audrey. Right from the beginning—or nearly the beginning. I used to feel her there in the house. It was as though it were *her* house, not mine. I changed the color scheme and did it all up but it was no good! I'd feel her there like a gray ghost creeping about. I knew Nevile worried because he thought he'd treated her badly. He couldn't quite forget about her—she was always there—a reproachful feeling at the back of his mind. There are people, you know, who are like that. They seem rather colorless and not very interesting—but they make themselves *felt*."

Battle nodded thoughtfully. He said:

"Well, thank you, Mrs. Strange. That's all at present. We have to ask—er—a good many questions—especially with your husband inheriting so much money from Lady Tressilian—fifty thousand pounds—"

"Is it as much as that? We get it from old Sir Matthew's will, don't we?"

"You know all about it?"

"Oh yes. He left it to be divided between Nevile and Nevile's wife after Lady Tressilian's death. Not that I'm glad the old thing is dead. I'm not. I didn't like her very much—probably because she didn't like me—but it's too horrible to think of some burglar coming along and cracking her head open."

She went out on that. Battle looked at Leach.

"What do you think of her? Good-looking bit of goods, I will say. A man could lose his head over her easy enough."

Leach agreed.

"Doesn't seem to me quite a lady, though," he said dubiously.

"They aren't nowadays," said Battle. "Shall we see No. 1? No, I think we'll have Miss Aldin next, and get an outside angle on this matrimonial business."

Mary Aldin came in composedly and sat down. Beneath her outward calmness her eyes looked worried.

She answered Leach's questions clearly enough, confirming Nevile's account of the evening. She had come up to bed about ten o'clock.

"Mr. Strange was then with Lady Tressilian?"

"Yes, I could hear them talking."

"Talking, Miss Aldin, or quarrelling?"

She flushed but answered quietly:

"Lady Tressilian, you know, was fond of discussion. She often sounded acrimonious when she was really nothing of the kind. Also, she was inclined to be autocratic and to domineer over people—and a man doesn't take that kind of thing as easily as a woman does."

"As you do, perhaps," thought Battle.

He looked at her intelligent face. It was she who broke the silence.

"I don't want to be stupid—but it really seems to me incredible—quite incredible, that you should suspect one of the people in this house. Why shouldn't it be an outsider?"

"For several reasons, Miss Aldin. For one thing, nothing was taken and no entry was forced. I needn't remind you of the geography of your own house and grounds, but just bear this in mind. On the west is a sheer cliff down to the sea, to the south are a couple of terraces with a wall and a drop to the sea, on the east the garden slopes down almost to the shore, but it is surrounded by a high wall. The only ways out are a small door leading through on to the road which was found bolted inside as usual this morning and the main door to the house, which is set on the road. I'm not saying no one could climb that wall, nor that they could not have got in by using a spare key to the front door or even a skeleton key—but I'm saying that as far as I can see no one did anything of the sort. Whoever committed this crime knew that Barrett took senna pod decoction every night, and doped it—that means someone in the house. The niblick was taken from the cupboard under the stairs. *It wasn't an outsider, Miss Aldin.*"

"It wasn't Nevile! I'm sure it wasn't Nevile!"

"Why are you so sure?"

She raised her hands hopelessly.

"It just isn't like him—that's why! He wouldn't kill a defenseless old woman in bed—*Nevile!*'

"It doesn't seem very likely," said Battle reasonably, "but you'd be surprised at the things people do when they've got a good enough reason. Mr. Strange may have wanted money very badly."

"I'm sure he didn't. He's not an extravagant person—he never has been."

"No, but his wife is."

"Kay? Yes, perhaps—but oh, it's too ridiculous. I'm sure the last thing Nevile has been thinking of lately is money."

Superintendent Battle coughed.

"He's had other worries, I understand?"

"Kay told you, I suppose? Yes, it really has been rather difficult. Still, it's nothing to do with this dreadful business."

"Probably not, but all the same I'd like to hear your version of the affair, Miss Aldin."

Mary said slowly: "Well, as I say, it has created a difficult—situation. Whosoever's idea it was to begin with—"

He interrupted her deftly.

"I understood it was Mr. Nevile Strange's idea?"

"He said it was."

"But you yourself don't think so?"

"I—no—it isn't like Nevile somehow. I've had a feeling all along that somebody else put the idea into his head."

"Mrs. Audrey Strange, perhaps?"

"It seems incredible that Audrey should do such a thing."

"Then who else could it have been?"

Mary raised her shoulders helplessly.

"I don't know. It's just—queer."

"Queer," said Battle thoughtfully. "That's what I feel about this case. It's queer."

"Everything's been queer. There's been a feeling—I can't describe it. Something in the air. A *menace*."

"Everybody strung up and on edge?'

"Yes, just that . . . We've all suffered from it. Even Mr. Latimer—" She stopped.

"I was just coming to Mr. Latimer. What can you tell me, Miss Aldin, about Mr. Latimer? Who is Mr. Latimer?"

"Well, really, I don't know much about him. He's a friend of Kay's."

"He's Mrs. Strange's friend. Known each other a long time?"

"Yes, she knew him before her marriage."

"Mr. Strange like him?"

"Quite well, I believe."

"No—trouble there?"

Battle put it delicately. Mary replied at once and emphatically: "Certainly not!"

"Did Lady Tressilian like Mr. Latimer?"

"Not very much."

Battle took warning from the aloof tone of her voice and changed the subject.

"This maid, now, Jane Barrett, she has been with Lady Tressilian a long time? You consider her trustworthy?"

"Oh absolutely. She was devoted to Lady Tressilian."

Battle leaned back in his chair.

"In fact you wouldn't consider for a moment the possibility that Barrett hit Lady Tressilian over the head and then doped herself to avoid being suspected?"

"Of course not. Why on earth should she?"

"She gets a legacy, you know."

"So do I," said Mary Aldin.

She looked at him steadily.

"Yes," said Battle. "So do you. Do you know how much?"

"Mr. Trelawny has just arrived. He told me."

"You didn't know about it beforehand?"

"No. I certainly assumed, from what Lady Tressilian occasionally let fall, that she had left me something. I have very little of my own, you know. Not enough to live on without getting work of some kind. I thought that Lady Tressilian would leave me at least a hundred a year—but she has some cousins, and I did not at all know how she proposed to leave that money which was hers to dispose of. I knew, of course, that Sir Matthew's estate went to Nevile and Audrey."

"So she didn't know what Lady Tressilian was leaving her," Leach said when Mary Aldin had been dismissed. "At least that's what she *says*."

"That's what she says," agreed Battle. "And now for Bluebeard's first wife."

VII

Audrey was wearing a pale grey flannel coat and skirt. In it she looked so pale and ghostlike that Battle was reminded of Kay's words, "A grey ghost creeping about the house."

She answered his questions simply and without any signs of emotion.

Yes, she had gone to bed at ten o'clock, the same time as Miss Aldin. She had heard nothing during the night.

"You'll excuse me butting into your private affairs," said Battle, "but will you explain just how it comes about that you are here in the house?"

"I always come to stay at this time. This year, my—my late husband wanted to come at the same time and asked me if I would mind."

"It was his suggestion?"

"Oh yes."

"Not yours?"

"Oh no."

"But you agreed?"

"Yes, I agreed . . . I didn't feel—that I could very well refuse."

"Why not, Mrs. Strange?"

But she was vague.

"One doesn't like to be disobliging."

"You were the injured party?"

"I beg your pardon?"

"It was you who divorced your husband?"

"Yes."

"Do you—excuse me—feel any rancour against him?"

"No—not at all."

"You have a very forgiving nature, Mrs. Strange."

She did not answer. He tried silence—but Audrey was not Kay, to be thus goaded into speech. She could remain silent without any hint of uneasiness. Battle acknowledged himself beaten.

"You are sure it was not your idea—this meeting?"

"Quite sure."

"You are on friendly terms with the present Mrs. Strange?"

"I don't think she likes me very much."

"Do you like her?"

"Yes. I think she is very beautiful."

"Well—thank you—I think that is all."

She got up and walked towards the door. Then she hesitated and came back.

"I would just like to say—" she spoke nervously and quickly. "You think Nevile did this—that he killed her because of the money. I'm quite sure that isn't so. Nevile has never cared much about money. I do know that. I was married to him for eight years, you know. I just can't see him killing anyone like that for money—it—it—isn't Nevile. I know my saying so isn't of any value as evidence—but I do wish you could believe it."

She turned and hurried out of the room.

"And what do you make of *her*?" asked Leach. "I've never seen anyone so—so devoid of emotion."

"She didn't show any," said Battle. "But it's there. Some very strong emotion. And I don't know what it is . . ."

VIII

Thomas Royde came last. He sat, solemn and stiff, blinking like a little owl.

He was home from Malaya—first time for eight years. Had been in the habit of staying at Gull's Point ever since he was a boy. Mrs. Audrey Strange was a distant cousin—and had been brought up by his family from the age of nine. On the preceding night he had gone to bed just before eleven. Yes, he had heard Mr. Nevile Strange leave the house but had not seen him. Nevile had left at about twenty past ten or perhaps a little later. He himself had heard nothing during the night. He was up and in the garden when the discovery of Lady Tressilian's body had been made. He was an early riser.

There was a pause.

"Miss Aldin has told us that there was a state of tension in the house. Did you notice this too?"

"I don't think so. Don't notice things much."

"That's a lie," thought Battle to himself. "You notice a good deal, I should say—more than most."

No, he didn't think Nevile Strange had been short of money in any way. He certainly had not seemed so. But he knew very little about Mr. Strange's affairs.

"How well did you know the second Mrs. Strange?"

"I met her here for the first time."

Battle played his last card.

"You may know, Mr. Royde, that we've found Mr. Nevile Strange's fingerprints on the weapon. And we've found blood on the sleeve of the coat he wore last night."

He paused. Royde nodded.

"He was telling us," he muttered.

"I'm asking you frankly: *Do you think he did it*?"

Thomas Royde never liked to be hurried. He waited for a minute— which is a very long time—before he answered:

"Don't see why you ask *me*! Not my business. It's yours. Should say myself—very unlikely."

"Can you think of anyone who seems to you more likely?"

Thomas shook his head.

"Only person I think likely, can't possibly have done it. So that's that."

"And who is that?"

But Royde shook his head more decidedly.

"Couldn't possibly say. Only my private opinion."

"It's your duty to assist the police."

"Tell you any facts. This isn't facts. Just an idea. And it's impossible, anyway."

"We didn't get much out of him," said Leach when Royde had gone.

Battle agreed.

"No, we didn't. He's got something in his mind—something quite definite. I'd like to know what it is. This is a very peculiar sort of crime, Jim, my boy—"

The telephone rang before Leach could answer. He took up the receiver and spoke. After a minute or two of listening he said "Good," and slammed it down.

"Blood on the coat sleeve is human," he announced. "Same blood group as Lady T's. Looks as though Nevile Strange is for it—"

Battle had walked over to the window and was looking out with considerable interest.

"A beautiful young man out there," he remarked. "Quite beautiful and a definite wrong 'un, I should say. It's a pity Mr. Latimer—for I feel that that's Mr. Latimer—was over at Easterhead Bay last night. He's the type that would smash in his own grandmother's head if he thought he could get away with it and if he knew he'd make something out of it."

"Well, there wasn't anything in it for him," said Leach. "Lady T's death doesn't benefit him in any way whatever." The telephone bell rang again. "Damn this phone, what's the matter now?"

He went to it.

"Hullo. Oh, it's you, Doctor. What? Come round, has she? What? *What?*"

He turned his head. "Uncle, just come and listen to this."

Battle came over and took the phone. He listened, his face as usual showing no expression. He said to Leach:

"Get Nevile Strange, Jim."

When Nevile came in, Battle was just replacing the phone on its hook.

Nevile, looking white and spent, stared curiously at the Scotland Yard superintendent, trying to read the emotion behind the wooden mask.

"Mr. Strange," said Battle. "Do you know anyone who dislikes you very much?"

Nevile stared and shook his head.

"Sure?" Battle was impressive. "I mean, sir, someone who does more than dislike you—someone who—frankly—hates your guts?"

Nevile sat bolt upright.

"No. No, certainly not. Nothing of the kind."

"Think, Mr. Strange. Is there no one you've injured in any way—?"

Nevile flushed.

"There's only one person I can be said to have injured, and she's not the kind who bears rancour. That's my first wife, when I left her for another woman. But I can assure you that she does't hate me. She's—she's been an angel."

The Superintendent leaned forward across the table.

"Let me tell you, Mr. Strange; you're a very lucky man. I don't say I liked the case against you—I didn't. But it *was* a case! It would have stood up all right, and unless the jury happened to have liked your personality, *it would have hanged you.*"

"You speak," said Nevile, "as though all that were past?"

"It is past," said Battle. "You've been saved, Mr. Strange, by pure chance."

Nevile still looked inquiringly at him.

"After you left her last night," said Battle, "Lady Tressilian rang the bell for her maid."

He watched whilst Nevile took it in.

"*After.* Then Barrett saw her—?"

"Yes. *Alive and well.* Barrett also saw you leave the house before she went in to her mistress."

Nevile said:

"But the niblick—my fingerprints—"

"She wasn't hit with that niblick. Dr. Lazenby didn't like it at the time. I saw that. She was killed with something else. That niblick was put there deliberately to throw suspicion on *you*. It may be by someone who overheard the quarrel and so selected you as a suitable victim, or it may be because—"

He paused, and then repeated his question:

"Who is there in this house that hates you, Mr. Strange?"

IX

"I've got a question for you, Doctor," said Battle.

They were in the doctor's house after returning from the nursing home, where they had had a short interview with Jane Barrett.

Barrett was weak and exhausted but quite clear in her statement.

She had just been getting into bed after drinking her senna when Lady Tressilian's bell had rung. She had glanced at the clock and seen the time—twenty-five minutes past ten.

She had put on her dressing-gown and come down. She had heard a noise in the hall below and had looked over the banisters.

"It was Mr. Nevile just going out. He was taking his raincoat down from the hook."

"What suit was he wearing?"

"His grey pinstripe. His face was very worried and unhappy looking. He shoved his arms into his coat as though he didn't care how he put it on. Then he went out and banged the front door behind him. I went on in to her ladyship. She was very drowsy, poor dear, and couldn't remember why she had rung for me—she couldn't always, poor lady. But I beat up her pillows and brought her a fresh glass of water and settled her comfortably."

"She didn't seem upset or afraid of anything?"

"Just tired, that's all. I was tired myself. Yawning. I went up and went right off to sleep."

That was Barrett's story, and it seemed impossible to doubt her genuine grief and horror at the news of her mistress's death.

They went back to Lazenby's house and it was then that Battle announced that he had a question to ask.

"Ask away," said Lazenby.

"What time do you think Lady Tressilian died?"

"I've told you. Between ten o'clock and midnight."

"I know that's what you said. But it wasn't my question. I asked you what you, personally, *thought.*"

"Off the record, eh?"

"Yes."

"All right. My guess would be in the neighborhood of eleven o'clock."

"That's what I wanted you to say," said Battle.

"Glad to oblige. Why?"

"Never did like the idea of her being killed before ten-twenty. Take Barrett's sleeping draught—it wouldn't have got to work by then. That sleeping draught shows that the murder was meant to be committed a good deal later—during the night. I prefer midnight, myself."

"Could be. Eleven is only a guess."

"But it definitely couldn't be later than midnight?"

"No."

"It couldn't be after two-thirty?"

"Good heavens, no."

"Well, that seems to let Strange out all right. I'll just have to check up on his movements after he left the house. If he's telling the truth he's washed out and we can go on to our other suspects."

"The other people who inherit money?" suggested Leach.

"Maybe," said Battle. "But somehow, I don't think so. Someone with a kink, I'm looking for."

"A kink?"

"A nasty kink."

When they left the doctor's house they went on to the ferry. The ferry consisted of a rowing boat operated by two brothers, Will and George Barnes. The Barnes brothers knew everybody in Saltcreek by sight and most of the people who came over from Easterhead Bay. George said at once that Mr. Strange from Gull's Point had gone across at ten-thirty on the preceding night. No, he had not brought Mr. Strange back again. Last ferry had gone at one-thirty from the Easterhead side and Mr. Strange wasn't on it.

Battle asked him if he knew Mr. Latimer.

"Latimer? Latimer? Tall handsome young gentleman? Comes over from the Hotel up to Gull's Point? Yes, I know him. Didn't see him at all last night, though. He's been over this morning. Went back last trip."

They crossed on the ferry and went up to the Easterhead Bay Hotel.

Here they found Mr. Latimer newly returned from the other side. He had crossed on the ferry before theirs.

Mr. Latimer was very anxious to do all he could to help.

"Yes, old Nevile came over last night. Looked very blue over something. Told me he'd had a row with the old lady. I hear he'd fallen out with Kay too, but he didn't tell me that, of course. Anyway, he was a bit down in the mouth. Seemed quite glad of my company for once in a way."

"He wasn't able to find you at once, I understand?"

Latimer said sharply:

"Don't know why. I was sitting in the lounge. Strange said he looked in and didn't see me, but he wasn't in a state to concentrate. Or I may have strolled out into the gardens for five minutes or so. Always get out when I can. Beastly smell in this Hotel. Noticed it last night in the Bar. Drains, I think! Strange mentioned it too! We both smelt it. Nasty decayed smell. Might be a dead rat under the billiard room floor."

"You played billiards, and after your game?"

"Oh we talked a bit, had another drink or two. Then Nevile said 'Hullo, I've missed the ferry,' so I said I'd get out my car and drive him back, which I did. We got there about two-thirty."

"And Mr. Strange was with you all the evening?"

"Oh yes. Ask anybody. They'll tell you."

"Thank you, Mr. Latimer. We have to be so careful."

Leach said as they left the smiling, self-possessed young man, "What's the idea of checking up so carefully on Nevile Strange?"

Battle smiled. Leach got it suddenly.

"Good lord, it's the *other* one you're checking up on. So that's your idea."

"It's too soon to have ideas," said Battle. "I've just got to know exactly where Mr. Ted Latimer was last night. We know that from quarter past eleven, say—to after midnight—he was with Nevile Strange. But where was he *before* that—when Strange arrived and couldn't find him?"

They pursued their inquiries doggedly—with bar attendants, waiters, lift boys. Latimer had been seen in the lounge between nine and ten. He had been in the bar at a quarter past ten. But between that time and eleven-thirty he seemed to have been singularly elusive. Then one of the maids was found who declared that Mr. Latimer had been "in one of the small writing-rooms with Mrs. Beddoes—that's the fat North country lady."

Pressed as to time, she said she thought it was about eleven o'clock.

"That tears it," said Battle gloomily. "He was here all right. Just didn't want attention drawn to his fat (and no doubt rich) lady friend. That throws us back on those others—the servants, Kay Strange, Audrey Strange, Mary Aldin and Thomas Royde. *One* of them killed the old lady, but which? If we could find the real weapon—"

He stopped, then slapped his thigh.

"Got it, Jim, my boy! I know now what made me think of Hercule Poirot. We'll have a spot of lunch and go back to Gull's Point and I'll show you something."

X

Mary Aldin was restless. She went in and out of the house, picked off a dead dahlia head here and there, went back into the drawing-room and shifted flower vases in an unmeaning fashion.

From the library came a vague murmur of voices. Mr. Trelawny was in there with Nevile. Kay and Audrey were nowhere to be seen.

Mary went out in the garden again. Down by the wall she spied Thomas Royde placidly smoking. She went and joined him.

"Oh dear." She sat down beside him with a deep perplexed sigh.

"Anything the matter?" Thomas asked.

Mary laughed with a slight note of hysteria in the laugh.

"Nobody but you would say a thing like that. A murder in the house and you just say 'Is anything the matter?' "

Looking a little surprised, Thomas said:

"I meant anything fresh?"

"Oh, I know what you meant. It's really a wonderful relief to find anyone so gloriously just-the-same-as-usual as you are!"

"Not much good, is it, getting all het up over things?"

"No, no. You're eminently sensible. It's how you manage to do it beats me."

"Well, I suppose I'm an outsider."

"That's true, of course. You can't feel the relief all the rest of us do that Nevile is cleared."

"I'm very pleased he is, of course," said Royde.

Mary shuddered.

"It was a very near thing. If Camilla hadn't taken it into her head to ring the bell for Barrett after Nevile had left her—"

She left the sentence unfinished. Thomas finished it for her.

"Then old Nevile would have been for it all right."

He spoke with a certain grim satisfaction, then shook his head with a slight smile, as he met Mary's reproachful gaze.

"I'm not really heartless, but now that Nevile's all right I can't help being pleased he had a bit of a shaking up. He's always so damned complacent."

"He isn't really, Thomas."

"Perhaps not. It's just his manner. Anyway he was looking scared as Hell this morning!"

"What a cruel streak you have!"

"Anyway it's all right now. You know, Mary, even here Nevile has had the devil's own luck. Some other poor beggar with all that evidence piled up against him mightn't have had such a break."

Mary shivered again. "Don't say that. I like to think the innocent are—protected."

"Do you, my dear?" His voice was gentle.

Mary burst out suddenly:

"Thomas, I'm worried. I'm frightfully worried."

"Yes?"

"It's about Mr. Treves."

Thomas dropped his pipe on the stones. His voice changed as he bent to pick it up.

"What about Mr. Treves?"

"That night he was here—that story he told—about a little murderer! I've been wondering, Thomas . . . Was it just a story? Or did he tell it with a purpose?"

"You mean," said Royde deliberately, "was it aimed at someone who was in the room?"

Mary whispered, "Yes."

Thomas said quietly:

"I've been wondering, too. As a matter of fact that was what I was thinking about when you came along just now."

Mary half closed her eyes.

"I've been trying to remember . . . He told it, you know, so very deliberately. He almost dragged it into the conversation. And he said he would recognize the person anywhere. He emphasized that. As though he *had* recognized him."

"Mm," said Thomas. "I've been through all that."

"But why should he do it? What was the point?"

"I suppose," said Royde, "it was a kind of warning. Not to try anything on."

"You mean that Mr. Treves knew then that Camilla was going to be murdered?"

"No-o. I think that's too fantastic. It may have been just a general warning."

"What I've been wondering is, do you think we ought to tell the police?"

To that Thomas again gave his thoughtful consideration.

"I think not," he said at last. "I don't see that it's relevant in any way. It's not as though Treves were alive and could tell them anything."

"No," said Mary. "He's dead!" She gave a quick shiver. "It's so odd, Thomas, the way he died."

"Heart attack. He had a bad heart."

"I mean that curious business about the lift being out of order. *I don't like it.*"

"I don't like it very much myself," said Thomas Royde.

XI

Superintendent Battle looked round the bedroom. The bed had been made. Otherwise the room was unchanged. It had been neat when they first looked round it. It was neat now.

"That's it," said Superintendent Battle, pointing to the old-fashioned steel fender. "Do you see anything odd about that fender?"

"Must take some cleaning," said Jim Leach. "It's well kept. Nothing odd about it that I can see, except—yes, the left-hand knob is brighter than the right-hand one."

"That's what put Hercule Poirot into my head," said Battle. "You know his fad about things not being quite symmetrical—gets him all worked up. I suppose I thought unconsciously, 'That would worry old Poirot,' and then I began talking about him. Get your fingerprint kit, Jones, we'll have a look at these two knobs."

Jones reported presently.

"There are prints on the right-hand knob, sir, none on the left."

"It's the left one we want, then. Those other prints are the housemaid's when she last cleaned it. That left-hand one has been cleaned twice."

"There was a bit of screwed-up emery paper in this waste paper basket," volunteered Jones. "I didn't think it meant anything."

"Because you didn't know what you were looking for, then. Gently now, I'll bet anything you like that knob unscrews—yes, I thought so."

Presently Jones held the knob up.

"It's a good weight," he said, weighing it in his hand.

Leach, bending over it, said:

"There's something dark—on the screw."

"Blood, as likely as not," said Battle. "Cleaned the knob itself and wiped it and that little stain on the screw wasn't noticed. I'll bet anything you like that's the weapon that caved the old lady's skull in. But there's more to find. It's up to you, Jones, to search the house again. This time, you'll know exactly what you're looking for."

He gave a few swift detailed instructions. Going to the window he put his head out.

"There's something yellow tucked into the ivy. That may be another piece of the puzzle. I rather think it is."

XII

Crossing the hall, Superintendent Battle was waylaid by Mary Aldin.

"Can I speak to you a minute, Superintendent?"

"Certainly, Miss Aldin. Shall we come in here?"

He threw open the dining-room door. Lunch had been cleared away by Hurstall.

"I want to ask you something, Superintendent. Surely you don't, you can't still think that this—this awful crime was done by one of us? It must have been someone from outside! Some maniac!"

"You may not be far wrong there, Miss Aldin. Maniac is a word that describes this criminal very well if I'm not mistaken. But not an outsider."

Her eyes opened very wide.

"Do you mean that someone in this houe is—is *mad?*"

"You're thinking," said the Superintendent, "of someone foaming at the mouth and rolling their eyes. Mania isn't like that. Some of the most dangerous criminal lunatics have looked as sane as you or I. It's a question, usually, of having an obsession. One idea, preying on the mind, gradually distorting it. Pathetic, reasonable people who come up to you and explain how they're being persecuted and how everyone is spying on them—and you sometimes feel it must all be true."

"I'm sure nobody here has any ideas of being persecuted."

"I only gave that as an instance. There are other forms of insanity. But I believe whoever committed this crime was under the domination of one fixed idea—an idea on which they had brooded until literally nothing else mattered or had any importance."

Mary shivered. She said:

"There's something I think you ought to know."

Concisely and clearly she told him of Mr. Treves' visit to dinner and of the story he had told. Superintendent Battle was deeply interested.

"He said he could recognize this person? Man or woman—by the way?"

"I took it that it was a boy the story was about—but it's true Mr. Treves didn't actually say so—in fact I remember now—he distinctly stated he would not give any particulars as to sex or age."

"Did he? Rather significant, perhaps. And he said there was a definite physical peculiarity by which he could be sure of knowing this child anywhere?"

" Yes."

"A scar, perhaps—has anybody here got a scar?"

He noticed the faint hesitation before Mary Aldin replied:

"Not that I have noticed."

"Come now, Miss Aldin," he smiled. "You *have* noticed something. If so, don't you think that I shall be able to notice it, too?"

She shook her head.

"I—I haven't noticed anything of the kind."

But he saw that she was startled and upset. His words had obviously suggested a very unpleasant train of thought to her. He wished he knew just what it was, but his experience made him aware that to press her at this minute would not yield any result.

He brought the conversation back to old Mr. Treves.

Mary told him of the tragic sequel to the evening.

Battle questioned her at some length. Then he said quietly:

"That's a new one on me. Never came across that before."

"What do you mean?"

"I've never come across a murder committed by the simple expedient of hanging a placard on a lift."

She looked horrified.

"You don't really think—?"

"That it was murder? Of course it was! Quick, resourceful murder. It might not have come off, of course—but it *did* come off."

"Just because Mr. Treves knew—?"

"Yes. Because he would have been able to direct our attention to one particular person in this house. As it is, we've started in the dark. But we've got a glimmer of light now, and every minute the case is getting clearer. I'll tell you this, Miss Aldin—this murder was very carefully planned beforehand down to the smallest detail. And I want to impress one thing on your mind—don't let anybody know that you've told me what you have. That is important. Don't tell *anyone*, mind."

Mary nodded. She was still looking dazed.

Superintendent Battle went out of the room and proceeded to do what he had been about to do when Mary Aldin intercepted him. He was a methodical man. He wanted certain information, and a new and promising hare did not distract him from the orderly performance of his duties, however tempting this new hare might be.

He tapped on the library door, and Nevile Strange's voice called, "Come in."

Battle was introduced to Mr. Trelawny, a tall distinguished-looking man with a keen dark eye.

"Sorry if I am butting in," said Superintendent Battle apologetically. "But there's something I haven't got clear. You, Mr. Strange, inherit half the late Sir Matthew's estate, but who inherits the other half?"

Nevile looked surprised.

"I told you. My wife."

"Yes. But—" Battle coughed in a deprecating manner, "which wife, Mr. Strange?"

"Oh, I see. Yes, I expressed myself badly. The money goes to Audrey, who was my wife at the time the will was made. That's right, Mr. Trelawny?"

The lawyer assented.

"The bequest is quite clearly worded. The estate is to be divided between Sir Matthew's ward, Nevile Henry Strange, and his wife, Audrey Elizabeth Strange, née Standish. The subsequent divorce makes no difference whatever."

"That's clear, then," said Battle. "I take it Mrs. Audrey Strange is fully aware of these facts?"

"Certainly," said Mr. Trelawny.

"And the present Mrs. Strange?"

"Kay?" Nevile looke slightly surprised. "Oh, I suppose so. At least—I've never talked much about it with her—"

"I think you'll find," said Battle, "that she's under a misapprehension. She thinks that the money on Lady Tressilian's death comes to you and your *present* wife. At least, that's what she gave me to understand this morning. That's why I came along to find out how the position really lay."

"How extraordinary," said Nevile. "Still, I suppose it might have happened quite easily. She has said once or twice, now that I think about it, 'We come into that money when Camilla dies,' but I suppose I assumed that she was just associating herself with me in my share of it."

"It's extraordinary," said Battle, "the amount of misunderstandings there are even between two people who discuss a thing quite often— both of them assuming different things and neither of them discovering the discrepancy."

"I suppose so," said Nevile, not sounding very interested. "It doesn't matter much in this case, anyway. It's not as though we're short of money at all. I'm very glad for Audrey. She has been very hard up and this will make a big difference to her."

Battle said bluntly: "But surely, sir, at the time of the divorce, she was entitled to an allowance from you?"

Nevile flushed. He said in a constrained voice:

"There is such a thing as—as pride, Superintendent. Audrey has always persistently refused to touch a penny of the allowance I wished to make her."

"A very generous allowance," put in Mr. Trelawny. "But Mrs. Audrey Strange has always returned it and refused to accept it."

"Very interesting," said Battle, and went out before anyone could ask him to elaborate that comment.

He went out and found his nephew.

"On its face value," he said, "there's a nice monetary motive for nearly everybody in this case. Nevile Strange and Audrey Strange get a cool fifty thousand each. Kay Strange thinks she's entitled to fifty thousand. Mary Aldin gets an income that frees her from having to earn her living. Thomas Royde, I'm bound to say, doesn't gain. But we can include Hurstall and even Barrett if we admit that she'd take the risk of finishing herself off to avoid suspicion. Yes, as I say, there are no lack of money motives. And yet, if I'm right, money doesn't enter into this at all. If there's such a thing as murder for pure hate, this is it. And if no one comes along and throws a spanner into the works, I'm going to get the person who did it!"

XIII

Angus MacWhirter sat on the terrace of the Easterhead Bay Hotel and stared across the river to the frowning height of Stark Head opposite.

He was engaged at the moment in a careful stock-taking of his thoughts and emotions.

He hardly knew what it was that had made him choose to spend his last few days of leisure where he now was. Yet something had drawn him there. Perhaps the wish to test himself—to see if there remained in his heart any of the old despair.

Mona? How little he cared now. She was married to the other man.

He had passed her in the street one day without feeling any emotion. He could remember his grief and bitterness when she left him, but they were past now and gone.

He was recalled from these thoughts by an impact of wet dog and the frenzied appeal of a newly made friend, Miss Diana Brinton, aged thirteen.

"Oh come away, Don. Come *away*. Isn't it awful? He's rolled on some fish or something down on the beach. You can smell him yards away. The fish was awfully dead, you know!"

MacWhirter's nose confirmed this assumption.

"In a sort of crevice on the rocks," said Miss Brinton. "I took him into the sea and tried to wash it off, but it doesn't seem to have done much good."

MacWhirter agreed. Don, a wire-haired terrier of amiable and loving disposition, was looking hurt by the tendency of his friends to keep him firmly at arm's lenghth.

"Sea water's no good," said MacWhirter. "Hot water and soap's the only thing."

"I know. But that's not so jolly easy in a Hotel. We haven't got a private bath."

In the end MacWhirter and Diana surreptitiously entered by the side door with Don on a lead, and smuggling him up to MacWhirter's bathroom, a thorough cleansing took place and both MacWhirter and Diana got very wet. Don was very sad when it was all over. That disgusting smell of soap again—just when he had found a really nice perfume such as any other dog would envy. Oh well, it was always the same with humans— they had no decent sense of smell.

The little incident had left MacWhirter in a more cheerful mood. He took the bus into Saltington, where he had left a suit to be cleaned.

The girl in charge of the 24-Hour Cleaners looked at him vacantly.

"MacWhirter, did you say? I'm afraid it isn't ready yet."

"It should be." He had been promised that suit the day before, and even that would have been 48 and not 24 hours. A woman might have said all this. MacWhirter merely scowled.

"There's not been time yet," said the girl, smiling indifferently.

"Nonsense."

The girl stopped smiling. She snapped.

"Anyway, it's not done," she said.

"Then I'll take it away as it is," said MacWhirter.

"Nothing's been done to it," the girl warned him.

"I'll take it away."

"I daresay we might get it done by tomorrow—as a special favor."

"I'm not in the habit of asking for special favors. Just give me the suit, please."

Giving him a bad-tempered look, the girl went into the back room. She returned with a clumsily done up parcel which she pushed across the counter.

MacWhirter took it and went out.

He felt, quite ridiculously, as though he had won a victory. Actually it merely meant that he would have to have the suit cleaned elsewhere!

He threw the parcel on his bed when he returned to the Hotel and looked at it with annoyance. Perhaps he could get it sponged and pressed in the Hotel. It was not really too bad—perhaps it didn't actually need cleaning?

He undid the parcel and gave vent to an expression of annoyance. Really, the 24-Hour Cleaners were too inefficient for words. This wasn't his suit. It wasn't even the same color. It had been a dark blue suit he had left with them. Impertinent, inefficient muddlers.

He glanced irritably at the label. It had the name MacWhirter all right. Another MacWhirter? Or some stupid interchange of labels?

Staring down vexedly at the crumpled heap, he suddenly sniffed.

Surely he knew that smell—a particularly unpleasant smell . . . connected somehow with a dog. Yes, that was it. Diana and her dog. Absolutely and literally stinking fish!

He bent down and examined the suit. There it was, a discolored patch on the shoulder of the coat. On the *shoulder*—

Now that, thought MacWhirter, is really very curious . . .

Anyway, next day, he would have a few grim words with the girl at the 24-Hour Cleaners. Gross mismanagement!

XIV

After dinner he strolled out of the Hotel and down the road to the Ferry. It was a clear night, but cold, with a sharp foretaste of winter. Summer was over.

MacWhirter crossed in the ferry to the Saltcreek side. It was the second time that he was revisiting Stark Head. The place had a fascination for him. He walked slowly up the hill, passing the Balmoral Court Hotel and then a big house set on the point of a cliff. Gull's Point—he read the name on the painted door. Of course, that was where the old lady had been murdered. There had been a lot of talk in the Hotel about it, his chambermaid had insisted on telling him all about it and the newspapers had given it a prominence which had annoyed MacWhirter, who preferred to read of world-wide affairs and who was not interested in crime.

He went on, downhill again to skirt a small beach and some old-fashioned fishing cottages that had been modernized. Then up again till the road ended and petered out into the track that led up on Stark Head.

It was grim and forbidding on Stark Head. MacWhirter stood on the cliff edge looking down to the sea. So he had stood on that other night. He tried to recapture some of the feeling he had had then—the desperation, anger, weariness—the longing to be out of it all. But there was nothing to recapture. All that had gone. There was instead a cold anger. Caught on that tree, rescued by coastguards, fussed over like a naughty child in hospital, a series of indignities and affronts. Why couldn't he have been *left alone*? He would rather, a thousand times rather, be out of it all. He still felt that. The only thing he had lost was the necessary impetus.

How it had hurt him then to think of Mona! He could think of her quite calmly now. She had always been rather a fool. Easily taken by anyone who flattered her or played up to her idea of herself. Very pretty. Yes, very pretty—but no mind, not the kind of woman he had once dreamed about.

But that was beauty, of course—some vague fancied picture of a woman flying through the night with white draperies streaming out behind her . . . Something like the figure-head of a ship—only not so solid . . . not nearly so solid . . .

And then, with dramatic suddenness, the incredible happened! Out of the night came a flying figure. One minute she was not there, the next minute she was—a white figure running—running—to the cliff's edge. A figure, beautiful and desperate, driven to destruction by pursuing Furies! Running with a terrible desperation . . . He knew that desperation. He knew what it meant . . .

He came with a rush out of the shadows and caught her just as she was about to go over the edge!

He said fiercely: "No you don't . . ."

It was just like holding a bird. She struggled—struggled silently, and then, again like a bird, was suddenly dead still.

He said urgently:

"Don't throw yourself over! Nothing's worth it. *Nothing*. Even if you are desperately unhappy—"

She made a sound. It was, perhaps, a far-off ghost of a laugh.

He said sharply:

"You're not unhappy? What is it then?"

She answered him at once with the low softly-breathed word:

"Afraid."

"Afraid?" He was so astonished that he let her go, standing back a pace to see her better.

He realized then the truth of her words. It was fear that had lent that urgency to her footsteps. It was fear that made her small white intelligent face blank and stupid. Fear that dilated those wide-apart eyes.

He said incredulously: "What are you afraid of?"

She replied so low that he hardly heard it.

"I'm afraid of being hanged . . ."

Yes, she had said just that. He stared and stared. He looked from her to the cliff's edge.

"So that's why?"

"Yes. A quick death instead of—" She closed her eyes and shivered. She went on shivering.

MacWhirter was piecing things together logically in his mind.

He said at last:

"Lady Tressilian? The old lady who was murdered?" Then, accusingly: "You'll be Mrs. Strange—the first Mrs. Strange."

Still shivering she nodded her head.

MacWhirter went on in his slow careful voice, trying to remember all that he had heard. Rumor had been incorporated with fact.

"They detained your husband—that's right, isn't it? A lot of evidence against him—and then they found that that evidence had been faked by someone . . ."

He stopped and looked at her. She wasn't shivering any longer. She was standing looking at him like a docile child. He found her attitude unendurably affecting.

His voice went on:

"I see . . . Yes, I see how it was . . . He left you for another woman, didn't he? And you loved him . . . That's why—" He broke off. He said, "I understand. My wife left me for another man . . ."

She flung out her arms. She began stammering wildy, hopelessly:

"It's n-n-not—it's n-n-not l-like that. N-not at all."

He cut her short. His voice was stern and commanding.

"Go home. *You needn't be afraid any longer.* D'you hear? *I'll* see that you're not hanged!"

XV

Mary Aldin was lying on the drawing-room sofa. Her head ached and her whole body felt worn out.

The inquest had taken place the day before and, after formal evidence of identification, had been adjourned for a week.

Lady Tressilian's funeral was to take place on the morrow. Audrey and Kay had gone into Saltington in the car to get some black clothes. Ted Latimer had gone with them. Nevile and Thomas Royde had gone for a walk, so except for the servants, Mary was alone in the house.

Superintendent Battle and Inspector Leach had been absent today, and that, too, was a relief. It seemed to Mary that with their absence a shadow had been lifted. They had been polite, quite pleasant, in fact, but the ceaseless questions, that quiet deliberate probing and sifting of every fact was the sort of thing that wore hardly on the nerves. By now that wooden-faced Superintendent must have learned of every incident, every word, every gesture, even, of the past ten days.

Now, with their going, there was peace. Mary let herself relax. She would forget everything—everything. Just lie back and rest.

"Excuse me, Madam—"

It was Hurstall in the doorway, looking apologetic.

"Yes, Hurstall?"

"A gentleman wishes to see you. I have put him in the study."

Mary looked at him in astonishment and some annoyance.

"Who is it?"

"He gave his name as Mr. MacWhirter, Miss."

"I've never heard of him."

"No, Miss."

"He must be a reporter. You shouldn't have let him in, Hurstall."

Hurstall coughed.

"I don't think he is a reporter, Miss. I think he is a friend of Miss Audrey's."

"Oh, that's different."

Smoothing her hair, Mary went wearily across the hall and into the small study. She was, somehow, a little surprised as the tall man standing by the window turned. He did not look in the least like a friend of Audrey's.

However, she said pleasantly:

"I'm sorry Mrs. Strange is out. You wanted to see her?"

He looked at her in a thoughtful, considering way.

"You'll be Miss Aldin?" he said.

"Yes."

"I daresay you can help me just as well. I want to find some rope."

"Rope?" said Mary in lively amazement.

"Yes, rope. Where would you be likey to keep a piece of rope?"

Afterwards Mary considered that she had been half-hypnotized. If this strange man had volunteered any explanation she might have resisted. But Angus MacWhirter, unable to think of a plausible explanation, decided, very wisely, to do without one. He just stated quite simply what he wanted. She found herself, semi-dazed, leading MacWhirter in search of rope.

"What kind of rope?" she had asked.

And he had replied: "Any rope will do."

She said doubtfully: "Perhaps in the potting shed—"

"Shall we go there?"

She led the way. There was twine and an odd bit of cord, but MacWhirter shook his head.

He wanted rope—a good-sized coil of rope.

"There's the boxroom," said Mary hesitatingly.

"Ay, that might be the place."

They went indoors and upstairs. Mary threw open the boxroom door. MacWhirter stood in the doorway looking in. He gave a curious sigh of contentment.

"There it is," he said.

There was a big coil of rope lying on a chest just inside the door, in company with old fishing tackle and some moth-eaten cushions. He laid a hand on her arm and impelled Mary gently forward until they stood looking down on the rope. He touched it and said:

"I'd like you to charge your memory with this, Miss Aldin. You'll notice that everything round about is covered with dust. *There's no dust on this rope.* Just feel it."

She said:

"It feels slightly damp," in a surprised tone.

"Just so."

He turned to go out again.

"But the rope? I thought you wanted it?" said Mary in surprise.

MacWhirter smiled.

"I just wanted to know it was there. That's all. Perhaps you wouldn't mind locking this door, Miss Aldin—and taking the key out? Yes. I'd be obliged if you'd hand the key to Superintendent Battle or Inspector Leach. It would be best in their keeping."

As they went downstairs, Mary made an effort to rally herself.

She protested as they reached the main hall:

"But really, I don't understand."

MacWhirter said firmly:

"There's no need for you to understand." He took her hand and shook it heartily. "I'm very much obliged to you for your co-operation."

Whereupon he went straight out of the front door. Mary wondered if she had been dreaming!

Nevile and Thomas came in presently and the car arrived back shortly afterwards and Mary Aldin found herself envying Kay and Ted for being able to look quite cheerful. They were laughing and joking together. After all, why not? she thought. Camilla Tressilian had been nothing to Kay. All this tragic business was very hard on a bright young creature.

They had just finished lunch when the police came. There was something scared in Hurstall's voice as he announced that Superintendent Battle and Inspector Leach were in the drawing-room.

Superintendent Battle's face was quite genial as he greeted them.

"Hope I haven't disturbed you all," he said apologetically. "But there are one or two things I'd like to know about. This glove, for instance, who does it belong to?"

He held it out, a small yellow chamois leather glove.

He addressed Audrey.

"Is it yours, Mrs. Strange?"

She shook her head.

"No—no, it isn't mine."

"Miss Aldin?"

"I don't think so. I have none of that color."

"May I see?" Kay held out her hand. "No."

"Perhaps you'd just slip it on."

Kay tried, but the glove was too small.

"Miss Aldin?"

Mary tried in her turn.

"It's too small for you also," said Battle. He turned back to Audrey.

"I think you'll find it fits you all right. Your hand is smaller than either of the other ladies."

Audrey took it from him and slipped it on over her right hand.

Nevile Strange said sharply:

"She's already told you, Battle, that it isn't her glove."

"Ah well," said Battle, "perhaps she made a mistake. Or forgot."

Audrey said: "It may be mine—gloves are so alike, aren't they?"

Battle said:

"At any rate it was found outside your window, Mrs. Strange, pushed down into the ivy—*with its fellow.*"

There was a pause. Audrey opened her mouth to speak, then closed it up again. Her eyes fell before the Superintendent's steady gaze.

Nevile sprang forward. "Look here, Superintendent—"

"Perhaps we might have a word with you, Mr. Strange, privately?" Battle said gravely.

"Certainly, Superintendent. Come into the library."

He led the way and the two police officers followed him.

As soon as the door had closed Nevile said sharply:

"What's this ridiculous story about gloves outside my wife's window?"

Battle said quietly: "Mr. Strange, we've found some very curious things in this house."

Nevile frowned.

"Curious? What do you mean by curious?"

"I'll show you."

In obedience to a nod, Leach left the room and came back holding a very strange implement.

Battle said:

"This consists, as you see, sir, of a steel ball taken from a Victorian fender—a heavy steel ball. Then the head has been sawed off a tennis racquet and the ball has been screwed into the handle of the racquet." He paused. "I think there can be no doubt that this is what was used to kill Lady Tressilian."

"Horrible!" said Nevile with a shudder. "But where did you find this— this nightmare?"

"The ball had been cleaned and put back on the fender. The murderer had, however, neglected to clean the screw. We found a trace of blood on that. In the same way the handle and the head of the racquet were joined together again by means of adhesive surgical plaster. It was then thrown carelessly back into the cupboard under the stairs, where it would probably have remained quite unnoticed amongst so many others if we hadn't happened to be looking for something of that kind."

"Smart of you, Superintendent."

"Just a matter of routine."

"No fingerprints, I suppose?"

"That racquet which belongs by its weight, I should say, to Mrs. Kay Strange, has been handled by her and also by you, and both your prints are on it. *But it also shows unmistakable signs that someone wearing gloves handled it after you did.* There was just one fingerprint—left this time in inadvertence, I think. That was on the surgical strapping that had been applied to bind the racquet together again. I'm not going for the moment to say whose print that was. I've got some other points to mention first."

Battle paused, then he said:

"I want you to prepare yourself for a shock, Mr. Strange. And first I want to ask you something. Are you quite sure that it was your own idea to have this meeting here and that it was not actually suggested to you by Mrs. Audrey Strange?"

"Audrey did nothing of the sort. Audrey—"

The door opened and Thomas Royde came in.

"Sorry to butt in," he said, "but I thought I'd like to be in on this."

Nevile turned a harassed face towards him.

"Do you mind, old fellow? This is all rather private."

"I'm afraid I don't care about that. You see, I heard a name outside." He paused. "Audrey's name."

"And what the Hell has Audrey's name got to do with you?" demanded Nevile, his temper rising.

"Well, what has it to do with you if it comes to that? I haven't said anything definite to Audrey, but I came here meaning to ask her to marry me, and I think she knows it. What's more, I mean to marry her."

Superintendent Battle coughed. Nevile turned to him with a start.

"Sorry, Superintendent. This interruption—"

Battle said:

"It doesn't matter to me, Mr. Strange. I've got one more question to ask you. That dark blue coat you wore at dinner the night of the murder, it's got fair hairs inside the collar and on the shoulders. Do you know how they got there?"

"I suppose they're my hairs."

"Oh no, they're not yours, sir. They're a lady's hairs, and there's a red hair on the sleeves."

"I suppose that's my wife's—Kay's. The others, you are suggesting, are Audrey's. Very likely they are. I caught my cuff button in her hair one night outside on the terrace, I remember."

"In that case," murmured Inspector Leach, "the fair hair would be on the cuff."

"What the devil are you suggesting?" cried Nevile.

"There's a trace of powder, too, inside the coat collar," said Battle. "Primavera Naturelle No. 1—a very pleasant-scented powder and expensive—but it's no good telling me that you use it, Mr. Strange, because I shan't believe you. And Mrs. Strange uses Orchid Sun Kiss. Mrs. Audrey Strange does use Primavera Naturelle No. 1."

"What are you suggesting?" repeated Nevile.

Battle leaned forward.

"I'm suggesting that—on some occasion *Mrs. Audrey Strange wore that coat.* It's the only reasonable way the hair and the powder could get where it did. Then you've seen that glove I produced just now? It's her glove all right. That was the right hand, *here's the left.*" He drew it out of his pocket and put it down on the table. It was crumpled and stained with rusty brown patches.

Nevile said with a note of fear in his voice: "What's that on it?"

"Blood, Mr. Strange," said Battle firmly. "And you'll note this, it's the *left* hand. Now Mrs. Audrey Strange is left-handed. I noted that first thing when I saw her sitting with her coffee cup in her right hand and her cigarette in her left at the breakfast table. And the pen tray on her writing table had been shifted to the lefthand side. It all fits in. The knob from her grate, the gloves outside her window, the hair and powder on the coat. Lady Tressilian was struck on the right temple—but the position of the bed made it impossible for anyone to have stood on the other side of it. It follows that to strike Lady Tressilian a blow with the right hand would be a very awkward thing to do—but it's the natural way to strike for a *left-handed* person . . ."

Nevile laughed scornfully.

"Are you suggesting that Audrey—*Audrey* would make all these elaborate preparations and strike down an old lady whom she had known for years in order to get her hands on that old lady's money?"

Battle shook his head.

"I'm suggesting nothing of the sort. I'm sorry, Mr. Strange, you've got to understand just how things are. This crime, first, last, and all the time was directed against you. Ever since you left her, Audrey Strange has been brooding over the possibilities of revenge. In the end she has become mentally unbalanced. Perhaps she was never mentally very strong. She thought, perhaps, of killing you but that wasn't enough. She chose an evening when she knew you had quarrelled with Lady Tressilian. She took the coat from your bedroom and wore it when she struck the old lady down so that it should be blood-stained. She put your niblick on the floor, knowing we would find your fingerprints on it, and smeared blood and hair on the head of the club. It was she who instilled into your mind the idea of coming here when she was here. And the thing that saved you was the one thing she couldn't count on—the fact that Lady Tressilian rang her bell for Barrett and that Barrett saw you leave the house."

Nevile had buried his face in his hands. He said now:

"It's not true. It's not true! Audrey's never borne a grudge against me. You've got the whole thing wrong. She's the straightest, truest creature—without thought of evil in her heart."

Battle sighed.

"It's not my business to argue with you, Mr. Strange. I only wanted to prepare you. I shall caution Mrs. Strange and ask her to accompany me. I've got the warrant. You'd better see about getting a solicitor for her."

"It's preposterous. Absolutely preposterous."

"Love turns to hate more easily than you think, Mr. Strange."

"I tell you it's all wrong—preposterous."

Thomas Royde broke in. His voice was quiet and pleasant.

"Do stop repeating that it's preposterous, Nevile. Pull yourself together. Don't you see that the only thing that can help Audrey now is for you to give up all your ideas of chivalry and come out with the truth?"

"The truth? You mean—"

"I mean the truth about Audrey and Adrian." Royde turned to the police officers. "You see, Superintendent, you've got the facts wrong. Nevile didn't leave Audrey. She left him. She ran away with my brother Adrian. Then Adrian was killed in a car accident. Nevile behaved with the utmost chivalry to Audrey. He arranged that she should divorce him and that he would take the blame."

"Didn't want her name dragged through the mud," murmured Nevile sulkily. "Didn't know anyone knew."

"Adrian wrote to me, just before," explained Thomas briefly. He went on: "Don't you see, Superintendent, that knocks your motive out! Audrey has no cause to hate Nevile. On the contrary, she has every reason to be grateful to him. He's tried to get her to accept an allowance which she wouldn't do. Naturally when he wanted her to come and meet Kay she didn't feel she could refuse."

"You see," Nevile put in eagerly. "That cuts out her motive. Thomas is right."

Battle's wooden face was immovable.

"Motive's only one thing," he said. "I may have been wrong about that. But facts are another. All the facts show that she's guilty."

Nevile said meaningly:

"All the facts showed that *I* was guilty two days ago!"

Battle seemed a little taken aback.

"That's true enough. But look here, Mr. Strange, at what you're asking me to believe. You're asking me to believe that there's someone who hates both of you—someone who, if the plot against you failed, had laid a second trail to lead to Audrey Strange. Now can you think of anyone, Mr. Strange, who hates both you *and* your former wife?"

Nevile's head had dropped into his hands again.

"When you say it like that you make it all sound fantastic!"

"Because it *is* fantastic. I've got to go by the facts. If Mrs. Strange has any explanation to offer—"

"Did I have any explanation?" asked Nevile.

"It's no good, Mr. Strange. I've got to do my duty."

Battle got up abruptly. He and Leach left the room first. Nevile and Royde came close behind them.

They went on across the hall into the drawing-room. There they stopped.

Audrey Strange got up. She walked forward to meet them. She looked straight at Battle, her lips parted in what was very nearly a smile.

She said very softly:

"You want me, don't you?"

Battle became very official.

"Mrs. Strange, I have a warrant here for your arrest on the charge of murdering Camilla Tressilian on Monday last, September 12th. I must caution you that anything you say will be written down and may be used in evidence at your trial."

Audrey gave a sigh. Her small clear-cut face was peaceful and pure as a cameo.

"It's almost a relief. I'm glad it's—over!"

Nevile sprang forward.

"Audrey—don't say anything—don't speak at all."

She smiled at him.

"But why not, Nevile? It's all true—and I'm so tired."

Leach drew a deep breath. Well, that was that. Mad as a hatter, of course, but it would save a lot of worry! He wondered what had happened to his uncle. The old boy was looking as though he had seen a ghost. Staring at the poor demented creature as though he couldn't believe his eyes. Oh well, it had been an interesting case, Leach thought comfortably.

And then, an almost grotesque anticlimax, Hurstall opened the drawing-room door and announced: "Mr. MacWhirter."

MacWhirter strode in purposefully. He went straight up to Battle. "Are you the police officer in charge of the Tressilian case?" he asked.

"I am."

"Then I have an important statement to make. I am sorry not to have come forward before, but the importance of something I happened to see on the night of Monday last has only just dawned on me." He gave a quick glance round the room. "If I can speak to you somewhere?"

Battle turned to Leach.

"Will you stay here with Mrs. Strange?"

Leach said officially: "Yes, sir."

Then he leaned forward and whispered something into the other's ear.

Battle turned to MacWhirter. "Come this way."

He led the way into the library.

"Now then; what's all this? My colleague tells me that he's seen you before—last winter?"

"Quite right," said MacWhirter. "Attempted suicide. That's part of my story."

"Go on, Mr. MacWhirter."

"Last January I attempted to kill myself by throwing myself off Stark Head. I walked up there on Monday night. I stood there for some time. I looked down at the sea and across to Easterhead Bay and I then looked to my left. That is to say I looked across towards this house. I could see it quite plainly in the moonlight."

"Yes."

"Until today I had not realized *that was the night when a murder was committed.*"

He leant forward. "I'll tell you what I saw."

XVI

It was really only about five minutes before Battle returned to the drawing-room, but to those there it seemed much longer.

Kay had suddenly lost control of herself. She had cried out to Audrey.

"I knew it was you. I always knew it was you. I knew you were up to something—"

Mary Aldin said quickly:

"Please, Kay."

Nevile said sharply:

"Shut up, Kay, for God's sake."

Ted Latimer came over to Kay, who had begun to cry.

"Get a grip on yourself," he said kindly.

He said to Nevile angrily:

"You don't seem to realize that Kay has been under a lot of strain! Why don't you look after her a bit, Strange?"

"I'm all right," said Kay.

"For two pins," said Ted, "I'd take you away from the lot of them!"

Inspector Leach cleared his throat. A lot of injudicious things were said at times like these, as he well knew. The unfortunate part was that they were usually remembered most inconveniently afterwards.

Battle came back into the room. His face was expressionless.

He said: "Will you put one or two things together, Mrs. Strange? I'm afraid Inspector Leach must come upstairs with you."

Mary Aldin said: "I'll come too."

When the two women had left the room with the Inspector, Nevile said anxiously: "Well, what did that chap want?"

Battle said slowly:

"Mr. MacWhirter tells a very odd story."

"Does it help Audrey? Are you still determined to arrest her?"

"I've told you, Mr. Strange. I've got to do my duty."

Nevile turned away, the eagerness dying out of his face.

He said:

"I'd better telephone Trelawny, I suppose."

"There's no immediate hurry for that, Mr. Strange. There's a certain experiment I want to make first as a result of Mr. MacWhirter's statement. I'll just see that Mrs. Strange gets off first."

Audrey was coming down the stairs, Inspector Leach beside her. Her face still had that remote detached composure.

Nevile came towards her, his hands outstretched.

"Audrey—"

Her colorless glance swept over him. She said:

"It's all right, Nevile. I don't mind. I don't mind anything."

Thomas Royde stood by the front door, almost as though he would bar the way out.

A very faint smile came to her lips.

" 'True Thomas,' " she murmured.

He mumbled: "If there's anything I can do—"

"No one can do anything," said Audrey.

She went out with her head high. A police car was waiting outside with Sergeant Jones in it. Audrey and Leach got in.

Ted Latimer murmured appreciatively:

"Lovely exit!"

Nevile turned on him furiously. Superintendent Battle dexterously interposed his bulk and raised a soothing voice:

"As I said, I've got an experiment to make. Mr. MacWhirter is waiting down at the ferry. We're to join him there in ten minutes' time. We shall be going out in a motor launch, so the ladies had better wrap up warmly. In ten minutes, please."

He might have been a stage manager ordering a company on to the stage. He took no notice at all of their puzzled faces.

Zero Hour

I

IT WAS CHILLY on the water and Kay hugged the little fur jacket she was wearing closer round her.

The launch chugged down the river below Gull's Point, and then swung round into the little bay that divided Gull's Point from the frowning mass of Stark Head.

Once or twice a question began to be asked, but each time Superintendent Battle held up a large hand rather like a cardboard ham, intimating that the time had not come yet. So the silence was unbroken save for the rushing of the water past them. Kay and Ted stood together looking down into the water. Nevile was slumped down, his legs stuck out. Mary Aldin and Thomas Royde sat up in the bows. And one and all glanced from time to time curiously at the tall aloof figure of MacWhirter by the stern. He looked at none of them, but stood with his back turned and his shoulders hunched up.

Not until they were under the frowning shadow of Stark Head did Battle throttle down the engine and begin to speak his piece. He spoke without self-consciousness and in a tone that was more reflective than anything else.

"This has been a very odd case—one of the oddest I've ever known, and I'd like to say something on the subject of murder generally. What I'm going to say is not original—actually I overheard young Mr. Daniels, the KC, say something of the kind, and I wouldn't be surprised if *he'd* got it from someone else—he's a trick of doing that!

"It's this! When you read the account of a murder—or say, a fiction story based on murder, you usually begin with the murder itself. That's all wrong. The murder begins a *long time beforehand*. A murder is the culmination of a lot of different circumstances, all converging at a given moment at a given point. People are brought into it from different parts of the globe and for unforeseen reasons. Mr. Royde is here from Malaya. Mr. MacWhirter is here because he wanted to revisit a spot where he once tried to commit suicide. The murder itself is the end of the story. It's Zero Hour."

He paused.

"It's Zero Hour now."

Five faces were turned to him—only five, for MacWhirter did not turn his head. Five puzzled faces.

Mary Aldin said:

"You mean that Lady Tressilian's death was the culmination of a long train of circumstances?"

"No, Miss Aldin, not Lady Tressilian's death. Lady Tressilian's death was only incidental to the main object of the murderer. The murder I am talking of *is the murder of Audrey Strange*."

He listened to the sharp indrawing of breath. He wondered if, suddenly, someone was afraid . . .

"This crime was planned quite a long time ago—probably as early as last winter. It was planned down to the smallest detail. It had one object, and one object only; that Audrey Strange should be hanged by the neck till she was dead . . .

"It was cunningly planned by someone who thought themselves very clever. Murderers are usually vain. There was first the superficial unsatisfactory evidence against Nevile Strange which we were meant to see through. But having been presented by one lot of faked evidence, it was not considered likely that we should consider a *second edition of the same thing*. And yet, if you come to look at it, all the evidence against Audrey Strange *could* be faked. The weapon taken from her fireplace, her gloves—the left-hand glove dipped in blood—hidden in the ivy outside her window. The powder she uses dusted on the inside of a coat collar, and a few hairs placed there too. Her own fingerprint, occurring quite naturally on a roll of adhesive plaster taken from her room. Even the left-handed nature of the blow.

"And there was the final damning evidence of Mrs. Strange herself—I don't believe there's one of you (except the one who *knows*) who can credit her innocence after the way she behaved when we took her into custody. Practically admitted her guilt, didn't she? I mightn't have believed in her being innocent myself if it hadn't been for a private experience of my own . . . Struck me right between the eyes it did, when I saw and heard her—because, you see, I'd known another girl who did that very same thing, who admitted guilt when she wasn't guilty—and Audrey Strange was looking at me *with that other girl's eyes* . . .

"I'd got to do my duty. I knew that. We police officers have to act on evidence—not on what we feel and think. But I can tell you that at that minute I prayed for a miracle—because I didn't see that anything but a miracle was going to help that poor lady.

"Well, I got my miracle. Got it right away!

"Mr. MacWhirter, here, turned up with his story."

He paused.

"Mr. MacWhirter, will you repeat what you told me up at the house?"

MacWhirter turned. He spoke in short sharp sentences that carried conviction just because of their conciseness.

He told of his rescue from the cliff the preceding January and of his wish to revisit the scene. He went on:

"I went up there on Monday night. I stood there lost in my own thoughts. It must have been, I suppose, in the neighborhood of eleven o'clock. I looked across at that house on the point—Gull's Point, as I know it now to be."

He paused and then went on.

"There was a rope hanging from a window of that house into the sea. I saw a man climbing up that rope . . ."

Just a moment elapsed before they took it in. Mary Aldin cried out:

"Then it *was* an outsider after all? It was nothing to do with any of us. It was an ordinary burglar!"

"Not quite so fast," said Battle. "It was someone who came from the other side of the river, yes, since he swam across. But someone in the house had to have the rope ready for him, therefore *someone inside* must have been concerned."

He went on slowly:

"And we know of someone who was on the other side of the river that night—someone who wasn't seen between ten-thirty and a quarter past eleven, and who might have been swimming over and back. Someone who might have had a friend on this side of the water."

He added: "Eh, Mr. Latimer?"

Ted took a step backward. He cried out shrilly:

"But I can't swim! Everybody knows I can't swim. Kay, tell them I can't swim."

"Of course Ted can't swim!" Kay said.

"Is that so?" asked Battle pleasantly.

He moved along the boat as Ted moved in the other direction. There was some clumsy movement and a splash.

"Dear me," said Superintendent Battle in deep concern. "Mr. Latimer's gone overboard."

His hand closed like a vice on Nevile's arm as the latter was preparing to jump in after him.

"No, no, Mr. Strange. No need for you to get yourself wet. There are

two of my men handy—fishing in the dinghy there." He peered over
the side of the boat. "It's quite true," he said with interest. "He can't
swim. It's all right. They've got him. I'll apologize presently, but really
there's only one way to make sure that a person can't swim and that's
to throw them in and watch. You see, Mr. Strange, I like to be thorough.
I had to eliminate Mr. Latimer first. Mr. Royde here has got a groggy
arm, he couldn't do any rope climbing."

Battle's voice took on a purring quality.

"So that brings us to *you*, doesn't it, Mr. Strange? A good athlete, a
mountain climber, a swimmer and all that. You went over on the ten-
thirty ferry all right but no one can swear to seeing you at the Easterhead
Hotel until a quarter past eleven in spite of your story of having been
looking for Mr. Latimer then."

Nevile jerked his arm away. He threw back his head and laughed.

"You suggest that *I* swam across the river and climbed up a rope—"

"Which you had left ready hanging from your window," said Battle.

"Killed Lady Tressilian and swam back again? Why should I do such
a fantastic thing? And who laid all those clues against me? I suppose *I*
laid them against *myself*?"

"Exactly," said Battle. "And not half a bad idea either."

"And why should I want to kill Camilla Tressilian?"

"You didn't," said Battle. "But you did want to hang the woman who
left you for another man. You're a bit unhinged mentally, you know.
Have been ever since you were a child—I've looked up that old bow and
arrow case, by the way. Anyone who does you an injury has to be punished—and death doesn't seem to you an excessive penalty for them to
pay. Death by itself wasn't enough for Audrey—*your* Audrey whom you
loved—oh, yes, you loved her all right before your love turned to hate.
You had to think of some special kind of death, some long drawn out
specialized death. And when you'd thought of it, the fact that it entailed
the killing of a woman who had been something like a mother to you
didn't worry you in the least . . ."

Nevile said, and his voice was quite gentle:

"All lies! All lies! And I'm not mad. I'm *not* mad."

Battle said contemptuously:

"Flicked you on the raw, didn't she, when she went off and left you
for another man? Hurt your vanity! To think *she* should walk out on
you. You salved your pride by pretending to the world at large that *you'd*
left *her* and you married another girl who was in love with you just to
bolster up that belief. But underneath you planned what you'd do to
Audrey. You couldn't think of anything worse than this—to get her
hanged. A fine idea—pity you hadn't the brains to carry it out better!"

Nevile's tweed-coated shoulders moved, a queer, wriggling movement.

Battle went on:

"Childish—all that niblick stuff! Those crude trails pointing to you!
Audrey must have known what you were after! She must have laughed
up her sleeve! Thinking *I* didn't suspect you! You murderers are funny

little fellows! So puffed up. Always thinking you've been clever and
resourceful and really being quite pitifully childish . . ."

It was a strange queer scream that came from Nevile.

"It *was* a clever idea—it *was*. You'd never have guessed. Never! Not if
it hadn't been for this interfering jackanapes, this pompous Scotch fool.
I'd thought out every detail—every *detail*! *I* can't help what went wrong.
How was I to know Royde knew the truth about Audrey and Adrian?
Audrey and Adrian . . . Curse Audrey—she *shall* hang—you've *got* to
hang her—I want her to die afraid—to die—to die . . . I hate her. I tell
you I want her to die . . ."

The high whinnying voice died away. Nevile slumped down and began
to cry quietly.

"Oh God," said Mary Aldin. She was white to the lips.

Battle said gently, in a low voice:

"I'm sorry, but I had to push him over the edge . . . There was precious
little evidence, you know."

Nevile was still whimpering. His voice was like a child's.

"*I want her to be hanged. I do want her to be hanged . . .*"

Mary Aldin shuddered and turned to Thomas Royde.

He took her hands in his.

II

"I was always frightened," said Audrey.

They were sitting on the terrace. Audrey sat close to Superintendent
Battle. Battle had resumed his holiday and was at Gull's Point as a friend.

"Always frightened—all the time," said Audrey.

Battle said, nodding his head:

"I knew you were dead scared first moment I saw you. And you'd got
that colorless reserved way people have who are holding some very
strong emotion in check. It might have been love or hate, but actually
it was *fear*, wasn't it?"

She nodded.

"I began to be afraid of Nevile soon after we were married. But the
awful thing is, you see, that I didn't know *why*. I began to think that *I*
was mad."

"It wasn't you," said Battle.

"Nevile seemed to me when I married him so particularly sane and
normal—always delightfully good-tempered and pleasant."

"Interesting," said Battle. "He played the part of the good sportsman,
you know. That's why he could keep his temper so well at tennis. His
rôle as a good sportsman was more important to him than winning
matches. But it put a strain upon him, of course; playing a part always
does. He got worse underneath."

"Underneath," whispered Audrey with a shudder. "Always *underneath*. Nothing you could get hold of. Just sometimes a word or a look and then I'd fancy I'd imagined it . . . Something queer. And then, as I say, I thought *I* must be queer. And I went on getting more and more afraid—the kind of unreasoning fear, you know, that makes you *sick*!

"I told myself I was going mad—but I couldn't help it. I felt I'd do anything in the world to get away! And then Adrian came and told me he loved me, and I thought it would be wonderful to go away with him, and he said . . ."

She stopped.

"You know what happened? I went off to meet Adrian—he never came . . . he was killed . . . I felt as though Nevile had managed it somehow."

"Perhaps he did," said Battle.

Audrey turned a startled face to him.

"Oh, do you think so?"

"We'll never know now. Motor accidents can be arranged. Don't brood on it, though, Mrs. Strange. As likely as not, it just happened naturally."

"I—I was all broken up. I went back to the Rectory—Adrian's home. We were going to have written to his mother, but as she didn't know about us, I thought I wouldn't tell her and give her pain. And Nevile came almost at once. He was very nice—and—kind—and all the time I talked to him I was quite sick with fear! He said no one need know about Adrian, that I could divorce him on evidence he would send me and that he was going to remarry afterwards. I felt so thankful. I knew he had thought Kay attractive and I hoped that everything would turn out right and that I should get over this queer obsession of mine. I still thought it must be *me*.

"But I couldn't get rid of it—quite. I never felt I'd really escaped. And then I met Nevile in the Park one day and he explained that he did so want me and Kay to be friends and suggested that we should all come here in September. I couldn't refuse, how could I? After all the kind things he'd done."

" 'Will you walk into my parlor? said the spider to the fly,' " remarked Superintendent Battle.

Audrey shivered.

"Yes, just that . . ."

"Very clever he was about that," said Battle. "Protested so loudly to everyone that it was *his* idea, that everyone at once got the impression that it wasn't."

Audrey said:

"And then I got here—and it was like a kind of nightmare. I *knew* something awful was going to happen—I *knew* Nevile meant it to happen—and that it was to happen to *me*. *But I didn't know what it was*. I think, you know, that I nearly *did* go off my head! I was just paralysed with fright—like you are in a dream when something's going to happen and you can't move . . ."

"I've always thought," said Superintendent Battle, "that I'd like to have seen a snake fascinate a bird so that it can't fly away—but now I'm not so sure."

Audrey went on:

"Even when Lady Tressilian was killed, I didn't realize what it *meant*. I was puzzled. I didn't even suspect Nevile. I knew he didn't care about money—it was absurd to think he'd killed her in order to inherit fifty thousand pounds.

"I thought over and over again about Mr. Treves and the story he had told that evening. Even then I didn't connect it with Nevile. Treves had mentioned some physical peculiarity by which he could recognize the child of long ago. I've got a scar on my ear but I don't think anyone else has any sign that you'd notice."

Battle said: "Miss Aldin has a lock of white hair. Thomas Royde has a stiff arm which might not have been only the result of an earthquake. Mr. Ted Latimer has rather an odd shaped skull. And Nevile Strange—" He paused.

"Surely there was no physical peculiarity about Nevile?"

"Oh yes, there was. His left-hand little finger is shorter than his right. That's very unusual, Mrs. Strange—very unusual indeed."

"So *that* was it?"

"That was it."

"And Nevile hung that sign on the lift?"

"Yes. Nipped down there and back whilst Royde and Latimer were giving the old boy drinks. Clever and simple—doubt if we could ever prove *that* was murder."

Audrey shivered again.

"Now, now," said Battle. "It's all over now, my dear. Go on talking."

"You're very clever . . . I haven't talked so much for years!"

"No! That's what's been wrong. When did it first dawn on you what Master Nevile's game was?"

"I don't know exactly. It came to me all at once. He himself had been cleared and that left all of *us*. And then, suddenly, I saw him looking at me—a sort of gloating look. And I *knew*! That was when—"

She stopped abruptly.

"That was when what?"

Audrey said slowly:

"When I thought a quick way out would be—best."

Superintendent Battle shook his head.

"Never give in. That's my motto."

"Oh, you're quite right. But you don't know what it does to you being so afraid for so long. It paralyses you—you can't think—you can't plan—you just wait for something awful to happen. And then, when it does happen"—she gave a sudden quick smile—"you'd be surprised at the *relief*! No more waiting and fearing—it's *come*. You'll think I'm quite demented, I suppose, if I tell you that when you came to arrest me for murder I didn't mind at all. Nevile had done his worst and it was over. I felt so safe going off with Inspector Leach."

"That's partly why we did it," said Battle. "I wanted you out of that madman's reach. And besides, if I wanted to break him down I wanted to be able to count on the shock of the reaction. He'd seen his plan come off, as he thought—so the jolt would be all the greater."

Audrey said in a low voice:

"If he hadn't broken down would there have been any evidence?"

"Not too much. There was MacWhirter's story of seeing a man climb up a rope in the moonlight. And there was the rope itself confirming his story, coiled up in the attic and still faintly damp. It was raining that night, you know."

He paused and stared hard at Audrey as though he were expecting her to say something.

As she merely looked interested he went on:

"And there was the pinstripe suit. He stripped, of course, in the dark at that rocky point on the Easterhead Bay side, and thrust his suit into a niche in the rock. As it happened he put it down on a decayed bit of fish washed up by the flood tide. It made a stained patch on the shoulder—and it smelt. There was some talk, I found out, about the drains being wrong in the Hotel. Nevile himself put that story about. He'd got his raincoat on over his suit, but the smell was a pervasive one. Then he got the wind up about that suit afterwards and at the first opportunity he took it off to the cleaners and like a fool, didn't give his own name. Took a name at random, actually one he'd seen in the Hotel register. That's how your friend got hold of it and, having a good head on him, he linked it up with the man climbing up the rope. You *step* on decayed fish but you don't put your *shoulder* down on it *unless you have taken your clothes off to bathe at night*, and no one would bathe for pleasure on a wet night in September. He fitted the whole thing together. Very ingenious man, Mr. MacWhirter."

"More than ingenious," said Audrey.

"Mm, well, perhaps. Like to know about him? I can tell you something of his history."

Audrey listened attentively. Battle found her a good listener.

She said:

"I owe a lot to him—and to you."

"Don't owe very much to me," said Superintendent Battle. "If I hadn't been a fool I'd have seen the point of that bell."

"Bell? What bell?"

"The bell in Lady Tressilian's room. Always did feel there was something wrong about that bell. I nearly got it, too, when I came down the stairs from the top floor and saw one of those poles you open windows with."

"That was the whole point of the bell, see—to give Nevile Strange an alibi. Lady T. didn't remember what she had rung for—of course she didn't, because *she hadn't rung at all*! Nevile rang the bell from outside in the passage with that long pole, the wires ran along the ceiling. So down comes Barrett and sees Mr. Nevile Strange go downstairs and out, and she finds Lady Tressilian alive and well. The whole business of the maid was fishy. What's the good of doping her for a murder *that's going to be committed before midnight?* Ten to one she won't have gone off properly by then. But it fixes the murder as an inside job, and it allows a little time for Nevile to play his rôle of first suspect—then Barrett speaks and Nevile is so triumphantly cleared that no one is going to inquire very closely as to exactly what time he got to the Hotel. We know he didn't cross back by ferry, and no boats had been taken. There remained the possibility of swimming. He was a powerful swimmer, but even then the time must have been short. Up the rope he's left hanging into his bedroom and a good deal of water on the floor as we noticed (but without seeing the point, I'm sorry to say). Then into his blue coat and trousers, along to Lady Tressilian's room—we won't go into that—wouldn't have taken more than a couple of minutes, he'd fixed that steel ball beforehand— then back, out of his clothes, down the rope and back to Easterhead."

"Suppose Kay had come in?"

"She'd been mildly doped, I'll bet. She was yawning from dinner on, so they tell me. Besides he'd taken care to have a quarrel with her so that she'd lock her door and keep out of his way."

"I'm trying to think if I noticed the ball was gone from the fender. I don't think I did. When did he put it back?"

"Next morning when all the hullabaloo arose. Once he got back in Ted Latimer's car, he had all night to clear up his traces and fix things, mend the tennis racquet, etc. By the way, he hit the old lady *backhanded*, you know. That's why the crime appeared to be left-handed. Strange's backhand was always his strong point, remember!"

"Don't—*don't*—" Audrey put up her hands. "I can't bear any more." He smiled at her.

"All the same it's done you good to talk it all out. Mrs. Strange, may I be impertinent and give you some advice?"

"Yes, please."

"You lived for eight years with a criminal lunatic—that's enough to sap any woman's nerves. *But you've got to snap out of it now, Mrs. Strange.* You don't need to be afraid any more—and you've got to make yourself realize that."

Audrey smiled at him. The frozen look had gone from her face; it was a sweet, rather timid, but confiding face, with the wide-apart eyes full of gratitude.

She said, hesitating a little: "You told the others there was a girl—a girl who acted as I did?"

Battle slowly nodded his head.

"My own daughter," he said. "So you see, my dear, that miracle *had* to happen. These things are sent to teach us!"

III

Angus MacWhirter was packing.

He laid three shirts carefully in his suitcase, and then that dark blue suit which he had remembered to fetch from the cleaners. Two suits left by two different MacWhirters had been too much for the girl in charge.

There was a tap on the door and he called, "Come in."

Audrey Strange walked in. She said:

"I've come to thank you—are you packing?"

"Yes. I'm leaving here tonight. And sailing the day after tomorrow."

"For South America?"

"For Chile."

She said:

"I'll pack for you."

He protested, but she overbore him. He watched her as she worked deftly and methodically.

"There," she said when she had finished.

"You did that well," said MacWhirter.

There was a silence. Then Audrey said:

"You saved my life. If you hadn't happened to see what you did see—"

She broke off.

Then she said: "Did you realize at once, that night on the cliff when you—you stopped me going over—when you said 'Go home, I'll see that you're not hanged'—did you realize *then* that you'd got some important evidence?"

"Not precisely," said MacWhirter. "I had to think it out."

"Then how could you say—what you did say?"

MacWhirter always felt annoyed when he had to explain the intense simplicity of his thought processes.

"I meant just precisely that—that I intended to prevent you from being hanged."

The color came up in Audrey's cheeks.

"Supposing I had done it?"

"That would have made no difference."

"Did you think I *had* done it, then?"

"I didn't speculate on the matter overmuch. I was inclined to believe you were innocent, but it would have made no difference to my course of action."

"And then you remembered the man on the rope?"

MacWhirter was silent for a few moments. Then he cleared his throat.

"You may as well know, I suppose. I did not actually see a man climbing up a rope—indeed I could not have done so, for I was up on Stark Head on Sunday night, not on Monday. I deduced what must have happened from the evidence of the suit and my suppositions were confirmed by the finding of a wet rope in the attic."

From red Audrey had gone white. She said incredulously:

"Your story was all a lie?"

"Deductions would not have carried weight with the police. I had to say I saw what happened."

"But—you might have had to swear to it at my trial."

"Yes."

"You would have done that?"

"I would."

Audrey cried incredulously: "And you—you are the man who lost his job and came down to throwing himself off a cliff because he wouldn't tamper with the truth!"

"I have a great regard for the truth. But I've discovered there are things that matter more."

"Such as?"

"You," said MacWhirter.

Audrey's eyes dropped. MacWhirter cleared his throat in an embarrassed manner.

"There's no need for you to feel under a great obligation or anything of that kind. You'll never hear of me again after today. The police have got Strange's confession and they'll not need my evidence. In any case I hear he's so bad he'll maybe not live to come to trial."

"I'm glad of that," said Audrey.

"You were fond of him once?"

"Of the man I thought he was."

MacWhirter nodded. "We've all felt that way, maybe." He went on: "Everything's turned out well. Superintendent Battle was able to act upon my story and break down the man—"

Audrey interrupted. She said:

"He worked upon your story, yes. But I don't believe you fooled him. He deliberately shut his eyes."

"Why do you say that?"

"When he was talking to me he mentioned it was lucky you saw what you did in the moonlight, and then added something—a sentence or two later—about its being a *rainy night*."

MacWhirter was taken aback. "That's true. On Monday night I doubt if I'd have seen anything at all."

"It doesn't matter," said Audrey.

"He knew that what you pretended to have seen was what had really happened. But it explains why he worked on Nevile to break him down. He suspected Nevile as soon as Thomas told him about me and Adrian. He knew then that if he was right about the kind of crime—he had fixed on the wrong person—what he wanted was some kind of evidence to use on Nevile. He wanted, as he said, a miracle—you were Superintendent Battle's answer to prayer."

"That's a curious thing for him to say," said MacWhirter dryly.

"So you see," said Audrey, "you are a miracle. My special miracle."

MacWhirter said earnestly:

"I'd not like you to feel you're under an obligation to me. I'm going right out of your life—"

"Must you?" said Audrey.

He stared at her. The color came up, flooding her ears and temples. She said:

"Won't you take me with you?"

"You don't know what you're saying!"

"Yes, I do. I'm doing something very difficult—but that matters to me more than life or death. I know the time is very short. By the way, I'm conventional. I should like to be married before we go!"

"Naturally," said MacWhirter, deeply shocked. "You don't imagine I'd suggest anything else."

"I'm sure you wouldn't," said Audrey.

MacWhirter said:

"I'm not your kind. I thought you'd marry that quiet fellow who's cared for you so long."

"Thomas? Dear True Thomas. He's too true. He's faithful to the image of a girl he loved years ago. But the person he really cares for is Mary Aldin, though he doesn't know it yet himself."

MacWhirter took a step towards her. He spoke sternly.

"Do you mean what you're saying?"

"Yes . . . I want to be with you always, never to leave you. If you go I shall never find anybody like you, and I shall go lonely all my days."

MacWhirter sighed. He took out his wallet and carefully examined its contents.

He murmured:

"A special licence comes expensive. I'll need to go to the bank first thing tomorrow."

"I could lend you some money," murmured Audrey.

"You'll do nothing of the kind. If I marry a woman, I pay for the licence. You understand?"

"You needn't," said Audrey softly, "look so stern."

He said gently as he came towards her:

"Last time I had my hands on you, you felt like a bird—struggling to escape. You'll never escape now . . ."

She said:

"I shall never want to escape."

N or M?

1

I

TOMMY BERESFORD REMOVED his overcoat in the hall of the flat. He hung it up with some care, taking time over it. His hat went carefully on the next peg.

He squared his shoulders, affixed a resolute smile to his face and walked into the sitting-room, where his wife sat knitting a Balaclava helmet in khaki wool.

It was the spring of 1940.

Mrs. Beresford gave him a quick glance and then busied herself by knitting at a furious rate. She said after a minute or two:

"Any news in the evening paper?"

Tommy said:

"The Blitzkrieg is coming, hurray, hurray! Things look bad in France."

Tuppence said:

"It's a depressing world at the moment."

There was a pause and then Tommy said:

"Well, why don't you ask? No need to be so damned tactful."

"I know," admitted Tuppence. "There is something about conscious tact that is very irritating. But then it irritates you if I do ask. And anyway I don't *need* to ask. It's written all over you."

"I wasn't conscious of looking a Dismal Desmond."

"No, darling," said Tuppence. "You had a kind of nailed to the mast smile which was one of the most heart-rending things I have ever seen."

Tommy said with a grin:

"No, was it really as bad as all that?"

"And more! Well, come on, out with it. Nothing doing?"

"Nothing doing. They don't want me in any capacity. I tell you, Tuppence, it's pretty thick when a man of forty-six is made to feel like a doddering grandfather. Army, Navy, Air Force, Foreign Office, one and all say the same thing—I'm too old. I *may* be required later."

Tuppence said:

"Well, it's the same for me. They don't want people of my age for nursing—no, thank you. Nor for anything else. They'd rather have a fluffy chit who's never seen a wound, or sterilised a dressing than they would have me who worked for three years, 1915 to 1918, in various capacities, nurse in the surgical ward and operating theatre, driver of a trade delivery van and later of a general. This, that and the other—all, I assert firmly, with conspicuous success. And now I'm a poor, pushing, tiresome, middle-aged woman who won't sit at home quietly and knit as she ought to do."

Tommy said gloomily:

"This war is hell."

"It's bad enough having a war," said Tuppence, "but not being allowed to do anything in it just puts the lid on."

Tommy said consolingly:

"Well, at any rate Deborah has got a job."

Deborah's mother said:

"Oh, she's all right. I expect she's good at it, too. But I still think, Tommy, that I could hold my own with Deborah."

Tommy grinned.

"She wouldn't think so."

Tuppence said:

"Daughters can be very trying. Especially when they *will* be so kind to you."

Tommy murmured:

"The way young Derek makes allowances for me is sometimes rather hard to bear. That 'poor old Dad' look in his eye."

"In fact," said Tuppence, "our children, although quite adorable, are also quite maddening."

But at the mention of the twins, Derek and Deborah, her eyes were very tender.

"I suppose," said Tommy thoughtfully, "that it's always hard for people themselves to realise that they're getting middle-aged and past doing things."

Tuppence gave a snort of rage, tossed her glossy dark head, and sent her ball of khaki wool spinning from her lap.

"Are we past doing things? *Are* we? Or is it only that every one keeps insinuating that we are? Sometimes I feel that we never were any use."

"Quite likely," said Tommy.

"Perhaps so. But at any rate we did once feel important. And now I'm beginning to feel that all that never really happened. Did it happen, Tommy? Is it true that you were once crashed on the head and kidnapped by German agents? Is it true that we once tracked down a dangerous criminal—and got him! Is it true that we rescued a girl and got hold of important secret papers, and were practically thanked by a grateful country? Us! You and me! Despised, unwanted Mr. and Mrs. Beresford."

"Now dry up, darling. All this does no good."

"All the same," said Tuppence, blinking back a tear, "I'm disappointed in our Mr. Carter."

"He wrote us a very nice letter."

"He didn't *do* anything—he didn't even hold out any hope."

"Well, he's out of it all nowadays. Like us. He's quite old. Lives in Scotland and fishes."

Tuppence said wistfully:

"They might have let us do *something* in the Intelligence."

"Perhaps we couldn't," said Tommy. "Perhaps, nowadays, we wouldn't have the nerve."

"I wonder," said Tuppence. "One feels just the same. But perhaps, as you say, when it came to the point—"

She sighed. She said:

"I wish we could find a job of some kind. It's so rotten when one has so much time to think."

Her eyes rested just for a minute on the photograph of the very young man in the Air Force uniform, with the wide grinning smile so like Tommy's.

Tommy said:

"It's worse for a man. Women can knit, after all—and do up parcels and help at canteens."

Tuppence said:

"I can do all that twenty years from now. I'm not old enough to be content with that. I'm neither one thing nor the other."

The front-door bell rang. Tuppence got up. The flat was a small service one.

She opened the door to find a broad-shouldered man with a big fair moustache and a cheerful red face, standing on the mat.

His glance, a quick one, took her in as he asked in a pleasant voice:

"Are you Mrs. Beresford?"

"Yes."

"My name's Grant. I'm a friend of Lord Easthampton's. He suggested I should look you and your husband up."

"Oh, how nice, do come in."

She preceded him into the sitting-room.

"My husband, er—Captain—"

"Mr."

"Mr. Grant. He's a friend of Mr. Car—of Lord Easthampton's."

The old *nom de guerre* of the former Chief of the Intelligence, "Mr. Carter," always came more easily to her lips than their old friend's proper title.

For a few minutes the three talked happily together. Grant was an attractive person with an easy manner.

Presently Tuppence left the room. She returned a few minutes later with the sherry and some glasses.

After a few minutes, when a pause came, Mr. Grant said to Tommy:

"I hear you're looking for a job, Beresford?"

An eager light came into Tommy's eye.

"Yes, indeed. You don't mean—"

Grant laughed, and shook his head.

"Oh, nothing of that kind. No, I'm afraid that has to be left to the young active men—or to those who've been at it for years. The only things I can suggest are rather stodgy, I'm afraid. Office work. Filing papers. Tying them up in red tape and pigeon-holing them. That sort of thing."

Tommy's face fell.

"Oh, I see!"

Grant said encouragingly:

"Oh well, it's better than nothing. Anyway, come and see me at my office one day. Ministry of Requirements. Room 22. We'll fix you up with something."

The telephone rang. Tuppence picked up the receiver.

"Hallo—yes—*what?*" A squeaky voice spoke agitatedly from the other end. Tuppence's face changed. "When?—Oh, my dear—of course—I'll come over right away. . . ."

She put back the receiver.

She said to Tommy:

"That was Maureen."

"I thought so—I recognised her voice from here."

Tuppence explained breathlessly:

"I'm so sorry, Mr. Grant. But I must go round to this friend of mine. She's fallen and twisted her ankle and there's no one with her but her little girl, so I must go round and fix up things for her and get hold of someone to come in and look after her. Do forgive me."

"Of course, Mrs. Beresford, I quite understand."

Tuppence smiled at him, picked up a coat which had been lying over the sofa, slipped her arms into it and hurried out. The flat door banged.

Tommy poured out another glass of sherry for his guest.

"Don't go yet," he said.

"Thank you." The other accepted the glass. He sipped it for a moment in silence. Then he said: "In a way, you know, your wife's being called away is a fortunate occurrence. It will save time."

Tommy stared.

"I don't understand."

Grant said deliberately:

"You see, Beresford, if you had come to see me at the Ministry, I was empowered to put a certain proposition before you."

The color came slowly up in Tommy's freckled face. He said:

"You don't mean—"

Grant nodded.

"Easthampton suggested you," he said. "He told us you were the man for the job."

Tommy gave a deep sigh.

"Tell me," he said.

"This is strictly confidential, of course."

Tommy nodded.

"Not even your wife must know. You understand?"

"Very well—if you say so. But we worked together before."

"Yes, I know. But this proposition is solely for you."

"I see. All right."

"Ostensibly you will be offered work—as I said just now—office work—in a branch of the Ministry functioning in Scotland—in a prohibited area where your wife cannot accompany you. Actually you will be somewhere very different."

Tommy merely waited.

Grant said:

"You've read in the newspapers of the Fifth Column. You know, roughly at any rate, just what that term implies."

Tommy murmured:

"The enemy within."

"Exactly. This war, Beresford, started in an optimistic spirit. Oh, I don't mean the people who really knew—we've known all along what we were up against—the efficiency of the enemy, his aerial strength, his deadly determination, and the coordination of his well-planned war machine. I mean the people as a whole. The good-hearted, muddle-headed democratic fellow who believes what he wants to believe—that Germany will crack up, that she's on the verge of revolution, that her weapons of war are made of tin and that her men are so underfed that they'll fall down if they try to march—all that sort of stuff. Wishful thinking as the saying goes.

"Well, the war didn't go that way. It started badly and it went on worse. The men were all right—the men on the battleships and in the planes and in the dug-outs. But there was mismanagement and unpreparedness—the defects, perhaps, of our qualities. We don't want war, haven't considered it seriously, weren't good at preparing for it.

"The worst of that is over. We've corrected our mistakes, we're slowly getting the right men in the right place. We're beginning to run the war as it should be run—and we can win the war—make no mistake about that—but only if we don't lose it first. And the danger of losing it comes, not from outside—not from the might of Germany's bombers, not from her seizure of neutral countries and fresh vantage points from which to attack—but from within. Our danger is the danger of Troy—the wooden horse within our walls. Call it the Fifth Column if you like. It is here, among us. Men and women, some of them highly placed, some of them obscure, but all believing genuinely in the Nazi aims and the Nazi creed and desiring to substitute that sternly efficient creed for the muddled easy-going liberty of our democratic institutions."

Grant leant forward. He said, still in that same pleasant unemotional voice:

"And we don't know who they are. . . ."

Tommy said: "But surely—"

Grant said with a touch of impatience:

"Oh, we can round up the small fry. That's easy enough. But it's the others. We know about them. We know that there are at least two highly placed in the Admiralty—that one must be a member of General G—'s staff—that there are three or more in the Air Force, and that two, at least, are members of the Intelligence, and have access to cabinet secrets. We know that because it must be so from the way things have happened. The leakage—a leakage from the top—of information to the enemy, show us that."

Tommy said helplessly, his pleasant face perplexed:

"But what good should I be to you? I don't know any of these people."

Grant nodded.

"Exactly. You don't know any of them—*and they don't know you.*"

He paused to let it sink in and then went on.

"These people, these high-up people, know most of our lot. Information can't be very well refused to them. I was at my wits' end. I went to Easthampton. He's out of it all now—a sick man—but his brain's the best I've ever known. He thought of you. Over twenty years since you worked for the department. Name quite unconnected with it. Your face not known. What do you say—will you take it on?"

Tommy's face was almost split in two by the magnitude of his ecstatic grin.

"Take it on? You bet I'll take it on. Though I can't see how I can be of any use. I'm just a blasted amateur."

"My dear Beresford, amateur status is just what is needed. The professional is handicapped here. You'll take on in place of the best man we had or are likely to have."

Tommy looked a question. Grant nodded.

"Yes. Died in St. Bridget's Hospital last Tuesday. Run down by a lorry—only lived a few hours. Accident case—but it wasn't an accident."

Tommy said slowly: "I see."

Grant said quietly:

"And that's why we have reason to believe that Farquhar was on to something—that he was getting somewhere at last. By his death that wasn't an accident."

Tommy looked a question.

Grant went on:

"Unfortunately we know next to nothing of what he had discovered. Farquhar had been methodically following up one line after another. Most of them led nowhere."

Grant paused and then went on:

"Farquhar was unconscious until a few minutes before he died. Then he tried to say something. What he said was this: *N. or M. Song Susie.*"

"That," said Tommy, "doesn't seem very illuminating."

Grant smiled.

"A little more so than you might think. N. or M., you see, is a term we have heard before. It refers to two of the most important and trusted German agents. We have come across their activities in other countries and we know just a little about them. It is their mission to organise a Fifth Column in foreign countries and to act as liaison officer between the country in question and Germany. N., we know, is a man. M. is a woman. All we know about them is that these two are Hitler's most highly trusted agents and that in a code message we managed to decipher towards the beginning of the war there occurred this phrase—*Suggest N. or M. for England. Full powers—*"

"I see. And Farquhar—"

"As I see it, Farquhar must have got on the track of one or other of them. Unfortunately we don't know *which*. Song Susie sounds very cryptic—but Farquhar hadn't a high-class French accent! There was a return ticket to Leahampton in his pocket which is suggestive. Leahampton is on the South coast—a budding Bournemouth or Torquay. Lots of private hotels and guest-houses. Amongst them is one called *Sans Souci—*"

Tommy said again:

"Song Susie—Sans Souci—I see."

Grant said: "Do you?"

"The idea is," Tommy said, "that I should go there and—well—ferret round."

"That is the idea."

Tommy's smile broke out again.

"A bit vague, isn't it?" he asked. "I don't even know what I'm looking for."

"And I can't tell you. I don't know. It's up to you."

Tommy sighed. He squared his shoulders.

"I can have a shot at it. But I'm not a very brainy sort of chap."

"You did pretty well in the old days, so I've heard."

"Oh, that was pure luck," said Tommy hastily.

"Well, luck is rather what we need."

Tommy considered a minute or two. Then he said:

"About this place, Sans Souci—"

Grant shrugged his shoulders.

"May be all a mare's nest. I can't tell. Farquhar may have been thinking of 'Sister Susie's sewing shirts for soldiers.' " It's all guesswork."

"And Leahampton itself?"

"Just like any other of these places. There are rows of them. Old ladies, old colonels, unimpeachable spinsters, dubious customers, fishy customers, a foreigner or two. In fact, a mixed bag."

"And N. or M. amongst them?"

"Not necessarily. Somebody, perhaps, who's in touch with N. or M. But it's quite likely to be N. or M. themselves. It's an inconspicuous sort of place, a boardinghouse at a seaside resort."

"You've no idea whether it's a man or a woman I've to look for?"

Grant shook his head.

Tommy said: "Well, I can but try."

"Good luck to your trying, Beresford. Now—to details—"

II

Half an hour later when Tuppence broke in, panting and eager with curiosity, Tommy was alone, whistling in an arm-chair with a doubtful expression on his face.

"Well?" demanded Tuppence, throwing an infinity of feeling into the monosyllable.

"Well," said Tommy with a somewhat doubtful air, "I've got a job—of kinds."

"What kind?"

Tommy made a suitable grimace.

"Office work in the wilds of Scotland. Hush-hush and all that, but doesn't sound very thrilling."

"Both of us, or only you?"

"Only me, I'm afraid."

"Blast and curse you. How *could* our Mr. Carter be so mean?"

"I imagine they segregate the sexes in these jobs. Otherwise too distracting for the mind."

"Is it coding—or code breaking? Is it like Deborah's job? Do be careful, Tommy, people go queer doing that and can't sleep and walk about all night groaning and repeating 978345286 or something like that and finally have nervous breakdowns and go into homes."

"Not me."

Tuppence said gloomily:

"I expect you will sooner or later. Can I come too—not to work but just as a wife. Slippers in front of the fire and a hot meal at the end of the day?"

Tommy looked uncomfortable.

"Sorry, old thing. I *am* sorry. I hate leaving you—"

"But you feel you ought to go," murmured Tuppence reminiscently.

"After all," said Tommy feebly, "you can knit, you know."

"Knit?" said Tuppence. *"Knit?"*

Seizing her Balaclava helmet she flung it on the ground.

"I hate khaki wool," said Tuppence, *"and* navy wool *and* air force blue. I should like to knit something *magenta!"*

"It has a fine military sound," said Tommy. "Almost a suggestion of Blitzkrieg."

He felt definitely very unhappy. Tuppence, however, was a Spartan and played up well, admitting freely that of course he had to take the job and that it didn't *really* matter about her. She added that she had heard they wanted someone to scrub down the First-Aid Post floors. She might possibly be found fit to do that.

Tommy departed for Aberdeen three days later. Tuppence saw him off at the station. Her eyes were bright and she blinked once or twice, but she kept resolutely cheerful.

Only as the train drew out of the station and Tommy saw the forlorn little figure walking away down the platform did he feel a lump in his own throat. War or no war he felt he was deserting Tuppence. . . .

He pulled himself together with an effort. Orders were orders.

Having duly arrived in Scotland, he took a train the next day to Manchester. On the third day a train deposited him at Leahampton. Here he went to the principal hotel and on the following day made a tour of various private hotels and guest houses, seeing rooms and inquiring terms for a long stay.

Sans Souci was a dark red Victorian villa, set on the side of a hill with a good view over the sea from its upper windows. There was a slight smell of dust and cooking in the hall and the carpet was worn, but it compared quite favorably with some of the other establishments Tommy had seen. He interviewed the proprietress, Mrs. Perenna, in her office, a small untidy room with a large desk covered with loose papers.

Mrs. Perenna herself was rather untidy-looking, a woman of middle-age with a large mop of fiercely curling black hair, some vaguely applied make-up and a determined smile showing a lot of very white teeth.

Tommy murmured a mention of his elderly cousin, Miss Meadowes, who had stayed at Sans Souci two years ago. Mrs. Perenna remembered Miss Meadowes quite well—such a dear old lady—at least perhaps not really old—very active and such a sense of humor.

Tommy agreed cautiously. There was, he knew, a real Miss Meadowes—the Department was careful about these points.

And how was dear Miss Meadowes?

Tommy explained sadly that Miss Meadowes was no more and Mrs. Perenna clicked her teeth sympathetically and made the proper noises and put on a correct mourning face.

She was soon talking volubly again. She had, she was sure, just the room that would suit Mr. Meadowes. A lovely sea view. She thought Mr. Meadowes was so right to want to get out of London. Very depressing nowadays, so she understood, and, of course, after such a bad go of influenza—

Still talking, Mrs. Perenna led Tommy upstairs and showed him various bedrooms. She mentioned a weekly sum. Tommy displayed dismay. Mrs. Perenna explained that prices had risen so appallingly. Tommy explained that his income had unfortunately decreased and what with taxation and one thing and another—

Mrs. Perenna groaned and said:

"This terrible war—"

Tommy agreed and said that in his opinion that fellow Hitler ought to be hanged. A madman, that's what he was, a madman.

Mrs. Perenna agreed and said that what with rations and the difficulty the butchers had in getting the meat they wanted—and sometimes too much and sweetbreads and liver practically disappeared, it all made housekeeping very difficult, but as Mr. Meadowes was a relation of Miss Meadowes, she would make it half a guinea less.

Tommy then beat a retreat with the promise to think it over and Mrs. Perenna pursued him to the gate, talking more volubly than ever and displaying an archness that Tommy found most alarming. She was, he admitted, quite a handsome woman in her way. He found himself wondering what her nationality was. Surely not quite English? The name was Spanish or Portuguese, but that would be her husband's nationality, not hers. She might, he thought, be Irish, though she had no brogue. But it would account for the vitality and the exuberance.

It was finally settled that Mr. Meadowes should move in the following day.

Tommy timed his arrival for six o'clock. Mrs. Perenna came out into the hall to greet him, threw a series of instructions about his luggage to an almost imbecile-looking maid, who goggled at Tommy with her mouth open, and then led him into what she called the lounge.

"I always introduce my guests," said Mrs. Perenna, beaming determinedly at the suspicious glares of five people. "This is our new arrival, Mr. Meadowes—Mrs. O'Rourke." A terrifying mountain of a woman with beady eyes and a moustache gave him a beaming smile.

"Major Bletchley." Major Bletchley eyed Tommy appraisingly and made a stiff inclination of the head.

"Mr. Von Deinim." A young man, very stiff, fair-haired and blue-eyed, got up and bowed.

"Miss Minton." An elderly woman with a lot of beads, knitting with khaki wool, smiled and tittered.

"And Mrs. Blenkensop." More knitting—an untidy dark head which lifted from an absorbed contemplation of a Balaclava helmet.

Tommy held his breath, the room spun round.

"Mr. von Deinim." A young man, very stiff, fair-possible and unbelievable—Tuppence, calmnly knitting in the lounge of Sans Souci.

Her eyes met his—polite, uninterested stranger's eyes.

His admiration rose.

Tuppence!

2

HOW TOMMY GOT through that evening he never quite knew. He dared not let his eyes stray too often in the direction of Mrs. Blenkensop. At dinner three more habitués of Sans Souci appeared—a middle-aged couple—Mr. and Mrs. Cayley and a young mother, Mrs. Sprot, who had come down with her baby girl from London and was clearly much bored by her enforced stay at Leahampton. She was placed next to Tommy and at intervals fixed him with a pair of pale gooseberry eyes and in a slightly adenoidal voice asked: "Don't you think it's really quite safe now? Everyone's going back, aren't they?"

Before Tommy could reply to these artless queries, his neighbor on the other side, the beaded lady, struck in:

"What I say is one mustn't risk anything with children. Your sweet little Betty. You'd never forgive yourself and you know that Hitler has said the Blitzkrieg on England is coming quite soon now—and quite a new kind of gas, I believe."

Major Bletchley cut in sharply:

"Lot of nonsense talked about gas. The fellows won't waste time fiddling round with gas. High explosive and incendiary bombs. That's what was done in Spain."

The whole table plunged into the argument with gusto. Tuppence's voice, high-pitched and slightly fatuous, piped out: "My son Douglas says—"

"Douglas, indeed," thought Tommy. "Why Douglas, I should like to know."

After dinner, a pretentious meal of several meagre courses, all of which were equally tasteless, every one drifted into the lounge. Knitting was resumed and Tommy was compelled to hear a long and extremely boring account of Major Bletchley's experiences on the North-West Frontier.

The fair young man with the bright blue eyes went out, executing a little bow on the threshold of the room.

Major Bletchley broke off his narrative and administered a kind of dig in the ribs to Tommy.

"That fellow who's just gone out. He's a refugee. Got out of Germany about a month before the war."

"He's a German?"

"Yes. Not a Jew either. His father got into trouble for criticising the Nazi régime. Two of his brothers are in concentration camps over there. This fellow got out just in time."

At this moment Tommy was taken possession of by Mr. Cayley, who told him at interminable length all about his health. So absorbing was the subject to the narrator that it was close upon bedtime before Tommy could escape.

On the following morning Tommy rose early and strolled down to the front. He walked briskly to the pier and was returning along the esplanade when he spied a familiar figure coming in the other direction. Tommy raised his hat.

"Good morning," he said pleasantly. "Er—Mrs. Blenkensop, isn't it?"

There was no one within earshot. Tuppence replied:

"Dr. Livingstone to you."

"How on earth did you get here, Tuppence?" murmured Tommy. "It's a miracle—an absolute miracle."

"It's not a miracle at all—just brains."

"Your brains, I suppose?"

"You suppose rightly. You and your uppish Mr. Grant. I hope this will teach him a lesson."

"It certainly ought to," said Tommy. "Come on, Tuppence, tell me how you managed it. I'm simply devoured with curiosity."

"It was quite simple. The moment Grant talked of our Mr. Carter I guessed what was up. I knew it wouldn't be just some miserable office job. But his manner showed me that I wasn't going to be allowed in on this. So I resolved to go one better. I went to fetch some sherry and, when I did, I nipped down to the Browns' flat and rang up Maureen. Told her to ring me up and what to say. She played up loyally—nice high squeaky voice—you could hear what she was saying all over the room. I did my stuff, registered annoyance, compulsion, distressed friend, and rushed off with every sign of vexation. Banged the hall door, carefully remaining inside it, and slipped into the bedroom and eased open the communicating door that's hidden by the tallboy."

"And you heard everything?"

"Everything," said Tuppence complacently.

Tommy said reproachfully:

"And you never let on?"

"Certainly not. I wished to teach you a lesson. You and your Mr. Grant."

"He's not exactly my Mr. Grant and I should say you have taught him a lesson."

"Mr. Carter wouldn't have treated me so shabbily," said Tuppence. "I don't think the Intelligence is anything like what it was in our day."

Tommy said gravely: "It will attain its former brilliance now we're back in it. But why Blenkensop?"

"Why not?"

"It seems such an odd name to choose."

"It was the first one I thought of and it's handy for underclothes."

"What do you mean, Tuppence?"

"B., you idiot. B. for Beresford, B. for Blenkensop. Embroidered on my cami-knickers. Patricia Blenkensop. Prudence Beresford. Why did you choose Meadowes? It's a silly name."

"To begin with," said Tommy, "I don't have large Bs embroidered on my pants. And to continue, I didn't choose it. I was told to call myself Meadowes. Mr. Meadowes is a gentleman with a respectable past—all of which I've learnt by heart."

"Very nice," said Tuppence. "Are you married or single?"

"I'm a widower," said Tommy with dignity. "My wife died ten years ago at Singapore."

"Why at Singapore?"

"We've all got to die somewhere. What's wrong with Singapore?"

"Oh, nothing. It's probably a most suitable place to die. I'm a widow."

"Where did your husband die?"

"Does it matter? Probably in a nursing home. I rather fancy he died of cirrhosis of the liver."

"I see. A painful subject. And what about your son Douglas?"

"Douglas is in the Navy."

"So I heard last night."

"And I've got two other sons. Raymond is in the Air Force and Cyril, my baby, is in the Territorials."

"And suppose someone takes the trouble to check up on these imaginary Blenkensops?"

"They're not Blenkensops. Blenkensop was my second husband. My first husband's name was Hill. There are three pages of Hills in the telephone book. You couldn't check up on all the Hills if you tried."

Tommy sighed.

"It's the old trouble with you, Tuppence. You *will* overdo things. Two husbands and three sons. It's too much. You'll contradict yourself over the details."

"No, I shan't. And I rather fancy the sons may come in useful. I'm not under orders, remember. I'm a freelance. I'm in this to enjoy myself and I'm going to enjoy myself."

"So it seems," said Tommy. He added gloomily: "If you ask me the whole thing's a farce."

"Why do you say that?"

"Well, you've been at Sans Souci longer than I have. Can you honestly say you think any of these people who were there last night could be a dangerous enemy agent?"

Tuppence said thoughtfully:

"It does seem a little incredible. There's the young man, of course."

"Carl von Deinim. The police check up on refugees, don't they?"

"I suppose so. Still, it might be managed. He's an attractive young man, you know."

"Meaning, the girls will tell him things? But what girls? No generals' or admirals' daughters floating around here. Perhaps he walks out with a Company Commander in the ATS."

"Be quiet, Tommy. We ought to be taking this seriously."

"I am taking it seriously. It's just that I feel we're on a wild-goose chase."

Tuppence said seriously:

"It's too early to say that. After all, nothing's going to be obvious about this business. What about Mrs. Perenna?"

"Yes," said Tommy thoughtfully. "There's Mrs. Perenna, I admit—she does want explaining."

Tuppence said in a business-like tone:

"What about us? I mean, how are we going to cooperate?"

Tommy said thoughtfully:

"We mustn't be seen about too much together."

"No, it would be fatal to suggest we know each other better than we appear to do. What we want to decide is the attitude. I think—yes, I think—pursuit is the best angle."

"Pursuit?"

"Exactly. I pursue you. You do your best to escape, but being a mere chivalrous male don't always succeed. I've had two husbands and I'm on the lookout for a third. You act the part of the hunted widower. Every now and then I pin you down somewhere, pen you in a café, catch you walking on the front. Every one sniggers and thinks it very funny."

"Sounds feasible," agreed Tommy.

Tuppence said: "There's a kind of age-long humor about the chased male. That ought to stand us in good stead. If we are seen together, all any one will do is to snigger and say 'Look at poor old Meadowes.' "

Tommy gripped her arm suddenly.

"Look," he said. "Look ahead of you."

By the corner of one of the shelters a young man stood talking to a girl. They were both very earnest, very wrapped up in what they were saying.

Tuppence said gently:

"Carl von Deinim. Who's the girl, I wonder?"

"She's remarkably good-looking, whoever she is."

Tuppence nodded. Her eyes dwelt thoughtfully on the dark passionate face, and on the tight-fitting pullover that revealed the lines of the girl's figure. She was talking earnestly, with emphasis. Carl von Deinim was listening to her.

Tuppence murmured:

"I think this is where you leave me."

"Right," agreed Tommy.

He turned and strolled in the opposite direction.

At the end of the promenade he encountered Major Bletchley. The latter peered at him suspiciously and then grunted out, "Good morning."

"Good morning."

"See you're like me, an early riser," remarked Bletchley.

Tommy said:

"One gets in the habit of it out East. Of course, that's many years ago now, but I still wake early."

"Quite right, too," said Major Bletchley with approval. "God, these young fellows nowadays make me sick. Hot baths—coming down to breakfast at ten o'clock or later. No wonder the Germans have been putting it over on us. No stamina. Soft lot of young pups. Army's not what it was, anyway. Coddle 'em, that's what they do nowadays. Tuck 'em up at night with hot-water bottles. Faugh! Makes me sick!"

Tommy shook his head in melancholy fashion and Major Bletchley, thus encouraged, went on.

"Discipline, that's what we need. Discipline. How are we going to win the war without discipline? Do you know, sir, some of these fellows come on parade in slacks—so I've been told. Can't expect to win a war that way. Slacks! My God!"

Mr. Meadowes hazarded the opinion that things were very different from what they had been.

"It's all this democracy," said Major Bletchley gloomily. "You can overdo anything. In my opinion they're overdoing the democratic business. Mixing up the officers and the men, feeding together in restaurants—Faugh!— the men don't like it, Meadowes. The troops know. The troops always know."

"Of course," said Mr. Meadowes, "I have no real knowledge of Army matters myself—"

The Major interrupted him, shooting a quick sideways glance. "In the show in the last war?"

"Oh yes."

"Thought so. Saw you'd been drilled. Shoulders. What regiment?"

"Fifth Corfeshires." Tommy remembered to produce Meadowes's military record.

"Ah yes, Salonica!"

"Yes."

"I was in Mespot."

Bletchley plunged into reminiscences. Tommy listened politely. Bletchley ended up wrathfully.

"And will they make use of me now? No, they will not. Too old. Too old be damned. I could teach one or two of these young cubs something about war."

"Even if it's only what not to do?" suggested Tommy with a smile.

"Eh, what's that?"

A sense of humor was clearly not Major Bletchley's strong suit. He peered suspiciously at his companion. Tommy hastened to change the conversation.

"Know anything about that Mrs.—Blenkensop, I think her name is?"

"That's right, Blenkensop. Not a bad-looking woman—bit long in the tooth—talks too much. Nice woman, but foolish. No, I don't know her. She's only been at Sans Souci a couple of days." He added: "Why do you ask?"

Tommy explained.

"Happened to meet her just now. Wondered if she was always out as early as this?"

"Don't know, I'm sure. Women aren't usually given to walking before breakfast—thank God," he added.

"Amen," said Tommy. He went on: "I'm not much good at making polite conversation before breakfast. Hope I wasn't rude to the woman, but I wanted my exercise."

Major Bletchley displayed instant sympathy.

"I'm with you, Meadowes. I'm with you. Women are all very well in their place, but not before breakfast." He chuckled a little. "Better be careful, old man. She's a widow, you know."

"Is she?"

The major dug him cheerfully in the ribs.

"*We* know what widows are. She's buried two husbands and if you ask me she's on the lookout for number three. Keep a very wary eye open, Meadowes. A wary eye. That's my advice."

And in high good humor Major Bletchley wheeled about at the end of the parade and set the pace for a smart walk back to breakfast at Sans Souci.

In the meantime, Tuppence had gently continued her walk along the Esplanade, passing quite close to the shelter and the young couple talking there. As she passed she caught a few words. It was the girl speaking.

"But you must be careful, Carl. The very least suspicion—"

Tuppence was out of earshot. Suggestive words? Yes, but capable of any number of harmless interpretations. Unobtrusively she turned and again passed the two. Again words floated to her.

"Smug, detestable English. . . ."

The eyebrows of Mrs. Blenkensop rose ever so slightly. Carl von Deinim was a refugee from Nazi persecution, given asylum and shelter by English. Neither wise nor grateful to listen assentingly to such words.

Again Tuppence turned. But this time before she reached the shelter, the couple had parted abruptly, the girl to cross the road leaving the sea front, Carl von Deinim to come along in Tuppence's direction.

He would not, perhaps, have recognised her but for her own pause and hesitation. Then quickly, he brought his heels together and bowed.

Tuppence twittered at him:

"Good morning, Mr. von Deinim, isn't it? Such a lovely morning."

"Ah, yes. The weather is fine."

Tuppence ran on.

"It quite tempted me. I don't often come out before breakfast. But this morning, what with not sleeping very well—one often doesn't sleep well in a strange place, I find. It takes a day or two to accustom oneself, I always say."

"Oh yes, no doubt that is so."

"And really this little walk has quite given me an appetite for breakfast."

"You go back to Sans Souci now? If you permit I will walk with you." He walked gravely by her side.

Tuppence said:

"You also are out to get an appetite?"

Gravely, he shook his head.

"Oh no. My breakfast I have already had it. I am on my way to work."

" Work?"

"I am a research chemist."

So that's what you are, thought Tuppence, stealing a quick glance at him.

Carl von Deinim went on, his voice stiff.

"I came to this country to escape Nazi persecution. I had very little money—no friends. I do now what useful work I can."

He stared straight ahead of him. Tuppence was conscious of some undercurrent of strong feeling moving him powerfully.

She murmured vaguely:

"Oh yes, I see. I see. Very creditable, I am sure."

Carl von Deinim said:

"My two brothers are in concentration camps. My father died in one. My mother died of sorrow and fear."

Tuppence thought:

"The way he says that—as though he had learned it by heart."

Again she stole a quick glance at him. He was still staring ahead of him, his face impassive.

They walked in silence for some moments. Two men passed them. One of them shot a quick glance at Carl. She heard him mutter to his companion:

"Bet you that fellow is a German."

Tuppence saw the color rise in Carl von Deinim's cheeks.

Suddenly he lost command of himself. That tide of hidden emotion came to the surface. He stammered:

"You heard—you heard—that is what they say—I—"

"My dear boy," Tuppence reverted suddenly to her real self. Her voice was crisp and compelling. "Don't be an idiot. You can't have it both ways."

He turned his head and stared at her.

"What do you mean?"

"You're a refugee. You have to take the rough with the smooth. You're alive, that's the main thing. Alive and free. For the other—realise that it's inevitable. This country's at war. You're a German." She smiled suddenly. "You can't expect the mere man in the street—literally the man in the street—to distinguish between bad Germans and good Germans, if I may put it so crudely."

He still stared at her. His eyes, so very blue, were poignant with suppressed feeling. Then suddenly, he too smiled. He said:

"They said of Red Indians, did they not, that a good Indian was a dead Indian." He laughed. "To be a good German I must be on time at my work. Please. Good morning."

Again that stiff bow. Tuppence stared after his retreating figure. She said to herself:

"Mrs. Blenkensop, you had a lapse then. Strict attention to business in future. Now for breakfast at Sans Souci."

The hall door of Sans Souci was open. Inside, Mrs. Perenna was conducting a vigorous conversation with someone.

"And you'll tell him what I think of that last lot of margarine. Get the cooked ham at Quillers—it was twopence cheaper last time there, and be careful about the cabbages—" She broke off as Tuppence entered.

"Oh, good morning, Mrs. Blenkensop, you are an early bird. You haven't had breakfast yet. It's all ready in the dining-room." She added, indicating her companion: "My daughter Sheila. You haven't met her.

She's been away and only came home last night."

Tuppence looked with interest at the vivid, handsome face. No longer full of tragic energy, bored now and resentful. "My daughter Sheila." Sheila Perenna.

Tuppence murmured a few pleasant words and went into the dining-room. There were three people breakfasting—Mrs. Sprot and her baby girl, and big Mrs. O'Rourke. Tuppence said "Good morning," and Mrs. O'Rourke replied with a hearty "The top of the morning to you" that quite drowned Mrs. Sprot's more anemic salutation.

The old woman stared at Tuppence with a kind of devouring interest.

" 'Tis a fine thing to be out walking before breakfast," she observed. "A grand appetite it gives you."

Mrs. Sprot said to her offspring:

"*Nice* bread and milk, darling," and endeavoured to insinuate a spoonful into Miss Betty Sprot's mouth.

The latter cleverly circumvented this endeavour by an adroit movement of her head, and continued to stare at Tuppence with large round eyes.

She pointed a milky finger at the newcomer, gave her a dazzling smile and observed in gurgling tones: "Ga—Ga Bouch."

"She likes you," cried Mrs. Sprot, beaming on Tuppence as on one marked out for favor. "Sometimes she's so shy with strangers."

"Bouch," said Betty Sprot. "Ah pooth ah bag," she added with emphasis.

"And what would she be meaning by that?" demanded Mrs. O'Rourke, with interest.

"She doesn't speak awfully clearly yet," confessed Mrs. Sprot. "She's only just over two, you know. I'm afraid most of what she says is just bosh. She can say Mama, though, can't you, darling?"

Betty looked thoughtfully at her mother and remarked with an air of finality:

"Cuggle bick."

" 'Tis a language of their own they have, the little angels," boomed out Mrs. O'Rourke. "Betty, darling, say Mama now."

Betty looked hard at Mrs. O'Rourke, frowned and observed with terrific emphasis: "Nazer—"

"There now, if she isn't doing her best! And a lovely sweet girl she is."

Mrs. O'Rourke rose, beamed in a ferocious manner at Betty, and waddled heavily out of the room.

"Ga, ga, ga," said Betty with enornmous satisfaction, and beat with a spoon on the table.

Tuppence said with a twinkle:

"What does Na-zer really mean?"

Mrs. Sprot said with a flush: "I'm afraid, you know, it's what Betty says when she doesn't like anyone or anything."

"I rather thought so," said Tuppence.

Both women laughed.

"After all," said Mrs. Sprot, "Mrs. O'Rourke means to be kind but she is rather alarming—with that deep voice and the beard and—and everything."

With her head on one side Betty made a cooing noise at Tuppence.

"She has taken to you, Mrs. Blenkensop," said Mrs. Sprot.

There was a slight jealous chill, Tuppence fancied, in her voice. Tuppence hastened to adjust matters.

"They always like a new face, don't they?" she said easily.

The door opened and Major Bletchley and Tommy appeared. Tuppence became arch.

"Ah, Mr. Meadowes," she called out. "I've beaten you, you see. First past the post. But I've left you just a *little* breakfast!"

She indicated with the faintest of gestures the seat beside her.

Tommy, muttering vaguely: "Oh—er—rather—thanks," sat down at the other end of the table.

Betty Sprot said *"Putch!"* with a fine splutter of milk at Major Bletchley, whose face instantly assumed a sheepish but delighted expression.

"And how's little Miss Bo Peep this morning?" he asked fatuously. "Bo Peep!" He enacted the play with a newspaper.

Betty crowed with delight.

Serious misgivings shook Tuppence. She thought:

"There must be some mistake. There *can't* be anything going on here. There simply can't!"

To believe in Sans Souci as a headquarters of the Fifth Column needed the mental equipment of the White Queen in "Alice."

3

I

ON THE SHELTERED terrace outside, Miss Minton was knitting.

Miss Minton was thin and angular, but her neck was stringy. She wore pale sky blue jumpers, and chains or bead necklaces. Her skirts were tweedy and had a depressed droop at the back. She greeted Tuppence with alacrity.

"Good morning, Mrs. Blenkensop. I do hope you slept well."

Mrs. Blenkensop confessed that she never slept very well the first night or two in a strange bed. Miss Minton said, Now, wasn't that curious? It was exactly the same with *her*.

Mrs. Blenkensop said, "What a coincidence, and what a very pretty stitch that was." Miss Minton, flushing with pleasure, displayed it. Yes, it was rather uncommon, and really quite simple. She could easily show it to Mrs. Blenkensop if Mrs. Blenkensop liked. Oh, that was very kind of Miss Minton, but Mrs. Blenkensop was so stupid, she wasn't really very good at knitting, not at following patterns, that was to say. She could only do simple things like Balaclava helmets, and even now she was afraid she had gone wrong somewhere. It didn't look *right*, somehow, did it?

Miss Minton cast an expert eye over the khaki mass. Gently she pointed out just what had gone wrong. Thankfully, Tuppence handed the faulty helmet over. Miss Minton exuded kindness and patronage. "Oh, no, it wasn't a trouble at all. She had knitted for so many years."

"I'm afraid I've never done any before this dreadful war," confessed Tuppence. "But one feels so terribly, doesn't one, that one must do *something*."

"Oh yes, indeed. And you actually have a boy in the Navy, I think I heard you say last night?"

"Yes, my eldest boy. Such a splendid boy he is—though I suppose a mother shouldn't say so. Then I have a boy in the Air Force and Cyril, my baby, is out in France."

"Oh dear, dear, how terribly anxious you must be."

Tuppence thought:

"Oh Derek, my darling Derek . . . Out in the hell and mess—and here I am playing the fool—acting the thing I'm really feeling. . . ."

She said in her most righteous voice:

"We must all be brave, mustn't we? Let's hope it will all be over soon. I was told the other day on very high authority indeed that the Germans can't possibly last out more than another two months."

Miss Minton nodded with so much vigor that all her bead chains rattled and shook.

"Yes, indeed, and I believe"—(her voice lowered mysteriously)—"that Hitler is suffering from a *disease*—absolutely fatal—he'll be raving mad by August."

Tuppence replied briskly:

"All this Blitzkrieg is just the Germans' last effort. I believe the shortage is something frightful in Germany. The men in the factories are very dissatisfied. The whole thing will crack up."

"What's this? What's all this?"

Mr. and Mrs. Cayley came out on the terrace, Mr. Cayley putting his questions fretfully. He settled himself in a chair and his wife put a rug over his knees. He repeated fretfully:

"What's that you are saying?"

"We're saying," said Miss Minton, "that it will all be over by the autumn."

"Nonsense," said Mr. Cayley, "This war is going to last at least six years."

"Oh, Mr. Cayley," protested Tuppence. "You don't really think so?"

Mr. Cayley was peering about him suspiciously.

"Now I wonder," he murmured. "Is there a draft? Perhaps it would be better if I moved my chair back into the corner."

The resettlement of Mr. Cayley took place. His wife, an anxious-faced woman who seemed to have no other aim in life than to minister to Mr. Cayley's wants, manipulating cushions and rugs, asking from time to time: "Now how is that, Alfred? Do you think that will be all right? Ought you, perhaps, to have your sunglasses? There is rather a glare this morning."

Mr. Cayley said irritably:

"No, no. Don't fuss, Elizabeth. Have you got my muffler? No, no, my silk muffler. Oh well, it doesn't matter. I dare say this will do—for once. But I don't want to get my throat overheated, and wool—in this sunlight—well, perhaps you *had* better fetch the other." He turned his attention back to matters of public interest. "Yes," he said. "I give it six years."

He listened with pleasure to the protests of the two women.

"You dear ladies are just indulging in what we call wishful thinking. Now I know Germany. I may say I know Germany extremely well. In the course of my business before I retired I used to be constantly to and fro. Berlin, Hamburg, Munich, I know them all. I can assure you that Germany can hold out practically indefinitely. With Russia behind her—"

Mr. Cayley plunged triumphantly on, his voice rising and falling in pleasurably melancholy cadences, only interrupted when he paused to receive the silk muffler his wife brought him and wind it round his throat.

Mrs. Sprot brought out Betty and plumped her down with a small woollen dog that lacked an ear and a woolly doll's jacket.

"There, Betty," she said. "You dress up Bonzo ready for his walk while Mummy gets ready to go out."

Mr. Cayley's voice droned on, reciting statistics and figures, all of a depressing character. The monologue was punctuated by a cheerful twittering from Betty talking busily to Bonzo in her own language.

"Truckle—truckly—pah bat," said Betty. Then, as a bird alighted near her, she stretched out loving hands to it and gurgled. The bird flew away and Betty glanced round the assembled company and remarked clearly:

"Dicky," and nodded her head with great satisfaction.

"That child is learning to talk in the most wonderful way," said Miss Minton. "Say 'Ta ta', Betty. 'Ta ta'."

Betty looked at her coldly and remarked:

"Gluck!"

Then she forced Bonzo's one arm into his woolly coat and, toddling over to a chair, picked up the cushion and pushed Bonzo behind it. Chuckling gleefully, she said:

"Hide! Bow wow. Hide!"

Miss Minton, acting as a kind of interpreter, said with vicarious pride:

"She loves hide-and-seek. She's always hiding things." She cried out with exaggerated surprise:

"*Where* is Bonzo? Where *is* Bonzo? Where *can* Bonzo have gone?"

Betty flung herself down and went into ecstasies of mirth.

Mr. Cayley, finding attention diverted from his explanation of Germany's methods of substitution of raw materials, looked put out and coughed aggressively.

Mrs. Sprot came in with her hat on and picked up Betty.

Attention returned to Mr. Cayley.

"You were saying, Mr. Cayley?" said Tuppence.

But Mr. Cayley was affronted. He said coldly:

"That woman is always plumping that child down and expecting people to look after it. I think I'll have the woollen muffler after all, dear. The sun is going in."

"Oh, but, Mr. Cayley, do go on with what you were telling us. It was so interesting," said Miss Minton.

Mollified, Mr. Cayley weightily resumed his discourse, drawing the folds of the woolly muffler closer round his stringy neck.

"As I was saying, Germany has so perfected her system of—"

Tuppence turned to Mrs. Cayley, and asked:

"What do you think about the war, Mrs. Cayley?"

Mrs. Cayley jumped.

"Oh, what do I think? What—what do you mean?"

"Do you think it will last as long as six years?"

Mrs. Cayley said doubtfully:

"Oh, I hope not. It's a very long time, isn't it?"

"Yes. A long time. What do you really think?"

Mrs. Cayley seemed quite alarmed by the question. She said:

"Oh, I—I don't know. I don't know at all. Alfred says it will."

"But you don't think so?"

"Oh, I don't know. It's difficult to say, isn't it?"

Tuppence felt a wave of exasperation. The chirruping Miss Minton, the dictatorial Mr. Cayley, the nitwitted Mrs. Cayley—were these people really typical of her fellow countrymen? Was Mrs. Sprot any better with her slightly vacant face and boiled gooseberry eyes? What could she, Tuppence, ever find out here? Not one of these people, surely—

Her thought was checked. She was aware of a shadow. Someone behind her who stood between her and the sun. She turned her head.

Mrs. Perenna, standing on the terrace, her eyes on the group. And something in those eyes—scorn, was it? A kind of withering contempt. Tuppence thought:

I must find out more about Mrs. Perenna.

II

Tommy was establishing the happiest of relationships with Major Bletchley.

"Brought down some golf clubs with you, didn't you, Meadowes?"

Tommy pleaded guilty.

"Ha! I can tell you, *my* eyes don't miss much. Splendid! We must have a game together. Ever played on the links here?"

Tommy replied in the negative.

"They're not bad—not bad at all. Bit on the short side, perhaps, but lovely view over the sea and all that. And never crowded. Look here, what about coming along with me this morning? We might have a game."

"Thanks very much. I'd like it."

"Must say I'm glad you've arrived," remarked Bletchley as they were trudging up the hill. "Too many women in that place. Gets on one's nerves. Glad I've got another fellow to keep me in countenance. You can't count Cayley—the man's a kind of walking chemist's shop. Talks of nothing but his health and the treatment he's tried and the drugs he's taking. If he threw away all his little pillboxes and went out for a good ten-mile walk every day he'd be a different man. The only other male in the place is von Deinim, and to tell you the truth, Meadowes, I'm not too easy in my mind about him."

"No?" said Tommy.

"No. You take my word for it, this refugee business is dangerous. If I had my way I'd intern the lot of them. Safety first."

"A bit drastic, perhaps."

"Not at all. War's war. And I've got my suspicions of Master Carl. For one thing he's clearly not a Jew. Then he came over here just a month—only a month, mind you, before war broke out. That's a bit suspicious."

Tommy said invitingly:

"Then you think—"

"*Spying*—that's his little game!"

"But surely there's nothing of great military or naval importance hereabouts?"

"Ah, old man, that's where the artfulness comes in! If he were anywhere near Plymouth or Portsmouth he'd be under supervision. In a sleepy place like this, nobody bothers. But it's on the coast, isn't it? The truth of it is the Government is a great deal too easy with these enemy aliens. Anyone who cared could come over here and pull a long face and talk about their brothers in concentration camps. Look at that young man—arrogance in every line of him. He's a Nazi—that's what he is—a Nazi."

"What we really need in this country is a witch doctor or two," said Tommy pleasantly.

"Eh, what's that?"

"To smell out the spies," Tommy explained gravely.

"Ha, very good that—very good. Smell 'em out—yes, of course."

Further conversation was brought to an end, for they had arrived at the clubhouse.

Tommy's name was put down as a temporary member, he was introduced to the secretary, a vacant-looking elderly man, and the subscription duly paid. Tommy and the Major started on their round.

Tommy was a mediocre golfer. He was glad to find that his standard of play was just about right for his new friend. The Major won by two up and one to play, a very happy state of events.

"Good match, Meadowes, very good match—you had bad luck with that mashie shot, just turned off at the last minute. We must have a game fairly often. Come along and I'll introduce you to some of the fellows. Nice lot on the whole, some of them inclined to be rather old women, if you know what I mean? Ah, here's Haydock—you'll like Haydock. Retired naval wallah. Has that house on the cliff next door to us. He's our local ARP warden."

Commander Haydock was a big hearty man with a weather-beaten face, intensely blue eyes, and a habit of shouting most of his remarks.

He greeted Tommy with friendliness.

"So you're going to keep Bletchley countenance at Sans Souci? He'll be glad of another man. Rather swamped by female society, eh, Bletchley?"

"I'm not much of a ladies' man," said Major Bletchley.

"Nonsense," said Haydock. "Not your type of lady, my boy, that's it. Old boarding-house pussies. Nothing to do but gossip and knit."

"You're forgetting Miss Perenna," said Bletchley.

"Ah, Sheila—she's an attractive girl all right. Regular beauty if you ask me."

"I'm a bit worried about her," said Bletchley.

"What do you mean? Have a drink, Meadowes? What's yours, Major?"

The drinks ordered and the men settled on the veranda of the clubhouse, Haydock repeated his question.

Major Bletchley said with some violence:

"That German chap. She's seeing too much of him."

"Getting sweet on him, you mean? H'm, that's bad. Of course he's a good-looking young chap in his way. But it won't do. It won't do, Bletchley. We can't have that sort of thing. Trading with the enemy, that's what it amounts to. These girls—where's their proper spirit? Plenty of decent young English fellows about."

Bletchley said:

"Sheila's a queer girl—she gets odd sullen fits when she will hardly speak to any one."

"Spanish blood," said the Commander. "Her father was half Spanish, wasn't he?"

"Don't know. It's a Spanish name, I should think."

The Commander glanced at his watch.

"About time for the news. We'd better go in and listen to it."

The news was meagre that day, little more in it than had been already in the morning papers. After commenting with approval on the latest exploits of the Air Force—first-rate chaps, brave as lions, the Commander went on to develop his own pet theory—that sooner or later the Germans would attempt a landing at Leahampton itself—his argument being that it was such an unimportant spot.

"Not even an anti-aircraft gun in the place! Disgraceful!"

The argumet was not developed, for Tommy and the Major had to hurry back to lunch at Sans Souci. Haydock extended a cordial invitation to Tommy to come and see his little place, Smugglers' Rest. "Marvelous view—my own beach—every kind of handy gadget in the house. Bring him along, Bletchley."

It was settled that Tommy and Major Bletchley should come in for drinks on the evening of the following day.

III

After lunch was a peaceful time at Sans Souci. Mr. Cayley went to have his "rest" with the devoted Mrs. Cayley in attendance. Mrs. Blenkensop was conducted by Miss Minton to a depot to pack and address parcels for the Front.

Mr. Meadowes strolled gently out into Leahampton and along the front. He bought a few cigarettes, stopped at Smith's to purchase the latest number of *Punch*, then after a few minutes of apparent irresolution, he entered a bus bearing the legend, "OLD PIER".

The old pier was at the extreme end of the promenade. That part of Leahampton was known to house agents as the least desirable end. It was West Leahampton and poorly thought of. Tommy paid 2d. and strolled up the pier. It was a flimsy and weather-worn affair, with a few moribund penny-in-the-slot machines placed at far distant intervals. There was no one on it but some children running up and down and screaming in voices that matched quite accurately the screaming of the gulls, and one solitary man sitting on the end fishing.

Mr. Meadowes strolled up to the end and gazed down into the water. Then he asked gently:

"Caught anything?"

The fisherman shook his head.

"Don't often get a bite." Mr. Grant reeled in his line a bit. He said without turning his head:

"What about you, Meadowes?"

Tommy said:

"Nothing much to report as yet, sir. I'm digging myself in."

"Good. Tell me."

Tommy sat on an adjacent bollard, so placed that he commanded the length of the pier. Then he began:

"I've gone down quite all right, I think. I gather you've already got a list of the people there?" Grant nodded. "There's nothing to report as yet. I've struck up a friendship with Major Bletchley. We played golf this morning. He seems the ordinary type of retired officer. If anything, a shade too typical. Cayley seems a genuine hypochondriacal invalid. That, again, would be an easy part to act. He has, by his own admission, been a good deal in Germany during the last few years."

"A point," said Grant laconically.

"Then there's von Deinim."

"Yes. I don't need to tell you, Meadowes, that von Deinim's the one I'm most interested in."

"You think he's N.?"

Grant shook his head.

"No, I don't. As I see it, N. couldn't afford to be a German."

"Not a refugee from Nazi persecution, even?"

"Not even that. We watch, and they know we watch all the enemy aliens in this country. Moreover—this is in confidence, Beresford—very nearly all enemy aliens between 16 and 60 will be interned. Whether our adversaries are aware of that fact or not, they can at any rate anticipate that such a thing might happen. They would never risk the head of their organisation being interned. N. therefore must be either a neutral—or else he is (apparently) an Englishman. The same, of course, applies to M. No, my meaning about von Deinim is this. He may be a link in the chain. N. or M. may not be at Sans Souci, it may be Carl von Deinim who is there and through him we may be led to our objective. That does seem to me highly possible. The more so as I cannot very well see that any of the other inmates of Sans Souci are likely to be the person we are seeking."

"You've had them more or less vetted, I suppose, sir?"

Grant sighed—a sharp, quick sigh of vexation.

"No, that's just what it's impossible for me to do. I could have them looked up by the department easily enough—*but I can't risk it, Beresford.* For, you see, the rot is in the department itself. One hint that I've got my eye on Sans Souci for any reason—and the organisation may be put wise. That's where *you* come in, the outsider. That's why you've got to work in the dark, without help from us. It's our only chance—and I daren't risk alarming them. There's only one person I've been able to check up on."

"Who's that, sir?"

"Carl von Deinim himself. That's easy enough. Routine. I can have him looked up—not from the Sans Souci angle, but from the enemy alien angle."

Tommy asked curiously:

"And the result?"

A curious smile came over the other's face.

"Master Carl is exactly what he says he is. His father was indiscreet, was arrested and died in a concentration camp. Carl's elder brothers are in camps. His mother died in great distress of mind a year ago. He escaped to England a month before war broke out. Von Deinim has professed himself anxious to help this country. His work in a chemical research laboratory has been excellent and most helpful on the problem of immunising certain gases and in general decontamination experiments."

Tommy said:

"Then he's all right?"

"Not necessarily. Our German friends are notorious for their thoroughness. If von Deinim was sent as an agent to England, special care would be taken that his record should be consistent with his own account of himself. There are two possibilities. The whole von Deinim family may be parties to the arrangement—not improbable under the painstaking Nazi regime. Or else this is not really Carl von Deinim but a *man playing the part of Carl von Deinim.*"

Tommy said slowly: "I see." He added inconsequently:

"He seems an awfully nice young fellow."

Sighing, Grant said: "They are—they nearly always are. It's an odd life this service of ours. We respect our adversaries and they respect us. You usually like your opposite number, you know—even when you're doing your best to down him."

There was a silence as Tommy thought over the strange anomaly of war. Grant's voice broke into his musings.

"But there are those for whom we've neither respect nor liking—and those are the traitors within our own ranks—the men who are willing to betray their country and accept office and promotion from the foreigner who has conquered it."

Tommy said with feeling:

"My God, I'm with you, sir. That's a skunk's trick."

"And deserves a skunk's end."

Tommy said incredulously:

"And there really are these—these swine?"

"Everywhere. As I told you. In our service. In the fighting forces. On Parliamentary benches. High up in the Ministries. We've got to comb them out—we've *got* to! And we must do it quickly. It can't be done from the bottom—the small fry, the people who speak in the parks, who sell their wretched little news-sheets, they don't know who the big bugs are. It's the big bugs we want, they're the people who can do untold damage—and will do it unless we're in time."

Tommy said confidently:

"We shall be in time, sir."

Grant asked:

"What makes you say that?"

Tommy said:

"You've just said it—we've *got* to be!"

The man with the fishing line turned and looked full at his subordinate for a minute or two, taking in anew the quiet resolute line of the jaw. He had a new liking and appreciation of what he saw. He said quietly:

"Good man."

He went on:

"What about the women in this place? Anything strike you as suspicious there?"

"I think there's something odd about the woman who runs it."

"Mrs. Perenna?"

"Yes. You don't—know anything about her?"

Grant said slowly:

"I might see what I could do about checking her antecedents, but as I told you, it's risky."

"Yes, better not take any chances. She's the only one who strikes me as suspicious in any way. There's a young mother, a fussy spinster, the hypochondriac's brainless wife, and a rather fearsome-looking old Irishwoman. All seem harmless enough on the face of it."

"That's the lot, is it?"

"No. There's a Mrs. Blenkensop—arrived three days ago."

"Well?"

Tommy said: "Mrs. Blenkensop is my wife."

"*What?*"

In the surprise of the announcement Grant's voice was raised. He spun round, sharp anger in his gaze. "I thought I told you, Beresford, not to breath a word to your wife!"

"Quite right, sir, and I didn't. If you'll just listen—"

Succinctly, Tommy narrated what had occurred. He did not dare look at the other. He carefully kept out of his voice the pride that he secretly felt.

There was a silence when he brought the story to an end. Then a queer noise escaped from the other. Grant was laughing. He laughed for some minutes.

He said: "I take my hat off to the woman! She's one in a thousand!"

"I agree," said Tommy.

"Easthampton will laugh when I tell him this. He warned me not to leave her out. Said she'd get the better of me if I did. I wouldn't listen to him. It shows you, though, how damned careful you've got to be. I thought I'd taken every precaution against being overheard. I'd satisfied myself beforehand that you and your wife were alone in the flat. I actually heard the voice in the telephone asking your wife to come round at once, and so—and so I was tricked by the old simple device of the banged door. Yes, she's a smart woman, your wife."

He was silent for a minute, then he said:

"Tell her from me, will you, that I eat dirt?"

"And I suppose, now, she's in on this?"

Mr. Grant made an expressive grimace.

"She's in on it whether we like it or not. Tell her the department will esteem it an honour if she will condescend to work with us over the matter."

"I'll tell her," said Tommy with a faint grin.

Grant said seriously:

"You couldn't persuade her, I suppose, to go home and stay home?"

Tommy shook his head.

"You don't know Tuppence."

"I think I am beginning to. I said that because—well, it's a dangerous business. If they get wise to you or to her—"

He left the sentence unfinished.

Tommy said gravely: "I do understand that, sir."

"But I suppose even you couldn't persuade your wife to keep out of danger."

Tommy said slowly:

"I don't know that I really would want to do that ... Tuppence and I, you see, aren't on those terms. We go into things—together!"

In his mind was that phrase, uttered years ago, at the close of an earlier war. A *joint venture. . . .*

That was what his life with Tuppence had been and would always be—a Joint Venture. . . .

4

I

WHEN TUPPENCE ENTERED the lounge at Sans Souci just before dinner, the only occupant of the room was the monumental Mrs. O'Rourke, who was sitting by the window looking like some gigantic Buddha.

She greeted Tuppence with a lot of geniality and verve.

"Ah now, if it isn't Mrs. Blenkensop! You're like myself; it pleases you to be down to time and get a quiet minute or two here before going into the dining-room, and a pleasant room this is in good weather with the windows open in the way that you'll not be noticing the smell of cooking. Terrible that is, in all of these places, and more especially if it's onion or cabbage that's on the fire. Sit here now, Mrs. Blenkensop, and tell me what you've been doing with yourself this fine day and how you like Leahampton."

There was something about Mrs. O'Rourke that had an unholy fascination for Tuppence. She was rather like an ogress dimly remembered from early fairy tales. With her bulk, her deep voice, her unabashed beard and moustache, her deep twinkling eyes and the impression she gave of being more than life-size, she was indeed not unlike some childhood's fantasy.

Tuppence replied that she thought she was going to like Leahampton very much, and be happy there.

"That is," she added in a melancholy voice, "as happy as I can be anywhere with this terrible anxiety weighing on me all the time."

"Ah now, don't you be worrying yourself," Mrs. O'Rourke advised comfortably. "Those fine boys of yours will come back to you safe and sound. Not a doubt of it. One of them's in the Air Force, so I think you said?"

"Yes, Raymond."

"And is he in France now, or in England?"

"He's in Egypt at the moment, but from what he said in his last letter—not exactly *said*—but we have a little private code if you know what I mean?—certain sentences mean certain things. I think that's quite justified, don't you?"

Mrs. O'Rourke replied promptly:

"Indeed I do. 'Tis a mother's privilege."

"Yes, you see I feel I must know just where he is."

Mrs. O'Rourke nodded the Buddha-like head.

"I feel for you entirely, so I do. If I had a boy out there I'd be deceiving the censor the very same way, so I would. And your other boy, the one in the Navy?"

Tuppence entered obligingly upon a saga of Douglas.

"You see," she ended, "I feel so lost without my three boys. They've never been all away together from me before. They're all so sweet to me. I really do think they treat me more as a *friend* than a mother." She laughed self-consciously. "I have to scold them sometimes and *make* them go out without me."

("What a pestilential woman I sound," thought Tuppence to herself.) She went on aloud.

"And really I didn't know quite *what* to do or *where* to go. The lease of my house in London was up and it seemed so foolish to renew it, and I thought if I came somewhere quiet, and yet with a good train service—" She broke off.

Again the Buddha nodded.

"I agree with you entirely. London is no place at the present. Ah! the gloom of it! I've lived there myself for many a year now. I'm by way of being an antique dealer, you know. You may know my shop in Carnaby Street, Chelsea? Kate Kelly's the name over the door. Lovely stuff I had there too—oh, lovely stuff—mostly glass—Waterford, Cork—beautiful. Chandeliers and lustres and punchbowls and all the rest of it. Foreign glass, too. And small furniture—nothing large—just small period pieces—mostly walnut and oak. Oh, lovely stuff—and I had some good customers. But there, when there's a war on, all that goes west. I'm lucky to be out of it with as little loss as I've had."

A faint memory flickered through Tuppence's mind. A shop filled with glass, through which it was difficult to move, a rich persuasive voice, a compelling massive woman. Yes, surely, she had been into that shop.

Mrs. O'Rourke went on.

"I'm not one of those that like to be always complaining—not like some that's in this house. Mr. Cayley for one, with his muffler and his shawls and his moans about his business going to pieces. Of course it's to pieces, there's a war on—and his wife with never Boo to say to a goose. Then there's that little Mrs. Sprot, always fussing about her husband."

"Is he at the Front?"

"Not he. He's a tuppenny-halfpenny clerk in an Insurance office, that's all, and so terrified of air raids he's had his wife down here since the beginning of the war. Mind you, I think that's right where the child's concerned—and a nice wee mite she is—but Mrs. Sprot she frets, for all that her husband comes down when he can . . . Keeps saying Arthur must miss her so. But if you ask me Arthur's not missing her overmuch—maybe he's got other fish to fry."

Tuppence murmured:

"I'm terribly sorry for all these mothers. If you let your children go away without you, you never stop worrying. And if you go with them it's hard on the husbands being left."

"Ah! yes, and it comes expensive running two establishments."

"This place seems quite reasonable," said Tuppence.

"Yes, I'd say you get your money's worth. Mrs. Perenna's a good manager. There's a queer woman for you now."

"In what way?" asked Tuppence.

Mrs. O'Rourke said with a twinkle:

"You'll be thinking I'm a terrible talker. It's true. I'm interested in all my fellow-creatures, that's why I sit in this chair as often as I can. You see who goes in and who goes out and who's on the veranda and what goes on in the garden. What were we talking of now—ah yes, Mrs. Perenna, and the queerness of her. There's been a grand drama in that woman's life or I'm much mistaken."

"Do you really think so?"

"I do now. And the mystery she makes of herself! 'And where might you come from in Ireland?' I asked her. And would you believe it, she held out on me, declaring she was not from Ireland at all."

"You think she is Irish?"

"Of course she's Irish. I know my own countrywomen. I could name you the county she comes from. But there! 'I'm English,' she says. 'And my husband was a Spaniard'—"

Mrs. O'Rourke broke off abruptly as Mrs. Sprot came in, closely followed by Tommy.

Tuppence immediately assumed a sprightly manner.

"Good evening, Mr. Meadowes. You look very brisk this evening."

Tommy said:

"Plenty of exercise, that's the secret. A round of golf this morning and a walk along the front this afternoon—"

Millicent Sprot said:

"I took baby down to the beach this afternoon. She wanted to paddle but I really thought it was rather cold. I was helping her build a castle and a dog ran off with my knitting and pulled out yards of it. So annoying, and so difficult picking up all the stitches again. I'm such a bad knitter."

"You're getting along fine with that helmet, Mrs. Blenkensop," said Mrs. O'Rourke, suddenly turning her attention to Tuppence. "You've been just racing along. I thought Miss Minton said that you were an inexperienced knitter."

Tuppence flushed faintly. Mrs. O'Rourke's eyes were sharp. With a slightly vexed air, Tuppence said:

"I have really done quite a lot of knitting. I told Miss Minton so. But I think she likes teaching people."

Everybody laughed in agreement, and a few minutes later the rest of the party came in and the gong was sounded.

The conversation during the meal turned on the absorbing subject of spies. Well-known hoary chestnuts were retold. The nun with the muscular arm, the clergyman descending from his parachute and using unclergymanlike language as he landed with a bump, the Austrian cook who secreted a wireless in her bedroom chimney, and all the things that had happened or nearly happened to aunts and second cousins of those present. That led easily to Fifth Column activities. To denunciations of the British Fascists, of the Communists, of the Peace Party, of conscientious objectors. It was a very normal conversation of the kind that may be heard almost every day, nevertheless Tuppence watched keenly the faces and demeanor of the people as they talked, striving to catch some telltale expression or word. But there was nothing. Sheila Perenna alone took no part in the conversation, but that might be put down to her habitual taciturnity. She sat there, her dark rebellious face sullen and brooding.

Carl von Deinim was out tonight, so tongues could be quite unrestrained.

Sheila only spoke once towards the end of dinner.

Mrs. Sprot had just said in her thin fluting voice:

"Where I do think the Germans made such a mistake in the last war was to shoot Nurse Cavell. It turned everybody against them."

It was then that Sheila, flinging back her head, demanded in her fierce young voice: "Why shouldn't they shoot her? She was a spy, wasn't she?"

"Oh, no, not a spy."

"She helped English people to escape—in an enemy country. That's the same thing. Why shouldn't she be shot?"

"Oh, but shooting a woman—and a nurse."

Sheila got up.

"I think the Germans were quite right," she said.

She went out of the window into the garden.

Dessert, consisting of some under-ripe bananas, and some tired oranges, had been on the table some time. Everyone rose and adjourned to the lounge for coffee.

Only Tommy unobtrusively betook himself to the garden. He found Sheila Perenna leaning over the terrace wall staring out at the sea. He came and stood beside her.

By her hurried, quick breathing he knew that something had upset her badly. He offered her a cigarette, which she accepted.

He said: "Lovely night."

In a low intense voice the girl answered:

"It could be. . . ."

Tommy looked at her doubtfully. He felt, suddenly, the attraction and the vitality of this girl. There was a tumultuous life in her, a kind of compelling power. She was the kind of girl, he thought, that a man might easily lose his head over.

"If it weren't for the war, you mean?" he said.

"I don't mean that at all. I hate the war."

"So do we all."

"Not in the way I mean. I hate the cant about it, the smugness—the horrible, horrible patriotism."

"Patriotism?" Tommy was startled.

"Yes, I hate patriotism, do you understand? All this *country, country, country*! Betraying your country—dying for your country—serving your country. Why should one's country mean anything at all?"

Tommy said simply: "I don't know. It just does."

"Not to me! Oh, it would to you—you go abroad and buy and sell in the British Empire and come back bronzed and full of clichés, talking about the natives and calling for Chota Pegs and all that sort of thing."

Tommy said gently:

"I'm not quite as bad as that, I hope, my dear."

"I'm exaggerating a little—but you know what I mean. You believe in the British Empire—and—and—the stupidity of dying for one's country."

"My country," said Tommy drily, "doesn't seem particularly anxious to allow me to die for it."

"Yes, but you *want* to. And it's so *stupid*! *Nothing's* worth dying for. It's all an *idea*—talk—talk—talk—froth—high-flown idiocy. My country doesn't mean anything to me at all."

"Some day," said Tommy, "you'll be surprised to find that it does."

"No. Never. I've suffered—I've seen—"

She broke off—then turned suddenly and impetuously upon him.

"Do you know who my father was?"

"No?" Tommy's interest quickened.

"His name was Patrick Maguire. He—he was a follower of Casement in the last war. He was shot as a traitor! All for nothing! For an idea—he worked himself up with those other Irishmen. Why couldn't he just stay at home quietly and mind his own business? He's a martyr to some people and a traitor to others. I think he was just—*stupid*!"

Tommy could hear the note of pent-up rebellion coming out into the open. He said:

"So that's the shadow you've grown up with?"

"Shadow's right. Mother changed her name. We lived in Spain for some years. She always says that my father was half a Spaniard. We always tell lies wherever we go. We've been all over the Continent. Finally we came here and started this place. I think this is quite the most hateful thing we've done yet."

Tommy asked:

"How does your mother feel about—things?"

"You mean—about my father's death?" Sheila was silent a moment, frowning, puzzled. She said slowly, "I've never really known ... she never talks about it. It's not easy to know what Mother feels or thinks."

Tommy nodded his head thoughtfully.

Sheila said abruptly:

"I—I don't know why I've been telling you this. I got worked up. Where did it all start?"

"A discussion on Edith Cavell."

"Oh yes—patriotism. I said I hated it."

"Aren't you forgetting Nurse Cavell's own words?"

"What words?"

"Before she died. Don't you know what she said?"

He repeated the words:

"Patriotism is not enough . . . I must have no hatred in my heart."

"Oh." She stood there stricken for a moment.

Then, turning quickly, she wheeled away into the shadow of the garden.

II

"So you see, Tuppence, it would all fit in."

Tuppence nodded thoughtfully. The beach around them was empty. She herself leaned against a breakwater. Tommy sat above her, on the breakwater itself, from which post he could see any one who approached along the esplanade. Not that he expected to see anyone, having ascertained with a fair amount of accuracy where people would be this morning. In any case his rendezvous with Tuppence had borne all the signs of a casual meeting, pleasurable to the lady and slightly alarming to himself.

Tuppence said:

"Mrs. Perenna?"

"Yes. M. not N. She satisfies the requirements."

Tuppence nodded thoughtfully again.

"Yes. She's Irish—as spotted by Mrs. O'Rourke—won't admit the fact. Has done a good deal of coming and going on the Continent. Changed her name to Perenna, came here and started this boarding-house. A splendid bit of camouflage, full of innocuous bores. Her husband was shot as a traitor—she's got every incentive for running a Fifth Column show in this country. Yes, it fits. Is the girl in it too, do you think?"

Tommy said finally:

"Definitely not. She'd never have told me all this otherwise. I—I feel a bit of a cad, you know."

Tuppence nodded with complete understanding.

"Yes, one does. In a way it's a foul job, this."

"But very necessary."

"Oh, of course."

Tommy said, flushing slightly:

"I don't like lying any better than you do—"

Tuppence interrupted him.

"I don't mind lying in the least. To be quite honest I get a lot of artistic pleasure out of my lies. What gets me down is those moments when one forgets to lie—the times when one is just oneself—and gets results that way that you couldn't have got any other." She paused and went on: "That's what happened to you last night—with the girl. She responded to the *real* you—that's why you feel badly about it."

"I believe you're right, Tuppence."

"I know. Because I did the same thing myself—with the German boy." Tommy said:

"What do you think about him?"

Tuppence said quickly:

"If you ask me, I don't think he's got anything to do with it."

"Grant thinks he has."

"Your Mr. Grant!" Tuppence's mood changed. She chuckled. "How I'd like to have seen his face when you told him about me."

"At any rate, he's made the *amende honorable.* You're definitely on the job."

Tuppence nodded, but she looked a trifle abstracted.

She said:

"Do you remember after the last war—when we were hunting down Mr. Brown? Do you remember what fun it was? How excited we were?"

Tommy agreed, his face lighting up.

"Rather!"

"Tommy—why isn't it the same now?"

He considered the question, his quiet ugly face grave. Then he said:

"I suppose it's really—a question of age."

Tuppence said sharply:

"You don't think—we're too old?"

"No, I'm sure we're not. It's only that—this time—it won't be *fun.* It's the same in other ways. This is the second war we've been in—and we feel quite different about this one."

"I know—we see the pity of it and the waste—and the horror. All the things we were too young to think about before."

"That's it. In the last war I was scared every now and then—and had some pretty close shaves, and went through hell once or twice, but there were good times too."

Tuppence said:

"I suppose Derek feels like that?"

"Better not think about him, old thing," Tommy advised.

"You're right." Tuppence set her teeth. "We've got a job. We're going to *do* that job. Let's get on with it. Have we found what we're looking for in Mrs. Perenna?"

"We can at least say that she's strongly indicated. There's no one else, is there, Tuppence, that you've got your eye on?"

Tuppence considered.

"No, there isn't. The first thing I did when I arrived, of course, was to size them all up and assess, as it were, possibilities. Some of them seem quite impossible."

"Such as?"

"Well, Miss Minton for instance, the 'compleat' British spinster and Mrs. Sprot and her Betty, and the vacuous Mrs. Cayley."

"Yes, but nitwittishness can be assumed."

"Oh, quite, but the fussy spinster and the absorbed young mother are parts that would be fatally easy to overdo—and these people are quite natural. Then, where Mrs. Sprot is concerned, there's the child."

"I suppose," said Tommy, "that even a secret agent might have a child."

"Not with her on the job," said Tuppence. "It's not the kind of thing you'd bring a child into. I'm quite sure about that, Tommy. I *know*. You'd keep a child out of it."

"I withdraw," said Tommy. "I'll give you Mrs. Sprot and Miss Minton, but I'm not so sure about Mrs. Cayley."

"No, she might be a possibility. Because she really does overdo it. I mean there can't be many women *quite* as idiotic as she seems."

"I have often noticed that being a devoted wife saps the intellect," murmured Tommy.

"And where have you noticed that?" demanded Tuppence.

"Not from you, Tuppence. Your devotion has never reached those lengths."

"For a man," said Tuppence kindly, "you don't really make an undue fuss when you are ill."

Tommy reverted to a survey of possibilities.

"Cayley," said Tommy thoughtfully, "There might be something fishy about Cayley."

"Yes, there might. Then there's Mrs. O'Rourke?"

"What do you feel about her?"

"I don't quite know. She's disturbing. Rather *fee fo fum* if you know what I mean."

"Yes, I think I know. But I rather fancy that's just the predatory note. She's that kind of woman."

Tuppence said slowly:

"She notices things."

She was remembering the remark about knitting.

"Then there's Bletchley," said Tommy.

"I've hardly spoken to him. He's definitely your chicken."

"I *think* he's just the ordinary pukka old school tie. I *think so*."

"That's just it," said Tuppence, answering a stress rather than actual words. "The worst of this sort of show is that you look at quite ordinary everyday people and twist them to suit your morbid requirements."

"I've tried a few experiments on Bletchley," said Tommy.

"What sort of thing? I've got some experiments in mind myself."

"Well—just gentle ordinary little traps—about dates and places—all that sort of thing."

"Could you condescend from the general to the particular?"

"Well, say we're talking of duck-shooting. He mentions the Fayum—good sport there such and such a year, such and such a month. Some other time I mention Egypt in quite a diffferent connection. Mummies,

Tutankhamen, something like that—has he seen that stuff? When was he there? Check up on the answers. Or P. & O. boats—I mention the names of one or two, say so and so was a comfortable boat. He mentions some trip or other, later I check that. Nothing important, or anything that puts him, on his guard—just a check-up on accuracy."

"And so far he hasn't slipped up in any way?"

"Not once. And that's a pretty good test, let me tell you, Tuppence."

"Yes, but I suppose *if* he was N. he would have his story quite pat."

"Oh yes—the main outlines of it. But it's not so easy not to trip up on unimportant details. And then occasionally you remember too much—more, that is, than a bona fide person would do. An ordinary person doesn't usually remember off-hand whether they took a certain shooting trip in 1926 or 1927. They have to think a bit and search their memory."

"But so far you haven't caught Bletchley out?"

"So far he's responded in a perfectly normal manner."

"Result—negative."

"Exactly."

"Now," said Tuppence. "I'll tell you some of my ideas."

And she proceeded to do so.

III

On her way home, Mrs. Blenkensop stopped at the post office. She bought stamps and on her way out, went into one of the public call boxes. There she rang up a certain number, and asked for "Mr. Faraday". This was the accepted method of communication with Mr. Grant. She came out smiling and walked slowly homewards, stopping on the way to purchase some knitting wool.

It was a pleasant afternoon with a light breeze. Tuppence curbed the natural energy of her own brisk trot to that leisurely pace that accorded with her conception of the part of Mrs. Blenkensop. Mrs. Blenkensop had nothing on earth to do with herself except knit (not too well) and write letters to her boys. She was always writing letters to her boys—sometimes she left them about half finished.

Tuppence came slowly up the hill towards Sans Souci. Since it was not a through road (it ended at Smugglers' Rest, Commander Haydock's house) there was never much traffic—a few tradesmen's vans in the morning. Tuppence passed house after house, amusing herself by noting their names. Bella Vista (inaccurately named, since the merest glimpse of the sea was to be obtained, and the main view was the vast Victorian bulk of Edenholme on the other side of the road). Karachi was the next house. After that came Shirley Tower. Then Sea View (appropriate this time), Castle Clare (somewhat grandiloquent, since it was a small house),

Trelawney, a rival establishment to that of Mrs. Perenna, and finally the vast maroon bulk of Sans Souci.

It was just as she came near to it that Tuppence became aware of a woman standing by the gate peering inside. There was something tense and vigilant about the figure.

Almost unconsciously, Tuppence softened the sound of her own footsteps, stepping cautiously upon her toes.

It was not until she was close behind her, that the woman heard her and turned. Turned with a start.

She was a tall woman, poorly, even meanly dressed, but her face was unusual. She was not young—probably just under forty—but there was a contrast between her face and the way she was dressed. She was fair-haired, with wide cheekbones and had been—indeed still was—beautiful. Just for a minute Tuppence had a feeling that the woman's face was somehow familiar to her, but the feeling faded. It was not, she thought, a face easily forgotten.

The woman was obviously startled, and the flash of alarm that flitted across her face was not lost on Tuppence. (Something odd here?)

Tuppence said:

"Excuse me, are you looking for someone?"

The woman spoke in a slow, foreign voice, pronouncing the words carefully as though she had learned them by heart.

"This 'ouse is Sans Souci?"

"Yes. I live there. Did you want someone?"

There was an infinitesimal pause, then the woman said:

"You can tell me, please. There is a Mr. Rosenstein there, no?"

"Mr. Rosenstein?" Tuppence shook her head. "No. I'm afraid not. Perhaps he has been there and left. Shall I ask for you?"

But the strange woman made a quick gesture of refusal. She said:

"No—no. I make mistakes. Excuse, please."

Then, quickly, she turned and walked rapidly down the hill again.

Tuppence stood staring after her. For some reason, her suspicions were aroused. There was a contrast between the woman's manner and her words. Tuppence had an idea that "Mr. Rosenstein" was a fiction, that the woman had seized at the first name that came into her head.

Tuppence hesitated a minute, then she started down the hill after the other. What she could only describe as a "hunch" made her want to follow the woman.

Presently, however, she stopped. To follow would be to draw attention to herself in a rather marked manner. She had clearly been on the point of entering Sans Souci when she spoke to the woman, to reappear on her trail would be to arouse suspicion that Mrs. Blenkensop was something other than appeared on the surface—that is to say if this strange woman was indeed a member of the enemy plot.

No, at all costs Mrs. Blenkensop must remain what she seemed.

Tuppence turned and retraced her steps up the hill. She entered Sans Souci and paused in the hall. The house seemed deserted, as was usual

early in the afternoon. Betty was having her nap, the elder members
were either resting or had gone out.

Then, as Tuppence stood in the dim hall thinking over her recent
encounter, a faint sound came to her ears. It was a sound she knew quite
well—the faint echo of a ting.

The telephone at Sans Souci was in the hall. The sound that Tuppence
had just heard was the sound made when the receiver of an extension
is taken off or replaced. There was one extension in the house—in Mrs.
Perenna's bedroom.

Tommy might have hesitated. Tuppence did not hesitate for a minute.
Very gently and carefully she lifted off the receiver and put it to her
ear.

Someone was using the extension. It was a man's voice. Tuppence
heard:

"—everything going well. On the fourth, then, as arranged."

A woman's voice said: "Yes, carry on."

There was a click as the receiver was replaced.

Tuppence stood there, frowning. Was that Mrs. Perenna's voice? Difficult
to say with only those three words to go upon. If there had been only
a little more to the conversation. It might, of course, be quite an ordinary
conversation—certainly there was nothing in the words she had overheard
to indicate otherwise.

A shadow obscured the light from the door. Tuppence jumped and
replaced the receiver as Mrs. Perenna spoke.

"Such a pleasant afternoon. Are you going out, Mrs. Blenkensop, or
have you just come in?"

So it was not Mrs. Perenna who had been speaking from Mrs. Perenna's
room. Tuppence murmured something about having had a pleasant
walk and moved to the staircase.

Mrs. Perenna moved along the hall after her. She seemed bigger than
usual. Tuppence was conscious of her as a strong athletic woman.

She said:

"I must get my things off," and hurried up the stairs. As she turned
the corner of the landing she collided with Mrs. O'Rourke, whose vast
bulk barred the top of the stairs.

"Dear, dear, now, Mrs. Blenkensop, it's a great hurry you seem to be
in."

She did not move aside, just stood there smiling down at Tuppence
just below her. There was, as always, a frightening quality about Mrs.
O'Rourke's smile.

And suddenly, for no reason, Tuppence felt afraid.

The big smiling Irishwoman, with her deep voice, barring her way,
and below Mrs. Perenna closing in at the foot of the stairs.

Tuppence glanced over her shoulder. Was it her fancy that there was
something definitely menacing in Mrs. Perenna's upturned face? Absurd,
she told herself, absurd. In broad daylight—in a commonplace seaside
boarding-house. But the house was so very quiet. Not a sound. And she

herself here on the stairs between the two of them. Surely there *was* something a little queer in Mrs. O'Rourke's smile—some fixed ferocious quality about it, Tuppence thought wildly, "like a cat with a mouse".

And then suddenly the tension broke. A little figure darted along the top landing uttering shrill squeals of mirth. Little Betty Sprot in vest and knickers. Darting past Mrs. O'Rourke, shouting happily, "Peek bo," as she flung herself on Tuppence.

The atmosphere had changed, Mrs. O'Rourke, a big genial figure, was crying out:

"Ah the darlin'. It's a great girl she's getting."

Below, Mrs. Perenna had turned away to the door that led into the kitchen. Tuppence, Betty's hand clasped in hers, passed Mrs. O'Rourke and ran along the passage to where Mrs. Sprot was waiting to scold the truant.

Tuppence went in with the child.

She felt a queer sense of relief at the domestic atmosphere—the child's clothes lying about, the woolly toys, the painted crib, the sheeplike and somewhat unattractive face of Mr. Sprot in its frame on the dressing-table, the burble of Mrs. Sprot's denunciation of laundry prices and really she thought Mrs. Perenna was a little unfair in refusing to sanction guests having their own electric irons—

All so normal, so reassuring, so everyday.

And yet—just now—on the stairs.

"Nerves," said Tuppence to herself, "Just nerves!"

But had it been nerves? Someone *had* been telephoning from Mrs. Perenna's room. Mrs. O'Rourke? Surely a very odd thing to do. It ensured, of course, that you would not be overheard by the household.

It must have been, Tuppence thought, a very short conversation. The merest brief exchange of words.

"Everything going well. On the fourth, as arranged."

It might mean nothing—or a good deal.

The fourth. Was that a date? The fourth, say of a month?

Or it might mean the fourth seat, or the fourth lamppost, or the fourth breakwater—impossible to know.

It might just conceivably mean the Forth Bridge. There had been an attempt to blow that up in the last war.

Did it mean anything at all?

It might quite easily have been the confirmation of some perfectly ordinary appointment. Mrs. Perenna might have told Mrs. O'Rourke she could use the telephone in her bedroom any time she wanted to do so.

And the atmosphere on the stairs, that tense moment, might have been just her own overwrought nerves. . . .

The quiet house—the feeling that there was something sinister—something evil. . . .

"Stick to facts, Mrs. Blenkensop," said Tuppence sternly. "And get on with your job."

5

I

COMMANDER HAYDOCK TURNED out to be a most genial host. He welcomed Mr. Meadowes and Major Bletchley with enthusiasm, and insisted on showing the former "all over my little place".

Smugglers' Rest had been originally a couple of coastguards' cottages standing on the cliff overlooking the sea. There was a small cove below, but the access to it was perilous, only to be attempted by adventurous boys.

Then the cottages had been bought by a London businessman who had thrown them into one and attempted half-heartedly to make a garden. He had come down occasionally for short periods in summer.

After that, the cottages had remained empty for some years, being let with a modicum of furniture to summer visitors.

"Then, some years ago," explained Haydock, "it was sold to a man called Hahn. He was a German, and if you ask me, he was neither more nor less than a spy."

Tommy's ears quickened.

"That's interesting," he said, putting down the glass from which he had been sipping sherry.

"Damned thorough fellows they are," said Haydock. "Getting ready even then for this show—at least that is my opinion. Look at the situation of this place. Perfect for signalling out to sea. Cove below where you could land a motorboat. Completely isolated owing to the contour of the cliff. Oh, yes, don't tell me that fellow Hahn wasn't a German agent."

Major Bletchley said:

"Of course he was."

"What happened to him?" asked Tommy.

"Ah!" said Haydock. "Thereby hangs a tale. Hahn spent a lot of money on this place. He had a way cut down to the beach for one thing—concrete steps—expensive business. Then he had the whole of the house done over—bathrooms, every expensive gadget you can imagine. And who did he set to do all this? Not a local man. No, a firm from London, so it was said—but a lot of the men who came down were foreigners. Some of them *didn't speak a word of English*. Don't you agree with me that that sounds extremely fishy?"

"A little odd, certainly," agreed Tommy.

"I was in the neighborhood myself at the time, living in a bungalow and I got interested in what this fellow was up to. I used to hang about to watch the workmen. Now I'll tell you this—they didn't like it—they didn't like it at all. Once or twice they were quite threatening about it. Why should they be if everything was all square and above board?"

Bletchley nodded agreement.

"You ought to have gone to the authorities," he said.

"Just what I did do, my dear fellow. Made a positive nuisance of myself pestering the police."

He poured himself out another drink.

"And what did I get for my pains? Polite inattention. Blind and deaf, that's what we were in this country. Another war with Germany was out of the question—there was peace in Europe—our relations with Germany were excellent. Natural sympathy between us nowadays. I was regarded as an old fossil, a war maniac, a diehard old sailor. What was the good of pointing out to people that the Germans were building the finest Air Force in Europe and not just to fly round and have picnics!"

Major Bletchley said explosively:

"Nobody believed it! Damned fools! 'Peace in our time.' 'Appeasement.' All a lot of blah!"

Haydock said, his face redder than usual with suppressed anger: "A warmonger, that's what they called me. The sort of chap, they said, who was an obstacle to peace. Peace! I knew what our Hun friends were at! And mind this, they prepare things a long time beforehand. I was convinced that Mr. Hahn was up to no good. I didn't like his foreign workmen. I didn't like the way he was spending money on this place. I kept on badgering away at people."

"Stout fellow," said Bletchley appreciatively.

"And finally," said the Commander, "I began to make an impression. We had a new Chief Constable down here—retired soldier. And he had the sense to listen to me. His fellows began to nose around. Sure enough, Hahn decamped. Just slipped out and disappeared one fine night. The police went over this place with a search-warrant. In a safe which had been built-in in the dining-room they found a wireless transmitter and some pretty damaging documents. Also a big store place under the garage for petrol—great tanks. I can tell you I was cock-a-hoop over that. Fellows at the club used to rag me about my German spy complex. They dried up after that. Trouble with us in this country is that we're so absurdly unsuspicious."

"It's a crime. Fools—that's what we are—fools. Why don't we intern all these refugees?" Major Bletchley was well away.

"End of the story was I bought the place when it came into the market," continued the Commander, not to be side-tracked from his pet story. "Come and have a look round, Meadows?"

"Thanks. I'd like to."

Commander Haydock was as full of zest as a boy as he did the honors of the establishment. He threw open the big safe in the dining-room to show where the secret wireless had been found. Tommy was taken out to the garage and was shown where the big petrol tanks had lain concealed, and finally, after a superficial glance at the two excellent bathrooms, the

special lighting, and the various kitchen "gadgets", he was taken down
the steep concreted path to the little cove beneath, whilst Commander
Haydock told him all over again how extremely useful the whole lay-
out would be to an enemy in wartime.

He was taken into the cave which gave the place its name, and Haydock
pointed out enthusiastically how it could have been used.

Major Bletchley did not accompany the two men on their tour, but
remained peacefully sipping his drink on the terrace. Tommy gathered
that the Commander's spy hunt with its successful issue was that good
gentleman's principal topic of conversation, and that his friends had
heard it many times.

In fact, Major Bletchley said as much when they were walking down
to Sans Souci a little later.

"Good fellow, Haydock," he said. "But he's not content to let a good
thing alone. We've heard all about that business again and again until
we're sick of it. He's as proud of the whole bag of tricks up there as a
cat of its kittens."

The simile was not too far-fetched, and Tommy assented with a smile.

The conversation then turning to Major Bletchley's own successful
unmasking of a dishonest bearer in 1923, Tommy's attention was free
to pursue its own inward line of thought punctuated by sympathetic
"Not really?"—"You don't say so?" and "What an extraordinary business!"
which was all Major Bletchley needed in the way of encouragement.

More than ever now. Tommy felt that when the dying Farquhar had
mentioned Sans Souci he had been on the right track. Here, in this out
of the world spot, preparations had been made a long time beforehand.
The arrival of the German Hahn and his extensive installation showed
clearly enough that this particular part of the coast had been selected
for a rallying point, a focus of enemy activity.

That particular game had been defeated by the unexpected activity
of the suspicious Commander Haydock. Round one had gone to Britain.
But supposing that Smugglers' Rest had been only the first outpost of
a complicated scheme of attack? Smugglers' Rest, that is to say, had
represented sea communications. Its beach, inaccessible save for the path
down from above, would lend itself admirably to the plan. But it was
only a part of the whole.

Defeated on that part of the plan by Haydock, what had been the
enemy's response? Might not he have fallen back upon the next best
thing—that is to say, Sans Souci. The exposure of Hahn had come about
four years ago. Tommy had an idea, from what Sheila Perenna had said,
that it was very soon after that Mrs. Perenna had returned to England
and bought Sans Souci. The next move in the game?

It would seem therefore that Leahampton was definitely an enemy
centre—that there were already installations and affiliations in the neighborhood.

His spirits rose. The depression engendered by the harmless and futile
atmosphere of Sans Souci disappeared. Innocent as it seemed, that in-

nocence was no more than skin deep. Behind that innocuous mask things were going on.

And the focus of it all, so far as Tommy could judge, was Mrs. Perenna. The first thing to do was to know more about Mrs. Perenna, to penetrate behind her apparently simple routine of running her boarding establishment. Her correspondence, her acquaintances, her social or war working activities—somewhere in all these must lie the essence of her real activities. If Mrs. Perenna was the renowned woman agent—M.— then it was she who controlled the whole of the Fifth Column activities in this country. Her identity would be known to few—only to those at the top. But communications she must have with her chiefs of staff, and it was those communications that he and Tuppence had got to tap.

At the right moment, as Tommy saw well enough, Smugglers' Rest could be seized and held—by a few stalwarts operating from Sans Souci. That moment was not yet, but it might be very near.

Once the German army was established in control of the channel ports in France and Belgium, they could concentrate on the invasion and subjugation of Britain, and things were certainly going very badly in France at the moment.

Britain's Navy was all-powerful on the sea, so the attack must come by air and by internal treachery—and if the threads of internal treachery were in Mrs. Perenna's keeping there was no time to lose.

Major Bletchley's words chimed in with his thoughts:

"I saw, you know, that there was no time to lose. I got hold of Abdul, my syce—good fellow, Abdul—"

The story droned on.

Tommy was thinking:

"Why Leahampton? Any reason? It's out of the main stream—bit of a backwater. Conservative, old-fashioned. All those points make it desirable. Is there anything else?"

There was a stretch of flat agricultural country behind it running inland. A lot of pasture. Suitable, therefore, for the landing of troop-carrying airplanes or of parachute troops. But that was true of many other places. There was also a big chemical works where, it might be noted, Carl von Deinim was employed.

Carl von Deinim. How did he fit in? Only too well. He was not, as Grant had pointed out, the real head. A cog, only, in the machine. Liable to suspicion and internment at any moment. But in the meantime he might have accomplished what had been his task. He had mentioned to Tuppence that he was working on decontamination problems and on the immunising of certain gases. There were probabilities there—probabilities unpleasant to contemplate.

Carl, Tommy decided (a little reluctantly), was in it. A pity, because he rather liked the fellow. Well, he was working for his country—taking his life in his hands. Tommy had respect for such an adversary—down him by all means—a firing-party was the end, but you knew that when you took on your job.

It was the people who betrayed their own land—from within—that really roused a slow vindictive passion in him. By God, he'd get them!

"—And that's how I got them!" The Major wound up his story triumphantly. "Pretty smart bit of work, eh?"

Unblushingly Tommy said:

"Most ingenious thing I've heard in my life, Major."

II

Mrs. Blenkensop was reading a letter on thin foreign paper stamped outside with the censor's mark.

Incidentally the direct result of her conversation with "Mr. Faraday".

"Dear Raymond," she murmured. "I was so happy about him out in Egypt, and now, it seems, there is a big change round. All *very* secret, of course, and he can't *say* anything—just that there really is a marvelous plan and that I'm to be ready for some *big surprise* soon. I'm glad to know where he's being sent, but I really don't see why—"

Bletchley grunted.

"Surely he's not allowed to tell you that?"

Tuppence gave a deprecating laugh and looked round the breakfast table as she folded up her precious letter.

"Oh we have our methods," she said archly. "Dear Raymond knows that if only I know where he is or where he's going I don't worry quite so much. It's quite a simple way, too. Just a certain word, you know, and after it the initial letters of the next words spell out the place. Of course it makes rather a funny sentence sometimes—but Raymond is really most ingenious. I'm sure *nobody* would notice."

Little murmurs arose round the table. The moment was well chosen, everybody happened to be at the breakfast table together for once.

Bletchley, his face rather red, said:

"You'll excuse me, Mrs. Blenkensop, but that's a damn foolish thing to do. Movements of troops and air squadrons are just what the Germans want to know."

"Oh, but I never tell anyone," cried Tuppence. "I'm very, very careful."

"All the same it's an unwise thing to do—and your boy will get into trouble over it some day."

"Oh, I do hope not. I'm his *mother,* you see. A mother *ought* to know."

"Indeed and I think you're right," boomed out Mrs. O'Rourke. "Wild horses wouldn't drag the information from you—we know that."

"Letters can be read," said Bletchley.

"I'm very careful never to leave letters lying about," said Tuppence with an air of outraged dignity. "I always keep them locked up."

Bletchley shook his head doubtfully.

III

It was a grey morning with the wind blowing coldly from the sea. Tuppence was alone at the far end of the beach.

She took from her bag two letters that she had just called for at a small newsagent's in the town.

They had taken some time in coming since they had been readdressed there, the second time to a Mrs. Spender. Tuppence liked crossing her tracks. Her children believed her to be in Cornwall with an old aunt.

She opened the first letter.

"DEAREST MOTHER,

"Lots of funny things I could tell you only I mustn't. We're putting up a good show, I think. Five German planes before breakfast is today's market quotation. Bit of a mess at the moment and all that, but we'll get there all right in the end.

"It's the way they machine-gun the poor civilian devils on the roads that gets me. It makes us all see red. Gus and Trundles want to be remembered to you. They're still going strong.

"Don't worry about me. I'm all right. Wouldn't have missed this show for the world. Love to old Carrot Top—have the W.O. given him a job yet?

"Yours ever,
"DEREK."

Tuppence's eyes were very bright and shining as she read and re-read this.

Then she opened the other letter.

"DEAREST MUM,

"How's old Aunt Gracie? Going strong? I think you're wonderful to stick it. I couldn't.

"No news. My job is very interesting, but so hush-hush I can't tell you about it. But I really do feel I'm doing something worth while. Don't fret about not getting any war work to do—it's so silly all these elderly women rushing about wanting to *do* things. They only really want people who are young and efficient. I wonder how Carrots is getting on at his job up in Scotland? Just filling up forms, I suppose. Still he'll be happy to feel he is doing something.

"Lots of love,
"DEBORAH."

Tuppence smiled.

She folded the letters, smoothed them lovingly, and then under the shelter of a breakwater she struck a match and set them on fire. She waited until they were reduced to ashes.

Taking out her fountain pen and a small writing pad she wrote rapidly.

> "Langherne,
> Cornwall.

"DEAREST DEB,

"It seems so remote from the war here that I can hardly believe there is a war going on. Very glad to get your letter and know that your work is interesting.

"Auntie Gracie has grown much more feeble and very hazy in her mind. I think she is glad to have me here. She talks a good deal about the old days and sometimes, I think, confuses me with my own mother. They are growing more vegetables than usual— have turned the rose-garden into potatoes. I help old Sikes a bit. It makes me feel I am doing something in the war. Your father seems a bit disgruntled, but I think, as you say, he too is glad to be doing something.

> "Love from your
> "TUPPENNY MOTHER."

She took a fresh sheet.

"DARLING DEREK,

"A great comfort to get your letter. Send field postcards often if you haven't time to write.

"I've come down to be with Aunt Gracie a bit. She is very feeble. She will talk of you as though you were seven and gave me ten shillings yesterday to send you as a tip.

"I'm still on the shelf and nobody wants my invaluable services! Extraordinary! Your father, as I told you, has got a job in the Ministry of Requirements. He is up north somewhere. Better than nothing, but not what he wanted, poor old Carrot Top. Still I suppose we've got to be humble and take a back seat and leave the war to you young idiots.

"I won't say, 'Take care of yourself,' because I gather that the whole point is that you should do just the opposite. But don't go and be stupid.

> "Lots of love,
> "TUPPENCE.

She put the letters into envelopes, addressed and stamped them, and posted them on her way back to Sans Souci.

As she reached the bottom of the cliff her attention was caught by two figures standing talking a little way up.

Tuppence stopped dead. It was the same woman she had seen yesterday and talking to her was Carl von Deinim.

Regretfully Tuppence noted the fact that there was no cover. She could not get near them unseen and overhear what was being said.

Moreover, at that moment, the young German turned his head and saw her. Rather abruptly, the two figures parted. The woman came rapidly down the hill, crossing the road and passing Tuppence on the other side.

Carl von Deinim waited until Tuppence came up to him.

Then, gravely and politely, he wished her good morning.

Tuppence said immediately:

"What a very odd-looking woman that was to whom you were talking, Mr. Deinim."

"Yes. It is a Central European type. She is a Pole."

"Really? A—a friend of yours?"

Tuppence's tone was a very good copy of the inquisitive voice of Aunt Gracie in her younger days.

"Not at all," said Carl stiffly. "I never saw the woman before."

"Oh, really. I thought—" Tuppence paused artistically.

"She asks me only for a direction. I speak German to her because she does not understand much English."

"I see. And she was asking the way somewhere?"

"She asked me if I knew a Mrs. Gottlieb near here. I do not, and she says she has, perhaps, got the name of the house wrong."

"I see," said Tuppence thoughtfully.

Mr. Rosenstein. Mrs. Gottlieb.

She stole a swift glance at Carl von Deinim. He was walking beside her with a set stiff face.

Tuppence felt a definite suspicion of this strange woman. And she felt almost convinced that when she had first caught sight of them, the woman and Carl had been already talking some time together.

Carl von Deinim?

Carl and Sheila that morning. *"You must be careful . . ."*

Tuppence thought:

"I hope—I hope these young things *aren't* in it!"

Soft, she told herself, middle-aged and soft! That's what she was! The Nazi creed was a youth creed. Nazi agents would in all probability be young. Carl and Sheila. Tommy said Sheila wasn't in it. Yes, but Tommy was a man, and Sheila was beautiful with a queer breathtaking beauty.

Carl and Sheila, and behind them that enigmatic figure: Mrs. Perenna. Mrs. Perenna, sometimes the voluble commonplace guesthouse hostess, sometimes, for fleeting minutes, a tragic, violent personality.

Tuppence went slowly upstairs to her bedroom.

That evening, when she went to bed, she pulled out the long drawer of her bureau. At one side of it was a small japanned box with a flimsy cheap lock. Tuppence slipped on gloves, unlocked the box, and opened it. A pile of letters lay inside. On the top was the one received that morning from "Raymond". Tuppence unfolded it with due precautions.

Then her lips set grimly. There had been an eyelash in the fold of the paper this morning. The eyelash was not there now.

She went to the washstand. There was a little bottle labelled innocently: "Grey powder" with a dose.

Adroitly Tuppence dusted a little of the powder on to the letter and on to the surface of the glossy japanned enamel of the box.

There were no fingerprints on either of them.

Again Tuppence nodded her head with a certain grim satisfaction.

For there should have been fingerprints—her own.

A servant might have read letters out of curiosity, though it seemed unlikely—certainly unlikely that she should have gone to the trouble of finding a key to fit the box.

But a servant would not think of wiping off fingerprints.

Mrs. Perenna? Sheila? Somebody else? Somebody, at least, who was interested in the movements of British armed forces.

IV

Tuppence's plan of campaign had been simple in its outlines. First, a general sizing up of probabilities and possibilities. Second, an experiment to determine whether there was or was not an inmate of Sans Souci who was interested in troop movements and anxious to conceal the fact. Third—who that person was?

It was concerning that third operation that Tuppence pondered as she lay in bed the following morning. Her train of thought was slightly hampered by Betty Sprot, who had pranced in at an early hour, preceding indeed the cup of somewhat tepid inky liquid known as Morning Tea.

Betty was both active and voluble. She had taken a great fancy to Tuppence. She climbed up on the bed and thrust an extremely tattered picture-book under Tuppence's nose, commanding with brevity:

"Wead."

Tuppence read obediently.

"Goosey goosey gander, whither will you wander?

Upstairs, downstairs, in my lady's chamber."

Betty rolled with mirth—repeating in an ecstasy:

"Upstairs—upstairs—upstairs—" and then with a sudden climax: *"Down—"* and proceeded to roll off the bed with a thump.

This proceeding was repeated several times until it palled. Then Betty crawled about the floor, playing with Tuppence's shoes and muttering busily to herself in her own particular idiom:

"Ag do—bah pit—soo—soo dah—putch—"

Released to fly back to its own perplexities, Tuppence's mind forgot the child. The words of the nursery rhyme seemed to mock at her.

"Goosey—goosey, gander, whither shall ye wander?"

Whither indeed? Goosey, that was her, Gander was Tommy. It was at any rate, what they appeared to be! Tuppence had the heartiest contempt for Mrs. Blenkensop. Mr. Meadowes, she thought, was a little better—stolid, British, unimaginative—quite incredibly stupid. Both of them, she hoped, fitting nicely into the background of Sans Souci. Both such possible people to be there.

All the same, one must not relax—a slip was so easy. She had made one the other day—nothing that mattered, but just a sufficient indication to warn her to be careful. Such an easy approach to intimacy and good relations—an indifferent knitter asking for guidance. But she had forgotten that one evening, her fingers had slipped into their own practised efficiency, the needles clicking busily with the even note of the experienced knitter. Mrs. O'Rourke had noticed it. Since then, she had carefully struck a medium course—not so clumsy as she had been at first—but not so rapid as she could be.

"Ag boo bate?" demanded Betty. She reiterated the question: "Ag boo bate?"

"Lovely, darling," said Tuppence absently. "Beautiful."

Satisfied, Betty relapsed into murmurs again.

Her next step, Tuppence thought, could be managed easily enough. That is to say with the connivance of Tommy. She saw exactly how to do it—

Lying there planning, time slipped by. Mrs. Sprot came in, breathless, to seek for Betty.

"Oh, here she is. I couldn't think where she had got to. Oh, Betty, you naughty girl—oh, dear, Mrs. Blenkensop, I am so sorry."

Tuppence sat up in bed. Betty, with an angelic face, was contemplating her handiwork.

She had removed all the laces from Tuppence's shoes and had immersed them in a toothglass of water. She was prodding them now with a gleeful finger.

Tuppence laughed and cut short Mrs. Sprot's apologies.

"How frightfully funny. Don't worry, Mrs. Sprot, they'll recover all right. It's my fault. I should have noticed what she was doing. She was rather quiet."

"I know." Mrs. Sprot sighed. "Whenever they're quiet, it's a bad sign. I'll get you some more laces this morning, Mrs. Blenkensop."

"Don't bother," said Tuppence. "They'll dry none the worse."

Mrs. Sprot bore Betty away and Tuppence got up to put her plan into execution.

6

I

TOMMY LOOKED RATHER gingerly at the packet that Tuppence thrust upon him.

"Is this it?"

"Yes. Be careful. Don't get it over you."

Tommy took a delicate sniff at the packet and replied with energy.

"No, indeed. What is this frightful stuff?"

"Asafœtida," replied Tuppence. "A pinch of that and you will wonder why your boyfriend is no longer attentive, as the advertisements say."

"Shades of BO," murmured Tommy.

Shortly after that, various incidents occurred.

The first was the smell in Mr. Meadowes's room.

Mr. Meadowes, not a complaining man by nature, spoke about it mildly at first, then with increasing firmness.

Mrs. Perenna was summoned into conclave. With all the will to resist in the world, she had to admit that there was a smell. A pronounced unpleasant sell. Perhaps, she suggested, the gas tap of the fire was leaking.

Bending down and sniffing dubiously, Tommy remarked that he did not think the smell came from there. Nor from under the floor. He himself thought, definitely—a dead rat.

Mrs. Perenna admitted that she had heard of such things—but she was sure there were no rats at Sans Souci. Perhaps a mouse—though she herself had never seen a mouse.

Mr. Meadowes said with firmness that he thought the smell indicated at least a rat—and he added, still more firmly, that he was not going to sleep another night in the room until the matter had been seen to. He would ask Mrs. Perenna to change his room.

Mrs. Perenna said, "Of course, she had just been about to suggest the same thing. She was afraid that the only room vacant was rather a small one and unfortunately it had no sea view; but if Mr. Meadowes did not mind that—"

Mr. Meadowes did not. His only wish was to get away from the smell. Mrs. Perenna thereupon accompanied him to a small bedroom, the door of which happened to be just opposite the door of Mrs. Blenkensop's room, and summoned the adenoidal semi-idiotic Beatrice to "move Mr. Meadowes's things." She would, she explained, send for "a man" to take up the floor and search for the origin of the smell.

Matters were settled satisfactorily on this basis.

II

The second incident was Mr. Meadowes's hay fever. That was what he called it at first. Later he admitted doubtfully that he might just possibly have caught cold. He sneezed a good deal, and his eyes ran. If there was a faint elusive suggestion of raw onion floating in the breeze in the vicinity of Mr. Meadowes's large silk handkerchief nobody noticed the fact, and indeed a pungent amount of eau de cologne masked the more penetrating odor.

Finally, defeated by incessant sneezing and nose-blowing, Mr. Meadowes retired to bed for the day.

It was on the morning of that day that Mrs. Blenkensop received a letter from her son Douglas. So excited and thrilled was Mrs. Blenkensop that everybody at Sans Souci heard about it. The letter had not been censored at all, she explained, because fortunately one of Douglas's friends coming on leave had brought it so for once Douglas had been able to write quite fully.

"And it just shows," declared Mrs. Blenkensop, wagging her head sagely, "how little we know really of what is going on."

After breakfast she went upstairs to her room, opened the japanned box and put the letter away. Between the folded pages were some unnoticeable grains of rice powder. She closed the box again, pressing her fingers firmly on its surface.

As she left her room she coughed, and from opposite came the sound of a highly histrionic sneeze.

Tuppence smiled and proceeded downstairs.

She had already made known her intention of going up to London for the day—to see her lawyer on some business and to do a little shopping.

Now she was given a good send-off by the assembled boarders and entrusted with various commissions—"only if you have time, of course."

Major Bletchley held himself aloof from this female chatter. He was reading his paper and utturing appropriate comments aloud. "Damned swines of Germans. Machine-gunning civilian refugees on the roads. Damned brutes. If I were our people—"

Tuppence left him still outlining what *he* would do if he were in charge of operations.

She made a detour through the garden to ask Betty Sprot what she would like as a present from London.

Betty ecstatically clasping a snail in two hot hands gurgled appreciatively. In response to Tuppence's suggestions—"A pussy. A picture-book? Some colored chalks to draw with?"—Betty decided, "Betty dwar." So the colored chalks were noted down on Tuppence's list.

As she passed on meaning to rejoin the drive by the path at the end of the garden she came unexpectedly upon Carl von Deinim. He was standing leaning on the wall. His hands were clenched, and as Tuppence approached he turned on her, his usually impassive face convulsed with emotion.

Tuppence paused involuntarily and asked:

"Is anything the matter?"

"Ach, yes, everything is the matter." His voice was hoarse and unnatural. "You have a saying here that a thing is neither fish, flesh, fowl, nor good red herring, have you not?"

Tuppence nodded.

Carl went on bitterly:

"That is what I am. It cannot go on, that is what I say. It cannot go on. It would be best, I think, to end everything."

"What do you mean?"

The young man said:

"You have spoken kindly to me. You would, I think, understand. I fled from my own country because of injustice and cruelty. I came here to find freedom. I hated Nazi Germany. But, alas, I am still a German. Nothing can alter that."

Tuppence murmured:

"You may have difficulties, I know—"

"It is not that. I am a German, I tell you. In my heart—in my feeling. Germany is still my country. When I read of German cities bombed, of German soldiers dying, of German airplanes brought down—they are my people who die. When that old fire-eating Major reads out from his paper, when he say 'those swine'—I am moved to fury—I cannot bear it."

He added quietly:

"And so I think it would be best, perhaps, to end it all. Yes, to end it."

Tuppence took hold of him firmly by the arm.

"Nonsense," she said robustly, "Of course you feel as you do. Anyone would. But you've got to stick it."

"I wish they would intern me. It would be easier so."

"Yes, probably it would. But in the meantime you're doing useful work—or so I've heard. Useful not only to England but to humanity. You're working on decontamination problems, aren't you?"

His face lit up slightly.

"Ah, yes, and I begin to have much success. A process very simple, easily made and not complicated to apply."

"Well," said Tuppence, "that's worth doing. Anything that mitigates suffering is worth while—and anything that's constructive and not destructive. Naturally we've got to call the other side names. They're doing just the same in Germany. Hundreds of Major Bletchleys—foaming at the mouth. I hate the Germans myself. 'The Germans,' I say, and feel waves of loathing. But when I think of individual Germans, mothers sitting anxiously waiting for news of their sons, and boys leaving home to fight, and peasants getting in the harvests, and little shopkeepers and some of the nice kindly German people I know, I feel quite different. I know then that they are just human beings and that we're all feeling alike. That's the real thing. The other is just the war mask that you put on. It's a part of war—probably a necessary part—but it's ephemeral."

As she spoke she thought, as Tommy had done not long before, of Nurse Cavell's words. "Patriotism is not enough. I must have no hatred in my heart."

That saying of a most truly patriotic woman had always seemed to them both the high-water mark of sacrifice.

Carl von Deinim took her hand and kissed it. He said:

"I thank you. What you say is good and true. I will have more fortitude."

"Oh, dear," thought Tuppence as she walked down the road into the town. "How very unfortunate that the person I like best in this place should be a German. It makes everything cock-eyed!"

III

Tuppence was nothing if not thorough. Although she had no wish to go to London, she judged it wise to do exactly as she had said she was going to do. If she merely made an excursion somewhere for the day, somebody might see her and the fact would get round to Sans Souci.

No, Mrs. Blenkensop had said she was going to London, and to London she must go.

She purchased a third return, and was just leaving the booking-office window when she ran into Sheila Perenna.

"Hallo," said Sheila. "Where are you off to? I just came to see about a parcel which seems to have gone astray."

Tuppence explained her plans.

"Oh, yes, of course," said Sheila carelessly. "I do remember you saying something about it, but I hadn't realised it was today you were going. I'll come and see you into the train."

Sheila was more animated than usual. She looked neither bad-tempered nor sulky. She chatted quite amiably about small details of daily life at Sans Souci. She remained talking to Tuppence until the train left the station.

After waving from the window and watching the girl's figure recede, Tuppence sat down in her corner seat again and gave herself up to serious meditation,

Was it, she wondered, an accident that Sheila had happened to be at the station just at that time? Or was it a proof of enemy thoroughness? Did Mrs. Perenna want to make quite sure that the garrulous Mrs. Blenkensop really *had* gone to London?

It looked very much like it.

IV

It was not until the next day that Tuppence was able to have a conference with Tommy. They had agreed never to attempt to communicate with each other under the roof of Sans Souci.

Mrs. Blenkensop met Mr. Meadowes as the latter, his hay fever somewhat abated, was taking a gentle stroll on the front. They sat down on one of the promenade seats.

"Well?" said Tuppence.

Slowly, Tommy nodded his head. He looked rather unhappy.

"Yes," he said. "I got something. But Lord, what a day. Perpetually with an eye to the crack of the door. I've got quite a stiff neck."

"Never mind your neck," said Tuppence unfeelingly. "Tell me."

"Well, the maids went in to do the bed and the room, of course. And Mrs. Perenna went in—but that was when the maids were there and she was just blowing them up about something. And the kid ran in once and came out with a woolly dog."

"Yes, yes. Anyone else?"

"One person," said Tommy slowly.

"Who?"

"Carl von Deinim."

"Oh!" Tuppence felt a swift pang. So, after all—

"When?" she asked.

"Lunch time. He came out from the diningroom early came up to his room, then sneaked across the passage and into yours. He was there about a quarter of an hour."

He paused.

"That settles it, I think?"

Tuppence nodded.

Yes, it settled it all right. Carl von Deinim could have had no reason for going into Mrs. Blenkensop's bedroom and remaining there for a quarter of an hour save one. His complicity was proved. He must be, Tuppence thought, a marvelous actor. . . .

His words to her that morning had rung so very true. Well, perhaps they had been true in a way. To know when to use the truth was the essence of successful deception. Carl von Deinim was a patriot all right, he was an enemy agent working for his country. One could respect him for that. Yes—but destroy him too.

"I'm sorry," she said slowly.

"So am I," said Tommy. "He's a good chap."

Tuppence said:

"You and I might be doing the same thing in Germany."

Tommy nodded. Tuppence went on.

"Well, we know more or less where we are. Carl von Deinim working in with Sheila and her mother. Probably Mrs. Perenna is the big noise. Then there is that foreign woman who was talking to Carl yesterday. She's in it somehow."

"What do we do now?"

"We must go through Mrs. Perenna's room some time. There might be something there that would give us a hint. And we must tail her— see where she goes and whom she meets. Tommy, let's get Albert down here."

Tommy considered the point.

Many years ago Albert, a pageboy in a hotel, had joined forces with the young Beresfords and shared their adventures. Afterwards he had entered their service and been the sole domestic prop of the establishment. Some six years ago he had married and was now the proud proprietor of The Duck and Dog pub in South London.

Tuppence continued rapidly:

"Albert will be thrilled. We'll get him down here. He can stay at that pub near the station and he can shadow the Perennas for us—or anyone else."

"What about Mrs. Albert?"

"She was going to her mother in Wales with the children last Monday. Because of air raids. It all fits in perfectly."

"Yes, that's a good idea, Tuppence. Either of us following the woman about would be rather conspicuous. Albert will be perfect. Now another thing—I think we ought to watch out for that so-called Polish woman who was talking to Carl and hanging about here. It seems to me that she probably represents the other end of the business—and that's what we're anxious to find."

"Oh yes, I do agree. She comes here for orders, or to take messages. Next time we see her, one of us must follow her and find out more about her."

"What about looking through Mrs. Perenna's room—and Carl's too, I suppose?"

"I don't suppose you'll find anything in his. After all, as a German, the police are liable to search it and so he'd be careful not to have anything suspicious. Mrs. Perenna is going to be difficult. When she's out of the house, Sheila is often there, and there's Betty and Mrs. Sprot running about all over the landings, and Mrs. O'Rourke spends a lot of time in her bedroom."

She paused.

"Lunch time is the best."

"Master Carl's time?"

"Exactly. I could have a headache and go to my room—No, someone might come up and want to minister to me. I know, I'll just come in quietly before lunch and go up to my room without telling anyone. Then, after lunch, I can say I had a headache."

"Hadn't I better do it? My hay fever could recrudesce tomorrow."

"I think it had better be me. If I'm caught I could always say I was looking for aspirin or something. One of the gentlemen boarders in Mrs. Perenna's room would cause far more speculation."

Tommy grinned.

"Of a scandalous character."

Then the smile died. He looked grave and anxious.

"As soon as we can, old thing. The news is bad today. We must get on to something soon."

V

Tommy continued his walk and presently entered the post office, where he put through a call to Mr. Grant, and reported "the recent operation was successful and our friend *C.* is definitely involved."

Then he wrote a letter and posted it. It was addressed to Mr. Albert Batt, The Duck and Dog, Glamorgan St. Kennington.

Then he bought himself a weekly paper which professed to inform the English world of what was really going to happen and strolled innocently back in the direction of Sans Souci.

Presently he was hailed by the hearty voice of Commander Haydock leaning from his two-seater car and shouting "Hallo, Meadowes, want a lift?"

Tommy accepted a lift gratefully and got in.

"So you read that rag, do you?" demanded Haydock, glancing at the scarlet cover of the *Inside Weekly News.*

Mr. Meadowes displayed the slight confusion of all readers of the periodical in question when challenged.

"Awful rag," he agreed. "But sometimes, you know, they really do seem to know what's going on behind the scenes."

"And sometimes they're wrong."

"Oh, quite so."

"Truth of it is," said Commander Haydock, steering rather erratically round a one-way island and narrowly missing collision with a large van, "when the beggars are right, one remembers it, and when they're wrong you forget it."

"Do you think there's any truth in this rumor about Stalin having approached us?"

"Wishful thinking, my boy, wishful thinking," said Commander Haydock. "The Russkys are as crooked as hell and always have been. Don't trust 'em, that's what I say. Hear you've been under the weather?"

"Just a touch of hay fever. I get it about this time of year."

"Yes, of course. Never suffered from it myself, but I had a pal who did. Used to lay him out regularly every June. Feeling fit enough for a game of golf?"

Tommy said he'd like it very much.

"Right. What about tomorrow? Tell you what, I've got to go to a meeting about this Parashot business, raising a corps of local volunteers— jolly good idea if you ask me. Time we were all made to pull our weight. So shall we have a round about six?"

"Thanks very much. I'd like to."

"Good. Then that's settled."

The Commander drew up abruptly at the gate of Sans Souci.

"How's the fair Sheila?" he asked.

"Quite well, I think. I haven't seen much of her."

Haydock gave his loud barking laugh.

"Not as much as you'd like to, I bet! Good-looking girl that, but damned rude. She sees too much of that German fellow. Damned unpatriotic, I call it. Dare say she's got no use for old fogies like you and me, but there are plenty of nice lads going about in our own Services. Why take up with a bloody German? That sort of thing riles me."

Mr. Meadowes said:

"Be careful, he's just coming up the hill behind us."

"Don't care if he does hear! Rather hope he does. I'd like to kick Master Carl's behind for him. Any decent German's fighting for his country—not slinking over here to get out of it!"

"Well," said Tommy. "It's one less German to invade England at all events."

"You mean he's here already? Ha ha! rather good, Meadowes! Not that I believe this tommy rot about invasion. We never have been invaded and never will be. We've got a Navy, thank God!"

With which patriotic announcement the Commander let in his clutch with a jerk and the car leaped forward up the hill to Smugglers' Rest.

VI

Tuppence arrived at the gate of Sans Souci at twenty minutes to two. She turned off from the drive and went through the garden and into the house through the open drawing-room window. A smell of Irish stew and the clatter of plates and murmur of voices came from afar. Sans Souci was hard at work on its midday meal.

Tuppence waited by the drawing-room door until Martha, the maid, had passed across the hall and into the diningroom, then she ran quickly up the stairs, shoeless.

She went into her room, put on her soft felt bedroom slippers, and then went along the landing and into Mrs. Perenna's room.

Once inside she looked round her and felt a certain distaste sweep over her. Not a nice job, this. Quite unpardonable if Mrs. Perenna was simply Mrs. Perenna. Prying into people's private affairs—

Tuppence shook herself, an impatient terrier shake that was a reminiscence of her girlhood. *There was a war on!*

She went over to the dressing-table.

Quick and deft in her movements, she had soon gone through the contents of the drawers there. In the tall bureau, one of the drawers was locked. That seemed more promising.

Tommy had been entrusted with certain tools and had received some brief instruction on the manipulation of them. These indications he had passed on to Tuppence.

A deft twist or two of the wrist and the drawer yielded.

There was a cash box containing twenty pounds in notes and some piles of silver—also a jewel case. And there were a heap of papers. These last were what interested Tuppence most. Rapidly she went through them, necessarily it was a cursory glance. She could not afford time for more.

Papers relating to a mortgage on Sans Souci, a bank account, letters. Time flew past, Tuppence skimmed through the documents, concentrating furiously on anything that might bear a double meaning. Two letters from a friend in Italy, rambling discursive letters, seemingly quite harmless. But possibly not so harmless as they sounded. A letter from one Simon Mortimer, of London—a dry business-like letter containing so little of moment that Tuppence wondered why it had been kept. Was Mr. Mortimer not so harmless as he seemed? At the bottom of the pile a letter in faded ink signed Pat and beginning *"This will be the last letter I'll be writing you, Eileen my darling—"*

No, not that! Tuppence could not bring herself to read that! She refolded it, tidied the letters on top of it and then, suddenly alert, pushed the drawer to—no time to re-lock it—and when the door opened and Mrs. Perenna came in, she was searching vaguely amongst the bottles on the washstand.

Mrs. Blenkensop turned a flustered, but foolish face towards her hostess.

"Oh, Mrs. Perenna, do forgive me. I came in with such a blinding headache, and I thought I would lie down on my bed with a little aspirin, and I couldn't find mine, so I thought you wouldn't mind—I know you must have some because you offered it to Miss Minton the other day."

Mrs. Perenna swept into the room. There was a sharpness in her voice as she said:

"Why, of course, Mrs. Blenkensop, why ever didn't you come and ask me?"

"Well, of course, yes, I should have done really. But I knew you were all at lunch, and I do so hate, you know, making a *fuss*—"

Passing Tuppence, Mrs. Perenna caught up the bottle of aspirin from the washstand.

"How many would you like?" she demanded crisply.

Mrs. Blenkensop accepted three. Escorted by Mrs. Perenna she crossed to her own room and hastily demurred to the suggestion of a hot-water bottle.

Mrs. Perenna used her parting shot as she left the room.

"But you have some aspirin of your own, Mrs. Blenkensop. I've seen it."

Tuppence cried quickly:

"Oh, I know. I know I've got some somewhere, but, so stupid of me, I simply couldn't lay my hands on it."

Mrs. Perenna said with a flash of her big white teeth:

"Well, have a good rest until tea time."

She went out, closing the door behind her. Tuppence drew a deep breath, lying on her bed rigidly lest Mrs. Perenna should return.

Had the other suspected anything? Those teeth, so big and so white—

the better to eat you with, my dear. Tuppence always thought of that when she noticed those teeth. Mrs. Perenna's hands too, big cruel-looking hands.

She had appeared to accept Tuppence's presence in her bedroom quite naturally. But later she would find the bureau drawer unlocked. Would she suspect then? Or would she think she had left it unlocked herself by accident? One did do such things. Had Tuppence been able to replace the papers in such a way that they looked much the same as before?

Surely, even if Mrs. Perenna did notice anything amiss she would be more likely to suspect one of the servants than she would "Mrs. Blenkensop." And if she did suspect the latter, wouldn't it be a mere case of suspecting her of undue curiosity? There were people, Tuppence knew, who did poke and pry.

But then, if Mrs. Perenna were the renowned German agent M., she would be suspicious of counter-espionage.

Had anything in her bearing revealed undue alertness?

She had seemed natural enough—only that one sharply pointed remark about the aspirin.

Suddenly, Tuppence sat up on her bed. She remembered that her aspirin, together with some iodine and a bottle of soda mints were all together at the back of the writing table drawer where she had shoved them when unpacking.

It would seem, therefore, that she was not the only person to snoop in other people's rooms. Mrs. Perenna had got there first.

7

I

ON THE FOLLOWING day Mrs. Sprot went up to London.

A few tentative remarks on her part had led immediately to various offers on the part of the inhabitants of Sans Souci to look after Betty.

When Mrs. Sprot, with many final adjurations to Betty to be a very good girl, had departed, Betty attached herself to Tuppence, who had elected to take morning duty.

"Play," said Betty. "Play hide seek."

She was talking more easily every day and had adopted a most fetching habit, of laying her head on one side, fixing her interlocutor with a bewitching smile and murmuring: *"Peese."*

Tuppence had intended taking her for a walk, but it was raining hard, so the two of them adjourned to the bedroom where Betty led the way to the bottom drawer of the bureau where her playthings were kept.

"Hide Bonzo, shall we?" asked Tuppence.

But Betty had changed her mind and demanded instead:

"Wead me story."

Tuppence pulled out a rather tattered book from one end of the cupboard—to be interrupted by a squeal from Betty.

"No, no. Narsty . . . Bad . . ."

Tuppence stared at her in surprise and then down at the book, which was a colored version of Little Jack Horner.

"Was Jack a bad boy?" she asked. "Because he pulled out a plum?"

Betty reiterated with emphasis:

"B-a-a-ad!" and with a terrific effort. "Dirrrty!"

She seized the book from Tuppence and replaced it in the line, then tugged out an identical book from the other end of the shelf, announcing with a beaming smile:

"K-k-klean ni-t i ce Jackorner!"

Tuppence realised that the dirty and worn books had been replaced by new and cleaner editions and was rather amused. Mrs. Sprot was very much what Tuppence thought of as "the hygienic mother." Always terrified of germs, of impure food, or of the child sucking a soiled toy.

Tuppence, brought up in a free and easy Rectory life, was always rather contemptuous of exaggerated hygiene and had brought up her own two children to absorb what she called a "reasonable amount" of dirt. However, she obediently took out the clean copy of *Jack Horner* and read it to the child with the comments proper to the occasion. Betty murmuring *"That's* Jack!—Plum!—In a *Pie!"* pointing out these interesting objects with a sticky finger that bade fair to soon consign this second copy to the scrap heap. They proceeded to *Goosey Goosey Gander* and the *Old Woman Who Lived in a Shoe,* and then Betty hid the books and Tuppence took an amazingly long time to find each of them, to Betty's great glee, and so the morning passed rapidly away.

After lunch Betty had her rest and it was then that Mrs. O'Rourke invited Tuppence into her room.

Mrs. O'Rourke's room was very untidy and smelt strongly of peppermint and stale cake with a faint odor of moth balls added. There were photographs on every table of Mrs. O'Rourke's children and grandchildren and nieces and nephews and great-nieces and great-nephews. There were so many of them that Tuppence felt as though she were looking at a realistically produced play of the late Victorian period.

"'Tis a grand way you have with children, Mrs. Blenkensop," observed Mrs. O'Rourke genially.

"Oh, well," said Tuppence, "with my own two—"

Mrs. O'Rourke cut in quickly:

"Two? It was three boys I understood you had?"

"Oh yes, three. But two of them are very near in age and I was thinking of the days spent with them."

"Ah! I see. Sit down now, Mrs. Blenkensop. Make yourself at home."

Tuppence sat down obediently and wished that Mrs. O'Rourke did not always make her feel so uncomfortable. She felt now exactly like Hansel or Gretel accepting the witch's invitation.

"Tell me now," said Mrs. O'Rourke. "What do you think of Sans Souci?"

Tuppence began a somewhat gushing speech of eulogy, but Mrs. O'Rourke cut her short without ceremony.

"What I'd be asking you is if you don't feel there's something odd about the place?"

"Odd? No, I don't think so."

"Not about Mrs. Perenna? You're interested in her, you must allow. I've seen you watching her and watching her."

Tuppence flushed.

"She—she's—an interesting woman."

"She is not then," said Mrs. O'Rourke. "She's a commonplace woman enough—that is if she's what she seems. But perhaps she isn't. Is that your idea?"

"Really, Mrs. O'Rourke, I don't know *what* you mean."

"Have you ever stopped to think that many of us are that way— different to what we seem on the surface. Mr. Meadowes, now. He's a puzzling kind of man. Sometimes I'd say he was a typical Englishman, stupid to the core, and there's other times I'll catch a look or a word that's not stupid at all. It's odd that, don't you think so?"

Tuppence said firmly:

"Oh, I really think Mr. Meadowes is *very* typical."

"There are others. Perhaps you'll know who I'll be meaning?"

Tuppence shook her head.

"The name," said Mrs. O'Rourke encouragingly, "begins with an S."

She nodded her head several times.

With a sudden spark of anger and an obscure impulse to spring to the defense of something young and vulnerable, Tuppence said sharply:

"Sheila's just a rebel. One usually is, at that age."

Mrs. O'Rourke nodded her head several times, looking just like an obese china mandarin that Tuppence remembered on her Aunt Gracie's mantelpiece. A vast smile tilted up the corners of her mouth. She said softly:

"You mayn't know it, but Miss Minton's Christian name is Sophia."

"Oh," Tuppence was taken aback. "Was it Miss Minton you meant?"

"It was not," said Mrs. O'Rourke.

Tuppence turned away to the window. Queer how this old woman could affect her, spreading about her an atmosphere of unrest and fear. "Like a mouse between a cat's paws," thought Tuppence. "That's what I feel like . . ."

This vast smiling monumental old woman, sitting there, almost purring— and yet there was the pat pat of paws playing with something that wasn't, in spite of the purring, to be allowed to get away. . . .

Nonsense—all nonsense! I imagine these things, thought Tuppence, staring out of the window into the garden. The rain had stopped. There was a gentle patter of raindrops off the trees.

Tuppence thought: It isn't all my fancy. I'm not a fanciful person. There is something, some focus of evil there. If I could see—

Her thoughts broke off abruptly.

At the bottom of the garden the bushes parted slightly. In the gap a face appeared, staring stealthily up at the house. It was the face of the foreign woman who had stood talking to Carl von Deinim in the road.

It was so still, so unblinking in its regard, that it seemed to Tuppence as though it was not human. Staring, staring up at the windows of Sans Souci. It was devoid of expression, and yet there was—yes, undoubtedly there was menace about it. Immobile, implacable. It represented some spirit, some force, alien to Sans Souci and the commonplace banality of English guesthouse life. So, Tuppence thought, might Jael have looked, waiting to drive the nail through the forehead of sleeping Sisera.

These thoughts took only a second or two to flash through Tuppence's mind. Turning abruptly from the window, she murmured something to Mrs. O'Rourke, hurried out of the room and ran downstairs and out of the front door.

Turning to the right she ran down the side garden path to where she had seen the face. There was no one there now. Tuppence went through the shrubbery and out on to the road and looked up and down the hill. She could see no one. Where had the woman gone?

Vexed, she turned and went back into the grounds of Sans Souci. Could she have imagined the whole thing? No, the woman had been there.

Obstinately she wandered round the garden, peering behind bushes. She got very wet and found no trace of the strange woman. She retraced her steps to the house with a vague feeling of foreboding—a queer formless dread of something about to happen.

She did not guess, would never have guessed, what that something was going to be.

II

Now that the weather had cleared, Miss Minton was dressing Betty preparatory to taking her out for a walk. They were going down to the town to buy a Celluloid duck to sail in Betty's bath.

Betty was very excited and capered so violently that it was extremely difficult to insert her arms into her woolly pullover. The two set off together. Betty chattering violently: "Byaduck. Byaduck. For Bettibarf. For Bettibarf," and deriving great pleasure from a ceaseless reiteration of these important facts.

Two matches, left carefully crossed on the marble table in the hall, informed Tuppence that Mr. Meadowes was spending the afternoon on the trail of Mrs. Perenna. Tuppence betook herself to the drawing-room and the company of Mr. and Mrs. Cayley.

Mr. Cayley was in a fretful mood. He had come to Leahampton, he explained, for absolute rest and quiet, and what quiet could there be with a child in the house? All day long it went on, screaming and running about, jumping up and down on the floors—

His wife murmured pacifically that Betty was really a dear little mite, but the remark met with no favor.

"No doubt, no doubt," said Mr. Cayley, wriggling his long neck. "But her mother should keep her quiet. There are other people to consider. Invalids, people whose nerves need repose."

Tuppence said: "It's not easy to keep a child of that age quiet. It's not natural—there would be something wrong with the child if she was quiet."

Mr. Cayley gobbled angrily.

"Nonsense—nonsense—this foolish modern spirit. Letting children do exactly as they please. A child should be made to sit down quietly and— and nurse a doll—or read, or something."

"She's not three yet," said Tuppence smiling. "You can hardly expect her to be able to read."

"Well, something must be done about it. I shall speak to Mrs. Perenna. The child was singing, singing in her bed before seven o'clock this morning. I had had a bad night and just dropped off towards morning—and it woke me right up."

"It's very important that Mr. Cayley should get as much sleep as possible," said Mrs. Cayley anxiously. "The doctor said so."

"You should go to a nursing home," said Tuppence.

"My dear lady, such places are ruinously expensive and besides, it's not the right atmosphere. There is a suggestion of illness that reacts unfavorably on my subconscious."

"Bright society, the doctor said," Mrs. Cayley explained helpfully. "A normal life. He thought a guesthouse would be better than just taking a furnished house. Mr. Cayley would not be so likely to brood, and would be stimulated by exchanging ideas with other people."

Mr. Cayley's method of exchanging ideas was, so far as Tuppence could judge, a mere recital of his own ailments and symptoms and the exchange consisted in the sympathetic or unsympathetic reception of them.

Adroitly, Tuppence changed the subject.

"I wish you would tell me," she said, "of your own views on life in Germany. You told me you had travelled there a good deal in recent years. It would be interesting to have the point of view of an experienced man of the world like yourself. I can see you are the kind of man, quite unswayed by prejudice, who could really give a clear account of conditions there."

Flattery, in Tuppence's opinion, should always be laid on with a trowel where a man was concerned. Mr. Cayley rose at once to the bait.

"As you say, dear lady, I am capable of taking a clear unprejudiced view. Now, in my opinion—"

What followed constituted a monologue. Tuppence, throwing in an occasional "Now that's very interesting" or "What a shrewd observer you are," listened with an attention that was not assumed for the occasion. For Mr. Cayley, carried away by the sympathy of his listener, was displaying himself as a decided admirer of the Nazi system. How much better it would have been, he hinted, if did not say, for England and Germany to have allied themselves against the rest of Europe.

The return of Miss Minton and Betty, the Celluloid duck duly obtained, broke in upon the monologue, which had extended unbroken for nearly two hours. Looking up, Tuppence caught rather a curious expression on Mrs. Cayley's face. She found it hard to define. It might be merely pardonable wifely jealousy at the monopoly of her husband's attention by another woman. It might be alarm at the fact that Mr. Cayley was being too outspoken in his political views. It certainly expressed disatisfaction.

Tea was the next move and hard on that came the return of Mrs. Sprot from London exclaiming:

"I do hope Betty's been good and not troublesome? Have you been a good girl, Betty?" To which Betty replied laconically by the single word: "Dam!"

This, however, was not to be regarded as an expression of disapproval at her mother's return, but merely as a request for blackberry preserve.

It elicited a deep chuckle from Mrs. O'Rourke and a reproachful:

"Please, Betty dear," from the young lady's parent.

Mrs. Sprot then sat down, drank several cups of tea, and plunged into a spirited narrative of her purchases in London, the crowd on the train, what a soldier recently returned from France had told the occupants of her carriage, and what a girl behind the stocking counter had told her of a stocking shortage to come.

The conversation was, in fact, completely normal. It was prolonged afterwards on the terrace outside, for the sun was now shining and the wet day a thing of the past.

Betty rushed happily about, making mysterious expeditions into the bushes and returning with a laurel leaf, or a heap of pebbles which she placed in the lap of one of the grown-ups with a confused and unintelligible explanation of what it represented. Fortunately she required little co-operation in her game, being satisfied with an occasional "How nice, darling. Is it really?"

Never had there been an evening more typical of Sans Souci at its most harmless. Chatter, gossip, speculations as to the course of the war— Can France rally? Will Weygand pull things together? What is Russia likely to do? Could Hitler invade England if he tried? Will Paris fall if the "bulge" is not straightened out? Was it true that . . . ? It had been said that . . . And it was rumoured that . . .

Political and military scandal was happily bandied about.

Tuppence thought to herself: "Chatterbugs a danger? Nonsense, they're a safety valve. People *enjoy* these rumors. It gives them the stimulation to carry on with their own private worries and anxieties." She contributed a nice tit-bit prefixed by "My son told me—of course this is *quite* private, you understand—"

Suddenly, with a start, Mrs. Sprot glanced at her watch.

"Goodness, it's nearly seven. I ought to have put that child to bed hours ago. Betty—Betty!"

It was some time since Betty had returned to the terrace, though no one had noticed her defection.

Mrs. Sprot called her with rising impatience.

"Bett-eee! Where can the child be?"

Mrs. O'Rourke said with her deep laugh:

"Up to mischief, I've no doubt of it. 'Tis always the way when there's peace."

"Betty! I want you."

There was no answer and Mrs. Sprot rose impatiently.

"I suppose I must go and look for her. I wonder where she can be?"

Miss Minton suggested that she was hiding somewhere and Tuppence, with memories of her own childhood, suggested the kitchen. But Betty could not be found, either inside or outside the house. They went round the garden calling, looking all over the bedrooms. There was no Betty anywhere.

Mrs. Sprot began to get annoyed.

"It's very naughty of her—very naughty indeed! Do you think she can have gone out on the road?"

Together she and Tuppence went out to the gate and looked up and down the hill. There was no one in sight except a tradesman's boy with a bicycle standing talking to a maid at the door of St. Lucian's opposite.

On Tuppence's suggestion, she and Mrs. Sprot crossed the road and the latter asked if either of them had noticed a little girl. They both shook their heads and then the servant asked, with sudden recollection:

"A little girl in a green checked gingham dress?"

Mrs. Sprot said eagerly:

"That's right."

"I saw her about half an hour ago—going down the road with a woman."

Mrs. Sprot said with astonishment:

"With a woman? What sort of a woman?"

The girl seemed slightly embarrassed.

"Well, what I'd call an odd-looking kind of woman. A foreigner she was. Queer clothes. A kind of shawl thing and no hat, and a strange sort of face—queer like, if you know what I mean. I've seen her about once or twice lately, and to tell the truth I thought she was a bit wanting—If you know what I mean," she added helpfully.

In a flash Tuppence remembered the face she had seen that afternoon peering through the bushes and the foreboding that had swept over her.

But she had never thought of the woman in connection with the child, could not understand it now.

She had little time for meditation, however, Mrs. Sprot almost collapsed against her.

"Oh Betty, my little girl. She's been kidnapped. She—what did the woman look like—a gipsy?"

Tuppence shook her head energetically.

"No, she was fair, very fair, a broad face with high cheekbones and blue eyes set very far apart."

She saw Mrs. Sprot staring at her and hastened to explain.

"I saw the woman this afternoon—peering through the bushes at the bottom of the garden. And I've noticed her hanging about. Carl von Deinim was speaking to her one day. It must be the same woman."

The servant girl chimed in to say:

"That's right. Fair-haired she was. And wanting, if you ask me. Didn't understand nothing that was said to her."

"Oh God," moaned Mrs. Sprot. "What shall I do?"

Tuppence passed an arm round her.

"Come back to the house, have a little brandy and then we'll ring up the police. It's all right. We'll get her back."

Mrs. Sprot went with her meekly, murmuring in a dazed fashion:

"I can't imagine how Betty would go like that with a stranger."

"She's very young," said Tuppence. "Not old enough to be shy."

Mrs. Sprot cried out weakly:

"Some dreadful German woman, I expect. She'll kill my Betty."

"Nonsense," said Tuppence robustly. "It will be all right. I expect she's just some woman who's not quite right in her head." But she did not believe her own words—did not believe for one moment that that calm blonde woman was an irresponsible lunatic.

Carl! Would Carl know? Had Carl something to do with this?

A few minutes later she was inclined to doubt this. Carl von Deinim, like the rest, seemed amazed, unbelieving, completely surprised.

As soon as the facts were made plain, Major Bletchley assumed control.

"Now then, dear lady," he said to Mrs. Sprot. "Sit down here—just drink a little drop of this—brandy—it won't hurt you—and I'll get straight on to the police station."

Mrs. Sprot murmured:

"Wait a minute—there might be something—" She hurried up the stairs and along the passage to her and Betty's room.

A minute or two later they heard her footsteps running wildly along the landing. She rushed down the stairs like a demented woman and clutched Major Bletchley's hand from the telephone receiver, which he was just about to lift.

"No, no," she panted. "You mustn't—you mustn't. . . ."

And sobbing wildly, she collapsed into a chair.

They crowded round her. In a minute or two, she recovered her composure. Sitting up, with Mrs. Cayley's arm round her, she held something out for them to see.

"I found this on the floor of my room. It had been wrapped round a stone and thrown through the window. Look—look what it says."

Tommy took it from her and unfolded it.

It was a note, written in a queer stiff foreign handwriting, big and bold.

WE HAVE GOT YOUR CHILD IN SAFE KEEPING. YOU WILL BE TOLD WHAT TO DO IN DUE COURSE. IF YOU GO TO THE POLICE YOUR CHILD WILL BE KILLED. SAY NOTHING. WAIT FOR INSTRUCTIONS. IF NOT—

It was signed with a skull and crossbones.

Mrs. Sprot was moaning faintly:

"Betty—Betty—"

Everyone was talking at once. "The dirty murdering scoundrels" from Mrs. O'Rourke. "Brutes!" from Sheila Perenna. "Fantastic, fantastic—I don't believe a word of it. Silly practical joke" from Mr. Cayley. "Oh, the dear wee mite" from Miss Minton. "I do not understand. It is incredible' from Carl von Deinim. And above everyone else the stentorian voice of Major Bletchley.

"Damned nonsense. Intimidation. We must inform the police at once. They'll soon get to the bottom of it."

Once more he moved towards the telephone. This time a scream of outraged motherhood from Mrs. Sprot stopped him.

He shouted:

"But my dear madam, it's got to be done. This is only a crude device to prevent you getting on the track of these scoundrels."

"They'll kill her."

"Nonsense. They wouldn't dare."

"I won't have it, I tell you. I'm her mother. It's for me to say."

"I know. I know. That's what they're counting on—your feeling like that. Very natural. But you must take it from me, a soldier and an experienced man of the world, the police are what we need."

"*No!*"

Bletchley's eyes went round seeking allies.

"Meadowes, you agree with me?"

Slowly Tommy nodded.

"Cayley? Look, Mrs. Sprot, both Meadowes and Cayley agree."

Mrs. Sprot said with sudden energy:

"Men! All of you! Ask the women!"

Tommy's eyes sought Tuppence. Tuppence said, her voice low and shaken:

"I—I agree with Mrs. Sprot."

She was thinking "Deborah! Derek! If it were them. I'd feel like her.

Tommy and the others are right, I've no doubt, but all the same I couldn't do it. I couldn't risk it."

Mrs. O'Rourke was saying:

"No mother alive could risk it and that's a fact."

Mrs. Cayley murmured:

"I do think, you know, that—well—" and tailed off into incoherence.

Miss Minton said tremulously:

"Such awful things happen. We'd never forgive ourselves if anything happened to dear little Betty."

Tuppence said sharply:

"You haven't said anything, Mr. von Deinim?"

Carl's blue eyes were very bright. His face was a mask. He said slowly and stiffly:

"I am a foreigner. I do not know your English police. How competent they are—how quick."

Someone had come into the hall. It was Mrs. Perenna, her cheeks were flushed. Evidently she had been hurrying up the hill. She said:

"What's all this?" And her voice was commanding, imperious, not the complaisant guest-house hostess, but a woman of force.

They told her—a confused tale told by too many people, but she grasped it quickly.

And with her grasping of it, the whole thing seemed, in a way, to be passed up to her for judgment. She was the supreme Court.

She held the hastily scrawled note a minute, then she handed it back. Her words came sharp and authoritative.

"The police? They'll be no good. You can't risk their blundering. Take the law into your own hands. Go after the child yourselves."

Bletchley said, shrugging his shoulders:

"Very well. If you won't call in the police, it's the best thing to be done."

Tommy said:

"They can't have got much of a start."

"Half an hour, the maid said," Tuppence put in.

"Haydock," said Bletchley. "Haydock's the man to help us. He's got a car. The woman's unusual-looking, you say? And a foreigner? Ought to leave a trail that we can follow. Come on, there's no time to be lost. You'll come along, Meadowes?"

Mrs. Sprot got up.

"I'm coming too."

"Now, my dear lady, leave it to us—"

"I'm coming too."

"Oh well—"

He gave in—murmuring something about the female of the species being deadlier than the male.

III

In the end Commander Haydock, taking in the situation with commendable Naval rapidity, drove the car, Tommy sat beside him, and behind were Bletchley, Mrs. Sprot and Tuppence. Not only did Mrs. Sprot cling to her, but Tuppence was the only one (with the exception of Carl von Deinim) who knew the mysterious kidnapper by sight.

The Commander was a good organizer and a quick worker. In next to no time he had filled up the car with petrol, tossed a map of the district and a larger scale map of Leahampton itself to Bletchley and was ready to start off.

Mrs. Sprot had run upstairs again, presumably to her room to get a coat. But when she got into the car and they had started down the hill she disclosed to Tuppence something in her handbag. It was a small pistol.

She said quietly:

"I got it from Major Bletchley's room. I remember his mentioning one day that he had one."

Tuppence looked a little dubious.

"You don't think that—"

Mrs. Sprot said, her mouth a thin line:

"It may come in useful."

Tuppence sat marvelling at the strange forces maternity will set loose in an ordinary commonplace young woman. She could visualize Mrs. Sprot, the kind of woman who would normally declare herself frightened to death of firearms, coolly shooting down any person who had harmed her child.

They drove first, on the Commander's suggestion, to the railway station. A train had left Leahampton about twenty minutes earlier. Tuppence and Mrs. Sprot went into the Ladies' Room on the chance that the woman had gone in there to change her appearance before taking the train.

One and all drew a blank. It was now more difficult to shape a course. In all probability, as Haydock pointed out, the kidnappers had had a car waiting, and once Betty had been persuaded to come away with the woman, they had made their get-away in that. It was here, as Bletchley pointed out once more, that the co-operation of the police was so vital. It needed an organization of that kind who could send out messages all over the country, covering the different roads.

Mrs. Sprot merely shook her head, her lips pressed tightly together.

Tuppence said:

"We must put ourselves in their places. Where would they have waited in the car? Somewhere as near Sans Souci as possible, but where a car wouldn't be noticed. Now let's *think*. The woman and Betty walk down the hill together. At the bottom is the Esplanade. The car might have been drawn up there. So long as you don't leave it unattended you can stop there for quite a while. The only other places are the car park in

James's Square, also quite near, or else one of the small streets that lead
off from the Esplanade."

It was at that moment that a small man, with a diffident manner and
pince-nez, stepped up to them and said, stammering a little:

"Excuse me . . . No offence, I hope . . . but I c-c-couldn't help overhearing
what you were asking the porter just now" (he now directed his remarks
to Major Bletchley). "I was not listening, of course, just come down to
see about a parcel—extraordinary how long things are delayed just now—
movements of troops, they say—but really most difficult when it's per-
ishable—the parcel, I mean—and so, you see, I happened to overhear—
and really it did seem the most wonderful coincidence . . ."

Mrs. Sprot sprang forward. She seized him by the arm.

"You've seen her? You've seen my little girl?"

"Oh really, your little girl, you say? Now fancy that—"

Mrs. Sprot cried: "Tell me." And her fingers bit into the little man's
arm so that he winced.

Tuppence said quickly:

"Please tell us anything you have seen as quickly as you can. We shall
be most grateful if you would."

"Oh, well, really, of course, it may be nothing at all. But the description
fitted so well—"

Tuppence felt the woman beside her trembling, but she herself strove
to keep her manner calm and unhurried. She knew the type with which
they were dealing—fussy, muddle-headed, diffident, incapable of going
straight to the point and worse if hurried. She said:

"Please tell us."

"It was only—my name is Robbins, by the way, Edward Robbins—"

"Yes, Mr. Robbins?"

"I live at Whiteways, in Ernes Cliff Road, one of those new houses on
the new road—most labor saving, and really every convenience, and a
beautiful view and the downs only a stone's throw away."

Tuppence quelled Major Bletchley, who she saw was about to break
out, with a glance, and said:

"And you saw the little girl we are looking for?"

"Yes, I really think it *must* be. A little girl with a foreign-looking woman,
you said? It was really the woman I noticed. Because, of course, we are
all on the lookout nowadays for Fifth Columnists, aren't we? A sharp
lookout, that is what they say, and I always try to do so, and so, as I say,
I noticed this woman. A nurse, I thought, or a maid—a lot of spies came
over here in that capacity, and this woman was most unusual-looking
and walking up the road and on to the downs—with a little girl—and
the little girl seemed tired and rather lagging, and half-past seven, well,
most children go to bed then, so I looked at the woman pretty sharply.
I think it flustered her. She hurried up the road, pulling the child after
her, and finally picked her up and went on up the path out on the cliff,
which I thought *strange,* you know, because there are no houses there
at all—nothing—not until you get to Whitehaven—about five miles over

the downs—a favorite walk for hikers. But in this case I thought it odd. I wondered if the woman was going to signal, perhaps. One hears of so much enemy activity, and she certainly looked uneasy when she saw me staring at her."

Commander Haydock was back in the car and had started the engine. He said:

"Ernes Cliff Road, you say. That's right the other side of the town, isn't it?"

"Yes, you go along the Esplanade and past the old town—and then up—"

The others had jumped in, not listening further to Mr. Robbins.

Tuppence called out:

"Thank you, Mr. Robbins," and they drove off leaving him staring after them with his mouth open.

They drove rapidly through the town, avoiding accidents more by good luck than by skill. But the luck held. They came out at last at a mass of straggling building development, somewhat marred by proximity to the gas works. A series of little roads led up towards the downs, stopping abruptly a short way up the hill. Ernes Cliff Road was the third of these.

Commander Haydock turned smartly into it and drove up. At the end the road petered out on to bare hillside, up which a footpath meandered.

"Better get out and walk here," said Bletchley.

Haydock said dubiously:

"Could almost take the car up. Ground's firm enough. Bit bumpy but I think she could do it."

Mrs. Sprot cried:

"Oh yes, please, please . . . We must be quick."

The Commander murmured to himself:

"Hope to goodness we're after the right lot. That little pipsqueak may have seen any woman with a kid."

The car groaned uneasily as it plowed its way up over the rough ground. The gradient was severe, but the turf was short and springy. They came out without mishap on the top of the rise. Here the view was uninterrupted till it rested in the distance on the curve of Whitehaven Bay.

Bletchley said:

"Not a bad idea. The woman could spend the night up here if need be, drop down into Whitehaven tomorrow morning and take a train there."

Haydock said:

"No signs of them as far as I can see."

He was standing up holding some field glasses that he had thoughtfully brought with him to his eyes. Suddenly his figure became tense as he focused the glasses on two small moving dots.

"Got 'em, by Jove. . . ."

He dropped into the driver's seat again and the car bucketed forward.

The chase was a short one now. Shot up in the air, tossed from side to side, the occupants of the car gained rapidly on those two small dots. They could be distinguished now—a tall figure and a short one—nearer still, a woman holding a child by the hand—still nearer, yes, a child in a green gingham frock. Betty.

Mrs. Sprot gave a strangled cry.

"All right now, my dear," said Major Bletchley, patting her kindly. "We've got 'em."

They went on. Suddenly the woman turned and saw the car advancing towards her.

With a cry she caught up the child in her arms and began running.

She ran, not forward, but sideways towards the edge of the cliff.

The car, after a few yards, could not follow, the ground was too uneven and blocked with big boulders. It stopped and the occupants tumbled out.

Mrs. Sprot was out first and running wildly after the two fugitives.

The others followed her.

When they were within twenty yards, the other woman turned at bay. She was standing now at the very edge of the cliff. With a hoarse cry she clutched the child closer.

Haydock cried out:

"My God, she's going to throw the kid over the cliff . . ."

The woman stood there, clutching Betty tightly. Her face was disfigured with a frenzy of hate. She uttered a long hoarse sentence that none of them understood. And still she held the child and looked from time to time at the drop below—not a yard from where she stood.

It seemed clear that she was threatening to throw the child over the cliff.

All of them stood there, dazed, terrified, unable to move for fear of precipitating a catastrophe.

Haydock was tugging at his pocket. He pulled out a service revolver.

He shouted: "Put that child down—or I fire."

The foreign woman laughed. She held the child closer to her breast. The two figures were moulded into one.

Haydock muttered.

"I daren't shoot. I'd hit the child."

Tommy said:

"The woman's crazy. She'll jump over with the child in another moment."

Haydock said again, helplessly:

"I daren't shoot—"

But at that moment a shot rang out. The woman swayed and fell, the child still clasped in her arms.

The men ran forward. Mrs. Sprot stood swaying, the smoking pistol in her hands, her eyes dilated.

She took a few stiff steps forward.

Tommy was kneeling by the bodies. He turned them gently. He saw the woman's face—noted appreciatively its strange wild beauty. The eyes opened, looked at him, then went blank. With a little sigh, the woman died, shot through the head.

Unhurt, little Betty Sprot wriggled out and ran towards the woman standing like a statue.

Then, at last, Mrs. Sprot crumpled. She flung away the pistol and dropped down clutching the child to her.

She cried:

"She's safe—she's safe—Oh, Betty—*Betty.*" And then, in a low, awed whisper:

"Did I—did I—kill her?"

Tuppence said firmly:

"Don't think about it—don't think about it. Think about Betty. Just think about Betty."

Mrs. Sprot held the child close against her, sobbing.

Tuppence went forward to join the men.

Haydock murmured:

"Bloody miracle. I couldn't have brought off a shot like that. Don't believe the woman's ever handled a pistol before either—sheer instinct. A miracle, that's what it is."

Tuppence said:

"Thank God! It was a near thing!" And she looked down at the sheer drop to the sea below and shuddered.

8

I

THE INQUEST ON the dead woman was held some days later. There had been an adjournment while the police identified her as a certain Vanda Polonska, a Polish refugee.

After the dramatic scene on the cliffs, Mrs. Sprot and Betty, the former in a state of collapse, had been driven back to Sans Souci, where hot bottles, nice cups of tea, ample curiosity, and finally a stiff dollop of brandy had been administered to the half-fainting heroine of the night.

Commander Haydock had immediately got in touch with the police, and under his guidance they had gone out to the scene of the tragedy on the cliff.

But for the disturbing war news, the tragedy would probably have been given much greater space in the papers than it was. Actually it occupied only one small paragraph.

Both Tuppence and Tommy had to give evidence at the inquest, and

in case any reporters should think fit to take pictures of the more unimportant witnesses, Mr. Meadowes was unfortunate enough to get
something in his eye which necessitated a highly disfiguring eyeshade.
Mrs. Blenkensop was practically obliterated by her hat.

However, such interest as there was focused itself entirely on Mrs.
Sprot and Commander Haydock. Mr. Sprot, hysterically summoned by
telegraph, rushed down to see his wife, but had to go back again the
same day. He seemed an amiable but not very interesting young man.

The inquest opened with the formal identification of the body by a
certain Mrs. Calfont, a thin-lipped, gimlet-eyed woman who had been
dealing for some months with refugee relief.

Polonska, she said, had come to England in company with a cousin
and his wife who were her only relatives, so far as she knew. The woman,
in her opinion, was slightly mental. She understood from her that she
had been through scenes of great horror in Poland and that her family,
including several children, had all been killed. The woman seemed not
at all grateful for anything done for her, and was suspicious and taciturn.
She muttered to herself a lot and did not seem normal. A domestic post
was found for her, but she had left it without notice some weeks ago
and without reporting to the police.

The Coroner asked why the woman's relatives had not come forward,
and at this point Inspector Brassey made an explanation.

The couple in question were being detained under the Defense of the
Realm Act for an offense in connection with a Naval dockyard. He stated
that these two aliens had posed as refugees to enter the country, but
had immediately tried to obtain employment near a Naval base. The
whole family was looked upon with suspicion. They had had a larger
sum of money in their possession than could be accounted for. Nothing
was actually known against the deceased woman Polonska—except that
her sentiments were believed to have been anti-British. It was possible
that she also had been an enemy agent, and that her pretended stupidity
was assumed.

Mrs. Sprot, when called, dissolved at once into tears. The Coroner
was gentle with her, leading her tactfully along the path of what had
occurred.

"It's so awful," gasped Mrs. Sprot. "So awful to have killed someone.
I didn't mean to do that—I mean I never thought—but it was Betty—
and I thought that woman was going to throw her over the cliff and I
had to stop her—and oh, dear—I don't know how I did it."

"You are accustomed to the use of firearms?"

"Oh, no! Only those rifles at regattas—at fairs—when you shoot at
booths, and even then I never used to hit anything. Oh, dear—I feel as
though I'd *murdered* someone."

The Coroner soothed her and asked if she had ever come in contact
with the dead woman.

"Oh, *no*. I'd never seen her in my life. I think she must have been
quite mad—because she didn't even *know* me or Betty."

In reply to further questions, Mrs. Sprot said that she had attended a sewing party for comforts for Polish refugees, but that that was the extent of her connection with Poles in this country.

Haydock was the next witness, and he described the steps he had taken to track down the kidnapper and what had eventually happened.

"You are clear in your mind that the woman was definitely preparing to jump over the cliff?"

"Either that or to throw the child over. She seemed to me quite demented with hate. It would have been impossible to reason with her. It was a moment for immediate action. I myself conceived the idea of firing and crippling her, but she was holding up the child as a shield. I was afraid of killing the child if I fired. Mrs. Sprot took the risk and was successful in saving her little girl's life."

Mrs. Sprot began to cry again.

Mrs. Blenkensop's evidence was short—a mere confirming of the Commander's evidence.

Mr. Meadowes followed.

"You agree with Commander Haydock and Mrs. Blenkensop as to what occurred?"

"I do. The woman was definitely so distraught that it was impossible to get near her. She was about to throw herself and the child over the cliff."

There was little more evidence. The Coroner directed the jury that Vanda Polonska came to her death by the hand of Mrs. Sprot and formally exonerated the latter from blame. There was no evidence to show what was the state of the dead woman's mind. She might have been actuated by hate of England. Some of the Polish "comforts" distributed to refugees bore the names of the ladies sending them, and it was possible that the woman got Mrs. Sprot's name and address this way, but it was not easy to get at her reason for kidnapping the child—possibly some crazy motive quite incomprehensible to the normal mind. Polonska, according to her own story, had suffered great bereavement in her own country, and that might have turned her brain. On the other hand, she might be an enemy agent.

The verdict was in accordance with the Coroner's summing up.

II

On the day following the inquest Mrs. Blenkensop and Mr. Meadowes met to compare notes.

"Exit Vanda Polonska and a blank wall as usual," said Tommy gloomily.

Tuppence nodded.

"Yes, they seal up both ends, don't they? No papers, no hints of any kind as to where the money came from that she and her cousins had, no record of whom they had dealings with."

"Too damned efficient," said Tommy.

He added: "You know, Tuppence, I don't like the look of things."

Tuppence assented. The news was indeed far from reassuring.

The French Army was in retreat and it seemed doubtful if the tide could be turned. Evacuation from Dunkirk was in progress. It was clearly a matter of a few days only before Paris fell. There was a general dismay at the revelation of lack of equipment and of material for resisting the Germans' great mechanized units.

Tommy said:

"Is it only our usual muddling and slowness? Or has there been deliberate engineering behind this?"

"The latter, I think, but they'll never be able to prove it."

"No. Our adversaries are too darned clever for that."

"We are combing out a lot of the rot now."

"Oh, yes, we're rounding up the obvious people, but I don't believe we've got at the brains that are behind it all. Brains, organization, a whole carefully thought out plan—a plan which uses our habits of dilatoriness, and our petty feuds, and our slowness for its own ends."

Tuppence said:

"That's what we're here for—and we haven't got results."

"We've done something," Tommy reminded her.

"Carl von Deinim and Vanda Polonska, yes. The small fry."

"You think they were working together?"

"I think they must have been," said Tuppence thoughtfully. "Remember I saw them talking."

"Then Carl von Deinim must have engineered the kidnapping?"

"I suppose so."

"But why?"

"I know," said Tuppence. "That's what I keep thinking and thinking about. It doesn't make *sense.*"

"Why kidnap that particular child? Who are the Sprots? They've no money—so it isn't ransom. They're neither of them employed by Government in any capacity."

"I know, Tommy. It just doesn't make any sense at all."

"Hasn't Mrs. Sprot any idea herself?"

"That woman," said Tuppence scornfully, "hasn't got the brains of a hen. She doesn't think at all. Just says it's the sort of thing the wicked Germans would do."

"Silly ass," said Tommy. "The Germans are efficient. If they send one of their agents to kidnap a brat, it's for some reason."

"I've a feeling, you know," said Tuppence, "that Mrs. Sprot *could* get at the reason if only she'd *think* about it. There must be *something*—some piece of information that she herself has inadvertently got hold of, perhaps without knowing what it is exactly."

"*Say nothing. Wait for instructions,*" Tommy quoted from the note found on Mrs. Sprot's bedroom floor.

"Damn it all, that means *something.*"

"Of course it does—it must. The only thing I can think of is that Mrs.

Sprot, or her husband, has been given something to keep by someone else—given it, perhaps, just because they are such humdrum ordinary people that no one would ever suspect they had it—whatever 'it' may be."

"It's an idea, that."

"I know—but it's awfully like a spy story. It doesn't seem real somehow."

"Have you asked Mrs. Sprot to rack her brains a bit?"

"Yes, but the trouble is that she isn't really interested. All she cares about is getting Betty back—that, and having hysterics because she's shot someone."

"Funny creatures women," mused Tommy. "There was that woman, went out that day like an avenging fury, she'd have shot down a regiment in cold blood without turning a hair just to get her child back, and then, having shot the kidnapper by a perfectly incredible fluke, she breaks down and comes all over squeamish about it."

"The Coroner exonerated her all right," said Tuppence.

"Naturally. By Jove, I wouldn't have risked firing when she did."

Tuppence said:

"No more would she, probably, if she'd known more about it. It was sheer ignorance of the difficulty of the shot that made her bring it off."

Tommy nodded.

"Quite Biblical," he said. "David and Goliath."

"Oh!" said Tuppence.

"What is it, old thing?"

"I don't quite know. When you said that something twanged somewhere in my brain, and now it's gone again!"

"Very useful," said Tommy.

"Don't be scathing. That sort of thing does happen sometimes."

"Gentlemen who draw a bow at a venture, was that it?"

"No, it was—wait a minute—I think it was something to do with Solomon."

"Cedars, temples, a lot of wives and concubines?"

"Stop," said Tuppence, putting her hands to her ears. "You're making it worse."

"Jews?" said Tommy hopefully. "Tribes of Israel?"

But Tuppence shook her head. After a minute or two she said:

"I wish I could remember who it was that woman reminded me of."

"The late Vanda Polonska?"

"Yes. The first time I saw her, her face seemed vaguely familiar."

"Do you think you had come across her somewhere else?"

"No, I'm sure I hadn't."

"Mrs. Perenna and Sheila are a totally different type."

"Oh, yes, it wasn't them. You know, Tommy, about those two. I've been thinking."

"To any good purpose?"

"I'm not sure. It's about that note—the one Mrs. Sprot found on the floor in her room when Betty was kidnapped."

"Well?"

"All that about its being wrapped round a stone and thrown through the window is rubbish. It was put there by someone—ready for Mrs. Sprot to find—and I think it was Mrs. Perenna who put it there."

"Mrs. Perenna, Carl, Vanda Polonska—all working together."

"Yes. Did you notice how Mrs. Perenna came in just at the critical moment and clinched things—not to ring up the police? She took command of the whole situation."

"So she's still your selection for M."

"Yes, isn't she yours?"

"I suppose so," said Tommy slowly.

"Why, Tommy, have you got another idea?"

"It's probably an awfully dud one."

"Tell me."

"No, I'd rather not. I've nothing to go on. Nothing whatever. But if I'm right, it's not M. we're up against, but N."

He thought to himself.

"Bletchley. I suppose he's all right. Why shouldn't he be? He's a true enough type—almost too true, and after all, it was he who wanted to ring up the police. Yes, but he could have been pretty sure that the child's mother wouldn't stand for the idea. The threatening note made sure of that. He could afford to urge the opposite point of view—"

And that brought him back again to the vexing, teasing problem to which as yet he could find no answer.

Why kidnap Betty Sprot?

III

There was a car standing outside Sans Souci bearing the word Police on it.

Absorbed in her own thoughts Tuppence took little notice of that. She turned in at the drive, and entering the front door went straight upstairs to her own room.

She stopped, taken aback, on the threshold, as a tall figure turned away from the window.

"Dear me," said Tuppence. "Sheila?"

The girl came straight towards her. Now Tuppence saw her more clearly, saw the blazing eyes deep set in the white tragic face.

Sheila said:

"I'm glad you've come. I've been waiting for you."

"What's the matter?"

The girl's voice was quiet and devoid of emotion. She said:

"They have arrested Carl!"

"The police?"

"Yes."

"Oh, dear," said Tuppence. She felt inadequate to the situation. Quiet as Sheila's voice had been, Tuppence was under no apprehension as to what lay behind it.

Whether they were fellow-conspirators or not, this girl loved Carl von Deinim, and Tuppence felt her heart aching in sympathy with this tragic young creature.

Sheila said:

"What shall I do?"

The simple forlorn question made Tuppence wince. She said helplessly:

"Oh, my dear."

Sheila said, and her voice was like a mourning harp:

"They've taken him away. I shall never see him again."

She cried out:

"What shall I do? What shall I do?" And flinging herself down on her knees by the bed she wept her heart out.

Tuppence stroked the dark head. She said presently, in a weak voice:

"It—it may not be true. Perhaps they are only going to intern him. After all, he is an enemy alien, you know."

"That's not what they said. They're searching his room now."

Tuppence said slowly, "Well, if they find nothing—"

"They will find nothing, of course! What should they find?"

"I don't know. I thought perhaps you might?"

"I?"

Her scorn, her amazement were too real to be feigned. Any suspicions Tuppence had had that Sheila Perenna was involved died at this moment. The girl knew nothing, had never known anything.

Tuppence said:

"If he is innocent—"

Sheila interrupted her.

"What does that matter? The police will make a case against him."

Tuppence said sharply:

"Nonsense, my dear child, that really isn't true."

"The English police will do anything. My mother says so."

"Your mother may say so, but she's wrong. I assure you that it isn't so."

Sheila looked at her doubtfully for a minute or two. Then she said:

"Very well. If you say so. I trust you."

Tuppence felt very uncomfortable. She said sharply:

"You trust too much, Sheila. You may have been unwise to trust Carl."

"Are you against him too? I thought you liked him. He thinks so too,"

Touching young things—with their faith in one's liking for them. And it was true—she had liked Carl—she did like him.

Rather wearily she said:

"Listen, Sheila, liking or not liking has nothing to do with facts. This country and Germany are at war. There are many ways of serving one's country. One of them is to get information—and to work behind the lines. It is a brave thing to do, for when you are caught, it is"—her voice broke a little—"the end."

Sheila said:

"You think Carl—"

"Might be working for his country that way? It is a possibility, isn't it?"

"No," said Sheila.

"It would be his job, you see, to come over here as a refugee to appear to be violently anti-Nazi and then to gather information."

Sheila said quietly:

"It's not true. I know Carl. I know his heart and his mind. He cares most for science—for his work—for the truth and the knowledge in it. He is grateful to England for letting him work here. Sometimes, when people say cruel things, he feels German and bitter. But he hates the Nazis always, and what they stand for—their denial of freedom."

Tuppence said: "He would say so, of course."

Sheila turned reproachful eyes upon her.

"So you believe he is a spy?"

"I think it is"—Tuppence hesitated—"a possibility." Sheila walked to the door.

"I see. I'm sorry I came to ask you to help us."

"But what did you think I could do, dear child?"

"You know people. Your sons are in the Army and Navy, and I've heard you say more than once that they knew influential people. I thought perhaps you could get them to—to do—something?"

Tuppence thought of those mythical creatures. Douglas and Raymond and Cyril.

"I'm afraid," she said, "that they couldn't do anything."

Sheila flung her head up. She said passionately:

"Then there's no hope for us. They'll take him away and shut him up, and one day, early in the morning, they'll stand him against a wall and shoot him—and that will be the end."

She went out, shutting the door behind her.

"Oh, damn, damn, damn the Irish!" thought Tuppence in a fury of mixed feelings. "Why have they got that terrible power of twisting things until you don't know where you are? If Carl von Deinim's a spy, he deserves to be shot. I must hang on to that, not let that girl with her Irish voice bewitch me into thinking it's the tragedy of a hero and a martyr!"

She recalled the voice of a famous actress speaking a line from *Riders to the Sea*:

"It's the fine quiet time they'll be having . . ."

Poignant . . . carrying you away on a tide of feeling . . .

She thought: If it weren't true. Oh, if only it weren't true. . . .

Yet, knowing what she did, how could she doubt?

IV

The fisherman on the end of the Old Pier cast in his line and then reeled it cautiously in.

"No doubt whatever, I'm afraid," he said.

"You know," said Tommy, 'I'm sorry about it. He's—well, he's a nice chap."

"They are, my dear fellow, they usually are. It isn't the skunks and the rats of a land who volunteer to go to the enemy's country. It's the brave men. We know that well enough. But there it is, the case is proved."

"No doubt whatever, you say?"

"No doubt at all. Among his chemical formulæ was a list of people in the factory to be approached, as possible Fascist sympathizers. There was also a very clever scheme of sabotage and a chemical process that, applied to fertilizers, would have devastated large areas of food stocks. All well up Master Carl's street."

Rather unwillingly, Tommy said, secretly anathematizing Tuppence, who had made him promise to say it.

"I suppose it's not possible that these things could have been planted on him?"

Mr. Grant smiled, rather a diabolical smile.

"Oh," he said. "Your wife's idea, no doubt."

"Well—er—yes, as a matter of fact it is."

"He's an attractive lad," said Mr. Grant tolerantly.

Then he went on.

"No, seriously, I don't think we can take that suggestion into account. He'd got a supply of secret ink, you know. That's a pretty good clinching test. And it wasn't obvious as it would have been if planted. It wasn't 'The mixture to be taken when required' on the wash-hand stand, or anything like that. In fact, it was damned ingenious. Only came across the method once before, and then it was waistcoat buttons. Steeped in the stuff, you know. When the fellow wants to use it, he soaks a button in water. Carl von Deinim's wasn't buttons. It was a shoelace. Pretty neat."

"Oh!" Something stirred in Tommy's mind—vague—wholly nebulous . . .

Tuppence was quicker. As soon as he retailed the conversation to her, she seized on the salient point.

"A shoelace? Tommy, that explains it!"

"What?"

"Betty, you idiot! Don't you remember that funny thing she did in my room, taking out my laces and soaking them in water. I thought at the time it was a funny thing to think of doing. But, of course, she'd seen Carl do it and was imitating him. He couldn't risk her talking about it, and he arranged with that woman for her to be kidnapped."

Tommy said, "Then that's cleared up."

"Yes. It's nice when things begin to fall into shape. One can put them behind you and get on a bit."

"We need to get on."

Tuppence nodded.

The times were gloomy indeed. France had astonishingly and suddenly capitulated—to the bewilderment and dismay of her own people.

The destination of the French Navy was in doubt.

Now the coasts of France were entirely in the hands of Germany, and the talk of invasion was no longer a remote contingency.

Tommy said:

"Carl von Deinim was only a link in the chain. Mrs. Perenna's the fountainhead."

"Yes, we've got to get the goods on her. But it won't be easy."

"No. After all, if she's the brains of the whole thing one can't expect it to be."

"So M. is Mrs. Perenna?"

Tommy supposed she must be. He said slowly:

"You really think the girl isn't in this at all?"

"I'm quite sure of it."

Tommy sighed.

"Well, you should know. But if so, it's tough luck on her. First the man she loves—and then her mother. She's not going to have much left, is she?"

"We can't help that."

"Yes, but supposing we're wrong—that M. or N. is someone else?"

Tuppence said rather coldly:

"So you're still harping on that? Are you sure it isn't a case of wishful thinking?"

"What do you mean?"

"Sheila Perenna—that's what I mean."

"Aren't you being rather absurd, Tuppence?"

"No, I'm not. She's got round you, Tommy, just like any other man—"

Tommy replied angrily:

"Not at all. It's simply that I've got my own ideas."

"Which are?"

"I think I'll keep them to myself for a bit. We'll see which of us is right."

"Well, I think we've got to go all out after Mrs. Perenna. Find out where she goes, whom she meets—everything. There must be a link somewhere. You'd better put Albert on to her this afternoon."

"You can do that. I'm busy."

"Why, what are you doing?"

Tommy said:

"I'm playing golf."

9

I

"Seems quite like old times, doesn't it, madam?" said Albert. He beamed happily. Though now, in his middle years, running somewhat to fat, Albert had still the romantic boy's heart which had first led him into associations with Tommy and Tuppence in their young and adventurous days.

"Remember how you first came across me?" demanded Albert. "Cleanin' of the brasses, I was, in those top notch flats. Coo, wasn't that hall-porter a nasty bit of goods? Always on to me, he was. And the day you come along and strung me a tale! Pack of lies it was too, all about a crook called Ready Rita. Not but what some of it didn't turn out to be true. And since then, as you might say, I've never looked back. Many's the adventures we had afore we all settled down, so to speak."

Albert sighed, and, by a natural association of ideas, Tuppence inquired after the health of Mrs. Albert.

"Oh, the missus is all right—but she doesn't take to the Welsh much, she says. Thinks they ought to learn proper English, and as for raids— why, they've had two there already, and holes in the field what you could put a motor-car in, so she says. So—how's that for safety? Might as well be in Kennington, she says, where she wouldn't have to see all them melancholy trees and could get good clean milk in a bottle."

"I don't know," said Tuppence, suddenly stricken, "that we ought to get you into this, Albert."

"Nonsense, madam," said Albert. "Didn't I try and join up and they were so haughty they wouldn't look at me. Wait for my age-group to be called up, they said. And me in the pink of health and only too eager to get at them perishing Germans—if you'll excuse the language. You just tell me how I can put a spoke in their wheel and spoil their goings-on—and I'm there. Fifth Column, that's what we're up against, so the papers say—though what's happened to the other four they don't mention. But the long and short of it is, I'm ready to assist you and Captain Beresford in any way you like to indicate."

"Good. Now I'll tell you what we want you to do."

II

"How long have you known Bletchley?" asked Tommy as he stepped off the tee and watched with approval his ball leaping down the center of the fairway.

Commander Haydock, who had also done a good drive, had a pleased expression on his face as he shouldered his clubs and replied:

"Bletchley? Let me see. Oh! About nine months or so. He came here last autumn."

"Friends of friends of yours, I think you said?" Tommy suggested mendaciously.

"Did I?" The Commander looked a little surprised. "No, I don't think so. Rather fancy I met him here at the Club."

"Bit of a mystery man, I gather?"

The Commander was clearly surprised this time.

"Mystery man? Old Bletchley?" He sounded frankly incredulous.

Tommy sighed inwardly. He supposed he was imagining things.

He played his next shot and topped it. Haydock had a good iron shot that stopped just short of the green. As he rejoined the other, he said:

"What on earth makes you call Bletchley a mystery man? I should have said he was a painfully prosaic chap—typical Army. Bit set in his ideas and all that—narrow life, an Army life—but mystery!"

Tommy said vaguely:

"Oh, well, I just got the idea from something somebody said—"

They got down to the business of putting. The Commander won the hole.

"Three up and two to play," he remarked with satisfaction.

Then, as Tommy had hoped, his mind, free of the preoccupation of the match, harked back to what Tommy had said.

"What sort of mystery do you mean?" he asked.

Tommy shrugged his shoulders.

"Oh, it was just that nobody seemed to know much about him."

"He was in the Rugbyshires."

"Oh, you know that definitely?"

"Well, I—well, no, I don't know myself. I say, Meadowes, what's the idea? Nothing wrong about Bletchley, is there?"

"No, no, of course not." Tommy's disclaimer came hastily. He had started his hare. He could now sit back and watch the Commander's mind chasing after it.

"Always struck me as an almost absurdly typical sort of chap," said Haydock.

"Just so, just so."

"Ah, yes—see what you mean. Bit too much of a type perhaps?"

"I'm leading the witness," thought Tommy. "Still perhaps something may crop up out of the old boy's mind."

"Yes, I do see what you mean," the Commander went on thoughtfully. "And now I come to think of it I've never actually come across any one who knew Bletchley before he came down here. He doesn't have any old pals to stay—nothing of that kind."

"Ah!" said Tommy—and added, "Shall we play the bye? Might as well get a bit more exercise. It's a lovely evening."

They drove off, then separated to play their next shots. When they met again on the green, Haydock said abruptly:

"Tell me what you heard about him."

"Nothing—nothing at all."

"No need to be so cautious with me, Meadowes. I hear all sorts of rumors. You understand? Everyone comes to me. I'm known to be pretty keen on the subject. What's the idea—that Bletchley isn't what he seems to be?"

"It was only the merest suggestion."

"What do they think he is? A Hun? Nonsense, the man's as English as you and I."

"Oh, yes, I'm sure he's quite all right."

"Why, he's always yelling for more foreigners to be interned. Look how violent he was against that young German chap—and quite right, too, it seems. I heard unofficially from the Chief Constable that they found enough to hang von Deinim a dozen times over. He'd got a scheme to poison the water supply of the whole country and he was actually working out a new gas—working on it in one of our factories. My God, the short-sightedness of our people! Fancy letting the fellow inside the place to begin with. Believe anything, our Government would! A young fellow has only to come to this country just before war starts and whine a bit about persecution, and they shut both eyes and let him into all our secrets. They were just as dense about that fellow Hahn—"

Tommy had no intention of letting the Commander run ahead on the well-grooved track. He deliberately missed a putt.

"Hard lines," cried Haydock. He played a careful shot. The ball rolled into the hole.

"My hole. A bit off your game today. What were we talking about?"

Tommy said firmly:

"About Bletchley being perfectly all right."

"Of course. Of course. I wonder now—I did hear a rather funny story about him—didn't think anything of it at the time—"

Here, to Tommy's annoyance, they were hailed by two other men. The four returned to the clubhouse together and had drinks. After that, the Commander looked at his watch and remarked that he and Meadowes must be getting along. Tommy had accepted an invitation to supper with the Commander.

Smugglers' Rest was in its usual condition of apple-pie order. A tall middle-aged manservant waited on them with the professional deftness of a waiter. Such perfect service was somewhat unusual to find outside of a London restaurant.

When the man had left the room, Tommy commented on the fact.

"Yes, I was lucky to get Appledore."

"How did you get hold of him?"

"He answered an advertisement as a matter of fact. He had excellent references, was clearly far superior to any of the others who applied and asked remarkably low wages. I engaged him on the spot."

Tommy said with a laugh:

"The war has certainly robbed us of most of our good restaurant service. Practically all good waiters were foreigners. It doesn't seem to come naturally to the Englishman."

"Bit too servile, that's why. Bowing and scraping doesn't come kindly to the English bulldog."

Sitting outside, sipping coffee, Tommy gently asked:

"What was it you were going to say on the links? Something about a funny story—apropos of Bletchley."

"What was it now? Hallo, did you see that? Light being shown out at sea. Where's my telescope?"

Tommy sighed. The stars in their courses seemed to be fighting against him. The Commander fussed into the house and out again, swept the horizon with his glass, outlined a whole system of signalling by the enemy to likely spots on shore, most of the evidence for which seemed to be non-existent, and proceeded to give a gloomy picture of a successful invasion in the near future.

"No organization, no proper coordination. You're an LDV yourself, Meadowes—you know what it's like. With a man like old Andrews in charge—"

This was well-worn ground. It was Commander Haydock's pet grievance. He ought to be the man in command and he was quite determined to oust Col. Andrews if it could possibly be done.

The manservant brought out whisky and liqueurs while the Commander was still holding forth.

"—and we're still honeycombed with spies—riddled with 'em. It was the same in the last war—hairdressers, waiters—"

Tommy, leaning back, catching the profile of Appledore as the latter hovered deft-footed, thought—"Waiters? You could call that fellow Fritz easier than Appledore . . ."

Well, why not? The fellow spoke perfect English, true, but then many Germans did. They had perfected their English by years in English restaurants. And the racial type was not unlike. Fair-haired, blue-eyed— often betrayed by the shape of the head—yes, the head—where had he seen a head lately. . . .

He spoke on an impulse. The words fitted in appositely enough with what the Commander was just saying.

"All these damned forms to fill in. No good at all, Meadowes. Series of idiotic questions—"

Tommy said:

"I know. Such as—'What is your name? Answer N. or M.' "

There was a swerve—a crash. Appledore, the perfect servant, had blundered. A stream of crème de menthe soaked over Tommy's cuff and hand.

The man stammered, "Sorry, sir."

Haydock blazed out in fury.

"You damned clumsy fool! What the hell do you think you're doing?"

His usually red face was quite purple with anger. Tommy thought, "Talk of an Army temper—Navy beats it hollow!" Haydock continued with a stream of abuse. Appledore was abject in apologies.

Tommy felt uncomfortable for the man, but suddenly, as though by magic, the Commander's wrath passed and he was his hearty self again.

"Come along and have a wash. Beastly stuff. It would be the crème de menthe."

Tommy followed him indoors and was soon in the sumptuous bathroom with the innumerable gadgets. He carefully washed off the sticky sweet stuff. The Commander talked from the bedroom next door. He sounded a little shamefaced.

"Afraid I let myself go a bit. Poor old Appledore—he knows I let go a bit more than I mean always."

Tommy turned from the wash-basin drying his hands. He did not notice that a cake of soap had slipped on to the floor. His foot stepped on it. The linoleum was highly polished.

A moment later Tommy was doing a wild ballet dancer step. He shot across the bathroom, arms outstretched. One came up against the right-hand tap of the bath, the other pushed heavily against the side of a small bathroom cabinet. It was an extravagant gesture never likely to be achieved except by some catastrophe such as had just occurred.

His foot skidded heavily against the end panel of the bath.

The thing happened like a conjuring trick. The bath slid out from the wall, turning on a concealed pivot. Tommy found himself looking into a dim recess. He had no doubt whatever as to what occupied that recess. It contained a transmitting wireless apparatus.

The Commander's voice had ceased. He appeared suddenly in the doorway. And with a click, several things fell into place in Tommy's brain.

Had he been blind up to now? That jovial florid face—the face of a "hearty Englishman"—was only a mask. Why had he not seen it all along for what it was—the face of a bad-tempered overbearing Prussian Officer. Tommy was helped, no doubt, by the incident that had just happened. For it recalled to him another incident, a Prussian bully turning on a subordinate and rating him with the Junker's true insolence. So had Commander Haydock turned on his subordinate that evening when the latter had been taken unawares.

And it all fitted in—it fitted in like magic, The double bluff. The enemy agent Hahn, sent first, preparing the place, employing foreign workmen, drawing attention to himself and proceeding finally to the next stage in the plan, his own unmasking by the gallant British sailor Commander Haydock. And then how natural that the Englishman should buy the place and tell the story to every one, boring them by constant repetition. And so N., securely settled in his appointed place, with sea communications and his secret wireless and his staff officers at Sans Souci close at hand, is ready to carry out Germany's plan.

Tommy was unable to resist a flash of genuine admiration. The whole thing had been so perfectly planned. He himself had never suspected Haydock—he had accepted Haydock as the genuine article—only a completely unforeseen accident had given the show away.

All this passed through Tommy's mind in a few seconds. He knew, only too well, that he was, that he must necessarily be in deadly peril. If only he could act the part of the credulous thick-headed Englishman well enough.

He turned to Haydock with what he hoped was a natural-sounding laugh.

"By jove, one never stops getting surprises at your place. Was this another of Hahn's little gadgets? You didn't show me this the other day."

Haydock was standing still. There was a tensity about his big body as it stood there blocking the door.

"More than a match for me," Tommy thought. "And there's that confounded servant, too."

For an instant Haydock stood as though moulded in stone, then he relaxed. He said with a laugh:

"Damned funny, Meadowes. You went skating over the floor like a ballet dancer! Don't suppose a thing like that would happen once in a thousand times. Dry your hands and come into the other room."

Tommy followed him out of the bathroom. He was alert and tense in every muscle. Somehow or other he must get safely away from this house with his knowledge. Could he succeed in fooling Haydock? The latter's tone sounded natural enough.

With an arm round Tommy's shoulders, a casual arm, perhaps (or perhaps not) Haydock shepherded him into the sitting room. Turning, he shut the door behind them.

"Look here, old boy, I've got something to say to you."

His voice was friendly, natural—just a shade embarrassed. He motioned to Tommy to sit down.

"It's a bit awkward," he said. "Upon my word, it's a bit awkward! Nothing for it, though, but to take you into my confidence. Only you'll have to keep dark about it, Meadowes. You understand that?"

Tommy endeavored to throw an expression of eager interest upon his face.

Haydock sat down and drew his chair confidentially close.

"You see, Meadowes, it's like this. Nobody's supposed to know it but I'm working on Intelligence. MI_{42} BX—that's my department. Ever heard of it?"

Tommy shook his head and intensified the eager expression.

"Well, it's pretty secret. Kind of inner ring, if you know what I mean. We transmit certain information from here—but it would be absolutely fatal if that fact got out, you understand?"

"Of course, of course," said Mr. Meadowes. "Most interesting! Naturally you can count on me not to say a word."

"Yes, that's absolutely vital. The whole thing is extremely confidential."

"I quite understand. Your work must be most thrilling. Really most thrilling. I should like so much to know more about it—but I suppose I mustn't ask that?"

"No, I'm afraid not. It's very secret, you see."

"Oh yes, I see. I really do apologize—a most extraordinary accident—"

He thought to himself, "Surely he can't be taken in? He can't imagine I'd fall for this stuff?"

It seemed incredible to him. Then he reflected that vanity had been the undoing of many men. Commander Haydock was a clever man, a big fellow—this miserable chap Meadowes was a stupid Britisher—the sort of man who would believe anything! If only Haydock continued to think that.

Tommy went on talking. He displayed keen interest and curiosity. He knew he mustn't ask questions but— He supposed Commander Haydock's work must be very dangerous? Has he ever been in Germany, working there?

Haydock replied genially enough. He was intensely the British sailor now—the Prussian Officer had disappeared. But Tommy, watching him with a new vision, wondered how he could ever have been deceived. The shape of the head—the line of the jaw—nothing British about them.

Presently Mr. Meadowes rose. It was the supreme test. Would it go off all right?

"I really must be going now—getting quite late—feel terribly apologetic, but can assure you will not say a word to anybody."

("It's now or never. Will he let me go or not? I must be ready—a straight to his jaw would be best—"

Talking amiably and with pleasurable excitement, Mr. Meadowes edged towards the door.

He was in the hall . . . he had opened the front door. . . .

Through a door on the right he caught a glimpse of Appledore setting the breakfast things ready on a tray for the morning. (The damned fools were going to let him get away with it!)

The two men stood in the porch, chatting—fixing up another match for next Saturday.

Tommy thought grimly, "There'll be no next Saturday for you, my boy."

Voices came from the road outside. Two men returning from a tramp on the headland. They were men that both Tommy and the Commander knew slightly. Tommy hailed them. They stopped. Haydock and he exchanged a few words with them, all standing at the gate, then Tommy waved a genial farewell to his host and stepped off with the two men.

He had got away with it.

Haydock, damned fool, had been taken in!

He heard Haydock go back to his house, go in and shut the door. Tommy tramped cheerfully down the hill with his two new-found friends.

Weather looked likely to change.

Old Monroe was off his game again.

That fellow Ashby refused to join the LDV. Said it was no damned good. Pretty thick, that. Young Marsh, the assistant caddy master, was a conscientious objector. Didn't Meadowes think that matter ought to be put up to the committee. There had been a pretty bad raid on Southampton the night before last—quite a lot of damage done. What did Meadowes think about Spain? Were they turning nasty? Of course, ever since the French collapse—

Tommy could have shouted aloud. Such good casual normal talk. A stroke of providence that these two men had turned up just at that moment.

He said goodbye to them at the gate of Sans Souci and turned in.

He walked up the drive whistling softly to himself.

He had just turned the dark corner by the rhododendrons when something heavy descended on his head. He crashed forward, pitching into blackness and oblivion.

10

I

"DID YOU SAY three spades, Mrs. Blenkensop?"

Yes, Mrs. Blenkensop had said three spades. Mrs. Sprot, returning breathless from the telephone: "And they've changed the time of the ARP exam. again, it's *too* bad," demanded to have the bidding again.

Miss Minton, as usual, delayed things by ceaseless reiterations.

"Was it two clubs I said? Are you sure? I rather thought, you know, that it might have been one No Trump— Oh yes, of course, I remember now. Mrs. Cayley said one heart, didn't she? I was going to say one No Trump although I hadn't quite got the count, but I do think one should play a plucky game—and then Mrs. Cayley said one heart and I had to go two clubs. I always think it's so difficult when one has two short suits—"

Sometimes, Tuppence thought to herself, it would save time if Miss Minton just put her hand down on the table to show them all. She was quite incapable of not telling exactly what was in it.

"So now we've got it right," said Miss Minton triumphantly. "One heart, two clubs."

"Two spades," said Tuppence.

"I passed, didn't I?" said Mrs. Sprot.

They looked at Mrs. Cayley, who was leaning forward listening. Miss Minton took up the tale.

"Then Mrs. Cayley said two hearts and I said three diamonds."

"And I said three spades," said Tuppence.

"Pass," said Mrs. Sprot.

Mrs. Cayley sat in silence. At last she seemed to become aware that everyone was looking at her.

"Oh dear," she flushed. "I'm so sorry. I thought perhaps Mr. Cayley needed me. I hope he's all right out there on the terrace."

She looked from one to the other of them.

"Perhaps, if you don't mind, I'd better just go and *see*. I heard rather an odd noise. Perhaps he's dropped his book."

She fluttered out of the window. Tuppence gave an exasperated sigh.

"She ought to have a string tied to her wrist," she said. "Then he could pull it when he wanted her."

"Such a devoted wife," said Miss Minton. "It's very nice to see it, isn't it?"

"Is it?" said Tuppence, who was feeling far from good-tempered.

The three women sat in silence for a minute or two.

"Where's Sheila tonight?" asked Miss Minton.

"She went to the pictures," said Mrs. Sprot.

"Where's Mrs. Perenna?" asked Tuppence.

"She said she was going to do accounts in her room," said Miss Minton. "Poor dear. So tiring, doing accounts."

"She's not been doing accounts all the evening," said Mrs. Sprot, "because she came in just now when I was telephoning in the hall."

"I wonder where she'd been," said Miss Minton, whose life was taken up with such small wonderments. "Not to the pictures, they wouldn't be out yet."

"She hadn't got a hat on," said Mrs. Sprot. "Nor a coat. Her hair was all anyhow and I think she'd been running or something. Quite out of breath. She ran upstairs without a word and she glared—positively glared at me—and I'm sure *I* hadn't done anything."

Mrs. Cayley reappeared at the window.

"Fancy," she said. "Mr. Cayley has walked all round the garden by himself. He quite enjoyed it, he said. Such a mild night."

She sat down again.

"Let me see—oh, do you think we could have the bidding over again?"

Tuppence suppressed a rebellious sigh. They had the bidding all over again and she was left to play three spades.

Mrs. Perenna came in just as they were cutting for the next deal.

"Did you enjoy your walk?" asked Miss Minton.

Mrs. Perenna stared at her. It was a fierce and unpleasant stare. She said:

"I've not been out."

"Oh—oh—I thought Mrs. Sprot said you'd come in just now."

Mrs. Perenna said:

"I just went outside to look at the weather."

Her tone was disagreeable. She threw a hostile glance at the meek

Mrs. Sprot, who flushed and looked frightened.

"Just fancy," said Mrs. Cayley, contributing her item of news. "Mr. Cayley walked all round the garden."

Mrs. Perenna said sharply:

"Why did he do that?"

Mrs. Cayley said:

"It is such a mild night. He hasn't even put on his second muffler and he *still* doesn't want to come in. I do *hope* he won't get a chill."

Mrs. Perrenna said:

"There are worse things than chills. A bomb might come any minute and blow us all to bits!"

"Oh, dear, I hope it won't."

"Do you? *I* rather wish it would." Mrs. Perenna went out of the window. The four bridge players stared after her.

"She seems very *odd* tonight," said Mrs. Sprot.

Miss Minton leaned forward.

"You don't think, do you—" She looked from side to side. They all leaned nearer together. Miss Minton said in a sibilant whisper:

"You don't suspect, do you, that she drinks?"

"Oh, dear," said Mrs. Cayley. "I wonder now? That would explain it. She really is so—so unaccountable sometimes. What do you think, Mrs. Blenkensop?"

"Oh, I don't *really* think so. I think she's worried about something. Er—it's your call, Mrs. Sprot."

"Dear me, what shall I say?" asked Mrs. Sprot, surveying her hand.

Nobody volunteered to tell her, though Miss Minton, who had been gazing with unabashed interest into her hand might have been in a position to advise.

"That isn't Betty, is it?" demanded Mrs. Sprot, her head upraised.

"No, it isn't," said Tuppence firmly.

She felt that she might scream unless they could get on with the game.

Mrs. Sprot looked at her hand vaguely, her mind still apparently maternal. Then she said:

"Oh, one diamond, I *think*."

The call went round. Mrs. Cayley led.

"When in doubt lead a trump, they say," she twittered, and laid down the nine of diamonds.

A deep genial voice said:

" 'Tis the curse of Scotland that you've played there!"

Mrs. O'Rourke stood in the window. She was breathing deeply—her eyes were sparkling. She looked sly and malicious. She advanced into the room.

"Just a nice quiet game of bridge, is it?"

"What's that in your hand?" asked Mrs. Sprot, with interest.

" 'Tis a hammer," said Mrs. O'Rourke amiably. "I found it lying in the drive. No doubt someone left it there."

"It's a funny place to leave a hammer," said Mrs. Sprot doubtfully.

"It is that," agreed Mrs. O'Rourke.

She seemed in a particularly good humor. Swinging the hammer by its handle she went out into the hall.

"Let me see," said Miss Minton. "What's trumps?"

The game proceeded for five minutes without further interruption and then Major Bletchley came in. He had been to the pictures and proceeded to tell them in detail the plot of *Wandering Minstrel*, laid in the reign of Richard the First. The Major, as a military man, criticized at some length the Crusading battle scenes.

The rubber was not finished, for Mrs. Cayley looking at her watch discovered the lateness of the hour with shrill little cries of horror and rushed out to Mr. Cayley. The latter, as a neglected invalid, enjoyed himself a great deal, coughing in a sepulchral manner, shivering dramatically and saying several times:

"*Quite* all right, my dear. I hope you enjoyed your game. It doesn't matter about *me* at all. Even if I *have* caught a severe chill, what does it really matter? There's a war on!"

II

At breakfast the next morning, Tuppence was aware at once of a certain tension in the atmosphere.

Mrs. Perenna, her lips pursed very tightly together, was distinctly acrid in the few remarks she made. She left the room with what could only be described as a flounce.

Major Bletchley, spreading marmalade thickly on his toast, gave vent to a deep chuckle.

"Touch of frost in the air," he remarked. "Well, well! Only to be expected, I suppose."

"Why, what has happened?" demanded Miss Minton, leaning forward eagerly, her thin neck twitching with pleasurable anticipation.

"Don't know that I ought to tell tales out of school," replied the Major irritatingly.

"Oh! Major Bletchley!"

"*Do* tell us," said Tuppence.

Major Bletchley looked thoughtfully at his audience: Miss Minton, Mrs. Blenkensop, Mrs. Cayley and Mrs. O'Rourke. Mrs. Sprot and Betty had just left. He decided to talk.

"It's Meadowes," he said. "Been out on the tiles all night. Hasn't come home yet."

"*What?*' exclaimed Tuppence.

Major Bletchley threw her a pleased and malicious glance. He enjoyed the discomfiture of the designing widow.

"Bit of a gay dog, Meadowes," he chortled. "The Perenna's annoyed. Naturally."

"Oh dear," said Miss Minton, flushing painfully. Mrs. Cayley looked shocked. Mrs. O'Rourke merely chuckled.

"Mrs. Perenna told me already," she said. "Ah, well, the boys will be the boys."

Miss Minton said eagerly:

"Oh, but surely—perhaps Mr. Meadowes has met with an accident. In the blackout, you know."

"Good old blackout," said Major Bletchley. "Responsible for a lot. I can tell you, it's been an eye-opener being on patrol in the LDV. Stopping cars and all that. The amount of wives 'just seeing their husbands home.' And different names on their identity cards! And the wife or the husband coming back the other way alone a few hours later. Ha ha!" He chuckled, then quickly composed his face as he received the full blast of Mrs. Blenkensop's dispproving stare.

"Human nature—a bit humorous, eh?" he said appeasingly.

"Oh, but Mr. Meadowes," bleated Miss Minton. "He may really have met with an accident. Been knocked down by a car."

"That'll be his story, I expect," said the Major. "Car hit him and knocked him out and he came to in the morning."

"He may have been taken to hospital."

"They'd have let us know. After all, he's carrying his identity card, isn't he?"

"Oh dear," said Mrs. Cayley, "I wonder what Mr. Cayley will say?"

This rhetorical question remained unanswered. Tuppence, rising with an assumption of affronted dignity, got up and left the room.

Major Bletchley chuckled when the door closed behind her.

"Poor old Meadowes," he said. "The fair widow's annoyed about it. Thought she'd got her hooks into him."

"Oh, Major *Bletchley*," bleated Miss Minton.

Major Bletchley winked.

"Remember your Dickens? *Beware of widders, Sammy.*"

III

Tuppence was a little upset by Tommy's unannounced absence, but she tried to reassure herself. He might possibly have struck some hot trail and gone off upon it. The difficulties of communication with each other under such circumstances had been foreseen by them both, and they had agreed that the other one was not to be unduly perturbed by unexplained absences. They had arranged certain contrivances between them for such emergencies.

Mrs. Perenna had, according to Mrs. Sprot, been out last night. The vehemence of her own denial of the fact only made that absence of hers more interesting to speculate upon.

It was possible that Tommy had trailed her on her secret errand and had found something worth following up.

Doubtless he would communicate with Tuppence in his special way, or else turn up, very shortly.

Nevertheless, Tuppence was unable to avoid a certain feeling of uneasiness. She decided that in her role of Mrs. Blenkensop it would be perfectly natural to display some curiosity and even anxiety. She went without more ado in search of Mrs. Perenna.

Mrs. Perenna was inclined to be short with her upon the subject. She made it clear that such conduct on the part of one of her lodgers was not to be condoned or glosssed over. Tuppence exclaimed breathlessly:

"Oh, but he may have met with an *accident*. I'm sure he *must* have done. He's not at all that sort of man—not at all loose in his ideas, or *anything* of that kind. He must have been run down by a car or something."

"We shall probably soon hear one way or another," said Mrs. Perenna.

But the day wore on and there was no sign of Mr. Meadowes.

In the evening, Mrs. Perenna, urged on by the pleas of her boarders, agreed extremely reluctantly to ring up the police.

A sergeant called at the house with a notebook and took particulars. Certain facts were then elicited. Mr. Meadowes had left Commander Haydock's house at half-past ten. From there he had walked with a Mr. Walters and a Dr. Curtis as far as the gate of Sans Souci, where he had said goodbye to them and turned into the drive.

From that moment, Mr. Meadowes seemed to have disappeared into space.

In Tuppence's mind, two possibilities emerged from this.

When walking up the drive, Tommy may have seen Mrs. Perenna coming towards him, have slipped into the bushes and then have followed her. Having observed her rendezvous with some unknown person, he might then have followed the latter, while Mrs. Perenna returned to Sans Souci. In that case, he was probably very much alive, and busy on a trail. In which case the well-meant endeavors of the police to find him might prove most embarrassing.

The other possibility was not so pleasant. It resolved itself into two pictures—one that of Mrs. Perenna returning "out of breath and dishevelled"—the other, one that would not be laid aside, a picture of Mrs. O'Rourke standing smiling in the window, holding a heavy hammer.

That hammer had horrible possibilities.

For what should a hammer be doing lying outside?

As to who had wielded it, that was more difficult. A good deal depended on the exact time when Mrs. Perenna had re-entered the house. It was certainly somewhere in the neighborhood of half-past ten, but none of the bridge party happened to have noted the time exactly. Mrs. Perenna had declared vehemently that she had not been out except just to look at the weather. But one does not get out of breath just looking at the weather. It was clearly extremely vexing to her to have been seen by Mrs. Sprot. With ordinary luck the four ladies might have been safely accounted for as busy playing bridge.

What had the time been exactly?

Tuppence found everybody extremely vague on the subject.

If the time agreed, Mrs. Perenna was clearly the most likely suspect. But there were other possibilities. Of the inhabitants of Sans Souci, three had been out at the time of Tommy's return. Major Bletchley had been out at the cinema—but he had been to it alone, and the way that he had insisted on retailing the whole picture so meticulously might suggest to a suspicious mind that he was deliberately establishing an *alibi.*

Then there was the valetudinarian Mr. Cayley who had gone for a walk all round the garden? But for the accident of Mrs. Cayley's anxiety over her spouse, no one might have ever heard of that walk and might have imagined Mr. Cayley to have remained securely encased in rugs like a mummy in his chair on the terrace. (Rather unlike him, really, to risk the contamination of the night air so long.)

And there was Mrs. O'Rourke herself, swinging the hammer, and smiling. . . .

IV

"What's the matter, Deb? You're looking worried, my sweet."

Deborah Beresford started and then laughed, looking frankly into Tony Marsdon's sympathetic brown eyes. She liked Tony. He had brains—was one of the most brilliant beginners in the coding department—and was thought likely to go far.

Deborah enjoyed her job, though she found it made somewhat strenuous demands on her powers of concentration. It was tiring, but it was worth while and it gave her a pleasant feeling of importance. This was real work—not just hanging about a hospital waiting for a chance to nurse.

She said:

"Oh, nothing. Just *family!* You know."

"Families *are* a bit tiring. What's yours been up to?"

"It's my mother. To tell the truth I'm just a bit worried about her."

"Why? What's happened?"

"Well, you see, she went down to Cornwall to a frightfully trying old aunt of mine. Seventy-eight and completely ga ga."

"Sounds grim," commented the young man sympathetically.

"Yes, it was really very noble of Mother. But she was rather hipped anyway because nobody seemed to want her in this war. Of course, she nursed and did things in the last one—but it's all quite different now, and they don't want these middle-aged people. They want people who are young and on the spot. Well, as I say, Mother got a bit hipped over it all, and so she went off down to Cornwall to stay with Aunt Gracie, and she's been doing a bit in the garden, extra vegetable growing and all that."

"Quite sound," commented Tony.

"Yes, much the best thing she could do. She's quite active still, you know," said Deborah kindly.

"Well, that sounds all right."

"Oh yes, it isn't *that*. I was quite happy about her—had a letter only two days ago sounding quite cheerful."

"What's the trouble, then?"

"The trouble is that I told Charles, who was going down to see his people in that part of the world, to go and look her up. And he did. And she wasn't there."

"Wasn't *there?*"

"No. And she hadn't been there! Not at all apparently!"

Tony looked a little embarrassed.

"Rather odd," he murmured. "Where's—I mean—your father?"

"Carrot Top? Oh, he's in Scotland somewhere. In one of those dreadful Ministries where they file papers in triplicate all day long."

"Your mother hasn't gone to join him, perhaps?"

"She can't. He's in one of those area things where wives can't go."

"Oh—er—well, I suppose she's just sloped off somewhere."

Tony was decidedly embarrassed now—especially with Deborah's large worried eyes fixed plaintively upon him.

"Yes but why? It's so *queer*. All her letters—talking about Aunt Gracie and the garden and everything."

"I know, I know," said Tony hastily. "Of course, she'd want you to think—I mean—nowadays—well, people *do* slope off now and again if you know what I mean—"

Deborah's gaze, from being plaintive, became suddenly wrathful.

"If you think Mother's just gone off weekending with someone you're absolutely wrong. Absolutely. Mother and Father are devoted to each other—really devoted. It's quite a joke in the family. She'd never—"

Tony said hastily:

"Of course not. Sorry. I really didn't mean—"

Deborah, her wrath appeased, creased her forehead,

"The odd thing is that someone the other day said they'd seen Mother in Leahampton, of all places, and of course I said it couldn't be her because she was in Cornwall, but now I wonder—"

Tony, his match held to a cigarette, paused suddenly and the match went out.

"Leahampton?" he said sharply.

"Yes. Just the last place you could imagine Mother going off to. Nothing to do and all old Colonels and maiden ladies."

"Doesn't sound a likely spot, certainly," said Tony.

He lit his cigarette and asked casually:

"What did your mother do in the last war?"

Deborah answered mechanically:

"Oh, nursed a bit and drove a General—army, I mean, not a bus. All the usual sort of things."

"Oh, I thought perhaps she'd been like you—in the Intelligence."

"Oh, Mother would never have had the head for this sort of work. I believe, though, that she and Father did do something in the sleuthing line. Secret papers and master spies—that sort of thing. Of course, the darlings exaggerate it all a good deal and make it all sound as though it had been frightfully important. We don't really encourage them to talk about it much because you know what one's family is—the same old story over and over again."

"Oh, rather," said Tony Marsdon heartily. "I quite agree."

It was on the following day that Deborah, returning to her digs, was puzzled by something unfamiliar in the appearance of her room.

It took her a few minutes to fathom what it was. Then she rang the bell and demanded angrily of her landlady what had happened to the big photogaph that always stood on the top of the chest of drawers.

Mrs. Rowley was aggrieved and resentful.

She couldn't say, she was sure. She hadn't touched it herself. Maybe Gladys—

But Gladys also denied having removed it. The man had been about the gas, she said hopefully.

But Deborah declined to believe that an employee of the Gas Co. would have taken a fancy to and removed the portrait of a middle-aged lady.

Far more likely, in Deborah's opinion, that Gladys had smashed the photograph frame and had hastily removed all traces of the crime to the dustbin.

Deborah didn't make a fuss about it. Some time or other she'd get her mother to send her another photo.

She thought to herself with rising vexation:

"What's the old darling up to? She might tell me. Of course, it's absolute nonsense to suggest, as Tony did, that she's gone off with someone, but all the same it's very queer. . . ."

11

I

IT WAS TUPPENCE'S turn to talk to the fisherman on the end of the pier. She had hoped against hope that Mr. Grant might have had some comfort for her. But her hopes were soon dashed. He stated definitely that no news of any kind had come from Tommy.

Tuppence said, trying her best to make her voice assured and business-like:

"There's no reason to suppose that anything has happened to him?"

"None whatever. But let's suppose it has."

"*What?*"

"I'm saying—supposing it has. What about you?"

"Oh, I see—I—carry on, of course."

"That's the stuff. *There is time to weep after the battle.* We're in the thick of the battle now. And time is short. One piece of information you brought us has been proved correct. You overheard a reference to the *fourth.* The fourth referred to is the fourth of next month. It's the date fixed for the big attack on this country."

"You're sure?"

"Fairly sure. They're methodical people, our enemies, All their plans neatly made and worked out. Wish we could say the same of ourselves. Planning isn't our strong point. Yes, the fourth is The Day. All these raids aren't the real thing—they're mostly reconnaissance—testing our defenses and our reflexes to air attack. On the fourth comes the real thing."

"But if you know that—"

"We know The Day is fixed. We know, or think we know, roughly, *where* . . . (But we may be wrong there.) We're as ready as we can be. But it's the old story of the siege of Troy. They knew, as we know, all about the forces without. It's the forces within we want to know about. The men in the Wooden Horse! For they are the men who can deliver up the keys of the fortress. A dozen men in high places, in command, in vital spots, by issuing conflicting orders, can throw the country into just that state of confusion necessary for the German plan to succeed. We've *got* to have inside information in time."

Tuppence said despairingly:

"I feel so futile—so inexperienced."

"Oh, you needn't worry about that. We've got experienced people working, all the experience and talent we've got—but when there's treachery within we can't tell who to trust. You and Beresford are the irregular forces. Nobody knows about you. That's why you've got a chance to succeed—that's why you *have* succeeded up to a certain point."

"Can't you put some of your people on to Mrs. Perenna? There *must* be some of them you can trust absolutely?"

"Oh, we've done that. Working from 'information received that Mrs. Perenna is a member of the IRA with anti-British sympathies.' That's true enough, by the way—but we can't get proof of anything further. Not of the vital facts we want. So stick to it, Mrs. Beresford. Go on, and do your darnedest."

"The fourth," said Tuppence. "That's barely a week ahead?"

"It's a week exactly."

Tuppence clenched her hands.

"We *must* get *something!* I say *we* because I believe Tommy is on to something, and that that's why he hasn't come back. He's following up a lead. If I could only get something too. I wonder now. If I—"

She frowned, planning a new form of attack.

II

"You see, Albert, it's a possibility."

"I see what you mean, madam, of course. But I don't like the idea very much, I must say."

"I think it might work."

"Yes, madam, but it's exposing yourself to attack—that's what I don't like—and I'm sure the master wouldn't like it."

"We've tried all the usual ways. That is to say, we've done what we could keeping under cover. It seems to me that now the only chance is to come out into the open."

"You are aware, madam, that thereby you may be sacrificing an advantage?"

"You're frightfully BBC in your language this afternoon, Albert," said Tuppence, with some exasperation.

Albert looked slightly taken aback and reverted to a more natural form of speech.

"I was listening to a very interesting talk on pond life last night," he explained.

"We've no time to think about pond life now," said Tuppence.

"Where's Captain Beresford, that's what I'd like to know?"

"So should I," said Tuppence, with a pang.

"Don't seem natural, his disappearing without a word. He ought to have tipped you the wink by now. That's why—"

"Yes, Albert?"

"What I mean is, if *he's* come out in the open, perhaps *you'd* better not."

He paused to arrange his ideas and then went on.

"I mean, they've blown the gaff on *him,* but *they mayn't know about you*— and so it's up to you to keep under cover still."

"I wish I could make up my mind," sighed Tuppence.

"Which way were you thinking of managing it, madam?"

Tuppence murmured thoughtfully:

"I thought I might lose a letter I'd written—make a lot of fuss about it, seem very upset. Then it would be found in the hall and Beatrice would probably put it on the hall table. Then the right person would get a look at it."

"What would be in the letter?"

"Oh, roughly—that I'd been successful in discovering the *identity of the person in question* and that I was to make a full report personally tomorrow. Then, you see, Albert, N. or M. would have to come out in the open and have a shot at eliminating me."

"Yes, and maybe they'd manage it, too."

"Not if I was on my guard. They'd have, I think, to decoy me away somewhere—some lonely spot. That's where *you'd* come in—because they don't know about you."

"I'd follow them up and catch them red-handed, so to speak?"

Tuppence nodded.

"That's the idea. I must think it out carefully—I'll meet you tomorrow."

III

Tuppence was just emerging from the local lending library with what had been recommended to her as a "nice book" clasped under her arm when she was startled by a voice saying:

"Mrs. Beresford."

She turned abruptly to see a tall dark young man with an agreeable but slightly embarrassed smile.

He said:

"Er—I'm afraid you don't remember me?"

Tuppence was thoroughly used to the formula. She could have predicted with accuracy the words that were coming next.

"I—er—came to the flat with Deborah one day."

Deborah's friends! So many of them, and all, to Tuppence, looking singularly alike! Some dark like this young man, some fair, an occasional red-haired one—but all cast in the same mould—pleasant, well-mannered, their hair, in Tuppence's view, just slightly too long. (But when this was hinted, Deborah would say, "Oh, *Mother,* don't be so terribly 1916. I can't *stand* short hair.")

Annoying to have run across and been recognized by one of Deborah's young men just now. However, she could probably soon shake him off.

"I'm Antony Marsdon," explained the young man.

Tuppence murmured mendaciously, "Oh, of course," and shook hands.

Tony Marsdon went on:

"I'm awfully glad to have found you, Mrs. Beresford. You see, I'm working at the same job as Deborah, and as a matter of fact something rather awkward has happened."

"Yes?" said Tuppence. "What is it?"

"Well, you see, Deborah's found out that you're not down in Cornwall as she thought, and that makes it a bit awkward, doesn't it, for you?"

"Oh, bother," said Tuppence, concerned. "How did she find out?"

Tony Marsdon explained. He went on rather diffidently:

"Deborah, of course, has no idea of what you're really doing."

He paused discreetly, and then went on:

"It's important, I imagine, that she shouldn't know. My job, actually, is rather the same line. I'm supposed to be just a beginner in the coding department. Really my instructions are to express views that are mildly Fascist—admiration of the German system, insinuations that a working alliance with Hitler wouldn't be a bad thing—all that sort of thing—just to see what response I get. There's a good deal of rot going on, you see, and we want to find out who's at the bottom of it."

"Rot everywhere," thought Tuppence.

"But as soon as Deb told me about you," continued the young man, "I thought I'd better come straight down and warn you so that you could cook up a likely story. You see, I happen to know what you are doing and that it's of vital importance. It would be fatal if any hint of who you are got about. I thought perhaps you could make it seem as though you'd joined Captain Beresford in Scotland or wherever he is. You might say that you'd been allowed to work with him there."

"I might do that, certainly," said Tuppence thoughtfully.

Tony Marsdon said anxiously:

"You don't think I'm butting in?"

"No, no, I'm very grateful to you."

Tony said rather inconsequentially:

"I'm—well—you see—I'm rather fond of Deborah."

Tuppence flashed him an amused quick glance.

How far away it seemed, that world of attentive young men and Deb with her rudeness to them that never seemed to put them off. This young man was, she thought, quite an attractive specimen.

She put aside what she called to herself "peace-time thoughts" and concentrated on the present situation.

After a moment or two she said slowly:

"My husband isn't in Scotland."

"Isn't he?"

"No, he's down here with me. At least he was! Now—he's disappeared."

"I say, that's bad—or isn't it? Was he on to something?"

Tuppence nodded.

"I think so. That's why I don't think that his disappearing like this is really a bad sign. I think, sooner or later, he'll communicate with me—in his own way." She smiled a little.

Tony said, with some slight embarrassment:

"Of course, you know the game well, I expect. But you ought to be careful."

Tuppence nodded.

"I know what you mean. Beautiful heroines in books are always easily decoyed away. But Tommy and I have our methods. We've got a slogan," she smiled. *"Penny plain and tuppence colored."*

"What?" The young man stared at her as though she had gone mad.

"I ought to explain that my family nickname is Tuppence."

"Oh, I see." The young man's brow cleared. "Ingenious—what?"

"I hope so."

"I don't want to butt in—but couldn't I help in any way?"

"Yes," said Tuppence thoughtfully. "I think perhaps you might."

12

I

AFTER LONG EONS of unconsciousness, Tommy began to be aware of a fiery ball swimming in space. In the center of the fiery ball was a core of pain, the universe shrank, the fiery ball swung more slowly—he discovered suddenly that the nucleus of it was his own aching head.

Slowly he became aware of other things—of cold cramped limbs, of hunger, of an inability to move his lips.

Slower and slower swung the fiery ball. . . . It was now Thomas Beresford's head and it was resting on solid ground. Very solid ground. In fact on something suspiciously like stone.

Yes, he was lying on hard stones, and he was in pain, unable to move, extremely hungry, cold and uncomfortable.

Surely, although Mrs. Perenna's beds had never been unduly soft, this could not be—

Of course—Haydock! The wireless! The German waiter! Turning in at the gates of Sans Souci. . . .

Someone, creeping up behind him, had struck him down. That was the reason of his aching head.

And he'd thought he'd got away with it all right! So Haydock, after all, hadn't been quite such a fool?

Haydock? Haydock had gone back into Smugglers' Rest, and closed the door. How had he managed to get down the hill and be waiting for Tommy in the grounds of Sans Souci?

It couldn't be done. Not without Tommy seeing him.

The manservant, then? Had he been sent ahead to lie in wait? But surely, as Tommy had crossed the hall, he had seen Appledore in the kitchen, of which the door was slightly ajar. Or did he only fancy he had seen him? Perhaps that was the explanation.

Anyway it didn't matter. The thing to do was to find out where he was now.

His eyes, accustomed to the darkness, picked out a small rectangle of dim light. A window or small grating. The air smelt chill and musty. He was, he fancied, lying in a cellar. His hands and feet were tied and a gag in his mouth was secured by a bandage.

"Seems rather as though I'm for it," thought Tommy.

He tried gingerly to move his limbs or body, but he could not succeed.

At that moment, there was a faint creaking sound and a door somewhere behind him was pushed open. A man with a candle came in. He set down the candle on the ground. Tommy recognized Appledore. The latter disappeared again and then returned carrying a tray on which was a jug of water, a glass, and some bread and cheese.

Stooping down he first tested the cords binding the other limbs. He then touched the gag.

He said in a quiet level voice:

"I am about to take this off. You will then be able to eat and drink. If, however, you make the slightest sound, I shall replace it immediately."

Tommy tried to nod his head which proved impossible, so he opened and shut his eyes several times instead.

Appledore, taking this for consent, carefully unknotted the bandage.

His mouth freed, Tommy spent some few minutes easing his jaw. Appledore held the glass of water to his lips. He swallowed at first with difficulty, then more easily. The water did him a world of good.

He murmured stiffly:

"That's better. I'm not quite so young as I was. Now for the eats, Fritz—or is it Franz?"

The man said quietly:

"My name here is Appledore."

He held the slice of bread and cheese up and Tommy bit at it hungrily.

The meal washed down with water, he then asked:

"And what's the next part of the program?"

For answer, Appledore picked up the gag again.

Tommy said quickly:

"I want to see Commander Haydock."

Appledore shook his head. Deftly he replaced the gag and went out.

Tommy was left to meditate in darkness. He was awaked from a confused sleep by the sound of the door reopening. This time Haydock and Appledore came in together. The gag was removed and the cords that held his arms were loosened so that he could sit up and stretch his arms.

Haydock had an automatic pistol with him.

Tommy, without much inward confidence, began to play his part.

He said indignantly:

"Look here, Haydock, what's the meaning of all this? I've been set upon—kidnapped—"

The Commander was gently shaking his head.

He said:

"Don't waste your breath. It's not worth it."

"Just because you're a member of our Secret Service, you think you can—"

Again the other shook his head.

"No, no, Meadowes. You weren't taken in by that story. No need to keep up the pretence."

But Tommy showed no signs of discomfiture. He argued to himself that the other could not really be sure. If he continued to play his part—

"Who the devil do you think you are?" he demanded. "However great your powers you've no right to behave like this. I'm perfectly capable of holding my tongue about any of our vital secrets!"

The other said coldly:

"You do your stuff very well, but I may tell you that it's immaterial to me whether you're a member of the British Intelligence, or merely a muddling amateur—"

"Of all the darnned cheek—"

"Cut it out, Meadowes."

"I tell you—"

Haydock thrust a ferocious face forward.

"Be quiet, damn you. Earlier on it would have mattered to find out who you were and who sent you. Now it doesn't matter. The time's short, you see. And you didn't have the chance to report to anyone what you'd found out."

"The police will be looking for me as soon as I'm reported missing."

Haydock showed his teeth in a sudden gleam.

"I've had the police here this evening. Good fellows—both friends of mine. They asked me all about Mr. Meadowes. Very concerned about his disappearance. How he seemed that evening—what he said. They never dreamed, how should they, that the man they were talking about was practically underneath their feet where they were sitting. It's quite clear, you see, that you left this house well and alive. They'd never dream of looking for you here."

"You can't keep me here for ever," Tommy said vehemently.

Haydock said with a resumption of his most British manner:

"It won't be necessary, my dear fellow. Only until tomorrow night. There's a boat due in at my little cove—and we're thinking of sending you on a voyage for your health—though actually I don't think you'll be alive, or even on board, when they arrive at their destination."

"I wonder you didn't knock me on the head straight away."

"It's such hot weather, my dear fellow. Just occasionally our sea communications are interrupted, and if that were to be so—well, a dead body on the premises has a way of announcing its presence."

"I see," said Tommy.

He did see. The issue was perfectly clear. He was to be kept alive until the boat arrived. Then he would be killed, or drugged, and his dead body taken out to sea. Nothing would ever connect his body, when found, with Smugglers' Rest.

"I just came along," continued Haydock, speaking in the most natural manner, "to ask whether there is anything we could—er—do for you—afterwards?"

Tommy reflected. Then he said:

"Thanks—but I won't ask you to take a lock of my hair to the little woman in St. John's Wood, or anything of that kind. She'll miss me when pay day comes along—but I dare say she'll soon find a friend somewhere."

At all costs, he felt, he must create the impression that he was playing a lone hand. So long as no suspicion attached itself to Tuppence, then the game might still be won through, though he was not there to play it.

"As you please," said Haydock. "If you did care to send a message to—your friend—we would see that it was delivered."

So he was, after all, anxious to get a little information about this unknown Mrs. Meadowes? Very well, then, Tommy would keep him guessing.

He shook his head. "Nothing doing," he said.

"Very well." With an appearance of the utmost indifference Haydock nodded to Appledore. The latter replaced the bonds and the gag. The two men went out, locking the door behind them.

Left to his reflections, Tommy felt anything but cheerful. Not only was he faced with the prospect of rapidly approaching death, but he had no means of leaving any clue behind him as to the information he had discovered.

His body was completely helpless. His brain felt singularly inactive. Could he, he wondered, have utilized Haydock's suggestion of a message? Perhaps if his brain had been working better. . . . But he could think of nothing helpful.

There was, of course, still Tuppence. But what could Tuppence do? As Haydock had just pointed out, Tommy's disappearance would not be connected with him. Tommy had left Smugglers' Rest alive and well. The evidence of two independent witnesses would confirm that. Whoever Tuppence might suspect, it would not be Haydock. And she might not suspect at all. She might think that he was merely following up a trail.

Damn it all, if only he had been more on his guard—

There was a little light in the cellar. It came through the grating which was high up in one corner. If only he could get his mouth free, he could shout for help. Somebody might hear, though it was very unlikely.

For the next half-hour he busied himself straining at the cords that bound him, and trying to bite through the gag. It was all in vain, however. The people who had adjusted those things knew their business.

It was, he judged, late afternoon. Haydock, he fancied, had gone out, he had heard no sounds from overhead.

Confound it all, he was probably playing golf, speculating at the club-house over what could have happened to Meadowes!

"Dined with me night before last—seemed quite normal, then. Just vanished into the blue."

Tommy writhed with fury. That hearty English manner! Was everyone blind not to see that bullet-headed Prussian skull? He himself hadn't seen it. Wonderful what a first-class actor could get away with.

So here he was—a failure—an ignominious failure—trussed up like a chicken, with no one to guess where he was.

If only Tuppence could have second sight! She might suspect. She had, sometimes, an uncanny insight . . .

What was that?

He strained his ears listening to a far-off sound.

Only some man humming a tune.

And here he was, unable to make a sound to attract anyone's attention. The humming came nearer. A most untuneful noise.

But the tune, though mangled, was recognizable. It dated from the last war—had been revived for this one.

"If you were the only girl in the world and I was the only boy."

How often he had hummed that in 1917.

Dash this fellow. Why couldn't he sing in tune?

Suddenly Tommy's body grew taut and rigid. Those particular lapses were strangely familiar. Surely there was only one person who always went wrong in that one particular place and in that one particular way!

"Albert, by gosh!" thought Tommy.

Albert prowling round Smugglers' Rest. Albert quite close at hand, and here was he, trussed up, unable to move hand or foot, unable to make a sound. . . .

Wait a minute. Was he?

There was just one sound—not so easy with the mouth shut as with the mouth open, but it could be done.

Desperately Tommy began to snore. He kept his eyes closed, ready to feign a deep sleep if Appledore should come down, and he snored, he snored. . . .

Short snore, short snore, short snore—pause—long snore, long snore, long snore—pause—short snore, short snore, short snore . . .

II

Albert, when Tuppence had left him, was deeply perturbed.

With the advance of years he had become a person of slow mental processes, but those processes were tenacious.

The state of affairs in general seemed to him quite wrong.

The war was all wrong to begin with.

"Those Germans," thought Albert gloomily and almost without rancor. Heiling Hitler and goose-stepping and overrunning the world and bombing and machine-gunning, and generally making pestilential nuisances of themselves. They'd got to be stopped, no two ways about it—and so far it seemed as though nobody had been able to stop them.

And now here was Mrs. Beresford, a nice lady if there ever was one, getting herself mixed up in trouble and looking out for more trouble, and how was he going to stop her? Didn't look as though he could. Up against this Fifth Column and a nasty lot they must be. Some of 'em English-born, too! A disgrace, that was!

And the master, who was always the one to hold the missus back from her impetuous ways—the master was missing.

Albert didn't like that at all. It looked to him as though "those Germans" might be at the bottom of that.

Yes, it looked bad, it did. Looked as though he might have copped one.

Albert was not given to the exercise of deep reasoning. Like most Englishmen, he felt something strongly, and proceeded to muddle around until he had, somehow or other, cleared up the mess. Deciding that the master had got to be found, Albert, rather after the manner of a faithful dog, set out to find him.

He acted upon no settled plan, but proceeded in exactly the same way as he was wont to embark upon the search for his wife's missing handbag or his own spectacles when either of those essential articles were mislaid. That is to say, he went to the place where he had last seen the missing objects and started from there.

In this case, the last thing known about Tommy was that he had dined with Commander Haydock at Smugglers' Rest, and had then returned to Sans Souci and been last seen turning in at the gate.

Albert accordingly climbed the hill as far as the gate of Sans Souci, and spent some five minutes staring hopefully at the gate. Nothing of a scintillating character having occurred to him, he sighed and wandered slowly up the hill to Smugglers' Rest.

Albert, too, had visited the Ornate Cinema that week, and had been powerfully impressed by the theme of *Wandering Minstrel*. Romantic, it was! He could not but be struck by the similarity of his own predicament. He, like that hero of the screen, Larry Cooper, was a faithful Blondel seeking his imprisoned master. Like Blondel, he had fought at that master's side in bygone days. Now his master was betrayed by treachery, and there was none but his faithful Blondel to seek for him and restore him to the loving arms of Queen Berengaria.

Albert heaved a sigh as he remembered the melting strains of "Richard, O mon roi," which the faithful troubadour had crooned so feelingly beneath tower after tower.

Pity he himself wasn't better at picking up a tune.

Took him a long time to get hold of a tune, it did.

His lips shaped themselves into a tentative whistle.

Begun playing the old tunes again lately, they had.

"If you were the only girl in the world and I was the only boy—"

Albert paused to survey the near white-painted gate of Smugglers' Rest. That was it, that was where the master had gone to dinner.

He went up the hill a little farther and came out on the downs.

Nothing here. Nothing but grass and a few sheep.

The gate of Smugglers' Rest swung open and a car passed out. A big man in plus-fours with golf clubs drove out and down the hill.

"That would be Commander Haydock, that would," Albert deduced.

He wandered down again and stared at Smugglers' Rest. A tidy little place. Nice bit of garden. Nice view.

He eyed it benignly. "I would say such wonderful things to you," he hummed.

Through a side door of the house a man came out with a hoe and passed out of sight through a little gate.

Albert, who grew nasturtiums and a bit of lettuce in his back garden, was instantly interested.

He edged nearer to Smugglers' Rest and passed through the open gate. Yes, tidy little place.

He circled slowly round it. Some way below him, reached by steps, was a flat plateau planted as a vegetable garden. The man who had come out of the house was busy down there.

Albert watched him with interest for some minutes. Then he turned to contemplate the house.

Tidy little place, he thought for the third time. Just the sort of place a retired Naval gentleman would like to have. This was where the master had dined that night.

Slowly Albert circled round and round the house. He looked at it much as he had looked at the gate of Sans Souci—hopefully, as though asking it to tell him something.

And as he went he hummed softly to himself, a twentieth century Blondel in search of his master.

"There would be such wonderful things to do," hummed Albert. "I would say such wonderful things to you. There would be such wonderful things to do—" Gone wrong somewhere, hadn't he? He'd hummed that bit before.

Hallo, funny, so the Commander kept pigs, did he? A long-drawn grunt came to him. Funny—seemed almost as though it were underground. Funny place to keep pigs.

Couldn't be pigs. No, it was someone having a bit of shut-eye. Bit of shut-eye in the cellar, so it seemed. . . .

Right kind of day for a snooze, but funny place to go for it. Humming like a bumble bee Albert approached nearer.

That's where it was coming from—through that little grating. Grunt, grunt, grunt, snooooore. Snooooore, snoooooore—grunt, grunt, grunt. Funny sort of snore—reminded him of something. . . .

"Coo!" said Albert, "that's what it is—SOS. Dot, dot, dot, dash, dash, dash, dot, dot, dot."

He looked round him with a quick glance.

Then kneeling down, he tapped a soft message on the iron grill of the little window of the cellar.

13

I

ALTHOUGH TUPPENCE WENT to bed in an optimistic frame of mind, she suffered a severe reaction in those waning hours of early dawn when human morale sinks to its lowest.

On descending to breakfast, however, her spirits were raised by the sight of a letter sitting on her plate addressed in a painfully backhanded script.

This was no communication from Douglas, Raymond, or Cyril, or any other of the camouflaged correspondence that arrived punctually for her, and which included this morning a brightly-colored Bonzo postcard with a scrawled, "Sorry I haven't written before. All well, Maudie," on it.

Tuppence thrust this aside and opened the letter.

"DEAR PATRICIA (it ran),

"Aunt Gracie is, I am afraid, much worse today. The doctors do not actually say she is sinking, but I am afraid that there cannot be much hope. If you want to see her before the end I think it would be well to come today. If you will take the 10:20 train to Yarrow, a friend will meet you with his car.

"Shall look forward to seeing you again, dear, in spite of the melancholy reason.

"Yours ever,
"PENELOPE PLAYNE."

It was all Tuppence could do to restrain her jubilation.

Good old Penny Plain!

With some difficulty she assumed a mourning expression—and sighed heavily as she laid the letter down.

To the two sympathetic listeners present, Mrs. O'Rourke and Miss Minton, she imparted the contents of the letter, and enlarged freely on the personality of Aunt Gracie, her indomitable spirit, her indifference to air raids and danger, and her vanquishment by illness. Miss Minton tended to be curious as to the exact nature of Aunt Gracie's sufferings, and compared them interestedly with the diseases of her own cousin Selina. Tuppence, hovering slightly between dropsy and diabetes, found herself slightly confused, but compromised on complications with the kidneys. Mrs. O'Rourke displayed an avid interest as to whether Tuppence would benefit pecuniarily by the old lady's death and learned that dear Cyril had always been the old lady's favorite grandnephew as well as being her godson.

After breakfast, Tuppence rang up the tailor's and cancelled a fitting of a coat and skirt for that afternoon, and then sought out Mrs. Perenna and explained that she might be away from home for a night or two.

Mrs. Perenna expressed the usual conventional sentiments. She looked tired this morning, and had an anxious harassed expression.

"Still no news of Mr. Meadowes," she said. "It really is *most* odd, is it not?"

"I'm sure he must have met with an accident," sighed Mrs. Blenkensop. "I always said so."

"Oh, but surely, Mrs. Blenkensop, the accident would have been reported by this time."

"Well, what do you think?" asked Tuppence.

Mrs. Perenna shook her head.

"I really don't know *what* to say. I quite agree that he can't have gone away of his own free will. He would have sent word by now."

"It was always a most unjustified suggestion," said Mrs. Blenkensop warmly. "That horrid Major Bletchley started it. No, if it isn't an accident, it must be loss of memory. I believe that is far more common than is generally known, especially at times of stress like those we are living through now."

Mrs. Perenna nodded her head. She pursed up her lips with rather a doubtful expression. She shot a quick look at Tuppence.

"You know, Mrs. Blenkensop," she said, "we don't know very much *about* Mr. Meadowes, do we?"

Tuppence said sharply: "What do you mean?"

"Oh, please, don't take me up so sharply. *I* don't believe it—not for a minute."

"Don't believe what?"

"The story that's going round."

"What story? I haven't heard anything?"

"No—well—perhaps people wouldn't tell you. I don't really know how it started. I've an idea that Mr. Cayley mentioned it first. Of course he's rather a suspicious man, if you know what I mean?"

Tuppence contained herself with as much patience as possible.

"Please tell me," she said.

"Well, it was just a suggestion, you know, that Mr. Meadowes might be an enemy agent—one of these dreadful Fifth Golumn people."

Tuppence put all she could of an outraged Mrs. Blenkensop into her indignant:

"I never *heard* of such an absurd idea!"

"No. I don't think there's anything in it. But of course Mr. Meadowes was seen about a good deal with that German boy—and I believe he asked a lot of questions about the chemical processes at the factory—

and so people think that perhaps the two of them might have been working together."

Tuppence said:

"*You* don't think there's any doubt about Carl, do you, Mrs. Perenna?"

She saw a quick spasm distort the other woman's face.

"I wish I *could* think it was not true."

Tuppence said gently: "Poor Sheila . . ."

Mrs. Perenna's eyes flashed.

"Her heart's broken, the poor child. Why should it be that way? Why couldn't it be someone else she set her heart upon?"

Tuppence shook her head.

"Things don't happen that way."

"You're right." The other spoke in a deep, bitter voice. "It's got to be the way things tear you to pieces . . . It's got to be sorrow and bitterness and dust and ashes. I'm sick of the cruelty—the unfairness of this world. I'd like to smash it and break it—and let us all start again near to the earth and without these rules and laws and the tyranny of nation over nation. I'd like—"

A cough interrupted her. A deep, throaty cough. Mrs. O'Rourke was standing in the doorway, her vast bulk filling the aperture completely.

"Am I interrupting now?" she demanded.

Like a sponge across a slate, all evidence of Mrs. Perenna's outburst vanished from her face—leaving in their wake only the mild worried face of the proprietress of a guest-house whose guests were causing trouble.

"No, indeed, Mrs. O'Rourke," she said. "We were just talking about what had become of Mr. Meadowes. It's amazing the police can find no trace of him."

"Ah, the police!" said Mrs. O'Rourke in tones of easy contempt. "What good would they be? No good at all, at all! Only fit for fining motor-cars, and dropping on poor wretches who haven't taken out their dog licenses."

"What's your theory, Mrs. O'Rourke?" asked Tuppence.

"You'll have been hearing the story that's going about?"

"About his being a Fascist and an enemy agent—yes," said Tuppence coldly.

"It might be true now," said Mrs. O'Rourke thoughtfully. "For there's been something about the man that's intrigued me from the beginning. I've watched him, you know," she smiled directly at Tuppence—and like all Mrs. O'Rourke's smiles it had a vaguely terrifying quality—the smile of an ogress. "He'd not the look of a man who'd retired from business and had nothing to do with himself. If I was backing my judgment, I'd say he came here with a purpose."

"And when the police got on his track he disappeared, is that it?" demanded Tuppence.

"It might be so," said Mrs. O'Rourke. "What's your opinion, Mrs. Perenna?"

"I don't know," sighed Mrs. Perenna. "It's a most vexing thing to happen. It makes so much *talk*."

"Ah! talk won't hurt you. They're happy now out there on the terrace wondering and surmising. They'll have it in the end that the quiet, inoffensive man was going to blow us all up in our beds with bombs."

"You haven't told us what you think?" said Tuppence.

Mrs. O'Rourke smiled, that same slow ferocious smile.

"I'm thinking that the man is safe somewhere—quite safe . . ."

Tuppence thought:

"She might say that if she knew . . . But he isn't where she thinks he is!"

She went up to her room to get ready. Betty Sprot came running out of the Cayleys' bedroom with a smile of mischievous and impish glee on her face.

"What have you been up to, minx?" demanded Tuppence.

Betty gurgled:

"Goosey, goosey gander . . ."

Tuppence chanted:

"Whither will you wander? *Up*stairs!" She snatched up Betty high over her head. "*Down*stairs!" she rolled her on the floor—

At this minute Mrs. Sprot appeared and Betty was led off to be attired for her walk.

"Hide?" said Betty hopefully. "Hide?"

"You can't play hide-and-seek now," said Mrs. Sprot.

Tuppence went into her room, donned her hat (a nuisance having to wear a hat—Tuppence Beresford never did—but Patricia Blenkensop would certainly wear one, Tuppence felt).

Somebody, she noted, had altered the position of the hats in her hat-cupboard. Had someone been searching her room? Well, let them. They wouldn't find anything to cast doubt on blameless Mrs. Blenkensop.

She left Penelope Playne's letter artistically on the dressing-table and went downstairs and out of the house.

It was ten o'clock as she turned out of the gate. Plenty of time. She looked up at the sky, and in doing so stepped into a dark puddle by the gatepost, but without apparently noticing it she went on.

Her heart was dancing wildly. Success—success—they were going to succeed.

II

Yarrow was a small country station where the village was some distance from the railway.

Outside the station a car was waiting. A good-looking young man was driving it. He touched his peaked cap to Tuppence, but the gesture seemed hardly natural.

Tuppence kicked the off-side tire dubiously.

"Isn't this rather flat?"

"We haven't far to go, madam,"

She nodded and got in.

They drove, not towards the village, but towards the downs. After winding up over a hill, they took a side-track that dropped sharply into a deep cleft. From the shadow of a small copse of trees a figure stepped out to meet them.

The car stopped and Tuppence, getting out, went to meet Antony Marsdon.

"Beresford's all right," he said quickly. "We located him yesterday. He's a prisoner—the other side got him—and for good reasons he's remaining put for another twelve hours. You see, there's a small boat due in at a certain spot—and we want to catch her badly. That's why Beresford's lying low—we don't want to give the show away until the last minute."

He looked at her anxiously.

"You do understand, don't you?"

"Oh, yes!" Tuppence was staring at a curious tangled mass of canvas material half-hidden by the trees.

"He'll be absolutely all right," continued the young man earnestly.

"Of course Tommy will be all right," said Tuppence impatiently. "You needn't talk to me as though I were a child of two. We're both ready to run a few risks. What's that thing over there?"

"Well—" the young man hesitated. "That's just it. I've been ordered to put a certain proposition before you. But—but well, frankly, I don't like doing it. You see—"

Tuppence treated him to a cold stare.

"Why don't you like doing it?"

"Well—dash it—you're Deborah's mother. And I mean—what would Deb say to me if—if—"

"If I get it in the neck?" inquired Tuppence. "Personally, if I were you, I shouldn't mention it to her. The man who said explanations were a mistake was quite right."

Then she smiled kindly at him.

"My dear boy, I know exactly how you feel. That it's all very well for you and Deborah and the young generally to run risks, but that the mere middle-aged must be shielded. All complete nonsense, because if anyone is going to be liquidated it is much better it should be the middle-aged, who have had the best part of their lives. Anyway, stop looking upon me as that sacred object, Deborah's mother, and just tell me what dangerous and unpleasant job there is for me to do."

"You know," said the young man with enthusiasm, "I think you're splendid, simply splendid."

"Cut out the compliments," said Tuppence. "I'm admiring myself a good deal, so there's no need for you to chime in. What exactly *is* the big idea?"

Tony indicated the mass of crumpled material with a gesture.

"That," he said, "is the remains of a parachute."

"Aha," said Tuppence. Her eyes sparkled.

"There was just an isolated parachutist," went on Marsdon. "Fortunately the LDVs around here are quite a bright lot. The descent was spotted, and they got her."

"*Her?*"

"Yes, *her*! Woman dressed as a hospital nurse."

"I'm sorry she wasn't a nun," said Tuppence. "There have been so many good stories going around about nuns paying their fares in buses with hairy muscular arms."

"Well, she wasn't a nun and she wasn't a man in disguise. She was a woman of medium height, middle-aged, with dark hair and of slight build."

"In fact," said Tuppence, "a woman not unlike me?"

"You've hit it exactly," said Tony.

"Well?" said Tuppence.

Marsdon said slowly:

"The next part of it is up to you."

Tuppence smiled. She said:

"I'm *on* all right. Where do I go and what do I do?"

"I say, Mrs. Beresford, you really *are* a sport. Magnificent nerve you've got."

"Where do I go and what do I do?" repeated Tuppence, impatiently.

"The instructions are very meager, unfortunately. In the woman's pocket there was a piece of paper with these words on it in German. "Walk to Leatherbarrow—due east from the stone cross. 14 St. Asalph's Road. Dr. Binion.""

Tuppence looked up. On the hilltop nearby was a stone cross.

"That's it," said Tony. "Signposts have been removed, of course. But Leatherbarrow's a biggish place, and walking due east from the cross you're bound to strike it."

"How far?"

"Five miles at least."

Tuppence made a slight grimace.

"Healthy walking exercise before lunch," she commented. "I hope Dr. Binion offers me lunch when I get there."

"Do you know German, Mrs. Beresford?"

"Hotel variety only. I shall have to be firm about speaking English—say my instructions were to do so."

"It's an awful risk," said Marsdon.

"Nonsense. Who's to imagine there's been a substitution? Or does everyone know for miles round that there's been a parachutist brought down?"

"The two LDV men who reported it are being kept by the Chief

Constable. Don't want to risk their telling their friends how clever they have been!"

"Somebody else may have seen it—or heard about it?"

Tony smiled.

"My dear Mrs. Beresford, every single day, word goes round that one, two, three, four, up to a hundred parachutists have been seen!"

"That's probably quite true," agreed Tuppence. "Well, lead me to it."

Tony said:

"We've got the kit here—and a policewoman who's an expert in the art of make-up. Come with me."

Just inside the copse there was a tumble-down shed. At the door of it was a competent-looking middle-aged woman.

She looked at Tuppence and nodded approvingly.

Inside the shed, seated on an upturned packing-case, Tuppence submitted herself to expert ministrations. Finally the operator stood back, nodded approvingly and remarked:

"There, now, I think we've made a very nice job of it. What do you think, sir?"

"Very good indeed," said Tony.

Tuppence stretched out her hand and took the mirror the other woman held. She surveyed her own face earnestly and could hardly repress a cry of surprise.

The eyebrows had been trimmed to an entirely different shape, altering the whole expression. Small pieces of adhesive plaster hidden by curls pulled forward over the ears that tightened the skin of the face and altered its contours. A small amount of nose putty had altered the shape of the nose, giving Tuppence an unexpectedly beak-like profile. Skillful make-up had added several years to her age, with heavy lines running down each side of the mouth. The whole face had a complacent, rather foolish look.

"It's frightfully clever," said Tuppence admiringly. She touched her nose gingerly.

"You must be careful," the other woman warned her. She produced two slices of thin india-rubber. "Do you think you could bear to wear those in your cheeks?"

"I suppose I shall have to," said Tuppence gloomily.

She slipped them in and worked her jaws carefully.

"It's not really too uncomfortable," she had to admit.

Tony then discreetly left the shed and Tuppence shed her own clothing and got into the nurse's kit. It was not too bad a fit, though inclined to strain a little over the shoulders. The dark blue bonnet put the final touch to her new personality. She rejected, however, the stout square-toed shoes.

"If I've got to walk five miles," she said decidedly, "I do it in my own shoes."

They both agreed that this was reasonable—particularly as Tuppence's own shoes were dark blue brogues that went well with the uniform.

She looked with interest into the dark blue handbag—powder; no lipstick; two pounds fourteen and sixpence in English money; a handkerchief and an identity card in the name of Freda Elton, 4 Manchester Road, Sheffield.

Tuppence transferred her own powder and lipstick and stood up, prepared to set out.

Tony Marsdon turned his head away. He said gruffly:

"I feel a swine letting you do this."

"I know just how you feel."

"But, you see, it's absolutely vital—that we should get some idea of just where and how the attack will come."

Tuppence patted him on the arm. "Don't you worry, my child. Believe it or not, I'm enjoying myself."

Tony Marsdon said again:

"I think you're simply wonderful!"

III

Somewhat weary, Tuppence stood outside 14 St. Asalph's Road and noted that Dr. Binion was a dental surgeon and not a doctor.

From the corner of her eye she noted Tony Marsdon. He was sitting in a racy-looking car outside a house farther down the street.

It had been judged necessary for Tuppence to walk to Leatherbarrow exactly as instructed, since if she had been driven there in a car the fact might have been noted.

It was certainly true that two enemy aircraft had passed over the downs, circling low before making off, and they could have noted the nurse's lonely figure walking across country.

Tony, with the expert policewoman, had driven off in the opposite direction and had made a big detour before approaching Leatherbarrow and taking up his position in St. Asalph's Road. Everything was now set.

"The arena doors open," murmured Tuppence. "Enter one Christian *en route* for the lions. Oh, well, nobody can say I'm not seeing life."

She crossed the road and rang the bell, wondering as she did so, exactly how much Deborah liked that young man. The door was opened by an elderly woman with a stolid peasant face—not an English face.

"Dr. Binion?" said Tuppence.

The woman looked her slowly up and down.

"You will be Nurse Elton, I suppose."

"Yes."

"Then you will come up to the doctor's surgery."

She stood back, the door closed behind Tuppence, who found herself standing in a narrow linoleum-lined hall.

The maid preceded her upstairs and opened a door on the first floor.

"Please to wait. The doctor will come to you."

She went out, shutting the door behind her.

A very ordinary dentist's surgery—the appointments somewhat old and shabby.

Tuppence looked at the dentist's chair and smiled to think that for once it held none of the usual terrors. She had the "dentist feeling" all right—but from quite different causes.

Presently the door would open and "Dr. Binion" would come in. Who would Dr. Binion be? A stranger? Or someone she had seen before? If it was the person she was half expecting to see—

The door opened.

The man who entered was not at all the person Tuppence had half fancied she might see! It was someone she had never considered as a likely starter.

It was Commander Haydock.

14

I

A FLOOD OF wild surmises as to the part Commander Haydock had played in Tommy's disappearance surged through Tuppence's brain, but she thrust them resolutely aside. This was a moment for keeping all her wits about her.

Would or would not the Commander recognize her? It was an interesting question.

She had so steeled herself beforehand to display no recognition or surprise herself, no matter whom she might see, that she felt reasonably sure that she herself had displayed no signs untoward to the situation.

She rose now to her feet and stood there, standing in a respectable attitude, as befitted a mere German woman in the presence of a Lord of creation.

"So you have arrived," said the Commander.

He spoke in English and his manner was precisely the same as usual.

"Yes," said Tuppence, and added, as though presenting her credentials: "Nurse Elton."

Haydock smiled as though at a joke.

"Nurse Elton! Excellent."

He looked at her approvingly.

"You look absolutely right," he said kindly.

Tuppence inclined her head, but said nothing. She was leaving the initiative to him.

"You know, I suppose, what you have to do?" went on Haydock. "Sit down, please."

Tuppence sat down obediently. She replied:

"I was to take detailed instructions from you."

"Very proper," said Haydock. There was a faint suggestion of mockery in his voice.

He said:

"You know the day?"

"The fourth!"

Haydock looked startled. A heavy frown creased his forehead.

There was a pause, then Tuppence said:

"You will tell me, please, what I have to do?"

Haydock said:

"All in good time, my dear."

He paused a minute and then asked:

"You have heard, no doubt, of Sans Souci?"

"No," said Tuppence.

"You haven't?"

"No," said Tuppence firmly.

"Let's see how you deal with that one!" she thought.

There was a queer smile on the Commander's face. He said:

"So you haven't heard of Sans Souci? That surprises me very much—since I was under the impression, you know, *that you'd been living there for the last month. . . .*"

There was a dead silence. The Commander said:

"What about that, Mrs. Blenkensop?"

"I don't know what you mean, Dr. Binion. I landed by parachute this morning."

Again Haydock smiled—definitely an unpleasant smile.

He said:

"A few yards of canvas thrust into a bush create a wonderful illusion. And I am not Dr. Binion, dear lady. Dr. Binion is, officially, my dentist—he is good enough to lend me his surgery now and again."

"Indeed?" said Tuppence.

"Indeed, Mrs. Blenkensop! Or perhaps you would prefer me to address you by your real name of Beresford?"

Again there was a poignant silence. Tuppence drew a deep breath.

Haydock nodded.

"The game's up, you see. *'You've walked into my parlour,' said the spider to the fly.'* "

There was a faint click and a gleam of blue steel showed in his hand. His voice took on a grim note as he said:

"And I shouldn't advise you to make any noise or try to arouse the neighborhood! You'd be dead before you got so much as a yelp out, and even if you did manage to scream it wouldn't arouse attention. Patients under gas, you know, often cry out."

Tuppence said composedly:

"You seem to have thought of everything. Has it occurred to you that I have friends who know where I am?"

"Ah! Still harping on the blue-eyed boy—actually brown-eyed! Young Antony Marsdon. I'm sorry, Mrs. Beresford, but young Antony happens to be one of our most stalwart supporters in this country. As I said just now, a few yards of canvas creates a wonderful effect. You swallowed the parachute idea quite easily."

"I don't see the point of all this rigmarole!"

"Don't you? We don't want your friends to trace you too easily, you see. *If* they pick up your trail it will lead to Yarrow and to a man in a car. The fact that a hospital nurse, of quite different facial appearance, walked into Leatherbarrow between one and two will hardly be connected with your disappearance."

"Very elaborate," said Tuppence.

Haydock said:

"I admire your nerve, you know. I admire it very much. I'm sorry to have to coerce you—but it's vital that we should know just exactly how much you *did* discover at Sans Souci."

Tuppence did not answer.

Haydock said quietly:

"I'd advise you, you know, to come clean. There are certain—possibilities—in a dentist's chair and instruments."

Tuppence merely threw him a scornful look.

Haydock leaned back in his chair. He said slowly:

"Yes—I dare say you've got a lot of fortitude—your type often has. But what about the other half of the picture?"

"What do you mean?"

"I'm talking about Thomas Beresford, your husband, who has lately been living at Sans Souci under the name of Mr. Meadowes, and who is now very conveniently trussed up in the cellar of my house."

Tuppence said sharply:

"I don't believe it."

"Because of the Penny Plain letter? Don't you realize that that was just a smart bit of work on the part of young Antony? You played into his hands nicely when you gave him the code."

Tuppence's voice trembled.

"Then Tommy—then Tommy—"

"Tommy," said Commander Haydock, "is where he has been all along—completely in my power! It's up to you now. If you answer my questions satisfactorily, there's a chance for him. If you don't—well, the original plan holds. He'll be knocked on the head, taken out to sea and put overboard."

Tuppence was silent for a minute or two—then she said:

"What do you want to know?"

"I want to know who employed you, what your means of communication with that person or persons are, what you have reported so far, and exactly what you know?"

Tuppence shrugged her shoulders.

"I could tell you what lies I choose," she pointed out.

"No, because I shall proceed to test what you say." He drew his chair a little nearer. His manner was now definitely appealing. "My dear woman—I know just what you feel about it all, but do believe me when I say I really do admire both you and your husband immensely. You've got grit and pluck. It's people like you that will be needed in the new State—the State that will arise in this country when your present imbecile Government is vanquished. We want to turn some of our enemies into friends—those that are worth while. If I have to give the order that ends your husband's life, I shall do it—it's my duty—but I shall feel really badly about having to do it! He's a fine fellow—quiet, unassuming and clever. Let me impress upon you what so few people in this country seem to understand. Our Leader does not intend to conquer this country in the sense that you all think. He aims at creating a new Britain—a Britain strong in its own power—ruled over, *not* by Germans, but by *Englishmen.* And the best *type* of Englishmen—Englishmen with brains and breeding and courage. *A brave new world,* as Shakespeare put it."

He leaned forward.

"We want to do away with muddle and inefficiency. With bribery and corruption. With self-seeking and money-grabbing—*and in this new state we want people like you and your husband*—brave and resourceful—enemies that have been, friends to be. You would be surprised if you knew how many there are in this country, as in others, who have sympathy with and belief in our aims. Between us all we will create a new Europe—a Europe of peace and progress. Try and see it that way—because, I assure you—it *is* that way. . . ."

His voice was compelling, magnetic. Leaning forward, he looked the embodiment of a straightforward British sailor.

Tuppence looked at him and searched her mind for a telling phrase. She was only able to find one that was both childish and rude.

"Goosey, goosey gander!" said Tuppence. . . .

II

The effect was so magical that she was quite taken aback.

Haydock jumped to his feet, his face went dark purple with rage, and in a second all likeness to a hearty British sailor had vanished. She saw what Tommy had once seen—an infuriated Prussian.

He swore at her fluently in German. Then, changing to English, he shouted:

"You infernal little fool! Don't you realize you give yourself away completely answering like that? You've done for yourself now— you and your precious husband."

Raising his voice he called:

"Anna!"

The woman who had admitted Tuppence came into the room. Haydock thrust the pistol into her hand.

"Watch her. Shoot if necessary."

He stormed out of the room.

Tuppence looked appealingly at Anna, who stood in front of her with an impassive face.

"Would you really shoot me?" said Tuppence.

Anna answered quietly:

"You need not try to get round me. In the last war my son was killed, my Otto. I was thirty-eight, then—I am sixty-two now—but I have not forgotten."

Tuppence looked at the broad, impassive face. It reminded her of the polish woman, Vanda Polonska. That same frightening ferocity and singleness of purpose. Motherhood—unrelenting! So, no doubt, felt many quiet Mrs. Joneses and Mrs. Smiths all over England. There was no arguing with the female of the species—the mother deprived of her young.

Something stirred in the recesses of Tuppence's brain—some nagging recollection—something that she had always known but had never succeeded in getting into the forefront of her mind. Solomon—Solomon came into it somewhere. . . .

The door opened. Commander Haydock came back into the room.

He howled out, beside himself with rage:

"Where is it? Where have you hidden it?"

Tuppence stared at him. She was completely taken aback. What he was saying did not make sense to her.

She had taken nothing and hidden nothing.

Haydock said to Anna:

"Get out."

The woman handed the pistol to him and left the room promptly.

Haydock dropped into a chair and seemed to be striving to pull himself together. He said:

"You can't get away with it, you know. I've got you—and I've got ways of making people speak—not pretty ways. You'll have to tell the truth in the end. Now then, *what have you done with it?*"

Tuppence was quick to see that here, at least, was something that gave her the possibility of bargaining. If only she could find out what it was she was supposed to have in her possession.

She said cautiously:

"How do you know I've got it?"

"From what you said, you damned little fool. You haven't got it on you—that we know, since you changed completely into this kit."

"Suppose I posted it to someone?" said Tuppence.

"Don't be a fool. Everything you posted since yesterday has been examined. You didn't post it. No, there's only one thing you *could* have done. Hidden it in Sans Souci before you left this morning. I give you just three minutes to tell me where that hiding-place is."

He put his watch down on the table.

"Three minutes, Mrs. Thomas Beresford."

The clock on the mantelpiece ticked.

Tuppence sat quite still with a blank impassive face.

It revealed nothing of the racing thoughts behind it.

In a flash of bewildering light she saw everything—saw the whole business revealed in terms of blinding clarity and realized at last who was the center and pivot of the whole organization.

It came quite as a shock to her when Haydock said:

"Ten seconds more . . ."

Like one in a dream she watched him, saw the pistol arm rise, heard his count:

"One, two, three, four, five—"

He had reached *eight* when the shot rang out and he collapsed forward on his chair, an expression of bewilderment on his broad red face. So intent had he been on watching his victim that he had been unaware of the door behind him slowly opening.

In a flash Tuppence was on her feet. She pushed her way past the uniformed men in the doorway, and seized on a tweed-clad arm.

"Mr. Grant."

"Yes, yes, my dear, it's all right now—you've been wonderful—"

Tuppence brushed aside these reassurances.

"Quick! There's no time to lose. You've got a car here?"

"Yes." He stared.

"A fast one? We must get to Sans Souci *at once.* If only we're in time. Before they telephone here, and get no answer."

Two minutes later they were in the car, and it was threading its way through the streets of Leatherbarrow. Then they were out in the open country and the needle of the speedometer was rising.

Mr. Grant asked no questions. He was content to sit quietly whilst Tuppence watched the speedometer in an agony of apprehension. The chauffeur had been given his orders and he drove with all the speed of which the car was capable.

Tuppence only spoke once.

"Tommy?"

"Quite all right. Released half an hour ago."

She nodded.

Now, at last, they were nearing Leahampton. They darted and twisted through the town, up the hill.

Tuppence jumped out and she and Mr. Grant ran up the drive. The hall door, as usual, was open. There was no one in sight. Tuppence ran lightly up the stairs.

She just glanced inside her own room in passing, and noted the confusion of open drawers and disordered bed. She nodded and passed on, along the corridor and into the room occupied by Mr. and Mrs. Cayley.

The room was empty. It looked peaceful and smelt slightly of medicines. Tuppence ran across to the bed and pulled at the coverings.

They fell to the ground and Tuppence ran her hand under the mattress. She turned triumphantly to Mr. Grant with a tattered child's picture-book in her hand.

"Here you are. It's all in here—"

"What on—"

They turned. Mrs. Sprot was standing in the doorway staring.

"And now," said Tuppence, *"let me introduce you to M.*! Yes. *Mrs. Sprot!* I ought to have known it all along."

It was left to Mrs. Cayley arriving in the doorway a moment later to introduce the appropriate anti-climax.

"Oh *dear,*" said Mrs. Cayley, looking with dismay at her spouse's dismantled bed. "Whatever *will* Mr. Cayley say?"

15

"I OUGHT TO have known it all along," said Tuppence.

She was reviving her shattered nerves by a generous tot of old brandy, and was beaming alternately at Tommy and at Mr. Grant—and at Albert, who was sitting in front of a pint of beer and grinning from ear to ear.

"Tell us all about it, Tuppence," urged Tommy.

"You first," said Tuppence.

"There's not much for me to tell," said Tommy. "Sheer accident let me into the secret of the wireless transmitter. I thought I'd get away with it, but Haydock was too smart for me."

Tuppence nodded and said:

"He telephoned to Mrs. Sprot at once. And she ran out into the drive and laid in wait for you with the hammer. She was only away from the bridge table for about three minutes. I *did* notice she was a little out of breath—but I never suspected her."

"After that," said Tommy, "the credit belongs entirely to Albert. He came sniffing round like a faithful dog. I did some impassioned Morse snoring and he cottoned on to it. He went off to Mr. Grant with the news and the two of them came back late that night. More snoring! Result was, I agreed to remain put so as to catch the sea forces when they arrived."

Mr. Grant added his quota.

"When Haydock went off this morning, our people took charge at Smugglers' Rest. We nabbed the boat this evening."

"And now, Tuppence," said Tommy. "Your story."

"Well, to begin with, I've been the most frightful fool all along! I suspected everybody here except Mrs. Sprot! I *did* once have a terrible feeling of menace, as though I was in danger—that was after I overheard that telephone message about the fourth of the month. There were three people there at the time—I put down my feeling of apprehension to either Mrs. Perenna or Mrs. O'Rourke. Quite wrong—it was the colorless Mrs. Sprot who was the really dangerous personality.

"I went muddling on, as Tommy knows, until after he disappeared. Then I was just cooking up a plan with Albert when suddenly, out of the blue, Antony Marsdon turned up. It seemed all right to begin with— the usual sort of young man that Deb often has in tow. But two things made me think a bit. First I became more and more sure as I talked to him that I *hadn't* seen him before and that he never had been to the flat. The second was that, though he seemed to know all about my working at Leahampton, he assumed that *Tommy* was in Scotland. Now that seemed all wrong. If he knew about anyone, it would be *Tommy* he knew about, since I was more or less unofficial. That struck me as very odd.

"Mr. Grant had told me that Fifth Columnists were everywhere—in the most unlikely places. So why shouldn't one of them be working in Deborah's show? I wasn't convinced, but I was suspicious enough to lay a trap for him. I told him that Tommy and I had fixed up a code for communicating with each other. Our real one, of course, was a Bonzo postcard, but I told Antony a fairy tale about the Penny Plain, Twopence Colored saying.

"As I hoped, he rose to it beautifully! I got a letter this morning which gave him away completely.

"The arrangements had been all worked out before-hand. All I had to do was to ring up a tailor and cancel a fitting. That was an intimation that the fish had risen."

"Coo-er!" said Albert. "It didn't half give me a turn. I drove up with a baker's van and we dumped a pool of stuff just outside the gate. Aniseed, it was—or smelt like it."

"And then—" Tuppence took up the tale. "I came out and walked in it. Of course it was easy for the baker's van to follow me to the station and someone came up behind me and heard me book to Yarrow. It was after that that it might have been difficult."

"The dogs followed the scent well," said Mr. Grant. "They picked it up at Yarrow station and again on the track the tire had made after you rubbed your shoe on it. It led us down to the copse and up again to the stone cross and after you where you had walked over the downs. The enemy had no idea we could follow you easily after they themselves had seen you start and driven off themselves.

"All the same," said Albert, "it give me a turn. Knowing you were in that house and not knowing what might come to you. Got in a back window, we did, and nabbed the foreign woman as she came down the stairs. Come in just in the nick of time, we did."

"I knew you'd come," said Tuppence. "The thing was for me to spin things out as long as I could. I'd have pretended to tell if I hadn't seen the door opening. What was really exalting was the way I suddenly saw the whole thing and what a fool I'd been."

"How did you see it?" asked Tommy.

"Goosey, goosey, gander," said Tuppence promptly. "When I said that to Commander Haydock he went absolutely livid. And not just because it was silly and rude. No, I saw at once that it *meant* something to him. And then there was the expression on that woman's face—Anna—it was like the Polish woman's, and then, of course, I thought of Solomon and I saw the whole thing."

Tommy gave a sigh of exasperation.

"Tuppence, if you say that once again, I'll shoot you myself. Saw all *what?* And what on earth has Solomon got to do with it?"

"Do you remember that two women came to Solomon with a baby and both said it was hers, but Solomon said, 'Very well, cut it in two.' And the false mother said 'All right.' But the real mother said 'No, let the other woman have it.' You see, she couldn't face her child being killed. Well, that night that Mrs. Sprot shot the other woman, you all said what a miracle it was and how easily she might have shot the child. Of course, it ought to have been quite plain then! If it *had* been her child, she *couldn't* have risked that shot for a minute. It meant that Betty *wasn't* her child. And that's why she absolutely had to shoot the other woman."

"Why?"

"Because, of course, the other woman was *the child's real mother.*" Tuppence's voice shook a little.

"Poor thing—poor hunted thing. She came over a penniless refugee and gratefully agreed to let Mrs. Sprot adopt her baby."

"Why did Mrs. Sprot want to adopt the child?"

"Camouflage! Supreme psychological camouflage. You just can't conceive of a master spy dragging her kid into the business. That's the main reason why I never considered Mrs. Sprot seriously. Simply because of the child. But Betty's real mother had a terrible hankering for her baby and she found out Mrs. Sprot's address and came down here. She hung about waiting for her chance, and at last she got it and went off with the child.

"Mrs. Sprot, of course, was frantic. At all costs she didn't want the police. So she wrote that message and pretended she found it in her bedroom, and roped in Commander Haydock to help. Then, when we'd tracked down the wretched woman, she was taking no chances, and shot her . . . Far from not knowing anything about firearms, she was a very fine shot! Yes, she killed that wretched woman—and because of that I've no pity for her. She was bad through and through."

Tuppence paused, then she went on:

"Another thing that ought to have given me a hint was the likeness between Vanda Polonska and Betty. It was *Betty* the woman reminded me of all along. And then the child's absurd play with my shoelaces. How much more likely that she'd seen her so-called mother do that— not Carl von Deinim! But as soon as Mrs. Sprot saw what the child was doing, she planted a lot of evidence in Carl's room for us to find and added the master touch of a shoelace dipped in secret ink."

"I'm glad that Carl wasn't in it," said Tommy. "I liked him."

"He's not been shot, has he?" asked Tuppence anxiously, noting the past tense.

Mr. Grant shook his head.

"He's all right," he said. "As a matter of fact I've got a little surprise for you there."

Tuppence's face lit up as she said:

"I'm terribly glad—for Sheila's sake! Of course we were idiots to go on barking up the wrong tree after Mrs. Perenna."

"She was mixed up in some IRA activities, nothing more," said Mr. Grant.

"I suspected Mrs. O'Rourke a little—and sometimes the Cayleys—"

"And I suspected Bletchley," put in Tommy.

"And all the time," said Tuppence, "it was that milk and water creature we just thought of as—Betty's mother."

"Hardly milk and water," said Mr. Grant. "A very dangerous woman and a very clever actress. And, I'm sorry to say, English by birth."

Tuppence said:

"Then I've no pity or admiration for her—it wasn't even her country she was working for." She looked with fresh curiosity at Mr. Grant. "You found what you wanted?"

Mr. Grant nodded.

"It was all in that battered set of duplicate children's books."

"The ones that Betty said were 'narsty'," Tuppence exclaimed.

"They *were* nasty," said Mr. Grant drily. "Little Jack Horner contained very full details of our Naval dispositions. Johnny Head in Air did the same for the Air Force. Military matters were appropriately embodied in *There was a Little Man and he had a Little Gun.*"

"And *Goosey, Goosey, Gander*?" asked Tuppence.

Mr. Grant said:

"Treated with the appropriate reagent, that book contains written in invisible ink a full list of all prominent personages who are pledged to assist an invasion of this country. Amongst them were two Chief Constables, an Air Vice-Marshal, two Generals, the Head of an Armaments Works, a Cabinet Minister, many Police Superintendents, Commanders of Local Volunteer Defence Organizations, and various military and naval lesser fry, as well as members of our own Intelligence Force."

Tommy and Tuppence stared.

"Incredible!" said the former.

Grant shook his head.

"You do not know the force of the German propaganda. It appeals to something in man, some desire or lust for power. These people were ready to betray their country not for money, but in a kind of megalomaniacal pride in what they, *they* themselves, were going to achieve for that country. In every land it has been the same. It is the Cult of Lucifer— Lucifer, Son of the Morning. Pride and a desire for *personal glory*!"

He added:

"You can realize, with such persons to issue contradictory orders and confuse operations, how the threatened invasion would have had every chance to succeed."

"And now?" said Tuppence.

Mr. Grant smiled.

"And now," he said, *"let them come! We'll be ready* for them!"

16

"DARLING," SAID DEBORAH. "Do you know I almost thought the most terrible things about you?"

"Did you," said Tuppence. "When?"

Her eyes rested affectionately on her daughter's dark head.

"That time when you sloped off to Scotland to join father and I thought you were with Aunt Gracie. I almost thought you were having an affair with someone."

"Oh, Deb, did you?"

"Not really, of course. Not at your age. And of course I know you and Carrot Top are devoted to each other. It was really an idiot called Tony Marsdon who put it into my head. Do you know, Mother—I think I might tell you—he was found afterwards to be a Fifth Columnist. He always did talk rather oddly—how things would be just the same, perhaps better if Hitler did win."

"Did you—er—like him at all?"

"Tony? Oh no—he was always rather a bore. I must dance this."

She floated away in the arms of a fair-haired young man, smiling up at him sweetly. Tuppence followed their revolutions for a few minutes, then her eyes shifted to where a tall young man in Air Force uniform was dancing with a fair-haired slender girl.

"I do think, Tommy," said Tuppence, "that our children are rather nice."

"Here's Sheila," said Tommy.

He got up as Sheila Perenna came towards their table.

She was dressed in an emerald evening dress which showed up her dark beauty. It was a sullen beauty tonight and she greeted her host and hostess somewhat ungraciously.

"I've come, you see," she said, "as I promised. But I can't think why you wanted to ask me."

"Because we like you," said Tommy smiling.

"Do you really?" said Sheila. "I can't think why. I've been perfectly foul to you both."

She paused and murmured:

"But I am grateful."

Tuppence said:

"We must find a nice partner to dance with you."

"I don't want to dance. I loathe dancing. I came just to see you two."

"You will like the partner we've asked to meet you," said Tuppence smiling.

"I—" Sheila began. Then stopped—for Carl von Deinim was walking across the floor.

Sheila looked at him like one dazed. She muttered.

"You—"

"I, myself," said Carl.

There was something a little different about Carl von Deinim this evening. Sheila stared at him, a trifle perplexed. The color had come up in her cheeks, turning them a deep glowing red.

She said a little breathlessly:

"I knew that you would be all right now—but I thought they would still keep you interned?"

Carl shook his head.

"There is no reason to intern me."

He went on:

"You have got to forgive me, Sheila, for deceiving you. I am not, you see, Carl von Deinim at all. I took his name for reasons of my own."

He looked questioningly at Tuppence who said:

"Go ahead. Tell her."

"Carl von Deinim was my friend. I knew him in England some years ago. I renewed acquaintanceship with him in Germany just before the war. I was there then on special business for this country."

"You were in the Intelligence?" asked Sheila.

"Yes. When I was there, queer things began to happen. Once or twice I had some very near escapes. My plans were known when they should not have been known. I realized that there was something wrong and that 'the rot', to express it in their terms, had penetrated actually into the service in which I was. I had been let down by my own people. Carl and I had a certain superficial likeness (my grandmother was a German) hence my suitability for work in Germany. Carl was not a Nazi. He was interested solely in his job—a job I myself had also practised—research chemistry. He decided, shortly before war broke out, to escape to England. His brothers had been sent to concentration camps. There would, he thought, be great difficulties in the way of his own escape, but in an almost miraculous fashion all these difficulties smoothed themselves out. The fact, when he mentioned it to me, made me somewhat suspicious. Why were the authorities making it so easy for von Deinim to leave Germany when his brothers and other relations were in concentration camps and he himself was suspected because of his anti-Nazi sympathies? It seemed as though they wanted him in England for some reason. My own position was becoming increasingly precarious. Carl's lodgings were in the same house as mine and one day I found him, to my sorrow, lying dead in his bed. He had succumbed to depression and taken his own life, leaving a letter behind which I read and pocketed.

"I decided then to effect a substitution. I wanted to get out of Germany—and I wanted to know why Carl was being encouraged to do so. I dressed his body in my clothes and laid it on my bed. It was disfigured by the shot he had fired into his head. My landlady, I knew, was semi-blind.

"With Carl von Deinim's papers I travelled to England and went to the address to which he had been recommended to go. The address was Sans Souci.

"Whilst I was there I played the part of Carl von Deinim and never relaxed. I found arrangements had been made for me to work in the chemical factory there. At first I thought that the idea was I should be compelled to do work for the Nazis. I realized later that the part for which my poor friend had been cast was that of scapegoat.

"When I was arrested on faked evidence, I said nothing. I wanted to leave the revelation of my own identity as late as possible. I wanted to see what would happen.

"It was only a few days ago that I was recognized by one of our people and the truth came out."

Sheila said reproachfully:

"You should have told me."

He said gently:

"If you feel like that—I am sorry."

His eyes looked into hers. She looked at him angrily and proudly—then the anger melted. She said:

"I suppose you had to do what you did . . ."

"Darling—"

He caught himself up.

"Come and dance . . ."

They moved off together.

Tuppence sighed.

"What's the matter?" said Tommy.

"I do hope Sheila will go on caring for him now that he isn't a German outcast with everyone against him."

"She looks as though she cared all right."

"Yes, but the Irish are terribly perverse. And Sheila is a born rebel."

"Why did he search your room that day? That's what led us up the garden path so terribly."

Tommy gave a laugh.

"I gather he thought Mrs. Blenkensop wasn't a very convincing person. In fact—while we were suspecting him he was suspecting us."

"Hallo, you two," said Derek Beresford as he and his partner danced past his parents' table. "Why don't you come and dance?"

He smiled encouragingly at them.

"They are so kind to us, bless 'em," said Tuppence.

Presently the twins and their partners returned and sat down.

Derek said to his father:

"Glad you got a job all right. Not very interesting, I suppose?"

"Mainly routine," said Tommy.

"Never mind, you're doing something. That's the great thing."

"And I'm glad Mother was allowed to go and work too," said Deborah. "She looks ever so much happier. It wasn't too dull, was it, Mother?"

"I didn't find it at all dull," said Tuppence.

"Good," said Deborah. She added, "When the war's over, I'll be able to tell you something about my job. It's really frightfully interesting, but very confidential."

"How thrilling," said Tuppence.

"Oh it is! Of course, it's not so thrilling as flying—"

She looked enviously at Derek.

She said, "He's going to be recommended for—"

Derek said quickly:

"Shut up, Deb."

Tommy said:

"Hallo, Derek, what have you been up to?"

"Oh, nothing much—sort of show all of us are doing. Don't know why they pitched on me," murmured the young airman, his face scarlet. He looked as embarrassd as though he had been accused of the most deadly of sins.

He got up and the fair-haired girl got up too.

Derek said:

"Mustn't miss any of this—last night of my leave."

"Come on, Charles," said Deborah.

The two of them floated away with their partners.

Tuppence prayed inwardly:

"Oh let them be safe—don't let anything happen to them. . . ."

She looked up to meet Tommy's eyes. He said, "About that child—shall we?"

"Betty? Oh, Tommy, I'm glad you've thought of it, too! I thought it was just me being maternal. You really mean it?"

"That we should adopt her? Why not? She's had a raw deal, and it will be fun for us to have something young growing up."

"Oh Tommy!"

She stretched out her hand and squeezed his. They looked at each other.

"We always do want the same things," said Tuppence happily.

Deborah, passing Derek on the floor, murmured to him:

"Just look at those two—actually holding hands! They're rather sweet, aren't they? We must do all we can to make up to them for having such a dull time in this war. . . ."